PRAISE FOR
THE ROMANCES OF

Elizabeth Mansfield

"Once again, Ms. Mansfield turns an old plot upside down, bringing a fresh, irresistible sparkle guaranteed to brighten your day."
—*Romantic Times*

"Elizabeth Mansfield is one of the best-loved authors of Regency romances. . . . *Miscalculations* is purely and simply a typical Mansfield Regency. . . . It has an engaging hero and heroine, a delightful cast of secondary characters, an interesting plot, and an authentic feel for the era. In short, 'typical' for Mansfield means an entertaining read. . . . *Miscalculations* is a light and enjoyable book. It has humor, romance, and a bit of intrigue."
—*The Romance Reader*

"There are two romances in this story, and, as usual, Ms. Mansfield has created realistic characters and a humorous plotline."
—*Rendezvous*

"Elizabeth Mansfield's tale of lasting friendship and misplaced jealousy is well-done. . . . The characters are so enchanting, you can't wait to turn the next page."
—*Affaire de Coeur*

"Ms. Mansfield proves why she is one of the enduring names in romance with this sparkling traditional Regency tale brimming with lively dialogue and charming characters."
—*The Paperback Forum*

Lords and Ladies

A Very Dutiful Daughter

The Counterfeit Husband

AND

The Bartered Bride

ELIZABETH MANSFIELD

NEW AMERICAN LIBRARY

New American Library
Published by New American Library,
a division of Penguin Group (USA) Inc.,
375 Hudson Street, New York, New York 10014, USA
Penguin Group (Canada), 90 Eglinton Avenue East, Suite 700, Toronto,
Ontario M4P 2Y3, Canada (a division of Pearson Penguin Canada Inc.)
Penguin Books Ltd., 80 Strand, London WC2R 0RL, England
Penguin Ireland, 25 St. Stephen's Green, Dublin 2,
Ireland (a division of Penguin Books Ltd.)
Penguin Group (Australia), 250 Camberwell Road, Camberwell,
Victoria 3124, Australia (a division of Pearson Australia Group Pty. Ltd.)
Penguin Books India Pvt. Ltd., 11 Community Centre,
Panchsheel Park, New Delhi - 110 017, India
Penguin Group (NZ), 67 Apollo Drive, Rosedale, Auckland 0632,
New Zealand (a division of Pearson New Zealand Ltd.)
Penguin Books (South Africa) (Pty.) Ltd., 24 Sturdee Avenue,
Rosebank, Johannesburg 2196, South Africa

Penguin Books Ltd., Registered Offices:
80 Strand, London WC2R 0RL, England

Published by New American Library, a division of Penguin Group (USA) Inc.
A Very Dutiful Daughter, *The Counterfeit Husband*, and
The Bartered Bride were previously published in Jove editions.

First New American Library Printing, May 2012
1   3   5   7   9   10   8   6   4   2

A Very Dutiful Daughter copyright © Paula Schwartz, 1979
The Counterfeit Husband copyright © Paula Schwartz, 1982
The Bartered Bride copyright © Paula Schwartz, 1989

 REGISTERED TRADEMARK—MARCA REGISTRADA

Set in Adobe Garamond Pro
Designed by Elke Sigal

Printed in the United States of America

PUBLISHER'S NOTE
These are works of fiction. Names, characters, places, and incidents either are the product of the author's imagination or are used fictitiously, and any resemblance to actual persons, living or dead, business establishments, events, or locales is entirely coincidental.

The publisher does not have any control over and does not assume any responsibility for author or third-party Web sites or their content.

A Very Dutiful Daughter

Chapter One

"*I* think Mama is going to faint again," remarked Augusta from her position at the keyhole.

"Oh, Gussie, not again!" responded her older sister, Prudence, in tones of deep disgust. "Get away from the door and let me see."

"It's *my* turn," whined Clara, the youngest by several years. "I haven't had *one chance* to peek. You both have been positively piggish about that keyhole ever since Letty and Aunt Millicent came home and locked themselves up in there with Mama!"

The accusation, though totally ignored by the two older girls, was quite true. Gussie and Prue had taken alternate turns at the keyhole for the past half-hour, pushing aside the fourteen-year-old Clara heartlessly and ignoring her persistent questions as if she did not exist. Indeed, the entire morning had not been a good one for Clara. The day had begun with a message from their governess, Miss Dorrimore, to the effect that she intended to remain in bed to nurse her cold and that the girls were to spend the morning working on their French declensions. The older girls, ignoring these instructions, had spent most of the morning poring over the fashion plates in a treasured copy of *La Belle Assemblée*. Clara, not yet old enough to be concerned with modish gowns and the art of hairdressing, had threatened to report her sisters' transgressions to the indisposed Miss Dorrimore. Her sisters had responded with threats and jibes of such malignity that Clara had been reduced to tears. In the midst of this *contretemps,* they'd heard the sound of a carriage pulling up at their front door. They'd rushed to the window in time to see the door of their Aunt Millicent's impressively ancient equipage open to discharge their eldest sister, Letitia. Letty looked woebegone and red-eyed, and Gussie and Prue had exchanged looks of surprise. The surprise soon turned to consternation, for Letty had been followed out of the carriage by their

Aunt Millicent, whose customary cold, forbidding features were so distorted with suppressed anger as to make her ordinarily stern expression seem positively beneficent in comparison.

"Something's gone wrong," Prue had remarked, in sepulchral tones. "She must have botched it somehow."

"Oh, no!" Gussie had moaned. "It can't be! Prue, didn't you tell me that Lord Denham was *certain* to make an offer?"

"Yes, it *was* certain. I overheard Aunt Millicent telling Mama all about it. Lady Denham assured her that her son Roger was ready to take a wife, and Letty was the girl they wanted."

"You *overheard* all that? Ha!" sneered the put-upon Clara. "*Eavesdropped*, more likely."

"And who's eavesdropping now, may I ask?" Gussie had asked quellingly. "This conversation is not meant for the ears of *children*, if you please. So take yourself off to your bedroom, or the nursery, or somewhere out-of-the-way."

"Listen to you, Miss Augusta High-and-mighty Glendenning! Just because you're sixteen, don't think you can queen it over me!" Clara had declared bravely, sticking out her chin in defiance.

"Stop squabbling," Prue had demanded with all the authority of her seventeen years in her voice. "Letty is in some sort of fix, and we ought to find a way to help her, not stand here brangling." With a toss of her red-gold curls, she'd turned quickly to the door and run to the landing. The two younger girls had followed hastily behind, and the three had peered over the banister to the floor below. They were barely in time to see Mama, the epitome of confused alarm, following Letty and Aunt Millicent into the small sitting room and shutting the door behind her.

Prue had lost no time in getting to the door and kneeling down with her eye at the keyhole. Gussie had cupped her hand to her ear and pressed it against the door. And thus it had been ever since, the two of them changing places periodically and pushing poor Clara aside whenever she attempted to come close to the door.

Gussie now surrendered her place at the keyhole to Prue, who reported promptly that Aunt Millicent was holding a bottle of vinaigrette to Mama's nose. "Can you hear anything?" Gussie asked impatiently.

"No," Prue muttered, "but they've not permitted Letty even to take off her bonnet and pelisse. She's just sitting there, staring at the floor. Aunt Millicent appears to be furious with her. But I don't see *why*! Is it *her* fault that Lord Denham didn't come up to scratch?"

Gussie looked down at her sister questioningly. "Do you think that's what happened? That Denham didn't offer after all?"

Prue, without taking her eye from the keyhole, shrugged. "What else could it be?"

Further speculation was interrupted by the opening of the front door. Their brother, Edward, strode in, his riding boots clattering loudly on the worn marble of the entryway as he hurried to the stairs. But he stopped short at the sight of the three girls grouped before the sitting room door.

"What on earth are you doing?" he demanded suspiciously.

Two pairs of eyes looked at him guiltily. "Oh, Ned, it's Letty!" Gussie said breathlessly. "Aunt Millicent is furious with her, and Mama has fainted twice, and—"

"They're eavesdropping—that's what they're doing, Neddie," Clara declared self-righteously. "You ought to make them stop."

"That's just what I intend to do, infant," Ned said, looking down at his youngest sister with distaste, "though you needn't think I'm doing it as a result of your tattling."

Prue had returned to the keyhole and now made her report. "Aunt Millicent is pacing again. And Letty is biting her lip. That means she's about to cry, the poor thing."

Ned pretended a disinterest he was far from feeling. "Get up, Prue, before someone catches you! Hang it, it ain't the thing for a girl your age to behave like a parlormaid!" he scolded.

Prue rose calmly and brushed off her skirt. "And what do *you* know of parlormaids? Was *that* why you were sent down from Oxford? For shame, Ned!"

Ned took a threatening step toward her. "Mind your tongue, goosecap! Get back to the schoolroom at once, and take your sisters with you, or you'll have to deal with me!"

Prue regarded him speculatively. He was only one year her senior, and barely an inch taller than she, but although he had not yet reached his full height, his shoulders were broad and the muscles in his arms fully developed. Previous experience had taught her that he was not easily bested in a fight. Besides, now that she was seventeen, it was no longer seemly to engage in a tussle with her brother. She shrugged and marched in brave retreat to the stairs. Gussie, meeting his glare, took Clara's hand and ran quickly after Prue. Ned waited until they had disappeared around the bend in the stairs. Then he listened for the closing of the schoolroom door, after which he promptly knelt down and peered into the keyhole to see for himself what was going on.

Inside the room the tension was palpable. Letty, seated in the far corner of the room, seemed immobile, her back straight, the hands in her lap hidden inside her fur-trimmed muff, her head lowered, her face shaded by the brim of her plumed bonnet, her eyes fixed on a worn patch of carpet at her feet. Only the sharpest of observers could have detected the movement of her fingers inside the muff as they clenched and unclenched in distress, and the frequent flicker of her eyelids as she battled valiantly to keep the tears from flowing over.

Her aunt paced the room with an angry stride, the stiff silk of her rather old-fashioned skirts whispering with matching anger every time she turned about. Letty began to count her aunt's paces . . . eight steps to the window, swish . . . eight steps back to the sofa, swish . . . eight steps to the window, swish . . .

A groan from the sofa caused Letty and Aunt Millicent to turn their heads. Lady Glendenning, stretched out full-length, sighed and raised her hand from her eyes. Her arm made a tremblingly nervous arc through the air and fell to her side, where it dangled over the edge of the sofa in listless despair. "Whatever are we to do now, Millicent?" she asked in a quavering voice. "Whatever are we to do?"

"Ask your daughter!" Millicent said with asperity. "*She's* the one who whistled a fortune down the wind!"

"Letty, my love," her mama asked tearfully, "*how* could you have done it? How could you have *refused* him?"

Letty, her lovely hazel eyes filling with tears, merely shook her head. Her aunt looked at her closely. Aunt Millicent, the formidable Lady Upsham, was no fool. No girl in possession of her senses could turn down a man like Lord Denham without a very good reason. "There *must* be someone else," she said for the third time. "You've fixed your heart on some ineligible wastrel, no doubt, and hope to make a match of it, in spite of your mother's wishes and your family's need—isn't that it?"

Letty looked up, blinking, as two tears rolled down her cheeks. "I've told you and told you. There's no one else. N-no one. I j-just c-could not . . ."

"You could not accept an offer from the most eligible bachelor in England? I fail to understand you, Letitia. It is not as if we were marrying you to an ogre. Or even to an old dodderer with nothing to recommend him but his purse. Denham is *more* than a wealthy peer. He is nothing if not charming and witty. His address is excellent, his mind superior to most of the young men of your flibberty-gibbety generation, and God knows he's as handsome a man as I've ever seen, even if his complexion is darker than I like, and his eyebrows somewhat heavy . . ."

"Was *that* it, Letty dear?" her mother asked in concern. "Did you take an aversion to his eyebrows?"

Letty had to smile, even if somewhat tremulously. "Oh, Mama, of course not!"

"His complexion, then?"

Letty's smile faded, and she returned her eyes to the patch in the carpet.

"There's nothing at all amiss in Lord Denham's appearance," she said in a flat voice.

Lady Glendenning pulled herself up on one arm and peered closely at her daughter. She had never seen Letty in such distress. The poor girl looked positively hagged, although Lady Glendenning had to admit that even her excessive pallor failed to detract appreciably from the loveliness of Letty's face. Letty was blessed with thick auburn hair, high cheekbones, a clear complexion and a full, expressive mouth. And her eyes, even when red-rimmed and tearful, were large and lustrous and showed clearly the gentleness and intelligence that were her nature. Lady Glendenning had waited for two years, ever since Letty's come-out at eighteen under the auspices of her sister-in-law, Lady Millicent Upsham, for Letty to choose one of her rich suitors to marry. It was Letty who would save the family from sinking into a mire of debt. But Millicent had urged Lady Glendenning to curb her impatience. Millicent had a match in mind for Letty that would solve all their problems. Letty would marry the man most girls in London only *dreamed* of attaching. Millicent was saving Letty for Roger Denham, the Earl of Arneau.

Lady Glendenning sighed. Millicent's hopes for Letty had made her, Letty's own adoring mother, uneasy from the first. Lord Denham was past thirty and had never succumbed to matrimony. All Millicent's assurances that Roger Denham would come up to scratch failed to ease her mind. Lovely as her daughter was, Lady Glendenning knew that there were others more beautiful, more well-connected or more lively, and that Lord Denham had ignored them all. Letty, quiet and self-effacing, was not likely to catch quite so big a fish. Couldn't Millicent be content with a lesser prize?

But Millicent had been adamant. Her connection with the Dowager Lady Denham was very close, and she knew that she, Roger's mother, was quite taken with Letty. And, just as she had predicted, Lord Denham had taken an interest in Letty and had *offered*! Millicent and Lady Denham, between them, had done the trick. It was Letty herself who had ruined everything! What maggot had found its way into her devoted and very dutiful daughter's head to cause her to do such a terrible thing?

Lady Glendenning lay back on the pillows with a groan. "I don't understand you at all," she said tearfully. "If you don't hold his appearance in aversion, what *is* it that made you refuse him?"

Aunt Millicent snorted. "The answer is obvious. There's nothing about Lord Denham to revolt a girl. Why, there's not another girl in all of England who would refuse him. Your daughter has her eye on someone else. It's the only possible explanation."

Lady Glendenning shook her head. "No, Millicent. Letty wouldn't lie to us.

She has always been the most devoted, the most obedient, the best behaved of all my children. She's never lied to me or given me the slightest trouble. She would not ruin her family by refusing a fortune—not for such a reason as that. You are not in love with some penniless fellow, are you, my darling?"

"No, Mama," Letty said quietly. "I swear I'm not. I'll marry anyone else you say. *Anyone*." Her eyes filled with tears again. "But not Lord Denham."

"Then at least tell us *why*!" her aunt demanded impatiently.

She shook her head. "Please don't ask me to explain. I . . . can't explain it to you. I c-can't!" she answered in a choked voice.

"Don't you realize, you silly peagoose, that there's not much chance of finding someone else now?" Millicent asked in disgust. "No one will believe that you turned Denham down. They will all say that he found *you* unsatisfactory and did not come up to scratch."

"Oh, my God!" wailed Lady Glendenning from the sofa. "I'd never thought of that . . ."

"Neither had your daughter, apparently," Millicent muttered angrily. "Perhaps if she had, she would not have been so quick to refuse him."

"It would have made no difference. I would have refused him in any case," Letty said in a flat, dead voice that her mother barely recognized.

"Stop badgering the girl, Millicent," Lady Glendenning said helplessly. "I can't bear to see her so unhappy."

"What about *your* unhappiness? And the rest of the family's?" Millicent demanded. "Why didn't she think of *that*?"

There was no answer. Lady Glendenning covered her eyes with trembling hands, and Letty stared in miserable silence at the carpet. Finally, Millicent sighed in defeat. "Well, go up to your room, Miss. I want to talk to your mother in private."

Letty rose quickly and hurried out, almost colliding with her brother, who had not moved quickly enough from the door. "Ned!" she gasped.

"Quiet!" he hissed nervously, carefully shutting the door behind her. "Do you want Aunt Millicent to know I've been eavesdropping?"

"Then you heard—?"

"Most of it. Whatever made you do it, Letty? Do you really dislike him so much?"

"Oh, Neddie, don't *you* start on me, too!" Letty cried, and she burst into long-suppressed tears and fell against his shoulder.

Ned looked down at his sister's bonnet in perplexity. "There, now, don't cry," he said, patting her shoulder awkwardly. "You know I can't abide waterworks. Besides, there's no need for tears *now*. It's all over and done with."

"D-done with?" Letty raised her head from his shoulder. "W-what do you m-mean?"

"You've turned him down, haven't you? It's done with. However much they may scold, they can't make you marry him now."

This brought out a fresh flood of tears. "You d-don't understand," she sobbed against his shoulder. "You d-don't unders-stand at all!"

"What is there to understand? Lord Denham asked you to marry him. You didn't want to marry him, so you refused him. Let Aunt Millicent carry on all she likes. It's too late for her to force you to marry him now, isn't it?"

"Yes," his sister nodded, still sobbing.

"Then I'm dashed if I can see what you're crying about. Stop it, will you? You're soaking my riding coat. Here." He lifted her head and handed her his handkerchief. "Dry those eyes, you silly puss. Everything is going to be fine."

Letty took a deep breath and tried to control her tears. Sniffing bravely into his handkerchief, she muttered, "Everything is going to be dreadful."

"Nonsense," her brother said decidedly. "You've only to weather a little scolding. They're bound to give up sooner or later. And when the noise is all over, you'll no longer have to marry a man you dislike."

"That's just it," Letty said, gulping back her tears and thrusting his wet handkerchief into his hand. "I *don't* dislike him. In fact, if you want to know the truth, there's no man in the world I'd *rather* marry than Roger Denham!" And she fled up the stairs, leaving her brother staring after her in openmouthed bewilderment.

Chapter Two

The sight of his mother's blue-and-gold coach at his doorway caused Roger Denham, Fourth Earl of Arneau, to groan out loud. Lord Denham had not had a good day. First, his morning call at the home of his mother's bosom-bow, Lady Millicent Upsham, to make an offer for her good-looking but rather mousy niece, had ended in disaster. Not that his heart was in any way touched. (He sometimes wondered if he would ever learn to feel the tender emotions so rapturously described by the poets.) But he had certainly suffered in his self-esteem. He had been given to understand by his mother that the chit was more than eager to receive his addresses, but when he had made his speech to her (and it was in his most charmingly polished manner, too), she had looked up at him with eyes that he had to admit were remarkably lustrous and had stumblingly told him that she was very sorry for the inconvenience (as well she should be! He had wasted the entire morning!), but that she was unable to accept his very flattering offer. (If she had been in any way flattered, she certainly didn't show it.)

He had made a hasty retreat and had promptly repaired for solace to the residence of Mrs. Brownell. The captivating Kitty, a notorious widow whose opulent apartments and costly wardrobe he had been financing for some years now, was (as usual) completely compliant, but he found her practiced lovemaking neither stimulating to his depressed spirits, nor soothing to the wound which had been dealt to his consequence.

The evening had been as flat and dull as the afternoon. His club had seemed to be devoid of good company, and his usual luck at the card table had quite deserted him. He'd left early, hoping that a good night's sleep would wipe away the memory of this irritating day. Thus, as he approached his residence, the sight of his mother's carriage fixed at his front door struck him as a particularly treacherous twist of fate. This ill fate was intent on clogging his steps as closely at the end of the day as it had at the beginning.

With a sigh, he submitted to the inevitable and went in to face his mother. He found her seated in his study in his favorite wing chair, her eyes closed. But he knew she was not asleep. Her tapping foot, her frowning expression and the motion of her quizzing glass (which swung from a long chain which she dangled between her fingers) gave mute evidence that she was (1) wide awake and (2) quite angry. He smiled down at her affectionately. His mother sometimes enjoyed affecting an acerbic manner—her sharp tongue and aloof dignity brought her admiration and respect from her peers, her servants, and all who met her—but she couldn't hide from her son the deep warmth and affection she felt for him and which he returned in no small measure. He bent and kissed her cheek.

The Dowager Lady Denham opened her eyes, raised her quizzing glass and looked at her son coldly. "So, you're home. Quite early, too. I fully expected to have to wait for you at least another hour."

"Good evening, Mama. I suppose you will think me quite beetleheaded to be surprised to find you here."

"Beetle-headed, indeed, if you *truly* didn't expect me. Did you think that I would take no interest in the result of your interview with Miss Glendenning this morning?"

"I was persuaded that you'd have heard the result of that interview from other sources," Roger responded drily.

"And so I have. But I want to hear from *you* exactly what happened today."

"I've nothing to add that you've not already heard from your friend, Lady Upsham. I presented myself at her door promptly at the appointed hour. I made my speech to Miss Glendenning in my most charming style. She looked up at me with those remarkably speaking eyes of hers and told me bluntly that she was unable to accept me. I responded that I quite understood, hoped we might remain friends, made my bow and departed."

"And that's the whole of it?"

"I'm afraid so."

Lady Denham rose and began to pace with impatient strides. "The girl gave you no explanation for this astounding turn of events?" she asked incredulously.

Roger grinned at her affectionately. "How like a doting mother you sound."

She glared at him. "Doting? Balderdash! In what way am I doting?"

"In your ready assumption that any female's refusal of me is astounding," he answered promptly.

Lady Denham gave a ripple of laughter. "Obnoxious boy! Do you think I'm so besotted a mother as that? We are not speaking of *any* female. Only this one. I've met Letty Glendenning on more than one occasion, and I had the distinct impression that she was more than a little interested in you. And, in addition, her family has everything to gain by the match. The whole matter is quite puzzling."

"Not at all. The girl has simply taken me in dislike, or—"

"Taken you in dislike!" his mother cut in with asperity. "Rubbish! Why on earth should she?"

Roger's eyes twinkled. "I have no idea. Such a paragon as I am, it *does* seem incredible that a lady could bring herself to reject me."

Lady Denham did not deign to respond, but merely favored him with a glower and returned to her chair. Roger dropped onto an ottoman near the fire and settled himself comfortably. While he gazed into the flames, his mother studied him closely. Despite his denials, she was well aware of his desirability on the Marriage Mart. Besides the advantages of birth and wealth, which he had in abundance, he had a generous share of those personal qualities which women admire and men envy. She was by no means one of those foolishly fond parents who cannot see their children's faults. She looked at him now, closely and dispassionately, as a stranger might. There in the firelight, his face looked quite appealing. His eyes were intelligent, humorous and kind, his mouth generous, his dark hair thick and curly. He had placed one booted foot on the fender of the fireplace and was resting his elbow on the knee of the other leg. Tall and masculine as he was, his body in repose seemed surprisingly graceful. What on earth was there about him that Letty had found to dislike?

"The girl's behavior is completely bewildering," she said, voicing her thoughts aloud, "unless she was playing a skittish game with you."

Roger made a dismissive gesture with his head. "Skittish? Not she."

"Why not? Many girls believe they ought to refuse a man the first time he offers."

"Not this girl. There was nothing coy in her refusal. She meant it."

"How can you be sure?"

Roger turned and faced his mother squarely. "Listen to me, Mama," he told her firmly, "and believe what I tell you. I'm thirty-one years old. I know the way of the world. I'm neither a coxcomb nor an innocent babe. I know when a young lady is flirting with me and when she is not, when she wants my attentions and when she doesn't. Miss Glendenning was not flirting. She was not skittish. She was not coy. She obviously doesn't want to become my wife. So I'm afraid you'll have to look elsewhere for a daughter-in-law. Sorry, but that's the end of it."

His mother stared at him in frustration. Damn the boy, would he *never* marry? Lady Denham winced to remember all the ploys she had used to stimulate Roger's interest in various eligible females. And she had not been alone in the attempt. She couldn't *count* all the designing mothers who had thrust their daughters in Roger's path. Not one of those girls had made the slightest mark on him. When he had at last agreed that the time had come for him to take a wife, he'd admitted to her that there was no girl at all for whom he had the slightest preference. He'd been quite willing to let his mother handle the selection of a suitable bride.

The result of that selection process had been Letty Glendenning. Lady Denham's closest friend, Millicent Upsham, had long spoken of her niece and had finally brought her to Arneau House for Lady Denham's inspection. Lady Denham had been delighted with the girl. Not only was she lovely and well-bred, but Lady Denham saw that under her outer softness, Letty had a character of moral strength. In addition, she had recognized, by Letty's carefully phrased questions and the unmistakable gleam in the girl's eyes when Roger's name was mentioned, that Letty was strongly attracted to him. If any girl could entice her son from the joys of bachelorhood, Lady Denham was sure Letty was the one. The plan had seemed so perfect, so simple, so foolproof. What could have gone wrong?

But she would let the matter drop for the nonce. There were too many unanswered questions to form a coherent plan of action. She stood up and wordlessly reached for the pelisse she had thrown over the back of her chair. Roger jumped to his feet and put it over her shoulders. Rubbing her cheek with the back of his hand, he smiled at her comfortingly and said softly, "Don't feel so put out, my dear. I'm sure you'll find another candidate for the post before very long."

"I haven't given up on *this* one yet," she answered curtly.

"Now, Mama—!" Roger began in annoyance.

"You must have said or done *something*," his mother said, ignoring his disapproval. "*Think,* you irritating jackanapes! Are you sure you said or did nothing which could have offended or upset her?"

"What *could* I have said? We've barely exchanged a dozen sentences since we were introduced. And those exchanges were the merest commonplaces, I assure you."

"I see." She buttoned her pelisse and started for the door. "Well, ring for Trebbs, will you? There's no point in pursuing this subject any further tonight."

"There is no point in pursuing the subject at *any* time. Miss Glendenning has refused me, and the subject is closed. And I shall *not* ring for Trebbs. I shall see you out myself."

Lady Denham took his arm. "Don't think to deter me from my object by playing the gallant. You may accompany me to the door if you wish, but I will not refrain from pursuing the subject further. Millicent may have learned something from the girl herself. When I hear from her, we shall talk again. Please come to see me before the week is out."

"Mama—!" Roger exclaimed in disgust.

"No later than Saturday, if you please—or if you don't please!" his mother said firmly, and went out to her carriage without a further word.

The following morning the Glendenning household was as somberly quiet as if a death had occurred in the night. The servants moved about the house on tiptoe. Lady Glendenning, who had taken to her bed immediately after the departure of Aunt Millicent on the previous afternoon, had made no appearance at the breakfast table. The tray which had been brought to her door had been rejected with a moan. The rest of the family sat at the breakfast table, eating listlessly. They spoke to each other only in subdued whispers. Miss Dorrimore, who had emerged from the sickroom well before her symptoms had disappeared, because she felt that her presence was needed in this emergency, stifled her sneezes in the voluminous folds of a very large handkerchief. Ned had dared to guffaw at something in a note a friend had sent round, but he was quickly silenced by the glares of disapproval his sisters shot at him.

Letty, getting up to help herself to a second cup of tea from the pot on the sideboard, looked up from her cup to find every eye upon her. Her sisters, her brother and everyone in the household had been following her every movement with solemn, lugubrious stares. Since she had been doing her very best to maintain a cheerful countenance, and to behave in a normal way, their stares were irritating in the extreme. She heaved a sigh of disgust and faced them squarely. "Will you all stop looking at me in that apprehensive way? You watch me quite as if I were dying of consumption of the lungs!" she burst out.

"It would serve you right if you were," pouted Clara under her breath.

"*What* did you say, you noddy little brat?" her brother growled. "Take that back at once!"

"I won't. Why did she have to make all this trouble for us?"

"Trouble?" asked Letty in surprise. "What do you mean, Clara?"

"You've refused Lord Denham, haven't you? Now we shall have no money, and we shall have to give up Hinson and the other servants and Miss Dorrimore, too. And we shan't be able to buy coal for the fire, or new dresses, and we shall all starve!"

Prue looked up from her plate in shocked disgust. "I'd like to slap your silly face!" she said. "Wherever did you hear such nonsense? Besides, who told you that Letty refused Lord Denham?"

"Everyone knows it, even Katie."

"Katie? Who's Katie?" Ned demanded.

"Katie-in-the-kitchen. She helps Cook. She knows everything."

Miss Dorrimore rattled her cup with a nervous hand. "Is this true, Miss Letty?" she asked with a trembling underlip. "Shall I have to go?"

"No, of course not," Letty assured her. "Really, Clara, you are getting too old for such silliness. Mama has an adequate income, if only we are frugal."

"Frugal? What's frugal?" Clara asked.

"Why don't you ask Katie-in-the-kitchen?" Ned put in with a satiric grimace. "She knows everything."

Miss Dorrimore, not to be outdone by a kitchen maid, immediately offered instruction. "From the Latin, *frugalis,* meaning economical and prudent in expenditure."

"Yes, Miss Dorrimore, but what does it *mean*?" Clara persisted.

"It means, love," Letty explained, "that we can't spend money on fripperies or ball gowns or parties or such things."

"Do you mean we won't be able to go to balls and parties?" Gussie asked, the import of Letty's action belatedly dawning upon her. "Oh, Letty, perhaps Clara is right. You shouldn't have done it."

"Gussie," Prue frowned, "that's a dreadful thing to say! Would you want your sister to sacrifice herself on the Altar of Matrimony just so that you can buy ball gowns and go to parties?"

"Prue's right," Ned said, nodding agreement. Then, turning to Gussie and Clara, he added vehemently, "Dashed if I ain't ashamed that you two are my sisters. You ought to know that Letty would do anything for us if she could. This was something she couldn't do, that's all."

"But I don't understand *why* she couldn't," Gussie argued. "Lord Denham is the best catch in the world. And now everyone will be saying that *he* didn't want Letty, and nobody else will offer for her. And then what will become of us?"

"Really, Gussie, I suppose I could have expected this from Clara, but I never thought to hear *you* talk like such a ninny," Prue said. "Letty is the prettiest, most sensible girl any man's likely to find. Do you suppose a man worth his salt would keep from offering for her just because of rumors that the toplofty Earl of Arneau didn't want her?"

"The Earl of Arneau is *not* toplofty," Clara informed them smugly. "Katie-in-the-kitchen says he's very pleasant and kind, besides being handsome and rich as King Midas."

"Katie-in-the-kitchen seems to be a veritable fount of information," Letty said drily.

"So it would seem." Ned laughed. "Perhaps, Miss Nodcock, you could ask your Katie-in-the-kitchen to recommend another lord for Letty to marry."

"I already did," Clara responded promptly, "but the only other lord she knows anything about is the Marquis of Atherton. Her cousin works in Lord Atherton's stables, you see. But Lord Atherton is not in the least eligible."

"No?" Prue asked with heavy sarcasm. "Why not?"

"Because he is fatter than the Prince and at least seventy-five years old."

Gussie and Prue giggled, but Ned, keeping his face in rigid control, held up a restraining hand. "That doesn't seem so bad. He might do for your sister, mightn't he, Clara? Especially if the marriage would mean gobs of money for the family to spend on balls and such."

"That's what I thought," Clara agreed with perfect seriousness, "but Katie said that he's not nearly rich enough to make up for his other defects."

The laughter could no longer be held back, and it burst forth from everyone at the table but Clara and Miss Dorrimore, Clara because she failed to see anything at all funny in what she'd said, and Miss Dorrimore because she felt that the whole conversation was far from proper and had listened to all of it with an expression on her face of profound disapproval.

"Good for Katie-in-the-kitchen," Prue gasped as soon as she could catch her breath. "I think I'd prefer *her* to be my sister, Clara. She seems to have a great deal more sense than you do."

"Shall we put it to a vote?" Ned chortled. "All in favor of moving Clara down to the scullery and Katie up to Clara's room—"

"Now, that's enough, Neddie," Letty said calmly. "We've had a good laugh, Clara's frankness has given us a chance to clear the air, and you all have stopped looking at me in that odiously solemn way. So no harm has been done."

Gussie looked up at her sister guiltily. "I'm sorry for what I said, Letty. Neddie is right—you would have accepted him if you could. Mama always says that you are the best, the most obedient of us all. So if you couldn't do this, the most important thing she's ever asked you to do, you must have had a good reason."

Letty lowered her eyes to her cup. "I *think* I had," she said hesitantly.

Prue looked at her earnestly. "Aren't you sure, Letty? Maybe you should tell us why you rejected him. If we all understood—"

Letty shook her head. "I *can't*! Please don't ask me." She put down her cup and made for the door. "Miss Dorrimore, please excuse me. I'd like to go to my room."

"Of course, my dear," Miss Dorrimore said, sensing some romantic drama behind the tearful expression in Letty's eyes.

Gussie, too, seeing a look in her sister's face she had never seen before, was overcome with a wave of sympathy. She jumped up, ran to her sister and threw her arms about Letty's neck. "You're not upset with me, are you?" she asked in self-reproach. "I'm sorry I sounded so selfish. And Clara is sorry, too, aren't you, Clara?"

"I suppose so," the petulant Clara said reluctantly.

Letty forced a smile and looked down at her sister. "Of course I'm not upset with you, Gussie dear. Don't look so downcast. After all, Prue is the *real* beauty in the family. She'll have her come-out next year, and before she is on the town a month, she will have found a lord even richer and handsomer than Denham. And she'll marry him, and we shall all live happily ever after."

Ned snorted. "*Prue?* You must be blind!"

Gussie agreed. "You're being silly, Letty. With her freckles and her lack of height, any man who's at all up to the mark would be unlikely even to *look* at her."

Prue drew herself up proudly. "Is that so? Well, I've been told by several gentlemen already that one need not be tall to be fashionably elegant, and that freckles are very *comme-il-faut*! So there!"

And while the merry discussion over Prue's charms—or lack of them—ensued, Letty quietly slipped from the room, ran to her bedroom and barricaded herself behind her locked door for the rest of the morning.

Chapter Three

Alone in her room, Letty's outer cheerfulness dropped away. Poor Clara had been closer to the truth than Letty had wanted to admit. The future was indeed bleak for the family and for herself. Not only had she doomed herself to spinsterhood, but she had condemned the family to a life of near-poverty. She lay down on her bed and shut her eyes. Had she tossed away all their futures for a silly scruple?

She had met Roger Denham during the month of her come-out two years ago. From the moment she had been introduced to him at Almack's, she had adored him. He had seemed to her a model of masculine perfection—a top-of-the-trees Corinthian, Ned would have called him. His dark curls, his sardonic smile, his easy manner with his friends, his polished address with young ladies, the stories of his sporting exploits, which were repeated in all the drawing rooms with such admiration, even his reputation for immunity to the lures of ladies of quality—all these things combined to make him a hero in her eyes.

As a result of the worshipful adoration with which she viewed him, her one and only dance with him had been a complete disaster. He had stood up with her for an interminable country dance, during which she'd been completely tongue-tied and had kept her eyes fastened to the floor. Naturally, he did not again seek her companionship, and on those few occasions when they met again, she was favored with nothing more than a small bow. A puzzled expression would cross his face, as if he were trying to remember who she was.

This lack of interest on his part did nothing to diminish Letty's adoration. She would often daydream of attending a glittering ball, looking ravishing in green silk. He would see her and be irresistibly drawn to her. He would ask her to dance the evening's first waltz. She would grant his request, and they would float around the ballroom, the most beautiful couple in the room. Ignoring the eyes on them, they would exchange the most witty banter, each verbal riposte laughingly returned. He would become completely enchanted, and she, of all the lovely, brilliant women in London, would win his heart!

But her month in the midst of the London social scene soon came to an end. Aunt Millicent could not be expected to finance indefinitely the high costs of the social whirl which a young lady in her first year in society must necessarily undergo. Letty's time on the town had ended without a second chance to stand up with Lord Denham. She had returned to the quiet, withdrawn life in her mother's household without any further expectation of seeing the great Earl of Arneau again, except at a distance, at the opera or the theater. Nevertheless, her daydreams of him continued. Until that terrible night a few months later . . .

The memory of that night came flooding back to her. The night she had gone to Vauxhall Gardens. If only she'd obeyed her better instincts and stayed at home . . .

The weather had been fine, that autumn of 1805, and a group of Ned's cronies had decided to visit the Gardens. Several young ladies had been invited to join the expedition, and a Mrs. Lorimer, the mother of one of them, had been prevailed upon to accompany them as chaperone. When Ned invited Letty to make one of the party, she had been ecstatic. She'd never seen Vauxhall, but of course she'd heard a great deal about its wondrous charm. The Gardens were said to be spacious and picturesque, with delightful walks, magnificent hedges and greenery, and a wonderful assortment of pavilions, lodges, groves, grottoes, lawns, temples, cascades, porticoes and rotundas. It was crowded with gay company who strolled its walks, ate cold collations at its lodges, listened to the merry sounds of the musical bands and singers, and in general cavorted through its twelve acres with happy abandon.

One could not be sure of the quality of the people one might meet at Vauxhall, for anyone who could afford the one-shilling admission fee was welcome to roam its walks at will. Mixing freely with the *ton* were merchants, foreigners, farmers, servants, ruffians, robbers, pimps and prostitutes. The prospect was a bit frightening to a young girl of nineteen who had never gone on such an excursion before.

When Letty had applied to her mother for permission, half hoping that her mother would refuse to let her go, Lady Glendenning had acquiesced, feeling that the chaperonage of Mrs. Lorimer made the outing somewhat respectable. Besides, Ned had assured her that there was to be a masquerade that evening, so that, even if Letty were seen in such surroundings, she would not be recognized behind her mask.

By the time the evening had arrived, Letty had been quite eager for the excursion. She'd felt wildly adventurous as she covered herself with the green domino, which Ned had provided for her. Ned himself had chosen to dress as a character from literature. He looked quite convincing as Prince Hamlet in his dark-colored doublet and full-sleeved shirt. He'd asked her to dress as the Lady Ophelia, but Letty was too shy to dress in costume and had decided that a simple domino would be exciting enough. She tied the shimmering, cloaklike garment at the neck, raised the hood over her well-brushed auburn hair, put on the matching mask and gazed at herself in the mirror. She appeared strange to herself, taller and more sophisticated and mysterious. She smiled at herself in sheer pleasure. The smile remained on her face as her brother escorted her by coach to Westminster, where they joined the band of laughing companions with whom they were to spend the evening. The whole group boarded a wherry to take them across the Thames to the garden entrance.

The entrance to Vauxhall was at the foot of a dark alley, which made their first glimpse of the Gardens overwhelming. The prospect that greeted them seemed even more resplendent in contrast to the dim alley they had just passed through. The innumerable colored lamps, the music, the laughter, the gay crowds—it was all as she had dreamed. People romped by dressed in all manner of colorful costumes. There were a goodly number of King Arthurs and Guineveres, Robin Hoods and Maid Marians, Arabian Sheikhs and dancing girls from their harems, Roman Legionnaires, Romeos and their Juliets. There were animals of all sorts—several kittens, a few lions, and one rather lumpy-looking unicorn. Some of the costumes were as shocking as they were ingenious. One lady wore a gown made entirely of silk leaves. It reached only to her knees and exposed (for all the world to see) a pair of very shapely but very bare legs. One gentleman, who seemed to represent the sun, had gilded himself from top to toe, not only his shoes, trousers and coat, but the skin of his face and hands as well.

Letty and her party proceeded down the Grand Walk to the Grove, the central quadrangle, which held a large pavilion from which issued forth some lively music. A great number of indecorous dancers whirled about the Grove, and it was not long before Ned and his companions were tempted to join. Two by two they paired off to participate in the festivities. Even Mrs. Lorimer succumbed to the blandishments of a young buck and allowed herself to be led into the throng. Only Letty resisted the various requests for her participation. One young man, who had been at her side since they'd boarded the wherry and whose name she could not remember, pleaded with her to dance with him. She shook her head, telling him that she preferred to stand here on the sidelines and watch. The young man remained dutifully at her side for several minutes, but suddenly spied a friend across the quadrangle. Promising a quick return, he set out through the crowd and was soon lost from view.

Letty, realizing that she was quite alone and unprotected, experienced a complete change of mood. People who a moment ago had seemed happy and innocent suddenly appeared menacing and sinister. The eyes of strangers seemed to be watching her with mocking leers. A raucous burst of laughter from somewhere behind her made her jump. Her eyes searched the crowd of dancers for a glimpse of Ned, but she couldn't locate him. What if he never found her in this sea of people? What could she do? How would she find her way home?

Suddenly she felt a hand on her shoulder, and she was wrenched around to face a tall, dark gentleman in a silver domino who was frowning down at her. "So here you are, my dear," he said in a tone of icy contempt. "I had not thought to find you alone."

"Sir, I think you m-mistake me—" Letty said timidly, trying to back away from him.

"Let us not play any more games," the stranger said curtly, and, grasping her hand in an iron grip, he turned and pulled her behind him as he strode rapidly away from the Grove. She was dragged down a walk darkened by the interlacing trees which lined it. He walked so quickly that she had to run to keep up and had hardly breath enough to repeat her cry that he'd made a dreadful mistake. The walk was not as crowded with people as the wider, brighter thoroughfares had been, but occasionally a passerby appeared. Letty's feeble cries for help were either ignored or she was stared at with suspicion, amusement or distaste.

At last they arrived at a little alcove, surrounded by Greek pillars, in which she glimpsed a table set for two and covered with cold meats, cheeses, cakes and wine. Here she was unceremoniously thrust into a chair. The stranger loomed up before her and looked down at her threateningly. "I've told you, Madam, that I don't relish these lovers' games you so enjoy. These attempts to arouse my jealousy are worse than pointless—they degrade us. I've had no liking for such behavior in the past and see no prospect of changing my mind in the future. If you wish to continue under my protection—"

"*Sir,*" cried Letty in dismay, "please say no more! You've made a terrible mistake and—"

The gentleman's expression of disgust could be discerned even through his mask. "Do you think to disarm me by this *newest* charade? I've no stomach for games, I tell you, even this nonsense you're attempting now."

Letty, breathless and frightened, could scarcely hold back her tears. "Sir, I b-beg you to l-listen to me—" she pleaded, her voice choked with fear.

"If I were in a better mood," the gentleman said, the anger in his voice receding, "I might find this playacting of yours a bit amusing. I had no idea that you were so good at it." With these words he took a seat opposite her, threw back the hood of his domino and removed his mask, tossing it carelessly on the table. "There, now, let's forgo this wrangling and try to salvage what is left of the evening. Shall I pour you a glass of madeira?"

Letty stared at her abductor speechlessly. She had recognized him as soon as he'd removed his mask. It was Roger Denham! She could scarcely believe her eyes. For months she had daydreamed of meeting him again, and here he was. And in surroundings that could have been delightfully private and romantic. But there was nothing romantic about being abducted by a man who was behaving like a veritable lunatic. As she stared at him in horror, she was filled only with the desire to run away from the place as fast as her legs could carry her.

With shaking knees she rose from her chair and stood before him. "Sir, I cannot tell you my name or remove my mask—it would embarrass us both. But please believe that I am not the lady you think me. I beg you to excuse me and permit me to return to my friends—"

He looked up at her, a reluctantly admiring smile appearing at the corners of his mouth. "You've disguised your voice very well, my love. I'll say that for your performance," he remarked. "Come here. We'll try something you *can't* disguise." And with that, he reached out, pulled her on his lap, put a strong arm about her shoulders and, before her cry of "My lord—!" had left her lips, his mouth was pressed to hers.

Letty couldn't even struggle, so tight was the grip in which she was held. Powerless to move, she submitted to the most intimate embrace she had ever experienced. She felt her blood burning in her cheeks and pounding in her ears, while she shivered from head to toe. Lord Denham's head came up sharply. "My God!" he gasped. "*You're* not—! You're trembling! What have I done? Who . . . who are you?" And he reached for her mask.

Shaken and breathless, Letty knew only that she must not let him learn her identity. "No, please!" she gasped and tried to fend off his hand.

At that moment there was a cry behind them. "So, my lord," came the shrill voice of a woman standing like a fury at the entrance of the alcove, "*this* is what happens the moment my back is turned!"

Denham hastily set Letty on her feet and jumped up. He stared at the lady who stood before them with her arms akimbo and her mouth stretched into a caustic smile. "Kitty . . . ?" he asked in confusion.

At last Letty understood, for the lady wore a shiny green domino, the twin of her own, its hood covering a mass of auburn curls quite similar to her own hair in style and color. And the lady's height and girth, too, were remarkably like hers. There, however, the resemblance ended. From what she could see of the lady's face under the mask which obscured her eyes and nose, Letty was not a bit flattered by Lord Denham's mistake. The lady was years older than Letty, and, in Letty's opinion, not at all pretty. Her lips were too thin, and there were hard lines around her mouth.

Denham looked from one to the other in amazement. Turning to Letty, he said quietly and shamefacedly, "Madam, forgive me. I don't know what to say to you. I *have* made a dreadful mistake—"

"Well, how long do you intend to ignore me?" the lady demanded. "Introduce me to that slut you've been fondling."

Denham whirled around and grasped the lady by the shoulders. "Damn it, Kitty, take a damper! Can't you see I mistook the girl for *you*?"

Letty, her breast heaving with a host of tumultuous and conflicting emotions, desired only to be gone from this place. Taking advantage of the momentary diversion of Lord Denham's attention, she ran between the two closest pillars into the shrubbery behind them. She heard Lord Denham swear and start to follow. The lady tried to restrain him, but he told her curtly that he had to find the girl, to apologize and restore her to her friends. Letty did not wait to hear more. The lady had detained Lord Denham just long enough to permit her to escape. Silently she darted across the lawn in the direction of the Grove and did not stop running until she had come out on the brightly lit quadrangle.

Almost immediately, she saw her brother, who was searching about for her with an air of desperation. Near hysterics, she pleaded with him to take her home. It took only one look at her strained face to convince him, and without questioning her further, he sought out Mrs. Lorimer, explained that his sister had the headache, and the two departed.

Once safely on the way home in a hired hack, Ned had turned to Letty and demanded to know what had occurred. Letty would say only that a gentleman had mistaken her for another and had handled her rudely. Ned hotheadedly had demanded that they return to the Gardens, seek out the miscreant and demand satisfaction, but Letty would have none of it. "Only take me home, Neddie," she had pleaded, "and let me forget the entire incident. The sooner forgotten, the better."

Ned obligingly had forgotten it within a week. But Letty could not forget. Her hero, she'd discovered, had feet of clay. A shrew of a woman—someone named Kitty, with auburn hair and a shrill voice—was "under his protection." Letty was not such an innocent that she was unaware of the meaning of the phrase; Kitty was his mistress. Kitty was a woman whom he kissed with passionate intensity. Yes, she now knew how men kissed their mistresses. It was disgraceful, shocking, appalling! And if Roger Denham were ever to come near her again, *she would want him to kiss her again in that very same way*. It was *that* awareness that shocked her most of all.

She had not stopped dreaming of him, but her dreams had changed. She no longer saw them waltzing together in a brilliantly lit ballroom watched by hundreds of envious eyes. Now, she pictured them alone in a tree-shaded grove, imagining herself lying in his arms in an intimate, blood-tingling embrace. Just thinking of it made her blush with shame and cover her face with trembling hands. What had that dreadful man done to her?

What an ironic twist of fortune it had been to have him approach her again—this time as a suitor for her hand! If she did not feel so much like crying, she would laugh at the way her fate had mocked her. Roger's mother had no doubt convinced him that the time had come to take a wife, and she, Letty, had been chosen as a likely candidate. It had been done through the machinations of her Aunt Millicent, she had no doubt. She could almost hear her aunt and Lady Denham discussing the advantages of the match— "Oh, yes, Letitia Glendenning is a perfect choice. So properly reared, so unexceptional, so unexciting and un-demanding." To them she was Lady Glendenning's complaisant, dutiful daughter. *Ha!*

Roger had evidently been a dutiful son, for he had let his mother arrange everything. Letty, completely in the dark, had been invited—was it only three weeks ago?—to spend some time visiting her aunt at Lady Upsham's elegant town house in Jermyn Street. She had been stricken speechless when Aunt Millicent had informed her that she was soon to receive a call from none other than the elusive Earl of Arneau, who had expressed his intentions of offering for her. When she could find her tongue to express her objections, her aunt had summarily dismissed them as "nothing but missish nonsense." Roger had paid a polite morning call, had driven her about the park in his curricle several times, had escorted her aunt, his mother and her to a play at Drury Lane and had proposed.

As a dutiful daughter, she knew what was expected of her. She was to make the best match she could, marry the man no matter what she felt about him, ac-cept whatever connubial demands he would make upon her, bear his children, run his home and ask no questions about his activities and liaisons away from home. She was sure she could accept those conditions—with any man in the world but Roger Denham.

No one could deny that Roger was as good a catch as it was possible for a young lady in her position to capture. She owed it to her family to accept him. And she had tried. When his intentions had at first been made clear, she had al-lowed herself to hope that he had changed—that he had given up his paramour and intended to turn over a new leaf. But it had not been hard to ascertain, from the many acquaintances who were only too delighted to pass on such juicy tid-bits of gossip, that Mrs. Kitty Brownell was known to have rejected several re-cent overtures—one from a duke!—declaring that she was quite content with her "present arrangements" with her Earl.

Could Letty marry Lord Denham, accept his bored but polite presence at her dinner table, his bored but polite kisses on her cheek, his bored but polite excuses when he absented himself from home? Could she play the game without flinching when she knew she would find herself filled with jealousy, realizing that he was finding love in the not-very-polite but not-at-all-boring arms of Mrs. Kitty Brownell? Lady Glendenning's dutiful daughter thought long and hard, through many sleepless nights and agonizing days, and she had come to the inescapable realization that she could not. She could not sentence herself to a lifetime of the sort of pain she was feeling now. She could *not*.

She turned over and buried her head in her pillow. "Mama, please forgive me," she whispered tearfully. "Your daughter can't be dutiful this time. Let me be wayward, just this once!"

Chapter Four

$\mathcal{L}$etty was not permitted the luxury of private tears for very long. An urgent knock at her bedroom door cut short her gloomy musings and brought her reluctantly to her feet. A quick glance at her mirror showed her that her eyes were too red-rimmed and her nose too swollen to permit speedy repair, so she shrugged helplessly and went to the door. Prue bounced in excitedly. "Aunt Millicent is back," she announced and perched on the bed. "They want us both in Mama's room right away."

"Both of us?" Letty asked in surprise. "Whatever for?"

"I can't imagine. Unless they want Lord Denham to offer for *me*!" Prue suggested with a giggle.

"That would be very obliging of Lord Denham, wouldn't it?" Letty muttered sarcastically, turning back to the mirror to see if she could in some way disguise the ruin of her face.

Prue tucked her legs up under her contentedly. "*I* wouldn't mind accepting an offer from Denham. It might be fun to be mistress of an enormous country house and queen it over hordes of servants, to come to London every month for balls and theaters, to buy lots of exquisite bonnets and—" Catching her sister's eye in the mirror, she gasped, "Letty, for heaven's sake! Have you been here *crying* all morning?"

"Yes, I have, if you must know. And how am I to face Aunt Millicent looking like this?"

Prue regarded her sister in sympathy. "What's the matter, Letty? Can't you tell me?"

"It's nothing, Prue, really. I'm just being missish. Be a dear and pay me no mind."

"Well, if you're sure . . . But we mustn't stay here talking, in any case. Aunt Millicent is waiting."

Letty sighed. "I thought I'd heard everything she had to say already. What else has she thought of, I wonder."

"And how does it involve *me*! Well," Prue said, getting to her feet, "we may as well go and find out."

"Can I go looking like this? Am I presentable?" Letty asked.

"You look terrible, but there's no time to do anything about it now," Prue answered encouragingly. And the two girls left the room.

Mama was sitting up among a dozen pillows, her face pale and her eyes underlined with purple shadows. Millicent was sitting at her side on a spindly-legged chair, still wearing her hat and pelisse. "There you are at last," she said sourly as the girls entered.

"Good afternoon, Aunt Millicent," Prue said with a quick curtsy.

"Good day, Aunt," Letty echoed. Then turning to her mother, she smiled and went to sit beside her on the bed. "You look quite done in, dearest," she said, taking her mother's hand in hers. "I've made you ill with my disobedience, haven't I?"

"What did you expect, goosecap?" her aunt asked in irritation.

Lady Glendenning patted her daughter's hand soothingly. "Never mind, sweetheart," she said. "I shall be up and about tomorrow, I promise."

"May I take your hat and pelisse, Aunt?" Prue asked primly.

"No, you may not," was the curt reply. "I don't intend to remain above a few minutes."

"Your aunt has a rather pleasant surprise for you both," Lady Glendenning put in cheerfully. "I think you'll both be delighted with the news."

The two girls turned to their aunt questioningly. Millicent looked from one to the other, frowned and spoke. "I've come to offer you a temporary solution to the predicament which you, Letitia, have made for yourself. Your name is already the subject of gossip and conjecture in the salons of London. Your mother and I have decided that it will be to your advantage to remove you from London for a few months, until the talk has died down. Since I always spend the late summer months in Bath, I propose to take you and Prudence with me for a while."

"To Bath?" Letty asked bewilderedly.

"With *me*?" Prue added with delight. "Oh, my!"

Millicent grunted. "At least *Prudence* shows some gratitude."

Letty forced a smile. "I'm grateful too, Aunt. Most grateful. I'd be delighted to accept, if Mama thinks she can spare me."

"Of course I can spare you. It will be the very thing for both of you," Lady Glendenning assured her.

"Oh, Mama," beamed the overjoyed Prue. "Bath! Only think of it! I've never traveled anywhere in my life." And she ran and hugged her aunt in enthusiasm.

"Enough!" muttered Aunt Millicent sourly, pushing her niece away. "I intend to be on my way by noon tomorrow, so don't waste time in effusive demonstrations. Go and pack your things."

"Yes, of course, Aunt Millicent," Prue said, trying to contain her excitement.

"Will you excuse us, Mama?" Letty asked.

"Yes, dears, go along. I feel so much better that I shall get up and come to help you select some suitable clothes in a little while."

When the girls had closed the door behind them, Lady Glendenning looked at her sister-in-law with misgiving. "Are you sure it's wise not to tell her that Denham will be there?"

"Yes. Lady Denham and I agreed it would be best. She is convinced that the reason Letty refused him is that their acquaintance was too short. She feels—and I am quite inclined to agree—that Roger was too precipitous. Half-a-dozen meetings in three weeks—they scarcely had time to become acquainted. A month or two in Bath, with very few other young people about to distract them, should do the trick. Of course, Lady Denham has not yet broached Roger on the subject . . ."

"Suppose he refuses to go?"

"He may balk, but he won't refuse. The attachment between him and his mother is quite strong."

"As yours is to my girls," Lady Glendenning said, smiling affectionately at her sister-in-law, "though you pretend to be indifferent. I hope you know how grateful I am to you for all you've done for my children."

"Whom else have I to care for?" Millicent said gruffly, standing up and adjusting her bonnet. "They are my brother's children, after all." She held out her hand to her sister-in-law. "I don't despair. With luck, we shall have them married before the year is out."

Lady Glendenning's smile clouded over. "I hope we're doing the right thing. All I want is my children's happiness."

Millicent dismissed her qualms with a wave of her hand and went to the door. "I don't know what maggot has got into Letty's head," she said firmly, "but don't let it get into yours. If those two do not make a perfect couple, I know nothing of human nature."

Lady Glendenning, mysteriously cured of the ailment which had sent her to bed, appeared in Letty's doorway an hour later, fully clothed and looking surprisingly healthy and cheerful. There on Letty's bed lay a huge mound of garments of all colors and descriptions. Prue was sorting the clothing into piles, watched by an abstracted Letty and the two younger girls, who were observing the activity with envious faces. "I see you've made a good start," Lady Glendenning said optimistically and entered to lend assistance.

"Here," Prue said to Gussie, "fold these petticoats. You may as well make yourself useful if you're going to sit here with us."

"I won't," said Gussie with a pout. "You're the one going, so *you* do the folding."

"Gussie, you jealous cat," Prue said accusingly, "you sound just like Clara."

"I'm not a jealous cat," Clara said sullenly, but she was ignored, as usual.

Lady Glendenning patted Gussie's head. "Don't be envious, Augusta. Your time will come one day, you'll see."

"I don't see that there's anything to be envious of," Letty added with a small sigh. "Bath is no longer a very exciting place to visit, unless one is elderly or infirm."

"Why, Letty!" her mother said in mild reproach. "How can you say so, when your aunt has provided you with the constant companionship of your sister to sustain you, and has undoubtedly planned any number of amusements and outings for you both to enjoy?"

"I'm sorry, Mama," Letty said, lowering her eyes. "I don't mean to sound ungrateful. It's just that I'm tired of being grateful to Aunt Millicent for things I don't want. If she hadn't . . ." But here she stopped herself, bit her lip, turned and went to the window, where she stood staring out at the summer blooms with unseeing eyes.

"Hadn't *what,* Letty dear?" her mother asked in concern.

"If she hadn't pushed Lord Denham to offer," Letty said from the window, "I wouldn't be in this fix, and we wouldn't have to go to Bath at all."

Prue looked up from the red Norwich crepe gown she was folding carefully and frowned at Letty in annoyance. "Well, I, for one, am glad she did. There's nothing lost by it—you are not being forced to marry him against your will, are you?—and *I* have gained this chance to travel. I don't care what you say about Bath—I shall love it. I've never been beyond ten miles of this house and, as far as I'm concerned, this trip will be a great adventure."

Letty, on whom the strain of the last few weeks was beginning to tell, wheeled about and snapped back at Prue curtly, "An adventure? You'll see what a great adventure it will be! We shall be beholden to Aunt Millicent for every bite of food, every night's lodging, every penny of pin money. Wait until you try to thank her, and all you get in return is a cold grunt. Wait until you try to dress for dinner and her sour-faced abigail, Miss Tristle, comes in to dress your hair, grumbling that she's neglecting her generous mistress, who insists on indulging spoiled young ladies at her own expense. And if you tell her you will not need her, she will sniff and say, 'Lady Upsham insists!' "

Prue stared at her sister, shocked. It was not at all like Letty to burst out in complaints. Letty had always been so gentle, softspoken and accepting. "Oh, Letty," she asked contritely, "is it really going to be as bad as that?"

Ashamed at having made an outburst, Letty shrugged and turned back to the window. Lady Glendenning sighed. "I know it's difficult for you to have to accept so much from her," she said. "Would it make things easier to bear if I told you that your Aunt Millicent *loves* doing things for you? With no children of her own, she delights in being a surrogate parent to you all."

"Does she?" Gussie asked in disbelief. "She always seems so . . . gruff."

Letty turned around. "Does she *truly,* Mama?"

"Yes, she does. Truly. Her gruffness only covers up a tender heart. All the Glendennings are like that. Even your father spoke in that grunting way whenever his emotions were involved." She sighed in melancholy recollection. "Dear man, he so hated to be thought sentimental."

Letty, thoroughly contrite, ran to her mother and knelt down before her. "Oh, Mama," she said tearfully, "I'm an ungrateful wretch."

Lady Glendenning smiled down at the auburn head in her lap and gently smoothed her daughter's tousled curls. "How can you be a wretch, you silly goose, when you are the very *best* daughter a mother could want?"

"Well, I *say*!" Prudence declared in mock offense. "What are *we,* your other daughters, to think of that, pray?"

Lady Glendenning laughed. "You are *all* my best daughters, as well you know. But, Letty, I've been thinking about what you said, and in a way, you're right. One doesn't like to feel beholden to a benefactor for *everything.* Perhaps we can find a way to provide you with your own abigail."

"Our own abigail?" Prue gasped with delight.

Letty looked up at her mother hopefully. "Can we afford it? It would be heavenly not to have to face Miss Tristle every evening."

"We might spare one of the maids . . ." Lady Glendenning said dubiously. The house was large and already understaffed, but she couldn't bear to see Letty so unhappy.

The neglected Clara let out a cry of dismay. "No, that's not fair! With Prue and Letty gone, that would leave too much housework for Gussie and me."

The justice of the complaint was apparent to everybody. They all fell silent. Prue looked at Clara speculatively. Soon her eyes lit up, as a delicious idea dawned. "I have it!" she said with a giggle. "Let's take Katie-in-the-kitchen!"

"Katie-in-the-kitchen?" Letty laughed. "What an idea! Prue, you're a genius!"

Lady Glendenning looked at her daughters in confusion. "Who *is* this Katie? Are you speaking of Cook's little cousin—the scrawny little thing who helps out in the kitchen?"

Clara nodded. "She's the one."

"But . . . what makes you think she'd make a satisfactory abigail?"

"I'm sure she'll be fine. Clara says that she's very knowing," Prue said, winking at Clara like a conspirator.

"I never said anything of the sort," Clara said sullenly. "And if you take her with you, who will help Cook?"

"Cook won't mind," Prue said airily. "She'll have two fewer mouths to feed, when we go."

Clara pouted again and flounced to the door in disgust. "I might have known I'd get the worst of it," she muttered. "Now there'll be no one in this whole household who'll tell me *anything*."

Katie-in-the-kitchen was sent for. She was indeed a scrawny girl, undersized for her sixteen years, but with a pair of shrewd eyes that looked out from her peaked little face and seemed to tell the world that here was a person not easily daunted. She was never at a loss for words. Even the surprising news that she was being invited to accompany Miss Letty and Miss Prue to Bath did not discomfit her. She cocked her head and looked from one to the other suspiciously. "Are you tryin' to tip me a rise?" she asked.

"Not at all," Prue assured her, the expression having been made familiar to her by Ned's frequent use of it. "Why would we want to fool you?"

" 'Cause I ain't never been a abigail afore. And I don't look so nice or talk so nice neither."

"We shall give you a lovely blue bombazine dress and a brand new white cap, and you shall make a very fine appearance," Lady Glendenning said soothingly.

"And as for not having been an abigail," Letty added with a smile, "Clara tells us that you know everything, so you should have no trouble."

Katie didn't blink. "I ain't sayin' as how I know'd *everything*, but I don't miss much. I suppose I could pick up the way of it quick enough. Don't know that I'd be much good at dressin' 'air, though."

"That's all right," Letty said. "We're quite accustomed to dressing our own hair."

"Well? Are you willing to come along with us?" Prue demanded eagerly.

Katie smiled broadly. "Willin'? If you 'ad to work in a kitchen, you'd a know'd the answer to that. I'll say I'm willin'! When do we start?"

They started the following morning. An impressive number of trunks and boxes were tied to the top of the Upsham coach, and three young ladies were helped aboard: first, Prue hopped up, her red-gold hair bouncing and her spirits soaring in joyous anticipation; next, Letty stepped up, subdued, brave and determined to show a cheerful facade to the world and to make herself forget what might have been; and last, the diminutive Katie, dressed in the finest gown she'd ever worn, her head erect as a queen's, permitted herself to be helped aboard as if she'd been to the manor born. Right on schedule, as a nearby steeple bell chimed noon, the coach lumbered off down the street, bearing its occupants to adventures which would turn out to be quite different from their various expectations.

It was not until three days later that Roger Denham paid the promised call on his mother. She lost no time in informing him that she wanted his escort to Bath. He readily agreed to provide it, but when he realized that she expected him to remain with her for several weeks, he firmly declined. Bath, he told her, was a dowdy, outdated, stodgy locality where neither good sport nor good company could be found, and he had no intention of rusticating there when he had everything he needed for contentment and amusement right here at home.

His mother then launched into a full explanation of her reasons for asking him to remain at Bath for so long a time. She wanted him to see Letty again. She told him bluntly that his pursuit of Letty had been inadequate—if not downright insulting to the girl. He had accused his mother of believing that his charms were such that no girl could refuse him, but was *he* not guilty of the same sort of conceit if he expected a girl to fall into his arms after a mere three-week acquaintance? "Did you ever have a sincere conversation with the girl?" she asked. "Have you ever spent more than two hours at a time in her company?"

Roger had to admit that he had not.

"Then what was the poor child to think of your proposal? Only that you wanted a suitable wife and didn't care much who she was."

"Well, that's really the truth of the situation, is it not?" Roger reminded her reasonably.

His mother looked at him disapprovingly. "It needn't be, if you'd only try to know her better," she suggested.

"If you have any expectations of my falling in love like a schoolboy, you're out in your reckoning, Mama," he told her flatly.

She sighed in discouragement. "I suppose I cannot expect too much," she said, "but you needn't have let the girl know how completely indifferent you are."

"At least my approach was honest. You wouldn't want me to mislead her into expecting more of me than I can offer her. If she's looking for a love match, she is right to refuse me."

"She has a right to expect some interest and affection from a suitor, even if some elements of romance are lacking. Marriage requires intimacy, in any circumstances."

Roger had to admit she was right. He had not gone out of his way to attach Miss Glendenning or to convince her that he had every intention of being a gentle, thoughtful, generous husband. He was certainly aware that the prospect of marriage could be frightening for an innocent young woman, and the prospect of marriage to a stranger might well seem terrifying. He had been thoughtless and unfeeling.

Once his mother had won this point, she was able to convince him to reconsider. Bath was very small, by London standards, and people mingled with each other constantly. He would find many opportunities to see Miss Glendenning, to draw her into conversation, to develop an understanding, to teach her to trust him, and to permit them both to feel comfortable with each other. Surely, she argued, he owed this chance to the girl and to himself.

Reluctantly, he agreed to remain in Bath for a fortnight. If, as he suspected, Miss Glendenning was quite indifferent to him, he would then return to London and the subject would be dropped. If, on the other hand, his renewed suit showed promise, he would abide by his mother's judgment and remain until the time was ripe for him to make his offer again. He chaffed a bit at the terms, but he had to admit they were sensible.

Roger left his mother's house with a feeling of resentment against all women. How they managed to cut up a man's peace! Until the subject of marriage had come up, he had been quite content. What was wrong with a bachelor's existence? He had everything a man could want—his home was comfortable, he had an army of servants to minister to his every need, a host of friends to provide amusing conversation and companionship, a mistress who was available when he desired her, and the freedom to spend his time exactly as he chose. A wife would only complicate his days and disturb his routine. What could a wife provide that he did not already have? His mother had given him the answer to that question—an heir. A man must do his part for posterity. Unfortunately, for him that meant spending a fortnight or more of numbing boredom at Bath. Oh, well, if it couldn't be helped, he told himself, he might as well accept it with good grace. With a shrug, he hurried off to his club to make as merry an evening as possible of his last night in London.

Chapter Five

The Glendennings' arrival at Bath coincided with the arrival of a week of chilling rain, a circumstance which not only dampened considerably the town itself but the high spirits of its newest inhabitants as well. As a result, Prue, who could not be restrained from venturing out to do a bit of exploring of her new surroundings, shortly came down with a head cold and was confined to her room until, her aunt told her firmly, all her symptoms had disappeared.

When three days of gloomy downpour had passed without the least sign of clearing, Aunt Millicent decided to pay a visit to the Pump Room in spite of the weather. Prue, she felt, was not well enough to join her in this expedition, but there was no reason why Letty might not be cheered by the outing, and she had no doubt that a drink of Bath's mineral water, ill-tasting though it was, would be beneficial to her. Strictly admonishing Letty to don a pair of thick-soled galoshes, Millicent opened a large umbrella and the two ladies ventured forth under its protection. With the umbrella above and the galoshes below, they walked the short distance from their lodgings on the North Parade to the Pump Room without too serious a soaking.

The Pump Room was surprisingly full of people who had been tempted out of their houses by a need for social intercourse stronger than their instincts to stay warm and dry at home. Letty looked around the imposing room with interest. Opposite the entrance was the focal point of the room—the pump itself, set before a window so large it provided light for the entire room. In a recess of the wall at some distance from her on the left she could see the famous equation clock, which had been presented to Bath by its maker, Thomas Tompion, almost a hundred years earlier. In a matching recess in the wall to her right sat a small group of musicians playing a selection of country airs. The music, combined with the cheerful sound of voices echoing in the high reaches of the ceiling, made a very pleasant din, which did much to lift her spirits.

Millicent, after pressing Letty to drink a glass of the much-praised mineral water, took her arm and began to parade around the room searching among the other strollers for a familiar face. Letty had barely time enough to note that the occupants of the room were preponderantly of middle-age or older when a feminine voice was heard behind them calling, "Lady Upsham! Lady Upsham!"

They turned to find a large-bosomed, gray-haired matron approaching them with a look of eager recognition. Trailing reluctantly behind her was a short, spectacled, thin-faced though handsome youth looking decidedly embarrassed. Aunt Millicent's face broke into an unaccustomed smile. "Why, Mrs. Peake! How good to see you here!"

The two women touched cheeks, and Mrs. Peake turned to introduce the young man. "I don't believe you've met my son, Brandon, Lady Upsham," she said, pulling the young man forward.

"How do you do, Mr. Peake? I thought you were at Oxford," Lady Upsham observed. Brandon Peake opened his mouth to respond, but Millicent, not really interested, went on. "And I don't think you know my niece, Letitia Glendenning. My brother's eldest daughter, you know."

Before the two young people could bow, the ladies had linked arms and proceeded to circle the room. Brandon Peake and Letty fell in behind them, Brandon surveying Letty shyly from behind his spectacles. Letty, searching for something to say, noticed that the young man carried a book with his finger marking his place. "I'm afraid we've interrupted your reading," she remarked.

"Oh, no," he said earnestly. "Not at all. I had hoped to find . . . That is, by your leave . . . I mean, I'm delighted to discover someone like you to talk to."

"Like *me*?" Letty asked.

"Well, yes . . . I mean . . . By your leave, someone more in my . . . That is to say . . ."

Letty smiled. "I know what you mean. Someone under the age of fifty."

Brandon colored and smiled gratefully. "Yes, by your leave, that's *just* what I mean. We've been here for over a fortnight and you're the first person of my age I've met."

"How terrible," Letty said with real sympathy. "Do you not have a brother or sister to keep you company?"

"No, I have none. Have you?"

"Yes, indeed. I have three sisters and a brother. Although only one sister is here with me."

"You have a sister here in Bath?" he asked interestedly.

"Yes, my sister Prudence. She has a slight indisposition and had to stay indoors today, but I'm sure she'll be out as soon as the weather turns."

"Well, well," Brandon smiled, "there will be three of us. That *will* be a merry change, if I may say so." Then, realizing that he was perhaps taking too much for granted, he looked at Letty shamefacedly and added a stumbling, "By your leave, of course . . ."

Letty suppressed a laugh and asked him what he'd been reading. The young man explained that he'd been studying the classics at Oxford, but that he'd contracted a severe inflammation of the lungs and had been sent home to recover.

"I'm surprised, in that case," Letty said, "that your mother permits you to come out on a day like this."

"Oh, I'm quite recovered now," Brandon assured her. "Healthy as the proverbial horse, actually. I'm only marking time until I can get back to school next month."

"I see. So your reading is by way of preparation?"

"Yes. I've fallen a bit behind, you see, and I'm trying to catch up. Today, I've been going over Thucydides again."

"Really? Reading history in Greek doesn't sound like much fun for someone just recovering from a long illness," Letty said with both admiration and commiseration.

"Oh, by your leave, I beg to disagree," the young man said earnestly. "I love history, and the story of the Peloponnesian War is particularly fascinating."

"My!" Letty said with a smile, "I suppose it must be."

The admiring look was all the encouragement the pale young man needed. He launched into a detailed explanation of those parts of Thucydides which he found particularly exciting and only stopped when Letty saw that her aunt and Mrs. Peake were saying their adieus. Brandon took her hand, thanked her for listening, hoped he had not been a crashing bore, told her that she was "very easy to talk to, for a female," and hoped, by her leave, to see her again on the morrow.

Letty, walking home with her aunt through the continuing rain, felt quite content. Brandon Peake was small of stature, shy, gauche and somewhat pedantic—certainly not the sort of man about whom she could weave romantic dreams—but he was well educated, sweet-natured and interesting to listen to. He had helped her while away the morning so pleasantly that she had thought of Roger Denham scarcely more than half-a-dozen times. Perhaps her aunt was right—perhaps here she would recover from the depression which had enveloped her for so long.

The following morning, Letty and Lady Upsham returned to the Pump Room. Brandon Peake immediately appeared to take Letty for a stroll around the room, while his mother and Lady Upsham sipped the waters and enjoyed a cozy chat on one of the rout benches, which were placed in every convenient nook. No sooner had Brandon launched into his topic for the morning, which was to illustrate the greater objectivity and re-creative powers of Thucydides over Herodotus—a point which Letty had no intention of disputing—when he was interrupted by the appearance of the Master of Ceremonies, who begged leave to introduce Sir Ralph Gilliam to Miss Glendenning. Sir Ralph was a lad of twenty, with two large front teeth and an occasional stammer. He expressed his delight at having discovered "some k-kindred souls" at what had previously seemed an unconscionably dull resort, and he followed them around the room, staring at Letty in adoration and interrupting Brandon's lecture at the most crucial points to say how delighted he was to have made Miss Glendenning's acquaintance.

"I thought you said there were no other young people here," Letty remarked to Brandon when Sir Ralph had at last taken his departure.

"By your leave, that was certainly my impression," Brandon said, puzzled. "I wonder if there are any others lurking about."

There were indeed others, as the next morning was to prove. The threesome was further increased by the addition of two more gentlemen—one was Osbert Caswell, a London youth who affected the *dégagé* in his hairstyle and casual dress, and the other a Mr. William Woodward, the stocky, sturdy and serious son and heir of a Lincolnshire country squire—and a young lady named Gladys Summer-Smythe, whose large and somewhat vacuous blue eyes shone with joy as she declared her surprise at discovering so many young gentlemen sojourning in Bath. Letty, Brandon and Sir Ralph gathered with the three newcomers near the alcove which housed the clock and spent the morning exchanging foolish pleasantries. Only Brandon remained silent, glowering at the others helplessly. Letty, noticing his displeasure, took his arm and drew him aside to whisper, "I thought you would be delighted to have so many young persons with whom to consort."

"Not anymore," he said bluntly. "By your leave, Miss Glendenning, they are all too foolish to converse with on any worthwhile subject. I can only say, as did Dionysius the Elder, that 'unless speech be better than silence, one should be silent.' And where," he added somewhat jealously, "were they before *you* arrived? You seem to be the flame, if I have your leave to say so, which has attracted this group of moths."

Letty laughed and turned to Sir Ralph, who was so overjoyed by this bit of attention that he confided to her that his friends all called him "Rabbit," and he hoped she would do the same. Brandon, completely disgusted, announced at this point that he had promised to restore Miss Glendenning to her aunt and, ignoring the vociferous objections of the other gentlemen, bore her away.

But Letty's reign as the Queen of Bath was to be short-lived. At the end of the week, as soon as the sun made its appearance, Prue emerged from her "sick-room" and announced her intention of joining her aunt and her sister on their daily expedition to the Pump Room. After lengthy argument, she succeeded in convincing Aunt Millicent that she was indeed free of any significant symptoms (for anyone could see that the slight sniffle which still troubled her was the merest trifle and might well disappear after she'd drunk a few glasses of Bath's salubrious water), and she ran gleefully to her room to begin the arduous task of picking the perfect dress in which to make her first appearance in Bath society.

Katie, who had been taking care of her during her illness, was consulted at every step of the dressing process, and it was Katie who decided that the pink dimity was too schoolgirlish, the blue linen more suited for early spring and the red Norwich crepe too unflattering to her coloring. At last, bedecked in a new morning dress of green jaconet, tied tightly under the bosom with silver ribbons, peasant-style, and wearing a fetching bonnet of beige straw with the tiniest poke and a mass of green feathers, she won Katie's approving smile and set off with her sister and her aunt to set Bath afire.

Her entrance into the Pump Room caused all heads to turn, a situation which made Letty blush with embarrassment but which did not at all disturb Prue, who reveled in the attention. "It's better to be looked at than to be ignored," she whispered to her sister flippantly.

Mrs. Peake expressed the view of the majority of the onlookers when she remarked to Lady Upsham that her younger niece was a striking-looking young woman, "although perhaps not quite as lovely as the elder, who, being taller, slimmer and more subdued in coloring, has a beauty which is more haunting because it is more subtle."

The subtlety was lost on most of the young men, however, and the ease with which they dropped their hearts into Prue's hand boded ill for the development of her character. From the moment that Letty introduced her sister into their circle, Prue became the focus of their attentions. Unlike Letty, who had treated them all with equal and polite indifference, Prue smiled flirtatiously at each one of them, laughed at their quips, teased them out of their shyness and played one against the other with a skill that belied the fact that she was just out of the schoolroom and had never met a young man in her life before, if one didn't count the dolts her brother had brought home from time to time.

Brandon Peake, however, remained aloof. Prue had smiled and flirted with him at this first meeting as she had with the others, but Brandon had not responded. He remained at Letty's side, watching the little scene Prue was enacting. After a while, he drew Letty away from the others, led her to a bench and endeavored to entertain her by expounding on Plato's view of the immortality of the soul as set forth in the *Phaedo.* But while he spoke, his eyes flitted to Prue every few moments. Something about her behavior disturbed him, yet he couldn't help watching her. "By your leave, Miss Glendenning," he said to Letty after a while, "I hope you won't mind my remarking that I find your sister's behavior a little forward."

"Forward, Mr. Peake? I don't know what you mean."

"I mean . . . by your leave of course . . . that perhaps it will not be considered seemly—Bath being a rather respectable place, you know—for a young lady to flirt so obviously with three gentlemen at once."

Letty jumped up and frowned down at Brandon angrily. He had never seen her in such a mood before. "Oh . . . I . . . beg your pardon. Perhaps I should not have spoken . . ." he began.

"No, you should not have," Letty said coldly.

Brandon got to his feet awkwardly, realizing that his words had been ill-chosen. Letty, ignoring his embarrassment, drew herself up to her full height, which was a full three inches greater than his, and said curtly, "If Bath society finds anything objectionable in a young lady who is doing nothing more reprehensible than laughing with her acquaintances, then it is made up of more dowdy a group of gudgeons than I had supposed!"

"I . . . I did not mean to offend you, Miss Glendenning," Brandon said miserably. "I only meant . . . After all, even the great Sophocles said—in the *Ajax,* you may remember—that women should be seen and not heard."

"Well, I *don't* remember, not having read it. And it is an extremely silly statement, even if it *was* Sophocles who said it, and the Greek women were very wise to ignore it, which they certainly did, if I know anything about Greek history."

Brandon lowered his head. "I most humbly beg your pardon, Miss Glendenning. I should not have presumed . . . That is, it was not my place . . ."

Letty, observing his discomfiture, softened. "Very well, Mr. Peake. Let us speak of it no further. Now, please sit down again and continue with your description of Tartarus. I find it most interesting."

Brandon, sighing with relief, resumed his lecture. Her ready forgiveness and her sincere attention to a subject so close to his heart did much to restore the pleasant comfort of their relationship. By the time they parted, they had agreed to call each other by their given names. It was only when he had to take his leave of her sister, Prue, that his awkwardness reasserted itself. He colored, stumbled over his words, and he took Prue's proffered hand so gingerly that one would have thought she carried the plague. When Prue glanced at Letty with questioning eyes, Letty could scarcely refrain from giggling.

"What on earth was wrong with Mr. Peake?" Prue demanded as soon as Brandon had left, and they stood waiting for Aunt Millicent to accompany them home.

"I'm afraid, Prue," Letty said with a laugh, "that Brandon finds you a bit overwhelming. I think he finds you *fast*."

"Fast!" Prue repeated, coloring angrily. "Of all the nasty—! What a stuffed goose! If you ask me, I find *him* a slow-top! He and his incessant 'by-your-leaves' are the outside of enough!"

"Well, you needn't fire up at *me*. I'm not responsible for what he says and does."

"You spent the entire morning in his pocket! What you see in him I can't imagine. He may be somewhat handsome, if one ignores his horrid spectacles, but he is inches shorter than you, and such a bore besides—"

"That's not fair. *You* may find him a bore, but I do not. I admit that he may be somewhat stuffy, but his conversation is so scholarly that I can't help but learn a great deal from him."

"Honestly, Letty, what can you possibly learn from him that's interesting?" Prue demanded sceptically.

"Many things. For instance, did you know that the saying 'Children should be seen and not heard' originally referred to *women*? Sophocles wrote it, in the *Ajax*."

Prue glared at her sister. "*Women* should be seen and not heard? Hmmmph! I can well imagine in what context *that* was quoted! It was directed at me, I have no doubt. Thank you so much, Letitia, for your scholarly lesson-of-the-day. But if tomorrow's discourse is like today's, I hope you will spare me the recital of it!" And she flounced off to find her aunt.

With the Bath season already well under way, the Assembly Rooms were the scene of nightly activities of great variety and interest; yet circumstances had conspired to prevent Lady Upsham and her charges from attending a single play, concert or ball since their arrival. Therefore, Lady Upsham's announcement that they were to attend the evening's concert in the Upper Rooms so delighted her two nieces that their little tiff of the morning was forgotten. The afternoon was happily spent in a shopping expedition to Milsom Street where Aunt Millicent, in an unaccustomed burst of good spirits, insisted on buying a new pair of gloves for Letty and a Florentine shawl for Prue. "It will be a special evening," she said, as if in apology for her unwonted generosity, "for it is your first formal appearance in Bath society. And nothing makes an evening feel more special than wearing something new."

Her generosity was more than rewarded, not only by the sincere gratitude of her nieces, but by the looks of admiration the girls received on their entrance into the Upper Rooms that evening. Both girls had chosen to wear blue. Prue wore a graceful lustring with small puffed sleeves and a three-inch flounce at the bottom, and had thrown the new shawl lightly over her shoulders. Letty wore a Tiffany silk overdress, which was buttoned beneath the bust with a pearl clasp and revealed a glimpse of its white satin underdress when she walked. A large number of people had gathered to hear the concert, and the din of their voices was perceptibly lowered when Letty and Prue entered the room and stood hesitantly in the doorway. Heads turned and people stared. Had they been alone, Prue would have been strikingly attractive with her red-gold hair, diminutive figure and laughing eyes, and Letty, lovely with her auburn curls, willowy grace and serene expression. But together in the doorway, the girls made a breathtaking picture. Aunt Millicent, aware of the admiring attention her nieces had attracted, was content.

Letty and Prue were too fascinated by their surroundings to notice the stir caused by their entrance. The elegant room, with its impressively high ceilings, gracefully shaped windows and magnificent chandeliers, was as lovely as any that could be found in London. Letty, absorbed in admiration of a particularly fine lustre, was suddenly jolted by Prue, who whispered urgently, "Hurry, Letty! Aunt Millicent has found seats and is beckoning to us." And she hurried down the aisle, not aware that her shawl had slipped from her shoulders to the floor. Letty stooped to pick it up. At the same moment, a gentleman who had been sitting on the aisle jumped up from his seat and bent to pick it up for her. Kneeling, their hands touched, and Letty glanced up to find herself looking directly into the smiling eyes of Roger Denham.

Chapter Six

"Allow me, Miss Glendenning," Lord Denham said, helping her up.

"M-my lord!" Letty gasped. "I didn't know . . . That is, I didn't expect to s-see you here."

"But I expected to see *you* here," he said, smiling at her with polished aplomb, "and I hoped I should find an opportunity to renew our acquaintance."

His self-assurance only succeeded in shaking her own. "Thank you . . . I mean, I don't think . . . That is . . ." and her voice petered out in hopeless dismay. She had no idea of what to say. She was so startled by his unexpected appearance that her mind didn't seem to be functioning. What had brought him to Bath of all places? This was scarcely the sort of place to attract a Corinthian whose activities had always been at the very center of the fashionable circles. But there was no time now for puzzling over riddles. She must say something—anything!—and make her escape. "I believe," she murmured, "that my aunt is . . . er . . . waiting for me. Please excuse me, sir."

She glanced up at him to find him regarding her with a most disconcerting look of amusement in his eyes. "Of course, my dear," he said, "but can you not spare a moment to greet my mother? She's sitting right there, directly behind you, and is eager, I'm sure, to say hello to you."

"Your mother?" Letty wheeled around.

Lady Denham was smiling up at her warmly. "How do you do, Letitia, dear?" she asked, holding out her hand. "How very lovely you are looking this evening."

Letty took the proffered hand and made a nervous curtsy. "Good evening, Lady Denham," she said awkwardly, and relapsed into blushing silence. She knew she should make some response to Lady Denham's compliment, but something seemed to have happened to her wits. A few phrases flashed through her mind—"I didn't see you sitting there," or "How delightful to see you here in Bath," or, "You, too, are looking very well this evening"—all of which she rejected for the inanities they were. But before her silence had become noticeable, a movement at the front of the room drew their eyes. The musicians were making their entrance.

"Oh, dear," murmured Lady Denham, "we shall have to postpone our conversation. But never mind. You are with your aunt, are you not? Tell her that Roger and I shall look for you both at the intermission."

Letty bobbed another awkward curtsy, smiled weakly and started quickly down the aisle. Suddenly, realizing that she had not said good-bye to Roger Denham, she turned and glanced back over her shoulder. He was standing where she had left him, looking after her. Meeting his eyes, which seemed to her to have a rather unholy gleam of mischief in them, she gave him the briefest of nods and turned quickly to rejoin her aunt. So precipitous was she in turning away from his amused regard that she blundered into a gentleman who was proceeding up the aisle in the opposite direction. Ready to sink into the ground in mortification, she made a blushing and incoherent apology to the stranger, who smilingly assured her that it was all his fault.

To add to her chagrin, she had a feeling that Roger had witnessed the entire scene. Unable to keep herself from confirming her fear, she glanced back up the aisle and saw, to her horror, that not only had he been watching but that he was coming toward her again. What can he want *now*? she wondered as she watched his approach fearfully. But when he came up to her, he merely grinned and said, "I'm afraid I neglected to return this to you." And he held out Prue's forgotten shawl.

"Th-thank you," she murmured miserably and, taking the shawl, fled down the aisle.

Her cheeks burning with embarrassment, she slid into the seat beside Prue just as the first notes of Handel's *Water Music* sounded. Prue, not the least bit interested in the music, leaned toward Letty. "What kept you?" she asked in a loud whisper.

"This!" Letty hissed, and tossed the troublemaking shawl on Prue's lap.

Lady Upsham, on the other side of Prue, frowned and leaned forward. "Is there anything the matter, Letty?" she asked.

"No, no. Nothing," Letty whispered back. "But Lady Denham is here and said to tell you she will join us during the intermission."

Aunt Millicent nodded without any apparent surprise at the news and sat back to enjoy the music. Prue, sensing some drama behind the little announcement, looked at Letty questioningly. But Letty shook her head and put a finger to her lips. Then she turned to face the orchestra and tried to concentrate on the lovely strains that had won for their composer the affection and support of a previously angry king.

But Letty couldn't concentrate on the music. Her cheeks still burned in embarrassment at the memory of her mortifying performance, her heart still beat rapidly at the remembered gleam in Denham's eyes, and her head still reeled with unanswered questions. That look in his eyes, as if he were enjoying a joke at her expense, was only to be expected when one thought of her behavior. She had acted like a veritable ninnyhammer. Never before, even when she had danced with him at Almack's so long ago, had she felt so gawky and maladroit. Even more bothersome to her peace of mind was her inability to sift out the confusion of her own emotions about facing him again at intermission. She was well aware that her emotions were a chaos of contradictions. Mixed with her misery was a strong feeling of anticipation. Mixed with her fear was a tingle of excitement. Mixed with her pain was a very distinct element of joy. None of these feelings was appropriate to the situation. None was a sensible reaction to a chance encounter with a man who was little more than a stranger to her. Inexplicable as Denham's appearance at Bath might be, Letty was sure it had nothing whatever to do with her.

Handel's music had never seemed so interminable. She could not wait for it to end. Yet she dreaded the moment the last chord would be sounded. She needed every moment to compose her mind and still the racing of her pulse. For this, the *Water Music* proved to be an ally, for by the time the music had ended and the applause had faded, she had regained some semblance of composure and was able to face the approach of Lady Denham and her son with at least the *appearance* of equanimity.

Lady Upsham and Lady Denham greeted each other effusively, and Lord Denham was made known to Prue, who, when learning the identity of the splendid-looking nobleman who smiled down at her, did all but gape at him openmouthed. When he turned away to exchange some remarks with Lady Upsham, Prue drew Letty aside and whispered excitedly, "I never took you for a fool, Letty, but fool you must be! How could you have refused him? He's *devastating!*"

"Hush, you idiot! Do you want him to hear you?" Letty answered in irritation. "And if you find him so devastating, why don't you ask him to offer for *you?*"

Prue was given no opportunity to respond, for Denham was approaching. With his practiced smile, he asked to escort Letty to the Octagon Room, where a table of refreshments had been laid out. Letty was about to make a polite refusal when she caught her aunt's eye on her. There was no mistaking the order in that glance. Letty was to accept. She threw her aunt a look of desperate appeal, but the answering glance held a command of such ferocity that Letty knew she had better agree.

Diffidently, she took Denham's proffered arm and walked with him out of the room. Roger, who had missed nothing of the little byplay between Letty and her aunt, gave her hand a sympathetic squeeze. "I know you're quite reluctant to accept my company, Miss Glendenning," he said with disarming candor. "I can't say I blame you. I perfectly understand that our situation is somewhat awkward."

"Very awkward, my lord," Letty admitted.

"But it needn't be. Even though you won't marry me, you may still *talk* to me, you know. Accepting my company to the refreshment table won't commit you to accepting my offer of marriage."

He was smiling down at her with his roguish look. It made her feel foolish and naive, and she lowered her eyes and said nothing.

Denham tried again. "If I promise to say nothing of marriage, I'm sure you will find me quite easy to talk to," he assured her with his unnerving self-confidence.

Letty felt a wave of resentment. He was talking to her as if she were a wilful child—as if her awkwardness came from her own lack of spirit rather than a dreadful situation which was completely of *his* making! With an intake of breath, she made a decision to match his candor with a bit of her own. "*Will* I find you easy to talk to?" she asked in a tone that was decidedly challenging. "I have not hitherto found you so."

Lord Denham looked at her in astonishment. This was not the sort of answer he'd expected. "What did you say?" he asked doubtfully. "Have you found my conversation . . . er . . . troublesome in some way?"

Letty, realizing that the answer to his question might lead her in a direction that was much too dangerous to approach, tried to draw back. "I . . . We . . . I see that we've arrived at the Octagon Room. Do you suppose they serve ratafia?" she asked innocently.

Roger cocked an eyebrow and surveyed her suspiciously. "You are trying to put me off the scent, Miss Glendenning, and I'm much too good a hunter for that. But, to answer *your* question before we return to *mine,* yes, I'm sure I can procure a glass of ratafia for you, if you're sure you want the dreadful stuff."

"I think I should like some, if you please," she answered mendaciously, well aware that ratafia was the most insipid drink imaginable.

Roger led her into the room, brought her to an unoccupied bench, bowed and went to the refreshment table. But the short interruption did not suffice to make him forget the subject under discussion. He quickly returned, handed her the drink and seated himself beside her. She peeped up at him to find him staring at her with interest—more interest, she thought, than he had shown when he'd asked her to marry him. Meeting her eye, he repeated his question abruptly. "In what way has my conversation been troublesome to you, Miss Glendenning?"

Letty lowered her eyes. "I've been too frank, I fear."

"Not at all," he assured her. "Frankness is a quality I very much admire."

Letty looked at him earnestly. "I've no wish for you to reproach yourself about . . . about anything in regard to me. Indeed, you've been . . . almost always . . . quite proper and kind. I should not have said what I did just now."

"*Almost* always?" Lord Denham persisted. "That means that, at some time, I was *not* proper and kind. Can you tell me when I was not?"

"Oh, dear, I *have* gone too far. Please, Lord Denham, may we change the subject?"

"Of course, if you wish. I don't want to make *this* conversation troublesome." His disarming smile made a sudden reappearance. "But I shan't let the matter rest for long. You've stirred up my curiosity, my girl, and it must, sooner or later, be satisfied."

Letty couldn't resist an impulse to tease. "You see?" she accused, with an impish smile. "You've done it again."

"What have I done?"

"Said something troublesome."

"What?" he asked in puzzled amusement. "Now?"

"Yes, you have."

"I can't think what it could have been," he said, watching her intently. The girl was almost enchanting, and he was surprised that he had not noticed it before. He smiled at her challengingly. "Either I'm a complete clodpole, or you are oversensitive."

"I don't choose to call you a clodpole, sir, but you *did* call me 'my girl,' which you must admit is a troublesome epithet for a young lady who . . . who . . ."

Roger laughed appreciatively. "A young lady who refused to be my wife. You are quite right. I *am* a clodpole."

With that disturbing gleam back in his eyes, he kept them fixed on Letty's face while he removed the glass gently from her hand (having noted that she had not drunk a drop), held it out to a passing waiter without even glancing round, and took both her hands in his. "Were my other troublesome remarks of the same nature," he asked her softly, "or were they even worse?"

Letty's smile wavered, her eyes dropped and she tried in vain to remove her hands from his clasp. "I thought we were going to change the subject," she said, her heart beginning to race.

"Tell me," he demanded with a smiling urgency.

She looked up at him with a show of defiance in her eyes. "Much worse," she said bluntly.

His smile faded, and he stared at her in dismay. "You're quite serious, aren't you? I *have* offended you in some way."

"You are being troublesome again, my lord. And I think you'd better release my hands. I'm afraid that we're becoming the object of a few curious stares."

Roger looked round to find her accusation to be quite true. With real reluctance, he released her and helped her to her feet. "Very well, Miss Glendenning, you win this round," he said as he took her arm. "We shall go back, though I'll admit to you that my pleasure in the music is quite at an end. But I intend to get to the bottom of this, and in the very near future, so take warning."

"You make too much of my nonsensical remarks, my lord," she said in the colorless tone she had used when he'd met her in the past, and nothing he said could induce her to say another word.

Roger was rather silent on the walk back to their lodgings, so Lady Denham took the bull by the horns and broached the subject in a direct assault. "I trust you made some headway with Miss Glendenning this evening," she said candidly.

Roger, who had been in a brown study, started. "What did you say, Mama? Headway?" he asked abstractedly. "Oh, you mean to ask if I encouraged her to look upon my suit more favorably. No, my dear, I've made no headway at all."

Lady Denham sniffed disgustedly. "Nonsense, you *must* have. Why, you spent over half-an-hour with her. Everyone remarked upon it."

"Did they?" Roger asked drily. "How very delightful. Shall all our encounters be clocked and watched like that—as if we were a pair of racehorses?"

"Roger, I hope I need not remind you that I'm your mother and will brook no disrespect. You needn't get on your high ropes with me. And you can't disappear with a refined young lady for over half-an-hour without having it remarked upon."

"I have often disappeared with a young lady—and for much longer than half-an-hour—without any ill consequences," he insisted.

"In London, perhaps, in that fast set with whom you choose to hobnob. But here in Bath, with the daughter of Lionel Glendenning, no, my dear boy, no."

Roger snorted. "Fast? *My* set? Really, Mama, you can't mean it. Denny Wivilscombe and Stosh St. John and Marmaduke Shackleford *fast*?" He laughed loudly.

Lady Denham was not amused but regarded her son with sceptical disdain.

"If you think to put me off my question by this obvious irrelevancy, you're off the mark," she told him curtly.

"I thought I'd answered your question," Roger said with false innocence, "but, to repeat, I saw no sign—in our over-half-an-hour *assignation*—that Miss Glendenning was any nearer to accepting me than she'd been when I asked her before."

"But *something* must have transpired between you. You've been completely abstracted since you restored her to her aunt."

"Have I been?" Roger asked. "If I have, it's because I've discovered some surprising facets in the girl. I'll admit to you, Mama, that she is not at all mousy, as I'd first supposed. She's hidden herself behind a rather thick wall of reserve, but when she reveals what lies behind it, she is quite—"

His mother looked at him keenly. "Quite what?" she prodded.

He grinned down at her boyishly. "Quite enchanting," he admitted.

"Well!" sighed his mother in satisfaction. "That is a remarkable discovery to have made in a half-hour *tête-à-tête*."

Roger laughed. "I know. You needn't say it. You told me so."

"So I did. Over and over. I'm delighted, though, that you've discovered it for yourself. It's not the sort of thing one wants to take another's word for—even one's own mother's word."

"I've made another discovery, too, that proves I have a very shrewd mother," Roger said, his smile fading.

"As if that needed proof," she retorted quickly. But, seeing his changed expression, her own smile disappeared. "Oh, dear, what now?" she asked anxiously.

"I'm afraid you were right about my having offended her. She hinted as much to me."

"I knew it! What had you done, you scoundrel?"

"I don't know. She won't speak of it."

"Won't speak of it? Why, Roger, it sounds as if you've done something rather dreadful to the girl!" she said, aghast.

"It does, doesn't it," Roger muttered, rubbing his chin ruefully.

"She gave you no clue at all?"

"No, none. She was completely immovable in her refusal to reveal the circumstances to me."

They had, by this time, arrived at the house, and their conversation was interrupted while the butler took their wraps. Roger requested a brandy to be brought to the study, but Lady Denham chose to go directly to bed. With a hand on the banister, she turned to her son. "Roger, it's incredible to me that you could so offend a young lady and not realize it. Think! Try to remember everything of your courtship. What could you have said or done to her?"

Roger sighed. "I've tried, Mama, truly. I've gone over it and over it in my mind. I tell you, our conversation was made up of the most trivial of commonplaces. I paid her compliments, which she answered in monosyllables. I made little pleasantries, to which she smiled wanly. I can think of nothing—nothing!—at all out of the way."

"But the girl is neither stupid nor mad. She cannot have *imagined* a slight!"

"I agree completely. I must have done *something*. But what? The only thing I can think of is my offer itself. You said I was by far too precipitous."

Lady Denham rejected the idea. "An offer of marriage is not *offensive*, even if it *is* precipitous. Unwelcome, perhaps, but not offensive."

Roger could only shrug helplessly. Lady Denham shook her head, sighed and went up the stairs. Roger retreated to the study, where he sank into a comfortable chair and sipped his brandy thoughtfully. But brandy offered no answer either, and in due time he gave up the puzzle and went wearily to bed.

Letty, too, found herself being subjected to close questioning by her family when they returned home that evening. First, Aunt Millicent asked her what she and Lord Denham had talked about for upwards of half-an-hour. Getting little satisfaction from Letty's evasive answers, she gave up and retired. Then Katie came in to help her into her nightclothes and asked a number of questions which clearly indicated that the perspicacious abigail had already learned—from what source heaven only knew—that Lord Denham had been present at the concert and had spent some time with Letty. Letty refused to answer. She dismissed the girl, telling her to see to Prue and leave her alone. But just as she was brushing her hair, the last chore before she would blow out the candles and retire for the night, her door opened and Prue, dressed only in a muslin nightdress, tiptoed in. "Oh, you're still awake," she observed cheerfully. "Good. I want to talk to you."

"Not tonight, Prue, please. I'm worn to the bone. Go to bed."

Prue ignored these remarks with such complete indifference that her sister could not be sure she had heard them. She perched on the bed cheerfully and tucked her legs up under her comfortably. "I think you must be mad," she said. "He's everything Aunt Millicent said he was—handsome and charming and kind. And he likes you. Really. I could tell by the way he looks at you."

"Prue, go to bed," her sister pleaded wearily.

"Did he do something dreadful to you?" Prue persisted. "Did he fondle your breast or some such thing?"

"Fondle my breast!" gasped Letty incredulously. "Good God, Prue, wherever did you get such an idea?"

"Well, promise not to tell anyone, but I read all about such things in a most shocking book called *Pamela*. Neddie's friend, Tom Vanleigh—do you remember him? The one with the spots—well, he gave it to me. All eight volumes. And I've had a terrible time hiding them, especially from Gussie, I can tell you! Well, anyway, in the story, poor Pamela is pursued by a Mr. B. who loves her but doesn't want to offer wedlock. So she refuses his advances, but he keeps attempting to seduce her, and he always comes up behind her at the most unexpected times and puts his hand—"

"Prue, that's enough!" cried Letty, horrified. "Such a story is too shocking to *read*, much less to repeat, and—"

"It's a *wonderful* story to read," Prue said defiantly. "I loved every word of it!"

"For shame! If you were a lady, instead of a brazen little hoyden, you would not admit to being the least bit interested in such a tale! And to suggest that a gentleman like Lord Denham would even *think* of behaving in such a monstrously rude fash—" But a sudden recollection of an embrace, in which she had been held so closely that a hand on her breast would have seemed tame by comparison, brought her up short. She fell silent and colored to her ears.

Prue did not fail to note her sister's embarrassment. Her eyes opened wide and, in an awed whisper, she gasped, "Oh, Letty! *Did* he—?"

"No, he did *not*!" Letty almost shouted. "And I'd be obliged if you'd remove yourself and your vulgar suggestions from this room at once!"

"Very well," Prue said, tossing her head proudly and getting up from the bed. "I'll go. But I'm not too far off the mark. I'm sure of that. *Something* made you color up like that." She went to the door and paused. Looking back at her sister, she said in a knowing tone, "I wouldn't let myself be too angry with Denham if I were you. He *did* ask you to marry him, which is more than Mr. B. did for poor Pamela—until the end of the story, that is."

"Prudence Glendenning—!" her sister muttered warningly.

"I'm going, I'm going," Prue assured her. "But if you continue to behave like a prudish old cat, you'll *never* get married." And by darting quickly out the door, she managed to escape being struck by the hairbrush which her infuriated sister had thrown in her direction.

Chapter Seven

The altercation between the sisters could not be classified as more serious than a squabble, and since squabbles between sisters are quite frequent in occurrence and petty in nature, the irritations they generate are not likely to be lasting. So it is not surprising that the following morning, Prue and Letty greeted each other with smiles of perfect amicability. The clear, bright day had lightened Letty's spirits and, with Prue wisely refraining from any reference to the subject of the night before, they entered the breakfast room hand-in-hand, greeting their aunt with high-spirited warmth.

All three were agreed that this lovely day was to be spent outdoors, and soon they were happily engaged in making plans for a morning stroll through the famous Sydney Gardens. This was interrupted, however, by the announcement that a morning caller—none other than Lord Denham himself—waited below. Lady Upsham instructed her butler to show him up immediately. As soon as the butler left the room, Letty mumbled an excuse and made for the door, but Aunt Millicent ordered her to resume her seat and to refrain from such skittish behavior. "It's time you learned to behave like a lady, my dear," Millicent said implacably. "You should count yourself fortunate that Lord Denham bears you no ill will and is willing to seek your company."

"But why should he *want* my company?" Letty asked in desperation. "What purpose could there be—?"

But her question was not to be answered, for Lord Denham entered at that moment. With a charming smile for each of the ladies, he wished them good morning and delivered a message from his mother, inviting Lady Upsham to take luncheon with her. As for himself, he would be delighted to have the companionship of the Misses Glendenning for a ride in his curricle.

Letty opened her mouth to refuse, but Lady Upsham broke in before Letty could utter a sound. "How thoughtful of you, Lord Denham," she said effusively. "It is quite the perfect day for a drive. And although I'm afraid I cannot spare Prue this morning—I require her assistance on an errand of some urgency—I'm sure Letitia will be happy to accompany you." With that, she turned to Letty with a look that brooked no opposition and said with a meaningful smile, "*Won't* you, Letty dear?"

Letty met her Aunt's eye with a rebellious flicker in her own, but realizing that an unpleasant scene would undoubtedly follow if she disobeyed the unspoken command, she submitted. Dropping her eyes to the floor, she nodded and said meekly, "Yes, of course, if Lord Denham can wait until I change into something more appropriate."

"I'll wait as long as necessary, of course," Denham said promptly, "although I think you look charming just as you are."

Letty glanced up at him distrustfully but met a look of such sincere sympathy that she was quite disarmed. Nevertheless, it was with a great deal of trepidation that, a few minutes later, having put on a fetching bonnet of natural straw and a camlet shawl, she permitted herself to be handed up into his lordship's curricle.

Prue and Aunt Millicent watched their departure from an upstairs window. "There," Aunt Millicent said with a relieved sigh when the curricle had disappeared from view, "that's done."

"What do you mean, Aunt?" Prue demanded forthrightly. "Are you making a game of poor Letty?"

Millicent frowned at her niece quellingly. "Never mind, Miss. Your manners are sadly in need of mending. For one thing, I don't like your tone when you address your elders. For another, I don't like your asking questions about matters that are not your concern."

Prue, never one to quail before an attack, remained undaunted. "I beg your pardon, but if you're going to tell whiskers involving me, then perhaps I'd best be in on the plot."

"Whiskers!" her Aunt exclaimed furiously. "Prudence, do you accuse me of telling a *lie*?"

"Well, didn't you? Prue asked reasonably. "You don't *truly* need me for any errand, do you? You only said that so Denham would have Letty to himself."

Millicent Upsham fixed Prue with a level stare and, drawing herself up to her full height, declared with dignity, "I do *not* tell whiskers, young lady. And I *do* need you for an errand. I need your help to . . . to . . . ." She hesitated, waiting for some inspiration to assist her.

Prue grinned mischievously. "To do what, Aunt?"

"To help me choose a gown to wear for my luncheon with Lady Denham,"

Millicent responded, without so much as a flicker of her eyelashes to indicate that she knew Prue would not be taken in by such a ridiculous answer.

"Oh, Aunt Millicent, really! As if Miss Tristle would permit *me* to—"

"Never mind Miss Tristle. I say I need you, and I do. And I don't intend to stand about bandying words with a jingle-brained snip of a girl who has more tongue than manners." She marched firmly to the doorway. "Now come along. We have a great deal to do this morning." She left the room without a further word.

Prue made a grimace at her aunt's retreating back, which managed to combine annoyed impatience with saucy amusement. "Huh!" she snorted under her breath. "Jingle-brained snip, am I? Well, not so jingle-brained that I don't know a whisker when I hear one." And making one last, disrespectful face, she followed her aunt out of the room.

Prue had not minded in the least being excluded from the drive in Lord Denham's curricle. Since Letty had not seen fit to confide in her sister about the true nature of her feelings for Lord Denham, Prue could not conceive how her presence on the drive would have been any help to Letty. The thought had crossed Prue's mind that perhaps she should try to attach Lord Denham herself and thereby rescue Letty from her predicament, but she soon realized that the scheme was too far-fetched. Lord Denham had taken no special notice of her and, as much as she admired his looks and demeanor, Prue had no personal interest in him. She was only seventeen and had never before gone into society. She looked on Denham as a member of an older generation. Although Prue wished her sister well, she was quite willing to allow Letty to deal with her own problems.

What Prue really wanted was the opportunity to develop her skill at coquetry on young men closer to her own age. Therefore, when Aunt Millicent suggested that she spend the morning in the company of her young friends at the Pump Room, she was quite content.

Aunt Millicent accompanied Prue to the Pump Room, where she left her in the company of Miss Gladys Summer-Smythe while she went on to pay her call on Lady Denham. Prue, completely unchaperoned for the first time in her life, felt positively lightheaded with freedom.

Unfortunately, however, Miss Summer-Smythe, whose first few weeks in Bath had been depressingly uneventful and lonely, welcomed Prue's arrival with the enthusiasm of a lost puppy for the arrival of its master. She immediately drew Prue to a rout bench near the clock and eagerly attempted to establish an intimacy between them by confiding to Prue all manner of girlish secrets, in particular her newborn but overwhelming passion for one of the young men in their "circle." Prue, her eyes roaming the room in search of a rescuer to interrupt this *tête-à-tête,* answered in polite monosyllables, but these were evidently encouraging enough to Miss Summer-Smythe to make her reveal the identity of the object of her secret passion: Sir Ralph Gilliam.

"Rabbit?" Prue asked, staring at the girl incredulously.

"Yes," Miss Summer-Smythe admitted, lowering her eyes in maidenly bashfulness. "Don't you think he's . . . elegant?"

"Elegant?" Prue repeated, trying not to giggle. Sir Ralph was the most *in*elegant man Prue could imagine. It was not only his rabbity appearance which was inappropriate for elegance, but his entire demeanor. He wore his shirtpoints so high that he could barely turn his head, and he was so conscious of the fit of his clothes that he constantly tugged at his waistcoat or smoothed out his breeches. The stiffness of his carriage, combined with his incessant tugging and pulling, made him appear ludicrously uncomfortable. "I'm not sure I would have chosen *that* word to describe him," Prue ventured.

"Oh, yes, it's the very word," Miss Summer-Smythe insisted. "His manners, his address, his . . . waistcoats. Why, did you not see him last evening at the concert? He was wearing a waistcoat of puce satin with wide yellow stripes. I'm sure it must have been the most outstanding waistcoat in the room." She glanced up at Prue and, lowering her voice to a dramatic whisper, revealed (for Prue's ears only, of course) the most exciting tidbit she could offer. "I told him so! Truly. When he approached me at the intermission, I actually told him so! I know it was terribly daring of me, but I said it. 'Sir Ralph,' I said, 'yours is by far the most outstanding waistcoat in the room.' You don't think it was too forward of me, do you? Telling him that?"

Prue, accustomed to the outspoken style of a large family, could only stare at Miss Summer-Smythe in amazement. At length she managed to nod and say, "It certainly *was* an outstanding waistcoat. I . . . er . . . noticed it myself," and endeavored to change the subject. Again searching the room for a rescuer, her eyes met those of Brandon Peake, who had just entered. He came to them immediately. "Good morning, Miss Summer-Smythe, Miss Glendenning. By your leave, Miss Glendenning, may I ask where your sister is today? I don't see her anywhere about."

"She is otherwise occupied this morning, Mr. Peake. *Our* company will have to suffice, I'm afraid," Prue said, smiling at him teasingly, "unless you'd rather go off into a corner and read that book you've brought with you."

Before Brandon could answer, the other three gentlemen arrived and greeted them noisily. As soon as the greetings had been exchanged, Miss Summer-Smythe blinked up at Sir Ralph and, interspersing her words with a series of self-conscious giggles, told him that his waistcoat was again outstanding. Since Sir Ralph had buttoned his coat, covering over all but the very edges of his waistcoat (which, since he knew it would not show, was a rather innocuous one of pale blue loretto), he stared at her dumbfounded. Prue, to cover what she felt must be an awkward moment for poor Miss Summer-Smythe, immediately directed her most enticing smile at the three gentlemen and demanded to know what had kept them all away until this advanced hour. The three, delighted that they had been missed, eagerly surrounded Prue and jostled with each other for her attention. Brandon had no liking for superficialities of this kind. He caught Prue's eye and, with a brief by-your-leave, took himself off. Prue was the only one who took note of his abrupt departure, her eyes following him until he took a seat across the room and opened his book.

Osbert Caswell, the tallest of the young men and the one most casual in his dress, leaned toward Prue, pulled at the ends of the handkerchief he'd tied around his throat and announced proudly, "I've written a poem about you, Miss Glendenning."

Prue, aware that Brandon's withdrawal had irritated her unduly, tried to recapture her former good spirits. "Have you indeed?" she asked with eager insincerity.

"Yes. I sat up half the night composing it. It's somewhat in the manner of Ben Jonson's 'Celia.'"

A giggle and nudge from Miss Summer-Smythe reminded Prue of that neglected young lady's presence. In an unaccountable wave of generosity, Prue attempted to share with her the attentions of the young men. Slipping an arm around her, Prue drew Miss Summer-Smythe into the circle and said to her laughingly, "I'm not terribly fond of 'Celia,' are you, Miss Summer-Smythe?"

"I don't think I've ever met her," Miss Summer-Smythe answered blandly.

There was a stunned silence for a moment. Then Prue quickly attempted to cover the gaffe by requesting Mr. Caswell to read his lyric aloud. This Mr. Caswell refused to do. "It's for your ears alone, lovely lady," he insisted and would not be moved.

"I wonder where Mr. Peake has gone?" Miss Summer-Smythe asked suddenly.

Sir Ralph glanced around and spotted Brandon seated some distance behind them. "There he is. Shall I get him for you?"

"No, no," Prue said quickly. "He's deep in his heavy reading, as usual. We mustn't disturb him, must we, Miss Summer-Smythe?"

Miss Summer-Smythe looked around toward Brandon. "I don't think it's heavy reading," she declared seriously. "It's only a very *little* book."

For Prue, this was the last straw. While the gentlemen struggled to keep from laughing, Prue lowered her eyes demurely and said nothing. But her sympathetic feelings for Miss Summer-Smythe evaporated as suddenly as they'd come. The silly chit could manage for herself from now on. Prue washed her hands of her.

Sir Ralph restored the equilibrium of the group by referring again to Osbert's poem and demanding a reading. When Prue added her voice to the rest, Osbert weakened and took from his pocket his magnum opus, a poem of two eight-line stanzas which would have taken no more than two minutes to read had not every line been greeted with hoots, catcalls and derision. Every 'rosy lip,' every 'glance divine,' every 'coppery curl' was met with a loud laugh from the listeners. Every 'whilst' and 'beguil'st,' every 'lover pained' and 'kiss abstained' was ridiculed merrily. Before very long, even the poet himself had joined in the hilarity, for he was quick to learn what many writers had learned before him—that if one cannot move one's readers to tears, moving them to laughter is the next best thing. So successful was the comic rendering that his listeners demanded three readings before they were satisfied.

Prue, her sides aching from her laughter, looked up to find that Brandon had returned and was regarding her balefully. "Aha!" she clarioned. "You've returned! No doubt you've finished your book and, having nothing better to do, decided to rejoin us."

The others, their discrimination having been weakened by laughter, reacted as if Prue had said something of enormous wit. They roared. Brandon merely frowned and asked Prue if he might, by her leave, have a word with her in private. Prue raised her eyebrows in surprise, excused herself and walked away on Brandon's arm. "Well, sir," she asked when they were out of earshot, "what is it you wish to say to me?"

"I hope that you'll not take this amiss . . . That is, I realize that it is not my affair, but . . . by your leave . . ."

"I've given you my leave by accompanying you, sir. Please speak up," Prue said with a shade of impatience.

"With your own reputation as my only concern, Miss Glendenning, I merely wished to point out that you've been the object of some . . . er . . . disapproval from the . . . er . . ."

Prue frowned at him in dawning annoyance. "I think I begin to feel the direction of the wind," she said stiffly. "Are you about to offer me a scolding, Mr. Peake?"

"No, no, of course not. I would scarcely call it . . . No, indeed. Merely a cautionary word of advice from someone who—"

"Someone who is almost a stranger to me—isn't that right, Mr. Peake?"

"Perhaps. But, you see, my friendship with your sister is my justification for presuming to speak to you on a matter which I would otherwise not venture to broach."

"Indeed? Do you think my sister would countenance such presumption?" Prue asked angrily.

Brandon began to feel misgivings. "I suppose not," he admitted, "b-but I only wished to point out to you that your . . . by your leave . . . your beauty, if I may be blunt, is such that you attract many eyes, and therefore it behooves you to show even more restraint than is necessary for other young women—"

"I'm glad you find me beautiful, sir, but I fail to see—"

"I didn't say *I* find you beautiful, exactly. I mean, I do, of course . . . that is . . . I mean that *others* do, and therefore your rather unseemly conduct this morning seems all the more indecorous because people tend to keep their eyes on you . . ."

"I see," Prue said with dangerous restraint, her eyes giving off a steely glint. "Other people—but not you, of course—find me beautiful, and therefore I may not enjoy myself with my friends. Is that what you're saying?"

"I'm afraid I'm not expressing myself at all well, Miss Glendenning," Brandon said, beginning to feel acutely uncomfortable in his chosen role as protective uncle. "I only meant to remind you of the wisdom of Aesop when he said, 'Outward show is a poor substitute for inner worth.' "

"I was wondering when you would come forth with a quotation. That was the one thing this conversation lacked," Prue said nastily.

"I'm sorry if my tendency to rely on quotations offends you," he responded lamely.

"Your tendency to rely on quotations is the least of it!" Prue burst out. "Your temerity in speaking to me at *all* on this matter offends me! Your calling my behavior unseemly offends me! Your avuncular manner offends me! And even your calling me beautiful offends me!"

Brandon, unaccustomed to the emotional outbursts of women, was completely taken aback. "I . . . I'm . . . sorry," he stammered, backing away from the angry flash of her eyes. "I m-meant no harm . . ."

"Meant no harm? Meant no harm? You call me a vulgar hussy and then say you meant no harm?"

"V-Vulgar hus—? I never said . . . ! Miss Glendenning, please believe me! I never meant to imply—"

"How else am I to interpret what you said?"

"I merely indicated that your rather noisy frivolity was a bit unseemly, that's—"

"Unseemly! That, Mr. Peake, is not much better than *vulgar*!" Prue snapped and turned her back on him.

Brandon came up behind her and said placatingly, "Please forgive me, Miss Glendenning. I meant it for the best. As Sophocles said in his great *Antigone*, 'None love the messenger who brings bad news.' "

Prue wheeled around and found herself face to face with her accuser. Staring at him stonily, her mind made irrelevant note of the fact that, slight in stature as he was, he stood at least an inch taller than she. Summoning all the control she could muster, she said spitefully, "But you see, Mr. Peake, I don't consider you to be the messenger. As far as I'm concerned, you are the bad news!"

Poor Brandon was stunned. "By your leave, Miss Glen—" he began.

"By *your* leave, Mr. Peake, I don't wish to hear any more. I intend to return to my friends and comport myself exactly as I wish. And I'll thank you to take no further notice of my behavior. In fact, I'd be delighted if you took your by-your-leaves and your classical quotations and never spoke to me again!"

She turned on her heel and ran quickly back to her friends, leaving Brandon bemused, remorseful and miserable. To make matters worse, he looked around to find himself the object of several curious stares. There was nothing for him to do but take his leave. Prue, on the other hand, resumed her laughter and flirtations with more energy than before, until she realized that Brandon was no longer in the room. Then some of her spiritedness seemed to desert her, and although she continued to smile indiscriminately on her three swains, she noticed that somewhere at the back of her throat she felt very close to tears.

In the meantime, Lord Denham was doing his best to find a way to penetrate his companion's thick wall of reserve. He had set a course for Limpley Stoke, promising Letty that she would have much picturesque scenery to enjoy, for the road ran along the Avon's banks for several miles. For the first hour he engaged in the kind of polite and amiable exchanges which had marked their conversation during his brief "courtship," but as the distance from Bath increased and the traffic on the road became lighter, he gave the horses their heads and turned his attention to the girl beside him. "It is quite lowering to realize, Miss Glendenning," he said disarmingly, "that I owe your company today to the coercion of your aunt."

Her eyes flew to his face and, finding him smiling down at her kindly, she colored slightly. "I . . . I . . . would not call it coercion, exactly. My aunt, despite a rather forbidding exterior, is really very kind."

"I didn't mean to imply that she would *beat* you, my dear," Lord Denham said drily. "I only meant that, without her urging, you would not have come."

"You are embarrassingly direct, my lord."

"I'm sorry if I make you uncomfortable, but I know no other way to learn to understand you. Why did you not wish to ride with me today?"

"I should think the answer to that would be evident," Letty said, matching his directness with her own. "People in our . . . situation do not usually seek out each other's company, do they?"

"By 'our situation' you are no doubt referring to the fact that I am your rejected suitor. I can perfectly understand your reluctance to accept me as a husband, Miss Glendenning, but does it necessarily follow that I am unacceptable as a friend as well?"

She looked up at him candidly. "As a friend, my lord? Is that your purpose in seeking me out? To develop a friendship between us?"

"Yes, *one* of my purposes. Why not?"

"I know that friendships between men and women do exist, but I can't believe they can come about after such a beginning as ours," Letty said sceptically.

"I don't think there are any immutable rules governing the conditions in which friendships can develop," he pointed out reasonably.

"Perhaps not, but in our case, there are . . . certain blocks . . ."

"Such as?" he asked intently.

She lowered her eyes. "Such as a feeling of discomfort . . . about the past."

"But I assured you last night that we need think no more about the past. I promise to avoid the subject of marriage completely—at least until or unless you give me leave to reopen it. Doesn't that dispense with the embarrassment of the past?"

Letty, intensely aware of a greater embarrassment by far than his rather uninspired proposal, did not answer.

"Doesn't it?" he insisted, looking at her closely.

She knew that a negative answer would prompt closer inquiries, and a positive one would be tantamount to giving him permission to pursue their relationship. Either course of action would give her pain. How like him to place her in this untenable position!

Before she could decide what to say, he abruptly steered the horses to the side of the road and brought them to a halt. He threw down the reins and turned to her, grasping her shoulder and turning her so that she had no choice but to face him squarely. "Letty, let's be honest with each other," he said earnestly. "I know I thrust upon you an unwanted proposal of marriage, and that I've said or done something that offended you. But please believe that I wish nothing more than to make amends."

Letty raised her eyes and looked at him levelly. "That is not honest. It's your *mother's* wish, not yours."

Roger dropped his hold on her and stared in astonishment. He had not expected quite so much honesty as that. "My mother's wish?" he asked awkwardly.

"Your mother's and my aunt's," she said calmly.

Roger smiled ruefully and rubbed his chin. "That's a leveler," he admitted. "You have me there."

"Then there isn't any more to be said, is there? I think you'd best turn the horses around and take me home."

"No, not quite yet, young lady," Roger said, undaunted. "There is still a great deal to be said. I admit that, at first, my interest in you was inspired by my mother. But since last night my interest has needed no outside prodding. In fact, I've been wishing that both your aunt and my mother would, in future, stay out of our affairs. I hope you believe me."

"It makes no difference whether I do or not," Letty told him bluntly. "A friendship between us is impossible in any case."

Roger shook his head. "If we were to be completely honest, my girl, we'd admit that even the things we've just been saying are nothing but subterfuge and nonsense. There can be only *one* real barrier to a friendship between us."

"Oh?" Letty couldn't resist asking. "And what's that?"

He took her chin in his hand and tilted up her face. "That you hold me in dislike," he said simply, his eyes fixed on her. "Only tell me *that,* and I shall disturb you no further."

Letty, forced to meet his dark, questioning regard, felt herself freeze. Tell him you dislike him, she told herself. It was much the simplest solution to this tangle. One simple little sentence—I cannot like you, sir—and he would be gone from her life. But her throat was constricted, and she could scarcely breathe. She couldn't even lower her eyes to escape his penetrating look. No words came.

The look in his eyes changed. Without taking his eyes from her face or releasing her chin, he slipped his free arm around her and gently drew her to him. "Does your silence mean that you *don't* dislike me?" he asked softly, his eyes glinting with a smiling warmth. "That you feel *some* little liking?"

Her heart was racing. He was too close, his look too intimate. She had to put an end to this—now! But still she couldn't speak.

"Say something, girl," he urged, smiling. "Just say that you feel enough liking to pursue a friendship. Just a *little* would be enough."

He had had no intention of kissing her. She was so young and looked so frightened, he knew that she would require the most gentle, sensitive handling. But at that moment her bonnet slipped back, and her face, which had been partially shadowed, was suddenly fully exposed. He was struck forcibly by its surprising sweetness and something that was not sweet—something unfathomable and mysteriously challenging—lurking in her eyes behind the fear, and he forgot himself. Almost without realizing it, he bent his head to hers.

Sensing his intention, she found her voice. "No!" she gasped, trying to push herself away from him. "No—!"

But it was a gentle kiss, soft and undemanding, and she realized that she could pull away easily if she wished. She felt dizzy, however, and everything seemed to be spinning around, requiring that she shut her eyes and cling to him for support. After a while, he let her go, but it took a moment more before she felt steady enough to open her eyes. When she did, she found him looking down at her with just the merest hint of a smile in his eyes and at the corners of his mouth. He leaned over to her, replaced her bonnet firmly on her head, then stooped and picked up the reins. She stared at him wordlessly as he calmly turned the horses around. Then he turned to her. "I think we may safely say," he said, his hint-of-a-smile broadening into an infuriatingly exultant grin, "that you like me enough."

Chapter Eight

$\mathcal{L}$etty knew she was not in her best looks when she entered the Pump Room with her aunt and her sister the following morning. The blue shadows beneath her eyes and the excessive pallor of her face could be directly attributed to the fact that she had spent another sleepless night. Even Aunt Millicent had noticed the ravages the night had wreaked in her appearance and had suggested that she return to bed. But Letty would not hear of it. She had an urgent need to visit the Pump Room this morning—a need which neither her aunt nor her sister could suspect. With luck, this morning's activities would bring a solution to her problem.

For Letty's sleepless night had not been in vain. With the early-morning light an idea had dawned—an idea of such audacity, deceit and cunning that she was dismayed that she had thought of it. It was an idea completely unworthy of Mama's sweet, obedient, well-behaved, dutiful daughter, and she laughed aloud in pure pleasure as she imagined putting it into action. It was shockingly dishonest and unladylike, but it was the very thing to put that unprincipled libertine, Roger Denham, in his place.

Letty knew that she should reject the idea out-of-hand. There was no doubt at all that it was highly improper and unworthy. But it was the only way she could think of to keep Roger at arm's length, and she knew that he must be kept away from her at all costs. She had spent the last few sleepless hours reliving the events of that morning, enduring the humiliation of realizing that she had behaved in the most spineless, weak-kneed, addlepated manner imaginable. Lord Denham had certainly carried the day. Not only had she not repulsed his brazen advances—she had met his embraces with only the flimsiest, the most feeble pretense at resistance. She had lain in his arms as bedazzled as a schoolgirl, unable to utter a word. She had been an easy conquest, an almost-willing victim of his practiced charm. But this idea—if she could put it to work—would be her armor against him in the future.

She looked around the Pump Room gingerly, hoping for a glimpse of Brandon Peake, the person who would be most instrumental in putting her plan into action. But he was not there. At that moment, she was startled to hear Prue whisper in her ear, "Thank goodness he isn't here!"

"Who?" Letty asked, confused.

"Mr. Peake," Prue said, making a face. "I hope he's broken a leg or something."

"Prue!" Letty exclaimed, shocked. She had an uneasy feeling that Prue had been reading her mind. "Why?"

"Why! Because he's an odious, spying, priggish fool, that's why!" Prue declared venomously.

"Has he done something to offend you, Prue?" Letty asked in surprise. "He seems to be a most docile, agreeable young man."

"Agreeable? Not to me," Prue said. "I hope I never see him again. I'll tell you about it later."

Fortunately for Prue, Letty was too preoccupied with her own thoughts to notice that, for the rest of the morning, Prue's eyes flicked to the doorway every few minutes, unconsciously watching for the appearance of the young man she hoped never to see again. Letty, too, watched the door for the very same young man, but Brandon Peake did not appear.

Brandon, chagrined and embarrassed by the scene with Prue the day before, had decided to avoid the Pump Room. Instead, he went for a stroll in the Parade Gardens. He paced its lanes until he had traversed every corner of the park, but his spirits remained downcast. Finally, weary and depressed, he sat down under a shady tree, pulled a book from his pocket and tried to lose himself in his reading. So quickly did the book absorb him that he didn't hear the clatter of approaching hooves until a horse and rider flew by him, liberally spraying him with a shower of pebbles and mud. With a sharp oath, he got to his feet, berating the careless horseman loudly and brushing himself off.

The horseman, however, had pulled up, dismounted and, leading his horse behind him, was walking quickly back in Brandon's direction. "I say, I'm terribly sorry," the rider said as soon as he came within earshot. "I didn't see you sitting there until I was almost upon you."

Brandon, not one to hold resentment long, was perfectly willing to forgive him. "Oh, it was nothing. No real harm done," he assured the rider, who had now come up to him.

"But your breeches are badly stained!" the rider said. "I am most truly sorry. If you'd care to step round to my rooms—they're only a short distance from here—my valet will see to them immediately."

"Thank you, but that won't be at all necessary. It's the merest trifle, sir, I assure you," Brandon told him. "Oh," he added, recognizing the rider, "you're Lord Denham."

"Why, yes," Roger said, putting out his hand with a ready smile, "but I don't think I—"

"I'm Brandon Peake. We haven't met, but I saw you the other evening at the concert. You were speaking to Miss Glendenning. Lady Upsham told me who you were."

The two men shook hands warmly. "Are you well acquainted with Miss Glendenning, Mr. Peake?" Roger asked.

"With Miss Letitia Glendenning, quite well. She has been kind enough to show an interest in my studies."

"Really? You are most fortunate," Roger remarked casually.

"Yes," Brandon agreed. "Not many young ladies are interested in the classics. Her sister, Prue, for instance, thinks my studies are the greatest bore."

"Oh? Does she?"

Brandon sighed. "I'm afraid so. She told me in so many words that my classical quotations were . . . were . . ."

"Were what, Mr. Peake?" Roger prodded, watching Brandon with amused curiosity.

"She said they were . . . *offensive*," Brandon admitted with a blush.

"Offensive! I'm sure you must have misunderstood—"

"No, I don't think so. Miss Prudence Glendenning doesn't mince words."

"It seems not," Roger said, trying to hide a smile. "I don't know her very well, but she seems a very lively girl. Sometimes lively young women are wont to say things they don't mean."

"Oh, well, I don't suppose it matters, one way or the other," Brandon said glumly.

"No, I suppose not, especially since the *other* sister is so encouraging," Roger ventured.

"Yes, the elder Miss Glendenning is quite interested. I've been thinking of reading some of *this* to her. Catullus, you know. I would like to hear her reactions to some of these lyrics—the more proper ones, of course."

"Are you reading Catullus?" Roger asked enthusiastically, reaching for the book and leafing through the pages. "I was quite fond of him, too, when I was your age."

"Oh, do you know the classics, Lord Denham?" Brandon asked in surprise. "I didn't think . . ."

Roger grinned at him. "Didn't think a man of my stamp would ever open a book—is that it?"

Brandon nodded guiltily. "I meant no disrespect, sir. It's only—by your leave—you Corinthians, especially those of note like yourself, are not usually known for your scholarly abilities."

"I don't claim to be a scholar, not by any means, but I did engage in serious study of the classics in my school days—with great enjoyment, I might add—and even now may be found in my library from time to time for purposes other than sitting by the fire with a glass of port."

"I do apologize, my lord," Brandon said in a chastened voice.

"Don't be a cawker. How would you be expected to know my interests?" Roger pointed out reasonably. "But to return to the subject of Catullus, what made you choose him to read to Miss Glendenning?"

"No special reason, exactly," Brandon said quickly. "It's only that it occurred to me today that he is the only Roman who knew anything about real love."

"You mean because he fell into it *per caputque pedesque*?" Roger asked with a small smile.

"Well, yes, for one thing. After all, 'head over heels' is the only way real love comes about, don't you think? Not casual and practiced, like Horace or Ovid," Brandon asked earnestly.

"I suppose, at your age, it is usual to think so," Roger answered thoughtfully. "Does it strike you that Miss Glendenning is especially interested in love poetry?"

Brandon seemed nonplussed by the question. "I thought *all* young ladies were interested in love poetry. Aren't they? Are you suggesting that you think she might not care for Catullus? I mean to read only the most proper and heart-felt of the poems, of course."

"No, I didn't mean to suggest anything at all," Roger assured him. "I'm sure she will enjoy the poems enormously. But I mustn't keep my horse standing any longer. Why don't you drop in to see me later on? I have a new translation of Horace that might interest you."

Brandon stammered an acceptance with obvious pleasure. He watched as Lord Denham mounted his horse, waved briskly and rode off. Brandon then walked back to his lodgings feeling more cheerful than he'd felt all day. How lucky he was to have found someone with whom he could talk!

To Brandon's surprise, his mother greeted him at the door, obviously in a flurry. She seemed quite overset by the fact that Brandon had received a note from Miss Glendenning. She handed it to him with a hand that shook with agitation. "What does Miss Glendenning want with *you*, my dear?" she inquired urgently.

Brandon stared at the note, feeling a little agitated himself. "I'm sure I couldn't say, Mama," he answered, unwilling to open it in front of her. "Did the messenger say which Miss Glendenning had sent it?"

"*Which* Miss Glendenning? Why, I never thought to ask. Are you on terms of such intimacy with *both* of them?"

"Intimacy?" Brandon said, looking at his mother with annoyance. "Of course not. Not with either of them. What sort of question is *that*?"

"Well, I'm sure that when *I* was a girl, I would never have been so forward as to send a note to a young man with whom I was barely acquainted," Mrs. Peake said with a scornful sniff.

"Never mind, Mama. I'm sure that it's nothing of importance. If you'll excuse me, I'll go to my room," Brandon said impatiently.

"Very well, I'm sure it's none of my business if young ladies choose to write to you. I only hope you realize that a connection with the Glendennings is not what I'd hoped for you. I have it on very good authority that poor Lady Glendenning has been left without a feather to fly with."

Brandon groaned under his breath and made a hasty escape. As soon as he'd closed his door, he opened the missive and read it eagerly. It was a briefly worded but urgent request that he pay a call at their house on the North Parade that afternoon at three. It was signed L.G.

Promptly at the appointed hour, Brandon reached for the door knocker at Lady Upsham's house on the North Parade. Before he could knock, however, the door was opened by Letty herself. "I've been watching for you," she said in a whisper. "Come in quickly. I don't want anyone to know you're here." Taking his hand, she led him to a small sitting room near the stairs and closed the door behind them. "There. We shall be safe now. Aunt Millicent and Prue have gone out, so we shan't be disturbed."

"By your leave, Letty, if you've asked me here to scold me about what I said to your sister yesterday," Brandon said quickly, "you needn't have gone to all this trouble. I've scolded myself enough already."

Letty looked at him in bewilderment. "What? I don't know what you're talking about. Did you say something dreadful to my sister?"

"Didn't she tell you?"

"No, not a word. Although, now you mention it, she did say something this morning about hoping you'd break a leg."

Brandon reddened. "Break a—?"

Letty laughed. "You mustn't take offense. That's just Prue's way. She doesn't really mean it, you know."

"Oh, she meant it," Brandon insisted glumly. "She's furious with me for criticizing her behavior in the Pump Room yesterday."

"Is that all? Well, I shouldn't give the matter a second thought, if I were you. She probably deserved it, anyway. Please, Brandon, I must speak to you about a matter of much greater importance."

"But Letty, she didn't deserve it. I mean, I had no right at all to comment on your sister's conduct."

"Brandon, you make a mountain of a molehill. Prue's temper can be volatile, I know, but she cools quickly. She's probably forgotten the whole incident by this time."

"Forgotten it? I can't believe—"

"But I'm sure of it. Don't let it worry you anymore. Come, sit down here. I have something to ask you of the utmost urgency." And she gently pulled him down on the sofa beside her.

Brandon, putting aside the subject of Prue with the greatest reluctance, looked at Letty dubiously. Something about the intensity of her manner made him distinctly uneasy. "Urgency?" he asked timidly.

"Yes. To me it is a matter of . . . of . . . my entire future. Brandon, will you do me the greatest favor?"

All Brandon's instincts set up loud warnings, but he hadn't the courage to be rude. "Well, if I can . . . of course. What is it you want of me?" he asked diffidently.

"I want you to be my . . . my betrothed . . . for just a little while."

"I don't understand, Letty. Your—?"

"My betrothed. My husband-to-be," she said distinctly, twisting her fingers in her lap nervously.

Brandon blinked at her in alarm. "Me? But . . . You don't . . . You can't mean that you—? I mean, by your leave, we are not so well acquainted that . . . I mean, do you think you know me well enough to . . . ?"

Letty smiled wanly. "Oh, Brandon, I don't mean it to be a *real* engagement! How can you think so? I could scarcely be the one to make such a proposal if I seriously wanted to marry you."

Brandon nodded thoughtfully. "Oh, I see what you mean. The gentleman is supposed to do the asking, I suppose. But if you *don't* want to marry me, then what *are* you asking?"

"Only that you *pretend* that we are promised. It would be very simple, really. We would pretend to have a secret understanding—secret because our families object to the match. We need tell no one at all about it, except—"

"Except?"

"Except . . . one person. In other words, we would go on exactly as before. Nothing at all would be changed, except that . . . if this person should ask you . . . you would say that I am indeed your betrothed, that we have had an understanding for several weeks, and that we hope to make the news public as soon as we win our families' approval."

"Letty, I hope you will forgive me for being quite dense, but I don't understand any of this."

Letty sighed. "I'm not explaining it at all well, I'm afraid. It's a rather complicated story. You see, before I came to Bath, a . . . gentleman of my acquaintance asked me to marry him. He had the support of my family but I . . . I cannot like the match. I could not accept him, as I told him. But he's come to Bath and has given me . . . er . . . signs that he doesn't believe my refusal is final."

"You mean that he persists in bothering you after you've refused him?" Brandon asked, shaking his head in outrage. "He sounds like the greatest of coxcombs! I don't blame you at all for refusing such a fellow."

"No, you mustn't be misled. He is not a coxcomb. He is a very . . . personable gentleman. That's what makes the matter so difficult. No one can understand why I don't think he'd make a suitable husband."

"But *I* understand," Brandon insisted loyally. "Any man who would thrust his attentions on a woman who doesn't want him must not be the right sort at all!"

"As to that, Brandon, I must be fair. My manner with him has not been. . . . Oh, how can I explain? . . . has not been as . . . er . . . discouraging as it should have been. I really cannot completely blame Lord Denham for—"

"Lord Denham!" Brandon gasped in astonishment. "*He* cannot be the one you mean!"

Letty raised an eyebrow. "No? And why not, pray?"

"But Letty, I've met him. Why, he's the kindest, most considerate, the *finest* man I've ever met!"

Letty frowned at him in annoyance. "What has that to say to anything?"

Brandon was completely at a loss. "But . . . but . . . I can't believe any young lady would . . . That is, are you *sure* you don't wish to marry him?"

"There! You see?" Letty burst out. "Even *you* won't accept my right to refuse him!"

"Well, I wouldn't say *that,* exactly. It's only that I don't understand—"

"But why *should* you understand? Why should *anyone* have to understand? *I* understand, and that should be enough!" she cried in desperation. Then, realizing that she was losing control of herself, she clenched her hands and blinked back the tears that she feared were about to make an appearance. "Oh, Brandon," she whispered helplessly, "if I'm forced to marry him, I think I'll die!"

Brandon looked at her miserably. "But, Letty, I still don't see what I can do . . ."

Letty looked up eagerly. "But you *can,* Brandon, don't you see? If he believes that I'm truly in love with someone else, he will surely go away and not trouble me again."

"Oh, I see. Yes, I suppose he will."

Brandon hesitated. He liked Lord Denham. He had intended to pay him a call that very afternoon. But how could he face him if he knew that sooner or later he would have to lie to him? Besides, what if the lie should be spread about, and his mother should hear of it? How could he explain? "By your leave, Letty," he asked worriedly, "have you given any thought to what would happen if word got out that you and I were betrothed? You might *have* to marry me! And I very much fear, my dear, that such an occurrence might turn out to be, as the great Sophocles said, 'a remedy too strong for the disease.' "

Letty laughed. "Oh, Brandon, as if I would do such a thing to you! No, have no fear on that score. If word should leak out—which I very much doubt—I would simply cry off. I assure you that I have no wish to be married—to *any-body*."

"I don't know," Brandon said, still reluctant, "it seems a very shaky plan to me."

"On the contrary," Letty insisted, "I'm sure it will work. If Lord Denham decides to give up his suit—which he might at any time, you know—we shall never have to use the plan at all. But if he persists, I'll simply tell him that my heart is otherwise engaged, and I'll name a man in whose company I've often been seen—*you*—and he'll be bound to believe me. If he goes to you, you'll support my story, leaving him no choice but to accept it. Then he'll go away, and we can forget all about it."

Brandon was silent for a moment. Finally he spoke up. "I cannot like it, Letty. Dishonesty makes me very uneasy."

"I know," Letty said, shamefacedly. "If I were not driven to desperate measures, I should never suggest such a thing. But what else am I to do?"

"Are you sure you cannot find it in your heart to like Lord Denham? I spoke to him just this morning and learned, to my surprise, that he is a classics scholar, in addition to his other accomplishments."

"If I wanted to marry a classics scholar," Letty said with asperity, "I would sooner marry *you*!"

Brandon, who had no answer to that, hung his head.

"Oh, Brandon, forgive me," Letty said contritely. "I'm so upset that I don't know what I'm saying. It's such a strain. Everyone thinks Lord Denham is such a paragon, it makes me want to scream in vexation."

"There's nothing to forgive," Brandon assured her, patting her hand comfortingly. "But should you not sleep on it tonight? Euripides tells us that second thoughts are ever wisest."

"I have slept on it, Brandon. My mind is quite made up. But if you wish to think it over, I must certainly allow you to do so. I just wish to point out to you that you once told me that Socrates said, 'Heaven ne'er helps the man who will not act.' "

Brandon could not help smiling at her proudly. "That's true! How clever of you to remember that. I would be a poor sort of man to refuse a favor to my most apt pupil."

"Then you'll do it?" Letty squealed in delight. "Oh, Brandon," she sighed in relief and threw her arms around his neck, "I don't know how to thank you!"

Brandon, blushing with pleasure at the feeling of self-satisfaction derived from the knowledge that he'd made a noble—indeed a knightly—sacrifice for a lady fair, permitted himself to be led to the door. His good-byes were said with a sincerely happy smile. His pleasure lasted until he reached the corner of the North Parade. There his sense of uneasiness assailed him again. Good God, what if his mother learned of this? What of his budding friendship with Denham? And what of Prue? What would *she* feel if she believed him to be in love with her sister? He didn't understand why the thought of Prue depressed his spirits, but he returned home filled with misgivings. Into what other difficulties, he wondered, would this devil's pact with Letty lead him?

Chapter Nine

The weather continued fine, luring the high-spirited youths of Bath to seek activities out of doors. Letty and Prue, often in the company of Brandon, the Rabbit, Osbert and the others, strolled the circuses, crescents and squares of Bath until the city was as familiar to them as to the natives. They explored the parks which liberally surrounded the town center, and they made special expeditions to the Sydney Gardens, where they blundered through the well-known labyrinth, laughing and shrieking until they had found their way out again. They even climbed up the high streets to a point above Lansdown Crescent, where, high over the lower city, they could make out through the trees the graceful curves of the city streets below.

On these bucolic rambles, Roger Denham rarely joined them, preferring to ride his horse through the countryside. But even he was soon tempted to explore more distant vistas, and when the young squire-to-be, the sober Mr. Woodward, undertook to organize an expedition to see the famous cathedral at Wells, some twenty-one miles to the south, Roger was prevailed upon to make one of the party. The group, which included (besides Woodward and Roger) both the Glendenning sisters, Miss Summer-Smythe, Sir Ralph and Osbert Caswell, was soon augmented when Lady Upsham and Lady Denham agreed to act as chaperones and Mrs. Peake declared her intense interest in making the trip with them. Lady Denham volunteered the use of her barouche, which, if one of the gentlemen rode with the driver, could seat five. This, with the addition of Roger's curricle and Mr. Woodward's phaeton, would be sufficient for transportation, and an early hour on the following Wednesday was decided upon for the start of the journey.

On the appointed morning, Katie-erstwhile-of-the-kitchen arose before the sun, picked up the two dresses she had chosen for her mistresses to wear—they had long since given such decisions into her forceful and capable hands—and made for the little room off the kitchen, where an ironing board was permanently set for use. To her chagrin (but not her surprise, since it had happened frequently before), Miss Tristle was there before her, busily pressing the ruffles on her mistress's voluminous traveling dress. "I might've know'd," Katie grumbled. "Don't you never sleep?"

Miss Tristle stared coldly at the diminutive wench whom she regarded as a vulgar, encroaching upstart, completely unfit for intimate service to ladies of quality and certainly not equal to herself in the household hierarchy. "You should have done your ironing last night," she said loftily, placing the flatiron she had been holding on a metal stand, which had been heated by a bed of hot coals, and picking up its twin, which had been warming on the stand.

"So could you," Katie came back disrespectfully. Miss Tristle was the only irritant in Katie's new, clean, pleasant existence. The woman had resented Katie's appearance in the household from the first, although Cook had told Katie how Miss Tristle had complained for days before they'd left London that she didn't like taking care of Lady Upsham's two nieces as well as her ladyship. But the moment the toplofty dresser had learned that the Misses Glendenning were arriving with an abigail of their own, her nose had been quite out of joint.

"I do not deign to bandy words with such as you," Miss Tristle said coldly, pursing her lips primly and speaking down her rather elongated nose to Katie. "I'm in no mood for squabbles, seeing as I'm not in the best of health this morning."

Katie pursed her lips and crossed her eyes in a satiric imitation of Miss Tristle's expression. "I do not deign to squabble wi' you neither," she said impertinently: "Howsomever, I 'ave two gowns 'ere what must be pressed, an' what am I s'posed to do about 'em, eh?"

Miss Tristle was about to retort when a sharp pain in a tooth which had been giving her severe discomfort for the past several hours caused her to drop the iron upon the dress and press both her hands against her cheek. Katie, with her usual presence of mind, snatched up the iron before it could do any damage and placed it on the stand. Then, looking at Miss Tristle with sympathetic interest, she asked, "Took wi' a toothache, are you?"

Miss Tristle only groaned.

"I know a good remedy for toothache," Katie suggested.

Miss Tristle sniffed disparagingly and picked up the cloth needed to grasp the iron's hot handle, the spasm of pain having passed. "I have my own remedy, thank you," she said slightingly, lifting the iron again.

"It don't seem to be doin' you no good, from what I can see," Katie remarked bluntly. "What is it you're usin'?"

Miss Tristle was forced to stop her work and clutch her face again. When the pain subsided, she turned to Katie with less assurance. "I learned the recipe from my mother," she said. "It is concocted of a mixture of honey, juniper root and rock alum. But I must admit," she added with a moan, "that it doesn't seem to be working a bit well."

"I ain't surprised. Honey is the most dimwittedest thing to put on a bad tooth. It's the sweetness, y'know, what makes the tooth feel worser."

"Is it indeed?" Miss Tristle asked contemptuously. "And how did you become so expert, may I ask?"

"I know a thing or two," Katie answered cryptically. "Do you want to 'ear my remedy or don't you?"

"If it's to lay roasted turnip parings behind the ear, I've already tried that, and it didn't help either," Miss Tristle told her, the discouragement and suffering in her voice softening the unfriendliness of her words.

"I ain't never 'eard such gammon as that!" Katie declared. "No, mine is a simple 'erb wash. I'll make it for you after we've got our ladies off, if you've a mind to try it."

A simple herb wash had a soothing sound. Miss Tristle nodded almost gratefully. She hastily completed her work on Lady Upsham's dress and turned the irons over to Katie with unmistakable eagerness, even offering to help by smoothing ruffles and folding ribbons. But Katie, her object won, generously urged Miss Tristle to snatch a few minutes rest before her mistress should wake and demand her services. Miss Tristle, feeling an unexpected spark of affection for the hitherto despised kitchen girl, smiled as warmly as her sour disposition and her aching tooth permitted, clutched her cheek and left Katie to her work.

The results of Katie's labors with the irons were much admired, first by Letty and Prue and then by their aunt. Lady Upsham smiled with satisfaction to see how fresh and lovely Letty looked in her dress of white cambric with its rows of red flowers embroidered at the hem and the red satin sash tied in a fetching bow at the back. And Prue, too, was a credit to her, looking charming in her yellow-and-white striped dimity with its perky ruffle at the neck. She was so pleased with her nieces that she uncharacteristically complimented them both on their appearance. Katie, who hovered near the door to see them off, grinned with pleasure when Letty waved a happy good-bye and Prue gave her a congratulatory wink. Then she hurried off to the kitchen to brew her herbal concoction for the suffering Miss Tristle.

The meeting place for the members of the expedition was the square at the back of Bath Abbey. Before the hour of eight had struck, a number of the adventurers had assembled, bearing baskets, parasols, lap robes and shawls in abundance, for early September weather was unpredictable. No sooner did Letty and

Prue make their appearance than everyone began a subtle but purposeful maneuvering for advantageous seating in the carriages. Lady Upsham immediately
claimed a place beside Lady Denham in the barouche. Letty, determined not to
ride with Roger, attempted to follow her aunt, but Millicent promptly declared
that she had promised the two remaining seats to Mrs. Peake and Brandon. To
Millicent's chagrin, however, Prue, with a mischievous twinkle (and blithely ignoring the pleas from all the gentlemen for her companionship), asked Roger if
she might join him in his curricle. Whether her motive was to tease her swains
or to help her sister, she was not sure. What Roger felt, no one could tell. He
merely threw Letty a quizzical look and smilingly helped Prue to climb into the
curricle.

Mrs. Peake took her place in the barouche, but before Brandon could follow
her, Roger approached him and offered to let him take the ribbons of the curricle. "What?" Brandon asked in pleased surprise. "Do you mean it? Would you
really let me handle your grays?"

"Why not? They are quite well trained, you know," Roger said.

"But . . . but they're the most beautiful set of matched grays I've ever seen,"
Brandon said in awe. "If they were mine, I don't think I could bear to let anyone
else touch them."

"I hope you're not trying to tell me that you're cow-handed with the ribbons," Roger said.

"Oh, no!" Brandon assured him hastily. "At Oxford, I'm considered to be
rather a creditable driver. I'd take very special care, if—by your leave—you are
truly in earnest about letting me take the reins."

Roger assured him of his sincerity with a warm smile and helped him into
the curricle. Brandon's face glowed with pleasure, not only at the prospect of
driving the beautiful grays but of showing off his prowess before none other
than Prudence Glendenning herself.

Lady Denham, meanwhile, enticed Sir Ralph to ride alongside her coachman with the promise that the coachman would give him the reins from time to
time. With excitement equal to Brandon's, Sir Ralph jumped up on the box in
happy anticipation. Gladys Summer-Smythe, who had been following Sir Ralph
around the square with doglike devotion, eagerly took the one vacant seat in the
barouche, having decided that being near her "rabbit" was worth enduring the
company of the three chaperones. That left Roger, Osbert and Letty to take
their seats in William Woodward's phaeton. Osbert helped Letty into the phaeton and followed after her. Roger took his place on her other side, Mr.
Woodward climbed onto the driver's seat and the entire cavalcade set off on the
twenty-one-mile trip to Wells.

Letty glanced surreptitiously at Roger settling himself comfortably beside her and was almost certain that his eyes held a mischievous gleam of triumph. But nothing in his manner or conversation was the least bit out-of-the-way. He complimented Mr. Woodward on the balance of his carriage, admired Osbert's yellow pantaloons, which he assured him were all the crack in London, and nodded in polite agreement when Osbert said in his flowery way that Letty was as pretty as the roses on her dress. Much of the conversation during the first hour of travel was made by Mr. Woodward who, because he had instigated the expedition, felt it incumbent upon him to point out the various places of interest along the way and to find something attractive about every vista they looked upon.

For a while, Osbert kept his eyes on the curricle just ahead of them, wishing it was he and not Brandon who sat beside Prue in that elegant, graceful curricle. But before long Brandon let the horses have their heads, and the curricle passed the barouche, which had led the way, and pulled out of sight. Having nothing better to do, Osbert found himself glancing more and more often at the subdued young lady seated beside him. The sun cast glinting highlights on Letty's hair, which was pulled back from her face and bound up in a knot at the back of her head, but Osbert noticed that little tendrils of sunlit curls had escaped their bonds and framed her face with entrancing charm. He noticed, too, the natural and delicate high color of her cheeks, the slender curve of her neck and the whiteness of the skin he could glimpse beneath her décolletage. Prue was quite forgotten as he gazed at Letty in dawning adoration. Suddenly he remembered a new poem he had composed the night before, which now rested in his coat pocket. It had been written to Prue, but if he remembered it rightly, it was general enough to apply to *any* lovely young lady. With a broad smile, he turned to Letty. "I say, Miss Glendenning, would you care to hear a poem I've penned just for you?"

Letty started. "For me?" she asked in surprise.

"Yes, indeed. I'm a great admirer of yours, you know."

At this, William Woodward turned around in disgust. "I thought it was Miss Prudence you was nutty on," he remarked forthrightly.

Osbert glared at William furiously. "Why don't you tend to your driving?" he muttered savagely.

Letty, suppressing a smile, looked down at her hands. But Roger was too amused to let the matter pass. "You are not being kind to our poet, Mr. Woodward," he said. "A true bard must be given the freedom to take inspiration from any number of sources. He needn't be inspired by only one female."

"Exactly so," Osbert agreed with alacrity.

Mr. Woodward shrugged. "If you want to encourage his nonsensical rhyming, it's nothing to me," he said placidly and turned back to his horses.

"I, for one, am quite agog to hear your verses, Caswell," Roger said encouragingly. "With Miss Glendenning's permission, of course."

"*By my leave,* Lord Denham?" Letty couldn't resist saying, hoping the teasing reference to Brandon's excessive formality would not be lost on Roger. They exchanged a smiling glance.

"By your leave, ma'am," he responded readily, with a nod of the head that signified *touché*.

"Of course you may read your poem, Mr. Caswell," Letty said, resuming her demure demeanor.

Osbert unfolded his paper and, enunciating carefully, gave his poem its first reading:

> "When in this Chariot of Love
>   We twain together ride,
>   I cannot voice my Ecstacy
>   When you are at my side.
>
> "Your copper Curls, your Skin so fair,
>   Your Smile that I adoreth—
>   I long to make them all My Own,
>   But dare not to imploreth.
>
> "From azure eyes one flashing Glance,
>   From ruby lips one Smile,
>   Then I, in fear, am stripped of words
>   Or Talent to Beguile.
>
> "So here in silent Misery
>   I gaze and yearn in vain,
>   And pray you'll turn those azure Orbs
>   To look on me again.

"Well, that's it. It don't do you justice, ma'am, of course, but I hope you liked it."

"Do her *justice*!" exclaimed William, turning around again. "It ain't got anything to *do* with her! Does she have copper curls? I ask you, does she?"

Roger's lips twitched. "It's . . . er . . . poetic license, Woodward. A poet may use poetic license in these matters."

"And how about 'azure orbs'?" Woodward demanded. "Are they poetic license, too?"

Roger was sure he heard a gurgle from Letty's throat. It took all his will-power to control the laughter welling up inside him. "Yes, indeed," he answered manfully.

"And how about 'imploreth'?" Woodward persisted, preferring the teasing they had given to Osbert at his last poetic reading to this politeness. "Are you trying to tell me you liked 'dare not to *imploreth*'?"

Roger choked. "It was . . . certainly ingenious," he managed.

"Thank you, Lord Denham," Osbert said, pleased. "Though I'll admit the last stanza is a little weak. I had a bit of trouble with that one."

"May I see it?" Roger offered. "Perhaps I can make a suggestion or two."

Osbert passed the paper to him, and Roger read the stanza carefully. Letty, her eyes brimming with suppressed amusement, looked over his shoulder. "Well, my lord, how do you propose to improve it?" she challenged.

"How about this?" he said promptly,

> "So here in silent misery
> I gaze and yearn in sorrow,
> And pray some *other* azure eyes
> Will smile on me tomorrow."

At this, Woodward gave a loud guffaw from his place on the box, slapping his knee in appreciation. This was too much for Letty, who burst into uncontrollable laughter. Roger tried for a moment to keep his expression serious but soon had to follow suit. Osbert, accustomed to hearing his verses greeted with merriment, good-naturedly joined in. The ice thus broken, the conversation in the phaeton became much less constrained, and by the time the halfway point had been reached, somewhere south of Midsomer Norton, the four were engaging in the comfortable raillery of old friends.

This was not the case in the curricle, where Prue had maintained her attitude of frigid indifference for almost two hours. Brandon had tried, at first, to maintain a stream of innocuous comments on the weather and the scenery, but her lack of response soon wearied him. He relapsed into silence and gave his attention to the magnificent horses. It was not long before he could drive the vehicle with skillful competence. He had left the other carriages far behind, and he bowled along the road at a pace lively enough to impress any young lady, but Prue showed no reaction. At length, he slowed the horses to a comfortable trot and settled back in his seat glumly. The ride, which had seemed at the outset to be so promising, was turning out in actuality to be a complete fiasco. Brandon turned to Prue in desperation. "Please, Miss Glendenning, won't you listen to me? I have apologized and apologized for my rudeness the other day. Can't you possibly forgive me—at least to the extent of speaking to me during this curst ride? We can't possibly travel all the way to Wells without saying a word to each other!"

"Yes, we can," Prue said coldly. "We'll be there in another hour."

"Nevertheless—by your leave—an hour can be interminable in these circumstances," Brandon pointed out.

"By your leave, I'm well aware of that," she answered drily.

"I seem to say 'by your leave' a bit too often, I suppose," Brandon said miserably.

"You say it every time you open your mouth," she told him in disgust.

"I'm sorry . . ."

Prue shrugged. "It doesn't matter to me," she said bluntly. "But while we're on the subject of your silly repetitions, I also find that you are always saying you're *sorry* about one thing or another."

"Really?" Brandon asked thoughtfully. "I'm sor—I mean, I didn't realize. Well, as the great Homer once said, 'A noble mind disdains not to repent.'"

Prue merely looked at him with her eyebrows raised.

Brandon colored. "Oh, I see. You are thinking that I'm too full of quotations also. I'm sor—"

A giggle escaped Prue. "It seems that, if we eliminate your by-your-leaves, your apologies and your quotations, you have nothing at all to say for yourself."

Brandon turned away. "If you choose to mock me, go ahead," he said, the epitome of injured dignity.

"If you ask me, a bit of mocking may be good for you," Prue said waspishly.

Brandon, nettled, turned to her. "If you ask *me,* a bit of—" But he cut himself off.

"What?" Prue asked curiously. "Go ahead and finish what you started to say."

Brandon shook his head and stared straight ahead, his mouth compressed in a straight line.

"Say it," she urged. "You were going to say that a bit of *something* would be good for me. Tell me what it is. Although I don't see why I bother to ask. I wouldn't take advice or counsel from a . . . a . . . stuffed prig."

"A stuffed—!" Brandon gasped. Pushed beyond endurance, he wheeled himself around and grasped her by the shoulders. "I'll tell you what would be good for you—*this!*" And he shook her so violently that her teeth rattled. After a moment, aghast at his loss of control, he stopped. His hands still grasping her shoulders, he stared at her in shamefaced remorse. "I'm . . . I'm . . . *sorry* . . ." he stammered breathlessly.

Prue stared back at him, her heart beating violently against her ribs. Adept as she was at coquetry and flirtation, she was really quite inexperienced in the feelings which come from intimate encounters between men and women. She knew that her feelings for Brandon were strangely ambivalent. He was often in her thoughts, and she knew that, of all the young men who circled about her, he was the one whose approval she most desired. Ironically, however, he had made his *dis*approval of her quite plain. First, he had criticized her to her sister, then to her face, and now this. She had a strong urge to burst into tears and collapse against his shoulder, but her pride and a fierce resentment which seemed to well up inside her kept her from succumbing to an urge which was nothing more than mawkish sentimentality. Instead, she shook his hands from her shoulders. "Sorry!" she cried out in fury. "Sorry! Here's what I think of your sorries!" She put her two hands flat against his chest and pushed him with such strength that he tumbled out of the carriage.

Frightened at the result of her impetuous act, Prue looked down at the road to see if he'd been hurt, but the horses, ignoring the drama being played behind them, continued to trot on. "Brandon! Are you hurt?" Prue called back in alarm.

Brandon sat up in the road and shook his head in confusion. Then, with a dawning realization of what was happening, he looked up and shouted frantically, "Prue, *wait*! Stop the horses!"

But she, now relieved of any guilt, since he was apparently unhurt, laughed wickedly. "I will not!" she called back. "You can jolly well *walk* to Wells!" With that, she picked up the reins, gave Brandon an insolent wave of her hand and drove off round a bend in the road.

In desperation, Brandon jumped to his feet, only to topple over on one knee. His ankle was sprained. "Prue, *Prue*," he shouted in anguish, "you must stop! The *horses*... I promised Lord Denham! Prue, come back!"

Once round the bend, Prue felt a twinge of fear. She had never driven a vehicle by herself before. Gingerly, she pulled the reins. Lord Denham's well-trained horses placidly slowed to a halt. She breathed a sigh of relief and decided to remain where she was. Brandon would come along soon. She would apologize, and all would be well.

It was a full quarter of an hour before the much-abused Brandon hobbled into view. The sight of him caused Prue to gasp. He was covered with dust, his face was streaked with perspiration and grime, and he winced in agony at every step. Prue leapt from the carriage and ran to him. "Oh, Brandon," she said in a voice of sincere self-reproach, "you *are* hurt. I'm a beast! I'll never forgive myself! Here, let me help you."

Brandon glared at the infuriating minx who stood so remorsefully before him, offering her arm. Even his sense of relief when he saw that she and the horses were safe was not strong enough to ease the wrath she had inspired in him. "Don't touch me," he snapped at her. Limping to the curricle, he painfully lifted himself into his seat.

Prue climbed up and seated herself beside him. She glanced covertly at his face, but one glimpse of his tense, frozen expression and the look in his eyes as he stared implacably at the road before him told her that any words of hers would fall on deaf ears. With a silent, rather pitiful sigh, she settled back to endure the rest of the ride. She knew in her bones that it would be passed in a silence more insupportable than before.

Chapter Ten

$\mathcal{D}$espite the temporary setback, Brandon's vehicle was the first to arrive at the King's Head Inn at Wells. Within half-an-hour the other carriages pulled into the courtyard. The gaiety of the four who spilled from Mr. Woodward's phaeton was so infectious that the whole group made a merry entrance into the inn and joined Prue and Brandon, who were sitting glumly at opposite sides of a tiny but cheerful dining room. Prue greeted them with an affected eagerness, but she was soon laughing with perfect and heartless sincerity over the fulsome compliments being paid to her by Sir Ralph. Brandon, who was determined not to spoil the outing for the others by bringing attention to his injured ankle, gave strained smiles to everyone, gritted his teeth and said nothing. And since Prue had no idea of the severity of his pain, she, too, said nothing about his accident. Thus no one else noticed that anything was at all amiss.

They sat down to a noisy luncheon, during which great quantities of country ham, cold mutton, coddled eggs, hot biscuits, currant pudding and home brew were consumed, after which they drifted out to take the short walk to the cathedral. Brandon, telling them that he would follow shortly, watched until they were out of sight and then hobbled to the innkeeper and asked for a room in which he could lie down for a while. The innkeeper helped him up to a small bedroom and offered to pull off his boots, but when they attempted to remove the boot from the injured foot, it caused such a spasm of pain that Brandon decided to leave it alone. The innkeeper shrugged and, not knowing what else to do for him, left him alone. Poor Brandon lay back against the pillows and surrendered to self-pity.

The rest of the party arrived at the cathedral and promptly separated into small groups, since some wanted to go first to the Chapel, some to the Chapter House and some straight to the famous Wells clock. Thus the fact that Brandon failed to arrive was not noticed.

When Letty became separated from her group, her absence was not noticed either. Fascinated by the sculpture that could be found embellishing the arches, the walls, the bosses and the tops of every column, Letty had stopped to study a charming lizard eating a bunch of grapes which was carved on the far side of an arch through which they had passed. When she looked up, the group had gone. Untroubled, she continued her rambles quite contentedly. Near the door to the cloisters, she discovered to her delight a number of little sculpted scenes depicting rather unusual subjects. One was of a man scowling at a thorn in his foot. Another scene showed a man suffering with a toothache. She was studying a third, in which a man appeared to be stealing fruit, when a voice behind her made her jump. "Did you know that this scene is one of a series?" Roger was remarking pleasantly.

"Series?" she asked stupidly, trying to hide the turmoil which his sudden appearance caused in the pit of her stomach.

"Yes. Here he is stealing the fruit. In this next scene, he is being apprehended, and here in the last he's being beaten."

"Oh, dear," Letty said with a rueful smile, "I wish you hadn't told me that. It seems a cruel punishment for so small a crime."

"So it is. Perhaps we should turn our backs on the whole scene and take a moment's respite out there in the sunshine. I see an ivy-covered wall that looks quite inviting."

"But . . . I've scarcely begun to see the sights—" Letty demurred.

"I know, but I've walked *miles* looking for the sight of you, and I'm exhausted," Roger countered, drawing her arm through his. "Besides, I've been waiting all day for the opportunity to talk to you alone."

Letty's heart began to beat in a disturbingly irregular fashion. "But, my lord," she said with a smile so broad she hoped it would cover her uneasiness, "what can you wish to speak to me about? *You* haven't composed a poem in my honor, have you?"

Roger grinned. "Well, no, I'm afraid not. But I would make the attempt, if it would please you."

"No, not today. One poem a day is quite enough. Any more would surely turn my head."

"No, we certainly must not have your head turned," Roger agreed, firmly leading her to the place he had indicated. "You've given me enough trouble with your head just as it is."

"Given you trouble, my lord? *I?*" she asked demurely.

"Don't play the innocent with me, my girl," Roger said, lifting her upon the wall and jumping up beside her. "You're quite well aware of the trouble you've been causing me."

"If the trouble to which you refer is related to a subject which is barred from discussion between us, you bring it on yourself, sir," Letty said with sudden seriousness.

"When do you think, *Miss Glendenning*," Roger demanded, "that you will feel friendly enough toward me to call me Roger? I find your endless 'my lords' very intimidating."

"Intimidating!" she said, outraged. "You wouldn't be intimidated if I had a . . . a . . . leopard alongside me!"

"You have a very flattering estimate of my courage, my dear," he laughed. "I think a leopard might well do the trick, if your object is to keep me at arm's length."

"Then perhaps I should investigate the possibilities of obtaining one," Letty said with a smile.

Roger's smile faded. "You needn't go to such lengths as that," he said, taking her hand in his and looking at her with sober affection. "I'm much more vulnerable to your slights than you think. One harsh word from you would be enough to send me to the grass."

Letty could not help but be touched. "I have no wish to . . . to send you to the grass . . ." she admitted in a tiny voice.

"I'm glad of that," he answered earnestly, his eyes fixed on her face. "I do love you, you know."

She felt her throat constrict. "Roger—!"

His clasp on her hand tightened. "Don't look so frightened. I know I'm being too precipitous again, but surely you can't be surprised. You must know how I feel. I've not tried to hide it from you—"

"No, no—!" Letty said tearfully, trying to remove her hand from his grasp. "I didn't think—"

"But you *must* have realized," he insisted. "And you must feel it, too. I cannot be so misguided as to have misunderstood—! Letty, dearest, what *is* it that makes you so afraid of me?"

Letty, her hand trembling in his grasp, stared up at him. How dear he looked to her now, how sincere and how deeply troubled. She longed to believe him, to trust him, to touch his face and soothe away the frown that creased his forehead. But she forced herself to remember that this very man whose eyes now searched hers with such tender concern had once shown quite another face. She had seen it at Vauxhall Gardens and she could not forget it. "It's not that I'm afraid of you, Roger," she said at last, "but that . . ."

"Yes?"

"That I am . . . promised . . . to someone else," she said hesitantly.

She saw his cheeks whiten. *"Promised—?"* He could barely say the word.

Letty nodded and removed her hand from his grasp, which had now grown slack. "Yes. I've been . . . betrothed for some weeks now."

"But you never . . . ! I had not heard a *word*—!"

"We've had to keep our plans secret. My family would oppose him, you see. They keep hoping that I . . ." She flicked a quick glance at his face.

Roger nodded in understanding. "That you will accept *me*," he finished for her.

Letty clasped her trembling hands together in her lap and lowered her eyes, aware that he was staring at her incredulously. "You know him, of course . . ." she said, to make sure he didn't doubt her word.

"Do I?" he asked in surprise.

"Yes. Brandon Peake."

"Brandon!" His voice was shocked.

"You needn't sound so surprised," she said defensively. "You'd find him an intelligent and thoughtful person, once you grew to know him."

"Yes, of course he is. I know that already," Roger assured her with perfect sincerity. "I find him a most admirable and likable young man. I . . . most earnestly wish you every happiness."

Letty murmured a thank-you and kept her eyes fixed on her hands. She had never felt so completely miserable. "F-forgive me for . . . for not telling you before," she said lamely.

"There's nothing to forgive. You owe me no explanations or apologies. It is *I* who should apologize for forcing my attentions on you."

Unwittingly, Letty's hand went out to him. "No, please," she said gently, "you mustn't think . . . I have never felt that you've been in any way . . . displeasing. You've always shown me the utmost courtesy and . . . and . . ."

"Thank you, my dear," Roger said with a wry smile, "but I have a very clear recollection of at least one time when my . . . er . . . attentions must have seemed in excess of what a betrothed young lady could consider desirable."

Letty, remembering that her *own* reactions to that kiss in the curricle were in excess of what would be considered desirable in a betrothed young lady, colored to her ears. But Roger, who was jumping down from the wall, did not notice. He stood in thought for a while and then seemed to pull himself together. Turning to her, he grasped her by the waist, lifted her gently and set her on the ground. For a moment he held her against him and smiled wistfully down at her. "Your Brandon is a damnably lucky fellow," he murmured and then abruptly let her go. He took her hand and led her to the Chapel, where they found Gladys Summer-Smythe on the arm of Mr. Woodward, examining with feigned interest the magnificent vaulted ceiling. Leaving Letty in Mr. Woodward's charge, Roger made a bow and left them. He was not seen by them again that afternoon.

More than an hour later, having somewhat dissipated his disappointment and frustration by striding through the narrow lanes and byways of the tiny city, Roger began to feel more in command of himself. Thinking longingly of the solace of a glass of good brandy, he made his way back to the inn, where he bespoke a private parlor and a glass of the best brandy in the house. The innkeeper complied in the leisurely style of country service, remarking as he poured the brandy that, "T'other young gent ain't come down from 'is room as yet."

"Other young gent?" Roger asked, puzzled. "Whom do you mean?"

"The gent 'oo come in with your party," the innkeeper explained. "The one wi' the bad leg."

"Bad leg? I can't imagine—" Then Roger realized that he had not seen Brandon all afternoon. "Are you speaking of a rather short young man with spectacles?"

"Yessir, that's the very one."

"You say he had a bad leg? You'd best take me to him at once," Roger said, rising hastily, his brandy forgotten.

He found Brandon stretched out on the bed, his brow wrinkled in pain, his arm thrown over his face. "Good Lord, Brandon," Roger said, dismayed, "what's amiss here?"

Brandon, startled, sat up abruptly and attempted to smile. "Oh, are you all back already? Don't look so troubled. It's nothing to speak of. I only twisted my ankle and decided not to march about the cathedral on it, that's all."

Roger took note of the whiteness of his lips and the tension in his face and was not taken in. "We are not *all* back, only I. So you needn't play the hero for my benefit. Let's have your boot off so that I can have a look at that ankle of yours."

Brandon was tremendously relieved to share his problem with someone as purposeful as Lord Denham, but he nevertheless was reluctant to make a fuss over what he knew was only a minor injury, the pain notwithstanding. "I don't think we should remove my boot," he demurred. "We won't be able to put it back on again, I'm afraid, and then everyone will see and make a great to-do—"

Roger had been feeling the ankle through the boot and shook his head in kind but firm disagreement. "I'm afraid you'll have to withstand a to-do, my boy. You've been subjecting yourself to needless suffering by keeping the boot on. Much as I admire your courage, I see no reason for you to endure unnecessary agony."

"But taking the boot off will be worse than anything," Brandon admitted fearfully. "Can't it wait until I get home?"

"Taking the boot off will be impossible now, I fear. Your ankle has become so swollen, we'll have to *cut* the boot off. But cutting it off won't cause you much discomfort, I promise, and the relief of removing it will be a positive blessing." With those comforting words, he turned to the landlord and ordered the necessary implements and the bottle of brandy.

When the innkeeper returned, Roger urged Brandon to drink a good quantity of brandy before he set to work cutting off the boot. But Brandon, not accustomed to drink, was reluctant. "I can bear it," he said manfully. "I don't need spirits to give me courage. Go ahead and cut."

Roger grinned at him. "Quite the hero, aren't you? No wonder Letty prefers you to me."

Brandon shot a startled glance at Roger's face. "Oh," he said with an agitated tremor in his voice, "did she . . . tell you about that?"

"Yes, she did. Do you mind?"

"Well, I had hoped she wouldn't have to—" Brandon began.

"But she *did* have to. I was forcing my attentions on her again, you see."

Brandon worriedly studied Roger's face, but Roger seemed to be quite calm and unconcerned. Nevertheless, a pervading sense of guilt depressed Brandon's spirits. Roger Denham had always been more than kind and generous to him, and even now was doing his best to help Brandon out of this fix that his ankle had caused. To repay Roger with a lie—to let him believe in this false betrothal to Letty—was beyond anything. He regretted with all his heart that he had given his word to Letty. But there was nothing he could do now. With a hopeless sigh, he reached for the brandy. "I think I *will* take that drink after all," he said.

By the time the others returned to the inn, Brandon was seated downstairs in the private parlor, his leg freed from the constricting boot and his ankle neatly bound with strips of cloth and propped up before him on a cushioned stool. The high color of his face, the foolishness of his smile and the brandy glass in his hand gave instant evidence that he was, if not quite cast away, at least gloriously tipsy. As he had predicted, a great fuss was made over him, especially by his mother, who, when they went to the carriages for their return to Bath, insisted that he sit next to her in the barouche to permit her to administer whatever aid he should require on the journey. Since the only aid she offered was to wring her hands and make repeated comments on the Peake family's tendency to adversity and misfortune, Brandon wisely turned away from her, closed his eyes and fell into a stertorous sleep.

The occupants of the other two carriages were not much more cheerful. Roger was forced to drive the vapid Miss Summer-Smythe in his curricle, and after responding to her inanities for half-an-hour he found himself gritting his teeth in impatience. As a result, he urged his horses into a wild gallop, frightening poor Miss Summer-Smythe into a frozen tension and completing the more-than-three-hour journey in less than two.

In the phaeton, Mr. Woodward and Osbert were at first overjoyed to find themselves squiring the two Misses Glendenning, but they soon noticed that their quips and pleasantries fell on deaf ears. The two girls sat side by side in a dismal, abstracted silence. Prue's thoughts were completely occupied with guilt and self-loathing. She had caused Brandon to sprain his ankle. She remembered saying to Letty one morning that she hoped he'd broken a leg. She hadn't meant it, of course, but it was as if she'd put a curse on him. And tonight, at the inn, when she'd tried to apologize to him, he'd turned away from her. She had ruined everything. Brandon, so serious, so sensible and reliable, was the only man whose good opinion she desired. For him, she would enjoy curbing her impetuosity and controlling her flirtatious behavior. But she had pushed him from the carriage and injured him. How could she expect him to forgive her when she could not forgive herself? She had lost forever the chance to show him what a truly lovable girl she could be if she tried.

Letty, too, was wrapped in misery. She could hear Roger's voice saying, "I do love you, you know." Even in her dreams she had not permitted herself to imagine his voice saying those words to her. But he'd said them. It had happened in a reality more wonderful and more terrible than any dream. His eyes had been lit with such warmth and confidence, and she had snuffed out that light with a couple of words. With a lie. It would have been so easy—so easy!—to have told him the truth, that she loved him to distraction, that she had never loved anyone else, that she wanted nothing more than the feeling of his arms around her. How different this ride home would have been if she had let herself say those things! At this very moment she would have been sitting beside him in the curricle, her head on his shoulder, his arm around her waist, blissfully whispering the sweet things that she imagined lovers say to each other when they are alone together.

But she could not let herself dwell on the might-have-been. She had thought the matter through clearly when she'd been calmer and more sensible. She had made what she was certain was the wisest decision under the circumstances. Everything had gone as she had planned. He would not ask her again. If the price she had to pay to see her plans fulfilled meant living in this utterly abject misery, well, she must pay it.

Thus three carriages returned from a pleasure trip with all the passengers disgruntled and more than half their number sunk in deep despond. When the good nights were finally said, there were not many among them who did not secretly vow to stay closer to home in the future.

Chapter Eleven

*R*oger had been at home an hour when Lady Denham wearily entered the house after the seemingly endless journey back from Wells. The first sight to greet her eye as she stepped in the door was Roger's man, Trebbs, climbing the stairs carrying a portmanteau and a small campaign trunk. "What on earth are you doing with those, Trebbs?" she inquired.

"Good evening, my lady," Trebbs said, turning and setting down the luggage. "I am carrying these up from the storeroom so that I can have them packed by morning."

"*Packed?* What for?"

"His lordship's orders, ma'am. He wishes to leave shortly after breakfast."

"Is his lordship leaving? He said nothing of it to me," the dowager said, puzzled. "Has he gone to bed?"

"No, my lady. He's in the study, I believe. Would you like me to find him and send him to you?"

"No, never mind, Trebbs. I'll find him myself."

Roger was indeed in the study, a glass of brandy in his hand and a half-empty bottle on the table at his elbow. Although he seemed to be staring at the glass with more-than-ordinary concentration, there was no other evidence that he had been imbibing too deeply. His mother stared at him for a moment with a troubled frown. "What's this Trebbs has been telling me?" she asked when it became apparent that he was not going to look up from his fascinated contemplation of the contents of his glass. "Do you truly intend to leave tomorrow?"

Roger looked up at her with a rather unfocused gaze. "Oh, there you are, Mama. Should stand up, o' course, but can't seem to use m' legs."

"Roger!" his mother said disapprovingly. "You're *foxed!*"

Roger nodded. "Drunk as a lord," he declared, and laughed. "Very appropriate saying, that. Drunk 's an earl might be even better. Tha's it. Drunk 's an earl."

"Well, if you're drunk, you should *not* be making decisions. Tell Trebbs to stop packing and to get you to bed. In the morning, when you're more yourself, you won't want to leave at all," Lady Denham said firmly, relieved that Roger's decision to depart was only the result of an alcohol-induced whim.

But Roger shook his head. "No. Made m' decision before I shot the cat. Cold-sober decision. No point staying here, y' know. She won't have me."

"What are you talking about? You aren't making a bit of sense. Roger, you sot, we can't have an intelligent conversation while you're in this condition."

"Nothing to discuss, Mama. 'S all very simple, really. She won't have me. Betrothed already. May 's well take myself back to London, see? Won't do any good staying here and brooding."

Lady Denham was beginning to understand. Her plan had apparently fallen apart. But she was too tired to probe further into the matter now—especially with Roger in this condition. "Take yourself to bed, my boy. That's my advice to you. We'll talk about this in the morning." She went to the door, but before she left the room, she stopped to give him one last warning. "Don't you try to steal away before I see you in the morning! Do you hear me, Roger? I want your word that you'll provide me with a coherent explanation before you desert me."

Roger lifted his glass in a salute. "Word of an Arneau. Promise. You may interog . . . inter . . . question me 's much 's y' like. But not now. In the morning."

Lady Denham shook her head compassionately. "Very well, my dear. In the morning."

Lady Denham had been awake for hours before her son made an appearance the following morning. It was after ten o'clock when she looked up from her coffee to find him looming in the doorway of the breakfast room, his eyes bloodshot, his brow furrowed and his mouth grim. But he was dressed for travel, and his mother saw at once that his present sobriety had not caused him to change his mind. She smiled at him over her coffee cup and beckoned to him to join her. Roger came in, bent to kiss her cheek and sat down. Before he uttered a word, he reached for the coffee pot and poured himself a cup with a hand that trembled slightly. Then he faced his mother with a rueful smile. "It seems that your son is a curst rum touch," he said. "I'm sorry you had to see it."

She patted his hand. "Don't underestimate me, my dear—or overestimate your own proclivities toward sin. I've lived a long time and seen a great deal worse."

He smiled at her. "Have you really? What a game old girl you are!"

"I suppose that is meant to be a compliment," she responded drily. "Roger, you do look awful. Do you feel well enough to travel today?"

"I feel like the devil," he answered bluntly. "I'm neither well enough to travel nor to answer the questions I know you're agog to ask me, but I intend to do both. Pluck to the backbone, that's the sort I am."

"Will you have time to see Brandon Peake before you go?" Lady Denham inquired. "He sent a message begging you to drop in for a moment this morning."

Roger raised his eyebrow. "Did he? Well, I suppose I . . ." He looked at his mother sharply. "Did he say anything else?"

Lady Denham looked puzzled. "No. Were you expecting something more?"

"I wasn't expecting anything at all. Now let's get to the inquisition. What is it you want to know that I haven't already spilled out in my drunken stupor?"

"*My son* was not in a stupor! And I will not subject you to an inquisition. I only want to know why Letty refused you again."

"I'm sure I've told you. She is betrothed to someone else. I believe that is the sort of news which we must accept as final," Roger said flatly.

"Oh, dear. *Betrothed!* And under our very noses! I was so *sure* that the child was quite besotted over you."

"It seems that *we* are the ones who were besotted."

"*We?* Did *you* believe she cared for you, Roger?"

"Yes, I did. I would not have asked her, otherwise. It seems I'm quite a coxcomb after all."

"No, you're anything but that," his mother insisted. "Her behavior is inexplicable. I can't help feeling that there's more to this affair than we know."

"Don't start that again, Mama, please," Roger begged, putting a hand to his throbbing temple. "She is attached to someone else. Let that be the end of the matter."

"Attached to someone else? I can scarcely credit it. Who, pray, *is* the gentleman?"

"Sorry, but I'm not at liberty to say."

"I see. Not that it matters, anyway. If she won't have *you,* I don't much care *whom* she marries."

"That sounds a bit churlish, doesn't it? *I* at least wished her well."

"It's too much to ask of *me,* I'm afraid. I suppose I shall *have* to wish her well when she tells me about it openly and frankly," Lady Denham said grudgingly. "I only wish she had done so earlier."

"So do I. Although, to be fair, this fix is more our fault than hers. We should have accepted her word when she first refused me. I could have walked away *then* without a backward look. *Now,* however—"

Lady Denham peered at her son with an expression which combined dismay and pity. "Oh, my dear, have you learned to care for her so much?"

Roger merely studied the coffee in his cup.

His mother pressed her hands against her mouth. "To what dreadful pass have I brought you?" she murmured heartbrokenly.

"Don't be so tragic, Mama," Roger said with a smile. "You've always wanted me to learn what love is. And now I have." His smile broadened as he added reflectively, "I had never quite believed in the kind of love about which the poets like to rhapsodize. But now I feel almost like one of them—the new romantical ones who are causing such a stir. Don't be surprised if you discover that I am busily composing tragic love ballads during the dark hours of the night."

She sighed. "You may joke about it if you wish, but it's quite true that I've wanted you to learn about love. I never wished you to suffer, of course, but this experience may be good for you nevertheless."

Roger gave a snort of laughter. "How easily you are consoled, Mama! In less than a minute a 'dreadful pass' has become a 'good experience.' If I stay here and continue this conversation, another minute may bring us to celebrating this whole disaster with a drink of champagne! If you don't mind, I'd rather endure my poetic suffering alone than share your satisfaction at the broadening of my experience. If you'll excuse me, I shall trot out to see what young Peake wants of me."

Lady Denham didn't try to hold him. She knew better than to press him further. His wound was too raw to permit much probing. Perhaps, in time, when the entire experience was well behind him, they would be able to talk about it more dispassionately and come to some understanding of what had gone wrong. For the time being, she had no choice but to let him go.

Roger found Brandon ensconced on a chaise lounge before a sunny window, desultorily attempting to read the *Philoctetes*. At the sight of his visitor, Brandon's face brightened. He tossed his book aside and held out his hand. "I'm so glad you came, Roger," he said in greeting. "I've been wanting to thank you properly for what you did for me yesterday."

"If that's why you asked me here, I shall go away at once. You must have thanked me at least a dozen times already," Roger responded in disgust.

"If I had, I don't remember it. All I remember is taking my first sip of brandy. Everything else is rather hazy in my mind."

"Yes, you were quite well to live by the time I'd gotten your boot off. I must say you look none the worse for it this morning," Roger said enviously. "I wish I could say the same for myself. My head feels as if someone had hammered a row of nails into it."

"Were you foxed too? I felt the same way earlier today, but I'm now feeling much more the thing," Brandon said cheerfully.

"Good. Then there's hope for me, I suppose. How's the ankle?"

"Fine, as long as I remain off my feet. I shall probably be hobbling around for weeks. But, please, let me say how very grateful I am for—"

"One more word of gratitude, my boy, and I shall walk out that door! By the way, Brandon, you never did tell me how you came to sprain your ankle. You obviously never went to the cathedral, so you couldn't have done it there. And you couldn't have done it while driving the curricle, so I can't imagine when or how it could have come to pass."

Brandon looked away in embarrassment. "I was hoping you wouldn't ask. It was the stupidest thing. I . . . I . . . er . . . fell off the curricle."

"Fell off the—? See here, old fellow, do you think to run sly with me? No one with sense would credit such a tale."

Brandon grimaced. "I was afraid of that," he said worriedly. "I've been avoiding the question so far—Mama has asked me at least fifty times how I came to do such a thing—but sooner or later I shall have to give some sort of explanation . . ."

"What's wrong with the truth?" Roger asked reasonably.

"The truth is rather awkward. I would be grateful for your advice, Roger, but as there is a lady involved, I . . . er . . . by your leave . . . will have to ask you—"

"Not to tell your story to anyone? You need have no worry on that score. Your secret will be absolutely safe with me, I promise you. There's a lady involved, you say? Are you referring to Letty?"

"Letty?" Brandon asked, looking at Roger in surprise. "Why, no. What made you think this has anything to do with *her*?"

Roger shrugged. "Nothing, really, except that I learned yesterday about your betrothal, so I assumed . . ."

"Oh, yes," Brandon mumbled, belatedly remembering his conversation on the matter with Roger the day before, "the betrothal. Yes, I see."

"But Letty had nothing to do with the accident?" Roger inquired curiously.

"No, oh no! Nothing at all. It was her sister Prue," Brandon explained hurriedly, happy to avoid the subject of the betrothal. "She was in the curricle with me, if you recall."

"Yes, now that you mention it, I do."

"Well, the truth of the matter is . . ." Brandon began, then lapsed into awkward silence.

"Go on. The story can't be as difficult to tell as all that."

"No, I suppose not, but . . . Why don't you sit down, Roger? It makes me uneasy having you stand over me like this."

Roger smiled. "Like a disapproving schoolmaster, is that it?" He pulled over the nearest chair and sat down. "There, now, I'm seated. Can you find any other excuses to postpone your tale? If not, please proceed. You were driving with Prue. And then—?"

"Well, the truth of the matter is," Brandon repeated shamefacedly, "that she pushed me out of the curricle."

"*Pushed* you? Hang it, Peake, is this another hum?" Roger demanded, trying his best to hide his amusement.

Brandon looked at him askance. "Go ahead and laugh. It's true!"

Roger permitted himself to grin. "You're not seriously expecting me to believe that a tiny chit is strong enough to push a full-grown man like you out of a carriage."

"Well, I wasn't expecting it, you see . . ." Brandon said defensively.

"I should think not!" Roger laughed. "Why in earth did she want to do such a thing to you?"

Brandon sighed. "That's the hardest part to explain."

Roger cocked his brow with a sudden suspicion. "Brandon, you're not trying to tell me that you behaved in some sort of ungentlemanly way, are you?"

"Ungentlemanly?" Brandon asked in complete innocence. "I suppose you could call it that. I shook her."

Roger, who had begun to believe that Brandon had attempted to seduce the sister of the girl to whom he was engaged, had been almost ready to give Brandon a facer. But the answer to his accusation was so unexpected and naive that Roger gaped. "Sh-shook her?" he asked in confusion.

Brandon nodded. "I'm afraid so."

Roger put his hand to his forehead unsteadily. "All this is a bit beyond me today, Brandon," he said. "Perhaps you'd better begin at the beginning."

"I'm not sure where to begin. I suppose the best way would be to say that she hates me."

"Hates you? *Prue* does? But why?"

"Because I tried to tell her that her flirtatious behavior was . . . er . . . unseemly."

"Did you indeed? That was not very wise. If I were a girl, I wouldn't feel very kindly toward you myself," Roger said frankly.

"I realize that now. I could bite out my tongue. But I've apologized and apologized, to no avail. She wouldn't say a word to me almost all the way to Wells!"

The tone of these remarks arrested Roger's attention. Until this point, Roger had assumed that Brandon had taken a brotherly interest in his betrothed's sister. But Brandon's concern was beginning to seem a bit beyond the brotherly. Observing Brandon closely, he remarked casually, "That must have been a bore."

"Not a bore, but a . . . a . . . strain," Brandon explained. "And then, when finally she *did* speak, it was only to criticize me."

"Oh? And what could she find to criticize?"

"You might better ask what could she *not* find to criticize! My speech, my manners, my . . . er . . . tendency to quote the classics, everything!"

"How very galling," Roger sympathized. "No wonder you shook her."

Brandon looked at him gratefully. "You *do* understand. But I didn't shake her until she . . . she . . . called me a . . . a . . ."

"A *what*, Brandon?"

"A stuffed prig."

Roger choked. "No, really? That was quite dreadful of her. I must admit she seems really to have *deserved* the shaking."

"Exactly!" Brandon agreed with satisfaction.

"And then she pushed you out of the carriage?"

"Yes. And *then* the vixen made off with the curricle! It must have been half a mile before she brought it to a halt. And I had to hobble after it on my twisted ankle, all the while terrified that she would do some damage to the grays!"

Roger shook his head compassionately. "Dreadful! I'd say she's a veritable hoyden."

"Well, not really," Brandon said hastily. "She only needs someone to give her a strong guiding hand, wouldn't you say?"

"I suppose so," Roger answered, watching Brandon carefully. "It's fortunate, however, that you've chosen the *sister* to marry."

Brandon, his imagination dwelling on a vision of himself offering a firm, guiding hand to Prue, did not readily follow the turn in conversation that Roger had made. "Marry? What do you mean?" he asked innocently.

"I mean Letty. Prue's sister. The girl you intend to wed."

"Oh, Letty. Yes, of course. I'm very fortunate. Very," Brandon said, the feeling of acute discomfort which had assailed him before returning with even stronger pangs.

"Yes, you're a most fortunate fellow," Roger repeated. "Can you imagine the turmoil of your life if you had to marry the younger sister? If you dared to tell her one morning that you didn't like the breakfast biscuits, she might push you from the window!"

Brandon smiled, but Roger noted that the smile was wan and unconvincing. "I . . . don't like you to think that of Prue," Brandon said hesitantly. "After all, she only pushed me because I shook her so hard. You mustn't think she's a termagant. I didn't mean to malign her to you."

"Of course you didn't," Roger said agreeably, rising to leave. "Give it no further thought. There's no permanent harm done, after all. No doubt the whole incident will be forgotten in a month."

"I suppose so," Brandon said somewhat glumly. Then realizing that his guest was about to leave, he said quickly, "Wait, Roger. You mustn't go yet. I wanted, by your leave, to have your suggestion concerning the story—Oh, dash it, I did it again!"

"Did what?"

"Said 'by your leave.' I've been trying to break myself of the habit."

"Why? I see nothing wrong with it."

"Prue says I say it every time I open my mouth."

"Does she?" Roger asked, looking at Brandon shrewdly. Then he turned to the door. "I think she exaggerates."

"You can't leave yet, Roger. You haven't told me what to say to people who ask me how I came to injure my ankle."

"Just tell them what you told me at first—that you fell out of the curricle."

"But . . . but *you* didn't believe me—!"

"They'll believe you if you tell it with conviction. And who cares if they don't? If I were you, I wouldn't give a hang if they believed me or not."

Roger walked to his mother's lodgings slowly. Brandon's artless story had given him much food for thought. The boy had spoken of no one but Prue. Prue seemed to occupy all his thoughts. Roger had tried repeatedly to bring Letty into the conversation, but Brandon had not seemed interested in discussing her. His embarrassment over the subject of Letty could, of course, be explained by his realization that he and Roger had been unwitting rivals for Letty's hand, but that embarrassment did not explain his inability to stop talking about *Prue*. If Roger's conclusions had any validity at all, Brandon was in love, *not* with his betrothed, but with her sister.

He began to recollect little signs that Prue had shown—unobtrusive glances, eyes which brightened when Brandon appeared in a doorway, overly animated flirtations with other men when his eyes were on her, and exaggerated indifference when he spoke to her—all indicating that she, too, was feeling the early pangs of love. If Brandon and Prue were, as he suspected, attracted to each other, what place had *Letty* in the situation? Was Letty about to be hurt?

The more Roger thought about the matter, the more convinced he became that Letty's heart was not involved in her betrothal. He was not a schoolboy, and he did not believe himself to be so foolish as to have mistaken Letty's response to his kiss or the look in her eyes whenever he came upon her unaware. He also was quite sure that she had an inexplicable but deep-seated fear of him. There was something havey-cavey about the entire business, and the more he thought about it, the more curious he became. He had to get to the bottom of it.

When he arrived at the lodgings, he found Trebbs in the hallway, dressed for travel and surrounded by a pile of neatly packed luggage. Roger winced. "I'm afraid you'll have to unpack again, Trebbs. We're not leaving after all."

Trebbs had been well schooled in the impassivity which was deemed appropriate for the demeanor of a gentleman's man; therefore, he merely nodded, murmured a soft, "Yes, my lord," picked up a piece of luggage and headed for the stairs. Lady Denham, however, who chose just this moment to make an appearance, was not so schooled. She gaped.

"What is going on *now*?" she demanded. "Why are you taking that portmanteau upstairs, Trebbs?"

"His lordship has asked me to unpack, my lady," Trebbs said with a barely noticeable quiver of disapproval in his tone. Before continuing up the stairs, he permitted himself to flick an accusing look at his lordship, who stood just inside the doorway, rubbing his chin sheepishly.

Lady Denham wheeled about to face her son. "Unpack? But why?"

Roger grinned, shrugged and walked quickly to the stairs. "I've decided to stay after all," he said and quickly started up.

"Just a minute, jackanapes. Come down here! I want an explanation," his mother demanded.

Roger came down again. "The only explanation I can give you is that I've changed my mind," he said, kissing her cheek.

"But *why*?" she insisted curiously.

"Mama," Roger said with his most charming, winning smile, "you know you are my dearest love, so I hope you will not take offense when I tell you that I think it would be best if you permitted me to manage my own affairs from now on."

"B-but, Roger—" she began, "you know I never—"

He placed his hand gently on her mouth. "Don't say anything for a moment, please, and listen to me. I agreed to permit you to find a suitable lady for me to marry. That was a mistake, and it has not ended well. Oh, I don't blame *you*— not at all! The mistake was all mine. I intend to rectify that error by taking the matter back into my own hands, as I should have done from the start. So, if you don't mind, I'd prefer not to discuss the matter with you. I promise that, when I find a girl and she has accepted me, you will be the very first person to be told." With that, he removed his hand.

"But Roger, my dear," she said as soon as she regained her breath, "I only want to know—"

"Mama!" he said warningly.

"But I can tell that something's happened. Have you found another girl already? Is that it? Just answer *that* and I promise to ask nothing else."

"I have nothing to tell you, ma'am," Roger said firmly. "And I want you to say nothing else but that I'm welcome to remain."

"But, Roger—" she pleaded.

Roger frowned at her sternly. "Very well, my dear," he said, "I shall tell Trebbs to repack and find lodgings elsewhere." And he started up the stairs again.

"Roger—!" Lady Denham cried.

He turned. "Yes, Mama?"

She raised her hand and opened her mouth to scold, hesitated, made a little helpless gesture and closed her mouth again. She drew in her breath and let it out in a long sigh. "Very well, my dear, you are welcome to remain," she said, defeated.

Chapter Twelve

The news had reached Bath that Charles James Fox had died, and the subject of his loss to Parliament and to England was discussed in the Pump Room, on every street and in all the drawing rooms of the city. But the members of Lady Upsham's domestic staff had something closer to their interests to discuss. Miss Tristle had taken Katie-from-the-kitchen under her wing! This surprising turn-about caused such endless expression of surprise and speculation that the topic drove all other matters from their conversation. All of the servants—even the butler—had felt a touch of Miss Tristle's spleen from time to time, but none of them had had to endure the verbal slights, the frequent criticism, the constant interference and the venomous disparagement which she had vented on poor Katie. Her sudden about-face on the subject of the rival abigail was nothing short of sensational. The death of Fox, famous though he was, had no power to drive from their minds and their tongues the subject of Miss Tristle's change of attitude toward the girl who she had once said was an ignorant and vulgar ur-chin trying to encroach on her position in the domestic domain.

Ever since the morning Katie had prepared a herb wash for her toothache, Miss Tristle had begun to look upon the girl with new eyes. The wash had been surprisingly efficacious. For the first time in days, Miss Tristle had found herself free of pain, and repeated rinsings with Katie's concoction had virtually cured the problem. She began to feel a new respect for Katie. She suddenly began to see the native intelligence and shrewdness which lay beneath Katie's unpolished surface. Everything Katie said made good sense, and she had somehow acquired an astonishing fund of interesting and useful information on all sorts of sub-jects. Miss Tristle was impressed. Grudgingly at first, but soon more readily, she began to ask the girl's opinion on matters she would never have deigned to ask before. Did Katie prefer the fichu or a Norwich shawl for Madam's plum-colored evening dress? Did the London ladies still lean toward tight curls hanging over their ears for daytime wear? Could Katie recommend a recipe for removing freckles? For all these, Katie had a ready—and usually original and sensible—answer.

By the time three days of this testing had passed, Miss Tristle had been won over. She made what was, for her, an amazing condescension—she invited Katie to spend the evening in her room so that they both could do their mending while enjoying a companiable coz together. Since it was much discussed among the servants that Miss Tristle's room was one of the largest and best lit of the servants' rooms, and that she kept it well supplied with tea, cakes and sherry, Katie readily accepted. The evening proved to be a great success. The two abigails discovered that they each had something to teach the other—Katie could teach Miss Tristle all manner of recipes for medications and cosmetic lotions (useful secrets she had learned from her many relatives in service) and Miss Tristle could teach Katie the rules of proper speech. They discovered, too, a shared interest in the strange and ever-fascinating doings of the *ton,* and when the educational part of the conversation had begun to pall, they turned to gossip.

Here, too, Miss Tristle found Katie surprisingly knowing. Her retentive memory stored away such interesting tidbits as the number of husbands that Lady Hester Houghton had managed to acquire before she passed away; the name of the fancy piece currently under the protection of the Marquis of Atherton; and the exact cost of the jeweled pendant the Prince had presented to Princess Caroline when he married her. In fact, Miss Tristle could rarely offer a juicy morsel that Katie did not already know.

However, she did manage to do so once or twice. One bit of news in particular seemed to be of great interest to Katie. Miss Tristle said she had heard that the elegant, vacant house on the Paragon had been let to a lady from London.

"Really?" Katie asked. "And who might she be?"

"I think Mrs. Besterbent said the name was Brownell," Miss Tristle said, knotting her thread and cutting it off with her teeth.

Katie eyed Miss Tristle with interest. "Brownell? Not Mrs. *Kitty* Brownell?"

Miss Tristle looked up with arched eyebrows. "Well, yes, I believe that was the very name. Why? Do you know of the lady?"

"Blimey if I don't," Katie said darkly. "I'd go bail that this means there's trouble brewin'."

"You don't say," Miss Tristle said eagerly, leaning forward with her mouth agape. "Why? Who is she?"

"I don't like bein' a chaffer-mouth, so I best not say nothin'. However, I don't think nobody what knows 'er 'll be glad she come'd."

"Came, my dear, *came*," Miss Tristle corrected condescendingly.

"Oh, is she 'ere a'ready?" Katie asked.

Miss Tristle was not gifted with a sense of humor, and so she merely looked at Katie with a confused expression. "No, I don't think so," she answered seriously. "Mrs. Besterbent said she's not due to arrive for yet a fortnight."

Katie leaned her elbows on the petticoat she had been trying to mend and propped her chin in her hands. "It queers me what 'er lay is," she muttered thoughtfully.

"I don't know what you're saying with those dreadful street words," Miss Tristle said testily, bursting with curiosity about Mrs. Brownell's identity but too proud to ask, "but you're making a mess of that petticoat. Here, give it to me. I'll finish it for you."

Katie, who had a distinct distaste and lack of talent for sewing fine stitches, gave over the petticoat with alacrity. "I'm only puzzlin' over what she's comin' 'ere for," she explained.

"Well, I can't help you, since I never heard of the lady."

"Kitty Brownell ain't no more lady 'n me! Less, in fact," Katie declared with disgust. "I'll tell you 'oo she is if you promise not to tattle it about."

"I can keep my mouth shut as well as you," Miss Tristle declared with an offended sniff.

"Then keep this tight under y'r bonnet," Katie said dramatically. "Mrs. Brownell is none other than Lord Denham's game pullet."

Miss Tristle's busy needle stopped. "You don't mean—?" she asked, aghast.

"Yes, I do. She's 'is bit o' muslin, 'is doxie, 'is *ladybird*!"

"No!" breathed Miss Tristle in pop-eyed fashion. "How shocking!"

"So it is," Katie agreed. "I'd give a yellow boy to get wind of 'er game."

The two lapsed into silence, absorbed in contemplation of the problem, but since no solution presented itself to either one, they put the question aside. A fortnight would soon pass, they told themselves, and then they would see what they would see.

Unaware of the impending calamity about to descend upon their lives with the arrival of Mrs. Brownell, the Glendenning sisters were making preparations to attend a small dinner party arranged by Mrs. Peake to cheer her housebound son. Mrs. Peake's guest list was small and select. She had invited Lady Upsham and her nieces, Lady Denham and Roger, and a Mr. Eberly, a wealthy gentleman who had been associated with her husband in some business ventures and who now resided in one of the elegant apartments in Bathwick.

Letty had dressed early on the afternoon of the dinner party and then went to her sister's room to see if she could be of assistance to Prue. She found her sister in a state of high-strung nervousness, pulling off a gown with angry impatience. Katie stood beside her with at least half-a-dozen discarded gowns thrown over her arm. Katie greeted Letty with relief. "I'm so glad you come'd . . . *came, Miss Letty.* This sister o' yours can't make up 'er mind what to wear."

"Everything this goosecap of an abigail has brought me is too . . . too garish!" Prue burst out, tossing the dress she had just removed at Katie crossly.

"Garish!" Letty said in bewildered amusement. "Is this the same Prue who said to me not long ago that it is better to be stared at than ignored?"

"Did I say that? Well, never mind. Tonight I want to look . . . subdued."

"Subdued? Whatever for? You couldn't look subdued with that hair of yours if you were dressed in mourning," her sister told her flatly. "Here, Katie, let me see what you have there."

"I told 'er this 'ere rose-colored one is bang up to the mark," Katie suggested.

"No!" Prue shouted, grimacing at Katie. "It makes my hair look too glaringly red."

"Then how about this blue silk? You quite swooned over it when we chose the pattern," Letty reminded her.

"The bodice is cut too low."

"Too low? What's the matter with you, Prue? You nagged Mama incessantly until she agreed to permit the dress to be cut this way."

Prue hung her head. "I don't care," she pouted. "I'm not in the mood for it today."

"I know!" Letty said with sudden inspiration. "Katie, bring her my lilac lustring. The color is so dusky, she's bound to find it subdued."

Prue's face brightened. "Your lustring would be perfect!" she cried, throwing her arms about her sister in gratitude. "Oh, Letty, you're an *angel*! But . . . you're so much taller than I . . . Don't you think it will be too long?"

"Perhaps? But if Katie pins it up at the shoulders, and you hold up the skirt just a bit when you walk, I think it should serve."

Prue's borrowed dress proved to be an excellent choice, for Brandon's eyes brightened perceptibly when she entered his mother's drawing room that evening. He was standing beside his mother, leaning on a sturdy stick and greeting her guests with an eager welcome. When Prue came up to him, he smiled at her uncertainly. "Good evening, Miss Glendenning," he said shyly. "By your leave, I'd like to say how lovely you l— Oh, hang it all!"

Prue looked up at him startled.

Brandon colored. "I do apologize. I didn't mean to say it, you know."

"Say what?" Prue asked, beginning to bristle. "That I look lovely?'

"Of course I meant to say *that*. It was the by-your-leave. It slipped out."

"Oh," said Prue. It was now her turn to blush. She turned away in embarrassment. She should never have said those cruel things to him. Now he would have to guard his tongue every time he spoke to her. Nevertheless, she was pleased to see that he apparently approved of her appearance. The look in his eyes when he saw her gave her the courage she needed to proceed on the course of action she had planned to undertake this evening; she had determined to find an opportunity to speak privately to him and apologize for causing his injury.

Roger, who had arrived some minutes earlier, did not fail to note Brandon's expression when he welcomed Prue. Roger was standing on the far side of the room, engaged in conversation with the one unfamiliar guest, Mr. Eberly. Eberly was not much older than Roger, but he appeared to be many years his senior. He was a heavyset, imposing gentleman who had lost much of the hair on his head and seemed to make up for it by the great amount of hair on his face. His eyebrows were remarkably thick and he sported a large and bushy mustache. He and Roger were discussing with approval the news which had just reached them of the passage in Parliament of a law which abolished the slave trade. Roger had managed to keep the conversation going while he observed Prue and Brandon in the doorway, but when Letty appeared, his concentration failed him.

Letty was indeed breathtaking this evening. Her thick auburn hair was loosely bound and fell in a soft curl over her shoulder. Her face glowed from the reflection of her burgundy-colored Belladine silk gown, which rippled gracefully as she moved. Mr. Eberly, following Roger's eye, smiled appreciatively. "What a lovely woman," he remarked.

"Yes," Roger said, the casual tone of his voice giving no indication of the pang the sight of her had caused in his chest. "Very lovely."

"She must be the Miss Glendenning I've been hearing so much about."

"Well," Roger explained with a smile, "she's one of them. She is here with her sister, who also has been turning the heads of the young Bath bucks."

"Do you mean that charming child over there with the red curls? I've noticed her myself. She seems always to be about to trip over her skirt."

"Yes, she's the one. Come along and let me introduce you to them."

When the introductions had been made and the guests had had their sherry, they moved into the dining room where, for more than two hours, they lingered over an excellent dinner, the highlights of which were a delectable veal ragout and a gooseberry trifle. The trifle was a culinary masterpiece concocted of cream, cake, wine, jam and almonds, but although the guests ate it with relish, they did not remark on it, so interested were they in the conversation which enlivened the dinner. Led by Roger and Mr. Eberly, the discussion centered on the part played by the late Mr. Fox in pushing the abolition bill through Parliament. Roger held that Fox had been a man of tremendous talent and great personal charm, while Mr. Eberly contended that Fox was basically a man of pathetically poor political judgment. Both Lady Upsham and Lady Denham agreed with Mr. Eberly, giving examples of many irresponsible acts Fox had committed in his political life. But Letty, who had been listening quietly through most of the talk, finally felt impelled to speak her mind. "You may be right about Mr. Fox's other failings," she said earnestly, "but I cannot help but feel that he deserves most of the credit for the abolition bill's passage, and I deem it a tragedy that he didn't live to see this fruition of his most commendable efforts."

"I think, Miss Glendenning," said Mr. Eberly, raising his glass to her, "that you've evaluated the matter most sensibly. I drink to you, my dear. As far as I'm concerned, you have quite won the day."

"Hear, hear!" Brandon added with enthusiasm, raising his glass as well.

Letty blushed at the unwonted attention and, quite despite her will, her eyes flew to Roger's face. His eyes were fixed on her, and they held a look of such unmistakable warmth and pride that her heart lurched. She quickly looked away and tried firmly but vainly to keep from glancing at him for the duration of the meal.

After the ladies had left the room, the men did not long linger over their port. When they rejoined the ladies in the drawing room, they found that Letty had been prevailed upon to play the piano. They took seats quietly and sat back to listen. Letty had chosen to play a simple country air to which she added impromptu variations, the sort of music with which she often entertained her young sisters. The small group of listeners enjoyed the unpretentious charm of the music as much as her sisters had. Prue, however, did not attend the music. Instead, she moved unobtrusively to the sofa where Brandon had seated himself and slipped into the seat beside him. "There's something I must say to you," she whispered.

"Is something the matter?" he whispered back.

"Yes, there is. *I'm* the matter. I'm terribly headstrong and thoughtless. It's all my fault that you're injured, and I just have to say how sorry I am that I pushed you out of the carriage."

Brandon reached impetuously for her hand. "You don't have to be sorry," he said, close to her ear. "It was more my fault than yours. I never should have shaken you like that."

"Well, I never should have been so rude and criticized you so dreadfully," she whispered into his ear, her breath tickling his neck and causing exquisitely agonizing bumps to form down his back and along his arms.

"Oh, Prue," he murmured with a catch in his voice, "I—"

But she was not to learn what he intended to say, for the music ended at that moment. He dropped her hand and they jumped apart, applauding enthusiastically for Letty's music as if they'd been listening as attentively as the rest. After that, Brandon, although incapacitated, had nevertheless to perform the duties of a host, making sure to give his attention to each of his guests and see that they were entertained and wanted for nothing. No further opportunity presented itself for him to complete the sentence he had started with such a burst of earnest feeling.

Roger, meanwhile, came up to the piano before Letty could leave and, leaning on the instrument, smiled affectionately at her. "You are full of surprises, my dear," he said. "I didn't know you were so accomplished a musician."

"You are surprised, my lord, only because you had prejudged me before we were fully acquainted and arrogantly decided that I *had* no accomplishments," she answered saucily, feeling more confident with him than she had before she was protected from him by her supposed betrothal.

"That is grossly unfair," he protested. "Experience had taught me that beautiful young women have little need for other accomplishments, and therefore don't trouble to develop them. How was I to know that you are the exception?"

"Stop, please," she said with a smile. "It is not like you to stoop to such wanton flattery."

"Do you think I offer you Spanish coin? Far from it, I assure you. Your playing was truly delightful. And your comments on Fox were quite impressive, too. I had no idea that you take an interest in politics."

"Any person of sense takes an interest in politics, my lord," she said, "although you must not conclude from one little remark of mine that I'm really knowledgeable."

"I insist on being permitted to draw my own conclusions, Miss Glendenning," Roger stated with a twinkle and helped her to rise from the piano stool. They turned and joined the others. Like Brandon and Prue, they found no other opportunity for private conversation.

Prue was feeling rather pleased with herself by the time Lady Upsham rose and indicated that it was time for them to take their leave. The entire evening had passed without a single instance of indecorous behavior on her part. She had sat politely beside her aunt, smiling and nodding and saying polite things to anyone who addressed her. She had neither giggled nor laughed loudly; she had not flirted; she had not drawn any attention to herself. In short, she had been a model of decorum, and she was sure that Brandon had noticed. Every time she'd met his eye, he had smiled at her approvingly.

Brandon rose and, leaning heavily on his stick, went to the entryway to bid the guests good night. Prue went up to him and held out her hand. "Do you truly forgive me, Brandon?" she asked in an undervoice.

"You know I do," he answered feelingly, squeezing her hand tightly.

She met his eye and felt a strange flutter inside her. Hurriedly, she turned to the door to join her aunt and Letty. In her confusion, she forgot to hold up the skirts of her borrowed gown. She stepped on the too-long hem and tripped clumsily. She would have fallen flat on her face had it not been for Mr. Eberly, who was standing nearby and swiftly reached out for her. She fell heavily against his chest and looked up at him in mortification. "Oh, how . . . how clumsy of me," she gasped. "I'm so sorry!"

Mr. Eberly laughed jovially and set her on her feet. "No need to be sorry," he said with a booming heartiness. "I quite enjoyed that! It's not every day that I can play the gallant to a charming young girl."

Prue glanced quickly around the foyer. Everyone was watching. She had made a fool of herself, and everyone had witnessed it. Her quick glance took in a glimpse of Brandon's face. He was frowning. In despair, she turned and ran to the door. She had made a spectacle of herself again. Her evening was ruined!

Lady Upsham and Letty, unperturbed at what Prue thought was a dreadful scene, said cheerful good nights, and the three departed. Mr. Eberly stood in the hallway smiling after them. "Charming little chit, Miss Prudence, don't you think?" he asked Brandon in a jolly man-to-man tone. He had no idea why Brandon chose to glare at him for saying it.

Chapter Thirteen

$\mathcal{R}$oger had been an interested observer of the little scene played at the doorway. The whole evening had done much to reinforce his feeling that, whatever tie had bound Letty and Brandon, it was not love. Brandon had been whispering in *Prue's* ear and had held her hand in a most loverlike fashion all the while that Letty had been at the piano. In Roger's view, Letty had looked so charming that any man who really loved her would not have been able to tear his eyes from her. And in addition, when Eberly had caught Prue in his arms (when the girl had tripped on her skirts), Brandon had looked as if he would like to call the fellow out. Brandon's interest in Prue was obvious. On the other hand, as far as Roger could tell, Brandon and *Letty* had not spent a moment in each other's company, nor had they exhibited an inclination to do so.

Of course, it was possible that Brandon and Letty had agreed to behave in this way to throw Lady Upsham off the scent, that they and Prue had conspired to enact a charade to confuse observers. But Roger's instincts told him that it was unlikely that Brandon's and Prue's behavior could be feigned. He was quite convinced that the two were strongly attracted to each other.

What he needed to ascertain was Letty's feeling for Brandon. He had never observed their behavior when they were together in private conversation. But he had a plan. He would arrange to take Brandon for a drive the very next day.

Brandon's gratitude to Roger for his invitation was so sincere that Roger felt a pang of guilt. Brandon, delighted to be freed from his imprisonment indoors on this beautiful late-September day, felt compelled to express his thanks all the while Roger helped him into his rented phaeton and during the first few minutes of the ride. But the subject of gratitude was completely forgotten when Roger suggested that they stop at Lady Upsham's to see if Letty would care to join them on the drive.

"Letty?" asked Brandon, taken aback. "But . . . Well, won't it be a bit awkward?"

"Awkward? Not at all. That's why I've rented this phaeton instead of taking out my curricle. I'll climb up on the box and leave you two lovebirds alone."

"That is most . . . er . . . thoughtful of you, Roger, but . . . I was thinking of Lady Upsham. She . . . er . . . mustn't see Letty and me together, you know."

"Oh, don't worry about that," Roger said airily. "I won't mention that you're here. You'll remain outside, waiting in the phaeton. I'll allow her to believe that I've come alone. Lady Upsham won't permit Letty to refuse me."

"I see . . ." Brandon said nervously. This situation was not at all to his liking. It was bad enough to have had to acknowledge Letty as his betrothed when it was not true, but it was even worse to have to enact a loverlike role before a witness. Especially before Roger. The fact that Roger was behaving in this excessively kind way made this predicament doubly painful. Besides, he had no skill at dissembling. He was sure to make a mull of it. He was being pulled deeper and deeper into an abyss of dishonesty and deceit. His mind searched desperately for a way of escape. But he could think of nothing except . . . Prue! Perhaps, with the addition of another person, he would not be forced to play the 'lovebird' role. "Er . . . Roger, do you think, perhaps, that you ought to ask Prue to come along too?" he suggested hesitantly.

"Prue?" asked Roger innocently. "I don't think so. I planned this so that you and Letty could have some time in each other's company. Prue would spoil everything. Besides, Lady Upsham never permits Prue to come along when Letty and I go riding."

Brandon could think of nothing else and relapsed into a worried silence. Roger whistled cheerfully until they drew up in front of Lady Upsham's residence. Promising Brandon a speedy return, he jumped down from the phaeton and went inside. In a few minutes he returned leading a puzzled-looking Letty to the carriage. She started at the sight of Brandon. "There!" Roger said in a self-satisfied way. "I told you I had a surprise for you."

"B-Brandon," Letty stammered uneasily, "what are you—? That is, how v-very nice to see you."

Roger helped Letty into the phaeton beside Brandon and vaulted up to the box. "It seems to me such a shame that a betrothed couple cannot spend any time together, so I made up my mind to give you both the opportunity to do so. You needn't mind me, you know. I'll just drive and think my own thoughts. Just pretend I'm not here."

Brandon and Letty exchanged helpless looks behind Roger's back, and Brandon shrugged to indicate that he couldn't have done anything to avoid the situation. Letty tried to fill in the dismaying silence by asking loudly how

Brandon's ankle was getting on. Brandon answered in such complete detail that Letty could find nothing more to say on the subject, and another interminable silence ensued. Finally Letty asked brightly if Brandon had had any time to pursue his studies. To this Brandon responded that he'd had little time since his accident to spend on his books because of all the callers who had come to pay their condolences and because of the assistance his mother had required in preparation for her dinner party. "However," he added, "I did manage to read the translation of Horace that Roger was good enough to lend me."

"Oh, yes," Letty said with sudden interest, "you *did* tell me that Lord Denham is a scholar of the classics. I didn't think you had interests along those lines, Lord Denham."

"Are you speaking to me?" Roger asked guilelessly, turning around to look at them.

"Yes, I am," Letty said. "Brandon tells me you've studied the classics. I was surprised to learn that you have interests in that direction."

Roger's eyes twinkled maliciously. "You are surprised, Miss Glendenning," he said, parroting her words of the night before, "only because you had prejudged me before we were fully acquainted and arrogantly decided that I had no accomplishments."

Brandon was appalled. "Oh, I say, Roger," he objected vehemently, "you can't call Letty arrogant! That's coming it a bit too strong, isn't it?"

Letty laughed and put a restraining hand on Brandon's arm. "He's only teasing, Brandon. That's what I said about *him* last night. And besides, I can now toss his reply to *me* right back at him."

"What reply was that, Miss Glendenning?" Roger asked.

"Experience has taught *me,* my dear sir," she replied archly, "that noted Corinthians like yourself, who spend their time in gaming, in sporting pursuits or in . . . er . . . other adventures, have little time for books."

"Touché," Roger admitted with a grin. "It would seem, ma'am, that we *both* have been guilty of misjudgment."

Roger turned back to his horses, leaving Letty and Brandon with the problem of finding something else to talk about. They succeeded in finding only the merest commonplaces, and both of them took every possible opportunity to draw Roger into the conversation. The halting and stilted exchanges were so amusing to the eavesdropper on the box that he had a difficult time keeping his shoulders from shaking.

After a while, Roger discovered that he'd taken a wrong turning. Seeing a cottage near by, he excused himself and climbed down to seek assistance from the inhabitants. Letty seized the moments of privacy to ask Brandon how this terrible state of affairs had come about. "I don't know," Brandon said miserably.

"He acted as if he were doing me the greatest favor. I didn't know how to refuse him."

"Do you think he's testing our story?" Letty asked worriedly.

Brandon shook his head. "Confound it, Letty," he groaned, "I wish I'd never agreed to your silly scheme. He's the best of good fellows, and I hate to play him false in this way."

Letty couldn't dispute him. "I know," she said disconsolately. "I don't like it either. But we've gone too far to deny it now. There's nothing for it but to play the game out."

"Very well, if we must. But Letty, I don't even know what to say to sound like a man betrothed to a girl. What do betrothed people talk about to each other?"

"I don't know," Letty said, chewing a nail nervously. "How much they love each other, I suppose. Fulsome compliments, dreams and plans for the future . . . But Lord Denham will not expect us to talk about such things when he's seated right there within earshot."

"Then what *can* we talk about to each other?" Brandon asked in desperation.

"Well, I have an idea. There's to be a ball at the Upper Rooms next week. Ask me if I intend to go and suggest ways that we might be together without calling attention to ourselves."

"But, Letty, I can't attend a ball with a sprained ankle," he objected.

"There comes Roger now," Letty said hurriedly. "You *can* attend if you don't dance. There's no time to think of anything else. Please, Brandon, do the best you can!"

The conversation between them, after Roget's return, did not differ in quality from their earlier attempts. Although they discussed the ball at great length, Brandon showed rather too much un-loverlike politeness in his oft-repeated request that Letty spend some time at the ball sitting out the dances at his side. Letty, realizing that the conversation between them lacked the sparkle of a couple in love, cast a number of agitated glances at Roger's unresponsive back, but in truth, Roger had long since given up paying any attention to what his passengers were saying to each other. The lack of intimacy in their tone of conversation had already convinced him that his estimate of the situation was correct—their betrothal was not based on love. His mind was grappling with a more perplexing problem.

Now that he was convinced that their betrothal was not a love match, he had to determine what had brought it about. The most obvious solution was that it was nothing but a ruse, designed to keep *him* from pursuing Letty. He spent the remainder of the ride trying to understand why a girl whose eyes brightened when she looked at him, whose mind seemed closely attuned to his, who so delightfully responded to his quips, his tastes, and even his kiss, should go to such lengths to keep him at a distance. He could find no answer.

But one fact was glaringly, upsettingly clear. Letty was firmly fixed on preventing him from making her another proposal of marriage. The girl, for all the signs of her attraction to him, did not want Roger for a husband. He sighed in discouragement and wondered how he had permitted himself to occupy this position of humiliation—the position of *an unwanted suitor who has not the sense to take himself off.* Perhaps he should oblige Letty and restore his self-esteem by giving up the pursuit. With every day that he lingered in her vicinity, he found himself more deeply attached to her. The longer he remained, the greater would be the pain if he ultimately failed to win her. Perhaps now was the time to give up the struggle and return to London.

They drew up outside Lady Upsham's lodgings. He jumped down from the box while Letty said her good-byes to Brandon. Then he reached for her hands to help her down. She paused on the carriage step and looked down at him, her eyes searching his face for a clue to his thoughts. For that moment, time seemed to stop for him. What was it he read in her expressive face? Fear and uncertainty, surely, but just as surely there was something else. Without conscious awareness, Roger smiled comfortingly at her and was rewarded by a sudden glimmer of luminescent gratitude which sprang into her unbelievably speaking eyes. Confound it, he thought, why did he always feel that they could converse with eyes alone? Fool that he was, he knew that he would not go away just yet. He would play out the game until the bitter end.

As if she had read his thoughts, her eyes dropped, her cheeks crimsoned and she withdrew her hands from his clasp. Without a word, she ran to the door and disappeared inside. He stood there staring after her long after she'd gone, and it was not until Brandon gave an awkward cough that he was brought back to consciousness of where he was.

"My very first ball, and I don't even want to go," Prue said glumly to her reflection in the mirror as she sat brushing her curls into a sophisticated hairstyle known as the *Sappho.* Katie stood behind her, watching admiringly and making herself useful by handing Prue hairpins and combs as they were called for. "'Course you want to go," she said sensibly. "You'll be in high leg soon as you're tiffled up and see how pretty you look."

"I *won't* be in high leg, as you call it. I'm in the dismals and will probably remain there all evening. The ball is bound to be deadly dull. I know every young man in Bath, and none of them is capable of brightening a girl's disposition."

Katie looked at her archly. "Not even a certain Mr. Peake?" she asked with brazen insolence.

Prue frowned at her. "You go too far, Miss Katie-from-the-kitchen. One of these days, I'll box your ears and send you back to the scullery."

Katie, having heard those threats many times before, merely ignored them. "If you know'd what I know'd," she said tauntingly, "you'd be took out o' the dismals like a shot."

"What's that?" Prue asked curiously.

"That Mr. Peake will be there this night."

"Don't be silly. He can barely walk with a stick, so why would he come to a dance?" Prudence asked logically.

" 'E'll be there. You ain't never knowed Katie to bamboozle you, 'ave you?"

Prue stared at her abigail suspiciously. "How do you know? Who told you?"

"Oh, I 'as my ways," Katie said superciliously, having learned to enjoy her reputation as a "knowing one."

Prue, convinced, found that, as Katie had predicted, she was rapidly becoming quite cheerful about the prospects for the evening. The blue silk, which had been rejected on the night of Mrs. Peake's dinner party because of its low *décolletage,* was deemed suitable for a ball, and by the time the dress had been donned, Prue's mood had changed from dismal to radiant.

Letty, on the other hand, saw no prospect of anything but a dull evening. She had determined to spend a good part of it at Brandon's side, for she was sure the two of them would be observed by the omnipresent Lord Denham. She knew that *she* could summon up the spirit to smile and flirt with Brandon with enough enthusiasm to confound Roger, but she had no confidence in Brandon's ability to be equally convincing. Brandon had no ability to act a role. Naive, innocent and straightforward, Brandon showed discomfort when forced to practice deception, which was obvious to any observer, and a man of Roger's perspicacity would never be fooled.

The two sisters arrived at the Assembly Rooms in completely opposite states of mind. Their eyes searched the room for the same young man, but one looked with eyes of eagerness and the other with eyes of dread.

Brandon, even with the assistance of his mother, was not able to make his way to the Upper Rooms easily. Therefore, it was quite late when they made their appearance in the ballroom. Mrs. Peake helped her son to a vacant chair and left him to join the elderly ladies who spent their time at dances watching and gossiping. Brandon sat back as comfortably as he could on the spindly chair and looked at the dance floor. The first thing to attract his eye was Prue's red-gold hair. She was spinning by on the arm of Sir Ralph, who was whirling her around the floor in a waltz with rather unexpected expertise. The waltz, while still restricted at Almack's in London to couples under the sanction of the patronesses, was indulged in quite freely in the more limited society of Bath. Brandon had never thought about it before, but now he was struck with disapproval. It was, he decided, a tasteless, indecent display, and Prue should have known better than to permit herself to indulge in it.

When Letty came up to him a few moments later, he greeted her with a strong reproof, blaming her for neglecting her sisterly duties. "How could you have permitted your sister to make a spectacle of herself on the dance floor?" he demanded.

Letty, taken aback, responded with annoyance. "You are being positively gothic, Brandon," she told him shortly. "*Everyone* dances the waltz in Bath. Even my aunt sees nothing objectionable in it, so I don't see why you should disapprove. Of what concern can it be to you, in any case?"

Brandon, having no answer, lapsed into a glum silence. Letty would have liked to walk away from him, but she caught a glimpse of Roger across the room, talking to Mr. Eberly but looking directly at them. She pulled up a chair and sat down beside Brandon with a sigh. "Don't glower so, Brandon," she begged. "Roger is looking at us."

"Bother Roger and bother this ball," Brandon said pettishly. "I wish I hadn't let you talk me into coming. By your leave, Letty, I'm bound to tell you that every time I let you persuade me to do anything, I soon regret it."

"Of all the ungallant things I've ever heard you say," Letty said in chagrin, "that is the worst. I never thought, Brandon Peake, that you could be so churlish and unkind. I thought you were my *friend*!"

Brandon, completely unequal to feminine attacks, completely unable to withstand their flashing eyes and quivering voices, subsided at once. "I . . . I'm sorry, Letty," he mumbled uneasily. "I didn't mean—"

"For heaven's sake, don't look so miserable," Letty said uncomfortably, keeping her eye on Roger as she spoke. "How can Lord Denham possibly believe that we're lovers when you look so glum in my company."

"Lovers!" Brandon groaned. "How does one look like a lover?"

"Stop asking me those silly questions. Just look at me and *smile*. Talk to me! Say something . . . anything! We used to have very interesting conversations when we first met. Can't we do so now?"

"I don't know," Brandon said bitterly. "We weren't involved in such deception then. How can I concentrate on anything when I know we're being watched?"

"Can't you forget that we're being watched? Can't you tell me about your precious Greeks? Once you spent *hours* telling me about Thucydides!"

"Well," Brandon said, grasping at a straw, "I *had* once planned on talking to you about Catullus. He's not a Greek, of course, but a Roman."

"Oh, Brandon," Letty laughed in relief, "as if *that* matters."

"I don't have the book with me, however. I don't know many of the verses by memory. But he'd make an excellent subject. He wrote love poetry, you see."

"Then we'll manage without the book. He'll make the perfect subject," Letty said encouragingly, leaning close to him.

By the time Prue extricated herself from the attentions of the Rabbit and came up to them, Letty and Brandon seemed quite happily absorbed in conversation. At the same moment, Roger approached the little group. After the greetings were exchanged, he turned to Letty. "Would you care to stand up with me, Letty? A set is just now forming for a country dance."

"Thank you," Letty answered pleasantly but with a negative shake of her head, "but I don't wish to leave Brandon sitting here alone."

Prue, with full realization that she was behaving in an unladylike manner, spoke up brazenly. "I'll keep Brandon company, Letty, if you wish to dance."

Letty cast a look of irritation at her sister. Why couldn't Prue mind her own business? But she knew she was being unreasonable. Prue had no idea of what was going on. So she smiled brightly at Prue but said in a determined voice, "No, thank you, Prue dear. Brandon has been reciting to me the love poetry of Catullus." Here she flashed a challenging glance at Roger. "I've been finding it delightful. Besides, I've *promised* this dance to Brandon, so to speak, haven't I, Brandon?"

Brandon cast a glance at Prue and nodded miserably. Prue, feeling the rejection like a sudden douse of cold water, recoiled. Roger, on the other hand, merely smiled jauntily. "I can quite understand your preferring Catullus to my dancing," he said, "but I don't think 'delightful' is the right word for his poetry. 'Passionate,' or 'frenzied,' even 'bitter,' but *not* 'delightful.'" With that, he made a little bow and left.

Prue gave a stammering, incoherent little apology and backed away. Unfortunately, she did not notice that Mr. Eberly had come up behind her, and she blundered into him. She lost her balance and fell against him, but he held her easily and restored her to her feet. She looked at him in agony and mumbled, "Oh, Mr. Eberly! I'm so sorry . . . !"

Mr. Eberly smiled down at her fondly. "My dear girl," he said in playful admonition, "have you blundered into me *again*? What am I to make of that, may I ask? Can it be that you are endeavoring to attract the attention of an old bachelor like myself?"

This flirtatious raillery did much to restore Prue's self-esteem. She threw Brandon a triumphant glance and smiled winningly at her rescuer. "Old bachelor, pooh!" she said with an enchanting giggle. "You are just the right age."

"The right age for what, you little minx?" Mr. Eberly inquired.

"For dancing with clumsy little minxes," Prue answered with a rather too-loud laugh. "Don't you agree, sir?"

"I most certainly do," Mr. Eberly said warmly and drew her arm through his. They walked off without a backward look, and only a toss of her head in Brandon's direction gave any sign that she had given him another thought.

"Did you mark that?" Brandon demanded of Letty as soon as they were out of earshot. "Is *that* the sort of behavior of which your aunt approves?"

"What are you talking about now, Brandon?" Letty asked, perplexed.

"Is it now considered permissible for a young lady to ask a gentleman to dance with her? It was my understanding that it is the gentleman's place to do the asking."

"If you are referring to Prue's suggestion that she sit here with you while I dance, I find nothing reprehensible about that."

"I am not referring to that at all. I am referring to her behavior with Eberly just now!" Brandon said in disgust.

"Oh, that," Letty said, dismissing it curtly. "That was only a bit of innocent flirting. Anyone with half an eye could see he was delighted with her."

"That's just it!" Brandon insisted. "She shouldn't be permitted to encourage an elderly man like Eberly to leer at her in that odious way."

"He's not elderly. And he did not leer. Really, Brandon, you are becoming quite tedious. I'm beginning to wish that we *were* betrothed, so I could have the pleasure of breaking it off!" And she walked away and left him to mope alone.

Prue, her self-esteem restored by the flattering attentions of Mr. Eberly, returned to Brandon's side when the dance ended. She had made up her mind to try again. Finding him alone, she dropped into the chair vacated by Letty and smiled at him brightly. "It's good to sit down," she said cheerfully. "My feet positively ache."

"I'm not a bit surprised," Brandon muttered sullenly. "What else should one expect when one has been bouncing around the floor as you've been doing?"

Prue blinked at him in surprise. "Whatever do you mean, Brandon? I can't say I like your tone."

"I can't say I like the way you *danced,* either," Brandon could not restrain himself from saying. He was feeling used, abused and neglected. He had sat in lonely misery, watching the dancers whirl about the room happily oblivious of his discomfort. He felt very, very sorry for himself.

Prue drew herself up stiffly. "What was wrong with the way I danced?" she asked, her voice taking on an ominous formality.

"The way you waltzed around with Sir Ralph was unquestionably the most tasteless, indecent exhibition I've ever seen," Brandon said heedlessly, his sullen mood driving him on, "and the way you encouraged Eberly to ogle you must have caused any observers to turn away in acute embarrassment!"

Prue whitened in fury. "How dare you!" she gasped in a horrified whisper, her lips trembling. "How *d-dare* you speak to me in such a way! I wouldn't permit my own b-brother to say such th-things to me! *Indecent?* A little waltz? And accusing Mr. Eberly of *ogling* me? I have a good mind to tell him what you've said! He'd probably call you out and *horsewhip* you. If only I were a man, I'd do it *myself*!"

She got to her feet and glared down at him, biting her underlip to keep back her tears and clenching and unclenching the hands held stiffly at her sides. Brandon looked up at her in shock. He had gone too far, and he knew it. He had no idea what had made him say those dreadful things. He didn't even believe those accusations himself. Disregarding his ankle, he struggled to his feet. "Prue . . ." he began pleadingly, "Prue—!"

"Don't speak to me," she said between clenched teeth. "Don't *ever* speak to me, Brandon Peake. I don't want to see you, or hear you, or know anything about you from this day forward! Do you hear? From now on, as far as I'm concerned, *you don't even exist!*"

She turned on her heel and walked rapidly away. He sank back on his chair and let his misery envelop him. This time, the misery was not self-induced. It came from the destruction of his dreams, and its painful reality made his earlier self-indulgence seem positively pleasurable in comparison.

Chapter Fourteen

$\mathcal{L}$ady Denham, in response to an urgent note from Lady Upsham, met her friend at the library on Milsom Street on an afternoon three days after the ball. As soon as the ladies had greeted each other, Lady Upsham embarked on the problem which occupied their thoughts. Circumstances beyond the knowledge or control of either one of them seemed to be destroying their hopes, and Lady Upsham wondered aloud if there was not some action they should take.

Lady Denham had confided in Lady Upsham earlier that, although Roger had masterfully taken matters out of her hands, she had every confidence that he would manage successfully on his own. Roger, she had said, was a man of amazing perception, competence and charm—facts which, of course, were obvious to anyone, not only his mother—and she had assured Lady Upsham that it was only a question of time before the entire affair would be settled. But now, Lady Upsham reported, there were unmistakable signs that matters were not going at all well. Both Letty and Prue were sunk in the doldrums. They remained abed until late, and when they finally made their appearances, they both looked hagged. Their eyes were circled, as if they'd not slept well. They resisted her repeated suggestions to visit the Pump Room or meet with their friends. They seemed to prefer to mope about the house. It was only with the strongest urging that she could prevail upon them to take the air briefly by strolling about in the Parade Gardens opposite their lodgings. Lady Upsham had no idea what had happened or why the doldrums seemed to beset both girls at once.

With arms linked, the two friends strolled up Milsom Street abstractedly. Each put forth various theories to explain what might have happened, but these were rejected. There was only one encouraging note in their entire conversation: Lady Denham noted that Roger did not seem unduly depressed. His mother could not go so far as to say that he actually was cheerful, but he was active, went riding daily, attended some of the evening functions at the Upper Rooms and, most significant of all, made no reference to returning to London. If Roger did not have expectations of success, why was he remaining fixed in a place which he normally abhorred?

With this slight bit of encouragement, the ladies considered what action they might take to move things forward. "Our first objective must be to find a way to shake my nieces from their lethargy," Millicent said shrewdly. "Nothing will happen while they remain hidden away at home."

They walked on in silence. Suddenly, Lady Denham stopped and smiled. "I think I have a suggestion," she said. "The fireworks."

"Fireworks?" Lady Upsham asked, regarding her friend with an arrested look. "Are you speaking of the display in the Sydney Gardens?"

"Yes, exactly," Lady Denham answered. "I hear that a display will be held tomorrow. I have not previously attended, but I understand that they are quite breathtaking. I shall make up a party for tomorrow evening. We shall have an alfresco dinner right there in the park. With the promise of music and merriment, and a most attractive fireworks display, your nieces will not be able to resist my invitation."

Lady Denham's prediction did not turn out to be quite accurate. Both girls looked decidedly dubious when Roger appeared at the house on the North Parade bearing his mother's invitation. In fact, they showed every indication that they intended to resist vigorously. Roger, recognizing the signs, remarked that the party would be very small—Lady Denham was inviting only Lady Upsham, her two nieces and himself—and that, under those circumstances, their absence would be disastrous to her plans. At this, Letty weakened perceptibly, and Prue looked thoughtful. After he left, Aunt Millicent made it quite plain that they would face her severe displeasure if they refused. So, in the end, the two sisters wrote a gracious note to Lady Denham accepting her kind invitation with thanks.

If the truth were told, it was the information that Brandon would not make one of the party that had decided the matter in the minds of both Letty and Prue. Letty would have been hard-pressed to spend another evening in Brandon's company. It was not that she was angry with him any longer, but she had had quite enough of dissembling. She could not have endured spending another evening pretending closeness to Brandon while Roger watched them with his shrewd and ironic eyes. She was quite relieved at the prospect of a temporary respite from the problems which her deceit had caused. She could look forward, instead, to an evening relaxed and at peace, knowing that Brandon would not be present to remind her of her foolish trickery and that Roger's friendship could be enjoyed without concern that he would press her for anything more.

As for Prue, she would not have agreed to go to the Gardens at all if Brandon had been included in the party. Her pain at his cruel and unjustified criticism of her behavior had not abated, and her determination to avoid him at all costs remained firm. As it was, however, she could look forward to a comfortable, if not a joyous, evening.

Of course, there was nothing to prevent their running into Brandon at the Gardens. The fireworks and gala festivities were open to the public, and often the entire population of Bath turned out for the display. There was no certainty that they would not come face-to-face with him. But since he was not to be one of their party, they would be under no obligation to associate with him.

Once the objections to their attendance at the Sydney Gardens were rationalized away, the mood of both girls brightened perceptibly. For the three days since the disastrous ball they had, each for her own reasons, been indulging in bouts of depression. But it is not in the nature of healthy young women to steep themselves in depression for very long. Their natures are amply supplied with qualities like hope and anticipation, which gather strength like antitoxins to fight the gloom. These hopeful feelings had lain dormant under the depression, waiting for an excuse to burst forth into the open. The prospect of the evening at the Gardens provided just such an excuse. What healthy, pretty, spirited young lady could remain gloomy with the prospect of a gala evening of music, lights and spectacular fireworks before her? Both Letty and Prue quickly became aware that their dismals seemed miraculously to disappear, and the world suddenly became a much more cheerful place.

On the afternoon of the gala, Lady Upsham ordered them both to return to their rooms for a nap before dressing. The fireworks would not begin before complete darkness had fallen, she explained, and they were bound to be out until late. Therefore, a nap in the afternoon was advisable. The girls complied, but neither one could sleep. Prue dug her face into her pillow and concocted daydreams in which she received elaborately worded offers of marriage from Osbert, the Rabbit, Mr. Woodward and Mr. Eberly, all of which were overheard by a jealous and tortured Brandon, who gnashed his teeth and clenched his fists in helpless agony.

Letty's mind was occupied with even more nonsensical fancies. She dreamed that she had become Roger's *cher amie* in place of Kitty Brownell, and she tried to imagine what it would be like to be with Roger in such a situation. She would, no doubt, have to appear before him quite scantily clad, and to permit him to handle her with disrespectful and passionate abandon. She covered her face in shame, but try as she would, her thoughts refused to take a more proper course, and she finally admitted to herself that, deep down, she was convinced that it was more appealing to be a man's mistress than his wife!

She was roused by a knock at the door, and Katie came in with two white dresses laid carefully over her arm. The abigail had decided that white was the most effective color without bothering to discuss the matter with either Letty or Prue. Letty took her dress from Katie's arm without objection. But Prue, when Katie delivered the other dress to her bedroom door, set up an instant outcry. She would wear a bright color—crimson, perhaps—no matter what *certain people* would say if they saw her. It was better to be stared at than ignored. Hadn't she always said so? But Katie was adamant. This was the dress she had prepared, and this was the dress Prue would wear.

When Lady Denham and Roger called for them in the barouche, Letty and Prue looked fresh, bright and lovely in their gowns of crisp white cambric. Their eyes sparkled in anticipation, their complexions glowed and their smiles were bright. No one would have guessed that they had spent the last few days sunk in gloom.

But Letty's high spirits seemed to disappear as soon as they entered the Sydney Gardens. The carriage had brought them to the entrance at the foot of Pulteney Street, and no sooner had they descended and entered the main pathway when Letty uttered an involuntary gasp. The Sydney Gardens had been completely transformed from their daytime appearance. There was music and singing everywhere, with the tinkle of high laughter combining with the music. The fountains and cascades sparkled, and the illuminations were superb. It was another *Vauxhall!* She shivered as the memory of that other night struck her with an almost tangible reality.

Lady Denham noticed the shiver. "Letty, my dear, you're cold," she said with concern. "Here. Take my shawl and put it over you." And she draped a magnificent green fringed shawl over Letty's shoulders. Letty, noticing with horror that it was the same bright green of her domino, wanted to snatch it off, but she merely shook her head and let it slip from her shoulders. "Th-thank you, Lady Denham," she said hastily, handing it back, "but I'm not at all cold. Please keep it for yourself."

Lady Denham's butler had set up the table on a grassy knoll protected from the breeze by a row of trees. The pickled salmon, the cold chicken and ham, the Highland creams were all delectable and served with the same elegance that would have marked the service in her ladyship's dining room. The champagne, chilled to perfection, had a beneficial effect on Letty. Her spirits rose again, and she and Roger indulged in lighthearted badinage with all the comfort and intimacy of old friends, while Lady Denham and Millicent watched with satisfied smiles.

After the dinner had been consumed, Lady Denham and Lady Upsham turned their chairs about to watch the parade of passersby. Although full darkness would not fall for another hour or more, the elderly ladies intended to pass the time seated comfortably where they were. The younger people, however, were more eager for activity, and Roger offered each girl an arm, suggesting that they stroll about the gardens to admire the illuminations. This they agreed to eagerly. Lady Upsham warned them absently to stay together, Lady Denham insisted that Letty take her green shawl, and the three set off.

After spending more than half-an-hour exploring the once-familiar paths, which had been so stunningly transformed by the ingenious lights, they came upon the entrance to the labyrinth. Although illumination had been provided here and there, the paths inside seemed rather frighteningly dusky in the gathering gloom. "Well, ladies," Roger said challengingly, "are you courageous enough to walk through these paths in the dark of night?"

"Oh, yes! Let's!" Prue responded eagerly.

"I don't know," Letty said hesitantly. "I've been told that, with all the ins and outs, one must walk half-a-mile before finding the way out. We may be late for the fireworks."

"I don't think it will take as long as that," Roger assured her. "But you must both agree to hold on tightly to my hands. I don't want us to separate. We *will* be late if we have to waste time looking for each other."

The labyrinth proved to be even greater fun in the darkness than it had been in daylight. They ran down the pathways hand-in-hand, turned the dark corners with a great pretense of fear and a great deal of sincere laughter, pulled poor Roger in opposite directions at each intersection, and indulged in many boisterous arguments over directions. When the sisters were in disagreement, Roger asserted his authority as the eldest of the three and made the final decision. At one point, however, he sided with Letty when Prue was convinced that she was right. "I *know* the exit is down there to the right," she declared stubbornly. She twisted her hand out of Roger's grasp and ran to the right. Calling over her shoulder, "I'll meet you at the exit," she disappeared around the bend.

"Prue, come back here!" Roger demanded, but she did not come. Letty and Roger exchanged helpless glances and turned to follow her. But when they rounded the bend, she was nowhere in sight. They called her name in vain. They peered into all the nearby paths of the maze but couldn't find her.

Prue, meanwhile, had run down the path she was convinced led to the exit, but it proved to be a dead end. Annoyed, but without real concern, she tried to retrace her steps, but the paths were confusing and not the same as they had seemed before. It was now quite dark, for the gardens' bright illumination could not penetrate the thick, tall shrubs which lined the paths of the maze. She called Roger's name, but there was no answer. Suddenly frightened, she called even louder for Letty. In response, she heard a raucous, drunken laugh. "'Ere, dearie, 'ere! I ain't no Letty, but won't I do?" came a drunken voice, and two hulking youths appeared from around a corner and stood blocking her path. From the look of their clothing she took them to be farmers, but they stood unsteadily on their feet and reeked of drink.

"Look, now," one of them said drunkenly, "we found oursel's a right pretty little straw hat."

The other nodded enthusiastically, his tongue licking a slack, leering mouth. "For once you ain't bammin'," he grinned. "Come 'ere, little poppet, and give us a kiss."

Prue, her heart hammering in her chest and her blood turning to ice, drew herself up proudly. "Stand aside, sir, and let me pass," she demanded with as much dignity as she could command.

The two men laughed. "Well, well—will y'listen to the dolly? Givin' 'ersel' airs like a lady," said one of them, coming a step closer to her.

"Ain't never know'd a dollymop what didn't want to pass fer a lady," the other said scornfully.

The first man reached for Prue and pulled her to him. Prue, in desperate fear, pushed against him with all her might. Already unsteady with drink, the fellow fell backward and dropped to the ground heavily. The other man grasped Prue's arm and laughed heartily. "You're as lushy as an old elbow-crooker," he said to his friend on the ground. "Go put your noddle under the pump and leave this 'ere morsel fer—" But he never finished his sentence, for Prue bit his hand and went flying down the path. The sounds of their grunts and shouts followed her, and she ran even faster, rounding a turn without slowing her step. A large pebble in her path caused her to lose her balance, and she fell flat on her face. She could hear the heavy pounding of their footsteps, and she jumped to her feet and ran on.

Rounding the next corner, she found to her intense relief that she had come to the exit. She noticed as she stumbled out of the labyrinth that the path was reassuringly bright, but to her dismay, Letty and Roger were not there. Somewhere just inside, she could still hear the shouts of her attackers. Would they follow her even here on the open path? Breathless and exhausted, she lifted her skirts and ran down the path, hoping to find safety among the crowds that must be milling about somewhere. At that moment, a sound like a cannon shot broke through the air, causing her to scream out loud. The boom was followed by a burst of light. She looked up in alarm to see a cascade of colored sparks wheeling about in the sky above her head, and she realized that the fireworks had begun. The unexpected display seemed eerily frightening, and the terrified girl continued to race down the path. Suddenly, just ahead, she saw a familiar figure leaning on a walking stick, his eyes turned up to the sky, absorbed in the spectacle now dwindling into darkness above them. "Mr. Eberly! Oh, Mr. Eberly!" she cried out in intense relief.

Mr. Eberly looked round abruptly and gaped in alarm as Prue, her hair disheveled and falling about her shoulders, her dress torn and covered with dust, came stumbling down the path. "Why, Miss Prue! What has happened to you?" he asked, holding out his arms to catch her. She tumbled into them, gasping and trembling, unable to speak. "There, there, child," he said soothingly, patting her back with avuncular kindness, "you're quite safe now."

The awkwardness of his gestures and the fatherliness of his voice were utterly comforting, and Prue responded with a flood of tears. Slowly and haltingly, she managed to convey to him an account of her ordeal, and after repeated assurances from him that she was now safe, her sobs subsided. He withdrew a large handkerchief from the pocket of his coat and dabbed at her cheeks. She looked up at him with gratitude. "I d-don't know how t-to thank you, s-sir," she said tremulously. "You seem always to b-be on hand when I have need of rescuing."

At that moment, Brandon Peake came hobbling along the path, supported by the cane in his right hand and his mother at his left. The sight that met his horrified eyes caused him to stop in his tracks. There stood Prue in a public embrace! She was dusty, tousled and disordered from head to toe, yet she was standing there shamelessly, for all the world to see, in Mr. Eberly's arms. He could feel his mother's arm tighten as she, too, came to a comprehension of what she was seeing. Just as Mr. Eberly became aware of their presence and seemed about to step forward and greet them, Mrs. Peake gave him a curt, dismissive nod, clutched Brandon's arm and hurried him off.

"Did you ever see anything so shocking?" Mrs. Peake hissed as they turned onto another path. "Embracing in public that way! The girl looked a veritable wanton!"

His mother's words so appalled Brandon that their lack of justice—and the injustice of his own impression of what he'd seen—burst upon him. "That is not fair, Mama," he said coldly. "They were not embracing. She looked upset about something."

"How can you be so naive?" his mother demanded. "That was an embrace if ever I saw—"

"By your leave, Mama," Brandon interrupted firmly, "I would rather not talk about it. We blundered into what was meant to be a private matter. We do not know what was going on, nor is it any affair of ours. I wish you would refrain from referring to this matter again, either to me or to anyone else."

Mrs. Peake sniffed indignantly and relapsed into offended silence, leaving Brandon free to reflect on the mixture of feelings which warred within him. One part of him was furious with Prue for permitting herself to appear wanton, her hair unkempt, her dress soiled, her face streaked with tears. Another part of him rejected this interpretation of her appearance. Prue was headstrong, short-tempered and stubborn, but she was not a wanton. There was undoubtedly an explanation for her appearance. But this restrained and temperate feeling did not soothe the anguish that continued to wash over him. The source of that anguish was not hard to determine. It was the look on Prue's face as she looked up at Mr. Eberly. The anguish he was feeling was an emotion he had never felt before but had read of often. Homer had written of it. Sophocles had written of it. And Catullus too. It was jealousy—naked, ugly, raging, murderous jealousy. He would have liked to knock Mr. Eberly down with his bare fists for the pure joy of lifting him up to knock him down again. And when Mr. Eberly would be lying on the ground senseless, his blood slowly dripping into the grass, Brandon would have liked nothing more than to pull Prue into his arms, to have her look up at him with just such a look as he had seen on her face tonight.

Meanwhile, the subjects of his reverie were standing where he had left them, looking after Brandon and Mrs. Peake with expressions of startled embarrassment. "Well," said Mr. Eberly ruefully, "I believe Mrs. Peake and her son have given us the cut direct."

"So it would seem," Prue said in innocent bewilderment. "I wonder why."

"I believe they misunderstood what they saw," Mr. Eberly explained gently. "After all, I had been holding you in a position of . . . er . . . shall we say *intimacy*?"

Prue stared at him. "Intimacy? Do you mean they thought we were *lovers*?" she asked in astonishment. "Of all the . . . the . . . presumption! Why, you're old enough to be my *father*!"

If poor Mr. Eberly's recent encounters with the unpredictable Prue had encouraged any flights of fancy in his bachelor's heart, if he had permitted himself to dream of romance with a red-headed chit barely out of the schoolroom, if he had indulged in even the *merest* hope of the possibility of making this bewitching child his own, her blunt words were a sufficient set-down to kill those illusions forever. He looked down at her, not knowing whether to laugh or scold. But he merely smiled wryly. "Well, not your father, perhaps," he said in his gentle way, "but certainly your uncle." With a sigh, he took her arm and escorted her back to the knoll where Lady Denham and Lady Upsham sat waiting. When the exclamations and explanations had been made, Mr. Eberly accepted their invitation to watch the fireworks with them, but he admitted that his enjoyment of them was somewhat diminished from what it had been earlier.

Roger and Letty had searched the maze without success until the first burst of fireworks lit up the sky. "They've started," Roger remarked. "She cannot still be here. She must have gone back to your aunt by this time."

"I hope so," Letty said, troubled. "Do you think she can have found her way back alone?"

Roger smiled at her comfortingly. "She is quite resourceful. I'm sure she can." Seeing that Letty still looked dubious, he pulled her arm through his and led her to the exit of the maze. When they came out to the open pathway, there was no one to be seen. A second burst of fireworks crackled in the air, causing Letty to jump nervously. Roger turned to her, took the green shawl from her arm and draped it over her shoulders. "Come along, my dear," he said. "I'll have you back with our party in a moment, and you'll see for yourself that Prue is safe and sound and undoubtedly enjoying the fireworks without a care in the world for *you*."

They hurried along the pathway and turned into the brightly illuminated lane which led to the knoll where their party waited. This lane was crowded with people moving in both directions, laughing, carousing and looking up at the sky. Passage was difficult, and even with Roger's expert maneuvering, their progress was slow. At one point, their way was completely blocked by three people who walked abreast, preventing any passage around them. The three persons, a tall woman wearing a poke bonnet trimmed with enormous feathers and a gentleman on each side of her, were proceeding so slowly that Roger became impatient. Tapping one of the gentlemen on the shoulder, he begged pardon for disturbing him, requested passage room, and guided Letty through the space he had arranged between the bonneted lady and the gentleman.

They walked on for only a step or two when the lady's voice stopped them. "This is fine treatment, I must say, Lord Denham," she said with a ringing laugh. "Is this the way you treat old friends?"

Roger seemed to stiffen at the first words, and he and Letty turned around. "Kitty!" he said, his voice shocked and edged with steel.

The lady was indeed Kitty Brownell. Ignoring the coldness in his voice, she came purposefully toward him, a bright smile fixed on her face, her hand extended for him to kiss. But a choked gasp from Letty diverted Roger's attention, and he quickly turned to her. Her face was white, and as he watched, her trembling hand flew to her mouth as she stared at the approaching woman with horrified eyes. For the briefest of moments, Roger was puzzled. She didn't know Kitty—they *couldn't* be acquainted! Then why was Letty reacting so strangely to the sight of Kitty? He glanced quickly at Kitty, who had heard Letty's gasp and was looking at her with cool curiosity, and then he looked back at Letty. A glimmer of a memory struck him. But even before his *mind* was able to grasp what it was that he'd remembered, his *feelings* grasped it. He felt a sharp contraction in his throat. There was something terribly disturbing about this scene. Disturbing and *familiar*. Letty's horrified eyes . . . her green shawl . . . the bright garden lights all around them . . . Kitty. He had seen all this before. *Good Lord!* he thought, gasping audibly, *the girl at Vauxhall!*

For a frozen moment they all stared at each other. Then Kitty, her eyebrows raised quizzically, turned to Roger. "Really, my dear, what—?" she began.

But Roger did not heed her. He was staring at Letty, agonized. With an urgent movement of his hand, he took a step toward her and clutched her shoulder. "Letty—?" he asked, pleading.

But Letty took a step back, shaking off his hand and leaving only the shawl in his grasp. With one last, horrified look at him, she turned and fled, brushing by the startled strollers without stopping, blundering into people like someone blind, on and on down the path until at last she was lost from his view.

Chapter Fifteen

*K*itty Brownell surveyed Roger curiously. He was staring down the road after the disappearing girl, his brow furrowed, his mouth in a tight line, his eyes unreadable. The fist in which he clutched the green shawl was clenched so tightly that the knuckles showed white. "Who was that peculiar girl?" she asked bluntly.

Roger forced himself to attention. "Good evening, ma'am," he said with cool formality. "I had no idea that Bath still had attraction for the fashionable set."

"You, my lord, are the attraction. I had intended to surprise you," she said with a teasing smile. "I seem to have succeeded beyond my expectations."

Lord Denham ignored the hints of intimacy in her tone and asked in a businesslike manner, "Are you fixed in Bath or just passing through?"

"Oh, I'm quite fixed. I've taken a house in the Paragon," she answered. "Number twelve," she added, her voice lowered. "Perhaps you would care to call on me there tonight."

Roger made a gesture toward the two gentlemen who escorted her. They had stepped aside as soon as they had become aware that some private drama was being played, but remained waiting for Mrs. Brownell to acknowledge them. "I see you are well provided with company for the evening. You won't have need of me."

"The gentlemen with me tonight? Oh, my dear, you're not going to pretend to be jealous of *them*," she said archly. "They are old friends who insisted on accompanying me on my journey from London. We only arrived today, you know."

"No, I'm not going to pretend to be jealous, ma'am," Roger said shortly. "Nor am I going to pretend to be pleased at your decision to take up residence here—a decision which I consider greatly lacking in both propriety and taste."

Kitty's smile grew strained. In an attempt to change the subject, she said hurriedly, "May I present my escorts to you?"

"Spare me, Kitty, please," he said in an undertone that brooked no argument. "I'm in quite a hurry and must instantly take my leave of you."

Unmindful of observers, she clutched his arm. "You can't go like this, Roger. Do you think I've come for any reason but to see you?"

"I will call on you," he said stiffly.

"Tonight?" she pressed.

He frowned at her in irritation. "Not tonight. You did notice, did you not, that I am otherwise engaged this evening?"

"Later tonight, when you have finished with that strange creature?"

"Damn it, Kitty, not tonight," he said between clenched teeth.

"Tomorrow, then."

He bowed in cold acquiescence and walked off quickly. She watched him for a moment with eyes that smoldered. Then, taking the arm of each of her escorts, she favored them with a smile as vivacious as it was false.

Roger hurried away down the path, dismissing Kitty from his mind. She presented a problem that he knew he must solve, but a solution would not be difficult to find. He would deal with her in due course. It was this new revelation about Letty that worried him. He needed time to think, to remember, to understand what he had done to her and how to make amends. He looked down at the green scarf in his hand. For a moment it had seemed to be a green domino.

The incident at Vauxhall was merely a blur in his memory, but he had no doubt that it was the clue to Letty's fear of him and to those occasional moments when she seemed to view him with aversion. He must have treated her dreadfully if the incident had lingered in her mind with such painful intensity. He flushed with humiliation to think that he could ever have used his lovely Letty as if she'd been nothing more than a bit of muslin! Gentle, sweet, sensitive Letty. What had he done to her?

The sky above him burst into spectacular brightness and the air boomed with the sound of dozens of fireworks being set off at once. The display had no doubt reached its climax and would be ending shortly. There was no time for him to think. He needed solitude and quiet in order to prod his memory. But there would be no solitude until he returned his guests safely to their home. And there would be no quiet until he could calm the turmoil inside him. At the moment, nothing was clear except that he loved Letty with an aching certainty. He had the terrible feeling that his whole life was falling down around him, and the falling shower of sparkles from dozens of fireworks only seemed to add to that illusion.

Letty had run down the path in heedless misery, not knowing where she was fleeing or what she was to do. It was only when she almost blundered into a tree that she stopped running and began to return to awareness of her surroundings. She was gasping for breath and sobbing. People on the path were looking at her curiously. She knew she must contain her emotions and return to her aunt. She moved around the tree so that it hid her from the lane and leaned against it until her breath was regained. Pressing her hands tightly against her chest, she forced her sobs to cease. What was there to cry about? she asked herself. She had known for a long time that Roger had a mistress. She had even seen Mrs. Brownell before. Of course, she had had no idea that Roger had installed her *right here in Bath*! That fact was indeed shocking, but certainly not something to cry about.

She realized bitterly that she had behaved like a child instead of a woman of sense and dignity. She should have pretended to be ignorant of Kitty's identity, permitted Roger to introduce them, and continued the evening as if nothing had happened. Instead she had behaved as if the world had come to an end. She had embarrassed Roger, made a fool of herself, and now had to face the others looking red-eyed and distraught.

She sighed tremulously and a fresh spring of tears spilled from her eyes. She had really believed he loved her. During these past few weeks in Bath, Roger had been so attentive, so charming, so . . . loving. When he had sat beside her on the churchyard wall and said those beautiful words, she would have sworn he was utterly sincere. What a fool she was. He had probably had his mistress conveniently established in Bath *all that time*!

But she could not dwell on the matter now. She had to compose herself. No matter how difficult, she was determined to pass off the rest of the evening with some vestige of self-respect and dignity. She wiped her eyes, forced herself to breathe deeply and evenly, and hurried off down the path to find her party.

When she came to the place where the Lady Denham and her guests were ensconced, the first person she laid eyes on was Prue, sitting beside Mr. Eberly, gazing up at the fireworks with childish absorption. Letty felt a twinge of shame. *Prue* . . . She had completely forgotten her! "There you are, Prue," she said with all the cheerfulness she could muster. "We looked all over the maze for you. You alarmed us greatly, you naughty puss!"

"Don't scold me, Letty," Prue pleaded. "I've had the most dreadful time. You see, as soon as I'd left you—"

"Before you hear the tale," Lady Denham interrupted, "please tell us what has become of my irresponsible son. It was unforgivable of him to permit you both to go about alone!"

Letty, living up to the promise she had made to herself, answered pleasantly, "He was not irresponsible, ma'am, I assure you. Prue ran away from us—you cannot blame Lord Denham for that. And as for me, I have only walked on ahead of him. He met a . . . a friend a little way back on the path and stopped to exchange greetings."

Satisfied with Letty's explanation, Lady Denham allowed Prue to relate the horrifying tale of her misadventures in the labyrinth, a tale to which Letty reacted with consternation and sympathy. Roger made his appearance shortly thereafter. His eyes immediately sought Letty's face, but she did not look at him. He was greeted eagerly by Prue and the others, so he concluded that Letty had not revealed anything about Kitty's appearance. Following her example, he pretended to a nonchalance he was far from feeling and turned to Prue, demanding an accounting of her whereabouts. The story was then repeated for his benefit with all the dramatic details included. While Prue told it, he moved unobtrusively behind Letty and put the shawl around her shoulders. She shuddered and pulled it off, but gave no other sign that she was aware of his existence.

At the conclusion of Prue's tale, Roger admitted to being much abashed by his failure to care for her properly. He thanked Mr. Eberly profusely for his aid to Prue in those dire circumstances. "No need for thanks," Mr. Eberly said, smoothing down his mustache in a deprecating manner. "I've been thanked quite enough by the young lady herself. To be cast in the role of rescuer is quite a romantic adventure for an old codger like myself."

Roger looked at him askance. "Old codger? You can't be more than eight and thirty."

"Thirty-seven, actually," he sighed. "I didn't consider myself elderly, either, until Miss Prue pointed out to me that I'm old enough to be her father."

"Oh, I see," Roger said, smiling at him with quick and sympathetic understanding. "So that's the way it was."

Mr. Eberly's eyes met Roger's, and he shrugged ruefully. "I'm afraid so."

"You shouldn't let it weigh with you, you know. The perspective of seventeen years is a distorted one when it looks toward thirty."

"Oh, it doesn't weigh with me, my boy. Not at all," Eberly assured him with a wry smile. "The fact that I'm suddenly quite tired and shall have to lean heavily on my cane on my way back to my bedroom does not signify at all." He bid his good nights to the ladies and, with a wink at Roger, hobbled off, leaning on his cane in an exaggeratedly elderly manner.

To Letty's relief, Roger did not go to her but sat down next to Prue. He spent the rest of the evening trying to explain to that heartless young vixen that telling a man he is old enough to be her father was a worse than tactless way of thanking him for his gallantry. Prue merely shrugged and said that since he *was* old enough to be her father (or at least *looked* so) she had only spoken honestly.

Not long afterward, Lady Denham led her guests back along the path to the waiting carriage. In the brightness of the illuminated lane, Prue noticed the redness of Letty's eyes. "Letty," she cried in another tactless act, "have you been *crying!*"

"Of course not, silly," Letty said quickly, trying with a quelling glance to silence her sister. But both Lady Denham arid Millicent had heard. In the carriage, the strained silence between Roger and Letty was noticed, and the redness around Letty's eyes could easily be discerned by Aunt Millicent's sharp eyes. "I hope you will find time to meet me at the library on Milsom Street tomorrow," Millicent said to Lady Denham in discouraged tones when the carriage arrived at her door.

Lady Denham nodded with the same feeling of despair. Somehow her party had become a dismal failure. "Yes, of course, Millicent," she said with a deep sigh.

Something forbidding in Letty's eyes kept Aunt Millicent and Prue from prying further into the cause of her red eyes and strained expression, and she was permitted to retire without delay. She hurried upstairs to her bedroom, only to find Katie waiting for her. Turning away so that Katie would not get a good look at her face, she said, "Please, Katie, go to Prue. I don't need you, but she's had a difficult evening and will be very grateful for your assistance." And she sank down on the edge of her bed.

Katie did as she was bid, but after she'd heard Prue's story, helped her wash the dirt away and tucked her into her bed, she returned to Letty's room and peeped in to see if anything needed doing. To her surprise, Letty was still sitting on the edge of her bed. She apparently had not moved for almost an hour. Her hands lay slackly in her lap and her eyes were fixed on the middle distance with an unseeing stare. Katie crept in, shut the door gently and knelt down before her. "Miss Letty, nothin' in the world can be bad enough to make you look so," she whispered worriedly.

Letty focused her abstracted eyes on Katie's face. The abigail was looking up at her with unmistakable affection and concern. It was the first sign of real sympathy Letty had had since Roger had come into her life. Because she had so determinedly kept her problems secret, the warmth and compassion that normally would have been offered by her mother, her sisters, and probably her Aunt Millicent had not been given. For months she had had to keep her own counsel and to weep into a lonely pillow. There had been no ear into which she could pour her troubles, no shoulder on which she could find comfort. So the troubled look on Katie's face undid her. "Oh, Katie," she whispered tremulously, the tears spilling from her eyes. The tiny abigail did not need to hear more. She jumped up beside her mistress and put a supporting arm around her. Letty's head dropped against the girl's shoulder, and she wept in great, gulping sobs. Katie rocked her gently, cooing soft, comforting sounds into Letty's ear. She continued her gentle rocking until Letty's sobs had worn themselves out. Then she washed Letty's face, undressed her and put her to bed. She blew out the candles and sat at the side of the bed until Letty had fallen asleep. She had asked no questions and had learned nothing of the cause of her mistress's anguish. But Katie had, as usual, learned *something* from the experience; she hadn't realized until tonight that anyone but scullery maids could cry that way.

Lady Denham kept silent until she and Roger had returned home and dismissed the servants. "I suppose you're going to tell me now," she said to her son furiously, "that you did nothing tonight to upset Letty. Do you intend to tell me that you exchanged nothing but the merest commonplaces again tonight?"

"I am not going to tell you anything tonight, Mama," Roger said wearily, "except to wish you a very good night."

She glanced up at him, ready to make a sharp retort, when she caught sight of his face. He was quite pale, his lips compressed, the line of his jaw tight and tense. Motherlike, she immediately softened. She reached up, drew his head down and kissed him lightly on the cheek. "A very good night to you, too, my dear," she said gently and went off to bed.

Roger dropped onto his bed without bothering to undress. He needed to think, to reconstruct that evening at Vauxhall, and he wanted to do it without delay. It must have occurred more than a year ago. He doubted if he could remember.

Lying in the darkness, he stared unseeing at the ceiling and tried to reproduce the evening in his mind. There was to be a masquerade at the gardens, he recalled, and even weeks before, Kitty had teased to be taken. But he disliked Vauxhall and he disliked masquerades. He had given in to her wishes, of course, but with ill grace. And he'd refused to wear a costume. A domino would suffice, he had told her with finality. Strange how it was coming back to him. He remembered that she'd decided to dress as Little Bo Peep. She had beautiful ankles, and the costume would give her an opportunity to display them to the world. The costume had been copied from a picture in a book of nursery rhymes and had looked quite charming. But when it had arrived from her dressmaker's, and she had put it on to show it to him, she had looked at herself with disgust. The very high waist and the short, full skirt had not flattered her. "I look as if I were *breeding*!" she'd said in revulsion. In the end, she'd worn a domino—a bright green domino.

He tried without success to remember the color of his own domino. It was not important, but he wanted to remember every detail. He didn't think it had been green. Whatever the color, he'd been wearing it when they'd arrived at the gardens. He had put on the mask, but he now remembered that he'd found it annoying—it was somewhat too narrow for his face and his vision had been partially blocked because of it. His groom had set up a table in a pleasant, Grecian-like alcove set within white pillars. Kitty had complained that the situation was not to her liking—too far from the bustle—but he'd ignored her complaints. Thinking back on it, he realized that he'd been a most ungracious host. She'd wanted him to take her to the rotunda to dance, but he'd refused. He was not overly fond of dancing, even in the best of circumstances, but to be milling about in the throng at the rotunda struck him as the very *worst* of circumstances. She had flounced off in annoyance, threatening to take up with the first familiar face she could find.

He remembered sitting alone for a long time, his feelings alternating between a desire to throttle her and guilt that he'd been so surly. But when more than half-an-hour had passed, he had begun to feel concerned. While it was true that Kitty was not a simpering little innocent and could easily take care of herself, this was a place which attracted all manner of ruffians, and the lady *was* there under his protection. He'd roused himself from his musings and had gone off to look for her.

Here Roger tried to envision every detail. He had come to the rotunda and looked over the crowd. At first, he'd been dismayed by the number of revelers who thronged the area. He'd feared that he never would find her in the mob. But almost at once, he'd seen the bright green domino and the auburn curls peeping out from under the hood, and he'd felt a wave of relief. Like a worried parent who finds a lost child, his relief had been followed by an explosion of fury. A parent would shout, slapping the child's face, "How *dared* you to be so naughty!" His feelings were quite the same. He would have liked to beat her! Instead, he'd dragged her ruthlessly behind him all the way back to the table.

But—good God!—*that* had been *Letty*! The memory of it made him groan aloud. The poor child had stumbled along behind him, terror-stricken, and he had callously ignored her cries. He had been completely convinced that it was Kitty whose hand he clutched. He'd thought that her cries were *playacting*—in fact, the choking sounds he'd heard behind him had seemed like suppressed laughter and had only increased his fury.

He closed his eyes and tried to imagine Letty's feelings. The girl was being abducted by a complete stranger and dragged to God-knew-where. Perhaps even to rape and murder, for all she knew! Roger felt sick with self-revulsion. But he knew there was more to remember, and reluctantly he forced himself to recall the rest.

They had returned to his table, and he had unceremoniously dumped her into a chair. She had said something about a mistake—*I am not the lady you think me,* or some such expression. He had not paid attention. He'd believed that Kitty was being coy—teasing him out of his anger. He'd said something curt to prevent her from continuing the nonsense. What had he said? He couldn't recall it at all. Try as he would, he could re-create none of the conversation that must have passed between them. He remembered only that she'd made a rather pretty, pleading speech, in a voice much lighter than Kitty's, and he'd been struck by what he thought was Kitty's talented acting. *Acting!* Lord, what a fool he'd been! The "acting" had seemed to give Kitty an unexpected charm, and he remembered feeling a surge of desire for her. He'd tossed off his mask to see her more clearly. She'd stood up before him, the curves of her body smooth, lithe and enticing under the domino, and he'd pulled her into his arms.

He shut his eyes in pain. How roughly had he handled her? He could not—or would not—recall. But he remembered how she'd felt in his arms. She had been unexpectedly light and soft, and for a moment he'd enjoyed the sensation without thought. Then he'd kissed her. She'd been pliant and unresisting, but also unresponsive. It was the unresponsiveness which had set off the warning bell in his head. He suddenly became aware that the girl in his arms was trembling from top to toe. That could *not* be Kitty!

The rest was easy to recall. Kitty had arrived, the two women had looked at each other carefully, and it was clear that both had understood what had happened. Then the girl—Letty—had darted off into the underbrush and made her escape. He'd tried to find her—to apologize—but she'd disappeared. He had felt guilty and uneasy for a brief while, but (he admitted to himself with shame) he had soon forgotten her. He'd returned to Kitty. That lady, probably because of an instinctive jealousy, had suddenly become so enticingly complaisant that the entire incident had gone completely out of his mind.

Lying there in the darkness, Roger felt himself flush hotly in mortification. He pulled off his neckcloth and tossed it to the floor. He pulled himself to his feet and strode about the room. But he could not shake off his feelings of humiliation and self-disgust. Damnation, he thought, I should be horsewhipped! Letty had a brother, hadn't she? Why hadn't *he* come looking for Roger, demanding satisfaction? London was supposed to be civilized—men could not go about abducting and abusing innocent girls without castigation! If he'd been properly taken to task at that time, he wouldn't now be in this impossible muddle.

It was clear that he'd taken off his mask and that Letty had recognized him. Why, then, had her family done nothing? And why, one year later, did they encourage him to pay his addresses to the girl he had so abused? The answer was obvious. *Letty had never told anyone.* The family did not know. The realization that she had confided in no one—not even Prue—made him sink down on the bed, his brow furrowed in deep speculation. She had kept the whole terrible story to herself. Why? His spirit leaped up at a ray of hope. Had Letty cared enough about him, even then, to protect his name?

No, the thought was ridiculous. They had barely been acquainted at the time. And after his gross mishandling of her at Vauxhall, it was scarcely likely that she could have any feeling for him but the deepest loathing. She had probably kept her peace and told no one because she wanted to forget the whole sordid affair. It was no wonder that she later refused to marry him. She had seen a side of him that no innocent girl should see. Letty had been gently reared—a sensitive, chaste, refined, obedient, ingenuous girl. How could she agree to wed a man she knew to be a vulgar, lustful, brutish lout?

He lay back on the bed and threw his arm across his forehead in a gesture of despair. At last he understood the nature of the obstacle which he had sensed lay between them from the first. But it was a sizeable obstacle indeed. He had badly botched his hopes. He'd done it unwittingly, but, he feared, irrevocably. Even if he were to assure her that he would never again treat her with anything but the most gentle understanding, would she be likely to believe him? Of course she wouldn't, he realized with a jolt, sitting up abruptly and staring out into the darkness in chagrin—she'd seen Kitty again tonight! She must have thought—Good Lord!—that *he* had brought her here! If he had in any way softened her resistance to him during all these weeks in Bath, the meeting with Kitty would surely have hardened it again to a rocklike, impenetrable solidity.

No, she would never take him now. Feeling drained and empty, without hope, and moving with the abstracted air of a somnambulist, he bent down and removed a boot. How ironical, he thought, that the artificial relationship he'd had with Kitty should appear to Letty more real than the agonizing genuineness of the love he felt for *her*. In a burst of anger at the helplessness and futility of his position, he stood up and flung his boot to the far corner of the room. Furiously, he repeated the act with the other boot. This conduct failed to relieve his frustrations but only succeeded in making him feel quite foolish. Without undressing further, he threw himself upon the bed, folded his hands beneath his head and stared up at the ceiling. Dawn would come eventually. In the meantime, he permitted himself an unaccustomed indulgence in self-pity, during which he glumly rejected even the small comfort his mother had once offered—when she'd said that a bit of suffering over a love affair would be good for his character. He very much doubted that this agony was good for anything—not his character, not his future, not even his immortal soul.

Chapter Sixteen

$\mathcal{T}$he morning should have dawned in gray and drizzly gloom, but Mother Nature, with her usual callousness and lack of sensitivity to human moods, brought forth a day of such sparkling brightness as to be considered singularly inappropriate by a good number of Bath's inhabitants. Roger, for one, buried his head in his pillow when Trebbs came in and threw back the curtains. "Shut those things!" he muttered hoarsely. "And Trebbs, be a good fellow and take yourself off. Don't come back until I call you. Sunshine! Faugh!"

Prue observed the sunlight spilling into her bedroom window and making lopsided rectangles on her carpet with a frown. "Doesn't it ever rain in this benighted place?" she asked no one in particular.

Her sister stood before the window in *her* bedroom studying her face in a hand mirror. The puffy redness of her eyes was quite unmistakable in the revealing glare of the sunlight. A grayer day would have made the morning—and the sight of her face—a little more bearable. She, too, drew the curtains against the relentless brightness.

Brandon also viewed the day with distaste. He stood leaning his forehead against the windowpane, watching two children play a game of hopscotch on the walkway below. He envied them their agile limbs and carefree hearts. From his window, he could see a bit of Union Street, which was already busy with strollers. That meant that the square before the Pump Room would by now be thronged with cheerful crowds, and he envied them, too. Only *he*, he felt, burdened with an injured leg and a bruised heart, was isolated from the laughing world and bereft of even the comfort that drops of rain upon the glass would have offered him. On a rainy day, one was less apt to be aware of a bustling, cheerful world outside one's window. Brandon realized that his thoughts were selfish and petty. He tried to turn them in a nobler direction. "Waste not tears

over old griefs," Euripides had written. "No human thing is of serious importance," Plato had said. Why, today, did he feel that his Greeks were not as wise
as he once had thought?

Even Mr. Eberly found the sun irritating. While he stood at his shaving mirror, a ray of sunshine, reflected in the glass, found its way to the left point of his
mustache, emphasizing the fact that an increasing number of gray hairs lodged
among the brown. "I'm well aware of them," he said to the streak of light in disgust. "I don't need you to point them out to me!" With a glance at the window
and the glorious day which lay beyond, he sighed and asked whatever gods
might be listening in, "Don't you think the time has come for a little rain?"

The morning was quite well advanced when Letty knocked at the Peakes' door.
Her knock was answered by the elderly butler, who informed Miss Glendenning
that Mrs. Peake was not at home. Letty, who had already peeped into the Pump
Room to make certain that Mrs. Peake was there and therefore surely not at
home, pretended to be disappointed. "Oh, dear, that *is* too bad. However, you
may announce me to *Mr.* Peake if you please. I have found a book I feel sure will
amuse him during his convalescence and am most eager to show it to him."

The butler pursed his lips in disapproval, but Letty put up her chin and
stared at him firmly, and the old man, shaking his head in a manner which
clearly revealed his low opinion of the manners of the younger generation, led
her to the library. There they found Mr. Peake, seated in a wing chair, a book
unopened on his lap, staring moodily into space. At the sight of Letty his eyes
brightened perceptibly, but they quickly took on a look of wary concern. He
struggled to his feet. "Letty! How . . . how nice," he said awkwardly.

The butler showed an inclination to linger in the doorway. Letty glanced at
him over her shoulder, wondering what to do to arrange a private conversation
with Brandon. It was not *her* place to dismiss the man. She smiled weakly at
Brandon and said in as cheerful a voice as she could summon up, "Good morning, Brandon. Look at the book I found for you at the library. It's the Thomas
Bowdler edition of Gibbons's *Decline and Fall of the Roman Empire*. I thought it
would be of interest to you."

Brandon made a face. "Thank you, Letty. That was quite thoughtful, but I'm
familiar with the edition, and, by your leave, I think it silly beyond anything.
Mr. Bowdler is a womanish old prude who becomes distressed with any word
even vaguely connected with the human body. Why the word *body* itself offends
him. He goes through the texts and changes it to *person!*"

"That does sound silly," Letty agreed absently. "I'll take it back and change it
for something else." She looked back at the butler watching them in the doorway

and threw Brandon a helpless look. Brandon, at last realizing that Letty wanted to talk to him, and that the book was just a ruse, told the man to close the door. With raised eyebrows and definite reluctance, the butler did as he was bid.

"Sit down, Letty, sit down. By your leave, I don't know where my manners have gone." Letty sank gratefully into an armchair and Brandon took his seat in the wing chair. "You wish to see me about something? I should have realized that old Bowdler was only a stratagem."

"Yes," Letty nodded, "and when you dispensed with him so quickly, I didn't know what to do!"

"I'm sorry. It's hard for a man to realize, sometimes, how difficult it is for a lady to pay a call on a gentleman when she's unaccompanied. What did you want to see me about? I hope you're not going to ask me to lie to Lord Denham again."

Letty bent her head. "I'm going to ask you something much, much more difficult, Brandon," she said.

Brandon eyed her warily. "See here, Letty," he said bluntly, "I don't wish to be rude, but, by your leave, I may as well be honest with you. I don't like deception. I most sincerely feel for you, and you know I would help you if I could, but I cannot—will not—lie anymore."

"But . . . no deception will be necessary, I assure you," she said earnestly, meeting his eye with a level gaze.

"In that case," Brandon said with relief, "I'll be glad to listen."

"First, I need some information from you, and I want you to be as frank and honest with me as you can."

"Fire away," he answered promptly. "I don't mind being truthful."

"Well, then," Letty said with some hesitation, "what I want to know is how . . . how you plan to spend your life."

This was unexpected. "Spend my life?" he echoed. "What do you mean?"

"Do you plan to live always with your mother? Do you plan to remain at Oxford? And most important, do you intend to marry, and if so, have you some young lady in mind?" Noticing how he gaped at her, Letty colored slightly. "I know these questions are most impertinent, but we *are* friends, after all, and the answers have great significance in determining how I shall proceed."

"I see," said Brandon, frowning. "Well, I suppose there can be no harm in discussing such things with a lady—"

"A friend," Letty emphasized.

"A friend, then. Let's see now. First, I do *not* plan to live with my mother. As for Oxford, my studies there will be concluded within a few months. I plan to take lodgings in London, to continue my studies, perhaps to publish some translations if they are good enough. I have friends, an adequate competence from my father and some property which comes to me when I'm twenty-five, which—"

"I didn't mean to pry into your financial affairs," she cut in, blushing.

"No, no, I don't mind. I only want to explain that my income will be more than adequate for me to live comfortably in London and to travel abroad from time to time—something I've always wanted to do."

"With a . . . a wife?"

Brandon looked at her in surprise, looked away and sighed. "Once I dreamed . . . of . . . of marrying. But no longer. I think I'm more suited to a bachelor life," he said grimly.

"Oh." Letty regarded him thoughtfully. "Are you *sure*, Brandon? You are very young, you know, and probably know very little of love."

"I know as much about it as I need," he declared bitterly, "and I don't want to feel it ever again!"

"I see. Then there *was* a young lady whom you loved. Is there a possibility— even a very remote one—that you may change your mind and wish to marry her after all?"

"No, none," he said flatly. "She is in love with another. I've no doubt an announcement of their betrothal will be forthcoming very soon."

"But, Brandon, if they are not yet betrothed, you may still have a chance—"

"No, I tell you! Even if she does *not* marry him, she is not for me. She is very volatile . . . and irresponsible . . . and would not be a suitable wife for a scholar. I want a quiet life, a withdrawn life. I have no great liking for balls and parties. Oh, the theater and the opera and small dinners with one's friends are pleasant enough, but the rest bear 'the evils of idleness,' to quote the great Seneca."

"Oh, Brandon," Letty breathed in relief, "that is exactly the sort of life *I* want! I shall make a very good wife for you, really I will!"

"Letty!" Brandon gasped. "What are you *saying*!"

Letty's eyes flickered up at him and then fell. She gave him an embarrassed smile. "Oh, dear, I didn't mean to say it so abruptly. It isn't easy to make a proposal of marriage, is it?"

"A proposal of *marriage*! Letty, have you lost your mind?"

"Brandon, hush! You are making me feel as if I'd said something *indecent*! You are not Thomas Bowdler, after all. You don't want me to think *you* a womanish old prude, do you?"

"No, but . . . but asking me a thing like that! It's not . . . it's not *done*!"

"How do you know? When people become close, they can say things to each other that may be unacceptable in the highest social intercourse. I would not be surprised to learn that *many* marriages were suggested by the woman of the pair!" Letty declared with conviction.

Brandon was not convinced. "I won't believe it," he said stubbornly.

Letty sighed. "Well, now that I've done it, shall I go on? Or are you so shocked that you want to call your old butler and have me shown the door?"

"Of course I don't," Brandon said impatiently. "I'm not such a prude as you seem to think. But this subject is—"

"This subject is why I came," Letty said bravely. "I must find a husband, and quickly! Lord Denham does not seem to take our betrothal very seriously. I thought he would return to London as soon as we told him about it, but he has remained here, persistent as ever. And everything has become worse! I'm at my wit's end, I can tell you, and I must do *something*!"

"I wish you could think of something to do that does *not* involve *me*," Brandon muttered ungraciously.

Letty looked at him with troubled eyes. "I'm sorry, Brandon, truly I am. But I believe my plan would be good for us both. I really *would* be a good wife to you. We have always got on well together. I could keep house for you in London and help you with your work. I could look things up for you and copy manuscripts and organize your library. And you could teach me Latin and Greek! I would love to learn. And we would be company for each other at the opera. And would it not be more cheerful to travel with a companion than to take your first look at the Acropolis alone?"

He leaned back and studied her with amazement. "Would you truly like to do those things?" he asked.

"Yes, I would. Truly." She leaned forward and reached out a hand to him. "Oh, Brandon, I'm sure we would learn to be content."

"Would you really like to study Greek?" he asked, moving to the edge of his chair and taking her hand. She truly was a lovely young woman, gentle and soft-spoken most of the time. She'd always shown an interest in his studies. It might be amusing to teach her the classics, to show her the famous shrines of Greece, to recite the great poems to her, to mold her mind. Prue would only have tortured him, led him a merry dance, laughed at his work, flirted with strangers under his very nose, teased him to take her to balls and festivities. She would have made an impossible wife. Yet he still felt a sharp sting of pain at the very thought of her. Perhaps Letty could help him ease that pain.

Letty watched him, her breath arrested. She had not really believed that he would seriously consider her proposal, but now it seemed that she had struck the right chord. She waited silently, her hand in his, for him to speak.

But after a moment, Brandon shook his head. "No, Letty, I don't think your plan will work. You are even younger than I, and know less of love. I would not wish to bind you to a loveless marriage."

Letty smiled sadly. "You're mistaken, Brandon. Women learn about love much sooner than men. I didn't ask you about the love you have put aside, and I hope you will not ask me about mine. But I can assure you that I am no more likely to succumb to love again than you are."

With this assurance, Brandon capitulated. They became betrothed in earnest. The only things remaining to be discussed were the details of the nuptials. In this matter, poor Brandon was to have another jolt.

"What? *Elope!* Letty, you cannot mean it!" he cried in alarm.

"Please, Brandon, don't be difficult. It's the only way. Think of the obstacles an elopement will avoid. We won't have to fight my family. I won't have to face Lord Denham ever again. And don't try to convince me that *your* mother will be happy about this. I have had the impression that she disapproves of my entire family."

Brandon colored. His mother would prove to be more difficult than even Letty's aunt. She had a point there. An elopement *would* permit them to escape family censure. Once the deed was done, their opposition would be pointless.

They finally agreed on Gretna, and, after much more persuasion by Letty, the date was set for dawn on the following morning. "It's an excellent time," Letty said with a teasing smile as she rose to leave, "for it gives you no time to reconsider."

Brandon hobbled to the library door with her and kissed her hand gallantly. "What a poor sort you must find me," he said ruefully. "But you needn't worry. We are truly betrothed now, and I am not likely to cry off. In fact, Letty, I'm rather looking forward to our marriage. I've had more adventures since I met you than ever before in my life. I suspect that our life together will not be dull."

"Thank you for saying that," Letty said gratefully. She leaned over, kissed his cheek, and with a quick reminder that she would watch for his carriage at dawn, she took her leave.

Lord Denham finally brought himself to face the day, and in the early afternoon, dressed impeccably in buff-colored breeches and a coat of blue superfine, he entered a jeweler's shop on Milsom Street. He emerged ten minutes later and slipped a small package into an inner pocket of his coat. Then, squaring his shoulders, he made his way to Number 12 on the Paragon.

He was admitted by a simpering maid and found Kitty standing before the window, the sunshine filtering through the sheer curtains and making dazzling highlights on her auburn hair and the curves of her white breast, which were tantalizingly revealed by the loose, low *décolletage* of her gown. She made a striking picture, as well she knew, but Denham was strangely unmoved. He smiled, took a step into the room and waited for the maid to close the door behind him. Then he carefully placed his hat and gloves on a table near the door, looked up at her and said admiringly, "You look like a painting by Van Dyke, my dear. Very sumptuous."

Kitty, having made the impression she wanted, walked quickly across the room and threw her arms around his neck. "Roger, you beast! You gave me a sleepless night with your coldness."

"Did I?" he asked coolly, removing her arms. "You look none the worse for it, I assure you. Come, sit down here with me. I want to talk to you."

She shook her head and slipped her arms around his waist. "But, love," she whispered into his ear, "we can talk later. I haven't seen you for almost a month."

"You are not trying to tell me that you've missed me, are you?" he asked, freeing himself from her embrace and leading her firmly to the sofa.

"But *of course* I've missed you, dearest. I've been so bored and lonely that I fell into flat despair! That's why I decided to come here. I was quite beside myself without you." She spoke with quavering sincerity and put her head on his shoulder.

Roger raised an eyebrow. "Oh? Then the news that I've had from London was no doubt false."

Her head came up abruptly. "News? What news?"

"The news that you were seen frequently in the company of your duke."

"*My* duke?" she exclaimed, drawing herself erect. "Roger, are you trying to pick a quarrel? If it is Eddington you are speaking of—"

"Oh? Have you *another* duke as well?"

"Really, my dear, you are being quite ridiculous. You cannot be jealous of Eddington! He is half bald, has a stomach as big as a barrel and is the greatest bore in Christendom."

"I am no more jealous of him than I was of your escorts last evening. I will admit that, in the past, I found it irksome to share your affection with other men while you openly declared that you were living under my protection. However, I no longer wish the right to feel irked. I think the time has come, my dear, to sever our connection."

Kitty whitened. "You can't mean it! Is it because I followed you?" She put a hand on his chest. "You cannot blame me, love. I *did* miss you so."

"I think it much more likely that you heard a rumor of my interest in matrimony. You *did* hear some gossip, did you not?"

"Well, I may have heard—"

"And you came to see if you could dissuade me—isn't that it?"

"Nonsense, Roger," Kitty said, getting to her feet and beginning to pace about the room. "I always knew you would marry eventually. What difference can it make to me? To us?"

Roger leaned back on the sofa and watched her agitated pacing unperturbed. "You always knew what my marriage would mean to us. I made my intentions quite plain. I never intended to play a wife false."

She halted her stride and stared at him. "Then you *are* to be married?" she asked tensely.

"I don't know," he answered frankly. "It seems unlikely." With a rueful smile, he added, "Not every woman finds me so good a catch as you do."

"Oh?" Kitty asked, brightening. She returned to the sofa and sat down close to him. "Is your courtship proving difficult?" She ran a finger affectionately along his jaw and the side of his face. "The girl must be a fool," she said in a low, provocative voice.

"Kitty, stop playing," he said brusquely, brushing her hand away. "Let's talk with gloves off. Whether I marry or not, it is *over* for us. It's been over for some time. Don't shake your head. You know it as well as I. Let's end what has become nothing more than a charade. Take your duke while you still can."

"No!" she said furiously, jumping up and turning her back on him. "He never meant anything to me! Your friends are *vicious* to have sent such gossip. You *know* you have always been first with me."

Roger rose and stood behind her. "First, perhaps, but never *only*," he said meaningfully. He reached into his pocket and took out the box. Turning her to face him, he placed it in her hand. She flicked him a sullen glance and then opened it. Against the black velvet lining of the box lay a magnificent diamond bracelet.

"Do you think to *buy* my complaisance?" she asked furiously, tossing the bracelet at him. It fell to the floor, where it lay unheeded.

"I have no need to buy your complaisance or anything else," Roger said gently. "I offer the gift to you only as a gesture of thanks for some pleasant memories." He went to the door, picked up his hat and gloves, and looked back at her. She stood in the middle of the room, her eyes stormy, her fingers clenched. "Try not to be angry," he said soothingly. "I think you and your duke will get on famously, especially now when you need no longer concern yourself about keeping that—and your other liaisons—secret from me. Good-bye, Kitty."

Kitty's color rose to an almost apoplectic red as the finality of his words struck her. A vase, filled with fresh flowers, was close at hand. She picked it up and hurled it against the door, which he had just closed behind him. It crashed noisily to the floor, spilling water and blooms in all directions. She next picked up a lovely and expensive Sevres bowl and was about to send it crashing to a similar fate when her eye fell on the bracelet. It was truly a magnificent piece. She replaced the bowl and knelt down. She picked up the bracelet and held it so that the light shone through. Her high color faded and her eyes narrowed as she observed the dazzling highlights of the multifaceted jewels. She sat back on her heels with a resigned sigh. He was right, of course. Everything he'd said was true. And even now, knowing her duplicity, he'd been more generous than she had any right to expect. With a shrug of acceptance, she began eagerly to count the diamonds.

Chapter Seventeen

*L*ady Denham sent round a note to Lady Upsham begging her forgiveness for being unable to keep their appointment for the afternoon. She was beset with a painfully nagging toothache, she wrote, and had taken to her bed. *I have learned nothing whatever from Roger,* she added, *about what transpired last night. Perhaps my discomfort with my tooth is the cause of my present mood, but I'm afraid, my dear Millicent, that I feel very little hope that our plans will ever come to fruition. I am much inclined to wash my hands of the entire matter. The young men and women of that generation behave in ways quite beyond my understanding.*

Lady Upsham read the note with sinking spirits, although the contents didn't really surprise her. She had been feeling, of late, that a match between Letty and Roger was not to be. Some serious impediment, the nature of which she could not guess, lay between them, and since neither of them saw fit to permit an outsider to assist them in overcoming it, the match was undoubtedly doomed. She knew she should accept that fact with resignation. But what she really felt was irritation.

To relieve that feeling, she sat down at her writing desk and penned a scathing letter to her sister-in-law. *Your daughters,* she wrote, *are quite impossible, and I seriously doubt if you should persist in the hope that they will make beneficial marriages. Letty remains unmoved in her position* vis-à-vis *Lord Denham. All our exertions in that direction have proved useless. And as for Prue, she continues to frustrate my hopes. She had attracted the attention of a mature and wealthy bachelor named Mr. Eberly. I was in transports, I can tell you. But last night the silly child blithely told him that he was old enough to be her father, and the poor man scurried off without a backward look. Although the little flirt has all the young men of Bath hanging at her heels, none of them can be considered marital prizes. The one ray of hope I can offer you is the prospect of a better choice when I bring Prue out next season. If, in the meantime, we can teach her to control her tongue—*

Her writing was interrupted by a tap at the door, and Miss Tristle came in to tell her that Lord Denham had called and was waiting below. "Lord Denham?" Millicent asked in delight. "Tell him I'll be right down." Hope sprang alive in her breast. If Lord Denham still cared to call, all was not lost. Perhaps her letter to Lady Glendenning had been hasty. She tore it up, straightened her hair and hurried downstairs.

Lord Denham had called to ask her permission to take Letty for a drive. This she gave with alacrity and sent Miss Tristle to fetch Letty at once. Miss Tristle returned alone and whispered in Lady Upsham's ear that Letty had sent her regrets to Lord Denham—she was feeling indisposed. Millicent could not permit Letty to ruin this opportunity. "Excuse me, Lord Denham," she said firmly. "Letty and I will return in a moment."

Millicent's resolve almost failed her when she entered Letty's room and confronted her. The expression in Letty's eyes was like that of a trapped rabbit. "Don't order me to go, Aunt Millicent," she pleaded. "I am not feeling at all the thing today."

"Of course I won't order you, my dear," Millicent said, offended. "I am not an ogre or the wicked stepmother in a fairy tale!" She took a seat and looked up at her niece in concern. "I only wish you would explain to me what it is about Lord Denham that makes you so eager to avoid him. Perhaps if I understood, I would refrain from giving him further encouragement," she said in as patient a tone as she could muster.

Letty shook her head and turned away. "It is not . . . There is nothing I can speak of, Aunt," she said in a muffled, quivering voice and went to the window.

A dreadful thought suddenly occurred to Millicent and caused her to rise quickly and follow Letty to the window. Putting her hands affectionately on Letty's shoulders, she asked gently, "Oh, my dear . . . It is not . . . Lord Denham cannot have behaved improperly toward you! Is that it? I should never forgive myself if—"

But Letty didn't let her finish. "No, no!" she said fervently. "You must not think such a thing! Lord Denham has never been anything but gentlemanly and proper in my company, I promise you. There is no blame to be placed on him or on you—or indeed on *anyone*!"

Millicent, much relieved, could not help but pursue her goal. "Then, Letty, what can be the harm of a little drive in his company?"

Letty turned away and stared out the window at Roger's curricle waiting below. "Tell him . . . tell him I'll ride with him *tomorrow*," she said in sudden inspiration.

Millicent smiled. At least her renewed hopes need not yet be dashed. "Very well," she said agreeably, and then added shrewdly, "but I would be obliged if you could go down and tell him so yourself."

Letty wheeled around, the frightened-rabbit look returning to her eyes. "No, please, don't ask me to do that!"

Millicent hardened her heart to Letty's look. What could be so dreadful about speaking briefly to Lord Denham? The girl was being too missish. Millicent told herself that such foolishness should not be encouraged. "I *do* ask it," she said coldly. "I am much too tired to climb down the stairs again. I'm going to my room to lie down."

"Then couldn't Miss Tristle—?" Letty asked desperately.

"Miss Tristle?" Millicent said in horrified accents. "Surely you cannot suggest that we treat Lord Denham in such cavalier style. Go down at once, and don't make a to-do over nothing."

With those quelling words she marched from the room. Letty had no choice but to obey.

Lord Denham was standing before the high, paned windows of the sitting room, his manner calm and cool, the picture of the impeccable and elegant Corinthian from the top of his curly hair, cut with a casual-seeming artistry, to his gleaming top boots, which gave a subtle emphasis to the excellent shape of his legs. The sight of his sartorial splendor reminded Letty that she had not even checked her appearance in the mirror before she had left her room, and her hand unwittingly flew to her hair, which she had loosened when she'd returned from her visit to Brandon and which now hung in unkempt abandon around her face. Her careless appearance gave her a decided feeling of disadvantage until she noticed that he was twisting his curly-brimmed beaver rather nervously in his hands.

His whole face brightened when he caught sight of her. "Letty!" he said in a voice vibrant with hope. "Are you coming with me, then?"

She gave him no answering smile but merely shook her head. "I hope you will forgive me, my lord," she said with excessive formality, "but I find I am rather indisposed this afternoon."

"I see," he said, deflated. There was a moment's pause. "Thank you for taking the trouble to inform me of your indisposition," he said carefully. "I hope it will not be of long duration. But since you're here, I wonder if you might spare me a moment or two. I have some matters of urgency to discuss with you."

Letty took a deep breath. "Lord Denham," she said with what she hoped was crushing dignity, "I don't believe there is *anything* which must be discussed between us."

"Letty, for heaven's sake!" he burst out impatiently, "must we hide behind these artificial attitudes? We've passed far beyond these formalities, you and I. You *know* there are matters to be discussed."

"You are mistaken, sir. The matters to which you refer are not my affair and of no concern to me."

He took a step toward her and looked at her intently. "Are you sure, my dear?"

She met his eyes unwaveringly. "Quite sure," she said.

They stared at each other, both of them pale and strained. His eyes fell first. Wordlessly, with a quick bow, he turned and went to the door. But there he hesitated. Without turning, he lowered his head and asked in a choked voice, "May I not even be permitted to apologize for . . . for Vauxhall?"

She felt her breath catch. "I . . . It is not at all necessary, my lord."

He turned and looked at her steadily. "It is necessary to me."

A pulse in her neck was beating wildly. Her knees felt weak and her determination to prevent any sort of intimate communication between them was weakening, too. But honest or meaningful conversations between them in the past had sometimes ended with an embrace, and she was well aware what his embrace could do to her resolve. "I am truly not up to exchanges of this kind today," she said helplessly.

Instantly he was struck with remorse. "I don't mean to press you," he said quickly. "Forgive me. Perhaps another time . . . ?"

She nodded. "Tomorrow," she said, her eyes downcast. "I'll . . . drive with you tomorrow."

His look of gratitude smote her like a blow. Then he bowed and was gone. She flew to the window and watched as he climbed into the curricle and drove off. By this time tomorrow she would be well on her way to Gretna Green. If she ever saw him again, it would be as a married woman, safely protected by wedlock against the temptations he represented. With her forehead pressed against the glass, she watched until the curricle had disappeared. Then she went up the stairs, feeling hopeless, empty and enveloped in a misery so acute it was beyond tears.

Lady Upsham stood behind her bedroom door, listening for the sound of Letty's step on the stairs. When she heard it, she opened a crack in her door and peeped out at her niece's face. What she saw was intensely discouraging, and she closed the door with a deep sigh. Perhaps she should not have sent the girl down after all. Deflated and worried, she sank down on a chair, completely absorbed in her concern for Letty. For several minutes her speculations occupied her attention, but soon she became aware that Miss Tristle was bustling about with her walking clothes. "What *are* you doing?" she inquired irritably.

Miss Tristle looked up in surprise. "Laying out your clothes, my lady. Are you not going out to meet Lady Denham this afternoon?"

"No, no. Put those things away. Lady Denham is laid up with a toothache."

"Oh, the poor dear," Miss Tristle murmured sympathetically, her own recent experience with the toothache fresh in her memory. "You should send Katie to her."

"Katie?" Lady Upsham asked, mystified.

"She's a wonder when it comes to concocting medicines and potions."

"Is she?" Lady Upsham asked with interest.

"Indeed she is," Miss Tristle said with enthusiasm. "She gave me an herb wash took my toothache off like *that!*"

"Is that so? Then you may be right—perhaps we should send her to Lady Denham." Lady Upsham paused thoughtfully. "But not today. Miss Letty may have need of her today. Remind me about it tomorrow."

The morrow brought the rain. In the early-morning hours the downpour began. Nature, in her contrary way, was responding to the wishes expressed by so many the day before—but much too late. Brandon in particular was struck by the spitefulness of the weather. He had risen before daybreak, dressed, picked up his packed cloak-bag and stolen from the house, to be greeted by the heaviest rainstorm he had known since his arrival. The air had a decided autumn rawness, and by the time he had limped to the stable he was thoroughly chilled and drenched. It was then he realized that he couldn't use his phaeton. Its light hood would be small protection against such a deluge. The only carriage in the stable which would be suitable was his mother's ponderous coach, and he could not in good conscience make off with that. Resigning himself to another soaking, he made his way as quickly as his slowly mending ankle permitted to the nearest livery stable, where he was forced to spend almost an hour under the narrow eaves waiting for the proprietor to make an appearance.

Letty viewed the rain with equal distress. It prevented her from seeing the road clearly from her window, and as the hour grew later, she wondered if it would be better for her to creep outside with her things and wait for him at the side of the road. While she vacillated, she heard the first stirrings of the servants in the hallway. She knew she had better leave at once.

She peeped out to make sure the hallway was clear. Then she lifted her overstuffed bandbox, took an umbrella and crept out. As she passed Prue's door she stopped in horror. She had left no word for Prue or anyone else in the family. Her thoughtlessness appalled her. She tiptoed back to her room, pulled off her gloves and found a pen and paper. *Dearest Prue,* she wrote hastily, *by the time you read this, I will be on my way to Gretna Green. I know that you, at least, who have been closest to me and have been most aware of my unwillingness to marry Lord D., will understand why I take this step. It will not be the sort of wedding I would have wished for myself, and I know Mama and Aunt Millicent will be very shocked at my reprehensible behavior, but I can find no other way. Do not tell Aunt Millicent* where I've gone until you can hold back no longer. Tell her that I am truly grateful for all she has tried to do for me and that my most painful regret is that I am forced to serve her what I am sure she will think is a backhanded turn. Tell Mama the same, and that I love her above all. And tell them that they will become more resigned to my marriage when they have learned to accept the fact that it is better so. They will grow to feel kindly toward Brandon, I am sure, once they recognize his admirable characteristics. Until we meet again, dearest, I remain your loving sister, Letty.

She folded the letter carefully, put on her gloves again and turned to go. But to her consternation, the door was opening. Katie stood in the doorway, gasping at the sight of her mistress, who was fully dressed and packed for a voyage. "Miss Letty! Wha—?"

"Hush, Katie," Letty whispered frantically, pulling the girl into the room and shutting the door.

"But, Miss Letty, what is it y're up to?" Katie demanded, her hands on her hips and her arms akimbo.

"I'm eloping," Letty said briefly. "And now that you've found me out, you can help me."

"I ain't helpin' till I know more about it," Katie said firmly. "Don' know yet if I hold wi' it."

"Oh, Katie," Letty laughed weakly, "you're impossible. You must take my word that what I'm doing is for the best."

"So *you* say," Katie replied sceptically. "Is it 'is lordship?"

Letty gave Katie a wondering glance. "What do you know of his lordship?" she asked.

"I ain't no slow-top. I know'd 'oo you was cryin' over that night."

Letty frowned at her. "Never mind that. I'm going to marry Mr. Peake."

Katie's brow wrinkled worriedly. "You're bammin' me! Tell me you're bammin' me!"

"It's true. So don't delay me further. Promise me you'll tell *no one*. And give this note to Miss Prue when she wakes."

"Does Miss Prue know what y're doin'?" Katie asked, looking at her narrowly.

"I've told her in the note."

Katie shook her head. "It's not right, Miss Letty. Y're makin' as big a mistake as a body can make."

Letty smiled at her indulgently and gave her a quick hug. "Don't worry, Katie dear. I know what I'm doing. Just be a good girl and do as I ask." She picked up her bag and ran out. Katie stood where Letty had left her, shaking her head in concern. "You don' know the 'alf, Miss Letty," she murmured. "You don' know the 'alf."

The rain had not abated when Letty came out, and by the time the hired coach came down the street, her bandbox and her shoes were sadly soaked. Brandon made profuse apologies for his lateness and tried his best to put on a cheerful aspect, but the bad start seemed to auger ill for their future, and though neither would admit it, they both were inwardly very depressed. Brandon could not help thinking of Euripides's words: *A bad beginning makes a bad ending.* And Letty, looking out the back window at her aunt's house, rapidly disappearing from view behind a thick curtain of rain, found that a little phrase kept repeating itself ironically in her brain: *Happy the bride the sun shines on.*

Chapter Eighteen

*K*atie went about her morning duties with an abstracted air. Miss Letty's note to her sister Prue was stowed in her apron pocket, ready to be delivered as soon as Prue should waken, but Katie dreaded the chore of delivering it. She knew that Prue would take the news hard. Mr. Peake seemed to occupy all Miss Prue's thoughts and dreams, and Katie knew that the news that he was to be her *brother-in-law* would be painful for the girl to bear. But half the morning went by without a sign of stirring from her bedroom.

On many mornings, Lady Upsham would ask Katie to wake the girls, but on this rainy day, her ladyship evidently had decided to permit the girls to stay abed. Katie paced the corridor outside Prue's bedroom anxiously. When the clock struck half after nine, she could bear it no longer. She opened the door and tiptoed in. Prue stirred and snuggled deeper into the pillows. "Are you awake, Miss Prue?" Katie asked tentatively.

"Mm. 'S raining," Prue mumbled.

"Yes'm, rainin' somethin' fierce. I never seen such a downpour," Katie said briskly, taking matters in hand. She pulled open the drapes and went over to the bed. "Do y'know it's half after nine?"

Prue yawned. "Is it?" she asked, stretching lazily.

"More'n time you turned yourself out," Katie said brusquely.

Prue sat back among the pillows and regarded Katie balefully. "You needn't sound so quarrelsome. I don't see why I should hurry to rise and dress on a morning like this. Is Letty up?"

Katie bit her lip. "Yes. Got up hours ago, she did. She's . . . gone out, y'know . . ."

"Gone out? In this weather? Where?"

"Can't say," Katie said shortly, "but she give'd me this for you." With a sur-reptitious glance at Prue's face, she handed over the letter.

"What on earth—?" Prue asked, perplexed, and opened the note. Her mouth dropped open as soon as she'd read the first sentence. "Gretna!" she gasped. "She must have lost her senses!" She looked up at Katie accusingly. "Do you know anything of this?"

Katie shrugged. "Is that all she says? That she's made off to Gretna?"

Prue scanned the rest of the letter quickly. Not until she'd read the last line was her eye arrested. "Oh, my God! Brandon! She hasn't gone off with *Brandon*! She *couldn't* . . . !"

Katie said nothing but watched Prue with concern. Prue had paled, and the hand holding the letter had begun to tremble. Prue turned to Katie suspiciously. "Is this some sort of hum? Is Letty trying to hoax me?"

Katie shook her head. "I ain't whiddled the whole scrap, but she's took off with Mr. Peake for sure. It ain't no whisker. I seen 'em leave."

"You *saw* them? Then for God's sake, why didn't you *stop* them?" Prue de-manded in a choked voice.

"It ain't my place to stop 'em, even if I could," Katie said reasonably.

"Then you should have called *me,*" Prue said furiously. "I would have found a way."

Katie looked dubious, and Prue, meeting her eye, was about to argue the point further when suddenly her face seemed to collapse, and she burst into tears. "Why did L-Letty do it?" she asked despairingly. "She d-doesn't even c-care for him!"

"Are you certain sure o' that?" Katie asked pointedly.

Prue angrily dashed the tears from her cheeks. "Yes, I'm sure! And he doesn't really c-care for her, either!"

"Then why did 'e go?"

Prue hesitated. "I . . . I don't know," she said pettishly. Then, with an angry hitch of her body, she cast herself down into the pillows, turning her head away from Katie's level-eyed, rational stare. "And I don't *care,* either!" she flung back over her shoulder. "Let them go. Let them marry. They m-made their beds . . . let them lie in them!"

"If you really think they mistook theirsel's," Katie suggested, "why don't you tell your aunt? Maybe they can be cotched . . ."

"No, I won't! I don't care if they're caught or not. I won't lift a *finger* to stop them! If Brandon wants Letty instead of . . . of . . . well, he can have her." She crushed the letter in her hand and threw it away.

"Miss Prue," Katie said soberly, sitting on the edge of the bed and patting Prue's shoulder, "Don't you think you should say *somethin'*? It ain't right to run sly about a thing like this."

"I don't care. Letty said not to tell until I must. I'll stay here as long as I can and say nothing till I'm asked. That's what Letty wants . . . and Brandon, too . . . so that's what I'll do. As far as I'm concerned," she added vehemently, her under-lip quivering and two large tears forming in the corners of her eyes, "I w-wish them h-happy!"

Katie tried to reason with her, but Prue dismissed the abigail coldly. Katie picked up the crushed letter, put it back in her pocket and left the room. Something told her to show the letter to Lady Upsham, but she could not bring herself to do so. "I ain't a tattlin' old chubb," she said to herself and, at last, she tore the letter to shreds and threw the pieces on the fire.

No sooner was this decision made than she was told by Miss Tristle that Lady Upsham wanted her to go to the Denham lodgings to help Lady Denham cure her toothache. With an unshakable feeling that she was going from the frying pan into the fire, she flung a shawl over her head and scurried off.

When she told Lady Denham why she had come, the dowager eyed her dubiously. Lady Denham had been seen by the most respected medical man in Bath, and the medication he had prescribed had not proved efficacious. Why, then, had Lady Upsham believed that this little maidservant, whose language reeked of the streets of London, would be of more help than the doctor?

Katie, with a professional air that belied her diminutive stature and humble position, took off her shawl and approached her patient, touching the swelling on Lady Denham's cheek with gently probing fingers. "What 'ave you took for it?" she inquired.

"This," Lady Denham said, handing a bottle of muddy-looking liquid to the girl and watching her with interest.

"What's in it?" Katie asked.

"I don't know," Lady Denham said with a shudder. "All I know is that it was too strong for my tooth to bear. I didn't even *try* to use it after the first experience."

Katie sniffed the liquid, then wet her finger with it and licked the finger with an exploring tongue. "I know'd it. Honey!" she declared.

"Honey?" Lady Denham repeated. "Is something wrong with that?"

"Everythin'," Katie declared with assurance. "Don' know why the doctors like this potion. It's made of juniper root, alum and honey, and maybe one or two other things. But honey ain't nowise good for bad teeth, ma'am. Take my word on it."

"I don't doubt you're right," Lady Denham said with a smile. The girl's air of authority had a winning charm and seemed to inspire confidence. "Doctors can be fools, you know. This silly man told me to soak my feet in hot water and rub them in bran at bedtime. I can't imagine how soaking my feet will be of any help to my tooth, can you?"

Katie grinned. "Sounds a queer start to me," she agreed.

The girl was given free rein. She made her herb wash, brought it to the patient, and after several applications a grateful Lady Denham was feeling some relief. Roger, entering his mother's bedroom in the early afternoon, was surprised to see her out of bed. She was sitting on a chaise, looking comfortably relaxed, while Katie applied cold compresses to her still-swollen cheek.

"Well, Mama," Roger greeted her, "you seem better this afternoon."

"Thanks to this child here," Lady Denham told him. "Lady Upsham sent her here to doctor me. Her name, she tells me, is Katie-from-the-kitchen."

Roger turned curiously and found himself regarded with equal interest by a pair of shrewd, bright eyes. Katie had heard a great deal about the fascinating Lord Denham and had even seen him once or twice from a discreet distance. This was the first time, however, that she could really look at him closely enough to make an evaluation. Roger could not help smiling at the intense scrutiny to which she was subjecting him. "How do you do, Katie-from-the-kitchen? How do you come by such a strange name?"

Katie curtsied awkwardly. "Miss Letty and Miss Prue like to call me that," she explained. "It's only a lark, y'know. That's where they come'd to find me."

"And a very good find it was, too," Lady Denham said affectionately. "I shall miss you when you leave me this afternoon. If ever you want a new place, child, come and see me."

Katie bobbed again. "Thank you, m'lady, but I like my place well enough." And she turned away to wring out a fresh compress.

Roger sat down beside his mother. "I've come to ask if I might use your carriage this afternoon," he said. "It's still raining too hard to permit me to use the curricle."

"Of course you may," Lady Denham said, "but I can't imagine why you should wish to drive out on such an afternoon."

"Because, my dear, I promised to take Letty for a drive," he told her with a smile.

Katie, who had heard every word, turned around abruptly. She had looked closely at this man for whom her sweet Miss Letty had sobbed so bitterly. If she was any judge—and Katie had no doubts of the perspicacity of her own judgment—this man was the one for Letty. Perhaps it was not too late to save Letty from the folly of her impetuous elopement. "Beg pardon, m'lord," she said bravely, "but if y're meanin' to drive Miss Letty today, you'll be bum-squabbled."

Roger looked at her sharply. "Why? Is she ill?"

"No, sir. She ain't at 'ome."

"Oh?" Roger asked, his eyebrows raised. "But I'm sure she'll return in time for our drive. We had an arrangement . . ."

"Yessir, but she's gone, you see."

"No, I'm afraid I don't see. Gone where?"

It took all Katie's courage to answer. "To Gretna Green, m'lord."

Roger stared at the girl, the color draining from his cheeks. His mother sat upright with a cry. "Katie, what are you saying? Has Letty eloped?"

Katie nodded humbly.

"I don't believe it!" Lady Denham declared, thunderstruck. "Not Letty. She has always been the most well-mannered, beautifully behaved—"

"Do you know with whom she has gone?" Roger asked intently, not even aware that he'd interrupted his mother's words.

"Yes, sir, I do. She went wi' Mr. Peake."

For a moment the two stared at Katie motionless. "Brandon?" Lady Denham gasped. "It's not possible!"

Roger got to his feet and went to the window. "Yes, it *is* possible," he said in a flat voice. "She *told* me they were betrothed."

"Roger! Are you saying that you *knew* something like this would happen?"

Roger stared out at the relentless rain. "No, for I refused to believe it. What a fool I've been! I could have *sworn* she didn't care a fig for him!"

"She don't," Katie said decidedly.

Lady Denham looked at Katie with disapproval. She had forgotten the girl was there. It was most improper for them to discuss the matter before a servant, and even more improper for the girl to interject her views. But Roger turned and was eyeing the girl with interest. "What do you mean, Katie? Explain yourself."

"I hardly think, Roger," his mother said in gentle rebuke, "that it is at all seemly to discuss this matter with Katie."

"Let's forget the proprieties, Mama. This is too important for me to worry about trivial conventions. Go on, Katie."

Katie looked at Lady Denham hesitantly, but Lady Denham shrugged and waved an approving hand at her. "My son is right, girl," she said. "Go ahead and tell us."

"I think Lord Denham 'ad the right of it," Katie explained. "Miss Letty never talked about Mr. Peake, nor thought about 'im, neither." She met Roger's eye and added challengingly, "She cried o' nights for some *other* gent, not 'im."

Roger's gaze wavered under Katie's forthright challenge. Lady Denham asked, "How do you know, Katie, that it was some 'other gent' for whom she cried?"

"She 'adn't no reason to cry over Mr. Peake," Katie said bluntly.

Roger gave a short, mirthless laugh. "You're quite a knowing one, aren't you, Katie?"

Katie smiled broadly. "That's what everyone says."

"And you didn't tell us all this just to poke bogey, did you, girl?"

"No, sir. I ain't no blabbin' chaffer-mouth."

"Then, if you didn't say all this to tell tales, you had another reason. You want something of me—isn't that it? Well, what is it you want me to do?"

"*Stop* 'er, o' course!"

"And how am I to do that?"

"It's a longish ride to Gretna, ain't it? And I don't suppose they call you a bruisin' rider for nothin'."

Roger rubbed his chin speculatively. "I have no rights in this—no claims," he murmured, half to himself. "She's given me no right to interfere—"

"Who's worried about trivial conventions now?" his mother asked, her eyes dancing in excitement.

"Mama!" Roger said in surprise. "Are *you* telling me to go after her?"

"Are *you* the 'other gent' who made her 'cry o' nights' ?" Lady Denham countered.

Roger looked from his mother to the abigail. They were both watching him intently. He colored. "I *think* I am," he admitted.

"Then stop her, Roger, before it's too late," his mother urged warmly.

"Come on then, Katie-from-the-kitchen. I'll take you back to Lady Upsham and tell her my intentions. Mama, I hope you can manage without your carriage for a day or two. This expedition may take quite a while." With a quick kiss on his mother's cheek, he strode out the door, pulling little Katie firmly behind him.

Lady Upsham's household was in a turmoil. Her ladyship had discovered the absence of her niece by late morning and had sent for Prue. The two had repaired to the sitting room where, for more than an hour, Prue had had to endure an emotional harangue. The word had spread among the servants that some crisis of an extremely delicate nature was transpiring, and each of them managed to find some excuse to linger about in the corridor outside the sitting room until Miss Tristle and the butler took stations at each end of the hallway and kept them away. In the midst of this *contretemps,* an agitated Mrs. Peake had made her appearance. She had been ushered into the sitting room, and from then on the sounds of her shrill and hysterical outbursts could be heard all the way down the corridor, making a dramatic contrast to the low, ironically bitter tones of Lady Upsham's voice.

It was at this awkward moment that Lord Denham and Katie arrived at the door. The butler tried to discourage his lordship from entering, but Lord

Denham ignored him and demanded to be announced to Lady Upsham at once. The butler tried to tell him that Lady Upsham was already engaged. "With Mrs. Peake, I presume," Lord Denham remarked drily, and walked past him into the sitting room, with Katie close behind.

The tension in the room was almost tangible. Lady Upsham stood near the fireplace, her cheeks pale and her lips compressed. Pacing about the room nervously was Mrs. Peake, her entire expression revealing the utmost agitation. In the corner farthest from the door sat Prue. Her hair had not been dressed, her eyes were stormy and red-rimmed, her face was strained and she twisted a handkerchief tightly through her fingers. Lady Upsham did not take kindly to the sight of the intruders. She fixed a cold eye on Roger and said curtly, "Lord Denham, I'm afraid you find me occupied with Mrs. Peake on pressing business. I must beg you to excuse us. I shall be happy to receive you at some future time."

"Forgive this intrusion, ma'am," Roger said, undeterred, "but your pressing business is also mine. I have some information for both you and Mrs. Peake and must advise you of it *at once.*"

Lady Upsham recognized the determination of his jaw and promptly waved the butler away. Then turning her eye on Katie, she tried to dismiss her as well. But Roger suggested that she might prove useful in their talk, and the girl was permitted to remain. "I stopped in to tell you, ma'am, that you need not worry about Letty. I leave immediately to follow the pair, and I hope to restore her to you safely before long."

Mrs. Peake gasped audibly. "How did you know?" she asked in a high, horrified voice. "Did Brandon tell you?"

"No, Mrs. Peake. It was Katie who brought me the information."

Lady Upsham's eyebrows shot up. "How dared you, Katie? Have you no loyalty? Is this how you repay Miss Letty's kindnesses to you—by spreading this terrible tale all over town?"

"No, Lady Upsham, you're out there," Roger intervened. "The girl is no gossip. She told only my mother and me, and you may surely count on our discretion."

"But she shouldn't have told *anybody!*" Lady Upsham said, unyielding. "Why didn't you come to *me*, you ninny?"

Prue spoke up from her corner in a tone of sullen disgust. "What good would it have done to come to *you*, Aunt Millicent? What could you have done about it?"

"That's exactly the point," Roger agreed. "You could not have ridden after her. That's why Katie thought of me."

"I don't see what *you* have to do with all this," Mrs. Peake said petulantly.

"These Glendenning girls have a way of embroiling outsiders into their affairs in a manner I cannot like."

"I'm afraid, Mrs. Peake, that this whole bumble-broth is more my doing than Miss Glendenning's. I suspect strongly that it was I who drove Letty to this pass. But I'm sure that I can straighten it all out, one way or another, and bring Letty back unharmed. Have I your permission to try, Lady Upsham?"

Lady Upsham looked up at him with such intense relief that her eyes became misty. Not given to sentiment, however, she did not shed a tear. She merely favored him with a tremulous smile and asked hopefully, "Are you sure you can catch them, Lord Denham? I believe they set out more than five hours ago."

"I'll catch them," Roger said reassuringly, "and before nightfall, too. So you may rest easy, ma'am." And with a quick bow to Mrs. Peake, he went quickly to the door. There he found his way blocked by a determined Prue.

"You shan't go," she declared. "Not without me."

"I'm touched by your concern for your sister," Roger said with gentle irony, "but there's no need for—"

"My sister? Do you think I'm concerned for my *sister*? You and Aunt Millicent have enough concern for her to make mine completely unnecessary. Letty, Letty, Letty—that's all I've heard! She's the only one you're worried about. What about *Brandon*? Has anyone given any thought to what *his* feelings might be when you ride up and wrest Letty away from him?"

"Well, *really,* Miss Glendenning!" Mrs. Peake declared coldly, "I fail to see how Brandon's feelings can be any concern of yours. I am his mother, after all, and *I* am convinced that a bit of humiliation will be an edifying lesson for him."

Prue stared, large-eyed, at Mrs. Peake and opened her mouth to remonstrate. Something made her change her mind. Brandon would not like it, she realized, if she engaged in a squabble with his mother. Ignoring her comment, she turned back to Roger and said in an urgent undervoice, "Please, Lord Denham, I *must* go! Take me with you!"

"I warn you, young lady, that it will not be a pleasure trip. We will not make any but the briefest stops, you will be jostled about unmercifully, and you will find me in no mood for idle conversation."

"Nothing you've said deters me in the least," she assured him.

"And I won't wait for you to change your clothes or dress your hair."

"I need only to put on a shawl."

Roger looked questioningly at Lady Upsham. Her ladyship, sore beset, put her hands to her forehead, sighed and made a helpless gesture of consent. Roger gave Prue a quick grin. "Come along then, minx. We've wasted too much time already."

Prue gave a little cry of joy and reached up to hug Roger gratefully.

"Lady Upsham," Mrs. Peake objected, "surely you don't intend to permit that child to involve herself in such a pursuit—!"

"Surely, Mrs. Peake, you do not mean to interfere with my judgment in—"

But Roger did not wait for more. With a wink and a wave to Katie, he grasped Prue's hand, and the two ran out to the carriage, leaving the ladies to continue their dispute without witnesses.

Chapter Nineteen

*I*n his hurried planning for the trip to Scotland, Brandon had anticipated reaching Wolverhampton by nightfall. But the rain had turned some of the roads to mud, had slowed the horses and had so dampened the spirits of the driver that, by four that afternoon, they were only a short way past Worcester. By this time, Letty and Brandon were both regretting the rashness of their decision to engage in this enterprise. Brandon had been shivering in his damp clothes and soggy boots all day. He was now chilled to the bone. His head had begun to ache, his eyes were clouded, and there was a persistent and painful tickle in his throat. He knew the signs—he would, by nightfall, be very sick indeed.

Letty was also damp and cold. Her shoes had been so badly soaked during her wait in the rain that they were quite ruined, the inner lining cracking and curling and causing her additional discomfort. Even more disturbing was the growing doubt in her mind of Brandon's ability to see to the practical matters involved in a long journey. She was depressed by the prospect of her future—a future which now seemed considerably less bearable than it had appeared when Brandon had described it. He'd spent the first four hours of the trip telling her about the dramatic intrigue of the *Choephoroe,* but the Greek names had so confused Letty that Brandon had felt it necessary to lecture at length on the genealogy of the House of Atreus. This only confused her further, and her mind wandered to other matters. She was beginning to realize that, while Brandon was brilliant on the subject of the classics, he was vague and absentminded about the practical matters of life. At a toll gate, he had caused a considerable delay while he searched through all his pockets for a coin (which Letty finally supplied from her reticule), and he would, more than once, have taken the wrong road had not Letty been watchful. But he had gone on and on about Agamemnon and Clytemnestra and their impossible offspring until Letty was sorely tempted to tell him that it was time for school to be out. At length, however, even *he* had tired of the subject. They had lapsed into silence—a brooding, empty, isolating silence.

They had gone a little way north of Ombersley when Letty noticed that Brandon looked ill. Over his objections, she insisted that they stop at the nearest inn for the night. They both needed rest and warmth, she pointed out, and she would prefer to *sleep* through the rain than *drive* through any more of it. Brandon, too weak to argue, turned the carriage into the courtyard of a small, thatched inn whose lights had beckoned invitingly to them through the gathering shadows.

From the curious and somewhat discourteous glance of the innkeeper when they entered, Letty became uncomfortably aware of the shabby appearance they made. Their clothes were badly wrinkled and soggy, their hair matted, and even their luggage was meagre and unprepossessing. Brandon wearily requested two bedrooms for the night and, turning to Letty, asked if she would mind dreadfully taking her dinner alone. He was not hungry. A warm bed was all he wanted. Letty assured him that she would manage well enough on her own. Brandon bespoke a private parlor for her and limped tiredly up the stairs.

A young boy brought in their things. Letty followed him up the stairs to see to the distribution of their boxes and to make sure that fires were lighted in their bedrooms. She told the boy to give Mr. Peake assistance in his undressing, and after settling everything upstairs to her satisfaction, she went down again to procure some hot soup for Brandon to drink before he fell asleep. This time she was greeted by the innkeeper's wife. The woman was robust and red-cheeked, and Letty would have assumed her to be a cheerful, warmhearted country wife except for her narrow eyes and thin lips, which combined to give her a sour expression strangely inappropriate when combined with her apple-dumpling appearance. The narrow eyes surveyed Letty with obvious suspicion and disdain, taking due note of the wrinkled gown and ruined shoes. Letty requested the soup. The woman, after a moment's hesitation, nodded a surly acquiescence and went off to prepare it, her reluctance apparent in every step she took.

Letty herself took the soup to Brandon and sat beside him while he drank. His cheeks were flushed and feverish, and though she kept up a flow of cheerful conversation, her heart failed her. What would she do if Brandon became seriously ill? He handed the bowl to her with a grateful smile and slid down under the covers. He was asleep almost at once.

She tiptoed from the room and, having two hours to wait before dinner, went to her room, removed her damp clothing with relief and lay down to rest. She, too, was soon asleep. She woke with a start to find the room in darkness. She didn't know how long she'd slept. Quickly she dressed in a fresh gown, brushed and tied back her hair and went out. She opened the door to Brandon's room. He was still asleep, and she was relieved to hear his steady, unobstructed breathing. Perhaps he was not as ill as she had feared. A good night's sleep might be sufficient to restore him to health. If he were sufficiently recovered by morning, and if the sun shone at last, the prospects for the future might seem a little brighter.

With the return of more hopeful spirits, Letty realized that she was very hungry. She went down the stairs and found the innkeeper in the taproom, where he was busily supplying tall mugs of home brew to a surprisingly large number of locals. Evidently the weather had not deterred his patrons from seeking their nightly refreshment. She learned from the innkeeper that it was after eight. Requesting her dinner, she went to the private parlor where she took a seat before the fire and tried to relax. After only a moment there was a tap on the door, and the innkeeper came in, followed closely by his wife. The innkeeper, embarrassed, took only a couple of awkward steps into the room. He stood blinking at Letty wordlessly. His wife, however, came in purposefully, closed the door and, with a deeper frown than was usual with her, poked her husband in the back with an angry forefinger.

"Excuse me, ma'am," the innkeeper said hesitantly, "but we was wonderin'— that is, my wife here was wonderin'—if you could see your way clear to . . . to . . ."

"Yes?" asked Letty encouragingly.

The innkeeper glanced dubiously at his wife. She glared at him in disgust and took over the matter herself. "We was wonderin' if you'd be so good as to pay yer shot now," she said grimly and shot a look at her husband which seemed to say that *that* was how to deal with suspicious-looking customers.

"Now?" Letty asked, nonplussed. "But . . . I don't understand. Is it customary to demand payment before the end of one's stay?"

"Well . . ." the innkeeper began.

"Don't care if it is or it ain't," his wife said flatly. "You come in 'ere wantin' two bedrooms 'stead of one and askin' fer the private parlor like you was a duchess. Well, how're we to know if you've so much as a copperjohn in yer pocket?"

"I can assure you, madam, that your reckoning will be paid in full," Letty said sternly.

"That's all well 'n good, but assurances don't ring near so good as brass," the woman said insolently. "A night like this'n is always busy fer us. We had *two parties* we turned away because you took the bedrooms, ain't I right, Joddy?"

The innkeeper nodded. "It *is* a busy night, ma'am," he said sheepishly.

"And now you want dinner, after I already let the fire die out," the woman complained. "This ain't the royal kitchen, y'know. We ain't inclined to 'ave dinner at all hours."

"There's no need to upset yourself over that," Letty said calmly. "Some cold meat and a piece of bread should do quite well."

"Cold meat or hot, I'd like to 'ear the clink o' yer guineas," she retorted.

"I'd be glad to oblige," Letty explained curtly, "but my . . . but Mr. Peake is not feeling well and is fast asleep. I would rather not disturb him just now. You shall have your money first thing in the morning."

The woman sneered and folded her arms across her chest adamantly. "It's now, my lady, or out you go," she declared.

Letty gasped and looked questioningly at the innkeeper. He shrugged helplessly. "Sorry, ma'am," was all he said.

Letty got stiffly to her feet and, with head erect, walked out of the room. She ran quickly up the stairs, tapped on Brandon's door and went in. He didn't stir. Reluctantly, she shook his shoulder. With a groan, he turned over and blinked up at her. "Letty," he mumbled hoarsely, "what—?"

"Sorry to wake you, Brandon, but I've just had a rather uncomfortable scene with the innkeepers. They want us to pay them *now.*"

Brandon rubbed his eyes and reached for the spectacles he had placed on a table near the bed. He put them on and peered at her, trying to get his brain to function. "Pay them?" he muttered thickly. "Yes, of course. Just take the—" Suddenly he sat bolt upright, his eyes wide awake and staring in alarm. "Money! Good God, Letty, I've forgotten to take any money!"

Letty paled. "Oh, Brandon, no!"

He clapped his hand to his aching forehead, and a croaking sound came from his throat. "What a complete *fool* I am! What are we to do now?"

For a moment Letty stared at him in disbelief. How *could* he have been so disordered? She felt a wave of revulsion for so muddleheaded a man. But immediately, the injustice of her feelings became apparent to her. She had *begged* him to do this for her. He had been safe and comfortable and content with his life. It was *she* who had turned his world upside down, brought him to this miserable inn, sick and penniless. *She* was the muddleheaded one. Whatever had possessed her to involve him in her life, to use him for her own selfish purposes? If she had any character at all, she would release him from his promise and set him free.

But this was not the time for such thoughts. He was sick, and his eyes were desperately worried. She bent over him and put a cool hand on his forehead. "There, now," she said soothingly, "don't look so alarmed. I shall simply tell the man to trust us for a while." She took off his spectacles and helped him to settle himself into the pillows again.

"Do you think he will?" Brandon asked, eager to believe that they were not so close to disaster as he had feared.

"Of course he will," Letty said with a cheerfulness she was far from feeling.

"But what about money? Where can we procure some money?"

"Don't worry about that now. Let's get a good night's sleep. We'll think of something in the morning."

Brandon sighed. "Very well, Letty. Sorry I'm such an absentminded idiot. Good night, my dear."

Letty went out and closed the door. She paused for a moment on the landing to brace herself for the ordeal ahead. Then she went firmly down the stairs. The innkeeper and his wife were waiting at the foot. "I'm sorry," she told them without mincing words, "but I'm afraid we could not put our hands on the money tonight. You will have to trust us until tomorrow."

"*Trust* you? Do y'think we're loobies? You can pack yer things right now and take yerselves off."

"What are you saying?" Letty asked, trying to control her agitation. "You cannot mean to put us out at this hour . . . and on such a night?"

The innkeeper turned to his wife diffidently. "She's right, pet. It ain't human to send 'em off in this downpour."

His wife fixed him with a glare of such animosity that Letty quailed. "Keep yer sneezer out o' this if you've nothing better to say, you cod's-head!" she sneered at him. "We ain't in the business o' givin' charity. If this fancy-piece and her chap upstairs ain't out o' here in a quarter-hour, you can pick 'em up by their tails and heave 'em out the door!"

A gust of wind and spray of rain behind them caused them to turn their heads toward the outer door. It had opened. Impressively filling the dimly lit doorway stood the most elegant gentleman the innkeepers had ever seen. His tall, rain-spattered beaver, his driving coat with its six capes, the high boots, which gleamed under a spattering of mud—all proclaimed the Corinthian. The innkeepers gaped, and even Letty was struck by the imposing figure before her. It wasn't until he spoke that she realized who he was. "Mind your malignant tongue, woman!" he was saying to the innkeeper's wife in coldly imperious accents. "Apologize to the lady *at once!*"

"*Roger!*" cried Letty joyously and, completely without thought but with a sensation of glorious relief at the sight of him, she ran to the door and flung herself into his arms. "I've never been so glad to see anyone in all my life!" The terror of the last few moments vanished like the remnants of a nightmare, and she clung to him with the instinctive wisdom of a drowning child for his rescuer. She had been battling an antagonistic world all day, a world which had persistently presented her with larger and larger obstacles. She had pushed herself and

Brandon into such deep waters that it had seemed they must drown, but Roger's sudden appearance had changed all that. Her prospects no longer had the power to overwhelm her. She was safe. With her head pressed against his shoulder, she surrendered to the tears that had been held just beneath the surface throughout this deplorable day.

Roger, amazed by the unexpected warmth of her welcome, held her closely to him in speechless gratification. He had no knowledge of the circumstances which had brought her to this pass, and he suspected that she would soon come to her senses and reconsider—with regret—her rash greeting. But in this brief, unguarded moment, she had revealed something of the depth of her feelings for him, and suddenly his prospects seemed brighter, too.

For an instant, he forgot his surroundings, the people who watched, the wind and the rain blowing at his back, and the reason why he came. His arms tightened around her, and he laid his cheek against her hair. Letty felt the movement of his arms and came to her senses with a jerk. She pulled herself from his arms and stammered guiltily, "Oh! I didn't mean to . . . that is I . . . I must explain why I—good God! *Prue!*"

Prue, who had been standing just behind Roger and watching the scene with fascination, could not help smiling. "I'm glad to find that *someone* has taken notice of me at last," she said. "I shall be drenched if I'm not permitted to come in out of the rain at once."

"Oh, indeed, come in, Miss," the innkeeper said hastily, ushering them all toward the private parlor with repeated and obsequious bows.

"I'm that upset that I disconstrued you, ma'am," the innkeeper's wife said to Letty with painful eagerness, "but I didn't know . . . I mean, if I'd know'd you was related to *this* gent 'ere . . ." But no one paid her any heed. With a great number of exclamations, gasps and half-uttered questions, they made their way into the private parlor.

"How did you find us?" Letty asked repeatedly. "And what are you doing here?"

Roger refused to discuss anything until he had disposed of the innkeeper and his wife, who remained at the door watching the goings-on with open-mouthed interest. "I shall leave Prue to explain how and why we're here," he said, "while I deal with our hosts and make arrangements for dinner and bed-chambers. But when I return, my girl," he added, taking Letty's chin in his hand and forcing her to look up at him, "you and I are going to have a long, long talk." Letty was disconcerted by the unmistakable twinkle in his eye. It was there for no good reason that she could ascertain, unless he had exaggerated the significance of her greeting. She would have some arduous explaining to do.

As soon as the parlor door closed behind him, Letty turned to her sister and hugged her effusively. "I never *dreamed* you'd come after me," she exclaimed in astonishment. "Whatever made you do such a foolhardy thing? And why did you persuade Lord Denham to accompany you? That was beyond anything! I should really be angry at you, you know, except that I am so glad to see you that I shan't scold at all."

"Scold!" Prue said contemptuously. "You are in no position to scold anyone, Letty Glendenning! Eloping in that wild way! Whatever possessed you?"

"I refuse to answer any of your questions until you answer mine. Why did you bring Lord Denham with you?"

"I didn't bring him—he brought me," Prue said, taking off her shawl and settling near the fire. "He was coming alone, but I begged him to let me come along."

"But why did he wish to—? And how did he learn that I—?"

"Katie told him."

"Katie?" Letty asked incredulously. "But . . . *why*?"

"She thinks Roger is the perfect man for you . . . and so do I."

Letty's expression clouded over, and she frowned at her sister in annoyance. "My thanks to you both," she said tartly. "You know nothing whatsoever about the matter, either of you. Therefore, your opinions are worthless, and I'd be obliged if you both would refrain from expressing them."

"And *I'd* be obliged if you'd refrain from running off with a man for whom you care nothing," Prue retorted.

Letty gave Prue a startled glance. "What do you mean? Why do you say *that*?"

"I can tell. You've never even talked to me about him."

"I may not talk about him," Letty said, trying to convince herself as much as her sister, "but that doesn't mean that I don't think highly of all his admirable qualities."'

"Well, *I* don't think of his 'admirable qualities' at all, and I—" She stopped, flushed and looked down at the floor.

Letty, arrested, stared at her sister. "Prue! What are you saying?"

Prue bit her lip. "I only mean that love doesn't have anything to do with *admirable qualities*. One can love someone without finding him so very admirable . . . I believe . . ."

Letty ran to her sister and knelt beside the chair. "Oh, Prue," she said softly, "you don't mean that you . . . you can't mean *Brandon*!"

Prue nodded and looked at her sister with a rueful smile. "Isn't it shocking? I know he's stodgy and stuffy and impossibly priggish, but . . . Oh, Letty, it's all midsummer moon with me!"

Letty looked up at her sister aghast. "But I had no *idea* . . . ! Why did you never *tell* me?"

"I wanted to, Letty, truly. I *longed* to talk to you about him. But you've been so abstracted . . . so troubled . . . and you didn't seem to want to talk to me about it . . ."

Letty was deeply shamed. She'd been so self-absorbed, she'd taken no notice of what had been happening to her sister. She rose and turned to the fire. "I've been completely selfish," she said, deeply humiliated. "I never even *noticed* . . . and you must have had a difficult time of it! Can you forgive me, Prue?"

Prue stood up and joined her sister at the fire. "Don't be a goosecap," she said, slipping an arm around her sister's waist. "Just tell me truly if *you* care for him."

Letty grinned. "If today was an indication of the sort of life Brandon and I would have together, we neither of us could have borne it for a week! No, my dear. I've been completely foolish to have imagined that the two of us could make a match." She glanced at her sister cautiously. "But, Prue, are you sure that *you* would be happy with him?"

"You're asking if I could bear his by-your-leaves and his quotations and his endless prosings about his old Greeks, is that it?" Prue laughed.

"Yes, dearest, I am. And his absentmindedness, and his disregard for the practicalities, and . . . Prue, to be truthful, he is so *different* from you," Letty said with a worried frown.

Prue gave her an affectionate squeeze. "I know all that," she said with a reassuring smile, "but he doesn't dare prose on to *me* about Euripides and Catullus. He needs someone like me to enliven him, Letty—really he does. And I need him to . . . settle me down."

Letty stared at her sister with dawning admiration. The girl was right. Prue had always been practical and down-to-earth. She would enjoy seeing to Brandon's mundane needs—making sure that his hat was firmly on his head, his spectacles on his nose and his money in his pocket. She would tease him into displaying the charm that lay beneath his scholarly disposition, and she would bring enchantment to his hitherto ordinary existence. And *he* would curb the excesses of her volatile nature. They would undoubtedly quarrel and rub against each other frequently, but they would never spend a day of tedium such as *she* and Brandon had endured today. And it was Prue herself, not yet eighteen, who had realized all this. She had grown up these past few weeks, right before Letty's eyes, and Letty, to her shame, had not noticed.

"What have you done with him, Letty?" Prue asked suddenly. "I haven't caught a glimpse of him. Why wasn't he with you while you were holding off that dragon of a woman at the door?"

"Oh, dear, I've forgotten to tell you. I'm afraid he's contracted a chill. He was quite feverish and went to bed immediately upon our arrival."

"Then I'll go to him at once," Prue said and started for the door.

But Letty suggested that this would not be the time for a meeting between them. He would be groggy, ill and bewildered. The morning would be soon enough, she reasoned, to confront him with the many surprises which he had in store. Prue, exhibiting the new maturity that had so amazed her sister, soon saw the wisdom of Letty's suggestion and agreed to curb her impatience.

Roger had been waiting outside to permit Letty and Prue to have their *tête-à-tête,* but now he entered and announced that all the arrangements had been made and that supper would immediately be served. Although the tiny inn contained no bedrooms other than the two that Brandon and Letty had taken, which meant that Roger would be forced to sleep on a narrow cot in Brandon's room and that Prue would share Letty's bed, Roger had managed to arrange a feast sumptuous enough to be worthy of a much grander establishment. The innkeeper's wife had evidently rekindled her fire without complaint, for she served them generously with steaming hot roast pork, a neck of mutton smothered in onions, a couple of small stuffed chickens, a currant pudding, a custard pudding and all the tea, hot punch and cool ale they could possibly want. These were served with such ingratiating smiles and affable manners that Letty could barely suppress her laughter at the woman's miraculous transformation.

When the meal was done, Prue tactfully excused herself and went to bed. Letty tried to follow, but Roger forcibly detained her. "I haven't driven all these miles to be cheated out of my chance to give you a proper scold, my girl," he said, taking her arm and leading her to the chair before the fire. "Why did you do such a shatterbrained thing?"

"It *was* shatterbrained, my lord. I'm most dreadfully sorry, and I can only express my gratitude to you for saving me from the consequences of my folly," she said carefully.

"Have we returned to 'my lord' again? If you really wish to express your gratitude, call me by my Christian name. You managed it quite beautifully, I thought, earlier this evening," he said with a mischievous gleam.

"As to that, my l— Roger," she said, coloring, "I wish you will not refine on it too much. I was most sorely pressed, as you saw. It was so horrible to contemplate being forcibly ejected from this place, with Brandon feverish and the rain pouring down, that the sight of . . . of a friendly face was an overwhelming relief. I . . . may have passed the bounds a bit in my gratitude . . ."

Roger sighed. "Are you going to pretend that the look on your face was *gratitude?*" Discouraged, he turned away, leaned on the mantel and stared into the fire. "Letty, when will you bring yourself to speak your mind to me, honestly and openly?"

"There are some things that cannot easily be spoken between us. Yet I've tried to be as honest with you as I could, sir."

"*Anything* can be spoken of between us, Letty," he said, turning to her with a compelling look. "And now must be the time. We've been moving at cross-purposes for too long. Both of us have been guilty of some dishonesty and evasion, and the problems between us have not been resolved. Perhaps it is time to try some frankness."

"Very well, you may be right. Where would you like to begin, sir?"

"Shall we begin with Brandon? Do you want to marry him?"

Letty lowered her eyes. "No," she said in a small voice. "I've behaved disgracefully in that respect. I made him lie to you about our betrothal. And this stupid elopement is all my doing. He never cared for me, except as a friend. In fact—" She looked up at him with a wry smile. "In fact, I shan't be surprised to learn that he has had a tendre for Prue all this time."

"I'm sure he does. I'm glad you've realized it. I didn't relish the idea of convincing you of the possibility."

"But, how did *you* realize it?" Letty asked in surprise.

"I watched and listened. I had to learn if you truly cared for him, you see. But when it comes to *you,* my wishes get in the way of my eyes. I was never certain. Tell me, my dear, *do* you care for him?"

Letty shook her head wordlessly.

"And I was right," Roger went on, "in assuming that the betrothal was concocted to keep *me* at arm's length?"

"Yes," Letty admitted shamefacedly.

"Don't look so miserable, my love," Roger said with an ironic smile. "The fact that you needed to trick me is more my fault than yours."

"Wh . . . What do you mean?" Letty asked falteringly. She knew that they now approached the subject that would be most painful for her to discuss. She didn't want to discuss it. She wanted, more than anything, to end this interview and go to bed. But she realized that there was no other way for her to make Roger understand that she could never marry him but to face the real reason for her refusal. So she clenched her hands in her lap and prepared herself for the ordeal to come.

"It is now *my* turn for honesty," he began. "I know the subject is a difficult one for a young lady as delicately reared and as sensitive as you, but you *must* let me explain my behavior." He turned back to the fire and spoke with some difficulty. "If, when I've finished, you still find the thought of marriage to me too . . . repellent, I shall not trouble you again."

For a moment he fell silent. She found that she was holding her breath. He didn't turn but spoke quietly into the fire, feeling that he could not face the look of revulsion he feared he might see in her eyes. "I didn't know you were aware that I had a mistress when I first asked you to marry me. I had no recollection of that night in Vauxhall, when you first learned of it. But you must believe that the liaison would not have continued once I had married. Kitty . . . Mrs. Brownell has always understood that my relationship with her would end when I married." He took a deep breath. "There is something even more important that I beg you will believe. I didn't bring her to Bath. Since my first evening here, I haven't given her a single thought. She arrived the day of the fireworks display and surprised me as much as she did you. And I didn't come to you again until I had severed all ties between us. The relationship never signified anything very important in my life, and its ending gave me great relief. It's not a thing I'm proud of, Letty, but I don't believe it means that I can never be a loyal, honest and faithful husband."

"Roger," Letty whispered shakily. "I . . . thank you for telling me, but . . ."

"There's something else," Roger said, turning and kneeling before her chair, "I must say *something* about my monstrous treatment of you at Vauxhall—"

Letty held up a restraining hand. "Roger, no—"

"I must. I know how the experience must have disturbed you. I've not been able to forgive myself since the moment I realized that it was you who—"

"Please don't go on. This isn't necessary, I promise you. It was a mistake. I don't blame you at all," she said earnestly.

He grasped her hands and looked at her closely. "But it *was* the barrier that kept you from accepting me, was it not? Tell me the truth, Letty."

She stared at him and then nodded slowly.

He winced. "Oh, my darling," he groaned, "what can I do? I cannot undo what I did that night. But listen to me, Letty, please! I promise you that I will never, never use you so again." He lowered his head until it rested on their clasped hands. "If we were wed," he said in a low voice, "I would treat you with the utmost gentleness. I need not be the kind of man whom you met that night in the gardens. I will be as tender and restrained as a bride could desire."

There was no answer. He looked up at her questioningly. She was staring at him with an enigmatic, wide-eyed expression he could not fathom, as if she were seeing him—or herself—for the first time. "No, Roger, no," she said in a voice that trembled in pain and surprise. "You don't understand. I'm not the girl you think me. I can't be the kind of wife you want. Please let me go. There's no use in talking anymore—I don't think I could ever explain it to you. I'm not sure I can explain it to myself. But I can't marry you."

She stood up and made for the door, but he jumped to his feet and caught her arm. "No!" he said, baffled. "You aren't making sense!" He whirled her around so that she fell against him, and he held her fast. "Look at me, Letty," he ordered, lifting her face and forcing her to meet his eyes. "Are you trying to tell me you don't love me? Is that it?"

She looked up with a level gaze. "I'm not trying to tell you anything," she said in a voice that strained to remain steady. "We've already said too much. Perhaps, sometimes, a man and a woman are not suited, no matter what they feel for one another. Let me go, Roger. It's for the best."

He stared at her uncomprehendingly, but the firmness in her eyes seemed unanswerable. There was a frightening finality in her expression. His arms dropped from her, and she stepped back. She took one last look at his face, which was clouded with bewilderment and a kind of numb despair, and she ran from the room.

But even when she had closed the door behind her, climbed the stairs to her room, undressed in the darkness and lain, wide-eyed, in her bed through the weary hours of the night, she could not erase from her mind the look of his face, staring at her with the haunting persistence of a reproachful ghost.

Chapter Twenty

*B*randon opened his eyes to bright sunlight streaming into the little window set in a dormer on the other side of his room. His head felt clearer than it had last night, and the sunlight seemed to offer some hope that today might turn out to be less wretched than yesterday. He yawned, stretched, and wondered how long he'd slept. He felt as if he'd slept a week. He raised himself on his elbow to see if he could ascertain the position of the sun to give himself some inkling of the time of day. In front of the window he saw a blur of something that looked like red-gold hair. Puzzled, he put out his hand, felt gingerly on the top of the table for his spectacles and carefully put them on. His vision cleared, and he looked again at the red-gold blur. "Prue!" he gasped.

She was sitting on the window seat, watching him with a half-smile. "Good morning, Brandon," she said with unusual sweetness.

"What on earth—?" He sat up in bed, pulling the blankets up to his neck. "What are you doing here?"

"Do you mean here, in your room, or here in an inn on the road to Gretna Green?"

"I don't know what I mean," he answered, bemused. "Does Letty know you're here?"

"Yes, indeed. We arrived last night and had dinner together."

"We?"

"Roger and I."

"Oh, is Roger with you?" Brandon asked with a feeling of relief. "Good. Then I'll be able to borrow some blunt." He put his hand to his forehead as his last conversation with Letty came back to him. "I was idiotic enough to go off on an elopement without a farthing in my pocket."

"I'm not at all surprised," Prue remarked cheerfully. "You need someone to remind you of such mundane matters. After all, you have more important things on your mind."

Brandon frowned and regarded her through narrowed eyes. "Even if that remark is meant as a slur on my studies, I shall ignore it. I have no wish to bandy words with you. Why have you come, anyway? Does Roger think he can stop our plans?"

"I believe he already has."

Brandon peered at her. "What? Is Letty going to marry him after all?"

"I don't know. But I believe she'd decided not to marry *you*," Prue explained matter-of-factly, though her eyes were fixed on his face attentively.

"Oh? She has? Why?"

"I think she feels that you don't quite suit."

"I see," Brandon said thoughtfully.

Prue came up to his bedside. "You don't seem very brokenhearted, Brandon," she remarked casually.

"I'm not. To be honest, it was to be a *mariage de convenance,* as the French say."

"And how would the Greeks say it?" Prue teased.

He glared at her for a moment and then returned to his train of thought. "I didn't think it a very good idea, even from the beginning. But since Letty and I had both decided we wanted no more of love, we thought we might brush through. But I think Letty is wise to change her mind. The affair augered ill, and it would not do to 'purchase regret at such a price,' to use the words of Demosthenes."

"Why do you want no more of love, Brandon?" Prue asked brazenly. "And don't answer in the words of Demosthenes, if you please. I'd like to hear your own words."

"I fell in love once," he said, with a sidelong glance at her face, "but I found the experience too painful."

"Did you? Why?"

"Because the young lady was frivolous, unpredictable and an incorrigible flirt," Brandon said sternly.

"Was she?" Prue said softly, sitting down on the edge of the bed.

"Yes, she was," Brandon declared, throwing caution to the winds. "She called me a stuffy prig, pushed me out of a carriage in the most callous way, and the last time I saw her, she was in the arms of a man-about-town old enough to be her father."

"Really?" Prue said, lowering her lashes in quite fetching remorse. "That was quite dreadful of her, and I'm sure she must be very sorry."

"Do you think so?" Brandon asked, his heart beginning to leap about in his chest in a most disturbing way.

The lowered lashes fluttered. "Oh, yes, I'm sure of it."

"But I thought . . . It seemed to me . . . that she had set her heart on becoming Mrs. Eberly."

"Gudgeon! How could she, when her heart has been set on a much more . . . scholarly type of gentleman?"

"Prue!" He grasped her hands. "You can't mean it!"

"Brandon," Prue said, her lips curled in a mischievous smile and her eyelids fluttering up at him distractingly, "have you ever . . . kissed anyone?"

He leaned toward her, pulse racing and mind bedazzled in a most unscholarly way. "I'm . . . afraid not," he admitted, somewhat breathlessly. "I've always been too preoccupied . . . with the Greeks . . . to kiss anyone."

"Neither have I," Prue said, her arms stealing around his neck, "but I don't think it can be very difficult . . ."

Letty had had a most troublesome night. She had reviewed her conversation with Roger over and over. The pain in his eyes had haunted her, but she could think of nothing she could have done to avoid the necessity of causing him pain, short of agreeing to marry him. That she couldn't do. Nothing had changed. It was still clear that he wanted a wife who was—how had he put it?—"delicately reared and sensitive." After all the talk, all their time together, all the occasions when they had seemed to be attuned to each other, he still expected her to be the girl her Aunt Millicent had described to his mother so many months ago— well-bred, gracious, serene, dutiful and obedient. To play that role, to live with Roger in the polite, indifferent manner of so many other "arranged" marriages, would be more than she could bear. But as the night had worn on, and she had tried to imagine what that life would be like, and to compare it to the life that now faced her—a life in which she would dwindle into an old maid, to play the fond aunt to her sisters' children, to be the "extra guest" at dinner parties, to take in cats to have something to love, and to spend her old age dreaming of what might have been—she couldn't help but wonder if the proper and discreet life offered by Roger might not be more bearable than *that*.

She couldn't answer. She was completely ignorant of married life, her father having died before she was old enough to have made sensible observations about her parents' life together, and Aunt Millicent, too, having been widowed early. Perhaps she should discuss the matter with Roger, openly and honestly, as he had suggested. They had been able to talk about Mrs. Brownell quite satisfactorily. Perhaps she could bring herself to explain to him that she was not the delicate, obedient, polite girl that he had supposed her to be. Even if he then decided that she was not a proper wife for him, she would at least have the satisfaction of seeing that haunting look of pain leave his eyes.

By the time the first faint light of dawn had crept into her window, she had decided that she would talk to him first thing in the morning. With a feeling of contentment such as she had not had in weeks, she'd closed her eyes and fallen into a peaceful sleep.

When she awakened, she knew at once that the morning was far advanced. The sun was high in the sky and the voices from the taproom below had the loud, bustling sound that comes when the whole world is wide awake. Guiltily, she washed and dressed and hurriedly went to find the others. Brandon's door was ajar, and she tapped and entered.

Brandon was still in his bed, Prue unnecessarily feeding him soup. When they looked up and saw Letty in the doorway, Brandon looked sheepish. "She insists on treating me like an invalid," he explained quickly. "I've told her repeatedly that my fever has quite gone."

"But a day of rest is very beneficial after a fever, is it not, Letty?" Prue asked. "Roger thinks that we may stay another day, if we wish."

"A day of rest is very beneficial," Letty concurred, and added with a grin, "It's so pleasant to see the two of you getting on so well."

"Wish us happy, Letty," Brandon announced, smiling shyly.

Letty looked from one to the other delightedly, and Prue ran to her and enveloped her in an excited embrace. "Oh, Prue," Letty sighed, "I *am* happy for you both."

Finally, Letty found an opportunity to refer to the subject that had brought her. "Where is Roger?" she asked.

"Oh, he's gone," Prue said, returning to her duties with the soup.

Letty's heart lurched. "G-Gone?" she managed.

"He thought *someone* should return to Bath as soon as possible, to inform the families that all is well. He said that he is impatient to return to London, at any rate, and saw no point in cooling his heels here."

All Letty's old misery descended on her again with a sickening thump. "When did he leave?" she asked in a voice she scarcely recognized.

Prue and Brandon, absorbed in their new happiness, did not notice her perturbation. "Not long ago," Prue answered absently. "Why?"

But Letty didn't answer. She turned and went quickly down the stairs. The innkeeper was clearing the remains of a single breakfast from the table in the private parlor. "Has Lord Denham gone?" she asked urgently.

The innkeeper turned and answered deferentially, "Yes, Miss, I b'lieve so. Just 'ad 'is 'orses put to, not two minutes since."

Letty, still hoping desperately that he had not yet gone, ran out the door. There in the courtyard, Roger was helping the boy who served as ostler, porter and errand boy to adjust the reins. She stopped in her tracks and took a quick breath of relief. Roger, not seeing her, was about to swing himself up to the box when she called his name. He turned and saw her running across the courtyard toward him with an expression of joy not unlike the look she had had on her face when she had discovered his presence the day before. Completely bemused, he stood and stared until she came up to him. "Oh," she sighed breathlessly, grasping his arm, "I'm so *glad* you haven't gone!"

He looked at her with a wry smile. "Your greetings could well become the delight of my life," he said drily, "if I hadn't been told that they have no significance and that I mustn't refine too much upon them. Is there something I can do for you before I leave?"

She cast him a sidelong glance. His eyes looked weary and his mouth strained. His hair had been carelessly combed, and a lock fell tantalizingly over his forehead. She itched to brush it away with her hand. But she merely cast her eyes to the ground. "Have you a few minutes to spare? I would like to talk to you."

She could see him stiffen. "I'm really rather pressed," he said coldly. "I'm eager to return to Bath and then to start for London before nightfall."

"I see."

He hesitated. "I thought you had said everything you could last night."

"Not everything."

"Very well, then, what is it?" he asked impatiently. Even to his own ears he sounded childishly sullen.

"May we walk a little way?" she asked shyly, with a glance at the ostler who suddenly began to polish a brass fitting energetically. "I noticed from my window that there's a pretty little garden at the back . . ."

"Of course," he said contritely and fell into step beside her.

For a while they walked in silence while Letty shored up her failing courage. "It's difficult for me to explain, Roger, but I want you to understand why I couldn't . . . why I can't . . ."

"It's not at all necessary, Letty," he said in a strange, detached way that pierced her heart. "You have finally convinced me that your refusal is final. There is not the slightest need for you to make me any explanations. Although I appreciate your kindness in wishing to do so."

He made a little bow and turned to go. Letty watched him, quite nonplussed. She could not let him go like this. "But, Roger," she said quickly, "I don't want to explain because of kindness. It's only because . . . I love you so very much . . ."

He stood stock still for a long, breathless moment. Then, running his fingers through his hair in a gesture of helplessness, he said in a tightly controlled voice, "Letty, all this is very confusing to me—"

"Yes, I know." She put out her hand. "Please come with me. There's a little wooden bench back there, just wide enough for the two of us . . ."

He took her hand and let her lead him to the bench. They sat down, and he faced her tensely. He couldn't wait to hear what she would say, even though he was convinced it would end with the same pain. Why, he asked himself, am I subjecting myself to further torture? But wild horses could not have dragged him away.

Still clinging to his hand, her eyes lowered, she began. "You've told me many times, my dear, that you think me delicately bred, refined and . . . obedient. That's what everyone thinks. Lady Glendenning's dutiful daughter." She turned her lustrous eyes to him in earnest appeal. "Roger, can't you see that I'm not that girl? Would Lady Glendenning's dutiful daughter refuse to marry the man her family so much desires for her? Would *she* lie, and evade, and make up false betrothals, and elope with the man her sister loves? And . . . and . . . would *she* feel as I do about . . . about what happened at Vauxhall?"

Roger was staring at her in puzzled fascination. "What *is* it you feel about Vauxhall?" he asked, his breath suspended in his throat.

Her eyes flickered down again. "Oh, Roger," she said in a very small voice, "how can I say this? Ever since that day at Vauxhall, I've known . . . I've known . . . that I am *not* the girl you all think me." With a shudder that passed over her whole body, she dropped her hold on him and covered her face with her hands. "I knew then," she said in a mortified voice, "that I didn't want to be your wife. That I couldn't be the dignified, polite, calm, bloodless sort of person that you and my aunt and your mother expect. You see, I would much rather be . . . much rather be . . ."

"Yes?"

"I would much rather be your *mistress!*"

There was no sound, no response. When she could stand the silence no longer, she peeped at him through her fingers. He was staring at her, stunned, trying to understand what she'd said. Then a light seemed to spring on in his eyes, and he threw back his head and gave a shout of laughter. As if a dam had given way inside him, he laughed and laughed until he doubled over in helpless merriment. When at last he could catch his breath, he turned to Letty, who was watching him in some dismay, and gathered her in his arms. "Oh, my sweet little *idiot!*" he said, still gasping with laughter. "My poor, foolish, absurd, adorable idiot!" And he tilted her head back and kissed her with such intensity that it reminded her thrillingly of that terrible kiss in the gardens so long ago. When he let her go, she looked up at him with wide, awed eyes. "Does this mean that I *am* to be your mistress?" she asked shyly.

"Of course you are," he said with a wide grin. "To all the world you will be my well-bred, refined, serene, dignified and dutiful wife. And when we are alone, you'll be the most beautiful, the most exciting, the most delightful mistress a man ever had."

From a window above them, Prue watched the activities on the bench shamelessly. "Oh, look, Brandon," she chortled happily, "they're kissing!"

Brandon knelt on the window seat beside her and peered out to the garden. "Good!" he said contentedly. "I always thought she should have him. 'Sweet is a grief well ended.'"

Prue frowned at him in mock-irritation. "Sophocles?" she asked disdainfully.

"Aeschylus," he retorted promptly.

"Well, I prefer the saying that goes, 'The learned man quotes well the words of others; the wise man quotes his own.'"

Brandon looked at her with a puzzled frown. "Who said *that*? I don't think I recognize the style."

"You'll learn to recognize it soon enough. It's only one of the many Witty Thoughts of Prudence Glendenning." And she stuck out her tongue at him saucily and ran laughing from the room.

The Counterfeit Husband

Prologue

⸌⸍

October, 1803

Thomas Collinson stood leaning on the rail of the merchant ship *Triton*, watching the waves slap away at the worn piles of the Southampton dock where the ship was moored. The wharf was dingy and rotting, but it was what the crew of a merchantman had come to expect in these days of war. Nelson's naval vessels had first choice of moorage space, and the vessels of the East India Company had their own prime anchorages. So ships like the *Triton* took what was left.

It was already dark; the sails had been furled and the rigging secured an hour earlier. The captain and most of the crew had already gone ashore, but a few stragglers were still making their way down the gangplank toward the waterfront taverns or, if they were lucky, a woman's bed. Most of these tag-tails were the ones who hadn't signed on for the next voyage and had spent the past hour packing their gear. Tom gave an occasional wave of the arm to a departing sailor. He, the ship's mate, had been given the watch, but he felt no resentment as his glance followed his shipmates, their seabags slung over their shoulders as they walked across the wharf and disappeared into the dark shadows beyond the dock where the light from the ship's forward lantern couldn't reach. He didn't mind having the watch. He was in no hurry to get ashore; there was no place on land for which he had any particular fancy.

A man came stealthily up behind him—a sailor, moving quietly toward the railing on tiptoe. He was not as tall as Tom but so powerfully built that the heavy seabag resting on his shoulder seemed a lightweight triviality. His approach was soundless, but some instinct made Tom whirl about. He gave a snorting laugh. "You didn't think you could sneak up behind me with success, did you, you whopstraw, with me waiting to see you off?"

The stocky sailor lowered his seabag to the deck and shrugged. "Tho't I'd give it one last try." He grinned at Tom with unabashed admiration. "I guess no pressman'll take *you* unawares."

Tom's answering grin soon died as the two men stared at each other in silent realization that it might be for the last time. "So you've packed, eh, Daniel? Ready at last?" He forced a smile. "It's good-bye, then."

Daniel pulled off his cap and ran his fingers through his shock of curly red hair. "It's the only thing I regret about leavin', y' know . . . sayin' good-bye to ye, Tommy lad." His soft brown eyes, usually gleaming with good cheer, now looked watery, as if the fellow was holding back tears. He thrust out his hand for a last farewell.

Tom ignored the hand and threw his arms about his friend in a warm embrace. "No need for the dismals, Daniel," he said softly, patting his friend's back with affection. "Where did you say Betsy is? Twyford, isn't it? That's less than a dozen miles north of here. We'll see each other from time to time."

"No, we won't," Daniel muttered, breaking out of the embrace and turning away his face. "Betsy an' me'll be movin' to God-knows-where, an' ye'll get yerself a berth with the John Company, an' we'll lose track—"

"Stow the gab," Tom ordered with an attempt at a laugh. "We can keep in touch if we try. There are letters . . ."

"I ain't much good at writin'."

"Then Betsy can do it for you. I've seen her letters . . . your wife writes a fine hand."

Daniel sighed and put on his cap. "Aye, I suppose so." He lifted his seabag to his shoulder and gave his friend a pathetic mockery of a grin. "Be seein' ye, then, eh? We'll let ye know where we'll be settlin'."

Tom nodded, finding himself suddenly too choked to speak. They walked together slowly toward the gangplank. "Are you sure you won't sign on again? Just one more voyage?" he asked at last.

"What's the use of it? Betsy's heart'd break fer sure. It's different fer you, Tommy. You haven't a wife t' cling to yer knees, sobbin' her eyes out every time ye make fer the door. Besides, one more voyage an' ye'll have yer master's papers. Why, next time I hear of ye, ye'll be mate on a John Company ship."

"Not very likely. East India Company berths are saved for rich men's sons, not for the vicar's daughter's bastard."

"You can try, can't ye? Ol' Aaron swears he heared that a mate on a company ship can pile up a couple o' thousand quid on a single voyage!"

Tom shook his head dubiously. "Two *thousand?* What gammon! Don't put your trust in those dreamers' yarns. Besides, if I get to captain a ship like this tub we're on, it'll be good enough for me."

"Aye, if that's the sort of life ye want."

"It is." Tom threw his friend a worried look. "But what about you? What will you do now, do you think?"

"I dunno. I'll find somethin'. I'll *have* to, y' know—what with Betsy makin' me a father by spring."

"Aye, you lucky bag-pudding," Tom chuckled. "A *father!* Before you know it, there'll be a strapping, redheaded whelp sitting astride your shoulder instead of that seabag. It's a sight I'd give a yellow boy to see."

Daniel's face clouded over. "Per'aps ye will," he muttered without much conviction. "Per'aps you will."

Tom felt a wave of depression spread over him. Daniel was probably right. They were about to set off on widely diverging paths, and the likelihood of ever meeting again was slim. And even if they did, the close camaraderie of the past months would have long since evaporated into the unreality of nostalgic memory.

Daniel stuck out his hand again, and Tom gripped it tightly. They held on for a long while, and then, by some manner of wordless communication, let go at the same moment. The redheaded man turned abruptly away and marched purposefully down the gangplank. Tom watched him from his place on the railing, feeling bereft. *A sailor's life is always leavetaking,* he told himself glumly as he watched his friend trudge stolidly across the wharf. Just before Daniel was completely swallowed up by the shadows, Tom saw him pause, turn and give one last wave of farewell.

Tom waved back, his throat tingling with unexpected emotion. He grunted in self-disgust, annoyed at this indulgence in sentiment. If there was one requirement for a ship's master, it was hardness—hardness of body and of feeling. If he was ever to become a master, he'd better learn to behave like one. He'd be—

"Tom! *Tom! Press-gang!*" came a shout from the shadows.

Tom felt the blood drain from his face. "Good God! *Daniel!*"

He could hear, above the noisy slap of the water against the side of the ship, the sounds of a violent scuffle in the dark of the dock. His heart began to hammer in his chest, for he knew that the worst had happened. An attack by a press-gang was a merchant seaman's direst fear. He glanced about him desperately for some sort of weapon. Snatching up a belaying pin, he vaulted over the railing onto the gangplank and dashed down.

The sounds from the shadows became louder and more alarming as he tore across the wharf and neared the shadowy part of the dock beyond. "No, no, don't use the cutlass," he heard a voice bark. "He's a good, stalwart specimen. I don't want him spoiled."

Tom raced round a mound of crates and gasped at the sight that met his eyes.

Daniel was struggling like a wild stallion against the tugs and blows of half-a-dozen ruffians armed with cutlasses and cudgels. Standing apart, his arms folded over his chest, was a King's officer watching the proceedings with dispassionate interest. Tom would have liked to land him a proper facer, but the six bruisers had to be tackled first. He threw himself headlong into the melee. "All right, Daniel," he shouted, "let's give it to 'em!"

There was no answer from the beleaguered Daniel, but he struggled against his attackers with renewed energy. Tom swung the belaying pin about in violent desperation, striking one pressman on the shoulder hard enough to make him squeal and drop his hold on Daniel's arm. Turning quickly about, he swung the pin at the head of another attacker and heard a very satisfactory crack of the skull as the fellow slumped to the ground.

The shouting was deafening as shadowy figures swirled about him. He swung his makeshift weapon wildly, hoping desperately that he wouldn't accidentally strike his friend. "Daniel, are you . . . there?"

"Aye, lad," came a breathless, discouraged answer from somewhere behind him.

"Don't despair," Tom urged, swinging the belaying pin vigorously about him, keeping two of the ruffians at bay. Just then, from behind, came a sharp blow. The flat side of a cutlass had struck powerfully and painfully against his ear. He swayed dizzily. The pin was wrenched from his weakened grasp, and three men jumped on him at once. He felt himself toppling over backwards, but he kept swinging his fists as he fell. With a string of curses, his assailants slammed his head down upon the cobbles. It struck with an agonizing thud. Streaks of red and yellow lightning seemed to obscure his vision and sear his brain with pain.

By the time he could see again, the fight was over. He lifted his head and looked about him. Two of the pressmen were leading Daniel off, his shoulders pathetically stooped and his hands bound behind his back. Three others of the gang, looking very much the worse for wear, were trussing up his own wrists with leather straps. And the sixth lay stretched out on the cobbles, blood trickling from his nose. Above it all, the King's officer stood apart, his hands unsullied by the struggle he'd just witnessed. Catching Tom's eye, the officer smiled in grim satisfaction. Tom well understood the expression. The man on the ground might be dead, and another of his gang might not have the use of his right arm for a long spell, but the two men the officer had caught were trained seamen. He and Daniel were the sort of catch the press-gangs most desired. This had been, for the officer, a very good night's work.

After having been alternately shoved and dragged along the waterfront for what seemed like miles, his head aching painfully and his spirits in despair, Tom was pushed into a longboat manned by eight uniformed sailors. Daniel was no-where in sight. The King's officer dismissed the ruffians of the press-gang and climbed into the boat, giving Tom a smug smile as he seated himself on a thwart facing his prisoner. Tom's fingers ached to choke that smile from his face.

The sailors began to row toward an imposing frigate (painted with the yellow and black stripes that Admiral Nelson required of naval vessels), which rode at anchor some distance from the dock. It was His Majesty's Ship *Undaunted,* and despite the darkness Tom could see that it carried at least fifty guns and floated in the water at over six hundred tons. As the longboat drew up alongside the ves-sel, a sailor prodded Tom with an oar, urging him to climb up the ladder to the upper deck.

Despite the desperation of his condition, Tom couldn't refrain from peering with considerable interest through the darkness at the activity on deck. While the King's officer, who had followed him up the ladder, held a whispered collo-quy with the vessel's first lieutenant, Tom looked around, marvelling at the pris-tine neatness of the ship. But before he had an opportunity to scrutinize what was a vastly different vessel from the one he'd just abandoned, the lieutenant, a stocky, balding man in his midtwenties, with a florid complexion that bespoke a hot temper, gave an order to the two sailors who were guarding him, and he was roughly dragged across the deck to the companionway.

At the end of the passage, he was unceremoniously ushered into what he in-stantly recognized was the captain's cabin. It was a low-ceilinged, unpretentious compartment with panelled walls and a row of wide windows (which usually graced the stern of a sailing ship) covering the far wall. The captain himself was nowhere in evidence, for the chair behind the huge desk (a piece of furniture which gleamed with polish and importance in its impressive position at the dead center of the room) was empty. The only sign of the cabin's inhabitant was a coat trimmed with gold braid, which had been thrown over a cabinet in the corner.

After his eyes became accustomed to the light—provided by a lamp swing-ing at eye level from the rafters on a long brass chain—he could see that the desk was covered with navigational charts and a heavily bound ship's log. But his eyes were immediately drawn to the group of men who had been standing at the desk when he'd entered. Two of them were uniformed sailors, set to guard the pris-oner standing between them. It was Daniel, his face chalky-white in the lamp-light, his hands still secured behind him and blood dripping from a cut on his upper lip. Tom felt his stomach lurch with nausea as their eyes met. Daniel's face was rigid with terror. *And no wonder,* Tom thought miserably. Daniel's life was no longer worth a brass farthing.

The worst circumstance that life could impose on Daniel had occurred: im-pressment. All through their sailing days, merchant seamen were edified with blood-chilling tales of the sort of life they could expect if they were so unfortunate as to be impressed into naval service. Service in His Majesty's Navy was hell for impressed seamen. They were forced to fill the most unwanted posts, to work at the dirtiest jobs and made to expose themselves to the greatest dangers. The food the King allotted for ordinary seamen was rotten beyond belief, and the pay a pittance. And the chance of coming out of the experience alive—after who-knew-how-many forced voyages—was slim indeed. The Navy, unable to recruit enough seamen to staff its ships because of this notorious mistreatment, had for centuries used the nightmarish device of impressment to fill its berths. And this time, Tom and his best friend had been caught in the net. For *him* there was a ray of hope—the shipmaster's apprentice papers in the pocket of his coat; but for Daniel there was no hope at all.

He started across the cabin to stand beside his friend, but he was jerked back to his place by the sailors who were guarding him. The lieutenant and the King's officer conferred again briefly, and then the lieutenant went to a door near the far corner of the wall at Tom's right and tapped gently. At the sound of a voice from within, the lieutenant opened the door and disappeared inside. He emerged a few moments later, followed by a tall, lean man of late middle age with a head of iron gray hair, a short beard and a pair of narrow, glinting eyes. The man was in his shirtsleeves, but Tom knew it was the captain even before he reached for the gold-trimmed coat and shrugged himself into it.

The lieutenant, meanwhile, came into the circle of light which surrounded the desk and, bending over, began to shuffle the papers about until he found what appeared to Tom to be a ship's roster.

"Sit down, Mr. Benson, sit down," the captain muttered from the shadows, where he stood leaning his elbow on the cabinet and looking from Tom to Daniel and back again.

"Aye, aye, Captain." Mr. Benson, the lieutenant, took the chair behind the desk, picked up a pen from the inkstand and wrote something on the paper. Then he looked up at the two prisoners coldly. "Which one of you is the murderer?" he asked.

"It's the taller one, of course," came the captain's voice from the shadows. "Isn't that so, Moresby?"

The King's officer chuckled. "You're right again, Captain Brock."

At the sound of the captain's name, Daniel's eyes flew to Tom's with a look of desperation. Sir Everard Brock was notorious. His reputation for cruelty was legendary among seamen.

"Start with the other one," the captain ordered.

Mr. Benson nodded. "What's your name, fellow?" he demanded of Daniel.

"Dan'l Hicks, sir."

"You were an ordinary seaman on the *Triton?*"

"Aye, sir, but . . . I . . ."

"Yes?"

"I've finished my time."

"Finished? Didn't sign up again, eh? Had enough of the old scow?" Mr. Benson asked with a sardonic grimace.

"Well, I . . . I suppose ye could say that."

"Good. If they're not expecting you back on board the *Triton,* no one will be looking for you." He dipped the pen carefully in the inkwell.

"But ye see, sir, there *will* be someone—"

"What?" the lieutenant asked, writing.

"Someone lookin' fer me. I have a wife, y' see, an' she—"

"Forget your wife, fellow. Can't worry about wives. Haven't you heard that the Prime Minister, Mr. Addington, declared war on Napoleon this past May? This is wartime," Mr. Benson said pompously, adding Daniel's name to the roster. "Cut his bonds," he ordered the guards.

"Y' don't understand, sir," Daniel pleaded as a sailor stepped behind him and sliced the cords at his wrists with a small, curved-bladed knife. "I—"

The lieutenant paid no attention but merely held out the pen. "Here. Put your X right here."

Daniel's hands were trembling. "But . . . y' see . . . I *can't* sign on. My wife's in the family way, if y' know what I mean. She'll starve t' death if I—"

Mr. Benson's eyes narrowed angrily. "Are you daring to contradict me, Hicks? If I don't have your X on this sheet at once, it'll be ten stripes for you!"

"Twenty," came the captain's voice ominously out of the shadows.

"Twenty!" Mr. Benson echoed.

Daniel cast Tom a look of stricken anguish. Tom, his mind racing about to think of a way out of this rattrap, could do nothing at the moment but signal with a blink of the eyes that Daniel should acquiesce. Poor Daniel groaned despairingly, stepped forward and took the pen from the lieutenant's hand. He knew well enough how to sign his name, but he wrote an X as a gesture to himself that he still had a spark of rebellious spirit within him.

Mr. Benson threw a look of satisfaction over his shoulder at the captain and turned to Tom. "Now *you,* murderer," he said with a kind of malicious enjoyment, "what's *your* name?"

"Collinson, sir. Thomas Collinson." Tom used the opportunity to move closer to the desk and Daniel's side.

"You don't appear to be overly disturbed about having killed a man," the lieutenant remarked, looking him over interestedly.

"If you're speaking of the pressman I laid low, he damn well deserved it."

Mr. Benson's self-satisfied expression changed to one of discomfort. He was not accustomed to backtalk. This fellow was a cool one, and that type could make him look foolish before the captain. "Watch your tongue, fellow," he growled threateningly, "if you know what's good for you."

Tom shrugged. "May as well be hanged for a sheep as a lamb," he said, brazenly directing his words to the captain.

Captain Brock said nothing, but he moved in closer to the light and peered at Tom intently. The lieutenant, meanwhile, jumped angrily to his feet. "Oh, you won't hang, fellow," he sneered, "but you'll wish by tomorrow that you had. Hanging's too good for the likes of you."

"Don't think to frighten me with this fustian," Tom retorted. "A civil trial might be more damaging to the Navy than to me, and *that's* why I won't hang."

The lieutenant, red-faced with fury, reached out and grasped Tom by the collar of his coat, but before he was able to do anything further, the captain's voice stopped him. "Hold on there, Mr. Benson. Let the fellow be for a moment." He walked into the circle of light and studied Tom's face before turning to the King's officer. "Speaks the King's English, Moresby, did you notice? You haven't made a mistake again, have you?"

The officer stepped forward, his brow wrinkled with sudden alarm. If a member of the nobility had been mistakenly caught in his net, he could find himself in a great deal of difficulty. He circled Tom slowly, looking carefully at his clothing, his hands and the careless way his hair had been cut. "I don't think so, Captain Brock," he said thoughtfully. "Looks all right to me. He came off the *Triton,* after all, and that's not the sort of berth a gentleman would seek."

"Where did you learn a gentleman's English, fellow?" the captain asked Tom.

"At Cambridge. Where else?" Tom responded flippantly.

The captain drew in his breath and nodded at the lieutenant.

Mr. Benson, who still clutched Tom's collar with one hand, smashed him in the mouth with the other. "The captain asked you a question, sailor. Answer him properly, or you'll feel the taste of wet leather!"

Tom pulled himself free of the lieutenant's grasp and licked the blood from his split lip before he answered. "I read a bit, that's all," he muttered.

"That's *not* all," the captain said in a voice so icy that Tom understood how he could command this ship with its crew of hundreds. "One doesn't learn to speak well only by reading. Well?"

Tom gave the captain a sardonic shrug. "I had a mother who set great store by appearances. She trained me. She thought that if her boy *appeared* to be a gentleman, he might be taken for one."

"How very interesting," the captain murmured, his voice, even while tinged with amusement, still chillingly cold. "And *were* you taken for one?"

Tom smiled wryly. "Not until now."

The captain let out a grudging laugh. "You've a sharp wit, Collinson, but you'll find that wit is no advantage here. Carry on, Mr. Benson." And he walked back out of the light.

The lieutenant sat down and leered up at Tom with satisfaction. "As I was saying, sailor, you're not going to hang. That would be too easy a punishment for you. You're going to serve on this ship. You're going to labor through two watches every day. *Two!* And once a week, the bo'sun will deliver upon your back at least . . . er . . ."

"Thirty-five," came the voice from the shadows.

"Thirty-five stripes. Do you understand, Collinson? *Thirty-five.* Every week. Why, when we put into port, you'll be so bone-weary and sore you'll be glad that you have to stay behind in the brig instead of going ashore with the rest of the scum you'll be calling your shipmates. What have you to say to *that* with your clever tongue, eh, Collinson?"

Tom moved close to the desk, carefully stepping on Daniel's foot and pressing down on it with just enough weight to indicate that the pressure was not accidental. He hoped Daniel would recognize it as a signal to stay alert. Meanwhile, he faced Mr. Benson with a leer of his own. "What I have to say, sir, is that you can't do it. I'm sorry to disappoint you . . . and you too, Captain Brock. You may be able to bring me to the magistrates on the charge of murder, but you can't make me sign on. I have papers."

"Papers?" The lieutenant looked nonplussed. "What papers?"

"If you'll permit your men to untie my hands, I'll show you."

Mr. Benson looked over his shoulder for guidance. The captain nodded, and the lieutenant motioned to the guard with the knife to slice the straps. Then Tom reached into his coat and pulled out an oilskin packet. He was about to untie the strings when the lieutenant reached out his hand. "Here, give it to me."

Mr. Benson nervously undid the strings as if he feared a snake might emerge and sting his finger. He pulled out the contract which Tom had signed with the captain of the *Triton,* and his eyes slid over the closely written words. Then, biting his lip, he looked hesitantly over his shoulder. With a sigh of annoyance, the captain came up behind him and picked up the document.

After a quick scan of the papers, the captain looked up at Tom, his lips twisted in a small smile. "So," he said with quiet menace, "you're a mate, are you? Well, well! You *have* brought me a good haul this time, Moresby. It's not often we get recruits who know the difference between main and mizzen."

"But you can't recruit me," Tom argued. "Those papers prove I'm exempted by law—"

"Papers?" the captain asked. "What papers?" He ripped the document in half and then in half again. "Did you see any papers, Mr. Benson?"

The lieutenant smirked. "No, Captain."

"Did anyone here see any papers?" Captain Brock asked, looking around at all the faces pleasantly, all the while tearing the precious sheets into shreds.

"No, Captain," the sailor-guards said in unison.

Captain Brock turned and walked back into the shadows, reappearing again with a washbowl in his hand. He placed the bowl on the deck before Mr. Benson and threw the shreds of paper into it. "Burn it," he said curtly, turned on his heel and strode off to his inner cabin, slamming the wooden door behind him.

Every man around the desk watched soundlessly as Tom's papers burned. They all knew that a man's future was going up in smoke. But Tom felt no emotion but a sharp, alert tension. *There'll never be a better time,* he thought, and he pressed down hard on Daniel's foot while, at the same moment, he snatched up the flaming washbowl and smashed it down on the lieutenant's head. "Use the log book!" he shouted to Daniel, and he ducked down and lunged at the legs of the guard closest to him.

Daniel, with a cry of elation, snatched up the heavy volume and swung it at the head of the guard at his right, while the other one was busily occupied putting out the fire on the desk. Tom, meanwhile, from his place at the top of his first guard, grabbed the legs of the second and pulled him down. Before they'd recovered from their surprise, he scrambled to his feet in time to see the King's officer advancing on him with a drawn cutlass. Again he ducked and dived for the fellow's midsection. They toppled over in a heap, the officer waving his deadly implement wildly in the air. Tom grabbed at his wrist, for the officer was trying urgently to hack him to pieces. Suddenly Daniel loomed above them and, using the log book as a broadsword, knocked the cutlass out of the officer's hand and sent it spinning across the floor. The fellow cried out in pain. Tom seized the moment and administered a smashing right to his jaw, while Daniel used the log book to good effect on the heads of the two tackled sailors, who were just getting to their feet again.

Tom leaped up, fists ready, but only Daniel was still erect, his breast heaving and his eyes shining with the glow of victory. Tom chortled in delighted surprise at the sight of six men sprawled about in various degrees of semiconsciousness. "We *did* it!" Daniel crowed, hugging Tom and slapping him on the back.

"Don't congratulate yourselves too soon," came the captain's icy voice from the shadows, and they wheeled about to see him step into the light, pointing at them with the black, ugly barrel of a very long pistol.

"Go ahead and shoot, Captain Brock," Tom said, moving in front of Daniel and motioning behind his back for Daniel to edge toward the cabin's outer door. "I'd rather be dead than serve under you."

"But you'll live," the captain muttered with chilling calm. "You'll live . . . and you'll serve!"

Tom wished he could look up at the lantern to gauge its distance accurately, but he knew that if he moved his eyes from the captain's face he'd give his scheme away. "*Duck,* Daniel!" he shouted and swung his arm at the lantern.

A shot rang out, and he felt the ball whiz by the side of his face as the lantern swung across the desk, a glowing missile aimed right for the captain's head.

They didn't stay to watch it reach its mark but bolted for the door. The companionway was already filling with sailors who'd heard the noises, but they were either too startled by the sudden appearance of the fleeing men or too sympathetic to their plight to grab hold of them. "Head starboard," Tom gasped as they broke onto the deck. They ran across the deck, meeting with no obstruction in the darkness, and came to the railing near the stern. With the sounds of shouts and running footsteps hot behind them, they climbed up on the railing and, with one quick look at one another, leaped overboard into the black water.

Chapter One

Camilla stared out of the library window at the sunny lawns and chaste gardens of Wyckfield Park (a vista which had been acclaimed for generations as the most beautiful in the county) and admitted to herself that she hated the very sight of the place. The entire world might admire the grounds—those lawns, which were mowed, edged and cultivated until they resembled lush velvet; the hedges, which were clipped, trimmed and manicured until there was not a twig that would dare to pop crookedly out of place; the fall flowers which were lined up below her window in rigid neatness, each row bearing blooms of only one color so that the rows of reds could never presume to mix with the pinks—but *she* found nothing admirable about the view.

The carefully tended, rich and spacious grounds of Wyckfield Park were an anathema to her. To her eyes they seemed a travesty of natural beauty—a place where the Goddess of Nature had been bound, shackled and restricted at every turn. Nowhere on the estate's vast acreage had any living thing been allowed to develop in its own way. Each hedge and shrub had been made to conform to the Wyckfields' grand plan, every natural instinct compelled to yield. That was why Camilla hated the grounds—they were a monument to repression. *Like my own life,* she thought, crossing her black-clad arms over her chest as if to ward off a cold draught.

"What's the matter, Mama?" came a child's voice behind her.

Camilla put on a smile and turned to face her ten-year-old daughter, who was curled up on the sofa with a copy of *Evelina* on her lap. "Matter? Nothing at all. What makes you ask?"

The child looked over the spectacles perched on her nose and fixed her blue eyes on her mother's face with a gaze that was unnervingly mature. "You sighed three times," she accused.

"Did I?" Camilla's smile lost its strained insincerity and widened into a grin. "Have you been sitting there counting my sighs?"

The child grinned back. "It's no great task to count to three, you know."

"True, but I thought you were absorbed in your reading."

"I was, until your heartrending breathing distracted me."

"Heartrending? *Really,* Pippa!" Camilla couldn't prevent a gurgling laugh from welling up into her throat. Her daughter, Philippa, was her joy—the only real joy that life had ever offered her. Small in size but gifted in intellect, the child was the only creature in the household whose development had been miraculously unaffected by the repressive atmosphere. Pippa was perhaps too bookish and precocious, but her nature had a pervasive serenity and self-confidence. She was capable of such outpourings of affection and good cheer that the cold aridity of the Wyckfields seemed unable to penetrate her spirit.

To Camilla, her daughter was a miracle. Pippa's father, now deceased, had been cold as steel, his sister Ethelyn rigid and forbidding and Oswald, Ethelyn's husband, weakly indifferent. Each of them had attempted to control the child's growth, yet Pippa had developed a clear-eyed optimism, an honest, straightforward way of thinking and an amazingly strong spirit. In this house of gloomy religiosity and fanatical repression, the little girl had learned to laugh.

Best of all, in Camilla's view, was the combination of precocity and innocence in Pippa's character. It was a combination so charming that even Ethelyn couldn't bring herself to scold the child with nearly the animosity with which she scolded the rest of the world. No matter how angry Ethelyn would become at one of Pippa's blithe infractions of the rules, Pippa could turn the wrath aside with her sturdy, unafraid, logical explanations. Camilla wished that she herself had been gifted with some small part of the child's courage and ability to adapt to these sterile surroundings.

Camilla sat down beside her daughter on the sofa. She hated to see the little girl clad in the depressing mourning dress, but Ethelyn insisted that they both wear black until the entire year of mourning had passed. Camilla put an arm about the little shoulders and drew Pippa close. "Why are you studying me so speculatively, love?" she asked. "Miss Burney's tale must be disappointing to you if your attention is so easily diverted by my sighs."

"I *love* Miss Burney's story," Pippa declared earnestly, snuggling into the crook of her mother's arm, "but I *don't* love to hear you sighing. You can tell me, you know, Mama, if something's troubling you. I'm quite good at understanding worldly problems."

"Are you indeed?" She squeezed Pippa's shoulders affectionately. "Are you trying to make a romance out of my breathing, my dear? If you're looking for worldly problems, stick to Miss Burney's book."

The bright, spectacled eyes turned up to Camilla's face with a look of disdain. "You needn't try to put me off, Mama. I know you're worrying about something."

"Perhaps I am, but even if I *did* have 'worldly problems,' I shouldn't wish to burden you with them. I've no intention of permitting you to grow old before your time." She planted a light kiss on the girl's brow. "You've plenty of time to cope with worldly problems when you're older."

"If your problem concerns Aunt Ethelyn, I can help, you know," the child insisted.

"Hush, dear. Do you want Uncle Oswald to hear us?"

Pippa and her mother both turned their eyes instinctively to the huge wing chair near the fireplace across the room. Oswald Falcombe, Lady Ethelyn's lethargic husband, was slumped upon it, fast asleep, the handkerchief still spread over his face as it had been for the past two hours. "He's sleeping quite soundly," Pippa whispered reassuringly. "You can see it in the way the handkerchief pops up and down with his breath."

"You seem to have made quite a study of breathing," her mother said drily.

Pippa giggled. "It's just observation, Mama. Keen observation." Her smile faded, and she sat up straight and looked at her mother in mild rebuke. "That's how I know that something is bothering you. Observation."

"You, my girl, are a persistent little *witch!* I've already told you that I don't intend to discuss my problems—if there *are* any—with you. You are not to worry about me, Pippa! I'm perfectly capable of handling my problems without the advice or assistance of a ten-year-old, even if she *is* a prodigy."

"I'm not certain you *are* capable of handling them, Mama, if they require facing up to Aunt Ethelyn."

Camilla drew herself up in mock affront. "Is that so?"

"Yes, it is. You've been trying for two months to convince her to let us put off these mourning clothes, and you still haven't succeeded," the girl pointed out frankly.

"I know."

"After all, it's been almost a year since Papa died—"

"Passed to his reward," Camilla corrected in perfect imitation of Ethelyn's words and manner.

Pippa laughed. "Passed to his *just* reward," she amended with an almost equal talent for mimicry. "Aunt Ethelyn is a great stickler for rules, isn't she? Everything must always be exactly proper . . . proper dress, proper demeanor, proper wording. I wonder why she thinks the longer phrase 'passed to his just reward' is better than just saying he died?"

"I don't know, love. Perhaps she thinks 'died' is too blunt . . . or too disrespectful to God."

"You mean 'Our Blessed Lord,'" Pippa quipped, using her aunt's tone again. "*Is* it disrespectful, Mama, to speak bluntly? To say 'God' or 'died' straight out?"

"I don't think so, dear. It's just that your aunt is . . . well, a stickler as you said."

Pippa made a face. "A *real* stickler. That's why we've had to wear black for so long. I wish she'd change her mind and let us put off full mourning. I don't think wearing black helps one to remember Papa any more than one would if one were wearing *pink*. To tell the truth, I barely remember his face anymore."

"*That*, Philippa Wyckfield," came an ominous voice from the doorway, "is a *sinful* thing to say!" And Lady Ethelyn Falcombe, her large frame draped in a round-gown of heavy black bombazine, her wiry gray hair rolled up in a knot at the back of her head and looking like a twenty-gun frigate ready for battle, sailed into the room.

"Eh? What's that?" muttered Oswald, shaken awake by his wife's booming voice and pulling the handkerchief from his face.

"Come now, Ethelyn," Camilla said placatingly, "what Pippa said was only natural—"

"As if that excuses it! If we all were permitted to give in to our natural instincts, we'd still be *savages*. How *dare* she say she's permitted herself to forget her father!"

"I'm sorry, Aunt Ethelyn," Pippa said, calmly cheerful. "I didn't say I'd forgotten Papa. I said I'd forgotten his *face*." She got up from the sofa and took her aunt's hand affectionately. "It's quite the truth, you know. I've tried to remember his face, but I can't seem to bring it to mind. Can you?"

"Can I what? Remember my beloved brother's face? What an absurd question."

"I mean actually *see* him in your mind whenever you wish to. Can you do it now, this moment? Close your eyes, Aunt Ethelyn, right now, and try to remember him. Tell me if you see him clearly, just as he was."

"But of *course* I . . ." Ethelyn stared at the child looking innocently up at her. Then she shut her eyes tightly. After a moment she blinked her eyes open and glanced down at her niece, who still held her hand and was watching her closely. "Well, I *think* I . . ." She shut her eyes again. Her heavy cheeks quivered, and her brow wrinkled as her effort intensified. "Isn't that strange?" she murmured. "I see the *portrait* of him that we've hung on the drawing room wall, but . . ."

"I remember his nose," Oswald put in reflectively. "Had a slight hook in it, from having been tossed from a horse during that hunt—"

"Oswald, don't speak like a fool!" Ethelyn barked, her eyes still shut. "Desmond's nose was perfect."

"Remembering that his nose had a hook doesn't count, Uncle Oswald," Pippa explained reasonably. "You're remembering a fact, not seeing a face."

"Ummm," he nodded, shutting his eyes to try again.

Camilla sank back against the sofa cushions and looked at the others in wonder. There they were, the three of them, trying to conjure up the face of the deceased Desmond in their minds merely at the behest of the little girl. Her ingenious daughter had managed to turn what could have been an unpleasant scene into a little game. Pippa was truly an amazing child.

Of course, Camilla herself could see Desmond's face all too clearly in her mind. She didn't even need to close her eyes to conjure up a vision of those steely eyes, that thin-lipped mouth, that wiry gray hair that had been steadily receding from his forehead in recent years. Even after almost a year, the memory of his face could make her blood run cold. In her dreams she still heard the cutting sarcasm of his voice and the sound of his icy scoldings. At unexpected times of the day she still found herself stiffening when she heard a certain sort of footstep on the stairs. And sometimes at night, when she blew out her bedside lamp, she had to remind herself to relax . . . to will herself to recall that he could no longer pay his devastating fortnightly visits to her bed.

"The child's right," Oswald admitted. "I can't bring his face to mind either."

"I think it's shocking!" Ethelyn muttered irritably. "We must ask our Blessed Lord's forgiveness this evening at prayers. Perhaps with His Divine Assistance we may find the strength to overcome this lapse in our mental powers. Meanwhile, Philippa, I will refrain from any further comment on the unfeeling words you spoke when I entered. I suppose you meant no harm."

"Thank you, Aunt Ethelyn," the child said pleasantly.

"Now, my dear, I desire you to run off and occupy yourself elsewhere," Ethelyn ordered. "I have something of importance to discuss with your mother."

Pippa, with a sidelong glance at her mother, bobbed obediently and turned to go. Her mother handed her her book with a reassuring smile.

"What have you there?" Ethelyn demanded as the girl skipped to the door. "I hope, Philippa, that it isn't one of those dreadful novels for which you seem to have such an appetite."

"It's only *Evelina*. And it can't be *very* dreadful, for it was written by Fanny Burney, whom you told me you'd met in your youth." With that the girl smiled, waved a cheery good-bye to her uncle, gave her mother an encouraging wink which seemed to say, *Don't let the old dragon bully you,* and whisked herself out of the room.

Lady Ethelyn glared at the door as if trying to decide whether to call the child back for a scold or let her go. After a moment, she wheeled about to face her sister-in-law on whom, she concluded, a scolding would have more effect. "Really, Camilla, how can you permit the child to read *novels?* If I know Miss Burney's interests, the book deals with nothing but flirtations and matchmaking and the like. I can't approve of so frivolous a piece of reading matter even for an adult, but to permit a mere *child* to—!"

Camilla clenched her fists in her lap and tried to keep Ethelyn's booming voice from overwhelming her courage. "I believe it best," she said quietly, "to let Pippa choose her own reading matter, since she is so advanced."

"Choose her own? Are you *mad?* A child, no matter how gifted, needs direction. She should be reading books which are *edifying* rather than entertaining—like Mr. Watt's *Divine and Moral Songs for Children.* Or, if she must read stories, let her peruse the one I gave her last week."

"If you mean the tale by Mrs. Sherwood called *The Fairchild Family,* she's already read it." Camilla's lips turned up in a tiny, almost unnoticeable smile. "She said it was excessively silly."

"Silly? It was recommended by Harriet More herself!" Ethelyn's breast heaved in outrage that anyone could question the judgment of the famous evangelical.

"Nevertheless," Camilla said, her chin coming up bravely, "Pippa said it's fit only to frighten little children, making them believe that at each and every second of their lives they are walking the tightrope between eternal bliss and eternal damnation. She said she's sorry for the little ones in the charity schools who have to read it, but that *she's* too old to be frightened by it."

"Shocking! The child's too clever for her own good!" Ethelyn frowned down at her sister-in-law darkly. "I suppose it's too much to hope that you took her to task for saying such sinful things."

"There was nothing sinful—!"

"You are as aware as I am that we *do* walk a tightrope, every moment of our lives, between bliss and damnation, and the sooner a child knows it the better. You, of all people, should show some concern for Philippa's immortal soul!"

A flash of anger seared through Camilla's chest. "There's not the least reason for me to have concern for her soul!" she retorted, a touch of waspishness in her voice. As if Pippa had anything in her soul but the purest, sweetest innocence!

But there was nothing to be gained by pursuing this subject with Ethelyn. Camilla had never been able to argue against either of the Wyckfields—Ethelyn or Desmond—with any degree of success. Even when she was in the right, they could put her on the defensive and make her feel inadequate. Often in the past, she would find herself at the end of a dispute defeated, choked with frustration and shamefully giving way to a flood of tears. Even now that Desmond was dead, and she was legally mistress of this house, she found herself intimidated by her sister-in-law's sheer forcefulness. She realized that she'd have to face up to Ethelyn one of these days, if she was ever to have any sort of life for herself. But it was silly to have an altercation now on so ludicrous a subject as the danger to her daughter's soul from a bit of innocuous reading. "Did you say earlier, Ethelyn, that you have something to discuss with me?" she asked, turning the subject.

"Yes, I did." Ethelyn seated herself imperiously on the chair facing the sofa and folded her hands in her lap primly. "It's the matter of *your* butler."

"Hicks? Again? What's he done?"

"The man actually uttered a foul blasphemy . . . and in my presence!"

"Oh, Ethelyn, he *couldn't* have," Camilla said, leaning forward worriedly. "I've known him all my life, and I've *never* heard him—"

"But *I* heard him!" Ethelyn retorted coldly. "I gave him an order, and I heard him mutter something under his breath."

Camilla felt her stomach tighten. The matter of Hicks had been a subject of contention between them for years, and Camilla instinctively felt that the matter was about to explode in her face. She got up from the sofa and returned to her place at the window. Staring out on the prim grounds with unseeing eyes, she said hesitantly, "Perhaps you misunderstood . . . or didn't hear him quite accurately . . . ?"

"Camilla, I am sick and tired of listening to your weak-kneed defense of that incompetent, disobedient, *godless* knave! While this is, of course, just as much your home as mine—and the Good Lord knows that you may have an equal say in running it—you cannot expect me to have to endure obscenity and blasphemy from the servants!"

Camilla's fingers clenched. *An equal say in running it, indeed!* she thought, gritting her teeth furiously. Never once in the eleven years since she'd come to this house as a bride had Ethelyn permitted her to make a decision regarding the running of the house. Everything from the planning of the week's menus to the decoration of the sitting room was decided by her sister-in-law. Even the servants knew whose word was law in this house. While Desmond had been alive, he'd been the undisputed master, but the domestic details had been the province of his sister, not his wife. And now that he was dead, nothing had changed. Even though he'd left everything to his only issue—his daughter Philippa—Ethelyn still ruled with an iron hand. Desmond had left both his wife and his sister generous independencies and had stipulated that the estate of Wyckfield Park should be open to them whenever they wished to reside therein, but Ethelyn still behaved as if the property were her own.

Only two members of the household staff considered Camilla to be mistress of the house—Hicks and Miss Ada Townley, her old governess. Camilla had brought them with her when she'd come to Wyckfield Park eleven years ago. During all those years, Ethelyn had attempted to oust the two servants whom Camilla had (as Ethelyn like to put it) "inflicted" on her. But Camilla, even though she'd been too young and frightened to take a stand on anything else, had been adamant about keeping them with her. She'd felt (and she *still* believed) that they were her only friends in the household of cold antagonists who surrounded her.

In defense against the houseful of indifferent or icy adversaries, Camilla, Miss Townley and Hicks seemed to form a small enclave of cheerfulness and affection which embraced little Pippa and protected them all from feelings of loneliness and ostracism. But Camilla soon realized that it was an enclave which Ethelyn was determined to break apart. Ethelyn had often and openly declared that Hicks and Miss Townley encouraged Camilla and even Pippa in keeping secrets, in scornful attitudes toward the rest of the household, in engaging in frivolous pursuits, and in latitudinarian—nay, *godless*—behavior. Ethelyn had long ago convinced herself that she and she alone was responsible for the welfare of the immortal soul of every member of the household, even the staff. Anything which interfered with that Godly Mission was sinful in the extreme.

Camilla knew that Ethelyn's resentment ran deeper than her repeated protestations that she was concerned only for the welfare of their souls. The little circle of four had managed, by sticking together, to keep from being completely dominated by the strong-willed, dictatorial woman. The truth was that Ethelyn had convinced herself that if she could rid the household of Hicks, she'd be able to control the others.

Camilla could feel, in the determined fury of Ethelyn's voice, that her sister-in-law had made up her mind to force a confrontation. Hicks's blunt, country honesty made it hard for him to hide his feelings, and his outspoken manner had always roused Ethelyn's ire. But Camilla had managed, until now, to keep matters from coming to a head. With her legs trembling under the black skirts, she turned to face her irate sister-in-law and try again. "I'll speak to him, Ethelyn," she offered with a sigh.

"You've spoken to him any number of times already, and it hasn't made one particle of difference in his manner."

"But I shall be . . . *most* severe," Camilla promised.

Ethelyn hooted. "It's not *in* you to be severe! You've never shown the servants that you have an ounce of strictness in you. It is your nature to be lenient and indulgent, and *this* is the result. I've warned you, Camilla, that softness of character eats away at the discipline of a human being as well as a household. If it weren't for my God-given strength, this house would be a shambles."

"If I've been lenient and indulgent," Camilla declared, lifting her chin in self-defense, "it's only because you've never given me the opportunity to—"

"Oh, how many times do I have to listen to *that* argument? It won't wash, Camilla. If you feel superseded in the running of this house, you have only yourself to blame. I've said to Oswald time and again—haven't I, my dear?—that if you'd shown any sign of the rigor and forcefulness needed to run an establishment of this sort, I would have gladly surrendered the responsibility into your hands. Just ask Oswald if those weren't my very words."

"I think, ladies," Oswald murmured, pulling his bulk from the wing chair awkwardly, "that I had better toddle off and let you pursue your discussion uninterruptedly."

Camilla frowned in disgust. It was just like Oswald to wish to evade the scene. She supposed that, many years ago, when he'd been with the Admiralty, he might have been a tolerable sort, but he'd long ago lost any vestige of purposefulness of character. Now he was careful only to avoid confrontation or any involvement in the stressful situation developing around him. He seemed to wish for nothing but peace and his daily allowance of sweets.

His wife fixed a firm eye on him. "Sit down and be still, Oswald! I want you to be a witness to this. I mean to settle this matter once and for all, and I want no recriminations later."

"I don't see what there is to settle," Camilla said with quiet constraint. "I know that Hicks's manner is annoying to you, but there doesn't seem to be any way to change him at his advanced age, so we may as well make the best of it."

"I *intend* to make the best of it, Camilla, by insisting that we get *rid* of him."

"Oh, Ethelyn, you can't mean that. Surely you see that I couldn't discharge a man who has been in my family's employ all his life."

"No, I *don't* see. You may pension him off or do anything else you wish, but you will direct him to *leave this house!*"

"Ethelyn, I can't do that. It would be the cruelest sort of blow to the old fellow. You mustn't ask it of me."

"I am not asking. I'm demanding. My brother made it clear in his will that this is where I'm to live, did he not? And since I cannot live in the same house with that *depraved* butler, there is nothing for it but to let him go."

Camilla's heart sank in her chest. There it was . . . an ultimatum. And although the impasse had been erected by her sister-in-law, she herself had made it mountainous by eleven years of evasion. Now she would either have to make a complete surrender or attempt to surmount it by having it out with Ethelyn once and for all.

She raised her eyes and met Ethelyn's cold, inflexible stare. Her spirit quailed, but she warned herself that the security of a beloved servant, the respect of her daughter and the hope of her own future contentment were at stake. She drew in a deep breath, clenched her fingers into tight fists and said firmly, "See here, Ethelyn, I—"

At that moment the door burst open. "Miss *Camilla!*" Miss Townley said breathlessly from the doorway, "the fat's in the fire this time. Hicks is packin' to *leave!*"

Chapter Two

$\mathcal{D}$inner that night was a strangely silent meal, in spite of the fact that everything in the household was at sixes and sevens. Ethelyn was not speaking to Camilla at all; Oswald had decided to keep his eyes on his plate and to use his tongue only for tasting; and Pippa, not having been told the details but aware that a crisis had struck, watched everyone carefully from the corners of her eyes but said nothing. Even the servants walked about as if on eggs, terrified that the least mischance would set off an explosion.

Camilla had managed to persuade Hicks (who had been pushed beyond his limit by what he said was "Lady Ethelyn's wrongful abuse") to retire to his room for the rest of the day until she could find time to think . . . and to decide what was best to be done. Ethelyn, feeling postponement to be "a most dastardly placating of a reprehensible servant," had fallen into a rage and had ranted at Camilla for almost the entire afternoon. When she'd finally realized that Camilla would make no decision until she could sleep on the matter, Ethelyn had stalked off, declaring furiously that Camilla would get "not one more word from me until the despicable fellow has been sent packing!"

Even Miss Townley had given Camilla a scold. The elderly governess, taking advantage of her lifelong intimacy with her mistress, told her roundly that she'd "better show Lady Ethelyn some backbone—and mighty soon!—if you ever intend to call your soul your own," and had marched off in a huff.

After dinner, Camilla accompanied her daughter to her room and, with Miss Townley's assistance, dressed the child in her nightclothes. "Aren't you going to tell me what's amiss?" Pippa asked when her mother tucked her into bed.

"No, I'm not," Camilla answered firmly.

"Then I'll coax Miss Townley to—"

"No, you won't, my girl," Miss Townley said briskly, folding away Pippa's mourning dress. "If your mother doesn't think you should know, then neither do I."

Pippa looked from one to the other. "I shall worry all the more if I'm kept in ignorance."

Camilla sat down at the edge of the bed and stroked her daughter's silky hair. "There's no need to worry, love. I promise you that all will be well by morning."

"I'd surely like to know," Miss Townley said disgustedly after they left Pippa's room, "what magic it is you'll use to get out of this fix by mornin'."

Camilla smiled with more reassurance than she felt. "Never mind, Ada. You can put off your Friday-faced frown. I shall think of something." And she walked airily away down the hall.

With Ada Townley thus dismissed, she had only her abigail to send to bed to be alone at last. When this had been done, she locked her door, took off her shoes and climbed into bed. She would really need an inspiration to solve this vexing problem, which she'd avoided for so long. Her avoidance and lack of firmness had enlarged the problem until it had become a true crisis, and she would need a veritable stroke of genius to solve it now. Here, in the comfortable silence of her bedroom, she hoped to find it. She sat back against the pillows, pulled an eiderdown quilt over her legs and tried to concentrate.

The problem was truly a knotty one, with ramifications beyond the obvious one—the antagonism between her sister-in-law and Hicks. First there was Hicks himself. All day he'd repeatedly declared he would not remain in this house, but Camilla was certain he'd be hurt beyond repair if she permitted him to leave. Even a generous pension would not salve the blow to his pride if she let him go. It would be, in his eyes, an admission that Camilla *agreed* with Lady Ethelyn's disdainful assessment of his worth.

Another ramification of the problem was its reflection on her own character. If Hicks left this house, both her daughter and Ada Townley would be justified in believing that she was completely lacking in backbone. And they would be quite right. Whenever there had been a confrontation with Ethelyn, Camilla had backed down. If she yielded again—especially over something as important as Hicks's future—they would despise her.

Yet she had to think of Ethelyn too. This *was* the only home that Ethelyn had ever known. Ethelyn had often remarked that it was unthinkable for her to live anywhere else but on the land that her family had owned for generations. Was it fair or just for Camilla to make her uncomfortable in a home to which she really had more right than Camilla?

She sighed again as she'd been sighing all day—helplessly. If only she could make her sister-in-law understand her attachment to the stubborn old butler.

But Ethelyn would never understand. Ethelyn had never been poor, and she didn't know anything of what Camilla's life had been like twelve years before. Twelve years ago . . . when her father had died. Camilla needed only to shut her eyes, and the scenes of that dreadful year would come crowding back to her mind . . .

They weren't memories so much as a series of sounds—voices, noises, cries. Her father's voice on his deathbed, muttering brokenly, "I'm sorry, dearest . . . forgive me." The solicitor's voice explaining why the home she'd always lived in was now no longer hers. She hadn't understood anything about the entail and the debts, but she'd understood, when Miss Townley had held her in her arms and crooned brokenly, "Oh, my little lamb, my poor little lamb," that at the age of seventeen she was orphaned, homeless and almost penniless.

Then Hicks's voice, gentle and optimistic, explaining that the shabby, ugly little cottage he'd found for them was only temporary . . . that as soon as she turned eighteen, she and Miss Townley could start a school for young ladies and that they would then make out very well. But she'd known that the school was only a dream.

And there'd been the sound of Miss Townley's clatter in the smoky cottage kitchen as she banged the pots in anguish over her meager talents in cookery, frustrated beyond words at being unable to turn oatmeal and turnips into a palatable meal. Worst of all had been the scratching of the rats behind the walls of her cottage bedroom as she lay sleepless during the dark, endless hours of the night.

And finally there'd been Desmond's voice. Desmond, the Earl of Wyckfield, one of her father's creditors, who'd come to collect an unpaid debt and remained to woo the terrified girl who was twenty years his junior. Oh, it had been a very mellow voice, well-modulated and velvet with promises. She would have everything, he'd said. All her dreams would be fulfilled. She'd be a Countess, with a magnificent home, a stable full of horses, her very own carriage, the Wyckfield Necklace made of emeralds and diamonds, and a cloak lined with sable . . .

Camilla gave her head an abrupt shake and opened her eyes, hoping to dissipate the sounds of those echoing voices from the past. But no mere movement, no matter how sharp or sudden, could dissipate the gloom that twelve years of painful regret had pressed upon her spirit. It had all been her own fault. It had been she who'd persuaded herself to marry Desmond in the first place. Miss Townley had warned her that his air of cold reserve might run deeper than mere outward manner. But Camilla had been too eager for the security of wealth; those months of poverty had been too terrifying.

She told herself that she would grow to love him, and she'd married Desmond in a self-deluding glow of optimism. It didn't take long to discover that the ice in his manner was an integral part of his nature. It took a bit longer to learn that wealth and security make inadequate substitutes for inner contentment, but she'd learned it well. She'd soon realized that she would never find contentment in this house. But when that realization had finally burst upon her, escape had become impossible—she was bearing his child.

The thought of the child immediately cheered her. Little Pippa had been a lifesaving gift—a sign of God's grace. It was as if she'd been forgiven for having married for the wrong reasons. From the child she'd learned that happiness was still possible. Every evening, at the family prayers, which Ethelyn's domination turned into a cold and almost meaningless ritual, Camilla sat apart and gave thanks for the miracle of her daughter's existence.

More for her daughter's sake than for any other reason, Camilla had to find a solution. Pippa could not be permitted to believe that her mother was a spineless jellyfish. Yet a bitter, recriminative collision with Ethelyn would be horrible. Even if she remained firm and refused to let Hicks go, Ethelyn would never back down, and life in this house would be even more unpleasant.

Camilla winced in self-disgust. Her thinking was as shillyshallying as her character. Here she was, a grown woman of twenty-nine, and no more capable of handling her problems than a child. Why, a child like Pippa could probably handle it without a blink!

She shut her eyes, wondering what Pippa would do in her place . . . and suddenly the answer came like a candle flame shining through the mist. Of *course!* How simple and how *perfect!* She threw off the coverlet, jumped out of bed and gleefully danced about the room in her stockinged feet, smiling broadly. She, Camilla Wyckfield, was not such a ninnyhammer after all.

Early the next morning, Camilla leaped out of bed and, without ringing for her abigail, hurried into her clothes. Halfway through buttoning the back of her mourning dress, she stayed her hands. *If I'm about to play the rebel,* she thought with amusement, *I may as well go all the way.* Quickly she stripped off the black dress and replaced it with a poplin gown of soft lilac. Thus attired, she sped quickly downstairs and hurried into the morning room. But she was not the first to arrive. Miss Townley was already there, setting a pot of tea in the center of the table. "What *is* this, Ada?" Camilla asked, pausing in the doorway. "Where's Hicks?"

Miss Townley didn't look up. "He asked me to set breakfast in his place," she said, her voice cold with disapproval. "He's packed his things and is all ready to leave."

"Good," Camilla said promptly. "Will you ask him to—

"*Good?*" Miss Townley's head came up angrily. "Are you backin' down, then, after—? *Good Lord!*" She gaped at her mistress openmouthed. "Where's your mournin'—"

"Hush, Ada, hush. Leave the breakfast things, and ask Hicks to come here to see me, will you, please?"

"Then you *do* have a plan!" The governess smiled at Camilla proudly. "I *knew* you'd think of some—"

"You knew no such thing, you humbug. Just a second ago you were ready to eat me whole."

Miss Townley ignored the chastisement and rubbed her hands eagerly. "You're goin' to have it out with her!" she chortled. "I can't wait to see—"

"Hush, I tell you! Please, Ada, don't jump to conclusions. Just do as I ask, and get Hicks for me. And don't say anything to anyone."

"Not even about the gown?" the governess asked as she scurried to the door.

"Not even about that."

Miss Townley nodded, gave Camilla an approving wink and left. Camilla seated herself at the table facing the door and, with hands that shook only slightly, filled her cup with tea. Bracing herself with a quick gulp of the steaming brew, she sat back and waited. She was quite ready.

The first to arrive was Pippa, who took immediate note of her mother's change of attire. "Oh, *my!*" she breathed in amazement, stopping in her tracks and gaping in admiration. "Does Aunt Ethelyn *know?*"

Camilla grinned. "Isn't it customary to say 'good morning' when you first come in?"

Pippa skipped around the table and flung her arms about her mother's neck. "Never mind the good mornings. You look *beautiful!* May I go up and change, too?"

"Perhaps later. Sit down, love, and have your breakfast."

Pippa threw herself upon a chair and reached for a biscuit. "I suppose there's a deeper meaning in this, isn't there, Mama?" Her eyes twinkled expectantly. "This has something to do with yesterday's crisis, hasn't it?"

"It's not a bit ladylike to speak with your mouth full, you know," her mother chided as a tactic of evasion.

"Very well, don't answer," Pippa said calmly, helping herself to tea. "I shan't leave your side until I learn for myself just what's going—"

"Good morning, good morning," came Oswald's voice from the doorway. "We have two early birds at the table, I s—" He was about to pull out a chair when he noticed Camilla's garb. "My *word!* You've put off mourning!"

"Yes, I have," she said, buttering a slice of toast.

"Does Ethelyn . . . that is, I mean to say . . . is everything—"

"If you are asking whether I've been given Ethelyn's *permission,* Oswald, the answer is no."

Pippa gave a little giggle, but Oswald stiffened. "I . . . er . . . think I'll put off breakfasting a little while," he mumbled, backing to the door. "Perhaps later, when—"

"Oh, do sit down, Oswald," Camilla said impatiently. "This has nothing to do with you. There's no reason for you to run off without your breakfast."

Trapped, Oswald clumsily sank into a chair, but it was clear to all of them that he would take no pleasure from this morning's meal. He was reaching half-heartedly for the covered platter containing the coddled eggs when Hicks tapped at the door and came in. He was dressed in his Sunday coat instead of his butler's garb, and he carried a shabby beaver in one hand and a stuffed portmanteau in the other. "I've come to say good-bye, Miss Camilla," he said stiffly.

"And a good riddance!" Ethelyn said, sailing into the room behind him. "Then this will be the last time I'll have to take you to task for calling her ladyship 'Miss Camilla.'" She breezed past the infuriated butler and took her place. "I'm delighted, Camilla, that you've come to your senses. Good heavens, *what* are you *wearing?*"

"Never mind that," Camilla said. "I've something important to say to Hicks before he leaves."

"Mama, you're not going to let Hicks *leave,* are you?" Pippa asked, jumping up and running to the butler's side in alarm.

"Don't worry, poppet," whispered Miss Townley, who was watching the proceedings from the open doorway. "Your mother has a plan."

"Don't care if she has," the butler muttered. "There's nothing she can devise to make me remain."

"Well, Camilla, say what it is you have to say, and let the fellow take his leave," Ethelyn ordered impatiently, "for I have a thing or two to say to *you,* and I don't want to wait all day to say it!"

Camilla folded her hands tightly in her lap and sat up very straight. "If you wish to say something about my putting off mourning, Ethelyn, you may as well save your breath. The length of my period of mourning is my own affair."

"I think, my dear," Oswald said uncomfortably, "that I'll just pop out for a . . . a stroll. Glorious morning, you know. Glorious. So if you'll excuse me—"

"Be quiet, Oswald," Ethelyn ordered, motioning him to remain in his chair. "Really, Camilla, you've no need to take that tone. If you wish to incur the disapproval of all our friends and neighbors by appearing in colors before the year has passed, I'm sure I wouldn't take it upon myself to chastise you."

"Thank you. Then I may speak to Hicks without further interruption." Camilla stood up and walked round the table to the butler. "I know you no longer wish to remain here in this house, Hicks, and I won't insist that you do, but—"

"Thank the Good Lord for *that,* at least," Ethelyn muttered.

"I've had quite enough breakfast, my dear," Oswald mumbled, "so if you don't mind—"

"Be *quiet,* I said!" his wife barked.

Camilla gave them both a look of reproval and turned back to Hicks. "As I was saying, I won't insist that you remain, but you wouldn't object to remaining in my employ, would you?"

The butler looked at her, puzzled. "Well, no, Miss Camilla, but I don't understand how—"

"I'd like you to execute a commission in London for me."

"Camilla, what is this all about?" Ethelyn asked, her brow wrinkled in annoyance. "Why do you want *him* to do it? We have any number of servants who would be much more capable—"

"Hicks is the perfect choice for *this* commission, I assure you."

"But what is it you want him to *do?*"

"I want him to find me a house. And since the house will be in his charge, he's the best one to find it."

"A *house?* What are you talking about?"

"I'd better take myself off to—" Oswald said in desperation.

"Oswald, will you be *still?* How can you wish to scurry off when Camilla has obviously lost her mind? Really, Camilla, it's the outside of enough to buy a house for the fellow in London! You can certainly find him a retirement abode in some less expensive—"

"But the house in London is not for *him* to live in . . . not alone, that is."

"Why . . . what on earth do you mean?" Ethelyn demanded, half rising from her chair.

"I've decided," Camilla said, turning to face them all and speaking with a tense firmness, "that Pippa and I shall be taking up residence in London."

There was a moment of complete silence, during which no one in the room seemed able to draw a breath. Then Oswald spoke up. "I really *must* ask to leave the room."

"Oh, *Mama!*" Pippa cried, jumping up and down jubilantly. "What a perfectly *splendid* notion!"

"Miss Camilla," Miss Townley exclaimed, "you're a *genius.*"

Hicks pumped her hand. "You've made me a happy man, Miss Camilla. A very happy man."

"Camilla!" The room fell silent as Ethelyn rose grandly to her feet. "You are speaking utter nonsense. You will do nothing of the sort."

Everyone watched intently while Ethelyn and Camilla faced each other. But for Camilla, the war was over. She'd made a decision she knew in her bones was right, and Ethelyn was powerless to stop her. Her trembling ceased. With a look of compassion, she crossed the room and put a light hand on her sister-in-law's arm. "I *will* do it, Ethelyn," she said quietly. "Don't look so thunderstruck. In a very short time you'll get used to the idea. And one day, much sooner than you think, you'll agree that I've made the very best decision for us all."

Chapter Three

$\mathcal{B}$y the time the last customer had stumbled out of the taproom of the Crown and Cloves, Twyford, and into the rain, it was well past midnight. But Betsy Hicks, the barmaid, still had the washing-up to do. The innkeeper's wife had, as usual, followed her husband up to bed, leaving every remaining chore to Betsy. Wearily, she washed and dried the glasses, wiped down the tables and swept the floor. Then, every bone aching, she got down on her knees, smothered the remainder of the fire with a bucketful of ashes and, patting her slightly swelling belly as if making a promise to the budding life within that only one more chore remained, swept the ashes back into the bucket and deposited it outside the back door.

The rain was coming down heavily now. Although her room over the stable was only a step away, she pulled off her apron and held it over her head as she dashed across the cobbled courtyard and into the stable door. Every step up the rickety ladder to her room seemed an enormous effort, and she was breathing heavily by the time she reached the top. She longed for sleep. Tonight she'd make only a hasty washing before throwing herself into bed. Usually she liked to daydream of Daniel when she snuggled under the blankets, but tonight she would probably be asleep before she could even bring his face to mind. It was cruel of Mrs. Crumley to keep her working so late, especially since she was four months pregnant. She limped down the short passageway with the painful shuffle of an aged crone. *If only Daniel would get home,* she prayed, *before these endless hours of work make an old woman of me.*

She'd barely opened the door and stepped over the threshold, wondering if she'd left herself a match with which to light the candle, when she was seized about the shoulders from behind, and a hand clamped down firmly on her mouth. Terrified, she struggled wildly. "Shhh, girl," a man's voice whispered in her ear, "it's only me. Don't make a noise when I let ye go."

"Daniel!" Betsy, trembling from head to toe, couldn't decide whether to kiss him or strike him. "How *could* ye—"

But he pulled her into his arms and kissed her with all the hunger that more than three months of separation had built up in him, and she forgot her fright and anger and let herself surrender to the urgency of his embrace. "Oh, Dan'l, love," she murmured breathlessly between kisses, "I thought ye'd never . . . I'm so *happy!*" It was not until she heard a match being struck by someone behind her that she realized there was someone else in the room. "Daniel," she asked with a troubled start, "who—"

The match flared up, revealing a shadowy figure on the other side of the room. "Don't make any noise, love," Daniel warned in a hissing whisper. "It's my friend, Tom, that I wrote ye of. We been sittin' here in the dark for three hours, waitin' fer you t' finish yer chores."

"Sorry we had to break in on you this way, Mrs. Hicks," Tom said quietly, lighting a candle on Betsy's bedside table.

Betsy put a hand to her heaving breast and sank down on the bed, looking from one man to the other. "Somethin's gone wrong, ain't it? That's why ye didn't come to the inn to fetch me. Somethin's terrible wrong. I've felt it in my bones all day."

Daniel sat down beside her, took her hand and stroked it gently. "Don't take on when I tell ye. I . . . can't stay with ye. We're on the run."

"On the *run?*" In the dim light of the candle she searched his face, taking agonized note of his puffed right eye and the ugly bruise on his left cheek and a bit of dried blood on his lip. "Oh, my God! What is it ye've *done?*"

Quickly, without going into minor details, he related to her the events of the evening before—the encounter with the press-gang and the struggle in the cabin of the *Undaunted.* "We're in fer it now, y' see," he concluded glumly. "They'll be lookin' fer us up and down the coast."

"But, why?" Betsy asked, fingering her husband's bruised face tenderly. "Ye've given them the slip, haven't ye? They'll forget all about ye as soon as they nab some other poor sot in yer place."

He shook his head. "I don't think so. That Captain Brock'll remember us, fer sure. And the officer—what was his name, Tom?"

"Moresby."

"Aye, Moresby. He'll not forget us, neither. We've got to get away, love." His voice choked. "We only waited so's I could say good-bye to ye."

"No!" the girl cried, flinging her arms round his neck. "Ye'll not go a step without me! I swore to myself ever since ye left that I'll never say good-bye to ye again."

Daniel buried his face in her neck. "Nay, love, don't be foolish," he murmured brokenly. "We don't know where we'll end. We can't—"

She put a hand to his mouth to stop his words and shook her head. They clung to each other for a long moment. Then she pushed him away and got to her feet. "Y're wet and cold and prob'ly hungry. We can't think straight in such a state." She wiped her eyes, sniffed bravely and tried to pull herself together. Straightening her shoulders, she looked at Tom shyly. "Excuse me, sir," she said, holding a hand out to him. "I been very rude. I'm most pleased t' meet ye after all Daniel's wrote me about ye."

Tom took her hand and smiled down at her. "Daniel told me about you, too, especially how pretty you are. I was sure the fellow was lying, but I see now that he didn't exaggerate a bit."

A pathetic little smile made an appearance at the corners of her mouth. "Oh, pooh, I must look a sight." She blushed and pushed aside a fallen lock of hair. "But I want t' thank ye, Mr. Collinson, for bein' such a good friend to my Daniel."

"I haven't been a very good friend in *this* matter," Tom muttered ruefully. "I'm afraid I've gotten him into deeper trouble than he'd have had without my interference."

"Belay that, Tom," Daniel ordered. "If it warn't fer you, I'd be prisoned on the *Undaunted* like a slavey, with no hope of any life at all, and no way t' get word to Betsy."

"And it was only t' help him that y're in this fix at all," Betsy added. "We'll always be grateful to ye."

"There's no earthly reason for that," Tom sighed, "for all the good my 'help' has done. But standing here talking won't pay the piper. We'd better be on our way."

"He's right, Betsy, love." Daniel got up from the bed reluctantly. "Laggin' in the valley won't get us over the hill."

"No, I won't have it," Betsy declared firmly. "Ye can't leave me behind, nor the baby neither. Besides, you'll never get away dressed in seamen's clothes and lookin' all battered, like ye do."

"But, Mrs. Hicks," Tom said gently, "there's nothing else to be done. We may even endanger *you* if we're caught in your company."

"My name is Betsy, if you please, and we're not *goin'* to be caught if we think of a good-enough plan. Y're both too cold and miserable to see things straight. I'll slip down t' the kitchen an' fetch some bread an' cold meat—"

"Nay, lass," Daniel cut in, although the prospect of food was painfully tempting, "someone might see ye."

"No one will see me, I promise," She wrapped a shawl around her and moved toward the door. "After ye've filled yer bellies, ye'll be able to think better on what t' do next."

Betsy proved to be right. A tray of food and a few mugs full of home brew made the whole world seem brighter. And after they'd discarded their damp clothes, wrapped themselves in dry blankets and permitted Betsy to tend their bruises, it became difficult to see how they could get along without her. Finally, she pointed out that they would look less suspicious travelling about with a woman, and they agreed that, wherever they should decide to go, she would be with them.

With that decided, they turned their attention to the problem of their destination. It had to be a place far from any seaport where press-gangs were likely to be active, yet somewhere which would offer opportunities to find work. Betsy, her weariness forgotten in the anticipation of the start of a new life in the company of her husband, was full of suggestions. But each one was ruled out by the men for being either too optimistic or too impractical.

She paced the tiny room animatedly, while the two men sat huddled near the fire staring discouragedly into the flames. Although their spirits were too depressed to permit their minds to function, *her* brain seethed with fertile imaginings. She would not permit herself to succumb to discouragement. "I have it!" she clarioned excitedly for the sixth time. "The perfect plan at last!"

"Now, love, don't carry on," Daniel admonished with gentle hopelessness. "Ye've said that about *all* yer ideas."

"But this one will work. I *know* it! I been thinkin' on it all these months, tryin' to puzzle out where we might go when ye returned from the sea. I put the idea out o' my head, figurin' ye wouldn't take kindly to it. But now it seems t' me to be just exac'ly what we need."

"Why? If I wouldn't take kindly to it afore—"

"Well, matters 'er different now. It'd be a perfect place to hide."

Daniel tried to stop her effusions, but Tom put a hand on his arm. "Let her talk, Daniel. She's the only one of us who's shown a spark of imagination. Perhaps she has something, this time."

"I do, Dan'l, truly. The best suggestion yet. Yer uncle Hicks."

"My uncle? What're ye talkin' about?"

"He's in Dorset, somewheres near Shillingstone, ain't he? That must be a goodish distance from the sea, and as good a place as any I can think of to—"

"But he's a butler, ain't he? On a grand estate. Workin' fer a duke or an earl. Wyckfield Park it's called, if I remember rightly. You ain't imaginin' he could take us in an' hide us, are ye?"

"No, but per'aps he could find us places there. To work, I mean. I could serve as a housemaid, couldn't I? At least 'til the baby comes. And you both could be gardeners or stable hands or footmen or somethin'."

"Nay, girl, ye're talkin' like a witlin'. What do we know about gardenin' or horses or household service?"

"What do ye know about *anythin'* save seafarin'?" she countered bluntly. "That sort of work's as easy t' learn as anythin' else."

Daniel was silenced but unconvinced. Dubiously, he looked at Tom. Tom shook his head. "She may be right, Daniel. Certainly no impressment officer would go seeking you in the house of a nobleman. It isn't the sort of work for *me,* but you and Betsy might do very well—"

Betsy planted herself before him, her eyes flashing and her arm akimbo. "We already decided we'll stick t'gether, so let's hear no more you-and-Betsys! An' if the work would do fer Daniel an' me, why wouldn't it do fer you?"

Tom made a face. "I'll be dashed if I want to be a footman for a puffed-up nobleman to step upon."

"Are ye tryin' to say ye're too good fer household service? Per'aps it'd be better t' be trussed up like a sack o' mutton and dumped on the deck o' that Navy ship ye spoke of, eh?" she demanded tartly.

Daniel grinned at his wife's spirit. "She has ye there, old man. An' she may be right. No King's officer would recognize us all spruced up in footmen's livery."

Tom looked from one to the other questioningly. "Are you seriously saying you want to go to Dorset and ask this uncle of yours for work as *servants?*"

"That's exac'ly what I'm sayin'," Betsy declared. "Nothin's wrong with bein' servants. The quarters are clean, the pay's reg'lar, and the food's always good an' plentiful."

"That's true enough," Daniel agreed. "You'll probably like it better 'n ye think, Tom, fer there's sure t' be a goodish number of pretty young maids about to kiss under the stairs—"

"Oh, hush, Dan'l! What a thing to say! Tom ain't the sort to maul the girls under the stairs," his wife objected. "He's far too gentlemanly."

Tom grinned at her. "No man's too gentlemanly for that, my dear. In fact, the promise of some pretty girls to cuddle is the only part of your plan which I find pleasing, if the truth were told."

"There, y' see?" Daniel chortled, pinching his wife's cheek. "I know this fellow better 'n you do, my girl. I seen 'im fondle and forsake more 'n one lass in our time together."

"Shame on ye, Dan'l, trying to make me b'lieve yer best friend is a rake! I don't want t' hear no more o' this. Besides, it ain't gettin' us no closer to solvin' our problem. Are we goin' to Dorset or ain't we?"

"But Betsy, love," Daniel said, his grin dying, "it ain't very likely, is it, that my uncle Hicks could find posts fer all three of us?"

"How can we tell 'til we try?" Betsy responded reasonably. "Stake nothin', draw nothin', as they say."

Daniel shrugged. "Well . . . it's the best scheme we've come up with so far. What do y' say, Tom? Shall we chance it?"

Tom stared into the fire. It *was* the best suggestion to come forth, yet it only served to deepen his despond. He suddenly perceived that his dreams of mastering a vessel were now completely beyond the possibility of fulfillment . . . and for the first time since they'd encountered the press-gang, that truth swept over him with the finality of death. No more would he feel the rocking of the deck beneath his feet, the salt wind cracking his lips, the wheel fighting for supremacy under his hands. No more would he wake up in the morning, climb up on deck and stare out at the gray mist rising from the immensity of gray sea. Now he'd probably wake up to the smell of horse dung in the stable, or, if he were housed in the servants' quarters, he'd probably look out on a backyard court piled with kitchen refuse waiting to be burned. At sea the work had seemed to him to be purposeful and important; the way he'd order the sails trimmed or how he'd chart a course would determine how quickly and safely the ship would reach its destination. He'd had rules to obey, but they'd made sense. Now his work would be trivial, and the rules would be made—and arbitrarily changed—at the whim of a spoiled nobleman with nothing more to do than give orders. At sea he'd had a chance to become a master. Now he'd be subjected to orders from an army of superior beings, and the hope of ever becoming his own man would be an empty dream.

A hand on his shoulder made him look up. Daniel was standing above him, looking down at him with eyes that revealed his complete understanding of his friend's feelings. "I'm . . . right sorry," he mumbled miserably. "Things shouldn't 've turned out like this fer ye . . ."

Filled with shame at his attack of self-pity, Tom forcibly shook off his dejection. "No, Daniel, don't mind me," he said, getting to his feet and smiling reassuringly. "Being sorry for myself won't buy any barley, as your sensible little wife would be quick to tell me. She seems to have more brains than the two of us together. Well, Betsy, it seems we're going to Dorset. What are your plans, then? Give us our orders, my dear. You're the captain of this voyage."

Betsy threw her arms around him in a grateful hug. Then, clapping her hands happily, she looked at them both with eyes shining in excited anticipation. "If I'm to be captain," she said, laughing, "my first order is to warn you, Tom, to stop usin' all that mariner's talk. Next, I say we should all go to sleep, fer there's nothin' more we can do tonight. We'll be able to think better after we've rested. Dan'l, you and Tom take the bed. I'll fix myself a pallet on the hearth—"

"Not on your life," Tom interrupted, grinning. "I'll obey your orders on almost anything, Betsy, but not on this. You and Daniel take the bed. I'll do very

well on the hay in the loft outside. Good night to you both." And with a wink at
his friend, he wrapped his blanket about him and fled.

Betsy proved more than equal to the task of organizing their departure. First
thing next morning, she had them pool their resources. Betsy had managed to
save—after months of slaving in the taproom—only a meager pile of coins, and
Tom, having left the *Triton* so abruptly, had only a few shillings in the pocket of
his coat. But Daniel had sewn into his coat lining the twenty pounds which the
paymaster had given him before his departure from the *Triton*. Betsy decided
that most of the money had to be spent on clothing. "We ain't likely to get posts
as respectable servants if we look like shabby beggars," she informed them.

To avoid arousing suspicion while they prepared themselves for the trip to
Dorset, the men kept hidden in the stable while Betsy took steps to procure the
items of clothing they would need. First she informed her employers at the
Crown and Cloves that she was leaving to live with distant relatives until her
child was born. Then, quite openly, she ordered a warm and amply cut gown for
herself from a seamstress in Twyford. An extra few shillings convinced the woman
to set aside her other work and stitch up the dress as soon as possible. Meanwhile,
Betsy unobtrusively made her way by cart, wagon and shank's mare to the town of
Winchester to buy clothing for the men. She waited until dark to make her way
back, and her husband was in a state of considerable agitation by the time she slipped
back into the room. "Where've ye been, woman?" he almost shouted when he saw
her safe. "Ye had me fearin' you'd been trampled by a horse or worse!"

"Hush, ye great looby, do ye want them t' hear ye in the taproom? I had to
wait 'til dark so no one'd see me carryin' these parcels. I'm fine, as ye can see.
And just wait 'til ye glimpse what I've bought fer ye."

The packages were eagerly unwrapped, and the merriment was hard to contain as they watched Daniel struggle into a pair of almost-new buff-colored
breeches which were much too tight for him. But they all roared aloud when
Tom stood before them fully dressed. The coat Betsy had purchased for him had
been cut for a much shorter man. The waist was too high, and his wrists hung
from the sleeves like those of a fifteen-year-old youth who'd grown too quickly.
And the high-crowned, curly-brimmed top hat she'd purchased, while certainly
fit for a gentleman, fit him not at all. It was so large that it slipped down over his
ears. The entire effect of his altered appearance in those ill-fitting clothes set
them all in stitches. But Betsy sat up all night, letting out the seams of Daniel's
"smalls" and lengthening the sleeves of Tom's new coat. And the next day, after
exchanging Tom's top hat for the low-crowned, soft-brimmed headpiece she'd
bought for Daniel, she was quite pleased with their appearances.

It took one more day for Betsy's dress to be ready, but they looked a very presentable trio when they finally set out, on foot, before the sun had risen the next morning. Daniel was surprisingly gentlemanly in his top hat (which Betsy had made to fit by stuffing paper into the inner hatband), Tom was quite "sporting" in his more informal headgear, and Betsy was neatly demure in her plum-colored kerseymere gown and black bonnet. All their extra linens were packed into one small parcel wrapped in brown paper and tied with a cord, which Tom and Daniel took turns carrying.

By midmorning they reached Winchester, where they boarded the stage bound for Bath. Although they were going only to Deptford—a distance the coach would cover in less than seven hours—they found the ride completely nerve-wracking, for the coach had started out from Southampton, and it seemed to them that every passenger who'd boarded before them was staring at them with suspicion. They disembarked at Deptford, however, without any untoward incident having occurred. In joyful relief, they squandered a large portion of their meager funds on a substantial dinner and lodgings at a respectable inn. And the next morning, after a whispered conference over the breakfast table, they decided to throw what remained of their finances into hiring a private carriage to take them the rest of the way to Wyckfield Park.

The carriage ride was a merry one, for the privacy was heady luxury. There was no one aboard to stare into their faces or eye their makeshift clothing with suspicion. Their spirits rose to dizzy heights as they laughed and joked and made optimistic predictions about their futures. "My uncle'll be delighted t' see us, don't ye think, Betsy, love?" Daniel asked. "He always like me as a boy. Tossed me up in the air and pinched my cheek . . ."

"I'm certain he'll be glad t' see you, my dear." His wife smiled confidently. "By tonight, we'll be comfortably moved into neat bedrooms, an' we'll be havin' our supper in a nice, warm kitchen with the rest o' the staff, all smilin' and friendly."

No cloud could be envisioned to dim their bright prospects. Betsy was convinced they were embarked on a promising new path. She painted a glowing picture of how she imagined their new mistress would be: a sweet, generous lady who'd be delighted that her new maid was with child, and who'd kindly provide a midwife to see her through the birthing safely. Daniel dreamed of the small apartment they would be given all for themselves, and of the kitchen gardens and the ample grounds where the child would be permitted to run and play quite freely.

Betsy and Daniel together made predictions even for *Tom's* future. Tom, because of his gentlemanly speech, would soon be promoted to the favored post of gentleman's gentleman. Tom laughed at the absurdity and acted out a comical pantomime in which he attempted to tie an impatient gentleman's neckcloth with staggering ineptitude. By keeping everyone laughing, he was able to mask, even to some extent from himself, the despair with which his altered prospects had overwhelmed his spirit.

The ride was briefer than they'd expected. By midmorning they'd arrived at the impressive gates of Wyckfield Park. They quickly sobered at the sight. Ordering the coachman to set them down just outside the gates, they climbed from the carriage and trudged along the drive leading to the great house. Silently, with unspoken fears beginning to hammer away at their previous optimism, they made their way round to the kitchen door. Before knocking, the men removed their hats, and Betsy nervously looked them over. She straightened Daniel's neckcloth, picked a piece of lint from Tom's shoulder and nodded. Daniel stepped forward and, with a deep breath, knocked firmly at the door.

It was opened by a plump, fuzzy-haired woman in a very large, stiffly starched white apron and neat cap. "Yes?" she asked, eyebrows raised.

Betsy dropped a quick curtsey. "Beg pardon, ma'am," she said politely, "but we was wonderin' if we could see Mr. Hicks."

The woman, taking note of their dusty shoes and strained expressions, looked at them with a twinge of sympathy. "Mr. Hicks? I'm sorry to have to disappoint you, but he ain't here no more. He's gone off to London, he has, not a se'ennight since. An' he ain't expected back."

Chapter Four

For three days following Camilla's announcement of her intention to leave Wyckfield Park for London, a painful war had ensued. Ethelyn had subjected her sister-in-law to a most trying ordeal, attacking Camilla repeatedly with every weapon of persuasion or coercion available to her. There had been hours of argument, during which Ethelyn described London as a place of vice and iniquity, declaring it to be completely unsuitable for a woman of Camilla's sensitivity and sheltered background, "and positively *unfit* for a child like Philippa!"

When the arguments had proved ineffective, Ethelyn had resorted to shouts, demands, threats, and even a shocking and most uncharacteristic flood of tears. Finally she'd taken to her bed, accusing Camilla of driving her to death's door. But Camilla, through it all, had remained adamant. Once she'd breathed the whiff of freedom . . . once she'd realized that escape from the repressive confines of her sister-in-law's domination was possible . . . once she had permitted herself to believe that a new life was within her grasp, she couldn't turn away from the joyful prospect.

Patiently, and with a quiet steadfastness that was as surprising to Ethelyn as it was irritating, Camilla tried to bring her sister-in-law to a calm acceptance of the inevitable separation. She explained that her decision to move to London was not a sign of depravity. They would choose a house in a quiet neighborhood. They would not indulge in hectic socializing but would keep very much to themselves. But they *would* avail themselves of the many cultural and artistic activities that London offered—the museums, the libraries, the opera, the shops and the parks. Pippa needed more intellectual stimulation than she could find in the country. "And I myself," she added gently, "need to get away from these surroundings which remind me so much of . . . of death and mourning."

Ethelyn remained unconvinced, but she was powerless to force her sister-in-law to accede to her will. Camilla was, after all, twenty-nine years old and possessed of more-than-adequate means. What Ethelyn would have found consoling would have been to remove Philippa from her mother's guardianship. She'd even consulted the family solicitor about the possibility. But there were no legal grounds on which they could build a case. Ethelyn, being female, had no stronger claim to the guardianship than the child's mother. If only she'd thought about it before her brother had died, she could have persuaded him to place the guardianship in Oswald's hands. Now, of course, it was too late . . .

Ethelyn had never set foot in London in her life and therefore despised the place with the unshakable conviction of prejudiced ignorance. She'd heard enough lurid tales and gossip to convince her that it was as iniquitous as Sodom, and she warned Camilla that she would never, as long as she lived, set foot in her sister-in-law's London establishment. "So you needn't expect any visits from *me!*" she warned. "Although I shall be willing to welcome you here. I shall expect you for all the important religious observances, of course, and for the warm-weather months as well." She fixed an eye on Camilla coldly. "And when you've realized that I am right about the unsuitability of those surroundings for your daughter, you will, of course, send her promptly home to me."

Camilla, who had chosen London as the locus of their new home for precisely the reason that Ethelyn never would visit there, merely lowered her eyes and kept silent. She'd won the war; there would be little harm in letting Ethelyn believe she'd won a small part of this last battle.

When they realized they'd been victorious, Camilla, Pippa and Miss Townley gathered behind the closed door of Camilla's bedroom and hugged each other in unrestrained elation. The future was suddenly wide open with exciting possibilities. "What wonderful adventures we'll have!" Pippa exclaimed, whirling about the room deliriously. "It will be like living a *novel!*"

Her mother tried to restrain the child's imagination from running riot. "It certainly will *not,*" she said, trying to frown. "We shall live in quiet modesty, just as we always have." But her imagination was scarcely less riotous than her daughter's, and she concluded her reprimand by lifting the child in her arms and spinning her about until, laughing and breathless, they both fell dizzily upon the bed.

While waiting to hear from Hicks that a house had been found and made ready for them, the three hurled themselves into a frenzy of packing. Besides their clothing and personal effects, there were some paintings, household articles, pieces of furniture and a great number of books which Camilla had purchased over the years that, if Ethelyn should not object, she wished to take with her. The next few days were spent going over lists of these items with her sour-faced sister-in-law and setting aside those things which Ethelyn agreed could be removed. Later, Miss Townley and Camilla packed the articles carefully with their own hands, and often with Pippa's assistance. It was the only activity which seemed to ease their impatience to be gone.

For Pippa, the waiting was almost unbearable. With typical childish avidity, she chaffed at the delay as day followed day without a word from the butler. "Why doesn't he write?" she asked nightly, when her mother tucked her into bed. "Why does it take so long to find a house?"

After several days, Camilla decided it was best to make it clear to the child that buying a house was not a task that could be easily concluded in a short time. "It's only been a week, dearest," she said soothingly. "We'll hear from Hicks before long."

"Yes, but *when?* A day? A week? A fortnight?"

"I don't know. Perhaps even longer."

Pippa winced. "*Longer?* Oh, no! I don't think I could *bear* it!"

"But why not, my love? You've lived here all your life in perfect contentment. Why does the prospect of spending a few more weeks under this roof seem suddenly unbearable to you?"

"I don't know," Pippa answered thoughtfully. "Perhaps it's because I never expected any sort of change before." She gave her mother a sudden, mischievous grin. "Now that I have the prospect of adventures, I just can't wait for them to begin to happen!"

"Oh, my *dearest*," Camilla admitted, enveloping the girl in a warm embrace, "neither can I!"

It was midmorning of the very next day that Mrs. Nyles, the fuzzy-haired cook, stood in the kitchen doorway staring interestedly at a trio of travelers who seemed inordinately disappointed at the news that Mr. Hicks had gone. The three, who'd introduced themselves as Betsy and Daniel Hicks and their friend Collinson, were gaping at her as if she'd announced the end of the world. "Ye've come a long way, I wager, and all for naught," the cook murmured sympathetically, tucking a crimped lock of hair under her cap. "Come in an' have a spot o' tea with me. It'll cheer ye som'at to rest yerselves a bit."

Betsy, the elected captain of this ill-fated expedition, tried to push aside her feeling of despair as she nodded gratefully. Mrs. Nyles seemed a woman of hearty good nature, and she and her companions needed to sit themselves down and think. They'd foolishly squandered all their money and were now stranded in the middle of Dorset with no resources and no plan. Why had they never even *considered* what to do if the first plan failed?

Mrs. Nyles ushered them into a huge, square kitchen, brightly lit by the

October sunshine streaming in through a row of windows in the south wall. The wall adjoining the windows contained two large ovens and an immense fireplace, and in the corner opposite was an open stairway which they surmised led up to the main part of the house. The cook led them to a long table in the center of the room and, as soon as they were seated, turned to two young kitchen maids who were lolling near the fire and ordered them into action. As the maids set plates and cups before the visitors, Mrs. Nyles took a seat beside Betsy and looked her over interestedly. "Did ye wish t' see Mr. Hicks fer some partic'lar reason?" she asked, turning away only to slice a loaf of bread, which one of the maids had set before her.

"Oh, yes," Betsy admitted, eyeing the large loaf, the wedge of cheddar cheese, the platter of cold, sliced ham and the basket full of warm raisin buns, which the maids set on the table, "he's my husband's uncle, y' see."

"His uncle, eh? My, my." Mrs. Nyles leaned toward Daniel and looked at him closely for a family resemblance. "Now you mention it, I mind as how he sometimes spoke of a nevvy he had as was a sailor. Is that you?"

Daniel cast Tom an uneasy glance, but Betsy covered quickly. "No, no," she said hastily. "Ye're thinkin' of his . . . er . . . brother."

"Right," Daniel said, nodding earnestly. "My brother. He's at sea."

"Ah, yes. Well, Mr. Hicks'll be sorry he missed ye, I'm sure."

"Not nearly as sorry as we are," Tom muttered.

Mrs. Nyles looked at him curiously. There was nothing she liked better than an opportunity for idle gossip. "Did ye have somethin' special ye wanted to see him about?" she asked, pouring out the tea.

Tom hesitated, but Betsy nodded frankly. "We was hopin' he could find us places here at Wyckfield Park," she admitted, hoping desperately that the friendly seeming cook could be of help. "I've had some years as a . . . a housemaid, y' see, and these two strong fellows could be of all sorts of use—"

"Ye weren't expectin' *Mr. Hicks* to find you places here, were ye?" The cook snorted in scornful amusement. "Ye're way out, if that's what ye come for."

The two kitchen maids, lingering about behind her and eyeing the two men covetously, giggled loudly.

Mrs. Nyles turned round. "What're ye doin' hangin' about here?" She swung her arm at them, catching one a good cuff at the hip. "Get about yer duties, both of ye!" The maids scurried off under Mrs. Nyles's glare. When they'd vanished, she sighed and shook her head. "Impudent snips! They'd rather stand about gossipin' than do anythin' else. If there's anythin' I can't abide, it's a lazy tittle-tattle."

"But, Mrs. Nyles, I don't understand why you all laughed," Betsy said, confused. "Mr. Hicks *is* the butler here, ain't he?"

"He *was* the butler. But her ladyship—Lady Ethelyn Falcombe, y' know—wouldn't never take on nobody of *his* recommendin'." She turned in her chair and leaned toward Betsy in eager confidentiality. "She never could abide him, y' know. If it wasn't fer the young Lady Wyckfield, Lady Ethelyn would've let him go years past."

"Are you saying that he's been given the *sack?*" Tom asked.

"In a manner o' speakin' he has."

"It's a fine kettle o' fish we're in," Daniel groaned, dropping his chin on his hand gloomily.

Tom studied the cook with a puzzled frown. "What do you mean, 'in a manner of speakin''? Has Mr. Hicks been sacked or hasn't he?"

"He still works fer the younger Lady Wyckfield. He's gone to find her a house in town. She's movin' away, y' see."

"And he won't be comin' back here?" Betsy queried.

"Not him. Swore he'd never set foot in this house again, he did. It was a reg'lar to-do he had with her ladyship afore he left, I can tell ye."

"Then we are in the soup an' no mistake," Betsy said, stirring her tea dispiritedly.

"Perhaps not." Tom eyed the cook speculatively. "Are you saying that Mr. Hicks is setting up a household for Lady Wyckfield in London? Won't he have to hire a number of servants to staff it?"

Mrs. Nyles's eyebrows rose delightedly. "O' *course!*" she exclaimed, clapping a hand to her forehead. "What a *codshead* I am! He'll need t' find parlormaids, an' a groom, an' footmen, an' a cook, an' all manner of help."

"That's right," Daniel chortled in relief. "He'll have a real *need* fer us."

"But Dan'l," Betsy murmured, frowning worriedly, "London . . . ?"

Daniel blinked. He'd completely forgotten the necessity for hiding. Would they be safe among the crowded masses of the city where, it was said, all roads cross? He looked over at Tom questioningly.

Tom shrugged. "I'd be willing to chance it, if you are," he murmured in an undervoice. "Now all we have to do is find the wherewithal to get there."

Daniel sagged in his chair. Life was one problem after the other. "That's the facer, ain't it?"

Mrs. Nyles looked from one to the other. "What's worryin' ye now?" she asked in her direct, curious way.

"We used all our blunt to get here," Betsy explained. "How are we to get to London without a shillin' in our pockets?"

"Is *that* all that troubles ye?" She got to her feet and, smiling broadly, went to the fire for the kettle. "Ye can catch a ride with my Henry. He's the coachman, y' see, an' he's settin' off this very afternoon to deliver some boxes fer Lady

Wyckfield to the new house. She got word this mornin' that Mr. Hicks has found a place on—where did she say?—Upper Seymour Street, if I remember rightly." She poured the boiling water into the teapot, feeling quite pleased with herself. "There, y' see?" She beamed at them, clapping Daniel on the shoulder with enthusiasm. "Ye haven't a care in the world. Now ye can drink yer tea without wearin' them long faces."

With the seemingly insoluble problem so easily dispensed with, the three travelers set upon the food before them with hearty appetites. Mrs. Nyles smiled encouragement and pressed them to refill their plates as often as they wished. It was not often she could welcome congenial visitors to her table, and she revelled in the opportunity to reveal tidbits of household gossip to strangers who hadn't heard the tales before. With an innate sense of the dramatic, she began to regale them with a detailed account of Lady Ethelyn's eleven-year battle with Mr. Hicks. She started with their initial encounter (a scene which Mrs. Nyles had been privileged to witness with her own eyes) when they'd taken an instant dislike to each other, and, providing her amused and fascinated listeners with almost verbatim accounts of the numerous altercations which followed, was just approaching her rendition of the final confrontation when her voice suddenly faded. With mouth open, she gaped up at the stairway in the corner of the kitchen. Her three guests, surprised at her change of expression, turned in the direction of her stare.

Coming down the stairs, her eyes fixed on a long sheet of paper in her hand, was a youngish woman whose appearance set Tom's pulse racing. She was slim as the stem of a seaweed, with a slightly pointed chin and a pale complexion. A mane of silky, light auburn hair was carelessly tied in a knot at the top of her head, but many strands spilled over her forehead in what Tom felt was enchanting disarray. Her face was smudged with dust, as was the voluminous apron which covered her dress. With her attention focussed on the paper she held, he couldn't see her eyes, but the hand which held lightly onto the banister to guide her down was as graceful as a gull. "Mrs. Nyles," she was saying in a soft, musical voice, "I wonder if you'd mind going over this list of equipment with me. Hicks writes that the kitchen in the London house is sadly lacking in—*oh!*"

Her eyes, as she looked up in startled embarrassment, were, Tom thought, beautifully dark in that pale face. "*Lord!*" he gasped, getting to his feet and moving trancelike toward the stairs, "someone should have told me household service could be like this!"

"*What?*" the woman on the stairs asked, blinking down at him in confusion.

A strangled gurgle came from deep within Mrs. Nyles's throat.

"The name is Tom," he said, taking her hand and helping her down the last two steps, "and I was saying that if I'd known there were housemaids like you on the premises, I should have entered service years ago." He grinned down at her, amused and delighted by her complete astonishment. He put one hand on the banister and the other on the wall, thus quite effectively preventing her from being able to move away from him.

"*Told* you that he'd like it," Daniel chortled, delighted at seeing his friend involved in a flirtation.

"Hush, Dain'l," Betsy murmured, an instinct warning her that something was wrong. "The poor lass looks frightened."

"Frightened?" Tom asked, glancing at Betsy over his shoulder. "Don't be foolish. I mean her no harm." Looking back at his prisoner, he took her chin in his hand. "You aren't afraid of me, are you, girl? Surely every fellow for miles about must be after you—and more forcefully than *this*. Why, I haven't even tried to *kiss* you yet."

The astonished woman gasped. "Mrs. Nyles!" she sputtered furiously. "Who *is* this person?"

Mrs. Nyles choked, unable to speak. "I . . . I . . ." she managed in a choking voice, her face reddening alarmingly.

"Go ahead and kiss 'er," Daniel urged, laughing. "There ain't a female in the world wouldn't prefer the deed to the word."

"You're quite right," Tom agreed, slipping an arm about his quarry and pulling her to him.

"Don't you *dare!*" the woman exclaimed in a voice of unmistakable authority. "I realize you've mistaken my identity, but even a *maid* ought to be safe in the kitchen of this house!"

Tom's grin faded. "Mistaken your identity?" he asked, his eyes narrowing.

"Oh, *heavens,*" Mrs. Nyles cried, finding her voice at last. "I'm so . . . I d-didn't *dream* . . . oh, yer *ladyship,* I—"

"Your *ladyship?*" Betsy gasped.

Daniel choked and Tom whitened. Dropping his hold, he backed away from her aghast.

"Yes, I'm Lady Wyckfield," Camilla said furiously. "And *who,* may I ask, are you?"

The three strangers, utterly confounded, stood rooted in their places. Mrs. Nyles rose from her chair and approached her mistress fearfully. "I don't know *how* t' apologize, your ladyship," she mumbled. "They're r-relations of Mr. Hicks, y' see, an'—"

"Relations of Hicks's? I don't believe it!" her ladyship said, looking at them sternly.

"It's true, ma'am," Daniel said, stepping forward with head lowered abjectly. "He's my uncle."

"*Is* he indeed! Well, he won't be very pleased with you when I report to him how you comported yourselves in my kitchen!"

"No, ma'am, he won't," Betsy said miserably. "We're dreadful ashamed. We never meant no harm, though. It was the apron, y' see."

"I see quite well. Is it your habit, young man, to accost everyone who wears an apron in that *libertinish* style?"

Tom, recovered from his initial shock at learning her identity, began to find the entire scene very amusing. "Not *every* one, my lady," he said, his lips twitching. "Only the very prettiest ones, I assure you."

"*Tom!*" Betsy protested in a hissing whisper.

Camilla flushed in irritation. "Oh, you find this incident amusing, do you?" she snapped. "You'd do better, fellow, to recognize the depravity of your character and attempt to mend your ways." *Good heavens,* she thought, surprised, *I sound just like Ethelyn.*

"Depravity, ma'am?" Tom regarded her with an irrepressible glint of humor. "If a pinch on the chin is depraved to you, you must be leading a saintly life. However, I'll try to mend my ways if you'll tell me how to go about it."

She frowned at him, not knowing what to make of his unchastened manner. "For one thing," she declared repressively, "you can try to show some sincere *regret*—"

"Am I *not* showing it? I assure you, ma'am, that I'm positively awash in regret."

"One would scarcely notice it," she said suspiciously. "But if you are *truly* sorry for that lecherous behavior, it's at least a beginning."

"Oh, it's not my *behavior* I'm sorry for, ma'am. It's my *lack* of it."

Something in his eyes told her that she would make no headway bandying words with him, but somehow she went on with it. "Lack of it? I don't understand."

He grinned broadly. "What I'm sorry for is that I didn't kiss you when I had the chance—before I found out who you were."

"*Tom!*" Betsy cried, appalled.

Tom kept his eyes on the lady's face. "Now, you see, my chance is gone forever."

"What I *see,* young man, is that you're quite incorrigible!" She gathered up her skirts and turned to mount the stairs. "I suggest, Mrs. Nyles, that you rid yourself of your 'guests' as soon as possible. When they've gone, please come up to the sitting room to go over this list with me. In the meantime, I hope you will make it clear to these . . . persons . . . that they will not be made welcome in this kitchen ever again!" With that, she marched up the stairs without a backward look and disappeared from view.

There was a moment of stunned silence in the kitchen. Then Mrs. Nyles stalked up to Tom and swatted him smartly on his backside. "You jackanapes! A fine stew ye've got me into!"

"Y' should've told us," Betsy piped up in his defense. "How was he to know?"

"Was *that* Lady Ethelyn?" Daniel asked. "Will she take it out on *you,* Mrs. Nyles, like she did on my uncle Hicks?"

Mrs. Nyles hooted scornfully. "Oh, no, don't worry yer head about *that.* It was only Lady Wyckfield. Camilla, y' know. She's the soft one."

"Camilla," Tom mumbled, staring up at the stairway. "Lovely name. Suits her."

Mrs. Nyles struck him another blow. "Never mind her name, ye great looby! That tongue o' yours'll get ye in fat trouble one o' these days."

She turned away and began busily to clear the table. Betsy, meanwhile, paced about before the fireplace. "Good God!" she exclaimed suddenly. "If that was the *other* lady . . . then *she's* the one goin' to be mistress of the London house!"

"My Lord!" Daniel stared at her in dawning alarm. "Ye mean—?"

Tom groaned and dropped into a chair, struck all at once with shame. "She means that, because of me, Mr. Hicks will never be able to hire us now."

Wordlessly, his friends sank down beside him. This latest blow was too great to permit them even to utter words of consolation to him. The last of the spirit that had sustained them all day deserted them, and they were aware only of the dire hopelessness of their situation.

Mrs. Nyles, crossing from the table to the larder with the leftovers, paused and squinted at them. "Why are ye sittin' about like three stones fer a passerby t' trip over?" she demanded. As far as she was concerned, the incident with her ladyship had been a momentary embarrassment and had passed without causing any permanent harm. She gave it no further thought. "My Henry'll be leavin' without ye if ye don't take yerselves over to the stables."

"No use goin' to London now," Betsy said, unable to keep her unshed tears from showing in her voice.

"No use?" Mrs. Nyles, stowing away the food, wrinkled her brow in confusion. "Why ever not?"

"Didn't ye hear what Tom just said?" Daniel asked morosely. "My uncle won't be able t' take us on now."

"Ye mean because of what just passed?" Mrs. Nyles strode back to them and, taking a stance in the middle of the room, glared at them with arms akimbo. "You three fall more easy into low tide than anyone ought! Don't make so much over nothin'. Just ferget all about that meetin' with her ladyship and go about yer business."

"Ferget it?" Betsy asked. "Ye can't mean it."

"O' course I mean it! Don't even think on it no more."

"But Mr. Hicks would never—"

"I wouldn't even *mention* it to Mr. Hicks, if I was you."

"Not mention it?" Betsy eyed the mettlesome cook dubiously. "But if he should engage us, and then the lady sees us, what then?"

"She won't even remember you, most likely. By tomorrow, she won't remember yer faces, and by the next day she'll have fergot the whole affair."

"Do ye really think so?" Daniel asked, his eyes brightening hopefully.

"I'm fair certain. Do y' think the lady has nothin' better on her mind than the likes o' *you?* Get along to the stables, now, afore ye miss my Henry altogether."

She shooed them cheerfully toward the door, fluttering her apron after them as if they were a brood of chickens.

"We don't know how t' thank ye, Mrs. Nyles, fer all yer kindnesses," Betsy said at the door. "We shan't ever forget ye."

Daniel leaned down and kissed the cook's cheek. "No, we shan't. We don't forget as easy as some."

"If it's her ladyship ye mean," Mrs. Nyles retorted with spirit, thwacking him on the arm with a combination of affection and reprimand, "she don't ferget the things she oughtn't. Ye should feel glad that y' ain't important enough fer her to remember. An' you, too, ye lummox," she added to Tom, swatting him on the backside for good measure.

Tom made a mock outcry of pain and rubbed his rear tenderly. Then, just before taking off after his friends down the path to the stables, he gave her a saucy grin. "It may be that her ladyship'll forget us, and it may be she won't," he tossed back, laughing, "but if I'd have kissed her, she'd have remembered me right enough!"

Chapter Five

$\mathcal{M}$r. Hicks was feeling nervous. It was a most unusual feeling for him; he was not the nervous sort at all. But today, for the first time in all the years he'd worked for Miss Camilla, he was conscious of strong pangs of insecurity and guilt. He and Miss Camilla had always been straight with each other, but now he was about to play her false.

He frowned resentfully at the three troublemakers lined up stiffly before him awaiting his inspection. *Damn* his nephew for placing this awkward situation in his lap! "Let's have a look at your fingernails," he barked irritably.

The three of them stuck out their hands, and Hicks gave them all a thorough inspection. "Very good. Now, stand up straight and let me make certain you look presentable."

If he hadn't been told the lurid tale that lay hidden behind the innocent faces they presented to the world, he'd have had to admit that their appearances were perfectly satisfactory. Collinson, his nephew's friend, was tall and quite prepossessing now that his lightish hair had been properly cut. Daniel, although perhaps a bit too stocky to make an ideal footman, was nevertheless strong and capable. And Betsy was an endearing little puss. Miss Camilla would undoubtedly take a shine to her, especially since she was so modest about the child she was carrying. Betsy had used good sense in decking herself out, for the dark, plum-colored dress she wore lay quite neatly over her swelling belly, and, although it didn't completely hide her condition, it didn't call undue attention to it either. Hicks would have been proud to recommend all three to Miss Camilla, if only he didn't have to hide from her the dark facts of their recent history.

If it weren't for his fond memory of his dead brother, Daniel's father, he'd never do it. As sympathetic as he was to their plight (for no one who'd ever heard an account of a victim of a press-gang could blame them for what they'd done—

not if he had a heart in his chest), he never, in ordinary circumstances, would get himself into a situation in which he'd have to lie to Miss Camilla. But these circumstances were different. Daniel was his only remaining relation—his own flesh and blood. Without his help, poor Daniel and his friend might even end up on the gibbet!

If only he didn't have to lie. But the two men had no letters of commendation and no one at all to vouch for them. So he, who had never before said or done a dishonest thing to his mistress, had concocted a fabric of lies and deceits to legitimize their backgrounds. And while one part of him was glad to assist them to start a new life, the other part writhed in remorse and guilt.

But there was nothing to be gained in dwelling on the matter. He'd made up his mind to recommend them, and he would go through with it, nervous or not. More than half-a-dozen candidates for posts on the household staff of Miss Camilla's new abode were probably already awaiting him in the corridor outside Miss Camilla's rooms in the Fenton Hotel. There was very little time left to make certain all would go well. "Let's get on with it," he muttered, looking them over with a last, critical appraisal. "Let's go over our stories once more, before we leave for the Fenton. Remember, I'll present you to her ladyship, and then she'll ask you a few questions. Shall we try it out? I'll be her ladyship. Let's say I turn to you first, Thomas. Step forward."

"A giant step or a baby step?" Tom asked, teasing.

"No levity, if you don't mind, Thomas," Hicks said reprovingly. "Remember that a footman attempts to be invisible and inaudible unless otherwise required."

"Invisible and inaudible, yes, sir," Thomas said agreeably.

"I am not 'sir,' I told you. I'm *Mr. Hicks* to the staff!" He rolled his grizzled eyebrows heavenward to beg for stamina. "May the Lord grant me the patience to deal with these loobies. Now, Thomas, I'm her ladyship, and I turn to you and say, 'What's your name, my good man?' "

"Thomas Collinson, your ladyship."

"And where did you work before?"

"I was underfootman to Dr. Newton Plumb of Derbyshire."

"And why haven't you a letter of commendation?"

"Because the fellow died before I could get one."

Hicks groaned and stamped his foot in annoyance. "Because the 'gentleman' *passed on* without warning and didn't make arrangements for your future, you idiot!"

"Sorry," Tom said with an abashed grin. "I didn't think I had to use those exact words."

"Well, you *do*, so let's hear 'em. Why haven't you a letter?"

Tom straightened, took on a stiff, footmanlike impassivity and repeated obediently, "Because the gentleman passed on without warning, your ladyship, and didn't make any arrangements for my future."

"Very well. And now you, fellow. Your name, please?"

"Daniel Hicks, ma'am."

"And your last employer?"

"I was gardener to the same gentleman as Thomas, here."

"Right. And therefore you couldn't get a letter either. As for you, Betsy Hicks, do *you* have a letter from your last employer?"

"Yes, ma'am, here it is."

"Good." He dropped the aloof manner and shook a warning finger at Betsy. "Now, girl, remember that since the letter says nothing about your last establishment being an inn, you needn't *volunteer* the information that you were a barmaid. But if Miss Camilla should ask, tell the truth. There's no use in lying more than absolutely necessary."

"Yes, sir."

"Yes, *Mr. Hicks!* How many times must I remind you? I'm not your master. And the same goes for Miss Townley. But be sure you always call Miss Camilla 'your ladyship' or 'my lady' or 'ma'am.'"

"Then how is it, Uncle, that ye call 'er Miss Camilla?" Daniel asked.

"Because I've known her since she was a babe. And, to speak the truth, I shouldn't call her that either. I only kept it up to spite Lady Ethelyn. It's a terrible habit with me now. But Daniel, how many times must I remind you not to call me Uncle? It must be *Mr. Hicks* at all times, so you fall into the habit of it."

"Aye, aye, Uncle," Daniel agreed readily.

Tom chortled, but Hicks groaned in irritation. *"Yes, Mr. Hicks!"* he corrected angrily, glaring at Tom for laughing. "Those aye-ayes'll give you both away one of these days. Silly tomdoodles, both of you!"

"Don't be nervous, Uncle," Betsy murmured comfortingly, coming up to him and planting a kiss on his cheek. "We won't joke in front of her ladyship, I promise." She gave Tom a reproving, meaningful look. "Isn't that right, Tom?"

"Aye, that's right, my dear. I'll be so inaudible and invisible that her ladyship'll think I'm only a piece of furniture."

"Me, too, Uncle," Daniel promised.

Hicks sighed deeply. Somehow he knew that the afternoon was going to be a terrible ordeal. He felt it in his bones.

Camilla had taken rooms in the Fenton on St. James Street so that she could oversee the final steps required to ready the house for their occupancy. The suite had two bedrooms (one for Pippa and Miss Townley and the other for herself) and a large sitting room. It was there that Hicks (who himself was already ensconced in the new house) was bringing the various candidates whom he'd chosen to make up the household staff. Camilla had permitted Pippa to run off to explore the neighborhood in the company of Miss Townley, while she herself was occupied with this household business.

It was a great bore to have to stay inside and interview servants when she could be strolling along the busy thoroughfares of London's most fashionable neighborhood, but Hicks seemed to feel that her approval of his choices was absolutely necessary. As a result, she'd moved a table from behind the sofa to a sunny spot before a pair of windows and taken a seat behind it. In the businesslike manner recommended by Miss Townley, she'd spoken briefly to each candidate Hicks had brought in, nodded her approval and then carefully entered into a large household-ledger book that person's name, the salary Hicks had promised, the name of the former employer and the title of the exact position for which the person had been engaged. It was all a rather mindless ritual, but it seemed to please Hicks greatly.

Camilla knew quite well that this was a futile exercise. Hicks had made his own records of the information she was recording, and Camilla was certain that all his decisions would be beyond reproach. The only thing that had been left to her discretion was the assigning of the rooms where the servants were to sleep, and even that could easily have been done by Hicks without her help. But both Hicks and Miss Townley had felt that the ritual was required in order to impress the staff. Since Camilla had made up her mind to be a firm and respected mistress of her new establishment, she'd agreed to do what was expected of her.

She had already interviewed and approved Hicks's choice of a cook, two parlormaids, a groom, two scullery maids, a gardener and a coachman, all of whom seemed perfectly suitable, and she would have become quite bored with the proceedings except that Hicks seemed increasingly nervous as the afternoon wore on. She wondered what was troubling him, and her curiosity sharpened her perceptions. When he brought in all three final candidates together, rather than one at a time, the change of routine made her suddenly alert. "Yes, Hicks, whom have we here?" she asked with more interest than she'd felt all afternoon.

"The two footmen and the upstairs maid, my lady. This one here and the woman are a couple, and the other fellow is their friend. That's why I've brought them in together. Here's a letter from the lady's former employer."

Camilla scanned the letter quickly. "Betsy *Hicks?*" she asked with a smile. "Are these people related to you, Hicks?"

He reddened. "Daniel, here, is my nephew, your ladyship."

"Is *that* why you've seemed so uncomfortable?" Camilla smiled in relief. "Did you think I would disapprove of your hiring your relations? You needn't worry on that score, Hicks. I don't mind at all. In fact, if your nephew is half as valuable to me as you've been, I shall be more than satisfied."

"Thank you, Miss Camilla," Hicks said, feeling more guilty than ever.

"Is your name Daniel? Why is there no letter here about you, Daniel?"

Daniel colored. "Well . . . y' see I was . . . er . . . gardener for . . . er . . . Dr. Newton Plumb of Derbyshire . . . an' he passed away sudden-like, y'see . . ."

Hicks felt like giving the slow-top a kick in his rear. "Dr. Plumb passed on before giving a thought to the future of any of his domestics," he offered in quick collaboration, throwing his nephew a look of annoyance.

"Oh, I see. But if Daniel is a gardener, Hicks, is there any special reason why you've made him a footman?"

"A couple of reasons, ma'am. One is that if he works indoors, he'll be close enough to his missus to be able to give her a hand with the heavy work when her time comes near. She's having a baby, you may have noticed. And second, he's worked close with this other fellow, back there, so I've kept them together."

"Very well, Hicks, you know best in these matters. I shall give your Daniel and his Betsy the corner room on the third floor. It's the most adequate room for a couple, I think, and shall afford them some privacy. And, Betsy, I believe it is large enough to be able to accommodate a cradle when you need it."

"Oh, *thank* you, my lady," Betsy murmured, bobbing gratefully.

"In the meantime, Hicks, you must be sure Betsy isn't given work which is too heavy for her, even if her husband *is* nearby."

"Yes, my lady. I had that in mind when I made her upstairs maid. So long as he does the fireplaces for her, she'll easily manage the rest."

"Good." Camilla made the appropriate entries in her ledger and then looked up at the third member of the group, who was hanging back in the shadows. "And what is the name of the other footman, Hicks?"

"Collinson, ma'am. Thomas Collinson," the butler answered.

"And he has no letter either?"

Hicks motioned with his head for Tom to step forward and speak his piece, but Tom hung back. Hicks clenched his fists in fury. "Since he was employed by the same Dr. Plumb, he's faced with the same problem," he responded, almost twitching with irritation at having to lie again, and without the assistance of the fellow who, more than the others, stood to gain from the subterfuge.

"Were you footman for this Dr. Plumb, Thomas?" Camilla asked, squinting into the shadows.

"Yes, my lady," he answered in almost a whisper.

"You needn't be afraid to speak up, fellow. Step forward, please. You seem to be unduly shy for a footman."

Tom took a step forward. "Not shy, ma'am. I'm just—" A glare from Hicks reminded him of his instructions to keep his answers as brief as possible, so he clamped his mouth shut. *A footman should attempt to be invisible and inaudible,* he reminded himself.

"You're just what, Thomas?" Camilla encouraged, looking at him curiously.

"Just self-effacing, as a footman should be," he responded, unable to treat the situation with proper seriousness. He couldn't seem to take any of what had happened to him in the past week seriously. He seemed to be living in some limbo-like state between the reality of his shipboard life and a nebulous future which he couldn't fathom. This footman business was somehow unreal—an enormous joke that life was playing on him, a temporary aberration that would right itself somehow . . . and some day soon. He couldn't *really* spend his life doing household service. Carrying wood for the fireplace, polishing silver, dressing up in livery to answer a door—those things were not serious work. They were parts of a children's game, like playing house. A man had to do the *real* work of the world—soldiering, or building roads, or sailing a vessel across an ocean.

Something of his inner feelings must have shown in the tone of his voice, because he became aware of Daniel's worried glance and a flashing glare from the eyes of the elderly butler, whose neck was growing red. Embarrassed, he tried to back surreptitiously into the shadows again.

But Lady Wyckfield (who was looking even more lovely than he remembered, sitting there in front of the windows with the sunlight etching magical highlights in her hair) was staring at him with an arrested look. Something in the ironic tone of his answer had triggered her memory. For a moment everything seemed to hang suspended—each person in the room watching unmoving, her ladyship's hand hanging in the air over her ledger halted on its way to her cheek. Then she blinked and gasped. "Good *God!* It's the *libertine* who accosted me in the *kitchen!*"

Betsy clapped her hands to her mouth in dismay. Daniel gulped. But Hicks could only gape at his mistress in utter confusion. "What's that you're saying, Miss Camilla?"

"Of *course!*" Camilla exclaimed, rising to her feet. "These are the three who came seeking you in Dorset. They invaded the kitchen at Wyckfield Park, and *that one* had the temerity to assault me on the stairs!"

Poor Hicks could scarcely believe his ears. It was bad enough that they were hiding from the authorities for having escaped from impressment, but this latest crime was too much! "Is this true?" he croaked, staring at the trio as if he'd just discovered they were lepers. "How could you have *done* such a thing?"

"It was all a . . . a misunderstandin', ye might say," Daniel mumbled miserably. "I'm truly sorry, Uncle. We thought she was a housemaid."

"Her ladyship a *housemaid?* Are you all *loony?*"

"Well, in fairness, Hicks," Camilla put in, already filled with sympathy for the pregnant girl, who was looking quite stricken, "I *was* wearing an apron—"

But Hicks was beside himself. Already having been functioning on the far edge of nervous balance, he was completely unsettled by this last blow. Hardly aware that he was interrupting his mistress in the middle of a sentence, he shouted, "That's not the least excuse! Any *fool* should be able to see that Miss Camilla is a lady no matter what she wears!" He waved his arms in the air, trying with gestures of frustration to express to each of the three his unmitigated revulsion. "And to think you let me recommend you to her ladyship, knowing all the while that this had taken place and not even telling me a *word*—"

"But, y' see, Uncle," Betsy said, the tears forming in the corners of her eyes, "the c-cook said that her l-ladyship'd never remember—"

"Never *remember?* Never remember being accosted on her own *stairs?*" Hicks, almost apoplectic, turned away in speechless chagrin.

Betsy came up behind him, the tears spilling down her cheeks. "Please, Uncle," she whispered tremulously, "don't take on so. We're terrible sorry . . ."

"Aye," Daniel sighed hopelessly, "we never meant to—"

"What good are your sorrys?" the old man burst out. "I can never face Miss Camilla again with my head up."

"Can't you now!" Tom snorted in sudden and violent disgust. "We've made you lose face, have we? What a terrible pass we've pushed you to. Perhaps we should all fall on our swords, like the Romans, or disembowel ourselves in shame, like the Orientals." He strode across the room and placed himself squarely in front of Camilla. "Put an end to this muddle, ma'am. Tell the old fellow you're not put out with him, and let him proceed with hiring his relations. *I* was the only one to blame in all this. I'll go at once and permit the rest of you to get on with your business."

He turned and started for the door, but Daniel blocked the way. "Shut up, can't ye?" he muttered in an angry whisper. "Y' ain't the mate here, y' know."

"I'm sorry, Daniel, but I've no patience with all this. I don't think I'm cut out for household service. You and Betsy'll do better without me."

"Well, we ain't goin' to do without ye. We've stood up together, an' we'll fall together. Come on, Betsy, we'd best take ourselves off."

"I tell you, there's no need to give up a good place," Tom insisted. "I'll find something—"

"I said no," Daniel retorted. "We been through this afore, an' ye know my feelin's. Come on, Betsy."

But Betsy, whose past experiences working for selfish and thoughtless mistresses had given her an insight into how decent this position might have been, burst into tears.

"There, now, see what you've done?" Tom muttered to Daniel angrily. "You've more to think of than just your own feelings. You've a wife to worry about. Look, man, I can find something on my own—"

"N-no, Tom," Betsy said bravely, wiping her eyes. "Dan'l's right. It's all of us, or none." She took her husband's arm and, before permitting him to lead her to the door, turned back to Camilla. "Ye'll not blame Mr. Hicks, will ye, yer ladyship?" she asked, her lips trembling. "He didn't know nothin' of what happened at Wyckfield Park."

Camilla, who'd been observing the dramatic scene with considerable fascination, gave the tearful young woman a sympathetic smile. "I understand that, Betsy. I don't blame Hicks in the least. In fact, Hicks, if you still want these people on your staff, I shall make no objection. The *contretemps* at Wyckfield *was* a misunderstanding, after all."

Hicks lifted his head and gawked at her. "Miss Camilla! You can't mean . . . after all this, you're *still* willing—"

"It's entirely up to you, Hicks. You are my steward in these matters."

"Thank you, your ladyship, for saying so, especially after seeing my humiliation. If it's up to me, then I say we should let 'em go. First they treated you with disrespect in Wyckfield, and then they kept the knowledge from me. I'm not sure they can be trusted."

"Betsy and Daniel are the most trustworthy pair you'll ever find!" Tom barked impatiently. "I don't see why they are included in this discussion at all. This entire matter is my fault and mine alone."

"That does seem to be true," Camilla said to the butler.

"But it was all *three of them* that didn't tell me what happened," Hicks said stubbornly.

"You're right about that," Camilla agreed thoughtfully, "but I imagine they've learned a lesson from all this."

"Oh, yes'm, we have," Betsy said earnestly.

"Are you saying, Miss Camilla, that you're willing to take all *three?*" Hicks asked in disbelief.

"Yes, if you are."

Hicks looked at Tom dubiously. The part of the story which Camilla did not know hung heavily on his conscience, and in that story as well as this one, Tom's part was most heinous. "I don't think I can recommend the third one, Miss Camilla. Not in good conscience."

"Then yer conscience has misled ye, Uncle," Daniel said firmly. "We thank ye fer yer kindness, my lady, but if ye can't take the three of us, we have t' ask fer permission to withdraw."

"Don't be a fool, Daniel," Tom muttered urgently.

Betsy put a restraining hand on Tom's arm. "It's a settled matter, Tom. Don't keep fightin' over it."

Camilla shook her head in grudging admiration over their loyalty to each other. "They seem to be an unbreakable set, Hicks. What do you think we should do?"

"I don't know, your ladyship," he said, troubled. "Let them all go, I suppose."

"But I hate to permit Betsy to go wandering about the streets looking for a place in her condition . . ."

Hicks sighed. "You're willing to take a chance on them all?"

"I don't see what else we can do, do you?"

Hicks shook his head dubiously. "Very well, my lady. We'll take them on. And I give you my word that I'll do everything in my power to see that you're not ill-served by your kindness."

Camilla nodded, sat down and entered the appropriate items in her ledger book, while Betsy and Daniel exchanged looks of relieved delight. But Hicks fixed a lugubrious eye on Tom. "I'm warning you, Thomas, that you'll get no further forgiveness if you use your free-and-easy ways as you've done today," he said sternly.

"That's quite true, young man," Camilla said, looking up at the tall, incorrigible fellow with a twinge of misgiving and attempting, by the coldness of her manner, to correct any impression of softness which her previous behavior had probably given. "From now on I shall expect you to behave with impeccable propriety, do you understand?"

"Yes, my lady," Tom assured her. "I shall be the most invisible and inaudible person on your staff, I promise you."

Somehow Camilla had an unshakable conviction that he would turn out to be quite the opposite. "I hope so," she said firmly, rising and dismissing them all with a wave of her hand, "because at the *first* infraction—the very slightest breach of discipline—*out you go!*"

Chapter Six

Dear Ethelyn, I have received your letter of 13 November and hasten to assure you that there has been no calamity. I am sorry that I neglected to write as often as you expected, but in the scramble to make things livable in the new house I was rather preoccupied. We have not fallen into any difficulties of the types you so dramatically suggest in your letter—there have been no robberies, no accidents and no descent into godlessness and sin. In truth, we do very well in all matters. The house is now fully staffed with efficient and respectable help, it is adequately spacious (although I will admit that it is tiny in comparison to Wyckfield), and our neighborhood is as quiet and proper as if it were located in a country town. We have even begun to make a few acquaintances. Pippa, in particular, is delighted to have found a friend her own age, about whom I am sure she will write to you herself. So I hope, my dear, that you will henceforth feel no need to trouble yourself and the Good Lord with concern for our health and happiness. Pippa and I think of you and speak of you often. With the most fond good wishes for your own and Oswald's well-being, I remain your most devoted, etc., Camilla.

Matters in the house on Upper Seymour Street were indeed going very well. It was a joy to Camilla to be able to rise each morning at any hour she wished, to take breakfast in bed if the inaction suited her mood, or to jump up and dress in the new (and shockingly fashionable) clothes she'd purchased. It was a delight to stroll along the streets with Pippa and Miss Townley (with one of the footmen following along a few paces behind to add an air of propriety to the outings and, incidentally, to carry whatever parcels they managed to acquire during the stroll) and look at the shop windows, the elegant town houses and the faces of hundreds of interesting passersby instead of the clipped hedges and rigid flowerbeds of Wyckfield Park. She felt a delicious, heady freedom. There was no one to account to, no one to give her orders, no one whose will was in combat with her own. The feeling was almost too wonderful to be true; sometimes she felt guilty to be so happy.

But every scolding letter from Ethelyn, every stricture, every reprimand, every bit of unsolicited advice which came regularly by post from Wyckfield made that guilt a little less severe. Her sister-in-law's letters merely served to remind her of what she'd escaped. The pleasure, the ease, the freedom of each passing day only confirmed her conviction that she'd done the right thing. She'd escaped from virtual confinement . . . and nothing or no one would ever prevail upon her to return to it.

Even Pippa seemed to be blossoming in the exhilarating atmosphere of what Ethelyn called "the city of sin." The child walked about with eyes wide in perpetual amazement. She drank in every detail of the new sights that greeted her every day. Every new experience filled her with the enthusiasm and excitement that come only to the very young. "Look, Mama," she would cry on a walk down Bond Street, "the lady on the other side of the street has a *finch* pinned to her hat. You don't suppose it's a real one that's been stuffed, do you? A milliner wouldn't—?"

And Camilla would reassure her that the finch had no more been a real bird than the doll in the window of a nearby shop had been a real baby.

Then Pippa's attention would turn to the carriages rattling by on the busy thoroughfare. "Have you ever seen so many different carriages?" she'd exclaim. "Barouches, and phaetons . . . and there's a cabriolet with the top raised! And that one, there—the one with the horses tandem—do you know what that's called?"

"No, I don't. Do you?"

"Yes. It's called a tim-whiskey. Thomas told me. And look over there, Mama—there's a post-chaise. Do you see the guard standing on the boot? That strange object he's carrying is a real blunderbuss. Thomas says it's a blunder every time someone tries to fire one."

"Thomas is a veritable fount of information, isn't he?" Camilla would murmur drily, unable to keep from throwing a backward glance over her shoulder to frown at him. He was performing his duties in a satisfactory way, as far as she could tell, but for someone who was supposed to be invisible and inaudible, he was certainly making himself noticed.

From the very first day the staff had moved into their new quarters, Thomas had been noticeable. She had called a staff meeting so that she and Hicks could acquaint them all with their duties, explain the rules for daily living and distribute their clothing and uniforms. She'd sat behind her desk and watched as Hicks had explained how they were to dress. Every member of the staff had been given several different costumes; some were for heavy work while others were to be worn when they had to appear at the front of the house. The footmen had three distinct sets of livery. The gold-braided, formal livery, Hicks had explained, was to be worn only when her ladyship held formal dinner parties. "Thank goodness," Thomas had muttered. "I'd hate to have to dress like a popinjay every day of the week." Hicks had delivered a brief scold, but a moment later, when he said that the footmen would not be required to powder their hair except when dressing in the formal livery, Thomas had objected vociferously. "Powder my *hair?*" he'd exclaimed. "Not on your life!" This type of behavior had become the fellow's style ever since.

She'd promised herself to become as good a manager of the household as Ethelyn was of Wyckfield, but she hadn't been able to control Thomas's excesses. Of course, he'd done nothing really reprehensible, and Pippa and Miss Townley seemed to admire what Miss Townley described as his "robust honesty," but he always made Camilla feel uncomfortable. She couldn't understand why she was always conscious of his presence . . . and discomfitted by it.

The trouble was, she supposed, that the fellow was not really like a servant at all. Everything about him, from his long-legged, self-assured stride to his polished speech, seemed more masterful than servantlike. There was nothing about Thomas that was humble or diffident. He behaved as if he were born to give orders rather than to take them. Sometimes she wondered if he weren't a gentleman of noble birth who was indulging in some sort of irritating masquerade, like certain members of the Corinthian set whom she'd heard of—wellborn gentlemen who dressed up like coachmen and drove stagecoaches for excitement.

She'd tried to query Betsy about Thomas's past, but everything she'd learned from the ingenuous girl gave support to the theory that Thomas was exactly what he claimed to be. There was nothing for it but to accept what appeared to be the facts.

But if any one factor could be singled out to be the primary cause of her discomfort in regard to Thomas, it was this very tendency of hers to think about him . . . to take notice of him, and to weave these "romances" about his background. She would have liked to dismiss him from her mind altogether. If only she had the character either to control his behavior with the proper detachment or to banish him from the premises.

Yes, there were problems in this new life, and Thomas was one of them. But there were several others which troubled her too, even though they were minor ones. The other servants still needed training, the household was not yet organized in a purposeful, daily routine, and Camilla suffered occasionally from bouts of loneliness. But for the most part, she was very pleased with her new surroundings. The atmosphere in the house on Upper Seymour Street was one of quiet contentment. Perhaps that contentment had about it an air of precariousness . . . perhaps things were too new and unstable to enable the inhabitants to feel completely relaxed . . . but that would come with time. And meanwhile, the very air was aglow with hopefulness.

Dear Ethelyn, your letter of 23 November was needlessly severe. I am not careless in matters concerning my daughter, and I would certainly not permit her to enter into an intimate friendship with a child whose family I did not know. As a matter of fact, little Sybil Sturtevant is a perfectly well-bred girl whose mother is Lady Sturtevant, wife of Edgar Sturtevant, who is a viscount and a member of Parliament. Even though Lady S. and I met during a morning walk through Hyde Park, it was quite obvious at once that she was eminently respectable (she has five children, and four of them were surrounding her that very morning, so she could hardly have been engaged in any activity of a reprehensible nature) and we took to each other at once. As for Pippa and Sybil, they make a wonderful pair, for Pippa is completely bookish and Sybil is completely active. Each one seems to exert a most beneficial influence on the other. I do not think that the fact that Sybil taught Pippa to play cards is a matter to arouse in you such violent antipathy. They play the most innocuous games, and it seems to me to be a perfectly permissible activity with which to pass a rainy afternoon. I think, Ethelyn, that you will feel much more reconciled to the situation if you disabuse yourself of your conviction that London is a hotbed of iniquity. I assure you, my dear, that it is not. With the fondest of good wishes for you and Oswald, I remain your devoted, etc., Camilla.

As a matter of fact, Camilla was not as certain that Sybil Sturtevant was as good an influence on Pippa as she'd claimed in her letter. Pippa was enchanted with her new friend, but Sybil had four brothers and had managed to reach the age of ten by learning the art of survival. She had made herself as agile and as strong as they. There was no little boy her age she couldn't outrun, outbox or outwit. She had a scorn of pretty dresses, the stride of a tomboy and a vocabulary of boxing terms that Camilla found a bit shocking. But Pippa was delighted with her. After the quiet, restricted years at Wyckfield, it was a revelation to Pippa to meet someone whose behavior was so completely uninhibited. Sybil sat on floors, climbed trees, dashed in and out of doors, tossed balls, engaged in fisticuffs, occasionally swore and hated to read. She taught Pippa how to shoot marbles, how to run like a boy and how to play cards. In return, Pippa told her stories. Sybil, who had never spent time with books, was unfamiliar with the most commonplace of fairy stories and was completely enthralled as Pippa regaled her by the hour with detailed accounts of *St. George and the Dragon, Caporushes,* or *The True History of Sir Thomas Thumb.* It was a friendship made in heaven, and the two little girls couldn't bear to be parted from one another.

For those times when the girls were not together, Pippa found herself another friend. It was the footman, Thomas, who (if he could be found without a pressing chore to do) would give her a good game of Hearts, make up riddles or tell her the most surprising tales of strange, exotic places like Barbados, Portugal, or India. On a particularly rainy, cold day in late November, when it became clear that Lady Sturtevant and Sybil would not be paying a call, Pippa roamed the house looking for her second-favorite companion. She found him in the warming room, a little room off the large dining room where the food which had cooled on its way up from the kitchen was reheated before being served. The room had a large fireplace, two warming ovens, a number of cupboards in which the large silver serving pieces were stored, and a long worktable at the center. It was at this table that Thomas, busily polishing an appalling number of trays, teapots and candlesticks, was found. "Are you very busy, Thomas," Pippa asked from the doorway.

Thomas looked up and grinned at her. "Busy? What a question, Miss Pippa. Of course I'm not busy. All I need do is say 'Rumplestiltskin,' and a little gnome will come and finish all this polishing in a twinkling."

Pippa giggled. "Wouldn't it be wonderful if you could? Then you'd be free to play cards with me."

"It wouldn't be wonderful at all," Thomas said severely. "I already owe you six hundred and forty-nine pounds for games I've lost to you."

"Six hundred and seventy. You're forgetting the twenty-one pounds I won yesterday."

"Six hundred and seventy, then. Do you realize, my lass, that if I spent not a penny of my wages, it would take me thirty-three-and-a-half years to pay you what I owe?"

"Oh, pooh! The debt is only pretend, as you very well know. Besides, you may be the one to win the next rubber or two, and our situations might well be completely reversed."

"That's true," Thomas agreed, rubbing at the rounded belly of an ornate teapot with energy. "I'm almost sorry, then, that our gambling is only pretend."

Pippa walked thoughtfully to the fire. "Thirty-three-and-a-half years?" She took off her spectacles and shut her eyes. "That means your wages for the year are twenty pounds."

Thomas stopped his work to stare at her admiringly. "That's very *good,* Miss Pippa!"

"Good? It seems to me to be a very paltry amount."

"I don't mean my wages. I mean the way you did that sum in your head."

"Oh, that." She put on her spectacles again and smiled at him. "That's nothing worth speaking of. I've always been very good at sums, you know."

"I *didn't* know. But I should have guessed. That's probably why you do so well at cards. But as for my wages being paltry, I'll have you know that I make three pounds per annum more than Lady Sturtevant's first footman, and I'm only an under."

"No, you're not. Mama says she doesn't approve of firsts and unders. But how can it be that my father left me twenty *thousand* pounds per annum while your wages are only twenty?"

Tom smiled ruefully. "It's the way of the world, Miss Pippa. But you shouldn't worry yourself about it. You should be pleased that you're such a rich little girl."

"Am I?"

"Indeed you are. I'm fair tempted to run off with you and wed you for your fortune."

Pippa studied him seriously. "No, I don't think you're the sort to make a mercenary match," she decided after brief reflection.

"Am I not? What makes you so certain? How, at your age, have you become so expert in these matters? Has someone tried to run off with you already?"

"What a jokester you are, Thomas," she giggled. "I learned from books, of course. There are many stories in which wicked men try to wed innocent damsels for their wealth. But those men aren't like you. They have narrow, glittering eyes, you see."

"Oh." He narrowed his eyes and leered at her. "Like this?"

She gurgled in amusement. "Not at *all* like that. You just aren't the sort."

He gave a lugubrious sigh. "Too bad. My one chance to become rich . . . gone through having the wrong sort of eyes!"

"But you have the right sort of eyes for gaming," the girl said with inspiration. "If you play cards with me, you may *win* yourself a fortune."

He made a face. "Only a pretend fortune. And I have all these very real trays to do."

"Can't you put off polishing some of them until tomorrow?" she pleaded.

"I'm sorry, Miss Pippa, but tomorrow's taken with other chores. Mr. Hicks has given us a daily schedule. I have it here." He put down his polishing cloth and took from his pocket a closely written sheet. "Let's see now . . . Thursday . . . Thursday . . . ah, here it is. Afternoon, after clearing away the luncheon, there's the stair rods and the brasses."

Poor Pippa's face fell. "Do you mean there's something on that list for *every* afternoon?"

"I'm afraid so. Monday the lamps, Tuesday the glassware, Wednesday the silver and so forth . . ."

"It's quite unfair! Why should *you* be required to do all the work? What about Mary, or Gladys, or Daniel?"

"They've all got their own lists, you know. Daniel, at this moment, is waxing all the oak. Now, don't look so crestfallen. You wouldn't wish me to neglect my duties and get the sack, would you?"

"Oh, you won't get the sack. In my opinion, you're the very best of all the servants."

"Thank you, Miss Pippa. Now if we could only convince Mr. Hicks and your mother of that very obvious truth, we'd have nothing to worry about. We could probably hide in here and play cards all day long."

"But I don't think I can manage it," Pippa admitted, turning with flagging steps to the door. "I don't think either one of them thinks as well of you as I do."

"I'm aware of that. But how did *you* know it?" Tom asked, looking at her curiously.

"I overheard them discussing you. They think you're too bold."

Tom grunted and returned to his polishing. "Hmm. Boldness . . . that's a lamentable flaw in a footman, you know."

The child paused at the door and looked back at him. "Yes, I suppose so. Though it sounds rather heroic to me." She sighed. "I hope there will be *some* time in the week when you can play with me, Thomas."

"Don't worry, lass, we'll manage something. Meanwhile, if you've nothing better to do, you can stay here and listen to me spin a yarn. I can talk and polish at the same time, after all."

The child's face brightened. "Oh, that will be *famous!* I love stories as well as cards, you know."

"Good, then. Here, let me lift you up on the table. It'll be more comfortable than standing about in the doorway."

He cleared away an area on the table to his right and lifted her up. She dangled her legs happily from her elevated perch. "Where are all the chairs?" she asked curiously. "Have they all been taken away somewhere?"

"Oh, there are no chairs in the warming room, ever. This is a workroom, you see. Chairs don't do in a workroom, because their presence might encourage a servant to sit down while working, and that is strictly forbidden. But never mind. You're comfortable up there on the table, aren't you?"

"Oh, yes, it's quite lovely up here," she assured him, picking up a polishing cloth and absently rubbing away at a tray. "What yarn will you spin today?"

"Have I told you the one about the stowaway? No? Well, it begins many years ago, on a schooner called the *Surprise,* when one of the crew who was laying up rigging heard a cough that seemed to come from under the taffrail, where the jollyboat was tied . . ."

The story was well along when Camilla appeared at the warming room door. "Oh, *there* you are, Pippa," she said in surprise. "I've been searching for you all over the house." She took due note of the tray and polishing cloth in her daughter's lap and the cozy intimacy of the scene before her. It was a scene which struck her as completely inappropriate, and she stiffened in irritation. "Come down from there at once!" she said sharply. "*Ladies* do not perch themselves on *tables.*"

"But Sybil would perch on a—"

"Never mind about Sybil. Perhaps Ethelyn is right, and you *are* seeing too much of that child."

"It was my idea to put Miss Philippa up there, ma'am," Tom ventured. "There isn't a single chair in here, you see—"

"Never mind. Just take her down," Camilla said coldly. "And in future, Thomas, I'd be greatly obliged if you'd do your *own* polishing without my daughter's help!"

"He didn't enlist my help," Pippa said quickly. "You're not being fair, Mama. I was only holding the tray in my lap. I don't think Thomas even noticed it."

Thomas, furious, clenched his fists. "Miss Pippa knows I don't approve of her polishing," he said sarcastically. "I only permit her to carry logs for me."

Pippa giggled, but her mother flushed. "Well, never mind. Just help her down. I want her to come along with me at once."

"But may I not stay for a few minutes more?" Pippa asked as Thomas helped her jump down from her perch. "Just to find out what the captain did to the stowaway?"

"No, you may not." Her mother took Pippa's hand and stalked to the door. "I don't think that fellow will ever learn to have a civil tongue in his head," she muttered. "Irritating rudesby!"

Pippa, just before she was pulled from the room, looked back at the chastised Thomas. *You're just too bold,* she mouthed with a teasing glint.

Thomas grinned and winked. *Much too bold,* he mouthed back.

Dear Ethelyn, I have your letter of 2 December before me, and I regret to have to refuse your kind invitation to return to Wyckfield for Christmas. Pippa has been invited to spend Christmas day at the home of her new friend (who, as I told you, has four siblings of assorted ages) and is quite looking forward to spending the holiday in the company of so many lively children. I, too, have been invited, of course, and I must admit that I share Pippa's eagerness to experience this new sort of holiday celebration. I hasten to assure you that there is nothing godless in the way our new London friends live. Lady Sturtevant, the hostess in question, is a person of whom you would surely approve.

I am sorry that the holiday will find us apart, but in any case, Ethelyn, I do not believe it would be wise to attempt such a long trip so soon after we've settled in, especially when the weather at this season is so uncertain. Please accept our very best wishes for your good health—and Oswald's, too, of course—and remember that I remain your most devoted, etc., Camilla.

Camilla reread the letter, chewing the tip of her pen worriedly. It was a poor letter in every respect. In the first place, it was awkwardly phrased. Her wording did nothing to hide the bald fact that both she and Pippa preferred to spend the holiday with their new acquaintances rather than return to Wyckfield. And, secondly, she'd added two other excuses—that the trip was too long and the weather uncertain—and anyone with an ounce of sense knew that three lame excuses were not nearly as effective as one good one. Ethelyn would be livid when she read this missive.

But Camilla had already written three earlier drafts. This was the best she could do. Perhaps there was no good way to phrase a refusal. But an acceptance was out of the question.

It was not that the London life was so completely joyful. On the contrary, there were many problems she had to face. She was still very insecure at playing the role of mistress of a household in which she had to make decisions for more than a dozen people. Her daughter was changing before her eyes, and Camilla was not sure the changes were all for the better. And, although she was making friends, she still felt lonely most of the time. No, things were not perfect. Life was teaching her that happiness, even in the best of circumstances, was not easy to achieve. But she did feel hopeful; she did feel alive; she did feel *free*. Those were feelings she'd never had at Wyckfield Park.

She'd had a bad dream just the other night, which had made her even more firm about refusing her sister-in-law's invitations. She'd dreamed that she'd returned to Wyckfield and was walking along a hedgerow in the garden, noting again, with distaste, the orderly decorousness of the hedge's shape. Not a twig nor leaf stuck out to mar the even perfection of the trim. Suddenly, however, the leaves withered and dropped off, and the bare twigs began to grow out in frightening, gnarled offshoots—woodsy, misshapen fingers which began to reach for and clutch at her hair, her arms, her dress. She tried to break free of their grasp, but although the branches appeared to be brittle, they did not break. Before she knew it, she was being held fast. The branches continued to grow and thicken and wind themselves about her. The light was soon blotted out; the hedge became an impenetrable cage, and she knew that she could never, even if she lived a hundred years, claw her way out . . .

With a decisive abruptness, she folded the third draft of the letter and sealed it. No matter how deplorable her sister-in-law would find it, the letter was going to be posted just the way it was, and the devil take the hindmost. She couldn't let it matter to her that her sister-in-law would be offended. She couldn't let herself be weakened by repeated urgings to return to Wyckfield. She couldn't let herself become disheartened, no matter how difficult life in London should become. She had to remember that London was freedom and Wyckfield a cage. No matter what happened, she was never, never going back to Wyckfield again.

Chapter Seven

There was no way in which the country-bred Camilla could have anticipated the excitement of spending the holidays in town. She was not prepared for the number of dinners, outings, balls, luncheons, fetes and routs which, under the aegis of Lady Sturtevant, she was encouraged to attend. By the time the new year had come, and the whirl of activities had finally subsided, Camilla and her daughter had gone through every item in their wardrobes, had been fully occupied every day for a fortnight, and were completely exhausted. It was Pippa who expressed aloud what Camilla felt: "Londoners are wonderful; they have time for everything but sleeping and reading."

They were both glad to be able to return to their previous, more placid routine, but Camilla soon learned that once the door to social life has been opened, it is difficult to close it again. A complete return to the quieter life was no longer possible. Lady Sturtevant, now a close friend, dropped by several times a week with at least two of her children in tow. And two gentlemen whom Camilla had met during the social whirl of the holidays became frequent callers. One was Lady Sturtevant's bachelor brother, Sir James Cambard, a cheerful, rotund, middle-aged man with a lethargic though generous disposition; and the other was a callow youth of twenty-two, Lord Earlywine, who had been a guest at one of the balls and had tumbled top-over-tail in love with the beautiful widow after merely holding Camilla's hand for one country dance.

It seemed to the servants that the knocker was never still. Unexpected guests were always being invited to stay to luncheon or to tea, thus throwing Mr. Hicks's carefully planned work schedule out of kilter. For all the staff, this meant a great deal of rushing about to catch up with the work, but none of them seemed to mind the extra effort so much as Thomas. Every time one or the other of the gentlemen paid a call, Tom had to grit his teeth to keep his disgust from showing in his face. They were a pair of fools, he thought, each one self-important and encroaching, and his mistress, who was far too good for them, saw them much too often.

Her ladyship usually greeted her callers in the library in the company of Miss Townley, but sometimes, if she were working at her desk in the sitting room, she would permit them to wait upon her there, and alone. It was at those times that Thomas would find an excuse to busy himself outside the door so that he would be at hand if needed. Even if it were Daniel's turn to assist Mr. Hicks in serving the wine or tea to the guest, Thomas would be somewhere in the vicinity. Mr. Hicks often glowered at him, but Thomas always made sure to be occupied with something useful and managed to escape a reprimand.

Thomas was the one on duty, however, the afternoon Lord Earlywine paid his third call in as many days. It was Thomas's task to assist Mr. Hicks to set up the tea things if her ladyship should request that tea be served. Her ladyship had evidently done so today, for Mr. Hicks came down to the kitchen and asked the cook to ready a tray. Thomas, carrying the tray on one shoulder, followed Mr. Hicks up the stairs. "Don't tell me it's Earlywine again," he muttered in disgust.

"It's none of your business, Thomas," Hicks said brusquely. "Just be sure you place the sugar tongs in *front* of the sugar bowl, not behind the scones as you did the last time. I was afraid her ladyship'd have to use her fingers."

"Aye, aye, sir," Tom said absently, standing aside as Mr. Hicks tapped at the sitting room door,

"Yes, Mr. Hicks," the butler growled as her ladyship's voice invited them to come in.

The butler entered first. "The tea, your ladyship," he said in his formal, company tone.

"Yes, put it on the table near the window, will you, Hicks?" she murmured and turned back to her guest with a fixed smile.

Thomas followed Mr. Hicks into the room and quickly assisted the butler to set up the table. While this was going on, Lord Earlywine, leaning his elbow on the mantelpiece as if he owned the place, prosed on and on about a horserace in which he'd been involved. Thomas, glancing at the lady's face, could see that she was bored and irritated. She even reminded her guest gently, twice, that he'd told her the story before. But the idiotic fellow merely smiled and said, "Yes? And did I tell you that . . ." and went on with his story in greater detail than before.

Lady Wyckfield, seated at the writing desk where she'd been working before her caller arrived, was turned about in her seat so that she could face him. It was an attitude that bespoke a feeling of impatience to have the visit brought to an end. When the tea table had been set, she rose from her place (reluctantly, it seemed to Thomas) and went to the table to pour. "Will you take sugar?" she asked her guest as Hicks handed her the empty cup.

Thomas, stationed behind the table at rigid attention, had nothing to do until it was time to gather up the tea things and remove them. From the corner of his eye, he watched his mistress go through the motions of entertaining her guest, but it was plain to the footman that she would have liked to get rid of Earlywine, and the sooner the better. Thomas racked his brain for some way to help her, but it was not until Lord Earlywine made his way to the tea table to help himself to a second buttered scone that Thomas got an idea. When his lordship drew close, Thomas leaned forward and whispered something into his ear. Then they both looked toward the window. Lord Earlywine nodded and put down his cup. "I think I'd better dash, ma'am," he said with a quick bow. "I hope, next time, that you'll agree to take a ride in my new phaeton. I promise to have a lap robe, some hot bricks and all sorts of things for your comfort."

"Thank you, my lord. We shall see," Lady Wyckfield said with a polite smile, holding out her hand.

Hicks motioned for Thomas to collect the cups while he led Lord Earlywine to the door. When the butler and the guest had departed, her ladyship sighed in obvious relief and went back to her writing table. Picking up her pen, she looked up at the busy footman curiously. "What did you say to his lordship, Thomas, to make him leave so abruptly?"

"Say, ma'm?" Thomas echoed innocently. "Nothing of any importance."

"That is no answer to my question. What did you say to him?"

"Only that his horses were standing, which everyone knows they shouldn't be doing on a cold day like this."

"But Lord Earlywine has a groom. He'd know enough to walk them, wouldn't he?"

"Yes, ma'am."

"Then why wasn't he?"

"Oh, he *was*." Thomas's eyes twinkled. "But not at that moment."

Camilla stiffened. "Are you saying that you *misled* Lord Earlywine into believing that his horses were being neglected?"

Thomas shrugged modestly. "I suppose you could say that."

"But . . . how *dared* you do such a thing? What did you expect to gain by it?" Camilla demanded, rising.

"Well, you wanted to be rid of him, didn't you?"

"I? I wanted—?" Camilla reddened in fury. "Really, Thomas, your presumption is beyond belief! What gave you the right—"

"Are you trying to say you *didn't* want to be rid of him?" Tom asked, bewildered.

Camilla's color deepened. "That has nothing to *do* with it! It's not your *place* to—"

"Oh, my *place*." He picked up the last cup and put it on the tray. "To be honest, your ladyship, I can't keep straight just what my place is. I thought it was my place to be of help to you."

"Well, it's *not* your place to help me unless I ask you!"

"That's the most confusing statement I've yet heard from you, ma'am. I don't wait for you to *ask* me to help you from the carriage or to polish the crystal. I don't have to be asked to perform ninety percent of the tasks I do. Shall I wait to do them, in the future, until I hear from you?"

"You are being purposely dense. You know perfectly well that I needn't give you specific orders when it comes to your routine tasks. Don't stand there and pretend that you don't know the difference between polishing the crystal and sending one of my guests flying out the door on a wild-goose chase!"

"I'm sorry, ma'am, if the young man's precipitous departure disturbed you," he muttered with a tinge of sarcasm as he lifted the loaded tray to his shoulder.

"Now you are being *impudent!*" she snapped. "It was not his departure but your *presumption* which disturbs me. And incidentally, in all the time you worked for that physician in Derbyshire, did he never tell you that it is improper to be lifting trays and fiddling about when your employer is speaking to you?"

"No, he never did. I'm sorry, ma'am. Shall I put the tray down?"

"Yes. And when you pick it up again, please carry it before you in both hands, with some semblance of dignity, instead of on your shoulder like a . . . a . . ."

"A seabag?" he supplied.

"Yes, exactly. I sometimes think, Thomas, that you are a complete fraud. You don't speak or act at all like a footman."

He tried to look crestfallen. "I know. Too bold."

"Bold is too mild a word. *Brazen* would be better."

Hicks came in just in time to hear the last few words. "Is anything wrong, Miss Camilla? Has this rogue been up to some deviltry?"

Thomas looked at her with something very like a challenge in his eyes. "Have I, your ladyship?"

She glared at him, but she was more angry with herself. Why could she not handle herself like a proper mistress with this fellow? From the first he'd had a free-and-easy attitude toward her that was completely inappropriate to their positions, yet instead of stifling him permanently and at once, she'd bandied words with him, often to her own disadvantage. By now he'd probably lost all sense of the reverence and awe which a servant should feel toward an employer. What she should do—right on the spot!—would be to dismiss him. He certainly deserved it. The fellow was rude, presumptuous, ill-mannered, forward and disrespectful. And he'd undoubtedly become worse if she let this situation pass unpunished.

This was just the sort of situation which Ethelyn could have handled without a bit of hesitation. If she were here, she would sneer at Camilla's "softness." And she would be quite right, for Camilla was already feeling squeamish about sending him out into the streets.

Her gaze flickered before the challenge in Thomas's eyes. The fellow was truly brazen, she knew . . . but had his infraction been great enough to warrant sending him packing? It had been a rather minor indelicacy, hadn't it? And she had to admit to herself that she was glad he'd done it. If he hadn't, the annoying Lord Earlywine might have remained for another hour or more!

"If Thomas has been overstepping again," Hicks was saying, "it'd please me mightily to cut him down to size."

Camilla dropped her eyes from those of her unrepentant footman and shook her head. "It was nothing worth discussing," she said, turning to her writing. "Just have him take up the tea things and go."

She would have liked to take another look at the footman's expression, but she wouldn't permit herself to do so. The brazen fellow was undoubtedly grinning in triumph, but at least he would not have the satisfaction of throwing that smirk in her face. She kept her eyes resolutely lowered on the paper before her and waited for the two servants to leave the room. She heard one man's footsteps recede and the door close, but the other seemed to be lingering behind. A cough sounded behind her, indicating that whichever one it was who remained was waiting for her attention. But she *knew* which one it was. "Yes?" she asked coldly, not looking up.

"Ma'am?" he asked in a voice unwontedly shy.

There was nothing for her to do but turn. He was standing a few paces away, carrying the loaded tray before him with both hands just as she'd instructed. And there was not a sign on his face of a smirk or grin. "Yes?" she asked again.

"I just wanted to . . . to say thank you."

She felt herself flushing. How was it that this fellow—a mere servant whose personality should be unknown to her and completely beneath her notice— could always manage to disconcert her? "Oh, go along, Thomas, go along!" she said in self-disgust and turned back to her letter. "Just try to remember that you promised to make yourself invisible and inaudible."

"Yes, ma'am," he mumbled with what seemed to be utmost sincerity, "I'll try. I'll certainly try."

Chapter Eight

The altercation with Thomas was still on Camilla's mind the next morning when, with a sigh, she entered the empty breakfast room. Pippa had already breakfasted and had gone off with Sybil Sturtevant for an outing in the park; and Miss Townley, despite the fact that Lady Sturtevant, two other Sturtevant offspring, their governess and a nursemaid were of the party, had insisted on going along to supervise her charge. (Miss Townley liked Lady Sturtevant well enough, but the lady's breezy, casual, unconcerned way of rearing children was not, in Miss Townley's view, good enough for Pippa.)

Camilla felt very much alone. She was not pleased with herself this morning (being struck with pangs of humiliation whenever she remembered her cowardly, weak-kneed performance of the day before), and the absence of company at the breakfast table only deepened her discontent. To make matters worse, a letter had been placed alongside her butter knife, which she instantly recognized had come from Wyckfield and which her instincts told her would *not* bring news to elevate her spirits.

The letter, written in Ethelyn's firm, decisive, heavy-on-the-downstroke hand, was not very different in substance from the other missives she'd received from her troublesome sister-in-law, but it was much more frightening in tone. Ethelyn insisted that a visit to Wyckfield was past due; this time she was not *requesting* Camilla's return—she was *demanding* it. She wrote that she found it "most peculiar" that Camilla had thus far been unable to arrange matters well enough to be able to spare her sister-in-law "at least a se'ennight's time" in Dorset. She and Philippa had now been gone from Wyckfield for three months, Ethelyn reminded her. Had she already forgotten her promise to return for frequent visits? *Was it fair,* Ethelyn had written, with underlines for emphasis, *to keep our dearest Philippa away from all intercourse with her father's family?*

There was a frightening little addition to all of this. *I have been thinking of something else, Camilla,* Ethelyn had appended in a postscript, *that will make it desirable for you to plan your visit for the week after next. That is the time that our vicar's brother will be visiting. I have met him on several occasions, since he is pastor to a flock located a few miles south of Deptford, and I have often heard him preach. He is filled with fiery conviction and has the same disdain for the comfortable latitudinarianism of some of the clergy which I hold. It seems that this gifted and respected clergyman has often taken notice of you when visiting his brother and has recently expressed an interest in offering for you. While I realize that it is just over a year since Desmond's passing and that it will be difficult for you to think so soon of a successor to my brother, I cannot imagine a more suitable candidate for the position of husband to you and stepfather to Philippa.*

Do not put on your missish airs in this matter, my dear. It is not often that such an opportunity comes along. Mr. Josiah Harbage, the gentleman in question, is not yet fifty, in excellent health and has a character both firm and godly. For Philippa's sake if not your own, you should consider this suggestion with all seriousness. At the very least, you must come for a visit at the time I suggest and permit me to introduce you. The possibilities of such a meeting are most promising. You may find yourself taking up residence in a parish just half an hour's ride from Wyckfield Park and embarked on a new, purposeful, spiritual rejuvenation. How delighted I should be never again to have to think of you residing in that place of sin and iniquity where you have, for the moment, so inexplicably chosen to bury yourself.

The hand holding the letter was trembling. Camilla could only be glad that she was alone at the table. She wouldn't have wanted Pippa to witness her agitation. Unable to eat a bite, she jumped up and strode across the hall to the sitting room. There she paced about, biting her lip, rereading the letter, crushing it into a ball, smoothing it out and reading it again. With each rereading, her agitation grew. It was in this state that Lady Sturtevant found her two hours later, when she brought Pippa home. The two girls had run up to Pippa's room, Miss Townley had gone to her room to lie down, and Lady Sturtevant, completely at home in Camilla's house, had told Hicks not to bother to announce her. In her usual breezy fashion, the feathers of her gaudy blue bonnet waving over her crimped red curls, she strode into the sitting room for a quick visit. The sight of Camilla's pale face and troubled eyes brought her to a standstill. "Good heavens, my dear, what's occurred to drain the color from your face?" she asked in instant sympathy.

"Oh, Georgie, I'm *so* glad to see you!" Camilla exclaimed with a tremulous smile. "I seem to have been working myself into a stew over nothing. Let's not even talk about it. Here, let me take your bonnet and pelisse."

"Never mind my bonnet and pelisse," Lady Sturtevant said firmly, seating herself on the sofa and pulling her friend down beside her. "Now, take a deep breath and tell me everything. What's happened to upset you so?"

Georgina Sturtevant was nothing if not motherly. Tall and large-bosomed, she looked capable of taking the world's troubles to her breast. At first meeting the well-known wife of the taciturn Whig, Lord Sturtevant, one might receive an impression of vulgarity, for she not only wore the brightest colors and the most outrageous hats, but she had a deep, full-throated laugh, a voice that carried across the most crowded of rooms and a way of gesturing with her hands that called immediate attention to the gesturer. On further acquaintance, however, it became clear that Georgina Sturtevant was a woman of remarkable common sense, a complete absence of pretension and an openhearted generosity of spirit. Camilla, quiet and self-effacing herself, was entirely won over by Georgie's spirited good nature. There was no one in the world in whom she would more readily confide. Wordlessly, she held out the crumpled letter to her friend.

Georgina's eyes flew over the sheet. "Is *this* what troubles you . . . this overbearing, presumptuous *rodomontade?*" She waved her hands in the air as if she were tossing all Camilla's worries to the wind. "Just tear this up, throw it out and forget it. It's nothing but bluster."

Camilla blinked. "But . . . you don't understand. It's from my *sister-in-law.*"

"I know who it's from. And I know that you're still in the habit of jumping when she snaps her fingers. You're independent of her now, Camilla, and you must try to remember it."

"But, you see, in some respects Ethelyn is quite right in what she says."

"Right? *Right?* In wishing you to wed a tub-thumping, hell-threatening, middle-aged country preacher?"

"No, not that. Of course not that. She's only right in the part about my keeping Pippa from her father's family. It *is* wrong of me, I suppose . . ."

Georgina cocked her head to one side to study her friend's face, causing her heavily feathered bonnet to fall slightly askew. "Well, if you truly believe it's wrong of you, go ahead and *spend* a week in Dorset."

Camilla bit her lip and dropped her eyes. "Yes, I thought you might say that. It would be the most direct . . . the most sensible action." She clenched her hands together but couldn't prevent a little shiver from spreading through her body. "Oh, Georgie, I . . ." She looked up at her friend fearfully. "I just *can't!*"

"But why ever not? It would be just for a week," the sensible Georgina asked, her brow knit in an effort to grasp the unspoken undercurrents.

Camilla got to her feet and resumed her pacing. "You'll think me a dreadful fool, I'm afraid . . ."

"That isn't very likely." Georgina's smile was reassuring. "Try me."

Camilla paused in her perambulations. "I'm quite ashamed to admit this to you, but I have this . . . this *feeling* about it. Ridiculous as it is, I can't shake it off."

"Feeling?"

"Yes. That if I once go back to Wyckfield, I shall never be able to leave."

"Good *God*, Camilla, do you think your sister-in-law would keep you *prisoner* or some such thing?"

Camilla shook her head, smiling a little at her friend's commonsensical literalness. "No, of course not. How could she? I *told* you it was foolish. But my feeling is very real, and I can't rid myself of it."

Georgina reached out her hand and drew Camilla back to the sofa. "My poor girl," she murmured in sudden understanding, "did you hate the place as much as that?"

Camilla lowered her head. "I was not . . . very happy there."

"Then I see no reason for you to go back," her friend said decisively.

"But what about Pippa?"

"Does Pippa feel the same way about Wyckfield as you do?"

"Oh, no, not Pippa. You know Pippa—she's happy anywhere. And it is her home . . . or it will be, when she's of age."

"Then it's all quite simple," Georgina declared, swinging her arms wide in proud acknowledgement of her brilliance in having solved everything. "Send Pippa to Wyckfield without you."

"Without me? Why, I *couldn't*—"

"But, Camilla, it's only for a week."

"But she'd be so *alone*."

"I'll let Sybil go with her, if you'd like. Miss Townley, who, I assume, will go with them, can be relied upon to see that your sister-in-law doesn't keep them beyond the allotted time."

Camilla gaped at her friend in awe. "Georgie! What a perfectly wonderful idea! The girls would have a marvelous time in the country together, and Ethelyn won't be able to say that I'm keeping Pippa from her." She threw her arms about her friend's neck. "You're a positive genius! And generous to a fault to let Sybil go off for a week. I don't know how to thank you."

Georgina returned the embrace, laughing. "Save your effusions for some other time, silly. It was a perfectly obvious solution, which you would have thought of yourself if you'd been less agitated. And as for letting Sybil go, I'm delighted to be rid of her. You've no idea how that tomboy can upset a household. Let your sister-in-law cope with *her* for a few days, and you'll see how quickly the children are sent home."

The vision of the rigid Ethelyn dealing with the mercurial Sybil kept them both laughing for a moment. Then, rising to leave, Georgina adjusted her bonnet and added with sudden seriousness, "I could solve your other problem, too, if you'd let me."

"My other problem?"

"About your sister-in-law's pressure on you to remarry."

"Oh, yes, I'd forgotten that for a moment." She got up to call for Hicks. "Ethelyn will be furious when she learns I won't be there to meet her Mr. Harbage." She smiled as she helped Georgina to straighten her pelisse. "And how, my wise and practical friend, do you think you might solve *that* problem?"

"Again the solution is simple. Just become betrothed to someone *else*— someone of your own choosing. Preferably a Londoner, so that I will always have you close by. As soon as you're betrothed, you know, your sister-in-law will have no reason for matchmaking."

"Oh, that's your 'simple' solution, is it?" Camilla grinned. "I suppose you have a candidate in mind?"

But Hicks came in at that moment. "Will you call Sybil for me, Hicks?" Georgina requested. "It's time we were getting home."

Hicks bowed out, and the two ladies followed him down the hall. Daniel, stationed at the bottom of the stairs, was sent up to fetch the girls, while Hicks sent for Thomas to alert the Sturtevant coachman.

The ladies waited in the entryway. "I don't have a candidate, my dear," Georgina said, picking up the threads of their interrupted conversation, "but I wish I did."

"Candidate?"

"For your hand, of course. I don't fancy myself as a matchmaker, but I wouldn't take it amiss if you showed an interest in my brother."

Camilla lowered her eyes in embarrassment. "I hope, Georgie, that you aren't entertaining serious hopes in that regard."

Georgina sighed. "No, I'm not so foolish. My brother is a dear, but I'm well aware that he's too old, too lazy and too complacent in his bachelorhood to make a satisfactory suitor for you."

Camilla put a hand on her friend's arm. "Your brother is a dear. And he does seem happy in his bachelorhood. That's why we get on so well. He understands that I have no wish to remarry, so he feels perfectly safe in my company."

"That may be, Camilla, but there are dozens of other men you might consider. I hate to hear you say you've no interest in remarriage. Just because your previous experience was unhappy is no reason to believe—"

Their conversation was again interrupted, this time by Thomas's return after fetching the Sturtevant carriage. At the same moment, Daniel's step was heard on the stairs. The two women looked up to see him descending rapidly, his face red with chagrin. "I beg yer pardon, yer ladyship, but Miss Sybil refuses to come down," he informed them.

"What?" Lady Sturtevant exclaimed angrily. "*Refuses?* Honestly, that child will drive me to madness! I suppose I'll have to go up and carry her down bodily."

Hicks came toward her from the door. "Is there anything *I* can do, your ladyship?"

Georgina put a hand to her forehead in an exaggerated gesture of helplessness. "I don't see what—"

"Permit me, your ladyship," Thomas offered. "I think I can persuade her to come down." And without waiting for an answer, he bounded up the stairs, taking them two at a time.

Lady Sturtevant stared after him in considerable astonishment. "Your footman seems very . . . er . . . energetic," she murmured to Camilla in some amusement.

"Yes," Camilla responded wryly as she watched Daniel and Hicks move away in perfect, mannerly dignity, "I've noticed, myself, that the fellow's behavior is a trifle . . . unorthodox. I don't know quite what to do about him. I've been thinking of giving him his notice."

"Oh, I wouldn't do that if I were you. I like the servants to be enterprising."

"I shall remember that, my dear," Camilla said with a laugh, "if I'm forced to let him go. In that event, I shall send him straight to you."

Georgina pulled on her gloves. "Why not? In my household of eccentrics, one more or less won't even be noticed. But if I may return to a more important matter, my love, I wish you will think about my suggestion to find yourself a betrothed. I would dearly love to see you happily wed."

"Don't press me on that subject, Georgie, please. I've made up my mind to remain as I am. But there's no need to look so glum about it. Your suggestion has given me a very good idea about what to do about Ethelyn's matchmaking. It's quite a splendid solution that I've thought of all by myself . . . and it will work without my having to become betrothed to accomplish it."

"Really? Then *tell* me—"

But there was no time for Camilla to explain, even if she'd wanted to. A murmur at the top of the stairs made them all look up. Sybil Sturtevant, her bonnet neatly tied on her head and her spencer buttoned, was marching down the stairs in slow, deliberate, completely unaccustomed dignity. Thomas and Pippa followed, both of them watching with interest as Sybil made her majestic descent. "I'm ready, Mama," the girl announced when she'd reached bottom, and, without breaking her even pace, she smiled at Camilla and went out the door to the carriage.

Georgina, her mouth open and her eyebrows raised, watched her daughter's exit with disbelief. "I don't think I've ever *seen* that child move in such a ladylike style!" she whispered to Camilla. "Your footman must have some sort of *gift!* Whenever you want to be rid of him, I'll take him in a snap."

When the visitors had gone and the servants had taken themselves back to their quarters, Camilla accosted her daughter. "What did Thomas *do* to make Sybil behave so well?"

Pippa giggled. "He made a wager with her. He wagered that she couldn't make it all the way down to the carriage without once breaking into a hop, skip or jump."

"Oh, so *that* was his ruse! What did he wager?"

"Nothing much," Pippa said, starting back up the stairs. "Only the four hundred and twenty pounds she owed him."

"Four hundred and twenty *pounds?*" Camilla stared after her daughter, aghast. "What are you *talking* about? Pippa Wyckfield, I see nothing in this matter to *laugh* about! Come back here at once! *Pippa!*"

Chapter Nine

*E*ven after she'd learned from her daughter (who parted with the information only after a prolonged indulgence in irritating and rowdyish hilarity) that the four-hundred-and-twenty-pound wager was only pretend money, Camilla had the feeling that Thomas ought to be scolded. There was something vaguely disquieting in what he'd done and in the fact that the girls and the footman were on so friendly a footing. It didn't seem right, somehow—but she couldn't put her finger on anything really *wrong* with it. According to Pippa, the footman was clever, humorous, friendly and kind. He was the only adult who was willing to spend time with them, telling them fascinating stories and playing cards with them when all the others—Miss Townley, Sybil's governess, Sybil's brothers, *everyone*—turned away in boredom. There was nothing in Pippa's account of the behavior of the footman toward the two girls to provoke a reprimand, but Camilla was uncomfortable nonetheless. The fellow didn't behave like a footman—that was the long and the short of it.

But she put the matter out of her mind and hurried back to her writing desk. She had to compose an answer to Ethelyn's letter, and, for once, she was able to frame her response with complete confidence. She knew just what she would say. Her conversation with Georgina had given her the inspiration, and she couldn't wait to put that inspired idea into execution.

At first, her pen flew over the page as she told her sister-in-law that "Philippa and her dear little friend" would be arriving at the suggested time for a brief visit to Wyckfield Park. But the writing slowed down considerably as she struggled to phrase the rest of her message. *I, however, will not be accompanying the girls on this visit,* she wrote, pausing frequently to ponder the effects of her words. *I am very much tied to London at this time. You see, Ethelyn, I've been thinking, just as you have, of the matter of remarriage. You will be pleased to learn that I am seriously considering taking your advice about finding a husband for myself and a father for Pippa.*

("It won't hurt to remind her that she made the suggestion herself," Camilla muttered with a small smile.) *As chance would have it, I have recently become acquainted with a gentleman who has many qualities which would make him suitable.* ("What qualities?" she asked herself, chewing the tip of her pen thoughtfully.) *In fact, I'm certain you would agree with me that he is in several ways more suitable than the vicar's brother, of whom you wrote so glowingly. For one thing, the gentleman I speak of is not so far into middle age as Mr. Harbage. The gentleman in question—*

(She scratched out the last phrase. She couldn't keep referring to her imaginary suitor as "the gentleman in question." She had better give him a name. This detail troubled her; she hadn't wanted to dip so deeply into deceit. Giving him a name imparted to the imaginary man a certain discomfiting reality. But there was no help for it. "Thus the liar becomes mired in her dishonesties," she sighed aloud as she pulled out a blank sheet of paper on which to scribble out some experimental names. *Mr. Jonathan Invention,* she began with a nervous giggle and then added, playfully. *Mr. Robert Fiction, Mr. John Ficsham, Mr. John Invensham, Mr. Robert Fabricaysham, Mr. Frederick Falsham, Mr. Peter Fablesham, Mr. Fable Petersham* . . . "Petersham," she mused aloud. That was not an unbelievable name. It had a rather honest sound, in fact, when one rolled it comfortably off the tongue. Mr. Petersham, her soon-to-be-betrothed. With a grin, she tore up the scratch sheet and proceeded with her letter.)

Mr. Petersham, the gentleman in question, is not above thirty-five, which you must agree is an age more suited to father a ten-year-old child than a man of fifty. As for his other qualities . . . (She nibbled the tip of her pen again, trying to think of the sort of qualities she would like in a husband.) . . . *As for his other qualities, he has a cheerful disposition, a keen sense of humor and a lack of pretension. These, in addition to some of the qualities you admire in your Mr. Harbage, like good health, firmness and godliness, make my Mr. Petersham an even more promising candidate than the vicar's brother.*

It is, of course, much too soon to make a final decision on this matter, and I know you will agree that the matter should not become a subject for public discussion but be kept strictly between the two of us. However, it seems to me that I should not absent myself from London at this delicate juncture in a budding relationship.

Feeling gleefully and mischievously wicked, Camilla reread what she'd written, added her usual wishes for her sister-in-law's good health and signed her name. Then she folded the sheet, sealed it and handed it over to Hicks for posting. The deed was done.

Camilla didn't think about her act of dishonesty during the next few days. She was busily occupied in preparing Pippa for her trip to Dorset, for one thing. And for another, she was somewhat eagerly making arrangements for the first formal dinner party to be held in her new home. It was to be a small gathering—only Lord and Lady Sturtevant and Sir James Cambard had been invited. (Sir James had arranged for the four of them to attend a performance of *Cosi Fan Tutte* at the King's Theatre in the Haymarket, and Camilla had invited them all to dine with her at Upper Seymour Street beforehand.) But although the number of guests would be small, it was to be the first time the Worcester Royal china and the new gold plate would be used, the first time the staff would be required to serve dinner guests and the first time the cook would be asked to put to use her talent in preparing creams and pastries. With the packing of Pippa's clothing and the readying of the formal dining room for guests, the household was humming with activity, in the midst of which Camilla forgot all about the imaginary Mr. Petersham . . . not dreaming how ominously his ghostly presence was looming over her future.

A prompt and scathing response from Ethelyn brought the entire matter forcibly back to her mind. With her sister-in-law's acrimonious letter held in a trembling hand, Camilla realized how shortsighted she'd been to have indulged herself in the hope that her invention of a London suitor would put to rest Ethelyn's urge to control her life. It was obvious, from the acerbic tone of the letter, that Ethelyn had no confidence whatever in Camilla's ability to choose a husband for herself. *How dared you take it on yourself to surmise,* Ethelyn demanded, the heavy downstrokes of her pen making the words almost shout in anger, *that your Mr. Petersham can in any way compare with the lofty, zealous, inspired Mr. Josiah Harbage? Who is this Mr. Petersham? From your inadequate characterization I have the impression that he is nondescript at best. What do you know of his family? If he were related to the Petershams of Lincolnshire he would have a title, wouldn't he? What is his income? Have you given a single thought to any of the practicalities of such a match? I very much fear, Camilla, that you are much too fanciful and bubble-headed to be trusted to make a decision of such importance as the choosing of a suitable mate. I therefore insist that you come to Wyckfield and meet Mr. Harbage before you become hopelessly involved in a situation which will lead to disaster.*

Camilla burned with fury. Fanciful and bubble-headed indeed! How dare her sister-in-law so contemptuously presume that she was incapable of choosing a husband for herself! Dashing away a few hot tears of anger, she stalked to her writing desk and penned an impassioned reply. *Even if I were as bubble-headed as you think me,* she scribbled in impulsive wrath, *my own decision in the choice of a marriage partner would be better than anyone else's. I have learned enough of the conditions of matrimony to understand what I require for my own happiness. I know that I need kindness more than firmness, laughter more than solemnity, and freedom more than repression. These are the qualities that I find in my Mr. Petersham, and besides these, the questions of his income and his family fade into insignificance.*

I have no wish to seem unappreciative of your concern for my happiness, but I cannot permit you to assume a parental role over me. I am of age and of sound mind. It is my considered opinion that I would not find happiness as the wife of a clergyman of the sort Mr. Harbage seems to be. Therefore I shall not subject myself nor Mr. Harbage to the embarrassment or discomfiture of a meeting. I hope you will respect my wishes in this matter and not refer to this subject again.

Since I know how much Pippa means to you, and how deep her affection for you and for Wyckfield remains, I shall not—as I was tempted to do—cancel our plans for her visit. I trust, however, that you will not discuss this matter with her while she is with you. My possible remarriage is a subject of the most delicate intimacy, and I shall confide my plans to my daughter if and when I believe the time is right. Any breach of this condition will certainly cause an estrangement between us, Ethelyn, and I am sure you do not wish to cause the severing of the slim ties which still hold us together as a family.

Without even a rereading, Camilla sealed the letter and sent it off. With considerable apprehension she waited for a reply. But the days passed with no response, and at last, when the day came for Pippa to leave, and there had been no word from Wyckfield, Camilla realized that her sister-in-law had, by her silence, indicated clearly that she wished to do nothing to jeopardize Pippa's visit. In a way, the silence revealed also that Camilla had achieved a victory in the clash of wills. But she felt no sense of triumph. She watched her daughter board the carriage with a heart fluttering with misgivings.

Before Miss Townley could follow her charge into the coach, Camilla drew her aside. "You'll be sure not to permit Lady Ethelyn to persuade you to extend the visit, won't you, Ada?"

"I've told you a dozen times, Miss Camilla, that you needn't trouble your head on that score. I won't stay in Dorset one minute longer than I have to."

"Good. But there's something else." She turned her head away so that Pippa, waving happily at her from the coach window, wouldn't see her troubled frown. "My sister-in-law may wish to engage you in conversation about . . . about my possible remarriage—"

"Remarriage?" The governess's eyes lit up with delighted speculation. "Miss *Camilla!* Are you—"

"No, I'm not, so you may wipe that expectant smile from your face. But if Lady Ethelyn presses on you the virtues of a certain clergyman—a Mr. Josiah Harbage by name—you are to give her no encouragement. Just tell her you're certain I would not be interested."

Miss Townley looked at her employer shrewdly and shrugged. "If that's what you wish me to say, that's what I'll say."

"Thank you. And there's . . . er . . . one other matter. She may ask you if you know anything about a . . . a Mr. Petersham."

"Petersham? Who's Mr. Petersham?"

"No one. That is, just say you haven't met him."

"Well, since I haven't, what else can I say?" the governess retorted.

"Exactly. Just remember to say you haven't met him, and change the subject."

"All this sounds very havey-cavey to me." Miss Townley squinted at Camilla suspiciously. "Are you up to somethin' smokey? Who *is* this Mr. Petersham?"

"No one. I'll tell you all about it . . . *him* . . . when you return. But for now you'd better go along. Sybil will be on tenterhooks by this time. Take good care of the girls, Ada. I'm counting on you."

Chapter Ten

*I*t was the first time Camilla had been separated from her daughter, and she was overwhelmed with despondency. To shake herself out of the doldrums, she threw herself into the preparations for the dinner party. She knew it was ridiculous to make so great a to-do over the prospect of a tiny party, but it was the very first such occasion she would be arranging completely on her own. For the sake of her self-esteem, she wanted everything to be planned and executed with perfection.

She and the cook had already planned a most sumptuous menu. They were to start with a soup of creamed cucumbers, followed by English turbot in lobster sauce, rolled veal, a timbale of macaroni *Napolitaine,* some poultry filets *à l'Orleans,* little mutton *pâtés,* orange biscuits, cabbage flowers, Spanish celery, other assorted vegetables and a complete array of cakes, *soufflés,* jellies and creams.

A magnificent Persian carpet had recently been laid in the hitherto-unused formal dining room, and although the room was somewhat large for such a small assemblage, Camilla was determined to use it. She had Hicks remove all the center leaves of the table to make the seating arrangement more intimate, and she ordered large pots of flowers to fill every corner. On the afternoon of the event, she herself arranged three huge bowls of fresh blooms—one for the entryway, one to set before the dining room windows and one for the center of the table.

Before she went upstairs to dress, she surveyed the scene with Hicks at her side. The dining room glowed from the efforts of a household of servants who'd scrubbed, aired, dusted and polished for two days. "Everything looks lovely, Hicks," she said with satisfaction, "and you are very impressive in your tails. Just make sure that Daniel and Thomas have done everything proper with their livery. And, Hicks, see that they don't overdo the hair powder. I have a nightmarish vision of Thomas clapping his hand to his head and loosing a cloud of white flour into the air! Warn him not to do anything the least bit out of the way, will you?"

By the time Betsy had dressed Camilla's hair and helped her into her favorite gown (a plum-colored creation of Genoa velvet with long sleeves and a positively wicked *décolletage),* Camilla was feeling festive, excited and optimistic. Everything had been arranged down to the last detail. Everything and everyone was prepared and ready. There was not a thing she could think of which could go wrong.

Her guests arrived promptly and were in the very best of spirits. Lady Sturtevant, sensing that this first dinner party was special to her friend, had seen to it that she and her two escorts were dressed with appropriate grandeur. They gathered, glittering with elegance, in Camilla's drawing room, where Sir James offered the ladies many effusive compliments on their outstandingly impressive looks. The wine, which was served by Hicks with flawless formality, was pronounced by Edgar (who considered himself a connoisseur in such matters) to be superior, and Sir James heartily seconded his brother-in-law's judgment. By the time dinner was announced, several glasses had been consumed and even the taciturn Edgar had unloosened enough to laugh at his wife's jokes and make one or two sallies of his own.

The first course passed with equal success. The food was much praised, and Sir James asked for his plate to be refilled so frequently that Camilla was convinced that his kind words were more than mere flattery. The two footmen, impeccable in their formal liveries, handled the serving without a slip, even Thomas behaving with such restraint that he was barely noticed. By the time the first course had been removed, Camilla knew that her party was a success. Edgar, surprising everyone by emerging from his usual reticence, took over the conversation, starting with a toast to his hostess. He lifted his wine glass and said, "To Camilla, who should teach my wife how to organize a dinner as memorable and free from disaster as this one."

Georgina laughed good-naturedly. "Never mind," she riposted. "When she has five children to get in her way, even Camilla will find it difficult to organize her dinners as well as she does now."

Camilla sat back and smiled contentedly. Everything was going just as she wished. There was nothing more to worry about.

Edgar, his tongue loosened by wine and good spirits, began to expound on the subject which occupied all his waking thoughts—politics. Prodded by the others (who eagerly grasped at this unwonted opportunity to learn about the situation in Parliament from an insider's point of view), he told them how discontent the house was with the leadership of Mr. Addington. "It looks more and more as if he will be stepping down before the year is out."

"Will he?" Georgina asked interestedly. "You don't think your Mr. Fox will succeed him, do you?"

"No, I'm afraid not. But I will not be sorry to see Pitt take over again. He's the best we have to lead us in time of war."

"Pitt?" Sir James asked, his mouth twisted into a cynical sneer. "If you ask me, he's too old and tired to be as effective as he once was."

"Perhaps," Sturtevant agreed, "but the country admires him. And he is perceived as being a strong leader."

"He *is* strong, when you compare him to Mr. Addington," Georgina said in support.

"Can't argue with that," Sir James laughed. "Have you heard the rhyme that's being bruited about?"

"You mean 'Pitt is to Addington as London is to Paddington,' don't you? We've been hearing that one for months."

"Are you saying, Edgar," Camilla asked shyly, never having had the opportunity before to discuss politics with men of power, "that you would *support* the return of Mr. Pitt? I thought you were a staunch supporter of Mr. Fox."

"I am, but these are unusual times. With Napoleon massing troops at Pas de Calais, we are being threatened on our own doorstep. We need a strong, *tried* hand at the helm. Already the talk of Pitt's possible return has caused an increase in the number of volunteers for the militia. I've heard rumors that the number may reach half a million."

"Half a million? Remarkable!" Sir James muttered, reaching for the port. "If only the Navy could inspire volunteers in such numbers."

"Perhaps they will," Edgar said optimistically. "We English are a surprising breed in time of crisis. Perhaps they will."

"Huh!" came a snort behind him.

Every head in the room turned toward the sound. It had obviously emanated from the throat of the footman standing just behind Lord Sturtevant, a decanter of wine in his hand. *"Thomas!"* Camilla exclaimed, shocked.

"Did you say something, fellow?" Sturtevant asked curiously.

"No, my lord," Thomas muttered and bent over to fill his glass.

"Yes, you did," Sir James accused, peering at him narrowly. "We all heard you."

Hicks stepped forward from his place at the sideboard. "I'm sure, sir, that Thomas was only . . . er . . . clearing his throat." He looked at Thomas threateningly. "Isn't that right, Thomas?"

Tom looked from Hicks to Lord Sturtevant, his face impassive. "I'm very sorry, your lordship," he murmured.

But Edgar's curiosity was piqued. "Never mind the apologies, fellow. What did you *mean* by that sound? I had the distinct impression that you were making a comment on my remark about volunteers for the Navy. Do you think I'm *mistaken?*"

"I'm sure that Thomas meant nothing at all," Camilla said, frowning at her footman with eyes flashing angrily.

"Of course he didn't," Sir James said flatly. "What does a footman know about such matters, anyway?"

"Don't jump to conclusions, James," Lady Sturtevant put in, grinning. "This fellow is a very unusual sort of footman."

Hicks came up behind his troublesome underling and gave him a shove in the back. "Take this tray of dishes to the warming room, you idiot," he hissed softly, "and *don't come back!*"

But Edgar wouldn't be put off. "Let the fellow speak," he insisted. "If he has an opinion, I'd like to hear it. Don't you believe that the Navy will get volunteers, fellow?"

"No, your lordship, I don't."

Sir James leaned forward. "What on earth do *you* know about it?"

"I know enough to remember the mutiny at Spithead, and how little has been done since to better a sailor's life," Tom retorted.

Hicks met Camilla's eye with a look of pained helplessness, a look that was returned in full measure.

"But improvements *have* been made since Spithead, haven't they?" Sturtevant asked, staring at the footman interestedly.

"Minuscule ones. Just ask yourself this, your lordship. With a man like Nelson as Admiral—a man who's a hero to every man and boy in the land— why is it still necessary to have press-gangs roaming the coastal towns for recruits?"

"Press-gangs!" Sir James snorted scornfully. "Nowadays there're no such things! They're just bogeymen, concocted from stories told at ale houses. We've the best Navy in all of Christendom, and every man of sense knows it."

"Bogeymen, eh? Let me tell you, sir, that—"

"Watch your tongue, Thomas," Hicks interrupted sharply. "Take this tray—!"

"Damnation," Thomas burst out, "I think these gentlemen ought to be *told* what goes on in the real world! Bogeymen, my *ass!*"

"*Thomas!*" Hicks, white-faced in fury and alarm, thrust the heavily laden tray into Tom's midsection. "Take this and *go!*"

While everyone watched in shocked silence, Tom took the tray to the door. But before he left, he looked back at Sturtevant and Sir James. "It would be better for the Navy and this country if you gentlemen stopped fooling yourselves. Go down to Southampton or Portsmouth and see for yourselves what goes on." With that he pushed the door open with his back, walked out and pulled the door closed behind him with his foot.

"Heavens, Camilla, where did you find that—" Sir James began.

But he was interrupted by a great crash of crockery. Out in the corridor, Thomas must have dropped the tray.

Camilla shuddered. With a wince, she put a shaking hand to her forehead. Her lovely dinner, ruined! She looked up at her dinner guests in humiliation and caught Georgina's eye. Georgina was trying very hard not to laugh. Suddenly Camilla felt herself relax. "So much for my well-organized, disaster-free dinner," she said with a rueful smile.

Everyone hooted with laughter. "But we can still say it was memorable," Edgar said when the laughter had died. "You seem to have learned Georgie's knack, Camilla, of finding eccentric servants."

"Eccentric is the word for him," Sir James put in. "Belligerent bloke, isn't he? What do you make of his remarks, Edgar?"

Sturtevant looked thoughtful. "I don't know what I make of them. They had a ring of truth. Don't know but that I won't do a little investigating of the matter, just as he suggests."

"Well, we'd better not think about it now," his wife pointed out. "We are already late for the opera."

The laughter and bustle of their departure didn't distract Camilla from her fury at her footman. Even though Thomas had cleared away any sign of broken china from the corridor by the time they'd emerged from the dining room, and even though he reappeared with Daniel at the front door, carrying the ladies' cloaks and looking as calm as if nothing untoward had occurred, Camilla had made up her mind. When he helped her on with her cloak, she whispered through clenched teeth, "I hope you realize, Thomas, that you've used your last chance. As of this moment, you have your notice. You are *sacked*."

The next morning, Hicks entered the breakfast room with an expression on his face of considerable agitation. Finding Camilla already there, he hastened to pour her tea. "Sorry I'm late, Miss Camilla," he apologized, "but the three of them are packing to leave, and I can't talk reason to any of 'em."

"By the three of them, I take it you mean Betsy, Daniel and Thomas?"

"Yes, ma'am. I knew from the first there'd be trouble with 'em. From the first moment they asked for places on this staff."

"But surely Daniel and Betsy have been satisfactory. They can't be so foolish as to wish to leave at this time. Betsy's baby will be coming in a couple of months."

"I know it. And they know it. But they won't listen." He sighed as he uncovered a dish of York ham and offered it to her. "Perhaps it's just as well they go, Miss Camilla. They've given you nothing but trouble."

"Daniel has given no trouble, and Betsy is a jewel. Really, Hicks, we *can't* let Betsy go. I'll talk to them. Send them all in to me at once."

She pushed aside her plate and sipped her tea thoughtfully, trying to find a way out of this sticky dilemma. Her mind was made up about Thomas—he had to go. But she was equally determined that Betsy should stay. The poor young woman would need care for the next few months, and Camilla was determined to see that she got it.

The three servants appeared before her in short order, dressed in the clothes in which Camilla had first seen them. "Hicks tells me," she said without round-aboutation, "that the three of you are packing to leave today. I'd like to know why."

Thomas and Daniel, both looking sullen, refused to answer. Betsy, after glancing quickly from one to the other of them, faced her mistress. "Please don't be angry at us, ma'am, but we're . . . er . . . sworn t' stick together."

"Rubbish!" Tom muttered disgustedly under his breath.

"That's a very foolish sort of pledge, my dear," Camilla said to her maid, trying to ignore Thomas. "The likelihood of your finding places in the same establishment—and soon—is very slim."

"We'll manage, m' lady," Daniel said, looking at Thomas with a stubborn set to his mouth, making Camilla suspect that the two men had been arguing the matter long and hard.

"I won't pursue the discussion for now. However, I do wish to remind you that, even if you're determined to stick together, you needn't leave at once. Thomas has the usual fortnight's notice."

"There, Tom, didn't I tell ye?" Betsy said with some satisfaction.

Tom made an impatient gesture with his hands. "I don't *want* her damned 'notice.' I won't remain on these premises another fortnight!"

"See here, Thomas," Camilla said angrily, getting to her feet, "I won't have you spewing out your vile curses in this house! It would be well to remember to guard your tongue when in the presence of ladies."

Thomas bit back a sharp retort and turned away. Betsy wheeled on him angrily. "Ye've no call t' talk to her ladyship that way, Tom, and you know it. We *need* that fortnight's grace, and if she's good enough t' give it to us, we'll take it. You turn around and thank her proper!"

Thomas's shoulders seemed to sag. He turned round as he was told. "Thank you, your ladyship," he said with glum reluctance.

Camilla nodded in disdainful acknowledgement of his surrender. "Do I take it, then, that the three of you will remain for the fortnight?"

"Yes, ma'am," Betsy said quickly, "we shall. You're bein' very kind, an' we're *all* grateful."

Camilla smiled at the young woman and put an arm around her shoulders. "Perhaps you'll change your minds before the fortnight is over, Betsy," she said comfortingly, walking with the maid to the door.

"I'd like t' say we will, ma'am," Betsy answered with a small sigh, "but I don't think so."

"Well, go along and don't worry about anything, my dear," Camilla said to her, throwing a look of disapproval at the two men who were following them out. "I won't permit these two brutes to force you to have your baby on the street. See her upstairs, Daniel. I want to speak to Thomas alone."

When Daniel and Betsy had closed the door behind them, Tom turned to face Camilla with a show of bravado. "If you think all this is my fault, you're mistaken, ma'am. I've argued myself blue in the face, begging Daniel to stay."

"I've no doubt you did. You needn't sound so defensively belligerent."

"Then why did you call me a brute?"

"I called *both* of you brutes. And it was only a . . . a figure of speech. Actually, I find Daniel's loyalty to you rather touching, even if I don't understand the reason. One would think you'd saved his life or some such thing."

His eyes dropped from her questioning gaze. "We . . . we've been through a great deal together, that's all."

"A great deal?" she echoed, puzzled. "At the home of that doctor in Derbyshire?"

Tom fidgeted in discomfort. "In many places," he answered evasively.

She studied him for a moment with wrinkled brows and then shrugged. "Well, if you don't choose to enlighten me, I shan't press you. I hope you realize, Thomas, that Betsy is in a difficult situation because of you. It's not just the birthing, you know. She'll be weak for quite a while afterwards, and she will have an infant to nurse and care for. Even if you *do* find posts together (which I very much doubt), your new employer may not be very sympathetic to the personal problems of the staff—"

"You needn't tell me that you're kinder than most. I'm not a fool," he interrupted brusquely.

"I didn't intend to flatter myself, and you know it! Really, Thomas, you can be the most irritating—! I only meant to make you see how difficult it might be for Betsy if you and Daniel insist on tearing her away from here."

"Do you think I don't know? Why do you suppose I've been arguing with Daniel all morning?"

Camilla bit her lip. "If you're trying to make me feel guilty for discharging you, you won't succeed, you know."

Thomas swore under his breath. "I *knew* you'd think this was a ruse! I *told* Daniel—!"

"Whether it's a ruse or not, I warn you that I won't be trapped into changing my mind about you, even for Betsy's sake. You're an *impossible* footman, and you should have been sacked weeks ago."

"I know it, ma'am. I agree with you."

"You agree with me?"

"Completely."

She stared at him in annoyance and dropped down on a chair. Shaking her head in bewilderment, she made a little, irritated rasp of sound in her throat. "Dash it all, why must you *agree* with me? Your agreement doesn't make me feel a whit better about this situation."

"Would it help if I disagreed?" he asked with an ironic smile. "If you like, I'll make some stupid defense of my behavior so that you can get angry at me and sack me all over again."

She gave a reluctant laugh. "You *are* an original—I'll say that for you. Perhaps I should send you to Lady Sturtevant. She indicated a willingness to take you on."

"No, thank you, ma'am. If I'm as impossible a footman as you say I am, I should soon be in Lady Sturtevant's black books as well as in yours. I've done with domestic service."

"Then what *will* you do?"

"I don't know. Something will turn up."

"That sounds much too vague a program for a man who has the responsibility of another couple on his shoulders . . . and one of them an expectant mother."

"You needn't remind me. I'm all too well aware of that responsibility."

"Then you do understand that you must convince Daniel and Betsy to remain in my employ, at least for a while."

"That's why I agreed to this blasted additional fortnight," he said frankly. "With the extra time at my disposal, I may be able to convince Daniel to let me go away alone. If I can convince him that this is the best place for the baby—"

"Yes, that's the best argument. Very well, Thomas, we'll see what happens. But you are not to think, if your arts of persuasion are ineffective, that I'll change my mind and keep you on. At the end of the fortnight, out you go. I'm determined on it."

"Don't worry, my lady," Tom said with a rather bitter smile. "You can't be more eager for my departure than I am."

She shot him an irritated glare and motioned with her hand for him to go. He bowed and turned to the door. But before his hand touched the knob she stopped him with a word. "Why?" she asked in plaintive curiosity.

He turned back, his brows raised. "Did you say something, ma'am?"

"I asked why you are so eager to leave these premises. You admitted before that I was kinder than most. You've been well treated here, haven't you? And until your dreadful exhibition in front of my guests last night, I've put up with all your . . . eccentricities. Haven't I?"

He stared at her for a moment, his eyes unreadable. "Yes, you're very kind. Yes, I've been well treated. Yes, you've put up with me with remarkable patience," he said flatly. "And I hate it here."

For some inexplicable reason, she felt stricken. "But . . . *why?*"

"Don't you know?"

"I wouldn't ask if I did."

His lips turned up in a sardonic smile—the kind she'd seen on his face before. "Because, ma'am," he said quietly, "while I remain in this house I have to see before me, every waking hour of every day, that which I can never have."

Without waiting for her acknowledgement or dismissal, he turned and left the room. She didn't call him back to reprimand him for that breach of protocol. She was glad he'd left. If he'd remained, he would have seen how burning hot her cheeks had become.

Chapter Eleven

$\mathcal{L}$ ady Sturtevant had been quite right in predicting that her little Sybil would prove to be too much for Lady Ethelyn to handle. Ethelyn took a dislike to the child from the moment of their arrival, a reaction not much to be wondered at, for Sybil had three traits which were immediately manifest and which seemed to be specifically designed to drive Ethelyn berserk: one, she never walked down the stairs—she slid down the wide banister of the main stairway as if it were her personal passageway; two, she peppered every sentence with such vile epithets as "Hang it all!" and "Egad!"; and, three, she ran, skipped or jumped about the house but never walked. And no one, not Miss Townley, nor Philippa nor Ethelyn herself seemed able to restrain her.

But what Ethelyn most disliked about the child was her influence on Philippa. It wasn't that Philippa had changed in any fundamental way—she was still perfectly ladylike, affable and polite. But she showered the most unaffected and warmhearted admiration on her friend, seeing nothing reprehensible in any of Sybil's pranks. "Don't take on so, Aunt Ethelyn," she would say to her aunt in her soothing, mature way. "It's only high-spiritedness. I think Sybil is wonderfully energetic and imaginative. She means no harm at all."

As a result, Philippa was led into the most shocking misdeeds, which would never otherwise have occurred. For example, when reading to Sybil a book about the Red Indians of America, Pippa agreed to Sybil's "imaginative" plan to paint their faces Indian-style with the pigments in Pippa's old box of watercolors. When they appeared in the drawing room to show the result to Aunt Ethelyn, the poor woman shrieked in fright. Another time, when the two girls went out riding, they outraced the groom, managed to escape from his supervision and rode off the property. They didn't return for four hours, during which time every servant in the household was enlisted to scour the countryside for their bodies, while Ethelyn took to her bed in hysterics despite Miss Townley's assurances that the girls were excellent horsewomen and would probably come to no harm. By the time the girls reappeared, perfectly safe and in time for dinner, Ethelyn was in need of the ministrations of a doctor.

But the straw which broke Ethelyn's spirit was the occasion of the curricle ride. The two girls stole into the stable, harnessed the curricle to a pair of chestnuts and tried to teach themselves to drive "a curricle and pair." Before anyone in the household even realized they'd gone out, they managed to drive the vehicle into a ditch, cracking the curricle beyond repair. (Fortunately, the chestnuts were a placid pair and didn't bolt.)

But the incident threw Ethelyn into trembling disorder. *Please send your carriage for the girls at once,* she wrote to Camilla, *for my nerves will not endure another day of their misconduct. I would send them home in my own coach if their behavior was the least bit reliable, but I cannot face shouldering the responsibility for their safety. Your Miss Townley, incidentally, does not seem any more capable of handling them than the rest of us, so I cannot count on her either. I trust your grooms and coachmen are more capable of dealing with such hoydenish behavior than mine have been.*

As a result, Camilla's coachman drew up at the Wyckfield Park gateway two days before the visit was scheduled to end, and Thomas, who had been selected to ride behind, climbed down to call for his charges. Camilla had given him the strictest of instructions. "Say as little as possible to Lady Ethelyn," she'd ordered, "for my sister-in-law is very short-tempered and is a high stickler in matters of decorum. If you should fall into verbal altercation with her, I shall be most provoked. So remember to say a simple 'Yes, your ladyship,' help Miss Townley to pack up the girls' things, and depart for home with as much dispatch as you can manage. I've chosen you to perform this vital errand for me merely because you seem to have a way with Sybil. But if you let me down by the *merest slip* of your unruly tongue, the *slightest* eccentricity or the *tiniest* dereliction of duty, I shall never forgive you nor shall I write a *single word* of commendation in your behalf. I hope you heed me, Thomas, for I was never more in earnest in my life."

With those words ringing in his ears, Tom presented himself at the door of the mansion at Wyckfield Park with considerable trepidation. After sternly warning himself not to talk back to Lady Ethelyn no matter what the provocation, he heard from her butler that the lady in question had taken herself to her bed and would not emerge until the girls had gone. With relief, he went up to the girls' room. They greeted him with the effusive delight of old friends, showed him their packed valises and declared themselves ready to start for home, a declaration heartily endorsed by Miss Townley, who had had quite enough of Lady Ethelyn's taunts and Sybil's unruliness.

Tom could scarcely believe his good luck. An errand that promised to be fraught with difficulty was turning out to be as easy as bowling down a hill. Cheerfully, he tucked the valises one under each arm, took the girls' hands and led them down to the waiting carriage, Miss Townley trailing along behind with her overstuffed bandbox. As they climbed aboard and tucked the lap robe about them, Tom took their luggage to stow away under the coachman's box. There his good spirits were given their first blow. The coachman stood leaning his forehead against the corner of the carriage, his shoulders sagging pathetically. "Is something wrong, Russ?" Thomas asked.

The coachman looked up. He was white about the mouth, and his cheeks were pale. "I dunno, Tom. Feel sum'at strange in me stomach. Do ye think we could wait round 'ere 'till tomorra?"

Tom scratched his chin worriedly. "Her ladyship's expecting us back by tonight. She'll be frantic if we don't appear until tomorrow afternoon. Is it very bad?"

Russ shrugged. "Bad enough. It ain't unbearable, I s'pose."

"Then why don't we start out. If you begin to feel worse, just pull over, and I'll take the reins myself."

"Mr. 'Icks wouldn't like that. 'E says a cook cooks, an' a butler butles. 'E wouldn't want t' see the footman take the reins."

"Even in an emergency?"

"I dunno. Can you handle four horses?"

"I don't know. I've never tried."

"Then we better not chance it."

"So you're saying we'd better stay here for the night, eh?" Tom couldn't help feeling dismayed at the prospect of disappointing the girls, causing Lady Ethelyn further displeasure and stirring up nightmares of alarm in Camilla's breast, alarm that was certain to beset her if the journey had to be delayed for eighteen hours.

"What's the trouble?" Miss Townley asked, lowering her window and peering out.

Tom went over to consult with her. "Russ is feeling poorly, Miss Townley. We were wondering if we should chance pushing on or postpone our departure until tomorrow."

The girls, overhearing, groaned loudly.

"Are you in very bad case, Russell?" the governess asked.

"Not very. I've felt sick afore an' managed to 'old the 'orses."

"Then I say let's get started. If you become worse, we'll find an inn somewhere. That will be more amusing for the girls than remaining here."

Russ nodded and climbed up on his box, while Tom walked to the rear of the carriage and climbed up on his stand. He was filled with disturbing apprehensions. If the carriage had been a ship, he'd have felt more sure of himself. On a ship, he knew what to do in an emergency. A ship started out on the tide even if the weather threatened. If the storm broke, he'd know how to trim the sails. But horses were something else again.

For more than an hour the carriage rolled along smoothly. Tom, feeling the sharp wind in his face, closed his eyes and pretended he was at sea. The smell was quite different from the sea winds, but the bite was not unlike them. With eyes closed he could almost imagine he was standing at the taffrail, the deck swaying beneath his feet and the polished wood of the railing under his hand. He felt the familiar lash of pain that struck every time he reminded himself that he'd never stand on a deck again. Riding the back of a shaking coach was a poor substitute for sailing.

But suddenly the rocking under him seemed to change its quality. He opened his eyes in instinctive alarm. The carriage seemed to be swaying more than before. He blinked into the wind to see if he could make out Russ's high hat over the top of the carriage. He was just in time to see the hat sink down and out of sight. *"Russ!"* he shouted, his chest constricting.

There was no answer. The carriage gathered speed and then, to Tom's horror, he saw Russ fall from his seat and roll to the side of the road. "Oh, God!" he muttered as the carriage rushed past the prostrate body. Tom's first instinct was to jump off and help the stricken coachman, but immediately he realized that there were two little girls and their governess inside the carriage and four horses running unguided along the road. There was nothing to do but to climb over the top of the coach and try to grasp the reins himself.

The horses, feeling the sudden lack of restraint, began to race wildly, and the lurching of the coach was sickening. Within, the two girls began to scream in fright. Tom, his blood turning to ice, tried to pull himself up on the roof, but there was nothing to hold on to. The swaying of the coach was worse than the rocking of the deck of any ship he'd ridden in a storm. If he didn't move quickly, he'd surely be thrown to the ground.

He could never have said later how he managed it. In mind-numbing terror, he heaved himself up on the roof and, flat on his stomach, he inched himself forward. When he reached the front, he let himself fall head first on the coachman's seat. As soon as he righted himself, he looked for the reins, but they were flapping on the ground completely out of his reach. The wind roared in his ears, not quite drowning out the screams of the girls, hanging out of the carriage windows behind him.

He stared for a moment at the dangling reins and the blurred hooves of the four wildly galloping horses. Then, in a last ditch act of desperation, he jumped for the yoke of the two horses closest to him. He hung from that for a moment, his legs dragging painfully on the ground, and then he heaved himself up so that he hung from the yoke by his midsection. The weight pained the horses, who reared up angrily, but Tom clung to his position. Holding himself in place with one hand, he reached out for the reins with the other. He grasped them after several attempts, quickly wound them tightly about one of his wrists to keep them secure, and pulled with all his might.

The rearing of the foremost pair pulled him right off his perch. He thought it was the end of him, but he managed to hook his free arm on the trace of one of the foremost horses as he fell. Even with his lower body dragging on the ground, he was able to keep hold of the reins, which were still twisted about his wrist. For a moment he felt paralyzed—fearful that he would never be able to move—but some inner force kept his mind alert. He began to inch his arm along the trace until he felt the buckle of the horse's bellyband under his fingers. With that hold secure, he focused on taking the slack out of the reins, which were still clutched in his other hand. By turning his arm in a kind of swimming motion, he twisted the reins round and round his wrist. He didn't feel any pain, so deep was his concentration on shortening the reins. Finally, when he'd tightened them sufficiently, he yanked on them as hard as he could, at the same time pulling down on the bellyband with his other arm. Miraculously, the horses responded. They slowed down sufficiently for him to draw himself erect and, by digging in his heels he was able at last to pull them to a stop.

With a shudder, he fell down on his knees in the dust, his legs seeming to give way beneath him. He sat there for a moment while he caught his breath, but the sound of sobbing from the carriage quickly shook him into action. He got unsteadily to his feet. With every muscle quivering, he unbound his wrist and ran to the carriage door. The moment he opened it, two weeping little girls threw themselves into his arms.

He could see, behind them, that their governess was slumped into a corner in a swoon but apparently unharmed. Pippa, her slim little body shaking, was clutching him tightly round the neck and sobbing into his shoulder, while Sybil, on his other side, was staring at him through red-rimmed eyes, her childish mouth agape and her lips trembling pathetically. He hugged the children to him with a convulsive groan of relief. Dropping down on the carriage step, he rocked them silently in his arms. It was a long time before any of them could speak.

By the time the carriage drew up at the door of the house in Upper Seymour Street, it was long after dark. Camilla flew down the steps, fire in her eyes. She'd spent three anxious hours pacing about the drawing room, the last one occupied with rehearsing the furious epithets she would hurl into Thomas's insolent face, for she had no doubt that whatever had happened was his fault. But the sight that greeted her eyes drove everything else from her mind.

First she noticed that there was no footman at the back of the coach. Next, Sybil's head appeared in the window, her bonnet askew and her hair alarmingly disheveled. Then she saw that it was Thomas on the coachman's seat instead of the coachman . . . a Thomas who'd been shockingly impaired. His livery was ripped and torn, his hat was gone, his nose mangled and bloody, and one of his eyes hideously blackened. "Oh, my God!" she cried out, "what's *happened?*"

Pippa opened the carriage door, jumped down and ran into her mother's embrace. "He saved our lives, Mama! You wouldn't have believed it could be done, but he really did it. He saved our lives!"

Sybil tumbled out close behind her. "It's true, Lady Wyckfield," she exclaimed excitedly. "Egad, I've never *seen* anything like it!"

Miss Townley tottered from the carriage and added her exclamations to theirs. Everyone was speaking at once. While Camilla tried to piece the story together from their incoherent ravings, Thomas slid down from the box and went round to the back. He ached in every bone and wanted only to stretch out on the bed in the narrow attic room that was his temporary home.

How he managed to climb the stairs he never knew. He let himself into his room, pulled off his ruined coat and threw it in a corner. He also tried to remove his shoes, but the effort proved too much for him. Gingerly, he laid himself down on the bed and shut his eyes. He thought fleetingly that he ought to wash himself and examine the extent of his wounds, but he didn't move. Of all the aches and pains he was aware of, he decided that his nose hurt him most. He wondered how badly mangled it was, and if he'd be disfigured for life, but he realized with surprise that he didn't much care. In truth, he felt wonderful. There was considerable satisfaction in having faced disaster head on and defeating it.

His mind roamed over the events of the day. Everything was quite clear except the struggle with the horses. That part was nothing but a blur. But the rest . . . the feel of the little girls' tears on his neck, the tension of the search for Russ in the hedges along the road, the relief when they'd brought him to the doctor in Aldershot (who'd said the coachman had had a heart seizure but would undoubtedly recover if he could remain in Aldershot in complete rest for a fortnight or so), the look on Camilla's face when her daughter had run into her arms . . . these were memories that would always give him a feeling of pride.

He was just drifting into sleep when he heard a tapping at his door. "Come in," he said, his tongue strangely thick.

The door opened, and Camilla, carrying a branched candlestick, came into the room, followed by Betsy, who carried a basin and a small pile of clean cloths. While Camilla placed the candlestick on the room's one table, Betsy grinned at him from the foot of the bed. "We heard ye acted the hero again, ye cawker," she whispered fondly.

"Oh, good heavens, look at his poor *face*," Camilla moaned, staring down at him in horror. "Betsy, let's have the basin, quickly!"

Ignoring his thickly muttered objections, they bathed the blood and dirt from his face. There were several cuts and bruises, and the nose was undoubtedly broken, but Camilla doubted that there would be permanent disfigurement. They were just about to leave and send Daniel in to undress him when Betsy gasped, "Oh, my lady, just look at his *wrist!*"

Camilla sank down on the edge of the bed, lifted his arm to her lap and pushed back his shirtsleeve. The sight of the raw wounds made her wince. "Oh, *Thomas!*" she whispered, the tears filling her eyes.

"Don't make a fuss, ma'am," he said tiredly. "They'll heal."

"Betsy, run and fetch the herb ointment in my m-medicine drawer. And I think we shall need some more b-bandages."

Betsy scurried out. Camilla sat staring at the lacerated wrist in her lap, the tears rolling down her cheeks. Tom, feeling a drop splash into his palm, pulled himself up on one elbow and stared at her. "Are you *crying* over me?" he asked in amazement.

"Yes, I c-certainly am," she stammered with a little sniff.

"But there's no need. I'll mend soon enough."

"I kn-know."

"Then, why—"

She turned to him, her tears sparkling in the candlelight. The look in her eyes gave him a twist of pain so strong that it made his broken nose seem like a tickle. "I was s-so cruel to you . . . and you have g-given me the greatest gift," she said tearfully. "I am more beholden to you than to anyone in the world. I d-don't know what you did for D-Daniel, but if it was something like this, I now fully understand why he is so loyal to you."

He groaned in disgust and threw himself down on his pillow. "I don't want your gratitude, nor Daniel's either. Gratitude is a . . . a damned *puny* little emotion. That's not what keeps Daniel and me together. It's something much stronger, something not possible between you and me. So don't waste your tears, ma'am."

She got up, placed his arm gently at his side and gazed down at him. "If not gratitude, what is it you *want* me to feel, Thomas?" she asked softly.

He stared up at her, his eyes lingering on the wet cheeks, the curve of her throat, the glow of the hair that had fallen over her shoulder. But after a moment, he shook his head and smiled the ironic smile she'd seen so many times before. "No, I won't tell you now. In your gratitude, you might offer it to me, and it's something that goes ill with gratitude."

Slowly, with trancelike gentleness, she reached out a hand and touched his cheek. Tom, with every intention of brushing it away, put his hand on hers, but before he realized what he'd done, he'd lifted it to his mouth and pressed his lips into her palm. The skin of her palm was soft and incredibly sweet-smelling, and his heart began to pound. He heard her make a small intake of breath, and he knew that, whatever the cost—in physical pain now and in anguish later—he was going to take her in his arms.

But the door banged open, and Betsy bustled in, Daniel at her heels. Camilla, shaken back to her senses, snatched her hand away. With eyes lowered, she sat down beside him and applied the salve to his wrist. While she busied herself bandaging it, Daniel chortled with such pride over his friend's performance that Tom growled at him to stop making such a bother.

The wrist bandaged, Camilla and Betsy went to the door. "You do realize, Thomas," Camilla said, pausing in the doorway, "that, under the circumstances, it will be quite impossible for me to sack you now."

Thomas lifted himself up on one elbow and fixed an enigmatic eye on her. "Will it, ma'am?"

"Of course." Her voice was unexpectedly choked and unsteady, and her eyes wavered from his discomfitting look. "You may remain in my employ for as long as you like."

There was a moment of awkward silence, during which Thomas peered at her outline silhouetted in the doorway. The candles at his bedside shone in his eyes, setting up a smokey barrier of light that obscured her face. He yearned to see her expression—to learn if a last, tiny remnant of that look he'd seen in her face a few moments ago still remained. But he could see only the halo that the light from the corridor made of her hair. *Damnation,* he thought, *it's the second time I've lost the opportunity to hold her in my arms.* He wondered if life would ever offer him another. The answer came to him in a wave of crushing despair; when, even if he remained in her employ forever, would there come another night like this?

Betsy, who'd been watching her mistress in immobile fascination, was the first to move. She made a motion of her hand to a puzzled, gaping Daniel to start taking off Tom's shoes. While Daniel bent to his work, Camilla raised her eyes and fixed them firmly on Thomas's face. "I shall bid you good night now, Thomas, because I . . . I don't know what else to say. But I hope you know that you will always have my gratitude . . . always . . . for what you did today . . . whether you wish for it or no. You may find it a puny emotion, but I am so . . . so filled with it that it doesn't seem at all puny to me."

She left the room, and Betsy followed, closing the door behind her. Tom fell back upon his pillow and stared up at the ceiling, letting Daniel remove his clothes and chatter away unheeded. *Gratitude!* he thought in disgust. She might be filled with it, but he didn't want it. Compared with what he wanted her to feel for him, gratitude was a crumb, a mote, a nothing!

She had offered it to him with a gentle, sweet generosity, and more than once. But the last time she'd offered it—there at the door, where he couldn't even see her face!—he recognized even without seeing her eyes that she'd bestowed it as a barrier—a wall she'd hastily erected to prevent any other emotion from finding its way inside her.

Well, he knew better than to butt against a wall. But as for her substitute of gratitude . . . let her keep it!

Chapter Twelve

*I*n the warming room, Pippa sat up on the table swinging her legs and reading aloud from her very own collection of the plays of Mr. William Shakespeare, while Thomas performed his Wednesday afternoon chore of polishing the silver. He had read some Shakespeare in his youth and had always carried a dog-eared copy of *The Tempest* in his seabag, but he'd never seen a performance on the stage. The precocious child, perched on the table next to him, was reading aloud from *King John* with an enchanting dramatic verve, and Thomas's polishing cloth grew still very often as he paused to watch the girl with amazed and admiring enjoyment.

"Then King Philip says, *'How much unlooked for is this expedition,'*" Pippa declaimed in tones of convincing alarm. "And then the King of Austria answers,

> By how much unexpected, by so much
> We must awake for defense,
> For courage mounteth with occasion."

She paused, looked up over her spectacles at the footman thoughtfully and asked, "What do you suppose he meant by that?"

"That courage mounts with the occasion? I suppose he means that one manages to act courageously when the situation demands it."

"Is that why *you* acted so bravely that day when we came home from Wyckfield? Because the situation demanded it?"

"Of course. Why else?"

"I don't know. It seems an inadequate explanation. *I* was in the same situation, and *my* courage didn't mount with the occasion. I was frightened to death."

"So was I, Miss Pippa, so was I! But you were much too little to do anything about the situation, and you knew it. I, on the other hand, am a rather big fellow—and I knew I was the only person on the scene who *could* do something. So I did it."

"Are you saying that *everyone* in such a situation would have acted as you did?"

"Most everyone. Isn't that what Mr. Shakespeare is saying as well?"

"It's what Mr. Shakespeare is saying that the Duke of Austria is saying. I don't believe that most everyone would have done it, and I don't think Mr. Shakespeare would think so either. After all, Miss Townley is a very good person, and *she* fainted dead away."

"That's not at all fair. Miss Townley was as helpless as you were," Thomas pointed out. He returned to his polishing with a troubled frown. "You mustn't make a hero of me, Miss Pippa. Heroes are for storybooks, not for real life."

Pippa grinned. "You're heroic to be so modest about it, you know."

He shook his head. "No, I don't want to joke about this. I think it's important that you understand. If you make an ordinary man into a hero, you'll expect him always to act heroically. But, since he's only ordinary, he'll be bound to let you down."

"You're not ordinary, Thomas. And you won't let me down." The little girl smiled at him with serene confidence and returned to her reading. But Thomas could no longer concentrate on her rendering of the drama. He was filled with misgivings. He didn't like being made a hero . . . not by Pippa nor by her mother. It made him deucedly uncomfortable. How would they feel if they knew the truth—that their hero was an escaped criminal with a charge of murder hanging over his head?

As the winter settled in with a dogged determination to keep the populace close to their firesides, the house in Upper Seymour Street became the quiet, comfortable haven that Camilla had envisioned. Callers stopped by when the weather permitted, and she and Pippa paid occasional visits to their new friends, but their social life was not as demanding as it had been during the holidays. As far as Camilla was concerned, this was just what she liked. Although the young Lord Earlywine still called more frequently than she wished, she'd learned that she could tell him flatly to go away, and the fellow would take himself off without offense. On the other hand, Sir James's attentions were just right for her purposes, for he was delighted to escort her to the theater and to parties without wishing for—or expecting—a real romance to develop between them. With Georgina as a friend and Sir James as an escort, Camilla's social life was as full as she wanted it to be.

There was only one fly in her ointment—the arrival twice weekly of letters from Wyckfield. There was not one which didn't mention the imaginary Mr. Petersham with disdain. Ethelyn wanted constant reports on the progress of the affair, obviously in the hope that matters would take a turn to cause Camilla to break off "this strange and suspect relationship." As a result, Camilla spent many hours at her desk, biting the tip of her pen as she concentrated her mind on the detailed creation of a perfect suitor.

She began to grow quite fond of her Mr. Petersham. She felt a bit like the author of a novel as she developed the details of his character and appearance. She made him very wise for his years, and very gentle in his dealings with others. She made him generous to a fault, telling Ethelyn that his friends frequently came to him to borrow money. *He even hands out sovereigns to beggars on the street,* she wrote, *which makes me believe (although of course I have not asked him) that he is very well to pass.*

She began to see him in her mind and even to hear the quality of his voice. He was tall, of course, with thick sandy hair and a charming mustache. He had a youthful swing to his walk, a ready smile and a way of making her laugh at the most unexpected times. *The other day,* she related to Ethelyn, *I remarked that I hadn't heard what he'd said because I'd been lost in thought. "Were you?" he quipped. "I didn't know you were a stranger there."* Actually it was a jibe that she'd overheard Thomas throw at Pippa, but it served her purpose very well.

As the weeks passed and Mr. Petersham's character became more distinct, Camilla found herself almost enjoying the letter writing. There was something pleasing about creating a character, making him both unique and believable, and imagining how he would behave in various situations. She wrote to her sister-in-law about a dinner party and included a detailed account of what Mr. Petersham had eaten. (He would enjoy the roasts and the fowl, she decided, but he'd spurn the fish and the sweetmeats.) She created a little drama in which she was strolling with him down Bond Street, which was crowded with people and carriages, and, right beside her, a pair of horses shied and broke into a gallop. *It was only by Mr. Petersham's quick thinking and adept manipulation in snatching me out of the way,* she wrote, *that I was saved from being hideously trampled to death.*

In response to that little tale, however, Ethelyn wrote frigidly that she remained unimpressed. *It is quite appropriate for you to feel grateful to Mr. Petersham, Camilla, but gratitude is scarcely a reason for betrothal. I have yet to read, in all the mass of detail you write about his character and manner, any proof of the rectitude of his morals, the depth of his religious convictions or the quality of his connections. Until these things are answered, I shall not feel easy in my mind about this association. Incidentally, Camilla, I hope that during that Bond Street stroll you and Mr.*

Petersham were not without chaperonage. Do not tell me again that you are of age. You are an unwed woman and should not be gallivanting about town with only a gentleman for company. I am assuming that a footman or some other servant was walking behind you, for otherwise you would have set tongues wagging. It can do you no service to be spoken of as fast. If ever that epithet attaches itself to your name, I shall not, even with my influence, be able to convince Mr. Harbage that you are suitable for him.

Camilla seethed with rage. There seemed to be no end to her sister-in-law's determination to run her life. Angrily, she paced about the sitting room, trying to find a way to end Ethelyn's irritating nagging. Suddenly a wicked smile lit her face. She ran over to her desk, trimmed a pen and impetuously dashed off a note to end these arguments over her suitor once and for all.

> *Dear Ethelyn,*
> *Your last letter arrived yesterday and gave me much amusement, especially the realization that you still had hopes of making a match between your Mr. Harbage and myself. You will be surprised, I am sure, to learn that I am no longer available for Mr. Harbage or any other gentleman you may find suitable for me. Have you guessed, my dear? Yes, Mr. Petersham and I are wed! It was a small, simple ceremony befitting my status as widow and mother of a ten-year-old child, and it was followed by a dinner in my own dining room at which nothing unusual was served except champagne. You, my dear Ethelyn, are the very first to know. I hope you will be as happy for me as I am for myself.*

It wasn't until she'd sent it off that Camilla began to feel misgivings. The letter had seemed, at first, like a little prank—a playful slap at Ethelyn's overweening presumption. But once the letter had been posted, she recognized that she'd indulged in an enormous, bald-faced, impulsive and shameful lie. It was so great a lie that she winced inside at the realization that she was capable of such deception. What if someone close to her, someone here in London, learned what she'd done? How could she face the world?

Worse than anything, what if *Pippa* learned of it? Pippa, to whom she'd never told a lie in all these years. How would Pippa regard a mother who'd erected a complete, elaborate structure of fabrications and deceits?

She would have to confess to Ethelyn, of course. That was the only solution. But a confession would have unbearable ramifications. Her head swam with sickening terror just thinking about them. First Ethelyn would write several vituperative, stinging letters about Camilla's sinfulness and depravity. Next would come the accusations that she'd fallen into corruption only since moving to

London. Then would follow the insistence that they return to Wyckfield. And when Ethelyn had achieved *that,* Camilla had the horrifying premonition that she would find herself *married to Mr. Harbage* just to expiate her sin!

For the next few days, Camilla moved about the house in a kind of trance. She was aware that Pippa and Miss Townley watched her with worried eyes, but she couldn't seem to rouse herself to make a decision on a course of action. The problem circled round and round her brain. On the one hand, the lie was too enormous to live with. On the other, Ethelyn's revenge was too unbearable to contemplate.

In her attack of guilt and fear, she didn't think about Ethelyn's more immediate reaction to the news of her supposed marriage. In her agony over what to do about the lie, it quite slipped her mind that, to Ethelyn, the news of her wedding at this time was still the *truth.* So when she came to the breakfast room one morning, only four days after the letter had been posted, she had no inkling that matters were about to be taken out of her hands.

She kissed Pippa on the cheek and said good morning to Miss Townley with forced good cheer. Pippa and Miss Townley exchanged worried glances. "Are you feeling well, Mama?" Pippa asked in concern.

"I'm fine, love. Why do you ask? Do I look hagged?"

"Not hagged," the girl said kindly. "Just a bit . . . tired."

"You look worse than hagged," Miss Townley contradicted bluntly. "I'd guess you haven't had a good night's sleep in a week. You can't make me believe, Miss Camilla, that there isn't somethin' amiss."

"Don't bully her, Miss Townley," Pippa said in staunch defense of her mother. "She'd tell us if there was something really wrong, wouldn't you, Mama?"

Camilla smiled at her daughter fondly and rumpled her hair. "I would if I felt it was your concern," she said, taking her place and reaching for the teapot.

"That's not right, Mama. Not right at all. If something was troubling *me,* you'd expect me to reveal it, even if it weren't your concern, wouldn't you?"

"But *everything* about you is my concern, dearest."

"And everything about you is mine," her daughter retorted promptly.

"The child is right," Miss Townley declared. "You've been wanderin' about this house like a frightened ghost for days now, and we think it's time you told us about it. But I won't bully you. Just want you to know we're more worried *not* knowin' than we'd be if we were told. That's all I'm goin' to say. Now drink your tea and read your letter in peace."

"Letter?" Camilla asked, the teacup beginning to shake in her hand.

"Right there beside you," Pippa said. "It's from Aunt Ethelyn. I recognize the hand."

Camilla slowly put down the cup. Aware that Miss Townley and Pippa were watching her, she concentrated on keeping up an appearance of calm. She picked up the letter, broke the seal and, with her lips pressed tightly together, she scanned the page.

Before Pippa's and the governess's horrified eyes, Camilla's face turned ash-white. "Mama! What *is* it?" Pippa cried.

"Good God!" Camilla gasped. "Ethelyn . . . she's *coming here!*"

Chapter Thirteen

$\mathcal{C}$amilla's announcement seemed to her listeners to be completely inadequate to explain her evident dismay. "Is Aunt Ethelyn coming for a visit?" Pippa asked, puzzled. "I don't see . . . Is there something troubling about that?"

But her mother didn't answer. She just stared straight ahead of her with unseeing eyes. Miss Townley, with the familiarity of lifelong closeness, reached over and pulled the letter from Camilla's nerveless hand. *"My dear Camilla,"* she read aloud, *"if you are expecting our good wishes, you will be disappointed. Oswald and I are shocked and offended that you saw fit to take such a step without first seeking our approval . . ."* She looked up at Camilla curiously. "What step?" she asked bluntly.

Camilla turned to her and made an attempt to answer. But her courage and her voice failed her, and she merely pressed her lips together and shook her head. With a helpless wave of her hand, she signaled her old governess to go on.

Miss Townley returned to her reading. *"Our first reaction after the shock of your announcement was anger. We almost decided to cut ourselves off from any connection with you at all. But after a night filled with prayer and meditation, I thought better of taking such a drastic step without seeking further enlightenment. After all, I do have Philippa to think about. Therefore, we have decided to meet your Mr. Petersham before we judge him . . ."*

"Who's Mr. Petersham?" Pippa asked.

Camilla cast her daughter a look of agonized shame and dropped her head in her hands.

"Petersham . . . Petersham . . ." Miss Townley mused. "You've mentioned that name to me. I remember! The day Pippa and I left for Wyckfield. Who *is* he, Miss Camilla? What sort of fix have you fallen into?"

"J-Just read the rest," Camilla mumbled from behind her hands.

"... *before we judge him. As much as I despise the prospect of setting foot within the environs of that loathsome city where you've chosen to reside, Oswald and I will pay a visit and see for ourselves what sort of husband you've chosen.* Good God! Husband?"

Pippa gasped. "Mama? Has Aunt Ethelyn gone mad?"

"No, dearest," Camilla said, lifting her head and throwing her daughter a glance of abject shame, "I think *I* have."

"Have you *married* someone?" Miss Townley asked, aghast.

"No, of course not. That is . . . not exactly."

"Not exactly?" Miss Townley frowned at her in disgust. "What sort of answer is that? Either one is married or one isn't."

"I'm not married. Surely you must know that." Camilla's cheeks became suffused with color. "But I've let Ethelyn believe I am."

"Good heavens! *How?*"

"I just wrote and told her I'd done it."

"But, Mama, do you mean to say that you concocted a *lie?*" Pippa stared at her mother with something akin to awe.

Camilla's eyes filled with tears, and she nodded in humiliation. "Yes, I did. Oh, Pippa, I'm so *ashamed*—"

"What I'd like to know," Miss Townley demanded, "is *why?* I've known you too long, Miss Camilla, to believe that you'd do such a thing without provocation."

Camilla shook her head. "Thank you for saying that, Ada. It's kind of you to try to find justification for what I've done. And I *did* have provocation, but it doesn't excuse—"

"I ain't impressed with self-flagellation," Miss Townley growled. "Just tell us why you did it."

"Well, you see, Ethelyn had taken it into her head that it was time for me to remarry. She'd even found someone whom she considered suitable. Pippa, my love, I hope you're able, at your tender age, to understand and forgive me for what I've done and what I'm going to say. I was not very happy in my marriage to your father, you see, and—"

"Oh, I knew that. I've always known. Papa was not the sort with whom one could be . . . well, comfortable."

"Pippa!" Camilla blinked at her daughter in astonishment. "I didn't dream you could discern—"

"Children can discern a great deal more than parents imagine. Sybil and I were talking about it just the other day. But do go on with your explanation, Mama. I'm all agog to learn who this Mr. Petersham is."

"He isn't anyone. That is, he isn't anyone real."

"I'm becomin' very muddled, Miss Camilla," the governess sighed. "I wish you'd tell the story straight."

"I'm trying to. Oh, dear, where was I?"

"You were saying that you weren't very happy in your marriage," Pippa reminded her.

"Yes. And I am determined not to marry again. Ever. I want us to be able to remain just as we are now, all by ourselves, with no one to order us about or dominate our lives. And things were going along so well for us when Ethelyn started to thrust her Mr. Harbage before me—"

"Harbage?" Pippa's eyebrows rose. "Mr. *Josiah* Harbage?"

"Yes." Camilla was baffled. "How did you know?"

"He came to dinner while Sybil and I were at Wyckfield. I *met* him. He *couldn't* be the man Aunt Ethelyn wants you to wed."

"But he is."

Pippa whooped. "Mr. *Harbage?* He's as fat as Uncle Oswald and as sour as a lemon! All he ever talks about is vice and sin. He lectured us on all of the deadly ones except gluttony, which is the sin he forgets about because he indulges in it all the time. Aunt Ethelyn must think you're past your last prayers."

For the first time that morning, Camilla laughed. "But I *am* past my last prayers, you goose. What sort of man besides the Josiah Harbages of this world would want to wed a thirty-year-old matron with a saucy daughter?"

"I'll wager there are scores of eligibles who'd jump at the chance. After all, you *are* beautiful, and Sybil says that *that* is what counts most with gentlemen."

"Be that as it may," Miss Townley interjected crisply, "I've yet to learn the identity of the mysterious Mr. Petersham."

"It's no mystery, Ada. I just made him up."

"What?"

"Well, what else was I to do? I didn't want Mr. Harbage foisted upon me— for I didn't need Pippa's description of him to guess what he was like—and I couldn't seem to convince Ethelyn that I wished to avoid wedlock at all costs. So I created a suitor for myself as a sort of protection. And, since I had to refer to him in my letters, I gave him a name. Mr. Petersham."

"Oh, Mama, *Petersham?*" The child giggled disparagingly. "You could have given yourself away right there. Didn't you see the *sham* in it?"

"Of course I did. It was there on purpose."

"Well," Pippa conceded, "it was an inventive plan, I'll grant you that."

"Thank you," her mother said drily.

"Very artful. I had no idea, Mama, that you were so ingenious."

"Does that mean," Camilla asked, eyeing her daughter hopefully, "that you don't despise me?"

"Despise you? How silly! I only wish I could have *helped* you. I might have thought of a better name than Petersham."

"No doubt you would, you little egotist," her governess said, "but we still haven't heard the whole. Miss Camilla, what gave Lady Ethelyn the impression that you've *wed* this nonexistent Mr. Petersham?"

Camilla's eyes clouded over, and she got wearily to her feet. "*I* gave her that impression. I announced my wedding in my last letter. It was a foolish and impulsive lie, and I don't know what to do about it." She walked to the window and looked out at the small, winter-browned garden below. "In a fit of pique, I wrote her that I'd wed him, hoping to silence her on the subject of Mr. Harbage once and for all. The moment I posted the letter I realized how stupid I'd been. Now I shall have to admit to her that I've been lying to her for months." Her head, lowered in dejection, rested on the glass, and her voice became choked with tears. "Heaven only knows *what* she'll demand of me in atonement. Nothing short of wedlock with the gluttonous Mr. Harbage, I suppose."

"Oh, Mama, no! You *wouldn't!*"

"Of course she wouldn't," Miss Townley snapped with asperity. "After all, Lady Ethelyn doesn't *own* her. I don't know why your mother can't seem to be able to stand up to that woman."

"You think me cowardly, don't you?" Camilla turned around to face her accuser. "But it's not as simple as that. Pippa is a Wyckfield, you know, and will be head of the family when she comes of age. If I permit a rift in the family now, it will be Pippa who'll have to mend it later."

"Rubbish. You're only looking for excuses. Pippa already handles Lady Ethelyn better than you do."

"Nevertheless, it will not serve my daughter well to antagonize her only family. She'd not thank me for it in years to come."

"But, Mama, you can't make a sacrifice of yourself just to keep peace in the family, you know."

Camilla sighed. "I know. That's why I made up that ridiculous lie. But I've only succeeded in making matters worse. Now it seems that my only alternatives are either a complete rift or complete self-sacrifice."

Pippa leaned her chin on her hand thoughtfully. "There *is* another way . . ."

"What other way?"

"We can find a Mr. Petersham for Aunt Ethelyn to meet."

Miss Townley and Camilla both turned to Pippa openmouthed. "What's that you say?" the governess asked in bewilderment.

"But Pippa, Mr. Petersham doesn't exist," her mother reminded her.

"I know he doesn't exist. But couldn't we find someone to play his part while Aunt Ethelyn is visiting?"

"Play his part?" Camilla came back to the table, peering at her daughter in fascination. "But that's . . . impossible . . ."

"I don't know, Miss Camilla. Per'aps the child has somethin' there. We *could* convince some gentleman to play the part, couldn't we?"

"I don't see how. And besides, what good would it do?"

"He could stay here for the length of Lady Ethelyn's stay. We'd coach him to behave in as proper and decorous a manner as possible, so that Lady Ethelyn would approve of him. Then, as soon as he's won her over, she will go home in perfect contentment, and we shall go on as before."

Camilla studied the two upturned faces that gazed at her expectantly. They seemed to her to have gone mad, both at the same time. "This is utterly ridiculous. That both of you, who are always so sensible and wise, should have agreed on so wild a plan quite amazes me."

"It's not so wild, Mama. We have to concoct *something,* you know. You've seemed so happy these last months. I don't want to see you sad again."

"Nor do I," Miss Townley agreed. "If it will take a Mr. Petersham to keep Ethelyn from making you miserable, a Mr. Petersham you shall have."

"But how? Where? *Who?*"

"How about your young caller, Lord Earlywine?" Miss Townley suggested.

"*Earlywine?* He's only a boy of twenty-two! Ethelyn would never believe—! I told her *all about* Mr. Petersham. I described him in every detail—how he looks, what he's like, even what he *eats!*"

"Well, what *is* he like? Describe him to us."

"He's thirty-five years old, for one thing. He's tall and sandy-haired, for another. And he's generous, kind, humorous, openhearted—"

"Quite a paragon," Miss Townley muttered drily. "You don't suppose Sir James might pass?"

"Sir *James?* Out of the question."

"Why? He's old enough, and his hair might pass for sandy—"

"He's *too* old. And much too stocky. And he's too hearty and boisterous to pass for my Mr. Petersham. Besides, I'd be much too embarrassed to ask such a thing of him."

Miss Townley drummed her fingers thoughtfully on the table. "Then I suppose the only thing to do would be to advertise for an actor—"

"An actor?" Camilla echoed in revulsion. "How can you suggest that we bring a stranger into the house? Really, Ada, you *must* see how impossible—"

A gasp from her daughter interrupted her. Pippa had been listening to the discussion with silent but rapt attention, her eyes growing wider and wider as an idea occurred to her. Now her whole face lit with excitement. "I know who'd be *perfect,*" she announced importantly.

"Who?" Miss Townley leaned forward in fascination.

"We need someone tall, right?"

"Yes," the governess prodded.

"Lean?"

"Yes . . ."

"With sandy hair . . . and just a few years older than Mama?"

"*Yes!* You can't mean that you know someone who *fits,* do you?"

"Don't be so silly, Ada." Camilla was finding the discussion ludicrous. The entire scheme was too far-fetched to consider seriously. "Who can the child know who has those attributes, as well as being generous—"

"Generous, kind, humorous and openhearted?" Pippa laughed triumphantly and jumped from her chair. She wheeled around to her mother and threw her arms about her waist in an effusive embrace. "He'd be *perfect,* Mama! Absolutely perfect!"

"Who, child, *who?*" her governess queried avidly.

"Thomas, of course!" The child whirled her mother about in dizzy delight. "Our *very own Thomas!*"

Chapter Fourteen

"Thomas?" Miss Townley knit her brows. "Thomas *who?*"

But Camilla knew, from the first mention of his name, whom Pippa meant. "She is referring, I believe, to our footman."

"Miss Pippa, you can't be serious. You can't expect your mother to embark on this plot with an ordinary *servant*."

Pippa drew up in offense. She couldn't see any validity in the objection. "I certainly do! Why shouldn't she? He has all the necessary qualities. Besides, Thomas *isn't* ordinary. He reads Shakespeare."

Miss Townley, on second thought, had to agree that he wasn't ordinary. "But . . . but it just isn't *done*," she muttered, trying to rationalize her objection.

Camilla had to laugh. "Making up a husband out of whole cloth isn't done either, for that matter."

"That's true enough," the governess conceded, trying to imagine Thomas as master of the house. "And the fellow certainly *looks* the part."

"And he speaks as well as Lord Earlywine," Pippa pointed out. "Better, if you ask me."

"And I wouldn't be surprised if he could charm Lady Ethelyn right out of her shoes with that crooked smile of his," Miss Townley mused. "Betsy says that half the maids are openly in love with him, and the other half pretend they're not."

"You don't say," Camilla muttered in disgust. "I'm surprised we get any work done in this house at all, with that sort of thing going on."

"But you do agree, don't you," Pippa insisted, "that he's the perfect choice?"

"Seems a good possibility to me," Miss Townley concurred.

"You are both being utterly nonsensical. Even if Thomas *were* suitable, which I don't agree at all that he is, the plan is still unworkable."

Miss Townley glowered at her. "I don't see why you say that."

"Look here. Suppose we do fool Ethelyn, and suppose she goes off convinced that I've made a satisfactory match. Don't you see that it's only a temporary reprieve? Sooner or later she's bound to learn the truth, and then I'll be in a worse case."

"Why would she be bound to learn it?" Pippa asked.

"Why indeed?" Miss Townley seconded. "All you need do is keep concocting stories about him."

"But what if Ethelyn asks to see him again?"

"You can make excuses," Miss Townley suggested. "Say he's gone abroad. Or he's engaged in important governmental activities."

"Or," Pippa added mischievously, "you can say he's 'passed to his reward,' just as Papa did."

"Pippa, what a shocking thing to say! Do you *see* what I've done, Ada? I've made a lying little devil out of my daughter!"

Pippa grinned. "Yes, isn't it appalling?"

"Pippa, this is no laughing matter! If Aunt Ethelyn had heard that last remark, she would have been quite justified in saying that I'm poisoning your immortal soul."

"Oh, stuff and nonsense!" Miss Townley declared. "No one can tell me that heaven wouldn't forgive a little girl for devisin' an innocent fabrication to protect her mother from the revenge of a domineerin' dragon."

"But I don't *wish* to be protected by my daughter. What sort of milksop do you take me for? I shall tell Ethelyn the truth and face whatever comes of it."

Pippa looked up at her mother with her calm, older-than-her-years directness. "And let Aunt Ethelyn bully you on the subject forever more?"

Camilla winced. "Do you think it will be as bad as that?"

"*I* think," Miss Townley declared, "that she'll be at you until you give in and wed someone she picks out for you."

"So do I," Pippa said.

Her mother glanced at the child and then at the governess, the frown lines deepening on her brow. "If you both have combined forces to unsettle me, you are succeeding very well," she muttered, sinking upon a chair.

"Let's try the ruse, Mama," her daughter urged.

"If it works, you may win yourself a long period of peace," Miss Townley pointed out. "And if it fails, you won't be in a worse case than you are now."

Pippa came up behind Camilla's chair and put an arm about her mother's sagging shoulders. "Don't be afraid, Mama. Thomas will make the scheme work, I know he will. But even if he doesn't, think how much fun we'll have had in the meantime."

"*Fun!*" Camilla gave a tearful little laugh and pulled her daughter into her lap. "You naughty puss! You've become so much like your friend Sybil that I almost can't tell you apart. When all this is over, you and I shall have to have a talk about your new attitudes. A *very long* talk!"

Pippa snuggled into her mother's embrace. "Does this mean you're going to *do* it?"

Camilla hesitated. "I don't know, Pippa. My Mr. Petersham is a very gentle sort . . ."

"So is Thomas."

"Thomas, *gentle?* Really, Pippa, I know he saved your life and all that, but you mustn't make a paragon of him."

"That's what Thomas tells me, too. But he's always very gentle with *me,* you know."

"And Lady Ethelyn won't know what a sharp tongue he can have when aroused. She's never seen him, after all," Miss Townley added.

"But what if he lets his spirit loosen his tongue in front of Ethelyn?" Camilla wondered.

"We'll train him not to. How much time do we have to prepare?"

"Not long. I believe Ethelyn said in the letter that they plan to arrive as soon as the weather eases. Mid-March, I expect."

"Mid-March? That gives us almost a month." Miss Townley rose briskly. "I should think that will be plenty of time in which to prepare ourselves. Meanwhile, Miss Pippa, I think it's time you and I made for the schoolroom. We are already late for your history lesson."

Pippa slipped from her mother's lap and followed her governess to the door, while Camilla reached for the teapot to try to soothe her upset nerves with a fresh cup of tea. "Good heavens!" she gasped suddenly. "I forgot!"

"Forgot what?" Miss Townley asked, turning in alarm.

"That my Mr. Petersham has a mustache. I wonder how long it takes for a man to grow one. Do you think, Ada, that Thomas will be able to grow one in a month?"

As far as Miss Townley was concerned, the mustache was the least of the problems. A more immediate concern was getting her mistress to generate enough courage to ask Thomas to participate in the masquerade. Somehow, Camilla kept postponing the task. The whole subject was so embarrassing to her that she felt too uncomfortable to tell the footman the details. Every day she promised Miss Townley that she would do it "tomorrow."

Finally, Miss Townley took matters into her own hands. One frigid evening, when dinner was over and Pippa had gone up to bed, Miss Townley sought the footman out in the servants' dining room. "Her ladyship'd like to see you, Thomas," she said mendaciously. "She's in the sittin' room."

But Camilla was not expecting to see anyone. She had settled into a comfortable easy chair with a copy of Maria Edgeworth's novel *Castle Rackrent*, which Georgina had given her. She'd taken off her shoes and was toasting her toes on the hearth, completely engrossed in the romantic tale with its unusual Irish setting, when the tap on her door distracted her. "Come in," she called, scarcely looking up.

"You wished to see me, ma'am," he asked.

She snatched her feet from the hearth. "I?"

"Yes, ma'am. Miss Townley said—"

"Oh, *did* she?" Camilla colored to her ears and tried to tuck her stockinged feet under her. "Then I suppose . . . yes, well, come in and . . . er . . . close the door, Thomas."

He did so with perfect, footmanlike precision and then stood erect at her elbow. She noticed with wry amusement that now, when it didn't matter, he was beginning to master the techniques of inaudible, invisible service. She cast him a sidelong glance, rubbed her forehead with nervous fingers, and sighed deeply. "I have something to ask of you, Thomas . . . a most enormous favor . . ."

"Yes, my lady?"

She hesitated. "Dash it all, I can't explain this to you while you're standing over me in that stiff, impersonal way. Do sit down."

"*Sit down,* ma'am? You can't mean it. Is this some sort of test of my sense of decorum? If there's anything I've learned since I've been in your service, it's that I must *not* sit down in the presence of my mistress."

"Yes, but I wish to ignore the rules this once. *Please* sit down."

"Very well, ma'am, but if Mr. Hicks should come in and see me, I hope you will explain to him that I'm doing it only in obedience to your orders."

"Good heavens, but you've become a stickler. Or else you're roasting me with decidedly malicious enjoyment. Are you going to sit down or not?"

"Where would you like me to sit, ma'am? On the floor at your feet?"

She glared at him. "Now I know you're roasting me. Sit down anywhere you like, and keep your barbs to yourself."

He sat down on the hearth before her and, with a kind of natural grace, stretched one long leg out before him. She couldn't help but notice how well it was shaped, for the tight breeches of his livery and the knit stockings revealed every curve and swell. She smiled to herself, remembering her conversation with the tradesman who'd sold her the servants' uniforms and liveries. He'd tried to sell her some special pads which, he explained, all the footmen in the great houses put in their stockings to make their calves appear well-developed. "Ye wouldn't want yer footmen to 'ave legs like sticks, would ye, me lady?" he'd asked. She'd responded that sticks would suit her well enough so long as the owner could walk on them. It was just as well she hadn't bought those pads. Thomas certainly had no need of them.

"Does this place suit you, ma'am?" Thomas asked from the hearth.

"Yes, that's fine." But it was not really fine, for his back was to the fire, and she had difficulty seeing his face. However, she didn't see how she could comfortably ask him to change his place after she'd given him free choice. "I asked to see you, Thomas, because I . . . I . . ." Her courage failed her. "How's your nose these days?" she asked, switching the subject abruptly.

"It's healed, ma'am. No pain anymore. Just this funny little knob on the bridge."

"And your wrist? Is it badly scarred?"

"No, my lady, it's not. And since I assume you didn't request my presence just to ask about my health, I'll save you the trouble of making further polite inquiry by telling you that the rest of my anatomy is in equally satisfactory condition."

She glared at him. "I sometimes wonder, Thomas, if your doctor in Derbyshire really died. He isn't dead at all, is he? If I wrote to him, I suspect I'd learn that he drove you out without a recommendation, because of your saucy tongue. It's hard for me to believe that your brazen wit hadn't landed you in trouble long before I came into contact with it."

"No one ever said, ma'am, that my tongue didn't land me in hot water before my meeting with you. It's gotten me into difficulty more times than I care to remember."

"Then one would think a person of your sense should have learned, by this time, to curb it."

"Yes, one would think so, wouldn't one?" He grinned up at her unabashed. "The answer must be that I'm not as sensible as you think. But about that favor you wished to ask of me . . ."

"Favor? Oh . . . yes." She closed the book on her lap and fiddled nervously with its ribbon, a device which should have been used to mark her place. "This is a very awkward subject to have to discuss with you, Thomas, and I don't know quite how to begin. It . . . concerns my . . . er . . . marital state."

"Yes?"

She wished desperately that she could get a better look at his face. Were his eyes mocking her? "I am, as you know, a widow, and my late husband's sister has taken it into her head that I should remarry." She paused awkwardly, wondering just how to phrase her synopsis of the whole, unpleasant situation, especially the humiliating request she had to make of him.

"You're surely not asking if I concur with your sister-in-law's suggestion, are you?"

"No, of course not! What an arrogant idea!"

"Then you probably want to know which of the current candidates I would recommend—is that it?"

She gasped in outrage. "*What* current candidates?"

"Lord Earlywine and Sir James. If you ask me, neither one is worth a second look."

"I was *not* asking you! How dare you assume that I would consult you on such a matter!"

"Were you not? I beg your pardon, ma'am. Then what *did* you wish to consult me about?"

"I didn't wish to 'consult' you at all! I only wished to . . . to . . ."

"To ask me a favor. An *enormous* favor, I think you said."

She could sense, even if she couldn't quite see his expression, that he was enjoying—even savoring—her awkwardness. She was most disconcertingly aware how easily he could put her at a disadvantage whenever they conversed, yet she never knew where she'd gone wrong or what she'd done amiss. And now that she was beholden to him for saving her daughter's life, she couldn't even *dismiss* the fellow. The situation was truly impossible. And if she compounded her errors by asking him to masquerade as her husband, wouldn't matters be even *worse* when the masquerade was over? The answer was plainly affirmative . . . if she had a grain of sense she would *not* go through with this.

As if he were reading her mind, Thomas said quietly, "You needn't hesitate to ask me, you know, ma'am. There's very little I wouldn't do for you."

Those soft-spoken words completely overturned her resolve. "I . . . er . . . thank you, Thomas. That was kind." She shook her head in confusion. "I don't know how you always manage to be both arrogant and kind at once."

"If I'm arrogant, ma'am," he said in a voice that was suddenly serious, "it's only to remind the world from time to time that behind the livery there's a living human being."

"In your case, Thomas, the world is not likely to forget it." She paused, twisting the little ribbon tightly around her fingers. "But to return to the subject of the favor . . ."

"Yes, ma'am?"

"I did a rather foolish thing, you see. In order to put my sister-in-law off from her matchmaking, I . . . I told her a dreadful lie. And now she intends to visit here, and I am forced to . . . make that lie appear to be true by staging a . . . a rather elaborate masquerade. And for that I need your help."

"What sort of help?"

"I need you to . . . to play a major role in the masquerade."

"I'm afraid I don't quite follow, ma'am. What was that 'dreadful lie'?"

Camilla felt her cheeks grow hot. "It's most awkward to have to reveal it to you. What I told my sister-in-law was . . . was . . ."

"Since it's so difficult for you to speak of, perhaps I can guess. You told her you'd contracted a fatal disease, and you want me to play the part of a physician to convince her that you have less than a year to live."

A nervous little laugh escaped her. "That's very ingenious, Thomas, but—"

"No? Then let me try again. You wrote her that you'd discovered in your family a ne'er-do-well relation—a brother, perhaps—who had so sullied the family name that no gentleman of respectability would marry you. And I'm to play the black sheep."

"I can see that you can invent much better lies than I. I should have consulted you before I first wrote to Lady Ethelyn."

"Do you mean that I'm wrong again? Well, I've run out of ideas. I'm afraid you'll have to tell me the tale yourself."

She took a faltering breath. "You'll have to understand, Thomas, that it started as a lark. A little private joke that I never dreamed would come to this. I wrote my sister that . . . that . . ."

"That you'd already remarried."

She gaped at him in relief. "Yes, that's *it!* However did you—" Her eager smile abruptly died, however, as a sharp perception of the truth burst upon her. "You *knew!* You knew all along!"

He laughed, a long, deep-throated, taunting laugh. "Miss Pippa told me days ago."

She jumped up from her chair in a rage. "And you let me go on . . . stammering and stuttering like an idiotic schoolgirl!" She heaved her book at him, but he shied away in time. "Why, you . . . you . . . !"

"Bounder? Jackanapes? Makebate? Muckworm? Dastard?" he supplied, laughing.

"All of them! Get out of my sight! I don't want to exchange another word with you!"

"Yes, ma'am." He got to his feet and backed to the door, the grin still wide on his face. "But don't you want to know if I'm willing to participate in your masquerade?"

"No, I don't." She turned her back on him. "I don't care whether you're willing or not. In fact, I don't care ever to speak to you again—or to my daughter either."

"Yes, ma'am. Then I'll just say good night."

She didn't turn until she heard him open the door. "Well, *will* you?" she asked, turning slowly, her head proudly erect.

"Play the role in your masquerade?" His broad grin had become a small half-smile, and his eyes held a warmth that made something in her chest clench. "I may have been deceitful in much of what I said tonight, my lady, but this one thing you may believe with absolute certainty: there's no role in the world I'd rather play than that of your husband."

Chapter Fifteen

*E*thelyn's letter had specified that her visit would last no longer than three days, "that length of time being the outward extent of my ability to exist in the atmosphere of filth and decadence which London generates." Since the visit was to be so short (the only blessing in this troublesome situation), Camilla decided that it would be unnecessary to take anyone outside the household into her confidence. She might tell Georgie, of course, when they had a moment of private conversation, but the wisest course seemed to be to tell as few people as possible. If, during those three days, Hicks informed all callers that his mistress was not at home, none of Camilla's friends would encounter her in the company of her counterfeit husband, and thus she could avoid embarrassing explanations later.

As for the household staff, only Hicks, Miss Townley and Thomas were to know the whole truth. Hicks, as soon as he understood the circumstances, called the staff together and explained to them that Lady Wyckfield was going to play a joke on her sister-in-law by passing the footman off as her husband. "It will be only for a short time, and she's asked that you all try your very best not to give the game away. As soon as the joke is over, Thomas will return to his post, and everything will go on as before."

Hicks was also assigned the task of escorting Thomas to Bond Street to see that he was appropriately outfitted. He was measured for three waistcoats, two coats, trousers, breeches, linens, a complete ensemble for dinner wear, two pair of boots and a pair of evening shoes. The question of a riding costume—at which Thomas balked, claiming that he was too awkward a horseman to pass as a gentleman in that setting—was discussed among the members of the full committee (Camilla, Miss Townley, Pippa and Hicks), who concluded that activities out of doors would be discouraged for the three days of the Falcombes' visit; and if Oswald or Ethelyn insisted on venturing out, Thomas would make some excuse and avoid the outing.

Tom had agreed to the ruse with gleeful nonchalance, but he soon learned that he'd accepted an awesome responsibility. There was a great deal for him to learn in order to be successful at the role. First, Camilla charted an entire family tree for him to memorize. "My sister-in-law is bound to question you about your family, and you must be familiar with your ancestry in every particular," she explained, showing him the long line of descent which she had carefully worked out to avoid any possible connection with the Petershams of Lincolnshire, with whom Ethelyn had indicated a familiarity.

Then he was given a comprehensive course in deportment by Miss Townley. Every day, at a preassigned hour, she met with him and drilled him in manners, particularly in rituals of behavior at the table. She reviewed the use of the fork, she taught him how to carve a roast, how to make a toast and how to converse with comfort with the lady on his right. "That will be Lady Ethelyn herself, you know, my lad. The host's right is the place of honor. Lord Falcombe will sit at Miss Camilla's right, and she'll attend to *him*. But he's easy goin'. It's *you* who'll have the hard part."

Thomas groaned. All this was much more than he'd bargained for. His head was swimming with the tedious minutiae of his role, and he began to fear that he'd make some hideous error and spoil everything for his lady. At first the task had seemed to be a great lark—a way to engage in flirtatious badinage, as well as a chance to live for a time the enviable life of a member of the upper classes. But he began to see that the style of life was not so very enviable. It began to seem trivial and dull. He couldn't envy the gentlemanly classes if all they had to keep in their heads were inanities like the proper method of introducing an older lady to a younger one.

Nevertheless, he realized that if he made a *faux pas* or erred in any of these trifles, he would cause Camilla a great deal of trouble and distress. So he tried his best to put his disgust from his mind and concentrate on learning the foolish and superficial rules of gentlemanly conduct.

The day that his evening clothes were delivered from the tailor, Pippa suggested that they hold a trial dinner. The suggestion was seized upon eagerly by everyone. Hicks helped Thomas put on his new clothes and did some mysterious, tedious things with his hair. After more than an hour of preparations, Hicks, filled with pride, led Thomas down to the drawing room, where the ladies had already gathered. "Your ladyship," he announced from the doorway with a grin, "may I present Mr. Petersham?"

Tom entered the room with studied nonchalance. "Good evening, my dear," he said, lifting Camilla's hand to his lips. "Good evening, ladies."

"Oh, Thomas, you look *splendid!*" Pippa cried.

He did indeed. Camilla and Miss Townley could only gape. This tall, lean, elegant creature looked every inch the gentleman. Hicks had curled and brushed his hair into the style of studied carelessness that was the height of fashion. His shirtpoints were high and stiffly starched, his coat (cut straight across the waist in the latest, double-breasted mode) was buttoned only at the lowest button and revealed a magnificent waistcoat of striped satin in two shades of gray. His gleaming neckcloth, although tied very simply, made his skin look attractively dark. He appeared to be, from his stylish haircomb to his patent leather shoes, a creature of taste, breeding and intelligence.

Camilla took note of the gleam of amusement in his eyes as they met hers. He was laughing at her again. Had he been able to read in her face her reaction to his altered appearance? Could he tell just by looking at her how impressed with him she was? She felt a telltale blush suffuse her cheeks, and she looked away, annoyed with herself for her inability to keep her feelings from showing. Nevertheless, she was proud of him. She became aware of a small thrill of pleasure glowing somewhere within her at the prospect of going through the pretense of marriage with him in the role of husband.

Miss Townley, meanwhile, was looking him over with sharp, critical eyes. "Needs a fob for his waistcoat pocket, I think. He looks too austere without a bit of jewelry, I'd say."

"Right," Hicks agreed, taking a folded sheet of paper and a stub of a pencil from a pocket and making a note. "Anything else?"

"I think he's perfect," Pippa said, running up and taking his hand. "Will you take me in to dinner, Thomas?"

"It'd be my pleasure, Miss Pippa, if the rules allow. Do they, Miss Townley?"

"You must call me Ada," the governess cautioned. "And call Pippa only by name, not with the 'Miss' in front of it."

"Yes, I know, but you don't want me to do it now, do you? I'm not playing my role yet, you know."

"You may as well become accustomed to it," Camilla said. "And you'd better begin to call me Camilla, too. If you slip and call me 'my lady,' we *shall* be in the soup."

"I won't slip, Camilla," he assured her, his eyes twinkling. "Not in that regard." He'd called her Camilla in his mind for so long, it was almost natural to do it aloud.

"I suppose I'd better call you . . ." She stopped and blinked at him with a momentary blankness. "Good gracious! I've never chosen a given name for Mr. Petersham."

"Then why not call me Thomas? It's as gentlemanly a name as any."

The "committee" voiced their agreement, and "Thomas Petersham" offered his arm to Pippa as they made their way into the small dining room. Pippa and Miss Townley took their accustomed places opposite each other, at the sides, while Camilla sat down at the foot. Thomas, eyeing the high-backed armchair at the head of the table, hesitated. "Go on," Hicks muttered *sotto voce*, digging Tom in the ribs with his elbow, "sit yourself down!"

Daniel, already in his place near the sideboard, waiting to assist in the serving, grinned at Tom as he passed. Tom answered with a wink and sauntered to his seat. But it was a strange sensation to sink down upon the massive chair. To Tom it was almost like a throne. He ran his hands over the carved wooden arms with a kind of proprietary pleasure before he settled back and looked down the length of the table at the faces staring at him expectantly. For a moment his mind went blank. Then he caught Miss Townley's eye. She gave him a little reminder by lowering her head, and he remembered that he was expected to say a grace. With unaccustomed shyness he recited a short one and looked up, wondering what he was supposed to do next.

Before he could begin to fidget, however, he found Hicks at his elbow, pouring a few drops of wine into his glass. "You needn't be so miserly, Mr. Hicks," he muttered. "I won't get drunk."

"I'm just plain Hicks to the master," was the hissed reply, "and you're supposed to taste the wine and give me the nod if you approve."

"Ah, yes, I forgot." He lifted the glass to his lips and sipped it with a pompous show of importance. "No, it won't do, my man," he said, playing the role to the hilt. "Take it away and open another."

Miss Townley whooped, but Hicks glared at him. "Just nod, you looby," he ordered, walking down the length of the table to pour the rejected wine for Miss Camilla. "Don't go putting on airs that don't suit you."

Camilla agreed. "He's right, you know, Thomas. You don't want to draw attention to yourself unnecessarily."

Thomas shrugged, but his lips twitched in amusement. "I can see that you're all determined to keep me from enjoying myself. Very well, ma'am, I'll only nod, even if the wine has turned to vinegar."

"There'll be no spoilt wine served in this house, of that you may be sure," Hicks said in high dudgeon.

"I think," Pippa pointed out mildly, "that if we all keep criticizing Thomas in this way, we won't be giving him the chance to act the master."

"That's quite true, Pippa, my love," Tom said brazenly. "You have more sense than the rest of us combined."

"That kind of talk will surely spoil the child, Mr. Petersham," Miss Townley said, settling into the pretense.

"I don't think so, Ada," he responded, watching Daniel serve him his soup with a feeling of distinct discomfort. "She's well aware that she's a very clever little thing, yet it hasn't seemed to spoil—"

The door opened at that moment, and the parlormaid hurried in. She whispered something of apparent urgency into Mr. Hicks's ear.

"No, Gladys, you must be mistaken," the butler murmured. He turned to Camilla with a puzzled frown. "There's a carriage at the door, ma'am, with two occupants and a load of baggage. Gladys says it bears the Wyckfield crest. If I may be excused, I'll see what's going on."

Camilla nodded her assent, but her eyes widened with alarm. "It *couldn't* be!" she said to Miss Townley after Hicks and the parlormaid had left. "It's been less than a fortnight since her letter came, hasn't it?"

"Don't fall into a taking," Miss Townley advised. "All crests look alike to a girl like that."

"But who else would be arriving at our door with baggage?" Pippa asked.

Belatedly, the realization of what they suspected was occurring outside the front door burst on Tom. "Do you mean," he asked, starting from his chair, "that Lady Ethelyn and her husband may have *arrived?*"

"No, no," Camilla said hurriedly, waving away the thought with a nervous gesture of her hand, "it simply couldn't be. Her letter distinctly said that she would not come until spring."

"It said," Pippa corrected, "when the weather eases."

"But this is still *February!* No one in his right mind would expect the weather to ease in Feb—"

The sound of the door interrupted her. Hicks stood on the threshold, trying to hide the dismay that was apparent in his eyes and his chalklike cheeks. "Lord Falcombe and Lady Ethelyn Falcombe," he announced in a voice of doom.

"My God!" Miss Townley groaned. "We're not *near* bein' ready!"

"Don't quail now," Pippa whispered confidently, getting up from her chair. "We shall brush through." With a bright smile, she ran to the door just in time to greet her relations, who were bustling in. "Aunt Ethelyn! Uncle Oswald! What an exciting surprise!"

Chapter Sixteen

*E*thelyn's large, black-clad frame filled the doorway. "Surprise?" she asked, bending stiffly to allow her niece to kiss her cheek. "I wrote that I was coming."

"But you didn't say exactly when," Camilla said, crossing the room to exchange greetings. "But never mind. It is good to see you, even unexpectedly."

"Thank you, m' dear," Oswald said, entering the room and enveloping her in a bearlike embrace. "I've missed you. I don't mind admitting it. You must forgive us for falling in on you in the midst of your dinner." He looked at the table longingly. "We had hoped to arrive earlier—so that we'd be in plenty of time to change for dinner, you know—but the thaw has made the roads so deucedly muddy—"

"It's only by the Good Lord's grace that we managed to avoid an accident," Ethelyn elaborated with a shudder. "A dreadful trip, dreadful!"

"But you're here now," Camilla said comfortingly, "and we don't care if you're dressed for dinner or not. We shall set two extra places at once. See to it, will you, Hicks?"

Ethelyn, having handed her black, plumed bonnet and heavy pelisse to the parlormaid, turned and looked about her. She fixed her eyes on Thomas at once. *"You,"* she said accusingly, "must be Mr. Petersham."

The room fell silent. Even Oswald, who was shrugging himself out of his greatcoat, stopped with his right arm still half buried in the coat's large sleeve to stare. Thomas crossed the room with a confident deliberation, a half-smile on his lips. "Yes, I'm Petersham, Lady Ethelyn," he said, raising her hand to his lips. "I've been anticipating this meeting for a long time, and with considerable interest."

"Have you indeed? You may be sure that your interest is not a bit greater than mine." She studied him with unsmiling directness. "You're younger than I expected. And where's your mustache?"

"Mustache?" He put a hand up to his face.

"Yes. I distinctly remember Camilla's writing to me that you had an impressive mustache."

Camilla and Miss Townley exchanged horrified glances. They'd completely forgotten the mustache! After the initial concern about the length of time necessary to grow one, the matter had completely slipped their minds!

"It's quite a coincidence that you should mention it," Thomas said, leading Ethelyn to the table. "I shaved it off just this week. Pippa didn't like it."

"No, I didn't," the child said with a giggle. "It tickled me when he kissed my cheek in the mornings."

"Should think it would," Oswald said, lowering himself into the chair at Camilla's right. "Plaguey nuisances, mustaches. Used to have one during my Admiralty days."

"Were you with the Admiralty?" Thomas asked, his eyes lighting with interest. "When was that?"

Oswald, flattered by the attention, embarked on a lengthy account of his earlier career. He was encouraged by the younger man's keen questions and obvious knowledge of ships and seamanship. Their conversation lasted through the second course and was only halted when Lady Ethelyn forcibly interrupted them to quiz Thomas about his family connections. But the gentlemen returned to the subject of the Navy after the ladies had left them to their ports, Oswald concluding the conversation by remarking that young Petersham should seriously consider embarking on such a career himself.

Camilla breathed a sigh of relief when Ethelyn declared herself too travel-weary to remain for long in the drawing room. As soon as they were joined by the gentlemen, she announced herself ready to retire. After Camilla had shown her sister-in-law and Oswald to their rooms and had tucked her incorrigibly optimistic daughter into bed ("I *told* you Thomas would be wonderful," Pippa had murmured as she'd snuggled into the pillows. "He can do anything!"), Camilla returned to the drawing room where Thomas, Hicks and Miss Townley waited, grouped round the fire. "Pippa thinks you were an enormous success," Camilla said when she'd shut the door behind her.

Thomas rubbed his chin warily. "Does that mean that you think otherwise?"

"I don't know what I think. We certainly haven't given ourselves away as yet, but I feel disturbingly apprehensive. We're not *at all* ready for this."

"I don't agree," Miss Townley declared, suddenly optimistic. "Everything went surprisingly well this evenin', despite the fact that we were taken completely unaware."

"But there are dozens of matters we haven't rehearsed . . . or even *discussed,* like choosing safe topics of conversation, or inventing a reason for Mr. Petersham to be living with us rather than we with him—"

"That's because he only had rooms in St. James," Miss Townley improvised promptly.

"Very well, but that still leaves matters like setting up a program of family prayers that Thomas should preside over—"

"Family prayers? But you don't hold family prayers," Thomas pointed out.

"I know, but Ethelyn will expect it of us."

"May I be permitted to make a suggestion, ma'am? I think it would be better to behave, not as Lady Ethelyn will expect, but as we would if I *were* your Mr. Petersham. Did you make him the sort of evangelical fanatic that Lady Ethelyn wished you to wed?"

"No, but—"

"Then you and Petersham wouldn't be holding household services, would you? It seems to me that we shall be more convincing if we act in a manner that would be natural to *us* rather than in an artificial way contrived to please your sister-in-law. Something as extraordinary as household prayers might even arouse her suspicions."

"But she's bound to disapprove of the lack of them."

"Let her. Our object is to make her believe you are well and truly wed, isn't it? You needn't win her approval to accomplish that."

"The fellow's right, Miss Camilla," Miss Townley said. "She's never approved of you anyway, and never will."

"But if she takes *Thomas* in dislike—"

"She won't," Miss Townley insisted. "I'm willin' to wager on it."

"Very well, Thomas, I'll take your advice. But that solves only one of our problems. I can't begin to enumerate all the others. There's your incompleted training, for one thing. For another, we haven't even *begun* to discuss how you and I are to behave toward each other—"

"Yes, and there's also the problem of where he's to sleep," Miss Townley added bluntly. "We can't have him sleepin' in the attic while Lady Ethelyn's here. She'll be bound to discover it."

"And there's something more," Hicks said worriedly. "His second coat hasn't yet arrived, nor his boots from Hoby's. He can't come down to breakfast tomorrow in his evening shoes."

"I can wear the shoes I've used with my livery. They'll do for a while. And the blue coat will do for tomorrow, won't it?"

"Yes, of course it will," Miss Townley said, nodding vigorously. "A little calm thinking is all we need to brush through."

"Right," the butler agreed, brightening. "I'll send Daniel out first thing in the morning to prod Hoby about the boots. Now what about his sleeping quarters?"

Camilla, pacing about the room thoughtfully, was so concerned about the possibility of forgetting some important detail (as she'd done about the mustache) that the butler's question failed to embarrass her. "With Ethelyn and Oswald occupying the two spare bedrooms, there isn't even a place for him upstairs."

"He ought to have a room adjoinin' yours," Miss Townley pointed out. "How about mine? I can have a bed set up in Miss Pippa's room."

It was an obvious and simple solution. "Of *course*," Camilla said with a relieved smile, pleased that a knotty problem had been so easily solved. But immediately after the words had left her tongue, a wave of mortification flooded over her. Miss Townley's room connected with hers through a door in her dressing room. Although it was inconceivable that Thomas would ever attempt to enter her bedroom that way (and besides, she could keep the door locked), the very thought of the *possibility* brought the color rushing up to her face. "That will do . . . er . . . nicely," she added lamely, turning her blushing face to the fire.

Miss Townley scurried off to arrange for a bed, and Hicks, declaring his intention to move all Thomas's things into his new quarters at once, followed the governess out. Camilla knew that it was up to her to deal with the largest remaining problem—how she and Thomas were to treat each other to give the appearance of a newly wed couple. She sank upon the sofa and looked up at him. "I don't suppose you've ever been married, have you, Thomas?"

"No. Why do you ask?"

She twisted her fingers together uneasily. "It would be helpful if *one* of us was familiar with the disposition and bearing of newlyweds . . ."

He studied her curiously. "But *you've* been married—"

"Yes, of course." Her eyes fell. "But it was a . . . a very long time ago."

So, he thought with a start, aware of a completely reprehensible feeling of satisfaction, *she wasn't happy in her marriage.* No wonder she didn't wish to be pushed into a second one. In wedlock, he suspected, even more than in other matters, once burned was twice shy. He looked down at her with a strong surge of sympathy. What suffering had her husband inflicted on her? he wondered. Sitting in the dim firelight, her eyes lowered shyly and her hands clenched in her lap like a frightened child's, she looked more vulnerable to the storms of life than the lowliest housemaid on the staff. This wasn't the first time he'd felt an urge to protect her from those storms, but tonight he felt it painfully. *He* could be a better husband to her than any nobleman he'd seen in her company (and evidently better than the one she'd had), but the conventions of society would never give him the chance to prove it. This game of pretense in which they were engaged was the closest approximation that life would ever offer him.

He sat down beside her, fighting the impulse to take one of her hands in his. "As to the disposition and bearing of newlyweds . . ." he began.

"Yes?" Her eyes flickered up to his face with a look of such hopefulness that it knotted his stomach.

"Their behavior shouldn't be very difficult to simulate. They'd behave like lovers, wouldn't they? Casting each other affectionate glances every now and again—"

"Yes," Camilla nodded, "and secret little smiles—"

"And slight touches of the hands as they pass each other on the stairs—"

She gave a flustered laugh. "Yes, that sort of thing. I suppose it will be quite awkward for us to have to engage in such goings-on—"

"Not for me." He grinned. "I shall not experience the least difficulty. And if it is difficult for you, an observer will only conclude that you are endowed with a most becoming modesty."

"Thank you for saying that," she murmured, getting to her feet and smiling down at him with greater warmth and relaxation than she'd been able to summon up since her sister-in-law had arrived. "You've been most helpful in this appalling muddle, Thomas—more than anyone could have had a right to expect. I am very grateful—"

He made a face at her as he rose. "Gratitude again! I wish to remind you, ma'am, that it's an offering which I don't prize."

"Very well, I'll try to leave it unsaid in the future. And now, I suppose, we may as well go up to bed. There isn't much else to be accomplished tonight."

They walked up the stairs in an uneasy silence. At the door to her room, they paused. "I suppose you know that the door to Miss Townley's room is the one just beyond," she whispered.

"Yes, I know."

"Good night, then, Thomas. I hope you sleep well."

But he didn't respond. He was staring at her with an unnerving intensity—a speculative look which, in the dim light of the corridor, she couldn't even begin to interpret. She blinked up at him questioningly, but before she could phrase an inquiry, she was pulled abruptly into his arms.

It had suddenly occurred to him that he'd almost kissed her twice before, yet each time he'd let the opportunity pass. Each time he'd hated himself for his vacillation. But now fate had provided him with an unprecedented third chance, and he was not going to miss it again. No vacillation nor hesitation this time. He tightened his arm about her waist, held her close and tilted her face up to his.

She stiffened in an involuntary, conditioned, immediate revulsion. "Desmond, *don't!*" she whispered, her eyes terrified.

He looked down at her, his eyes and voice gentle. "I'm not Desmond," he said and kissed her.

Slowly, firmly, with the mounting excitement caused by months of frustrated desire, he tightened his hold on her, his pulse racing. Not since the first time he'd thrilled to the effect of a wild wind on a schooner with fully expanded sails had he felt like this. Camilla, at first stiff and resistant in his arms, seemed slowly to melt in a sweet, heart-stopping submission, like a ship bending to the wind. *God, how I love her,* he thought exultantly.

At last he lifted his head, but he couldn't bring himself to let her go completely. She swayed in his arms, her eyes closed. After a moment the lids flickered open, her expression startled, as if she didn't know quite where she was. But almost immediately, she focused on his face and gasped. "Thomas! How *dare* you!"

He grinned and let her go. "Your Mr. Petersham is a fellow of rather warm affections," he said, his voice not quite steady. "You may as well get used to him."

He turned and proceeded down the hall with a step that was decidedly jaunty. She stared after him, openmouthed and breathless. When he reached his door, he looked back at her. "Good night," he sang out in a voice loud enough to be heard the entire length of the corridor. "Good night, Camilla, my love."

He disappeared into the room, leaving Camilla in a whirl of confusion. Was he being insolent or merely playing his role? Or was there, in his vexatious, troubling, utterly disturbing behavior, some other motive entirely?

Chapter Seventeen

$\mathcal{I}$t was immediately evident to Betsy, waiting for her mistress in the dressing room, that Miss Camilla was in a state. The lady's lips were pressed together in agitation, her nerves seemed overwrought, and she answered all Betsy's inquiries about the success of the evening with abstracted monosyllables. "Is anything wrong, my lady?" Betsy asked, bending clumsily to help Camilla take off her shoes.

Camilla, with an effort, forced herself to attend. "No, of course not," she muttered, blinking herself into concentration. "What are you doing, bending down like that? Betsy, you mustn't do such things! Your time is too close—"

Betsy smiled and pulled herself erect. "It's nothin', ma'am. I feel perfectly well."

"Nevertheless, I don't wish you to overexert yourself. Besides, you should be in bed at this hour. I told you not to wait up for me past ten—ever!"

"But, ma'am, who'd be here t' undo yer buttons?"

"I can undo my own buttons, thank you. Go to bed at once, woman. I shall manage without you."

The maid went reluctantly to the door. "I laid out yer nightdress, ma'am, and—"

"Good *night,* Betsy," Camilla said pointedly.

"Well, if ye're sure there's nothin'—"

"I'm sure."

Betsy, opening the door, threw Camilla a last, worried look. "G'night, then, Miss Camilla. I hope ye sleep well." With a troubled shake of her head, she closed the door behind her.

Camilla stripped off her gown and slipped into her nightdress without being aware of what she was doing. The scene in the corridor had shattered the last of her self-possession, and she felt frightened and confused. She crept into bed and drew up the covers to her neck, but she found herself shivering all the same. Thomas had shaken her to the core.

The truth was that she'd never, in all her life, been kissed in such a way. The kiss had profoundly disturbed her. Her husband's kisses had been cold, astringent things, calculatedly indulged in and hastily dispensed with, like small hurdles he'd had to step over on his way to his goal. She had never been stirred by them. But Thomas's kiss had been fraught with emotion. She'd felt the tremors in his arms, the pounding of his heart, the stoppage of his breathing. The kiss had been no small thing to him. Despite his taunting insolence after he'd let her go, he'd been deeply moved. That understanding moved her deeply, too.

But what did it mean? That he loved her? Perhaps he did, but such a love could only bring him pain. She was sorry for him. But even more disturbing to contemplate was her *own* reaction to the embrace. She should have been horrified, as any lady would be, at such an unthinkable liberty taken by a servant. Yet she'd felt . . . what? Not horror at all. Oh, at first she'd been seized with a sort of habitual terror, not because her servant was taking liberties but because for a moment she was reminded of Desmond. But after that brief panic, she'd found her fear dissipating into the most astounding and blissful lassitude. Desmond had been threatening, but Thomas had made her feel, somehow, *safe*. She'd let herself relax against him, her blood tingling with the most delightful sensations. It had been a dizzying, rapturous awakening of feelings she hadn't known existed inside her. She'd felt positively regretful when he'd let her go.

She lay awake, staring into the glowing embers in the fireplace, trying to understand what had happened to her. She couldn't be in love with her footman—that was unthinkable! Besides, she'd surmised when she lived with Desmond that she was probably incapable of loving a man. Then how was she to explain to herself this strange stirring of the blood? She was either a too-easily-unbalanced fool or an amoral sensualist, she supposed, and neither one of these designations was particularly pleasant to contemplate.

But if she *were* capable of that sort of love—if she were ever to consider remarriage—she had the disturbing perception that Thomas, her footman, would be nearer an embodiment of her ideal of a lover than any of the gentlemen she was likely to meet. That perception was both thrilling and depressing— thrilling because she was, perhaps, capable of love after all; and depressing because, if true, she would be as subject to pain as he was likely to be. After all, what future could there be for them?

With all these upsetting questions still swirling about in her head, she entered the breakfast room the next morning tired, heavy-eyed and cross. Her mood was not abated by finding that everyone had come down before her; Ada had evidently finished earlier, but Pippa, Ethelyn, Oswald and Thomas were all smiling up at her from their places at the table. She gave them a feeble greeting, took her place and lowered her eyes to her plate. Like an ostrich, she hoped that by avoiding the eyes of the others in the room she would make herself invisible.

She was in no condition to face up to the nerve-wracking challenges which the day would surely bring. It had been a terrible night and had left her with a number of unanswered questions, dismaying possibilities and a headache. She tried to ignore the sound of the voices eddying around her by concentrating on sipping her tea. But Thomas and Ethelyn seemed to be engaged in some sort of debate, and she surreptitiously lifted her eyes and looked over her cup to discover what was going on.

The faces were all quite cheerful. Ethelyn had apparently slept well, for she was smiling pleasantly at Thomas even though disagreeing with him. "But you must admit," she was saying, "that the draperies in this room, being made of that diaphanous material, are much too frivolous to be considered in good taste."

"I am no arbiter of taste, ma'am," Thomas responded, "but I find them most pleasing to the eye, besides permitting the light to filter in quite cheerfully. If you're saying that the choice of fabric is unconventional, I shall take your word for it, of course. But I'm not put off by unconventionality. Are you?"

"Well, I . . . I . . ." Ethelyn was at a sudden loss. She was, in reality, very uncomfortable with unconventionality, but she didn't like to admit it.

"I've heard Camilla's friends seek her advice very often on matters pertaining to the decoration of their establishments," Thomas said, pushing his advantage, "so I'm not alone in believing her taste to be admirable."

"What other opinion can I expect from a besotted newlywed?" Ethelyn said, smiling at him indulgently.

"Sybil says," Pippa volunteered, "that Lady Sturtevant and all her circle consider this house to be the most agreeably harmonious in decor of any in their set."

"You don't say," Ethelyn muttered, unconvinced. "Nonetheless, one must note that such draperies are woefully inadequate when drawn at night. How can they be expected to keep out draughts?"

"Since we never sit in here at night, that is a problem which doesn't much affect us," Thomas pointed out.

Camilla bent to her cup to keep her smile from showing. How delightful it was to have someone to fight her battles . . . someone at her side who could be counted on for support and protection! She felt her spirits rise and her tension ease. Ethelyn would have a difficult time winning an argument from her irrepressible footman.

It wasn't long before Ethelyn engaged him again in dispute, this time on a matter she considered much more serious than draperies. "Are you saying," she demanded in a voice choked with aversion, "that you don't hold family prayers *at all?*"

"No, we don't. I suppose you'll think us godless reprobates, ma'am, but—"

"I consider you to be a typical London *degenerate!*" she exclaimed. "Camilla, how *could* you—after all the warnings and instructions I gave you and the promises you made to me—permit such neglect of your child's moral upbringing, to say nothing of your own—"

"I assure you, ma'am, that Pippa's moral upbringing has not been neglected," Thomas said firmly, "and that—"

"The child's name is *Philippa!*" Ethelyn cut in coldly.

"I *like* to be called Pippa," the girl said in loyal defense.

"Yes, Ethelyn," Camilla supported quickly. "It's only an affectionate nickname. Thomas uses 'Philippa' on formal occasions, just as he ought."

"But we are moving from the point, ma'am," Thomas said. "In regard to family prayers, it is our belief that—"

"*Our* belief!" Ethelyn scoffed. "I am thoroughly familiar with *Camilla's* beliefs, so you needn't waste your breath. Camilla is the sort, I am sorry to say, who bends to the strongest wind. It's quite clear to me that you've coerced her to accept your undoubtedly latitudinarian views against her own better instincts."

"Ethelyn, that's not *true!*" Camilla cried. "You have no idea *what* my instincts are in this regard. You've never let me express them."

"And as to coercion, Lady Ethelyn," Thomas said calmly, "you completely misunderstand how we live in this house. There is no coercion here. We long ago discussed among ourselves (for Pippa's views are as important to us as our own) our feelings about religious observances, and we were unanimously agreed that—"

"Are you trying to make me believe that both Camilla *and* Philippa willingly agreed to forgo the very observances that had been so important a part of their former lives?"

"Not to forgo them, ma'am. Only to change the outward form." He passed a plate of biscuits to Ethelyn with a smile. "Daily family prayers are very public displays, you know. We prefer to perform our obeisances in private."

"In *private?* What's privacy to do with it?"

"Well, if one thinks about it," Oswald interjected with unaccustomed bravery, "praying in private is more . . . more straightforward."

"More sincere," Pippa amended.

"Yes, that's true," Camilla said with unusual assertiveness. "In private devotions, one is less apt to be swayed by the practices and opinions of others."

"And less likely to mouth words by rote," Thomas said. "Private prayers are less a matter of ritual and more a matter of honest faith."

"*Give me, kind heaven,*" Pippa recited a bit pompously, "*a private station,/ A mind serene for contemplation.*"

Ethelyn stared at the child, speechless. Philippa had even brought in poetry to join with the others at the table in giving support to a position which Ethelyn had, until this moment, found untenable. Now, however, she was quite at a loss as to how to argue the matter; one could hardly debate the value of attempting a private communion with one's God. She looked from one to the other of the faces surrounding her, shrugged and reached for the teapot. "Hummmph!" was all she said when she found her voice.

Thomas and Camilla exchanged looks of triumph, while Pippa squeezed her hero's hand under the table to show her pride in him. Thomas seemed never to let her down. She looked at her mother with an expression that said as clearly as words, *See? He's every bit as wonderful as I said he'd be.*

But Camilla, proud of his performance though she was, tempered her satisfaction with her awareness that she hadn't heard the last of the matter from Ethelyn. If she knew her sister-in-law at all, she was certain that Ethelyn would not let the subject of family prayers pass without further argumentation.

But the subject did not come up again. In fact, the day passed with surprisingly little strain. Ethelyn found nothing to complain about until teatime, when a small occurrence threatened to cause the break that Camilla had been fearfully anticipating all day.

Hicks, assisted by Daniel and the parlormaid, Gladys, had done the serving. The butler had not forgotten his former difficulties with the woman who was now a guest in the house, and he'd been particularly frozen-faced during the repast. After Pippa and Miss Townley had finished their tea and returned to the schoolroom, and the servants had taken their leave, Ethelyn remarked between bites of her sweet roll that she was surprised to see the butler still part of the household.

"Hicks?" Thomas asked in surprise. "Why should he not be?"

"The fellow is a dreadful incompetent, and rude in the bargain. Only Camilla's completely misguided loyalty explains his continued presence here," Ethelyn declared, brushing the crumbs from the impressive expanse of black bombazine that covered her bosom.

"But he's always seemed to me to be the most perfect of butlers," Thomas insisted.

"You are only a man. Men never take proper notice of the quality of their servants, except, of course, their valets."

"Hicks has doubled as valet for Thomas," Camilla said defensively, rising to her feet, "and he's never expressed the *slightest* dissatisfaction with him!"

"Pooh! That only proves that your husband is too easy to please. I'll have you know, Thomas, that your wife is notoriously incompetent in dealing with servants."

Camilla colored to her ears. "Really, Ethelyn!"

But Thomas, getting to his feet, couldn't help chuckling. "Is she indeed?" He crossed the room and put a comforting arm around Camilla's waist. "It has always seemed to me that she deals with her servants remarkably well," he said, looking down at her fondly.

Camilla's color heightened. To the onlookers they seemed the epitome of happy newlyweds. "That's because you're obviously bewitched," Ethelyn said placidly, helping herself to another bun.

Oswald chortled in agreement. "That much is quite plain. Smelling of April and May, the pair of you."

"But when the bloom wears off," Ethelyn predicted, "you'll discover for yourself what havoc a crew of incompetent servants can create."

Thomas looked down at the woman he held encircled in his arm. "I doubt that the bloom will ever wear off," he murmured. "Will it, my love?"

"Never," she answered, meeting his eyes with a wide-eyed glow in her own.

"So you see, ma'am," Thomas said to Ethelyn while bending to plant a kiss on Camilla's cheek, "the servants will never be a problem to us. We'll never bother to notice whether they're incompetent or not."

"That," Ethelyn responded acidly, "is nothing but foolishness. And I can't say I approve of such public snuggling and caressing, either."

"This isn't public," Oswald pointed out. "We're family."

"Nevertheless—"

"Nevertheless, Lady Ethelyn," Thomas said firmly, taking Camilla's hand and leading her to the sofa, "this is our home, where we can behave as we like. We shall hold hands if we like, hold prayer where we like, hire servants whom we like. This is a happy house, you see, and we intend to keep it that way. We shall always be glad of your approval, of course, but we can't permit ourselves to seek that approval at the expense of our own happiness. You yourself would not wish us to act otherwise."

Camilla stared up at him, her throat contracted. Those were the very words she herself would have liked to say to Ethelyn but had never found the courage to utter. She lifted a hand to his arm and drew him down beside her. "Thank you, my dear," she said softly.

Ethelyn looked from one to the other. "Hummmph!" she said and took another bite of her bun.

Later, on her way up to dress for dinner, Camilla came upon her sister-in-law on the stairs. It was the first time since Ethelyn's arrival that they'd been alone in each other's company, and Camilla held her breath and waited for what she was certain would be the inevitable diatribe against the manners and morals of the husband she'd dared to select without her sister-in-law's permission. But Ethelyn only said, "Your Thomas is a man of strong opinions."

"Yes, I . . . I suppose he is," Camilla murmured, bracing herself for the attack.

"I don't hold with all his views, of course, but he's a great deal more sensible than I'd expected him to be."

Camilla, though inwardly breathing a sigh of relief, was nonetheless offended. "What *did* you expect, my dear?" She asked with a wry smile. "That I would wed an imbecile?"

Ethelyn paid no heed to the sarcasm. "Perhaps not an imbecile, but I *did* expect a weakling. I didn't think your spiritlessness would attract any other sort."

"Thank you very much indeed!" Camilla said curtly. "Now that you see that you were mistaken, do you find it possible to admit that I am, perhaps, not as spiritless as you thought?"

"Now don't climb up on your high ropes. I meant no offense. I've always told you that you were too amenable—"

"I might have appeared so . . . but only because I didn't wish forever to be arguing with you."

"Be that as it may," Ethelyn said, strolling down the corridor beside the younger woman in complacent self-assurance, "I will admit that no one can say your husband is a milksop."

Camilla gave a dry little laugh. "No, one certainly can't. 'Milksop' is the *least* fitting of words to describe my hus—er . . . Thomas."

"All things considered," Ethelyn mused, patting Camilla's hand approvingly, "it seems to me that you haven't done badly for yourself. Not badly at all."

With a satisfactory verdict thus pronounced, Lady Ethelyn saw little reason to prolong her visit. She informed Camilla the next morning that she and Oswald would remain for one more night only. "No matter how pleasant the company, my dear," she said, "London is still London. It is, and always will be, a blemish on the English isles. Now that I've seen for myself that your situation is tenable as far as your marriage is concerned, I feel no need to remain. We shall leave tomorrow after breakfast."

Camilla could scarcely believe her ears. A wave of relief swept over her so strong that she felt almost giddy. What a triumph! They had *done* it; the ruse had succeeded. Thomas's wonderful performance had transformed her deceitful tale into a most believable performance. And now she would be free—free of

Ethelyn's interference, free of her past, free to live her life as she wished. She wanted to dance around the room in joy.

In the heady delight of the relief of her tension, she determined to make this last evening of her sister-in-law's stay as festive and enjoyable as possible. With Hicks and the cook, she devised a menu fit for royalty. Then, while Ethelyn took an afternoon nap and Oswald went out to stroll through the streets near Whitehall, where he'd once spent so much of his time, the staff went to work to ready the large dining room for its second use.

The entire household was in a flurry. Daniel and the housemaids dusted the chandeliers, polished the plate, waxed the floor, aired the room and set the table. The kitchen staff bustled about in a frenzy, for her ladyship had decided on serving not only partridge filets *à la Pompadour,* a veal ragout with onions, a roast of beef, a fish stew *Bordeaux,* three kinds of bread and six side dishes, but, to please Lord Falcombe's sweet tooth, a lemon gelatine mold, a "Turkish Mosque" cream, and some tiny apple-filled pastries, which took great effort to concoct.

Pippa was quite put out when she learned that she would not be permitted to attend the dinner party. "It will be Thomas's last dinner as your husband," she pouted, "and I had my heart set on observing him."

"I'm sorry, love," her mother explained gently, "but it is not appropriate for girls your age to attend such affairs. And besides, we shall take our places at the table at an hour much too late for you. I promise to observe everything very carefully and to tell you the whole tomorrow in great detail."

With that Pippa had to be content. But she instructed Miss Townley, who'd been invited to attend, to be equally observant. "I want to know *everything* that Thomas says and does," she requested, "so, please, Miss Townley, watch and listen as carefully as you can."

Miss Townley, who was busily letting out the waist of a gown which Miss Camilla had given her, merely grunted. "Ye'll turn into a regular busybody if you don't watch yourself," she said brusquely, biting off a thread. "Better get your nose back into that book and work on your French declensions."

By early evening, all was in readiness. But Camilla's careful plans were slightly disrupted when Oswald returned from his outing with the news that he'd met an old friend, Lord Jeffries, while walking near Whitehall. Lord Jeffries, who was still with the Admiralty, had been delighted to see him, and they'd spent more than an hour chatting about old times. Oswald had so enjoyed the encounter that he'd impulsively invited Jeffries and his lady to join them for dinner. "I hope, Camilla, my love," he apologized, puffing over his exertions to remove himself from his greatcoat, "that I haven't inconvenienced you."

"No, of course not, Oswald. I shall simply have Hicks set two more places. It will be very pleasant to expand our party. Let's see . . . with you, Ethelyn, Ada,

Thomas and me . . . that means we shall be seven all together. I'd better tell Cook at once."

But there were to be eight. When Lord Jeffries and his wife tapped at the door a little before nine that evening, they were accompanied by a naval officer in full dress uniform. "I hope your mistress won't mind my having brought an extra guest," Lord Jeffries said, handing his chapeaubras to Hicks.

Hicks, in turn, passed the chapeaubras to Daniel, who was standing just behind him, stiff and uncomfortable in his formal livery. The footman had put out his hand to take the hat when he saw the face of the "extra guest." The chapeaubras fell from his suddenly nerveless fingers. It was all he could do to keep from gasping.

"I'm sure my mistress will be delighted," Hicks said with a polite smile, bending down smoothly and retrieving the fallen headpiece. He thrust it into Daniel's hand with a warning glare and, his face restored to composure, turned to assist Lady Jeffries with her cloak.

The "extra guest" handed his hat to Daniel and turned away, but Daniel had gotten a close-enough look to be certain he wasn't mistaken. The gentleman was sickeningly familiar. He was tall, thin, with iron gray hair and a neatly trimmed beard. The only thing unfamiliar about his face was a livid scar which ran from the bridge of his nose diagonally across his forehead to the left corner of his hairline. But Daniel knew quite well how the scar had come there . . . and he felt his blood run cold. *Oh, God,* he thought wildly, *how can I warn Tom?*

Hicks had removed Lady Jeffries's cloak, and he tossed it to Daniel as he led the guests toward the drawing room, where the family waited. Daniel, in a helpless panic, followed them down the hall, hoping desperately for some sort of inspiration which would suggest a way out. But none came.

Hicks threw open the doors of the drawing room. "Lady Jeffries, Lord Jeffries, and Captain Everard Brock," he announced as the guests filed in.

While Oswald jumped to his feet (with all the alacrity that his huge bulk permitted) and began to make the introductions, Daniel peered over the butler's shoulder into the room. He spotted Tom almost at once and knew immediately that his friend had recognized the unexpected guest. Tom was poised, immobile, halfway between sitting and standing, his hand extended, a smile frozen on his face. Oswald was leading Captain Brock, of His Majesty's Ship *Undaunted,* across the room to meet him, but before the meeting took place, Tom's eyes met Daniel's. And, in that one timeless moment, each could read in the other's face the starkly terrifying certainty of impending doom.

Chapter Eighteen

"Captain Brock, may I present our host, Thomas Petersham? Thomas, the captain commands the *Undaunted,* which, you may know, distinguished itself at Camperdown."

Tom pulled himself erect and smiled. "Who doesn't know of the victory at Camperdown? This is indeed an honor, Captain Brock."

The men shook hands. Captain Brock squinted at Tom closely. "We haven't met before, have we? I have a feeling that—"

"I surely would have remembered meeting the captain of the *Undaunted,*" Thomas said smoothly. "But come and meet my wife, Captain. She won't forgive me if I keep you too long to myself."

As the rest of the introductions were made, Hicks and Daniel passed among the guests offering glasses of sherry. Tom, reaching for a glass from Daniel's tray, moved aside with him as inconspicuously as he could. "We're cooked fer sure," Daniel whispered through unmoving lips. "Let's make a run fer it."

"No, I can't do that to her ladyship. I'm going to play the game through to the finish. There's a chance we'll brush through. He hasn't been able to place where he's seen me."

"It's a dreadful chance t' take."

"I know." Tom looked round at the captain, sitting at his ease and chatting comfortably with Oswald. "You keep yourself out of sight if you can. No use both of us getting caught in this trap."

He moved back to the group and took a stance behind Camilla's chair. The conversation seemed to concentrate itself on the Navy, with Captain Brock at the center of attention. Even the ladies questioned him about his voyages and battles. Tom listened but didn't dare to contribute to the conversation. The less he drew attention to himself, the better. He only hoped that the conversation would veer in another direction; all this talk of ships and the Navy was decidedly dangerous.

Camilla, who was beginning to know him better than he dreamed, noticed his unusual silence. Just before dinner was announced, she managed to draw him aside. "Is anything amiss?" she asked nervously. "You've been very reserved."

"This is the first time I've heard you complain on *that* score," he said with a quick grin. But something in his eyes—a look of wary tension—troubled her, and she couldn't return his smile.

The dining room doors were thrown open at that moment, signaling the fact that dinner was ready to be served. "You haven't really answered me, Thomas," she whispered hastily. "Is there—"

"No, nothing. Don't trouble yourself about me," he assured her. "You'd better go along. Lord Jeffries is waiting to take your arm."

The dinner, served with inconspicuous efficiency by Hicks, Daniel and two parlormaids, was impressively lavish. To Thomas's relief, the food inspired a turn in the conversation. Lord Jeffries made a fuss over the fish stew, his wife sang the praises of the ragout and Oswald uttered effusive praise about everything. Lady Jeffries, a soft-spoken, fluttery woman with watery eyes and a way of hunching up her shoulders as if she were sitting in a perpetual draught, referred repeatedly to Camilla's remarkable ability to arrange so elaborate a dinner on such short notice. "And with an unexpected guest at the table as well!" she chirped in birdlike admiration. "You are much to be complimented."

"Yes, you do seem to have learned to set an admirable table, Camilla," Ethelyn admitted grudgingly. "I didn't dream you could manage so well."

While the guests continued to praise each dish set before them, a housemaid tiptoed in and spoke to Daniel. After a moment's exchange with Hicks, the footman followed the maid from the room. Tom, Camilla and Miss Townley all noted the occurrence and exchanged looks, but since Hicks did not appear to be perturbed by the defection, they did nothing about it.

The subject of food could not be expected to hold the attention of the diners indefinitely, and before Tom was quite aware of how it had happened, Oswald had turned the conversation back to the subject of the Navy. He spoke with patriotic optimism of the coming naval confrontations with Napoleon's fleet. "With men such as you in the Admiralty, Jeffries, with men like Nelson commanding the fleet, and with the like of Brock here captaining the ships of the line, we have nothing to fear," he declared expansively, lifting his glass.

"That's all very well," Jeffries said after swallowing his wine, "but the French have some ships of excellent design, very swift in the water—"

"Remarkably swift," Brock agreed. "I've seen them in action. They make many of ours seem like clumsy hulks."

"But we far outnumber them, don't we?" Oswald insisted. "And our men are better seamen. There's no fighter in the world like the British tar."

Tom felt himself stiffen, and his heart began to race. The closer they came to the subject of the recruitment of sailors, the more likely that Captain Brock's memory would be jogged. "Do you go to the theater a great deal, Lady Jeffries?" he asked abruptly, in a desperate attempt to turn the subject.

Lord Jeffries, about to embark on the subject of British seamen, blinked at his host in surprise. Falcombe had told him that afternoon that this Mr. Petersham had expressed some brilliant and original ideas about naval practices, and he'd looked forward to discussing those ideas with him. Yet the fellow had uttered hardly a word all evening and was now embarking on a completely irrelevant matter. What was wrong with the chap?

Lady Jeffries, accustomed to being overshadowed by her influential, opinionated husband, was taken aback by her host's unexpected interest. "Me?" she asked in her fluttery voice. "Why, no. I'm afraid not. My husband, you know, has little interest in drama and such fripperies."

"That's too bad," Tom murmured, seeing his heavy-handed maneuver about to fail. "I've become interested, of late, in seeing a performance of . . . of . . . *King John,* and I wondered . . ."

Everyone seemed to be staring at him. *"King John?"* Lady Jeffries inquired in confusion.

"Yes. Shakespeare, you know. I wondered if you'd ever seen it," he finished lamely.

"Oh, I see." She gave a helpless little giggle. "No, I'm afraid I'm totally unfamiliar with *King John.*"

"Silly play," Ethelyn said authoritatively, attacking the tender slice of beef on her plate with relish. "Full of illegitimacy and murder and pretenders-to-the-throne. I don't know why you wish to see it."

"Can't call it silly," Miss Townley objected, rushing to Thomas's defense. "After all, Shakespeare—"

"Don't know why you ladies always like to discuss plays and things when we can be speaking of really interesting matters like the naval war," Oswald said bluntly. "Didn't mean to cut you off, though, Miss Townley. If you want to prose on about Shakespeare, go right ahead."

"No, not at all, Lord Falcombe," Miss Townley said. "Don't mind droppin' the subject of Shakespeare for the Navy, if that suits you better."

"I must admit it does," Oswald said. "Couldn't ever understand why everyone's so fascinated with dead kings. I'd much rather talk about the here and now. Like what Jeffries here had to say about our British sailors. What were you saying, Jeffries?"

"I was about to say that our ships are grossly undermanned. The most serious problem is, was, and will probably always remain, recruitment."

"Yes, I agree," Oswald said eagerly. "That's why I'd like you to hear Petersham's ideas on the subject. Had me quite caught up when we discussed the subject yesterday. Tell him your analysis of the problem, Thomas."

Tom would have liked to wring Oswald's neck. "It wasn't much of an analysis," he said with a dismissive wave of his hand. "And I'd much rather talk about . . . about your stables, Oswald. How does one go about developing a reputable herd like the one at Wyckfield?"

Oswald's mouth dropped open. "Nothing particularly reputable about our stock at Wyckfield. Can't imagine what gave you such an idea. See here, old fellow, why are you suddenly becoming so modest about telling us your theory of naval re—"

He was interrupted by the sound of a female voice in the hallway outside the dining room. *"Hicks? Camilla?"*

"Good gracious, what was that?" Ethelyn asked, her head coming up with a start.

"Camilla, are you home? Where *is* everyone?" The voice was closer and clearer now.

"Oh, good God!" Camilla gasped, jumping from her chair. *"Georgie!* I completely *forgot!"*

The door of the dining room opened, and Lady Sturtevant, absorbed in the complicated process of removing the enormous, feathered hat she'd chosen to wear, strolled into the room. She glanced up as Camilla hurried up to her. "Ah, there you are, you beast. I've been waiting for you an *age.* Did you forget we were to go to—*Oh!"* She stared at the diners in amazement. "You have guests!"

"Yes, I—"

Georgina's eyebrows shot up. That she should have broken in unannounced upon a dinner party was humiliating in the extreme. "I'm terribly sorry. I had no *idea* that—! I seem to have intruded." She backed awkwardly to the door. "I thought we were going to the opera. I must have mistaken the date—"

"No, Georgie, it was *I* who mistook the date," Camilla said, putting a trembling hand on her friend's arm.

"Very rude sort of behavior, I must say," Ethelyn muttered.

Camilla cast an agitated glance over her shoulder at her sister-in-law and turned back to her friend. "Yes, it was. Please forgive me, Georgie. I've been at sixes and sevens for the past two days. Lady Ethelyn and Lord Falcombe arrived, you see, quite unexpectedly—"

Georgina, offended at having been forgotten and excluded from these festivities by the person she'd considered her very closest friend, was about to withdraw her arm from Camilla's clasp and stalk out of the room in high dudgeon when she became aware of the tension in her friend's face. Something was very much amiss here. The names she'd just heard clicked into recognition. "Your *sister-in-law?*" she asked in an undervoice, realizing that Camilla was in some sort of difficulty.

Camilla nodded. Georgina, her irritation forgotten, gave her friend a speaking look of compassion.

"Well, *really,* Camilla, don't just stand there like a gawk. Ask your friend to join us," Ethelyn ordered in disgust.

Camilla reddened. There was nothing for it but to do as Ethelyn said. She would have to introduce Georgie to everyone at the table. But, if the pretense of the last two days was to continue, Georgie would have to behave as if she were well acquainted with "Mr. Petersham." How could she warn her friend to assist her in the deception? If only she'd found time to confide in her friend beforehand! Well, it was too late now. Her house of lies was about to come tumbling down about her head. "Yes, Georgie," she said, swallowing courageously, "you must join us. Come and let me make you known to everyone."

"Well, I shouldn't. I should be on my way to the opera. But I'll stay for a little while."

"Good," Camilla said, but her heart sank. She took her friend's arm and led her to the table. "Lady Sturtevant, may I present Lady Jeffries, Lady Ethelyn Falcombe, Lord Jeffries, Lord Falcombe, Captain Brock and Miss Townley, whom you've met many times. And . . . and . . ." She gave her friend's arm a warning pinch. "And of course, you know my h-husband—"

This was too much for Georgina. In spite of the pinch, her mouth dropped open. "Your *husband?* But that's *Thomas!*"

"Yes, of course," Camilla said, pinching her with greater desperation. "Thomas. Who else? Bring Lady Sturtevant a chair, will you, Hicks? And, Gladys, take Lady Sturtevant's hat and pelisse."

"Why do you look so startled, Lady Sturtevant?" Ethelyn inquired. "One would think you didn't expect to see Thomas at his own table."

"She didn't," Thomas said, smiling at Georgina broadly. "I was to have gone to . . . to the country yesterday, to see about some matters on my . . . estates."

"Did you postpone your journey on our account? That was very good of you, old fellow," Oswald said cheerfully.

"I still don't see why Lady Sturtevant should look as if she's seen a ghost merely because Thomas postponed his trip for a day or two," Lady Ethelyn said, staring at Georgina suspiciously.

"Our Georgie doesn't react well to surprises, do you, my dear?" Thomas said, looking at her with an affectionate grin.

"Evidently not," Georgina muttered, trying to recover her equilibrium. If Camilla was playing some sort of havey-cavey game with her footman, it was not *her* place to give them away.

"Do sit down, my dear," Thomas urged her. "We gentlemen have been on our feet all this time, waiting for you to take your place."

Georgina speechlessly sank down on her chair. Camilla, waiting behind her, pressed her friend's shoulder thankfully. "I'll explain everything later," she whispered and turned to go back to her own place.

But just as she and the still-standing gentlemen were about to reseat themselves, the door burst open again. Daniel stood in the doorway, his face white. "My lady," he cried, "it's the baby! I think it's *comin'!*"

"Daniel!" Hicks barked, appalled.

"Is everyone in this house *demented?*" Ethelyn demanded.

"The *baby?*" Camilla, almost tottering, ran across the room to him. "But, Daniel, it's too early, isn't it? Are you sure you're not mistaken?"

"I don't think so, ma'am. She's got these seizin' pains, y' know, what make her shriek . . . every couple o' minutes, seems like."

"That sounds very much like birth-throes to me," Georgina said knowingly.

"Does it? Then someone ought to run for the midwife at once." Camilla put a shaking hand to her forehead. "Daniel—?"

"Yes, ma'am," he muttered dazedly. "The midwife . . ."

"Quite an interesting household you've brought us to, Falcombe," Lord Jeffries remarked, reaching for the wine.

"It's a veritable madhouse!" Ethelyn said icily.

"Who is it who's . . . er . . . expecting, if I may inquire?" Lady Jeffries asked timidly of Lady Sturtevant.

"Camilla's abigail, I believe. The footman's wife."

"Unheard of, disturbing a dinner party in this vulgar way!" Ethelyn muttered irritably.

"Now, now, my dear," Oswald temporized, "these things will happen when they will."

"Not much Miss Camilla could've done to prevent it," Miss Townley defended.

At the door, Daniel stood leaning dazedly against the frame. "The midwife," he was muttering. "Where . . . ?"

"Oh, dear," Camilla said, studying him worriedly, "I don't think *he* can be relied upon to fetch the midwife."

Georgina rose from her chair. "Let me do what I can until *someone* fetches her. After five hatchings of my own, I ought to be capable of offering some assistance."

"*Would* you, Georgie? I'd be eternally grateful."

"Shall *I* go for the midwife, Miss Camilla?" Hicks offered quietly.

Camilla threw a guilty look at her guests. "No, Hicks, I think we need you here."

Thomas, seeing an opportunity to escape from the nerve-wracking presence of Captain Brock (whom Daniel, in the shock of impending fatherhood, had apparently forgotten), jumped to his feet. "I'll go, my love. I can be spared more readily than our butler. Just give me the direction."

"Oh, yes, Thomas, that *is* the best solution," Camilla said in relief. "If you'll just settle Daniel into the sitting room before you go, Georgie and I can go up to Betsy, and all the others will be able to finish their dinners in peace."

Tom made his way across the room with alacrity, while Ethelyn shook her head in vehement disapproval. "In peace?" she said in tones of utter disparagement. "This is the least peaceful, the most disorganized dinner party I've ever attended in my life!"

Miss Townley frowned at her and got to her feet. "Miss Camilla, shall I—"

"No, Ada. Please stay here and play hostess in my stead."

"Come on, old man," Tom said to Daniel softly, putting a supporting arm about him, "let's get you down on the sitting room sofa."

"You and I had better be prepared," Georgina warned her friend. "If Betsy's 'seizures' were afflicting her every few minutes, it may be too late for the midwife."

"Oh, *L-Lord!*" Daniel stared at her in horror and swayed unsteadily. "Tom, I . . . think I'm goin' t' *faint* . . ."

Tom grabbed him with both arms. "Hold on, Daniel. It'll turn out all right." And bracing him up firmly, he tried desperately to hurry him out of the room.

"Hold on there!" came a sharp, cold command. "Don't either of you move another step!"

Everyone froze in his place. There was no mistaking the authoritative ring in that voice. It came from Captain Brock, who was leaning on the table with one hand and pointing at Tom with the other. Everyone in the room stared at him: Camilla and Georgina near the doorway, Hicks and the maids at their places near the server, the other diners surrounding the captain at the table, and Daniel and Tom framed in the doorway.

Oswald was the first to move. "Hang it, Captain, you've nearly made me jump out of my skin! What's the to-do *now?*"

"You, fellow—yes, *you,* the butler! Close the door! And Jeffries, you and Falcombe here, *seize that man!*"

"*Seize* him? Do you mean Thomas?" Oswald sputtered. "Have you lost your *wits?* That man is, roughly speaking, my *brother-in-law!*"

"I don't care if he's, roughly speaking, your *bastard son!* That's the murdering deserter who *cracked my skull!*"

Chapter Nineteen

*E*thelyn shrieked, Lady Jeffries gasped and Daniel, shocked into alertness by Captain Brock's accusation, groaned. There followed a veritable explosion of sound: exclamations, questions, expressions of disbelief, gasps and outcries. Ignoring the hubbub, Tom turned to face the agonized question in Camilla's eyes. In painful silence, they stared at each other until he could no longer bear it. His eyes flickered down in abject shame. He didn't see her cheeks whiten or her hand fly up to her mouth to press back the cry that came unbidden from her throat.

Lord Jeffries, who had also remained silent during the first chaotic reaction, now joined the others in throwing questions at the captain and Tom. But the noise made sensible communication impossible, and he threw up his hands in disgust.

"Will you all be quiet!" Tom ordered at last. "I'll answer all your questions and accusations in good time. But first I must remind you that there's a woman upstairs in labor. Go to her, Camilla. And you, too, Lady Sturtevant. We, none of us, would forgive ourselves if she suffered from neglect while we engaged in this pointless altercation."

"The altercation will not be pointless, I assure you," Captain Brock said threateningly.

"Nevertheless," Lord Jeffries said, "Mr. Petersham is quite right in advising the ladies to go at once."

Georgina hurried from the room, but Daniel stopped Camilla on the threshold. "Take care of 'em fer me, my lady, if . . . if I should be gone by the time the baby comes."

"Gone? Why should you be—" Her eyes widened in sudden understanding. Daniel, too was involved in this frightening turn of events. Was he—and Thomas, too—about to be *carted off in irons?*

Only by the sheerest effort of will—made possible by imagining her Betsy writhing in agony upstairs—was she able to keep hold of herself. She turned about to face her guests, all of whom were on their feet, staring at her with expressions which revealed shock, curiosity or concern. "Lord Jeffries," she said in a voice surprisingly firm and steady, "I appeal to you, as a member of the Admiralty and as the only gentleman here who can deal with this matter with some impartiality, to promise me that you will permit no one of this household to be removed from here until I return. What happens to persons living in my house is of vital concern to me, and it is simple justice that I be consulted before decisions relating to their futures are made. But I can only cope with one crisis at a time. This man's wife is about to have a baby. Therefore, until that baby is born, I insist that nothing—or no one—in this household be disturbed or uprooted. Will you see to it, my lord?"

"I would like very much to oblige you, my dear, but—" He turned a questioning eye to Captain Brock.

The captain shrugged. "If both these miscreants give their words not to make any attempt to escape, I'm willing to wait."

Tom and Daniel nodded their agreement.

"Very well, ma'am," Lord Jeffries said, "we'll take no action until the child is born."

Without another word, Camilla left the room.

"Now I think it's time we were given some sort of explanation," Ethelyn demanded as soon as the door had closed behind Camilla.

"The explanation is quite simple," Captain Brock said coldly. "These men were common sailors on my ship, brought before me for some infraction. They turned on their guards, knocked my mate senseless, swung a lantern against my head and jumped overboard. As brazen and revolting a pair of deserters as you're likely to find."

"That's nothin' but a pack o' lies," Daniel burst out.

"Is it, Petersham?" Jeffries asked.

"From start to finish."

"Are you trying to tell us," Brock sneered, "that you didn't give me this mark on my forehead?"

"Aye, I did. I won't deny that. But the circumstances leading up to it were not in any detail as you've related them, and you know it."

"All right, then, Petersham, let's hear *your* tale," Jeffries said, his voice tinged with suspicion.

"You won't like the truth any more than he does," Tom muttered, turning away, "so what's the good of telling it?"

"Why would I not? Your wife herself attested to my impartiality."

"No one of the Admiralty could be impartial, for my tale indicts you all."

"Does it indeed?" Jeffries said drily. "That's the sort of nonsense every criminal spouts, you know. It's never his fault—oh, no!—but only the fault of the system. Naval injustice, that's the cause. How sick I am of hearing *that*."

Thomas smiled grimly. "So you see, there's no point in my telling you the story, is there?"

"I suppose not," Jeffries said with a sigh. He peered at Thomas for a moment, wondering how an intelligent, audacious, personable young fellow like this had gotten himself into such a fix. "Well, if you don't wish to discuss the matter, we all may as well return to the table and finish our dinners, not that I myself have much appetite. Is there anything left that's edible—what's your name, fellow? Hicks?"

"Yes, my lord," Hicks said, clenching his fists to shake himself from the throes of a lethargy caused by his fear of impending tragedy, not only involving his nephew and Thomas but Miss Camilla as well. But he was head of the staff—he would carry on. "We've kept the beef warm . . . and the partridge filets. And we've still to serve the Turkish creams and the apple tartlets that Lord Falcombe likes so much."

Oswald shook his head glumly. He'd taken a strange fancy to Camilla's new husband, and this turn of events profoundly depressed him. His temporary return to the world of naval affairs had stimulated his spirit and roused him from his customary lethargy. Instead of wishing to run away from this situation, he wanted very much to be able to *do* something, but a course of action had not yet occurred to him. "No, no," he said with a sigh, "I don't want anything. Seem to have lost my appetite, too."

"The thought of returning to the table must be abhorrent to all of us," Ethelyn said, her mouth turning down in an expression of acute revulsion. "What I wish, Lord Jeffries, is to get to the bottom of this affair—one which, I might add, only serves to support my conviction that this city is a place of godlessness and corruption."

"I don't see how we're to get to the bottom of it, Lady Ethelyn, if Mr. Petersham refuses to discuss the matter."

"But the little I've heard makes no sense. How can a Petersham of the Sussex Petershams—it was Sussex, wasn't it, Thomas?—have been employed aboard Captain Brock's vessel as a common sailor?"

"Yes, I've been wondering about that myself," Jeffries said. "How did that happen, Petersham?"

Hicks and Miss Townley exchanged glances of alarm. Any revelations about the Petershams of Sussex were bound to bring the truth of Camilla's duplicity to light. Miss Townley bravely intervened. "If you are all determined not to return to the table," she said loudly, "may I suggest that we'll all be more comfortable seated in the drawing room? Hicks can bring in some tea, and the sweets and creams, and we shall all do nicely." *There!* she thought. *That will postpone these revelations for a while.*

For more than two hours, Camilla and Georgina were too busily occupied with assisting the birth to exchange a single word about the mysterious goings-on downstairs. A little before midnight Betsy gave birth to a beautiful little girl, healthy and perfect. Georgina sent a housemaid to fetch Daniel. It was fully fifteen minutes, however, before he came. (Evidently there had been some reluctance expressed by Captain Brock about letting the fellow out of his sight.) But his face, when he gazed at his wife in the candlelight holding the swaddled infant in her arms, showed nothing but a joyful awe. Both Camilla and Georgina were moved to tears. They led him to a chair beside the bed and tiptoed from the room.

"And now," Georgina demanded, throwing off a blood-besmirched apron and assisting Camilla to do the same, "will you please tell me what in the world is going *on* down there?"

"I wish I knew," Camilla answered, the exaltation of assisting with the birth fading from her face. "All I can tell you is that Thomas is evidently not what he professed to be."

"That much I surmised already. He's a sailor, not a footman. But, Camilla, have you *married* him?"

"Married him?" For a moment, Camilla blinked at her friend's confusion. "Oh, *that.* This new trouble has driven that from my mind."

"You must have a very spongelike mind to forget something like marriage to your footman!"

"I didn't marry him, you goose. It was only a pretense, to convince Ethelyn that her matchmaking scheme was quite hopeless. Strange, it seemed so important, just a little while ago, for my stupid hoax to succeed. Now I don't care a jot! All I can think of is . . . what I heard Captain Brock say. 'Murdering deserter.' My Thomas is a m-murdering deserter."

" '*My* Thomas'? Camilla! You're not in *love* with the fellow, are you?"

Camilla's eyes flew to her friend's face. "Would you think it . . . very dreadful . . . if I were?"

"Not dreadful. But . . . a bit tragic, under the circumstances." She peered at her friend closely. "You don't, do you? Love him, that is?"

"Oh, Georgie, I don't know! All I can say is that he's been more of a husband to me in the last two days than Desmond was in eleven years."

Georgina enveloped her in a tearful embrace. "Oh, my poor Camilla!" she murmured with deepest sympathy. "My poor, poor dear! Whatever shall we do now?"

They entered the drawing room to find the entire party waiting in glum silence. Hicks, Thomas and Captain Brock were the only three on their feet, Hicks standing in his place beside the tea service and the captain leaning on the mantel of the fireplace and glowering into the flames. On the sofa, Miss Townley was determinedly occupying herself with some embroidery, while Lady Jeffries was huddled in the corner, fast asleep. Ethelyn, sitting stiffly erect in one of the pair of wing chairs, was reading a book of sermons. In the other chair, Lord Jeffries lolled back against the cushion, his legs stretched out before him and his eyes half-closed in contemplation. Oswald had perched his expansive girth uncomfortably upon an ottoman and was staring with a worried frown at Thomas, who stood motionless in the window embrasure, looking out into the blackness of the night.

On the entrance of the two ladies, everyone but Thomas and the sleeping Lady Jeffries looked up. "The baby—?" Miss Townley asked.

Camilla gave her a smile. "A lovely girl. All is well there. No, don't get up, gentlemen. Let us not stand on points at this late hour." She took a chair beside the tea table, while Georgina sat down beside Miss Townley. "I'm quite ready now, Captain Brock, to hear what you have to say."

"There's nothing much to say, ma'am. The authorities have been searching for that fellow for months. He is a deserter from my ship, and I intend to take him back with me to the *Undaunted*. After a shipboard court-martial, I shall administer whatever punishment I deem suitable."

Both Lord Jeffries and Oswald voiced immediate objections, but it was Tom whose words rang loudest through the room. "Damnation, I'll not go! Try me in a civil court or not at all! I'm no cursed bluejacket trapped in the King's service. I'm a free Englishman and demand to be tried as such!"

"What nonsense is this?" Lord Jeffries asked. "If you're a seaman of the Navy, I'll see to it that you're tried fairly in an Admiralty court—you have my word."

"I am *not* a seaman of the Navy. I was the mate of the merchant ship *Triton* when they tried to impress me to serve on Captain Brock's vessel."

"Come now, Thomas," Oswald said, trying sympathetically to caution the young man to guard his tongue, "you can't expect us to believe that an experienced officer of Brock's stature would try to impress the mate of a merchant vessel."

"No, I can't expect you to believe it, but it's true nevertheless. The fact is that the press-gang didn't know I was the mate. They thought I was just another poor devil of a seaman like Daniel. But when I was dragged aboard the *Undaunted*, I showed the captain my papers. He knew full well who I was!"

"Is this true, Brock?" Jeffries asked, scowling.

"The man's lying," Brock said coldly. "Let him show you the papers, if they exist at all."

Tom laughed bitterly. "He knows they don't exist. He burned them."

"I can't *believe* he'd do such a thing," Jeffries said, troubled.

"You'd be well advised to believe it," Tom said earnestly, "unless you want to face more mutinies like Spithead and Nore. What have you done, you at the Admiralty, in the six years since but shut your eyes and drag your feet! Whatever victories the Navy's won have come about because a few commanders like Collingwood and Nelson know how to inspire men, and because the ordinary British sailor has a pride in his service and a love of country stronger than his self-interest. But don't push your luck too far. Don't shut your eyes to the abuses—and they are notorious to those of us who sail—of such men as Brock, for there is a limit even to your best sailors' patience."

Oswald stared at the younger man with wide eyes. "Good God, Jeffries," he said after a long silence, "are matters as rotten as this? What's the matter with you fellows at Whitehall? This impressment business is bad enough, but do our captains have to resort to destroying a merchantman's identity to fill their rosters?"

"You are assuming, Falcombe," Captain Brock said with icy sarcasm, "that your 'brother-in-law, roughly speaking' is telling the truth. I say I never saw any papers. Will you believe him or me?"

"I'll be blunt, Brock," Jeffries said. "I'm inclined to believe *him*. In your initial account, you said he was one of your sailors, brought before you for an infraction. You told us nothing of impressment. Sounds to me as if you were not giving an honest account from the first."

Brock made a dismissive, nonchalant wave of his hand. "You can't expect me to remember the minor details of one interview with an ordinary seaman. The only reason I remembered the fellow at all was that he struck me with the lantern."

"That may be, but Petersham seems to recall everything very well. I see no reason to doubt him."

"No? Well, I'll give you one: his name. I can't recall it right now, but I'd wager it wasn't Petersham. It was something like Collinge . . . or Collford . . ."

"Collinson," Tom supplied.

"Collinson?" Ethelyn gasped. "Do you mean to say that you're not a Petersham of Sussex at all?"

Tom threw Camilla a look of despair. "No, Lady Ethelyn, I'm not."

"I might have known!" Ethelyn fixed a disdainful eye on her sister-in-law. "It's just like you, Camilla, to be taken in. I warned you, but you took no heed. Now you find yourself married to a common criminal with, I'm certain, no family connections and no future. Serves you quite right, too!"

"See here, ma'am—!" Tom rounded on her angrily.

"No, Thomas, let me," Camilla said with calm astringency, rising and placing herself squarely before Ethelyn's chair. "Ethelyn, I've tried for years to maintain cordial relations with you, but tonight you've pushed me too far! I've been a coward long enough. Never again will I permit you to disparage me, insult me and manage me. The truth, my dear, is that I've know all along what Thomas's true name is. The name Petersham is *my* invention, not his. Thomas's only crime in this affair was to be kind enough to act the role of my husband for the length of your stay in this house."

"Do you mean," Ethelyn squeaked, aghast, "that you're *not married?*"

"Wha—? Who's no' married?" queried Lady Jeffries, waking with a start.

"No one. It's nothing, dear," Jeffries said, patting her hand. "Go back to sleep."

"Yes, Ethelyn," Camilla said, "that's what I mean. I'm not married at all."

Ethelyn fell back against the cushions, one hand clasped to her breast and the other to her forehead. "Oh, my heavens! This is worse than *anything!* The deceit! The *depravity!* You should be down on your *knees* asking the Good Lord's forgiveness for such sinfulness."

"Lady Ethelyn," Tom said furiously, "I can't remain silent when I hear such nonsense. There was no sinfulness and no depravity! Your sister-in-law's character is above reproach, and I won't stand here and listen to you villify her!"

"Hear, hear!" Lady Sturtevant cheered.

"I don't need lectures on morality from a common deserter," Ethelyn responded, drawing herself up in austere dignity. "You would be the *last* person to whom I'd listen when it comes to evaluating my sister-in-law's character."

"Ethelyn, be still!" her husband barked. So unaccustomed was he to use that tone of voice that not only Camilla, Miss Townley and Hicks looked up in astonishment but he himself seemed surprised.

"What was that?" Ethelyn asked him in disbelief.

"I said be still!" He rose from the ottoman with lumbering majesty. "What right have you to evaluate Camilla's character? Besides, we've been acquainted with her long enough to know, without Thomas having to tell us, what sort of person she is. It begins to be apparent to anyone with half an eye that much of this is *your own fault!* If you weren't so deucedly tyrannical, Camilla wouldn't have had to resort to subterfuge, we'd never have come to London at all, and

Thomas wouldn't have found himself at a dinner table facing Captain Brock. You've done enough damage for one night. Either sit here in silence or go up to your room. I'd like to try to see what I can do to *assist* this fellow, and it will be difficult enough without having the proceedings interrupted by your diatribes."

"Oh, Oswald!" Camilla cried tearfully, throwing her arms about his neck. "I never *dreamed* you could be so . . . so courageous."

"There, there, my dear," he said, patting her shoulder awkwardly. "No need to indulge in waterworks. I wasn't always a henpecked old pudding, you know."

"This is all very touching," Brock said drily, "but the hour grows late. Either let me take this makebate back to the ship or throw him in irons into Fleet prison."

"Don't see why we should do either," Oswald said, leading Camilla back to her chair. "It seems to me a matter that can be settled amicably right here. The way I see it, Thomas was caught in an impressment trap, and when you found you'd caught the wrong fish, you decided not to let him go. Burned his papers. A very embarrassing peccadillo for you to have to explain, if it should come out. True, he scarred your forehead—an equally embarrassing peccadillo for *him* to have to explain. If he forgets *his* grievance, can't you forget yours?"

"Oh, hear, hear!" Lady Sturtevant cried, applauding.

Everyone in the room gazed at him admiringly. No one had imagined that the huge, clumsy Lord Falcombe could conceive so cleverly diplomatic a scheme. Even Lord Jeffries was impressed. And Camilla let herself breathe deeply again in relief.

But Captain Brock came forward, his lips curved in an icy smile. "No, my lord," he said, crossing the room toward Thomas, "matters of this sort rarely can be settled so neatly. In the first place, I have never admitted that I'd burned any papers. In the second place, I do not consider this scar to be the result of a mere peccadillo. And lastly . . ." He put his hand on Thomas's shoulder and closed his fingers on it like a vise. ". . . lastly, you are quite forgetting about your man's most heinous crime of all."

"Oh?" Oswald asked, one eyebrow climbing up. "And what was that?"

"Murder, my lord. Nothing less than murder."

Chapter Twenty

$\mathscr{P}$ippa wandered about the house next morning, too ill at ease to settle down. She'd visited Betsy and seen the new baby, but Daniel was strangely subdued, as if something worrisome was on his mind and not permitting him to enjoy the birth of his first child with the proper enthusiasm. Aunt Ethelyn was locked in her room and had responded to her niece's knock with a curt command that she was to be left alone. Hicks, looking pale and heavy-eyed, had told her that her Uncle Oswald had left the house early this morning on a mysterious errand. Miss Townley and her mother had not yet made an appearance. And Thomas was nowhere to be found.

Pippa was far from being a fool; it was clear to her that something dreadful had happened at her mother's dinner party. Aunt Ethelyn had probably discovered the ruse, but Pippa could not believe that the mere unmasking of Thomas could so depress everyone in the house. It had been nothing but a little game. Even Aunt Ethelyn could be made to see the humor of it. Should she try again to talk to her aunt? Perhaps she could brighten up the situation.

But before she could put the thought into action, her mother emerged from her bedroom. One look at Camilla's red-rimmed eyes and wan cheeks and Pippa knew that matters were in a more serious state than she'd imagined. Without a word, she slipped her hand into her mother's and walked with her down to the breakfast room. She waited until her mother had drunk half a cup of tea before she spoke. "You promised me last night that you would tell me all. So, Mama, please—?"

Her mother put down the cup with a shaking hand. "Oh, Pippa, don't ask me!"

"I *must*. I know something terrible's happened. Do you want me to go about imagining all sorts of horrible falsehoods? Wouldn't it be better if I knew the truth?"

Camilla propped her elbows on the table and lowered her head to her hands. "Pippa, love, not now. I just can't."

"Then just tell me where Thomas is. He'll explain things to me. He always gives lovely, direct answers to my questions."

"But that's the problem, dearest. Thomas is . . . not here anymore."

"Not here? What do you mean? Where is he?"

"Well, you see, he's not really a footman at all."

"I surmised as much. He's a sailor, isn't he?"

Camilla looked up in surprise. "How did you know? Did he tell you?"

"No, but he always told sea stories so well. Full of details that a landlubber wouldn't know."

"Landlubber?"

"Yes. That's what he calls people who work on land. Has he gone back to sea, then? He wouldn't do that without saying good-bye to me, would he?"

"No, of course not. He's . . . oh, dear, I don't know how to tell you. He's been . . . taken into custody."

Pippa peered at her mother with stricken eyes. "Mama! You don't mean *prison!*"

Camilla tried to answer, but, afraid that she would burst into tears, put a hand to her mouth and merely nodded her answer.

Pippa drew in a breath. "But . . . *why?* What's he done?"

"I'm not completely sure," Camilla answered, choked. "The worst of it seems to be that . . . that, in a struggle with some men who were trying to kidnap him to serve on a naval vessel, he hit one of them so hard that . . . he d-died."

"Oh, Mama, *no!* What will they do to him?"

Again all Camilla could do was shake her head.

Pippa's eyes widened in horror. "Mama! They won't . . . they wouldn't . . . *hang* him!"

Camilla held out her arms to her daughter, and Pippa flew into them. They clung together for several minutes, too terrified even to weep. "Don't shiver so, love," Camilla said at last. "Your Uncle Oswald has gone to see what he can do to help. Perhaps he can find a way . . ."

Oswald returned late that afternoon and found Camilla sitting with Pippa near the fire in the sitting room. They both turned to him with faces of such eager hopefulness that he almost wanted to retreat. "My news is not all bad," he said in preparation, "but if you're hoping to see your Thomas come walking in that door, you'll be disappointed."

"Tell us what you've learned, Oswald. We can deal with disappointment, if we must, can't we, love?"

"You don't want Pippa here, do you?"

"Yes, she's all right. She loves Thomas very much, you see."

"Well, then," he said, seating himself on the edge of a chair and pulling a sheaf of notes from his coat, "let's see what I've accomplished thus far. First, there's some good news in Daniel's case. He's safely out of it. His papers were signed with an X, and when I showed the committee his real signature, they decided to rule that he had not legally been enlisted. Under the circumstances, no one seemed impelled to make an issue of his case, not even Brock. It's Thomas he wants."

"That *is* good news, Oswald. Betsy will be overjoyed."

"I wish I could say the same about Thomas's case. I discovered that the *Triton* is out to sea, which is a bit of bad luck because we won't be able to question the captain about Thomas's credentials until the ship returns. But most everyone I've spoken to on the Admiralty board seems inclined to believe that Thomas is telling the truth. Lord Jeffries is furious at this evidence of the continued activity of press-gangs—the Admiralty doesn't admit to sanctioning them, you know—and Lord Sturtevant is so angry about the incident that he threatens to bring the matter to the attention of Parliament if the Admiralty doesn't treat Thomas fairly. (He's quite impressed with Thomas, it seems, from some remarks he'd made at a dinner here. And Lady Sturtevant gave him a very dramatic account of everything that happened here last night.) I think Brock will find his friends at the Admiralty very cool to him as a result of all this. And if it turns out that Thomas has been telling the truth about being a mate on the *Triton*—"

"Don't worry, he has been," Pippa said confidently.

"If he has, then Brock will find himself in very hot water. But, of course, the murder is the sticking point for Thomas. Don't know what we can do about clearing him of that."

"But if he was defending himself, it isn't really murder, is it?" Camilla inquired, biting her lip.

"I don't know. Self-defense may not be applicable in this case." He looked down at his notes. "I've learned the name of the officer in charge of the press-gang, but no one seems to know the name of the deceased. Thought I'd ride down to Southampton and see if I can locate the officer. The prosecution will have to do it—they don't have a case without a victim—and I don't want them to have more information than we have. Don't know what good it will do, but there's no harm in learning all we can."

"When do you want to go?" Camilla asked.

"Right away. Why?"

"Because I'm going with you."

"I, too," said Pippa.

"No, dearest, you will stay right here. I'll give you a more difficult task to accomplish than chasing about with us in Southampton. Stay here and see if you can make matters right with your Aunt Ethelyn."

Moresby, the officer who'd led the press-gang, was not hard to find. But he seemed strangely reluctant to reveal the name of the murdered man. It was only after Oswald bribed him with a handful of sovereigns that the fellow managed to remember it was a Casper Jost who'd died that day.

"Where'd you bury him?" Oswald asked.

"I didn't bury him. It isn't my job," Moresby said.

"Who did, then?"

"How would I know that? Ask his widow."

"Where can we find her?" Oswald asked impatiently.

"Can't say. Jost was no friend of mine."

But with the help of an additional bribe, the officer remembered that Jost had mentioned having a place in Netley, a short distance south on the Portsmouth road.

On the way to Netley, Oswald castigated himself roundly. "Don't know why I dragged you on this goose chase. No point in it anyway. There's no good can come of it that I can see."

"Perhaps not," Camilla said, "but I'd like to talk to the widow anyway. It might ease her grief if I tell her that it was only an accident—that Thomas hadn't meant to kill her husband. And we can give her some money, too. Not that money could ever make up for . . . for . . ."

"I know," Oswald said, squeezing her hand.

The proprietor of the Netley Linendrapery pointed out the Jost domicile. It was the third from the corner of a long row of tiny, frame houses with identical front steps and little iron grillwork surrounding identical little front gardens. When the carriage drew up to the house, Camilla put a restraining hand on Oswald's arm. "Let me go alone," she begged. "I shall do better with the widow that way."

Oswald shrugged. She jumped out of the carriage and ran up to the front door. An ill-kempt, stoutish woman with a number of hairs on her chin answered the door. "Are you Mrs. Jost?" Camilla asked.

"That's 'oo I be. Whut ye want?"

"I . . . I've come to ask you some questions . . . about your late husband."

The woman squinted at her suspiciously. "Whut'd ye mean, me late husband? On'y got but one, an' he's sittin' back there in the kitchen, swillin' ale."

*   *   *

It was a jubilant Camilla who returned to Upper Seymour Street that night, and a jubilant Pippa she tucked into bed. "I *knew* my Thomas couldn't have killed anybody." The child grinned, hugging her mother tightly. "Will he be coming home tomorrow?"

Camilla eased her daughter on to the pillow and drew up the coverlet. "I don't know what will happen next, dearest. But I suspect Thomas will not be coming back here to live. He isn't a footman after all, you know, and we can't expect him to spend his life working at something for which he is unsuited."

"Yes, I understand that, but aren't you going to marry him?"

"*Marry* him? What gave you such an idea as that?"

"You did. When you invented a husband for yourself, you made him just like Thomas, didn't you?"

"No, I didn't. He wasn't like Thomas at all."

"Yes, he was. Tall, lean, sandy-haired, generous, kind and humorous. That's how you described Mr. Petersham, and that's just how Thomas is!"

Camilla flushed. "But, those are very general terms. They could equally apply to any number of people."

"I'll wager you can't name *one*."

"Really, Pippa, you are becoming much too cheeky. You must take my word for it that Thomas and I would not suit."

"I can't agree. When you pretended to be wed, it seemed to me that you suited each other very well."

"It was only pretense." She smoothed the hair from her daughter's brow tenderly. "I know you wish to have Thomas near you for always, dearest, but you mustn't let your desires run off with your reason. I can't be expected to marry everyone for whom you take a fancy, you know."

Pippa hitched to her side, turning her face away from her mother and pulling the coverlet up to her neck. "I thought you fancied him also," she said, her voice melancholy and suddenly very childlike.

"Well, I'm sorry to have to disappoint you, love. But isn't it enough that the man Thomas injured is fully recovered and that Thomas will soon be a free man? And that we can go on living contentedly here in London, near our friends the Sturtevants, just as before? Isn't that *enough* to be happy about?"

"I'm happy about Thomas being a free man, of course. About the rest, I shall have to think before I answer. For things will *not* be as they were before, with Thomas gone. Good night, Mama."

Camilla closed her daughter's door quietly behind her and walked thoughtfully down the hall, wondering why she'd been reluctant to reveal to the child how close her own desires were to Pippa's. But before she could find an answer, she thought she heard her name being called in a quavery voice. "Ethelyn?" she asked hesitantly, pausing before her sister-in-law's door. "Did you call?"

"Yes. Can you come in for a moment?"

She opened the door with considerable trepidation and looked in. Ethelyn was sitting up in bed, a prayer book in her lap. Camilla came in and stood at the foot of the bed, studying her sister-in-law curiously. Ethelyn was wearing only her nightdress. Somehow she looked much less formidable in the white muslin gown with its soft lace at the neck and with her graying hair loosened from its knot and falling round her shoulders with unaccustomed softness. It occurred to Camilla that she'd never seen Ethelyn except in the darkest of colors and the most formal of costumes. In this bedtime informality, her usually awesome sister-in-law looked almost frail. "Is there anything I can do for you, Ethelyn?"

"I wish to speak to you," Ethelyn said, her eyes lowered. "Will you sit down, please? Here at the side . . . that is, if you wish . . ."

"Yes, of course." Camilla took the chair indicated and waited for what she expected would be a long lecture on the blessings of redemption.

"I have had a number of long talks with Pippa since you left for Southampton," she said quietly, after a moment of silence. "Did the child tell you?"

"Pippa?" How had her ingenious daughter managed to convince her aunt to call her that? "No, she didn't tell me."

"She is quite remarkable, you know. She believes we . . . you and I . . . don't have an adequate understanding of one another."

"Oh?"

"She is probably right. It gave me pause, especially after what you had said . . . and Oswald, too. I've been thinking a great deal . . . and praying. And I've come to the conclusion, Camilla, that I have been . . . grossly at fault."

"Ethelyn, I didn't mean—"

"No, don't soften just because you see me shaken. I d-drove you to fabricate a large falsehood—"

"A very large falsehood."

"Yes, and I didn't want to admit that I knew . . . I *knew* . . . that lying is not characteristic of you. I knew it even when I accused you . . ."

"Please, Ethelyn, you don't have to—"

"But I *do*. You and Pippa and Oswald . . . you're all the family I *h-have!*" Astoundingly, she put her hands up to her face and burst into tears.

"Ethelyn!" Camilla gasped.

"I don't want to l-lose you!" the older woman wept.

"Oh, my dear," Camilla murmured, moving to the bed next to Ethelyn and putting an arm around her shoulders, "have no fear of that. I think Pippa was right. If we take the trouble to learn more about each other, instead of always judging each other, we shall do better."

"Then you . . . forgive me?"

"You don't need to ask."

"I shall not, ever again, give you orders, Camilla. I promise,"

Camilla laughed. "Then *I* promise, if ever I *do* find a suitor I wish to wed, to bring him round for your approval."

Ethelyn looked up in surprise. "What do you mean?" she asked, wiping the wetness from her cheeks with the back of her hand. "Aren't you going to wed Thomas?"

"*Thomas?*"

"Yes. Oswald told me it looks as though he'll be completely exonerated. I assumed, therefore—"

"Tell me, Ethelyn," Camilla said, watching her sister-in-law from the corner of her eye, "if I *did,* would you approve?"

"Well, I approved of him before, didn't I?"

"Yes, but you thought he was a Petersham. Of the Sussex Petershams."

"What difference does that make? A man is more than a pedigree."

Camilla, trying not to laugh, got up and looked down at her sister-in-law with hands on hips. "Did you know the fellow was my *footman?*"

Ethelyn's eyebrows rose. "What has *that* to say to anything? We are all equal in the eyes of God, you know. Really, Camilla, I hope your months in this mad, corrupt environment have not made a snob of you." She opened her prayer book and began searching for her place. "Thomas would be much more suitable for you than anyone I could think of, including Mr. Harbage. Good night, my dear."

Chapter Twenty-one

The *Triton* was rumored to be returning to port by the end of the month. As soon as it arrived, and Thomas's status could be verified by its captain, a final dispensation of his case would be made. In the meantime, Ethelyn and Oswald decided to return to Wyckfield. Ethelyn explained that she missed the sweet country air, and Oswald, whose increased activity had caused him to burn off a half-a-stone of fat, declared that if he stayed in town much longer he'd waste away. They therefore bid Camilla and Pippa a fond farewell, extracted a sincere promise from Camilla that she and Pippa would pay a visit to the country soon, and were embraced with a great deal more affection than they'd received on their arrival.

Camilla and Pippa, after a week of silence on the subject of Thomas's welfare, decided to pay a visit to Fleet prison. But a guard informed them that Thomas Collinson was no longer incarcerated behind those walls; he'd been released into the custody of Lord Jeffries. Camilla was hurt and angry that he'd sent her no word of his change of address, and she returned home feeling strangely empty. After all that had passed between them, was he now going to forget her existence?

There was nothing to do but wait and see. Despite Pippa's urging, her pride did not permit her to write to Lord Jeffries for information. If Thomas had wished them to know his whereabouts, he surely could have found a way to inform them of it.

Life returned to its previous pattern, but with a subtle difference. Camilla was aware of a certain joylessness, and it seemed to her that even Pippa had lost some of her serene good spirits. But a few weeks later, early in April, Oswald appeared without warning at the door of the breakfast room. "Put on your wraps, my dears. I'm going to take you both for a long ride."

"Oswald! What are you doing back in town? Is Ethelyn with you?"

"No questions now. We don't have time. Hurry, hurry, for you are about to have the most exciting surprise."

"You're not taking us off to Wyckfield, are you?" Camilla asked as he ushered them into his carriage. "I told you not to expect us until May or June."

"No, not Wyckfield. I'm taking you to Southampton."

"*Southampton!*" Pippa squealed in delight. "It's *Thomas!* You're taking us to Thomas!"

"That's right, you little magpie. You guessed it."

"Oswald! What's happened. How did you find him? And why have we not heard anything?"

"I didn't have to find him. I've been in touch with him all along. He didn't want to see you until everything had been cleared up. So that he could look you in the eye, he said."

"*Has* everything been cleared up, then?"

"Without a black mark remaining. The captain of the *Triton* not only vouched for him but said that he'd been unable to replace him with anyone of equal caliber. And Jeffries has taken the fellow under his wing. Trots him out to talk to everyone interested in naval matters. And the last surprise is that he's found him a berth on a John Company ship."

"John Company?" Pippa asked. "That's the East India Company, isn't it? Thomas told me they're the finest merchant ships afloat."

"So they are. As mate of the *Athena,* he'll have master's papers before he knows it. Jeffries hopes that, by that time, he'll have gotten over his prejudice against the Navy and will join up to captain a ship of the line. He has a very promising future, this lad of yours."

"Oh, fiddle-faddle, Oswald. He's no 'lad of mine,'" Camilla said with a toss of the head. But her heart was leaping about in her chest quite uncontrollably, and she had to turn her head to peer out of the window so that Oswald wouldn't see her cheeks.

The carriage rolled right on to the pier, and before it had come to a complete stop, Pippa jumped down. She stared in awe at the huge, three-masted ship *Athena,* anchored at the end of the pier and, spying Thomas waiting at the top of the gangplank, resplendent in a blue uniform with a cocked hat on his head, went flying aboard. She leaped right up into his arms. "Oh, Thomas, Thomas, I've missed you so!" she whispered into his neck.

"And I've missed you, Miss Pippa," he said hoarsely, squeezing her tightly.

His greeting to Camilla was much more subdued. Except for a certain tremulousness of the voice, his how-de-dos were very polite and formal. After shaking Oswald's hand warmly, he took them on a full tour of the ship, pointing out everything from the hold to the crow's nest and from the prow to the taffrail. He pointed out the Indian teak beams and the copper fastenings; he told them about the tonnage, the battery mounts, and the types of sail; he explained about the disposition of the crew of one-hundred-and-thirty-three men as well as a couple of dozen passengers. To Oswald and Pippa, it was all fascinating.

While he talked, Camilla studied him from under lowered lids. His blue uniform was trimmed with black velvet lapels and cuffs, and was embroidered with gold braid, not unlike officers of the Navy. It gave him a look of distinction that filled her with pride. And she was impressed by the diffident way in which the passing sailors greeted him. And the animation of his face while he spoke, and the way his hand lovingly caressed a rail or pole, completely revealed his feelings. He belonged here.

He took them to tea in the captain's quarters, where the bronzed, heavily jowled captain greeted them kindly and chatted with them for the better part of an hour. Before they'd realized it, the sun had begun to set. "Looks like it's time to disembark, as the sailors like to say," Oswald announced.

"Before you go, Lord Falcombe—" Thomas began.

"Lord Falcombe, is it? You called me Oswald easily enough when you were nothing more than a footman. Surely you can do so now."

"Oswald, then. Do you think you'd like to show Pippa the sailors' mess? And the galley?"

"Oh, *yes,* Uncle Oswald, I'd like that," Pippa said, her excitement boundless.

Oswald threw the young man a narrow-eyed look and laughed. "Come along then, Pippa. But I warn you that all this scurrying about is wearing me out."

As soon as they were out of sight, Thomas took Camilla's arm and led her across the deck to the port-side railing, where they could look out to the sea and watch the setting sun. Her heart began acting strangely again. What, she wondered, was he preparing to say to her?

"Oswald told me what you did for me, Miss Camilla, and I—"

"I did nothing, Thomas. Nothing at all."

"Nothing? You changed my condition of life from murderer to hero. From my point of view, that's a very great deal."

"Hero?"

He grinned. "Yes, so it seems. You should have seen me holding forth, spouting my views to all sorts of Important Personages—Admirals, MPs, even the Duke of York. Lord Jeffries couldn't seem to stop parading me before anyone and everyone with an interest in British seamanship. I'm thankful that this place was found for me before I'd become completely transformed from sailor to speaker."

"It's wonderful, Thomas. I . . . we're very proud of you."

"But it's all because of you. Oswald says he'd never have bothered about finding Jost if you hadn't persisted. I've been waiting all these weeks to tell you how . . . how grateful I am."

"Grateful?" She stared up at him, her heart sinking. "But you're the one who told me—a very long time ago, it seems—that gratitude is a very pallid emotion."

"I said it was a *damned puny* little emotion, and so it seemed when it was directed *at* me. But now, you see, it's turned the other way. Now I feel what you were feeling . . . and I find it quite overwhelming."

And now I feel what you were feeling, she thought, *and I hate it!* Gratitude! How very unsatisfactory it was when one wanted to inspire another type of emotion entirely. *Oh, Thomas,* she wanted to cry, *is this all you wish to tell me? Is this why you sent Pippa and Oswald away? Have we nothing else to say to each other?*

But she said nothing aloud, and they stood watching the sinking sun until Pippa and Oswald returned. Thomas escorted them to the gangplank, still sunk in silence. Oswald asked when the ship was to sail and how long the voyage was to be. Thomas answered, somewhat glumly, that they were to leave in a week for a three-month sail to the Indies. They shook hands vigorously, and Oswald wished him good fortune. Pippa kissed him good-bye and made him promise to visit them as soon as he returned. And, at the last, he kissed Camilla's hand. It seemed to her that he held it a bit longer than he should have, but perhaps the impression had been only the inaccurate measure of her aching heart, seeking some small sign of hope.

They went down the gangplank, Camilla in a bewildering fog of despair. All the way back to London she was unaware of her surroundings and what Pippa and Oswald were saying. She must have responded coherently, for they showed no signs of being disturbed by her behavior, but she was not aware of having spoken to them at all.

The fog in her brain persisted for two days. Then a question that Pippa put to her at the breakfast table brought her up sharply. "Are you *sure* you haven't taken a fancy to him?" the child asked.

"What?" Camilla asked, startled.

"I'm speaking of Thomas. Are you sure you haven't taken a fancy to him?"

Camilla frowned. "You asked something of this sort before. I thought I'd answered you. Why do you bring it up again?"

"Because you've been acting very strangely since we visited the *Athena*. I know this subject is not one on which I have any knowledge, but it does seem to me that you're in a state of confusion similar to lovers in books. They are always disturbed, distracted and distressed."

"Pippa, you can sometimes be a very irritating child." She propped her chin in her hands and looked at her daughter lugubriously. "But you're right, of course. I *am* in a state of confusion."

Pippa nodded knowingly. "I thought so. So is Thomas."

"Thomas? What do you mean?"

"He seemed similarly distracted when we saw him."

"Nonsense. I never noticed anything of the sort."

"Well, I did. So did Uncle Oswald. He said he thought Thomas was sick."

"Neither of you need worry," Camilla mumbled. "If he felt anything at all, it was *gratitude*."

Pippa shook her head dubiously. "I don't think gratitude can make one sick. Do you? He loves you, Mama, I'm sure of it."

"You, my love, are letting your wishes get the best of your judgment." She got up from her chair and began to wander absently round the room. "And even if he does, it makes little difference. He's off to sea on a three-month voyage."

"Not yet. They don't sail until Thursday."

She stopped in her tracks. "Pippa, you goose, what are you suggesting? That I rush back to Southampton and *throw* myself at him?"

Pippa considered the matter in all seriousness. "No," she said after due reflection, "that wouldn't be proper. But . . ." She looked up at her mother with a wicked glimmer. ". . . there's something you *can* do."

"Really?" Camilla asked with her eyebrows raised superciliously. "And what is that?"

"You could pack up some things and book passage on the ship. They take passengers, you know. Thomas said so."

"Book *passage?*" The idea was so unexpected that she could only gape at her daughter in awe. But then she shook her head impatiently. "I know what's in your mind, you little vixen. You'd like nothing better than to sail off to the Indies on Thomas's ship."

"I'd love it above anything, of course, Mama, but *this* time I think I'd better remain behind. You may take me on the *next* voyage, after your honeymoon is over."

"*Honeymoon!* Honestly, Pippa, I can't imagine where you pick up these ideas."

"Everyone knows about honeymoons, Mama, even Sybil. By the way, I think I'd like to stay with her while you're gone. Do you think Lady Sturtevant would permit it?"

"Yes, of course she would. Oh, good God, what am I *saying?* I really *must* be disturbed, distracted and distressed." She dropped down on her chair, giving a little shiver of excitement. "Oh, Pippa, love, do you really think I *should?* It seems the most impulsive, irresponsible, *wild* sort of plan."

Pippa grinned at her. "Yes, doesn't it? It's just the sort of thing Sybil might have thought of. I do believe I'm picking up some of her qualities at last. Isn't that *prodigious?*"

"Prodigious," Camilla agreed drily, making a face at her.

"Does that mean that you'll *do* it?" Pippa's face lit up with hope.

For a long moment her mother didn't answer but stared speculatively into space. Then, with a little shake of her head, she roused herself and jumped up. "Very well, I'll do it. I'll *go!* So don't just sit there, my girl. This is *your* idea, you know, and if it's to succeed, you haven't time to sit dawdling over breakfast. Come along. We have a thousand things to do!"

She seized her daughter's hand and, laughing, pulled her to the door. But as they crossed the threshold, Camilla stopped short. "I've just had the most mortifying thought. What if, after the ship has put to sea, I discover that Thomas doesn't want me after all?"

"He wants you. I'm sure of it."

"But what if you're mistaken? I know you're very gifted, but you *can* make mistakes, you know."

"Then, Mama," Pippa answered with her remarkable aplomb, "at least you'll see the Indies."

There followed a flurry of packing and preparation that was unprecedented in Camilla's experience. Miss Townley was convinced she'd lost her mind. Georgina, on the other hand, was enthusiastic. "It's just the sort of madcap adventure every woman ought to have. And don't worry about Pippa at all. After three months in my disorderly household, I'll return your admirably well-bred daughter to you healthy, unharmed and transformed into a wildcat."

Camilla felt as if she were living on the edge of hysteria. Her moods swung wildly between exhilaration and depression. In moments of optimism she packed her portmanteau with eager haste, only to pull everything out of it in fearful despondency a few moments later. She packed and unpacked three times in the next two days. But through it all, she knew she would go. For the first time she would gamble dangerously with life. The prospect made her blood dance in her veins. Never before had she felt so truly alive.

On the afternoon before her departure, while repacking the portmanteau for the fourth time, she realized that her favorite Norwich shawl was missing. Either Miss Townley or Betsy must have taken it to have it pressed. "Ada? Betsy?" she shouted like a hoyden. "Who's taken my shawl?"

There was no answer. Where were they? Unless the activities of the various members of the household could be better organized, she would never get off on time the next day. And if she departed late, she might arrive in Southampton and find that the ship had sailed without her!

Feeling more than ordinarily hysterical, she ran out of her room to the top of the stairs. "Hicks?" she called. "Can you come up here, please? I need some assistance."

Again there was no answer. "Where *is* everybody?" she snapped impatiently. "Will someone come upstairs to me?"

"Yes, ma'am," came a muffled voice from the nether region.

She sighed in relief. "Thank you, Daniel. And bring up the small hat box which I left on the table in the sitting room, will you?"

She dashed back to her bedroom and began to pull her hats and bonnets from her wardrobe. She tossed them, one after the other, on her bed. It was difficult to decide which headpieces would be most suitable for shipboard wear. After all, she'd never sailed to the Indies—or anywhere else—in her life and had no idea what the weather conditions would be. Small bonnets that could be firmly tied to the head would probably be best, she surmised.

There was a tap at the door. "Come in, Daniel," she said, not looking round. "Just put the box on my dressing table, and then come and see if you can close the portmanteau."

"Yes, ma'am."

The sound of the voice made her breath freeze in her chest. She wheeled around. *"T-Thomas!"*

He was standing in the doorway, dressed in his footman's everyday livery and holding her hatbox before him as if it were a present on a silver tray . . . the very model of footmanly decorum. "Yes, ma'am?" he asked politely.

"Wh-what are you *doing* here?"

"You called, I believe."

"Stop that!" she almost stamped her foot in impatience. "I don't want to joke. What are you doing here?"

"I'm employed here, am I not, ma'am? I don't believe I've been discharged. In fact, if I recall, you said I had a position here for as long as I wished."

"You are *not* employed here! You're the first mate of the *Athena,* and you are sailing tomorrow. Now what is this all *about?*"

"I *was* the first mate of the *Athena.* I've run off. I found that I couldn't sail with her."

"But that's nonsense! You love every plank and sail of that ship. You belong there."

"No, not after *you'd* been there." He tossed the hatbox on a chair and came up to her. "I kept seeing you on the deck . . . and remembering what a coward

I'd been that afternoon. I began to realize that there was no joy in it for me anymore. You weren't there, you see."

"I don't understand . . ."

"It became clear to me that I'd find life more bearable if I were close to you—even as your footman—than if I were far away as a seaman," he said softly, smiling down at her.

Her knees seemed to give way. "Oh, Thomas!" she breathed, sinking down upon the bed, ignoring the fact that at least two of her bonnets were being crushed beneath her.

"May I not come back on the staff, ma'am? I shall be the most invisible, inaudible footman that ever was."

She gave a tearful laugh. "A likely tale! You can't be invisible and inaudible to me anymore. I should always be watching you from the corner of my eye to see if you were going to pull me into your arms and kiss me, as you did so brazenly before."

He grinned. "I can see where that might present some difficulties. Then if I won't do as a footman, do you think you could try me as a husband? You've already given me a kind of trial. I didn't do badly, did I?"

"No, you didn't." She looked down at the hands clenched in her lap. "I . . . liked you as a husband very much indeed."

"Oh, Camilla!" He swept a few of the bonnets aside, sat down beside her and took her in his arms. "I do love you so," he murmured and kissed her hungrily.

"But, Thomas," she asked when she could speak again, "you cannot have been serious when you said that you'd run away from the *Athena*. You do want to sail on her, don't you?"

"I've taken a day's leave." A small, worried frown creased his forehead. "But I won't sail on her if you have objections to being a sailor's wife. Hang it, Camilla, let's not talk about it now. Ever since I let you leave the ship the other day, without telling you . . . I've been like a man possessed. I must kiss you again . . . just to convince myself that I really have you in my arms at last."

After a while, she put her hands to his chest and held him off. "We are really behaving in a shockingly disreputable way," she said, blushing. "This is my *bedroom!*"

"So it is." He lifted his head and looked about him happily. "Do you know, my love, that you are sitting on your hats?"

"Am I?"

"In fact, the room seems in an inordinate state of disorder. I think you *need* another footman, ma'am. From the look of things, you need all the assistance you can afford."

"I do *not* need another footman. I am going on a voyage, and a footman would be decidedly in the way. This confusion is only because I've been packing."

"Packing? For a voyage?" A light seemed to flare up at the back of his eyes. "A voyage where?"

"To the Indies, of course. Where else?"

He grasped her shoulders with eager intensity and pulled her to him. "Oh, God! Don't joke, woman! Were you *really* coming to me?"

"Yes, isn't it shameful? I couldn't bear to be without you either." She lifted a hand to his cheek. "Don't look at me in that adoring way, my love, or I shall cry. Do you think you might just . . . kiss me instead?"

Pippa and her friend Sybil, strolling down the corridor together, passed the open door and peered inside. "Egad!" Sybil exclaimed. "Who's that?"

Pippa beamed. "That's *Thomas!* I *knew* he fancied her."

"Your mother is sitting on her bonnets."

"Yes, I see. It's lovesickness, I believe. It makes one a bit confused."

"Does it? Then I hope I never catch it."

"Lovesickness? They say it's very enjoyable when you're older."

"It looks very dull to me. They haven't moved at all since we've been watching," Sybil observed in disgust.

"Well, I expect that kissing is more entertaining to *do* than to watch. Would you like to do something else?"

"Yes. Let's go back to your room and sit on your bonnets."

"All right. It will probably make them easier to pack." And the girls turned away from the still-embracing couple and strolled back down the hall.

The Bartered Bride

Chapter One

*T*he patrons of Hollings and Chast, Linendrapers, gasped audibly. One of the clerks had actually accused a young woman (who seemed the epitome of sweet-faced innocence) of trying to steal! He may not have said it in so many words, but his meaning was clear to everyone in the shop. They stared in speechless dismay as the color drained from the poor girl's face. Her lips turned so white that the onlookers feared she might swoon right then and there.

The incident would not have been quite so dreadful if the girl weren't so shy. Her shyness made everything worse, for it prevented her from speaking up for herself with any conviction. Never in her life before had Miss Cassandra Chivers been so horribly humiliated, but humiliation is the sort of emotion that makes shyness even more pronounced. The girl, who would never be described as outspoken even at the best of times, could not be expected to express herself well when things were at their worst. And what could be worse than hearing a booming-voiced clerk shatter the air of a large, busy, very fashionable shop with the accusation that one was *stealing*? It was no wonder the poor little chit became utterly tied of tongue. She could only stammer, "But I *p-paid* you!" in a small, unconvincing voice.

Mr. Dorking, the clerk behind the counter, sneered. He was the senior clerk, the most important of the fourteen clerks who handled sales for the firm of Hollings and Chast. Hollings and Chast, Linendrapers (established in 1790 and doing a thriving business at this, its original location on Wigmore Street, London, throughout the quarter century since its inception) was a favorite shop for members of the *ton* and ordinary citizens alike, for it was bountifully stocked with the widest possible selection of fabrics at all prices. At this very moment, for instance, all manner of patrons were making an amazing variety of purchases. At one counter a plainly dressed woman was examining a length of fine kentin for nightclothes; at another, a uniformed cavalry officer was selecting shirting. Here an overweight matron was bargaining for a remnant of muslin, and there a modish young lady was looking at a bolt of luxurious Persian silk. Every clerk was busy, and a number of customers were waiting to be served. And right before all these people, the shy Miss Chivers was being accused of thievery.

The clerk's loud accusation could be heard throughout the shop. All activity ceased. The clerks paused in their measurements or their cutting of the fabric or their rewinding of the bolts to watch Mr. Dorking "spear another sharper." Most of the patrons were too well-bred to stare, but they were not too well-bred to eavesdrop on the drama being enacted in their midst.

Dorking, the accusing clerk, was a long-nosed, thin-lipped, toplofty fellow who'd been employed by Hollings and Chast since he was a boy of fourteen. Hardened by his two decades of dealing with clutch-fisted, crafty, cunning, conniving customers, mostly female, he was convinced he'd seen every kind of swindle the human mind could devise. He liked to brag to his associates that he could sniff out a deceitful canary bird at twenty paces, so he was not going to be fooled by *this* little cheat, pretty though she was. She might look as innocent as a newborn babe, but he'd learned long ago that appearances could deceive. Therefore, he looked down his nose at the trembling girl with complete disdain. "I would remember if you'd paid me, wouldn't I?" he asked loudly.

"B-but I *did* pay you," the frightened Cassie Chivers whispered tearfully. "You *m-must* remember! You said the cambric was thirteen shillings fourpence, and I gave you a whole g-guinea!"

The clerk, aware that the scene he was playing was attracting the attention of the other customers (and pleased as punch to be performing the major role), smoothed his thinning hair in a gesture of pure arrogance and sneered again. "If you gave me a guinea, miss, then where is it, eh? Is it in my hand? No. Is it lying there on the counter? No. Is it on the floor? No. Is it in the parcel? No. Then where, I ask you, can it be?"

"I d-don't know," the girl murmured, her face painfully flushed. She tried to avert her head, as if to protect herself from the curious stares of the shop's patrons, but the self-effacing movement only made her seem more guilty. "But I *gave* it to you, t-truly! That guinea was all I had with m-me, except for a few pennies. Here! S-see for yourself!" And, her hands trembling, she turned the contents of her reticule out on the counter before him.

The contents were pathetically meager: only a handkerchief, a vial of smelling salts, a comb, an envelope on the back of which was scribbled a short shopping list and three pennies. The clerk eyed them with contempt. "And what do you think *that* proves, eh?" he asked scornfully. "You could have hidden your guinea anywhere on your person, if you ever had the guinea at all. Do you take me for a flat?"

"Hidden it on my *p-person?*" Cassie stammered, appalled. "Why, I would n- never *think* of such a—!"

"What on earth," came an angry voice from the back, "is going on there, Mr. Dorking? Do you realize you are creating a scene?"

It was Mr. Chast, the only partner of the partnership of Hollings and Chast still alive. He had emerged from his office at the rear of the shop and, in a stride befitting his importance, came marching across the floor to the counter where the scene was taking place. The other clerks immediately resumed their work, and the eavesdropping customers quickly turned their attention back to their own business, all except the cavalry officer, who continued to watch the proceedings with a troubled frown.

Miss Chivers lifted her head and glanced fearfully over her shoulder at the linendraper, who now loomed ominously behind her. She saw a tall, potbellied, dignified gentleman whose posture, expression and striped-satin waistcoat all contributed to his air of authority. It was plain that this gentleman was in charge of the shop. Was he going to clap her in irons, she wondered, her heart pounding in terror? "I . . . I—" she muttered helplessly.

Mr. Chast, ignoring her, frowned angrily at his clerk. "*Well,* Dorking?" he demanded in a tone that clearly revealed his dislike of public scenes.

"Sorry, Mr. Chast, but it's this ladybird," the clerk said, his demeanor suddenly becoming obsequious. "She's trying to—"

"Keep your voice down, man!" Mr. Chast chastized. "And you will *not* refer to any of our patrons as ladybirds—is that clear?"

The clerk bit his underlip in chagrin. "Yes, sir. Sorry, sir. But I do get so sick of these 'ladies' who try to filch goods. Thirteen an' four worth of cambric I cut for her, and now she says she handed me a guinea, which I swear on my mother's grave she never did."

"But I *did!*" Miss Chivers insisted, turning a pair of large, pleading eyes on the linendraper. "A whole guinea. All I had with me. I p-placed it right in his p- palm."

Mr. Chast studied the girl carefully. She was a small, pale-skinned creature with a pair of lovely, dark, expressive eyes and a wealth of curly auburn hair, which she'd crammed haphazardly into a dowdy brown bonnet. *At least she's not one of the nobs,* he told himself in relief. It would not have been the first time that a member of the *ton* tried to cheat one of his clerks. Bitter experience had proved that the nobility were just as prone to dishonesty as the rest of humanity. The difficulty was in getting justice when it was a nob you were dealing with. Mr. Chast had very painful memories of trying to exact payment from an earl whose daughter had filched a bolt of figured damask. He'd been thrown out on his ear! But *this* person, thank goodness, was not an earl's daughter . . . or even a baronet's. No baronet's daughter—or any young lady of the *ton*—would appear in public in such sturdy shoes and so drab a bonnet.

But she wasn't a street urchin either, he decided, for her dress was well-cut and her spencer was lined with a satin of excellent quality. She seemed a respectable type . . . not the sort who would perpetrate a fraud. Still, one could never be sure of a person's honesty by appearance. "Mr. Dorking has been with Hollings and Chast for twenty years, my girl," he said to the frightened creature before him. "I have never known him to lie. If he said you didn't give him the coin, then I must believe him."

"He may n-not be lying, s-sir," the girl managed, struggling to hold back her tears, "but he is s-surely m-mistaken."

"I certainly am not," the clerk insisted. "If I were, we would see the coin somewhere about, wouldn't we? And we'd see thirteen shillings fourpence entered here in my sales ledger, wouldn't we? But there's no such figure in the ledger—see for yourself, Mr. Chast!—and no such coin on the premises, either."

"Mr. Dorking does seem to be in the right of it, miss," Mr. Chast said to the girl in a voice that was firm though not unkind. "I'm sorry, but I don't see what else we can do but ask you to leave."

The beleaguered girl burst into tears. "But I *c-can't*. I live n-north of King's Cross. The ch-change from the g-guinea was to p-pay for a h-hack to t-take me *home!*"

"Enough of this," muttered the cavalry officer, who'd been watching the scene with mounting disgust. "Stop torturing the young lady. Anyone can see she's telling the truth."

Only one who knows the horror of being utterly alone in a sea of antagonists can guess the emotion that swept over Cassie Chivers at the sound of those trusting words. *Someone believed in her!* It was like rain to a dying bloom, a lifeline to a drowning swimmer, a gush of air to someone gasping for breath. Her heart leaped into her throat, and her eyes turned instinctively to see who it was who'd stepped forward to offer her aid. Whatever he looked like—old, ugly, scrawny, wizened or gross—she was quite prepared to find him beautiful. But she was not prepared for what she saw: a tall magnificence in a red coat blazoned with gold braid, tight-fitting white breeches and knee-high black boots, with a sword dangling at his side and a plumed shako held under his arm. He seemed quite literally to be a knight-in-arms. It was as if he'd ridden out of a medieval romance to enter the battle in her behalf. She could not believe her eyes. Perhaps she was not seeing clearly, she thought. After all, everything did look fuzzy through the tears that still clouded her eyes.

Meanwhile, the "knight," taking no notice of the astonishment in her face, strode past Mr. Chast and threw a guinea onto the counter. "Give the chit her goods and the change," he ordered, "and let her go."

Cassie Chivers blinked her eyes to clear her vision. But what she now saw—and with perfect clarity—made her rescuer seem even more unreal. This couldn't be happening to her, she thought. Not to Cassie Chivers. Cassie Chivers was not accustomed to miracles, yet here she was being championed by the handsomest man she'd ever in her life beheld.

Chapter Two

$\mathcal{M}$r. Chast's first instinct was to tell the interfering officer—tactfully, of course—to keep his sneezer out of shop business. But after taking a closer glance, he changed his mind. His eyebrows rose. He peered at the soldier in surprise. There was something about the fellow—an air of assurance, an ease of manner, a tone of command—that the linendraper had trained himself to recognize. He knew nobility when he saw it. The uniform of a cavalry officer might very well clothe a peer of the realm. This fellow was a nob, if he knew anything about it. Besides, there was something about the set of the officer's square chin that made one reluctant to cross him.

Mr. Chast had no intention of crossing him. Instead he bowed politely and said, "That is most gallant of you, sir. I'm sure this young lady will gratefully accept your kind assistance. Won't you, miss?"

Cassie's dark eyes flicked quickly from one face to the other before she lowered them and shook her head. "I do thank you," she murmured, "but . . . no."

"No?" Mr. Chast's temper flared up in irritation. Why was the girl prolonging the scene that was obviously more painful for her than for anyone else? "Did I hear you aright, ma'am? Did you say *no?*"

"Good God, man, don't bark at her!" the officer ordered. "Don't you see the young lady's frightened?" He turned to the girl and smiled down at her reassuringly. "You needn't fear my assistance, ma'am," he said softly. "I mean you no harm. May I introduce myself? I am Captain Rossiter. Robert Rossiter, of the Light Dragoons."

"Rossiter?" Mr. Chast tensed. "That's the family name of the Viscount Kittridge, is it not? Are you, perhaps, a relation to his lordship?"

"I *am* Lord Kittridge," the gentleman replied, "although I prefer to use my military rank while I still wear the uniform." A charmingly rueful grin appeared on his face. "Unfortunately I can only call myself Captain Rossiter until tomorrow. This is my last day in service."

Mr. Chast drew in a breath. The fellow was indeed a nob, just as he'd feared. In fact, the name was well known to him. The family of Viscount Kittridge had long been patrons of his establishment. This was the scion of a fine old family. Mr. Chast winced in annoyance. It was most unfortunate that so elevated a gentleman as the viscount had to involve himself in this sordid scene.

The girl, meanwhile, dropped a little curtsey. "Honored, my lord," she murmured, barely lifting her eyes.

"Captain, please, ma'am, captain. And let me assure you, ma'am," his lordship went on to explain, "that my only purpose in interfering in this matter is a desire to help you out of this ridiculous *contretemps*."

"Yes, Captain, I understand," the girl said shyly, keeping her head down and hoping that no one would notice the flush deepening in her cheeks. "I . . . I'm more grateful than I can say." She tried to speak calmly, but her heart was pounding loudly in her breast. The word *grateful* hardly expressed what she felt. She was aware of so great a sense of relief that words could scarcely describe her feelings. This magnificent knight—never mind that he was a mere cavalry officer to the rest of the world—had come to her aid. A moment ago she'd been more miserably helpless and alone than ever in her life before, terrified of being apprehended for thievery and sentenced to prison. But now, out of nowhere, had come this rescuer, tall and handsome and strong. An *ally* had risen up from among what had seemed to her a world full of enemies! It was miraculous! She could breathe again. His coming infused her blood with courage. With an ally, she could at last face her accusers with some semblance of confidence and stand up for her rights.

"You needn't be grateful, girl," her rescuer was saying. "You need only to accept the guinea I've offered you."

"Please . . ." She hated to refuse him anything, but she had to. She lifted her hand as if to ward off a blow. "Don't ask it of me. I . . . c-can't."

"But why can't you?" he demanded.

She twisted her fingers together. "It's a matter of . . . of principle."

"Principle?" The tall officer peered down at her lowered head, bemused. "I don't understand. What principle?"

She flicked another fleeting glance over his face before she dropped her eyes again. "It's a matter of . . . of honor, Captain. If I accepted your assistance, my innocence would not be proved." The words came slowly, as if the pronouncing of each one gave her pain. But she had to make this gentleman—this beautiful red and gold knight who'd inexplicably stood up in her behalf—understand why she was rejecting him. "Taking your money would be the same as admitting that I didn't p-pay in the first place, don't you see?"

The officer stared at her for a long moment. Then he shrugged. "I suppose I do," he admitted, picking up his guinea and pocketing it reluctantly. "You want your word to be affirmed. The Truth Made Manifest, is that it?"

"Yes," she admitted in her small voice. "Just so."

"Mmm." He rubbed his chin speculatively and then shrugged. "That means we shall have to *prove* your innocence somehow." He turned to the linendraper. "How do you suggest we begin?"

Mr. Chast was disgusted. He would have to deal with a nob after all. But viscount or not, the fellow was not going to weaken his stand. The linendraper's faith in his clerk was unshakable. "I'm afraid I haven't a suggestion, my lord. Mr. Dorking has been my clerk for two decades. In all that time, I've never known him to be dishonest. It is hardly likely that he would have pocketed a guinea."

"That's sure as check," the clerk muttered under his breath.

"On the other hand," the captain pointed out, "although I've known this young woman no more than a few minutes, I feel just as sure she isn't lying either. Let's assume for a moment that they're both telling the truth. In that case, the girl's guinea would be here somewhere. How can we go about finding it?"

Mr. Chast took a deep breath in surrender. "Oh, very well. Let's go over the incident in detail, Dorking. Tell us what happened, from the beginning."

Mr. Dorking, who'd been basking in the glow of his employer's support, suddenly began to feel put-upon. He didn't like being made to defend himself, but he had no choice but to swallow his pride. "Yes, sir. If you say so, sir. From the beginning. This here ladybird came up to m—"

"Dorking!" Mr. Chast admonished.

"Sorry. The young *lady* came up to me asking for cambric. I showed her three or four bolts, and she chose the stripes here. Said she needed five yards. I measured them off and cut the piece."

"Where did you do the cutting?" the officer asked.

"Right there, where the yardstick is."

Captain Rossiter carefully inspected the counter and the floor below. There was no coin. "Very well," he told the clerk. "Go on."

Dorking smirked. "*Told* you there's no guinea there."

"Go *on,* I said!" Captain Rossiter snapped.

The smirk on Dorking's face vanished at once. He'd finally perceived what Mr. Chast had noticed long before—that this gentleman was not one to cross. "Yes, m'lord. Sorry, m'lord," he mumbled hurriedly and proceeded with his tale. "After I cut the goods, I folded it like always and then I went to the table there, where we keep the wrapping paper, and I made up the parcel. Then I took it over to the lady, handed it over and asked for thirteen shillings fourpence. And that's when she said, I already gave you a guinea. But she never did."

"No," the girl said, glancing from one to the other fearfully. "It wasn't like that."

"Then give us *your* account, ma'am," the officer urged. "Go on. There's no need to be afraid."

The girl clenched her fists bravely. "He . . . he cut the cambric, brought it here where I was standing and folded it in front of me. It was then, you see, that I handed him the guinea. I *did, truly*! He took the coin and the fabric, turned and walked away to the wrapping table."

"Hang it," the clerk burst out, "it's a damn lie! She never—!"

"Dorking, watch your blasted tongue!" the linendraper hissed.

Captain Rossiter knit his brow in thought. "If she *had* given you the guinea, Mr. Dorking, what would you have done with it?" he asked.

"Dropped it in the cash box, of course," Dorking answered promptly. "But she didn't."

"But what if she did? Where is the cash box?"

"Right there, on the table near the wrapping things."

"Ah!" The captain's eyes lit. "Isn't it possible that you could have dropped the coin in the cash box before you wrapped the parcel? Without thinking about it?"

Mr. Dorking was not going to back down, even for a nob. Even for a nob as awesome as this one. He shook his head firmly. "No, my lord, not at all possible."

"But why not? What if you were thinking of something else? You could have dropped the coin in the cash box quite automatically, couldn't you? It *is* possible, I suspect. Dropping coins in the box must surely be a habit by this time. After all, it is something you do all day, every day."

"It isn't likely he wouldn't be aware of it," Mr. Chast put in. "You see, when he puts money in the cash box, he must note the amount on his ledger."

"But if his mind was preoccupied . . . if he wasn't thinking—"

Mr. Chast rubbed his fingers on the bridge of his nose. "Let's admit that there *is* a possibility that he dropped the coin into the box, my lord. I shall look into the matter. I give you my word that I shall personally tally up Mr. Dorking's cash box at the end of the day today, and if there is an overage of a guinea, I shall make restitution to the young lady myself."

Miss Chivers made a sound of despair in her throat. She couldn't help herself. The linendraper's words had upset her. So long a delay would spoil everything. If he didn't find her guinea until the end of the day, she would not be vindicated before the onlookers, and, what was worse, she would not be able to go home until terribly late.

Captain Rossiter fully understood her feelings. "Oh, no, Mr. Chast, that won't do," he said firmly, placing a reassuring hand on the girl's shoulder. "You shall tally up the cash box right now."

"But we can't do that, my lord. We are in the midst of a business day. Four other clerks use the same cash box. It is a complicated matter to tally the cash. We cannot disrupt our procedures for a mere guinea."

"But for a mere guinea you'd besmirch a young woman's honor—is that what you're saying?" the captain asked calmly.

"But, my *lord*—!" Mr. Chast objected.

"Captain, please, Mr. Chast. Call me captain." The officer looked the linen-draper squarely in the eye. "If you have any sense at all of fair play, you have no choice," he pointed out. "If a mistake *has* been made, you owe it to the young lady to clear her name right now, in front of all these witnesses. That is only just, is it not?"

See? Mr. Chast said to himself in disgust. *There's always trouble when you deal with nobs.* Aloud he said, "Very well, your lordsh— I mean, Captain Rossiter. We'll take the cash box to my office and tally up. It will take some time, I'm afraid. I'll have Dorking bring you a chair. And a cup of tea, if you wish."

"No, Mr. Chast, I care for neither chair nor tea. However, you may have them brought for the young lady, if she wishes. But you will tally the cash *right here,* in front of all of us."

The crowd broke into spontaneous applause. For Mr. Chast, that was the last straw. His face reddened alarmingly. "Are you implying, my lord," he demanded, drawing himself up to his full height and puffing out his chest belligerently, "that *I* would not make an honest accounting?"

"I am implying nothing," the captain retorted coolly. "I think, however, that a public reckoning is the only way that would show what happened and leave no questions remaining. It would clear up the matter once and for all. Do you agree, ma'am?"

Cassie Chivers looked up at her knight-at-arms adoringly. "Oh, yes, Captain! Yes, indeed."

Mr. Chast, realizing that what the captain was suggesting was probably best for business, swallowed his ire. "Very well, Captain Rossiter. As you wish. Bring the cash box here, Mr. Dorking," he ordered. "Let's get this over with."

Mr. Chast summoned two other clerks to his side with a crook of his index finger. Then, pulling the ledger from Dorking's hand, he dismissed the fellow with an abrupt flick of his wrist. He would not involve Dorking in the tally. The two clerks he'd chosen to assist him were completely objective; thus the captain would have no possible grounds for complaint that the tally was in any way tainted.

The linendraper and his two objective clerks bent over the cash box and all five sales ledgers. Meanwhile, Dorking himself supplied Miss Chivers with a chair and a cup of tea. He could afford to be gracious; he had no doubt that the tally would vindicate him completely. As soon as the girl (whom he still thought of as a cheating "canary bird") was comfortably seated, Dorking withdrew to the rear of the store and watched the accounting with the rest of the onlookers, a group which now included all the customers, even the well-bred ones.

The captain, having taken a stand beside the young lady's chair, kept his eyes fixed on the linendraper. Miss Chivers, on the other hand, took this opportunity to study her rescuer from the corner of her eye. Never in her wildest dreams could she have imagined that so breathtaking a hero would choose to enter the fray in her behalf. He was the sort one would expect to wear the colors for a great beauty, not for an ordinary mousy creature like herself. Robert Rossiter, Viscount Kittridge, was what the *haute ton* would call "top of the trees." He was tall and sinewy, with wide shoulders and large hands. His soldierly life had browned the skin of his face, but his weathered appearance only added to his attractiveness. His dark hair, as curly as her own, was clipped short in a soldierly style that she usually didn't like, but in Captain Rossiter's case she found it quite becoming. The short, tight curls that framed his face gave him the look of a Roman centurion. But what most entranced her were his eyes, the irises a light brown edged with yellow streaks. They gleamed with a piercing intelligence that seemed able to cut through any false facade and find the truth. The directness of his glance seemed capable of withering any opponent's will. The overwhelming impression one took away after meeting him was of a controlled strength, a power that was kept in tight restraint under a calm surface. It took no more than a glance at him to tell that he would not be easily bested in a fight. What a formidable ally she had found to fight her battle!

Meanwhile, business remained at a standstill while the customers watched the linendraper and his assistants count the coins and notes and pile them up on the counter in little stacks. An abnormal silence hovered in the air as Mr. Chast and the two clerks totalled and retotalled the figures in the ledgers and counted and recounted the money. Forty-five minutes passed. Finally Mr. Chast stood erect. "Dorking!" he shouted.

Mr. Dorking came running to his side. "Yes, Mr. Chast?"

"You're a damned fool!" the linendraper snapped under his breath. "You're a guinea over! The girl *did* give you the money, just as she claimed!"

The clerk winced. "Oh, my heavens!" he muttered, clapping a hand to his brow. "What've I done?"

"Come on, you idiot," his employer ordered, picking up the wrapped package of fabric before pulling the clerk after him, "let's go and apologize to the young lady."

They approached the seated girl and the officer who stood beside her chair. "You seem to be in the right of it, Captain," Mr. Chast announced shamefacedly. "We *have* found an extra guinea in the box."

The stillness of the air was rent with a cheer from the crowd. The observers had, in agreement with the officer, long ago decided that the sweet-faced girl had to be innocent. Now they were delighted to have their judgment validated, and they showed that delight with enthusiastic applause and cries of "Hear, hear!" and "Right-o!"

Miss Chivers, who'd been too deeply occupied with the problem of dealing with her own emotions to realize the extent of the interest she'd aroused in the crowd, leaped from her chair with a start. She stared at the cheering customers in shock. Then she turned back to find Dorking approaching her, his face ashen. "I can't tell you how sorry I am, miss," he began. "I've never done such a thing before in all my life."

"Your guinea, ma'am," the linendraper murmured, holding out the coin and the package as well. "We'd like you to have the fabric with our compliments."

The girl backed away from him, shuddering. For Miss Cassandra Chivers to find herself the center of so much attention was all too much. She could not bear to be the focus of so many eyes. She could not bear the misery on the clerk's face. She could not bear the ignominy of being offered the fabric as a gift—a sop for what they'd put her through! And she could not bear that her beautiful knight was witness to this cheap and tawdry scene. Her eyes flew from the clerk to Mr. Chast to Captain Rossiter to the crowd, and then, bursting into tears, she lowered her head and, pushing heedlessly through the crowd, ran to the door.

The humiliated clerk, not knowing what to do, gaped after her. Mr. Chast, too, seemed utterly nonplussed. The captain was the only one capable of action. Without a word, he strode through the throng after her.

He found the shaken young lady standing bewilderedly at the curb. "You'll be wanting a hackney, I imagine," he said calmly, taking her elbow and escorting her away from the store doorway, where curious gapers were beginning to gather.

"Yes, C-Captain," she stammered, "but you don't have to t-trouble. I c-can—"

"No trouble at all," he said, lifting his hand to signal a passing hack.

"You are t-too k-kind!"

The hack pulled to a stop. Cassie was not so agitated that she didn't realize she had only a moment in which to thank him properly for what he'd done for her. She tried desperately to overcome her timidity, but her tongue tripped awkwardly over the words. "I don't know how . . . to thank . . . I c-can't tell you . . ." she mumbled helplessly.

"There's no need to say anything, ma'am," the captain assured her as he threw the driver a coin and handed her into the carriage. "Anyone with half an eye could see you were innocent. It was a pleasure for me to see justice done."

Before she could utter another word, his lordship tipped his plumed shako and was off, striding away down the street with a long, loping step. Cassie Chivers peeped out the carriage window to watch him go. Her eyes held an unwonted intensity. She wanted to memorize the look of him—the set of his shoulders, the swing of his arms, the manly grace of his carriage. All too soon, however, the growing distance between them misted his outline until he became just a blur on the horizon. It was only when he'd completely disappeared from view that she signalled the driver to start the carriage.

She sat back against the cushions, an inexplicable shiver passing through her body. She had just lived through the worst and best morning of her life, and her emotions were churning within her. The expected emotion was relief—relief that her honor had been vindicated. And there was a feeling of triumph, too, in that vindication. But the surge of triumph could do nothing to assuage the sudden stab of despair that clenched her chest. The cause of the despair was obvious to her; she didn't have to spend a moment analyzing it. A lifelong dream had been granted this morning: Fate had brought a magnificent knight into her life in a time of dire need. But then, after only one joyful moment, it had taken him away again. There had hardly been any time at all to enjoy the meeting. After the merest of beginnings, it was all over.

Good-bye, Captain Rossiter, she said to herself sadly. She didn't need to look into a crystal ball to know that their paths would surely never cross again. Nor did she have to be a soothsayer to foretell that, though her meeting with her red-and-gold knight had been the briefest of encounters, she would love him as long as she lived.

Chapter Three

*I*t had grown quite dark and a chill wind was blowing up from the north when Mr. Oliver Chivers's phaeton pulled into the curved driveway in front of his home at King's Cross. He had just spent a long day at his office in the City and was looking forward to the warmth of his own fireside and a good dinner in the company of his daughter. Therefore, he was both surprised and annoyed when he discovered that another carriage had cut in ahead of his and was proceeding at a deucedly leisurely pace down his own driveway. He removed his spectacles (which made distant objects only a blur), rubbed his eyes and peered out the window at the other carriage. "Who the devil is that?" he asked his coachman querulously. He was tired, cold and hungry. He didn't want to have to delay his meal in order to deal with callers he hadn't invited.

"No one as I reco'nize," the coachman answered as he drew up at the door behind the unfamiliar carriage. "Per'aps Miss Cassie 'as a visitor."

"Cassie never 'as visitors," Mr. Chivers grumbled, climbing down from the phaeton. He looked over at the other carriage curiously. It was a businesslike vehicle with the words *Hollings and Chast, Linendrapers,* painted in gold leaf on its side. Was this some sort of delivery, Mr. Chivers wondered? If so, why were they making it at this time of night?

A large, potbellied fellow climbed down from the other carriage and surveyed the house. He seemed awestruck at its size and style. Oliver Chivers smirked inwardly. He loved to see strangers admire his home. He was very proud of the house he'd had built in this newly developed area of north London, and it always gave him enormous satisfaction when he caught an expression of admiration on the face of a passerby. The house, of pink brick and stone, was an architectural beauty, designed in the much-praised Adam style. It had a magnificent pedimented roof, a graceful fanlighted doorway and recessed arches for the windows. For Oliver Chivers the house was a personal triumph. No one looking at it could doubt that the owner was a person of taste and means.

The stranger who stood looking at it now was noticeably impressed. He turned at Mr. Chivers's approach and removed his hat. "Good evening, sir," he said, looking down at the smaller man curiously. "This cannot be—can it?—the residence of Miss Cassandra Chivers?"

"It is," Mr. Chivers replied. "I'm 'er father, Oliver Chivers."

The coachman, who followed closely behind Mr. Chivers, gave an I-told-ye-so snort. Mr. Chivers wheeled on him irritably. "Damnation, Measham, must ye be always eaves-droppin' on my conversations? Mind yer business and take care of the 'orses."

"Tole ye 'twas someone fer Miss Cassie," the coachman muttered as he walked away.

The stranger, meanwhile, eyed the house admiringly. "I had no *idea* the young lady's residence would be so . . . so . . . substantial," he murmured.

"Indeed?" Mr. Chivers retorted curtly. "An' who, may I ask, are you to be interested in my daughter's residence, substantial or no?"

The gentleman extended his hand. "George Chast, sir. Of Hollings and Chast, Linendrapers. You may have heard of my establishment."

"Can't say as I 'ave." Chivers shook the man's hand but peered at his face suspiciously. "Do ye 'ave some business with my daughter?"

"You could say that," the linendraper sighed. "Unfinished business. I've come to return her money, you see. And her reticule. And to give her this fabric. Gratis, of course. As a gesture of apology, you see."

The man's words were incomprehensible to Cassandra Chivers's father, but he found them troubling nevertheless. "You keep sayin' that I see, but I don't see," he said testily. "What are ye doin' with 'er reticule? Why should ye be givin' fabric to 'er gratis? And what do ye need to apologize *for?*"

Mr. Chast shifted his weight uncomfortably from one foot to the other. He was unhappy enough to have to face the girl again, but to have to face the father was even worse. And what made matters even more awkward was the fact that the father was obviously wealthy. The situation was becoming more mortifying every moment. This was turning out to be almost as bad as dealing with a nob. "It seems, Mr. Chivers," the linendraper said carefully, "that you haven't been told about the . . . er . . . occurrence this morning."

"Occurrence? What occurrence?" The worry in Mr. Chivers's chest expanded alarmingly.

"Perhaps it would be best," Mr. Chast suggested, trying valiantly to maintain his usual air of authority, "if I spoke directly to Miss Chivers."

"I'll decide what's best when I know what this is all about," Cassie's father snapped. "Let's 'ear it, man."

The linendraper's air of authority wilted before the other man's glare. "It was all a misunderstanding," he explained nervously. "One of my clerks—a very foolish fellow, I assure you, whom I would certainly dismiss out of hand if it weren't for the fact that he's been in my employ for twenty years or more—well, you see, he made the inexcusable blunder of accusing her—your daughter, sir, who, of course, in all fairness I must say we had no idea that she came from so, how shall I say, so substantial a family—"

"Will ye stop yer ditherin', Mr. Chast? This fool clerk of yours accused my daughter of *what*?"

Mr. Chast dropped his eyes in shame. "Of . . . er . . . trying to steal the goods."

"Tryin' to *steal*—? My *Cassie*?" Mr. Chivers felt his neck grow hot. "What blasted kind of idiocy is *that*? My Cassie wouldn't steal a blade of grass from a 'aystack! Yer clerk must be touched in his upper works!"

"Yes, sir. You're quite right. We were able to exonerate her completely. That's why I'm delivering these parcels myself. She ran out of the shop, you see, before we could apologize properly, so it seemed only right, after all that happened, that I should come myself—"

"She ran out of yer shop? Are you sayin', man, that you embarrassed 'er in yer place of business? That this . . . this *accusation* was made in *public*?"

Mr. Chast lowered his head miserably. "It happened in the shop, yes," he admitted, taking a step backward as if trying to escape from the ferocity of the smaller man's glare.

"Good God!" Oliver Chivers was beginning to feel quite sick. "Are you tellin' me that my little Cassie, who's so shy she can barely open 'er mouth in front of a stranger, was accused of thievery in a shop full of people?"

"Well, yes, sir, I'm afraid so. It was a dreadful misunderstanding. I myself had a suspicion—from the lining of her spencer, which was an excellent grade of satin—that she was well to pass, but my clerk is not very perceptive. And even the gentleman who aided her—a man of nobility, I assure you, although I don't believe I should take the liberty of revealing his identity—did not seem to have guessed that she was a young lady of quality. So, in a way, one can't fully blame my clerk. The girl was unescorted, after all. And all she had with her was the one guinea, you see, so—"

"Stop sayin' *you see* in that idiotic way!" Chivers shouted. "I *do not* see! I do not see 'ow anyone can accuse my Cassie of stealing! I do not see what she was doin' in your shop without 'er companion! I do not see why she 'ad only one guinea! I do not see *anythin*'!"

"I'm sorry, Mr. Chivers, sir, but I've tried to explain—"

"Then try *again,* confound it!" Mr. Chivers ordered, poking his index finger repeatedly into Mr. Chast's chest until the linendraper had backed up against his carriage and could escape no further. "An' tell it proper, do ye 'ear me? Step by step, from the beginning."

Chapter Four

Oliver Chivers found his daughter in the sitting room. She was curled up in a chair near the fire, engrossed in a novel. He stormed up to her chair (ignoring the approach of Miss Penicuick, his housekeeper and his daughter's companion, who was ready, as usual, with his preprandial sherry) and dropped a parcel in her lap. "Yer cambric, ma'am. It seems ye left it in the shop this morning."

Cassie started, her eyes flying from the package on her lap to her father's face. "Papa! How—?"

Miss Penicuick gasped. "Oh, heavens! He *knows*!"

"What do I know, Miss Penicuick?" Chivers asked in a tone heavy with sarcasm, glaring at his housekeeper over the spectacles that had slipped halfway down his nose. "That ye permitted my daughter to go into town in a rented 'ack without escort? Is that what ye think I know?"

Cassie put the package aside and rose from her chair. "Hush, Papa," she said quietly. "There's no need to make accusations. Drink your sherry, and let's go in to dinner. We'll talk over the soup."

Mr. Chivers had never been one to resist his daughter's gentle handling, so he permitted himself to be led into the dining room. But even when his hunger had been assuaged, his body warmed by good wine and his temper cooled by his daughter's calm manner, he was nevertheless very annoyed with her. When he had finished his second course, he pushed away his dinner plate and swore aloud that he would never, as long as he lived, understand the girl. "I 'ope ye see, Cassie Chivers, that the entire 'umiliatin' incident was somethin' ye brought on yerself."

He was distressed to his core. The incident at the linendraper's was simply another example of the way in which the girl's shyness, coupled with her lack of interest in financial matters, had brought her needless difficulty and pain.

Mr. Chivers had spent his entire life studying the intricacies of finance, with the result that he'd amassed a considerable fortune from the most modest of beginnings and that his financial advice was sought even by those who were financial experts in their own right. And yet his only offspring seemed to have no interest in the subject. Money was of no concern to her. Her complete indifference to the one subject that occupied his mind above all others hurt him deeply. But what was worse, it rendered her vulnerable to just such incidents as had occurred today.

He looked across the table to where his daughter sat picking away at her beef and glazed onions that their French cook had prepared and that he'd found delicious. But Cassie was evidently not interested in the food. The poor child had quite lost her appetite, but, considering the day's event, it was not surprising. He watched her as she absently moved a tiny onion back and forth across her plate. She seemed to him to be everything that was lovely in a young woman. Her oddly shaped face, with its full cheeks that narrowed down delicately to a charmingly pointed chin, had a unique beauty; her warm brown eyes were enormous and expressive; her hair was thick and seemed more abundant because of its profusely curled texture; her neck and shoulders were graceful and revealed the most perfect skin; and her figure was both slim and womanly. In addition, she had a quiet but delightful sense of humor and a quick mind. Why, under the circumstances, was she so shy and inept in public? "It's really beyond belief," he grumbled, unable to let the matter drop, "that a girl of sense would take 'erself into town with only one guinea on 'er person."

"I'm sorry, Papa," the girl said softly. "I didn't think I would require more than that."

"Ye didn't think at all!" Her father pushed his spectacles up on the bridge of his nose with a feeling of utter helplessness. "And that's only *part* of yer thoughtlessness. Ye went *alone*!" He turned his glare on Miss Penicuick, the middle-aged, angular woman who'd been Cassie's governess in her childhood and who now functioned not only as housekeeper but as Cassie's companion, chaperone, dresser, confidante and friend. "Where were *you*, Miss Penicuick, when all this was goin' on, may I ask?"

Miss Penicuick glanced guiltily at her employer from her place at the far end of the table and then lowered her eyes, sighed unhappily and stared miserably down at her own untouched dinner. "Well, sir, you see, I . . . I . . ."

"Don't blame Miss Penny, Papa," Cassie said, reaching across the table and patting her governess's hand gently. "I ran off behind her back."

"You did *what*?"

"Well, she *did* leave me a note," Miss Penicuick murmured in defense of her charge.

Cassie's father shook his head, deeply disturbed. He was about to utter a few nasty words about what he thought of the girl's running off, but he was stopped by the entrance of the butler with a tray of blancmange. Oliver Chivers glared at the bland white pudding the butler set down in front of him. "Not bla'mange again," he muttered angrily. "I don't pay a French chef an enormous salary to cook a deuced tasteless pudding! I thought I told ye to tell M'sieur Maurice I never want to see such 'orrid stuff on this table again!"

"Come, come, Papa, you never said any such thing," Cassie pointed out gently. "I know you're very angry at me, but you mustn't take it out on the rest of the household."

Her father grunted and relapsed into silence. The girl was right. It wasn't the chef's fault that he didn't know how to handle his daughter now that she was a grown woman. How he wished she were still a child! She'd been nothing but a joy to him in the early years, after her mother had passed away. Life would have been grim indeed if he had not had Cassie on whom to lavish his affection. And Cassie had responded to that affection as a flower does to sunshine. She'd been a charming, loving child. When he came home from the office every night, she'd brighten his arrival with her glad welcome. She always followed him about the house when he was home, sat on his lap while they read nursery rhymes together, told him wonderful, imaginary stories of her day's adventures, laughed at his jokes and filled his life with gaiety. Sometimes he let her visit him at his office, where she would sit for hours and watch him with quiet adoration as he worked. How happy she had made him then.

But now that she was grown she was greatly changed. Was it her schooling that had done it? He'd wanted to give her all the advantages that the most high-born of females were given, and he'd chosen a school for her that was much favored by the *haute ton*. But perhaps he'd been wrong. Her classmates at the Marchmont Academy for Young Ladies had been, for the most part, girls of noble birth. They soon discovered she was the daughter of a "cit," and they were quick to slight her. He'd hoped that his wealth would make up for his lack of a title—after all, he was richer than most of their fathers—but he should have known that Cassie was not the sort to flaunt her wealth. Shy to begin with, she grew positively invisible among the bright flowers of the *ton*. Even the few cits among the students did not make friends with her; they were too busy toadying up to the titles. Thus it was that her experiences at the Academy increased her tendency to withdraw into herself. Her schooling had given her polish, yes, but what good was that polish, and all her other excellent qualities, if they were obscured by her overwhelming shyness?

He had to admit that her shyness, so charming in the child, was a flaw in the woman. It became a screen that separated her from other people. She could be polite and mannerly in public, but she could not open herself enough to permit the slightest intimacy to develop. She had too much reserve to reveal her deepest self. Thus, she had no young ladies whom she could call friends; no young men whom she could call suitors. The veil of shyness even separated her from her own father. She did not share her thoughts with him as she used to do. Even the dreadful scene at Hollings and Chast's might have been kept from him if he hadn't come upon Mr. Chast in the driveway. Cassie seemed to live in her own world. And he, without a wife to advise him, did not know what to do to bring her out.

Yet, shy as she was, she had dared, today, to go shopping in the heart of London all by herself. And with only one guinea in her reticule. One guinea! He would have insisted on giving her *ten,* if she'd only told him she wished to shop for fabric for a gown. What was the matter with the girl? She was shy, yes, but she had a good share of common sense. How was he ever to learn to understand her?

He pushed his dessert away and looked at her sternly. "That ye went into town unescorted is bad enough," he scolded, "but that ye ventured forth without adequate funds was completely irresponsible. What is it, Cassie, that makes ye be'ave like a wet-goose? You know that ye 'ave only to ask, and ye can 'ave all the funds yer 'eart desires. Yet ye take yerself off on a shoppin' expedition with only a guinea. One would think ye were the daughter of a pauper! No wonder the blasted clerk took ye for a thief."

Cassie, too, lowered her eyes to her plate. "Yes, Papa. I'm sorry, Papa."

"There ain't no need to apologize to *me,* Cassie. I wasn't the one who 'ad to suffer 'umiliation in a crowded shop. You should apologize to *yerself* for subjecting yerself to such shame. If you'd 'ad Miss Penicuick with you, it would have been obvious that y're a young woman of substance. And if you'd 'ad sufficient funds in yer possession, ye could've thrown a guinea into that clerk's face an' left the premises with yer 'ead 'eld 'igh."

"No, Papa, I could not. Throwing out a second guinea would not have proved I'd given him the first."

"It would've at least proved that y're plump enough in the pocket to pay for the fabric easily enough and that therefore ye'd be unlikely to try to steal it."

"But, as it turned out, sir," Miss Penicuick offered, "the overage in the cash box was a much more definitive proof than an extra guinea in her reticule would have been."

"That may be," Oliver Chivers granted, "but if Cassie 'ad not been championed by that very kind stranger, I dread to think what might've become of 'er. How could she've faced the people in the store? How would she've made 'er way 'ome? The very thought of what she might've 'ad to endure makes me shudder."

"Yes, you're quite right there," Miss Penicuick agreed. "Thank the Lord for Captain Rossiter's presence. I shall remember him tonight in my prayers."

"Rossiter?" Mr. Chivers's eyes, behind their spectacles, blinked in astonishment. "Are you speakin' of Robert Rossiter, the Viscount Kittridge? Was 'e the officer who championed ye?"

"Why, Papa?" Cassie asked, her face coloring. "Are you acquainted with him?"

"No, not personally. But Delbert Jennings, who 'andled the financial affairs for the old viscount, is a good friend of mine. 'E's often spoken of the young man. Says 'e's a very good sort."

"He was certainly a 'good sort' to me today," Cassie murmured.

"Yes. It's too bad such a fine fellow 'ad a father as profligate as the old viscount. Now poor Rossiter'll find 'isself puntin' on tick. 'Asn't been left a feather to fly with, Jennings says."

Cassie stiffened in sudden attention. "What do you mean, Papa? Are you saying that the captain is in a bad way financially?"

"As bad as can be. 'Is father's gamblin' debts left 'im badly dipped. All the estates are mortgaged to the 'ilt. An' the poor fellow ain't yet been told. Far away, fightin' in the war with Nappy all these years, 'e don't know anythin' of the financial maneuverings that took place be'ind 'is back. Jennings says that when 'e learns the full extent of 'is indebtedness 'e'll be knocked off 'is pins."

Cassie stared at her father for a moment, a little cry escaping from her throat. The sound caught his attention. He peered at his daughter curiously through the thick lenses of his spectacles. "Ye seem unduly affected, Cassie. I thought financial affairs didn't 'old no interest for ye."

A blush suffused her face again. "I only . . . it's just that he was so very kind to me," she said. "I'm sorry to learn that so kind a gentleman will be so badly hurt."

Oliver Chivers didn't miss the flush on his daughter's cheeks. "*Liked* the fellow, eh, Cass?" he asked bluntly.

Cassie dropped her eyes, unable to reply. Miss Penicuick took it upon herself to answer for the girl. "How could she help but like him after his gallantry today?"

Cassie lifted her head. "Isn't there anything you can do for him, Papa?"

"Do for 'im? What can I do? I 'ave nothing to do with the Rossiters' finances."

"But couldn't you speak to—what was the name of the viscount's man of business? Jennings?—to Mr. Jennings? Make some suggestions, perhaps?"

"Really, Cassie, ye can sometimes be a complete green'ead. Don't ye know anythin' of the proprieties of business? I couldn't make suggestions to Jennings about the finances of one of 'is clients. That would imply that I believed myself to be more competent to 'andle the affair then 'e'd be. Besides, with all the viscount's properties encumbered, there ain't nothin' I *could* suggest that would get the fellow out of 'is fix, short of—" He stopped speaking abruptly, his mouth open and his eyes staring out at nothing, as if a dazzling idea had struck him with a clunk.

Cassie leaned forward eagerly. "Short of what, papa?"

Mr. Chivers blinked, his eyes focusing slowly on his daughter's face. Perhaps he *could* make a suggestion to Jennings about the viscount's finances. It was an off chance, an endeavor with a very low probability of success, but it just might work. He'd never before known Cassie to show so great an interest in a young man. If his suggestion were taken, it could benefit not only his lordship but Cassie as well. It was certainly worth a whack. He would put out a feeler and see what he could see.

"What *is* it, Papa?" Cassie asked, bursting with curiosity. "Why are you looking at me so strangely?"

"It's nothin', my love, nothin'," her father muttered, pulling his eyes from her and looking down at the dessert. "Eat yer blasted bla'mange."

Chapter Five

*S*ometimes it is hard to recognize the moment when one's life falls to pieces. Robert Rossiter, Viscount Kittridge, however, could give you the date, hour and minute when it happened to him.

His lordship was no fool. Although no one in his family—not his dithery mother, his young brother Gavin, nor his recently widowed sister, Lady Yarrow—had given him the slightest clue that anything was wrong with the family finances, it took no more than two days of civilian life for him to suspect that he was in trouble. But on the third day, an encounter with a wine merchant (who'd awaited him on the doorstep of the family town house in Portman Square and who'd asked point-blank for payment of a long-overdue bill for champagne) led him to seek out his father's man of business without further delay.

What he learned from Mr. Jennings sent him reeling. The news struck him like a blow to the stomach, knocking out his breath and causing him to fall back into the chair on the edge of which he'd been nervously perched. Mr. Jennings offered him a drink of brandy, which he downed without hesitation. "As bad as that?" he asked when he'd recovered his voice.

Mr. Jennings nodded. "I'm afraid so, my lord. I had warned your father repeatedly, during the last five years of his life, that this day of reckoning would come and that it might be his son—you, my lord—who'd have to face the consequences of a situation not of your making. But the gambling fever had too tight a hold on him. He didn't seem able to stop, even at the end when the pain of his illness was almost unendurable. Every day, rain or shine, in spite of his growing weakness, he had his man carry him to his club and seat him at the gaming table." He shook his head in dismal recollection.

Lord Kittridge shut his eyes. "That's not the man I remember," he muttered unhappily. "You've not painted a picture of a father of whom a son can feel proud."

"Nevertheless he loved you, my boy, as much as he could love anyone. I think one of the things that drove him on was the futile hope that he might make a killing and thus spare you some of this."

"Yes, the prayer of every man who ever rolled dice: *One killing, dear God, one killing, and I shall give up the game forever.*"

Delbert Jennings sighed. "Too true, my lord, unfortunately too true. A terrible disease, gaming. Your father is not the first, nor will he be the last to succumb to it." Sighing again, he gently pushed a folder across his desk toward the viscount. "I've worked out a plan of divestiture, which I've been waiting to go over with you—"

Lord Kittridge held up a restraining hand. "Not now, Jennings. I don't think I could make sense of anything right now. Let me go. I'll come back tomorrow, I promise. Tomorrow. Then we'll see what we can salvage from this fiasco."

"Yes, of course, my lord. I quite understand," the man of business said as both men rose. "But it need not be tomorrow. Take a few days to let the news sink in. Shall we say Monday?"

The day agreed on, Mr. Jennings led the viscount to the door, where they paused and shook hands. "Try not to fall into the dismals, my lord," the older man counselled. "Other men, many more than you dream, have managed to survive such blows as this."

Lord Kittridge emerged from Jennings's offices, his head in a whirl. It was hard for him to comprehend fully the extent of the disaster his father had left behind. But one thing was devastatingly clear: The future he'd imagined for himself was shattered. He knew that he was not the only soldier to return from the wars to find things at home devastatingly changed, but the knowledge that others had been struck with similar blows was not particularly comforting. No matter how often one hears that misery loves company, there are some miseries that can't be eased by the mere awareness that others have suffered a similar catastrophe.

He began to walk down the street, the cold wind buffeting his face. He couldn't help noticing that, although it was early afternoon, the day was as dark as twilight. The sky was a stormy gray, and the air had a bite that promised snow. He raised the collar of his greatcoat, thinking that the grim weather was deucedly appropriate to his mood. He didn't quite know where he was going. He knew only that he didn't want to go home. Facing his family would require more strength than he could now summon up. He turned up one street and down another until more than an hour had passed, but he still was not able to calm his inner perturbation.

But the wind nipped at his ears and his fingers tingled with the cold, so at last he hailed a hack and gave the address of the Fenton Hotel, where his friend Sandy was putting up. Sir Philip Sanford—Sandy to his friends—had been his comrade-in-arms through all his years of military service. Lord Kittridge had never had a better friend. Sandy was too short of stature and too moonfaced to be taken seriously as a military hero, but Kittridge knew that a braver, kinder, more loyal soldier never lived. There was hardly a time that Sandy would not show a cheerful face. No matter how grave the battle situation might seem, Sandy always had an optimistic outlook. He was the most warmhearted fellow in the world, and his broad-cheeked face was the only one Lord Kittridge wanted to see in this dark hour.

Besides, a visit with Sandy would bring back the feeling of being in military service. War was certainly as "grim-visaged" as Shakespeare said it was, but being a soldier had much to recommend it. Civilian life was messy and confusing. What Kittridge missed most at this moment was the clean, brave, unencumbered feeling he'd had as Robert Rossiter, cavalry officer. And that was something only Sandy would understand.

When Sandy's man admitted him to the sitting room of the rented suite on the Fenton's third floor, he found his friend lounging in a wing chair near the fire, his stockinged feet propped up on the hearth. Sandy looked up from the newspaper he'd been reading, peered at his friend for one long, silent moment and jumped to his feet. "Good God, man, what's amiss? You look as if you've lost your best friend, but that can't be, for here I am, quite alive and hale."

Rossiter acknowledged the quip with a mirthless imitation of a smile. "I'm glad to hear it," he said, throwing his greatcoat over a chair. "On top of the news I learned today, losing my best friend would be more than I could bear."

"Then what is it?" Sandy asked, his usually cheerful face clouding with the realization that his friend had suffered a severe blow. "Whatever it is, Robbie, old fellow, it can't be as bad as the look on your face."

Lord Kittridge turned to the fire and held out his hands to warm them. "I've just learned that I'm rolled up, that's all."

"Rolled up? How can that be? We've been back less than a week!" He pushed his friend into a chair and went to pour a couple of brandies. "How much blunt can you possibly have run through in so few days? What have you been up to, man?"

"Not I. My father. He performed the almost unbelievable feat of squandering the entire estate. The Suffolk property, Highlands—that's the family estate in Lincolnshire, you know—the London house, everything." And, taking the drink Sandy offered him, he began to relate the whole story.

At strategic moments during the recital of the details, Sandy refilled

Kittridge's glass, but even after the tale was fully told and the bottle stood empty on the floor beside their chairs, his lordship felt no effect from the drink. His spirit was so depressed that it seemed to leave no room for the brandy to do its work. "What am I to do, Sandy?" he asked miserably.

"Don't know, old fellow," Sandy admitted, taking the last swig left in his glass. "Haven't the foggiest. Finance is not a subject I've studied. But I know you, Robbie Rossiter. I've seen you lead a division across a ravine while three enemy regiments shot at us, and you, cool as ice, never hesitated or flinched. I've seen you land on your feet after your horse was shot from under you. I've seen you cut a piece of shrapnel from my thigh with the aplomb of a surgeon. I've seen you calm a brigade of terrified dragoons while a typhoon whistled round us like armageddon. If anyone can come through a crisis, it's you."

"Those crises were easy. I'd take any or all of them in place of this one. This one has me terrified. What will my mother say when I tell her we must sell the London house? How will I keep Gavin in school? And my sister will need help, too."

"Eunice?" Sandy's round face reddened, and he dropped his eyes from his friend's face. "Is something wrong with her?"

Kittridge was too absorbed in his own problems to notice Sandy's blush. "Her husband—you remember him, don't you? Henry Yarrow? He was at Eton with us when we were in our first year and he was in the upper fourth. Well, he died unexpectedly a few months ago—"

"Yes, I'd heard that," Sandy mumbled.

"His estate went to a distant cousin, because Eunice's babies are both girls. The heir is obligated, I believe, to supply her with some sort of allowance, but I shall have to provide housing for her and her children on top of the rest."

"That *is* too bad." Sandy fixed his eyes on his glass. "Is your sister still in mourning?" he asked with studied casualness.

"Half-mourning, I believe. Why?"

Sandy hesitated. "Never mind," he said. "It's not important."

Kittridge, who ordinarily would have exerted himself to draw out from Sandy what was on his mind, could not now concentrate on the matter. The thought of all his responsibilities—obligations which he had no idea how to discharge—was too overwhelming. He put his hand to his head and shut his eyes. "God! What am I to do?"

Sandy, unable to think of an optimistic answer, shook his head. Then he remembered that there *was* a bright side, a name the mere mention of which had always brought a light to Robbie's eyes. But it was a name that his friend seemed to have avoided all afternoon. "I say, old man, isn't there one person you've forgotten to speak of? Why haven't you mentioned Elinor?"

Kittridge's head came up slowly. "Oh, God! *Elinor!*" He stared at his friend, his eyes widening in horror. "I didn't even *think* of her!"

Sandy's round face took on a glow of hope. "Then think of her now, you clunch. At least you'll have Elinor to bring some light into your life."

"No," Kittridge groaned in despair. "Even *that* will be denied me."

Sandy's face fell. "Why? Do you think all this will affect her response to your proposal?"

"Affect her response? How can it *not*? But the question's moot. I can't ask her now."

Sandy gaped. "Can't ask her? But, Robbie, you *must*! She's expecting it, isn't she? The whole of London's expecting it. You and she have been smelling of April and May since the girl came out. She's waited all through the war for you!"

Kittridge, ashen-faced, stumbled to his feet. "You don't seem to realize the extent of my indebtedness, Sandy. I have *nothing*. No income, no prospects. Only debts. I don't know how I shall manage to support my family. In these circumstances, how can I ask *anyone* to be my wife?"

"Damn it, Robbie, we're speaking of *Elinor,* not some jingle-brained goose-cap. She's been loyal to you for six years. She has *character*. She will *want* to be at your side, to share in your deprivations, to help see you through."

"She may want to, but I won't let her. What sort of man would ask a woman to make such a sacrifice? Would you?"

Sandy blinked up at his friend, trying to answer honestly. "I don't know," he admitted at last. "No woman has ever loved me in that way."

Kittridge's eyes fell. He turned and stared into the fire. "I was going up to Suffolk on Saturday to see her. It was to be our grand reunion."

Sandy's face was a study in sympathy. "You'll still go, won't you? If she's expecting you—"

"Yes, I must, of course." Kittridge lowered his head until his forehead rested on the mantel. When he spoke again, his voice was hoarse. "I shall have to tell her that I won't be making an offer after all."

Sandy shook his head. He didn't believe matters would turn out as badly as that. The girl was much too fine—too loyal, too loving, too strong of character—to permit him to sacrifice their happiness. She would insist on their betrothal. Why, she might even convince her father to help Robbie with his finances! All might not be as black as Robbie imagined.

But Sandy didn't say anything of this aloud. Robbie was in no mood to believe him. All Sandy permitted himself to say was that he was glad Robbie still intended to call on the girl. "Be sure you don't permit the dismals to keep you from driving up there," he insisted.

"Yes, I shall go. But it will not be in any way the reunion I've been dreaming of."

"Don't be too sure," Sandy said cheerfully, unable to keep his optimism hidden. Then he added with a kind of raucous gaiety, "Do you know what I wish, Robbie?"

"What?" Robbie responded glumly, turning to stare at his ever-optimistic friend.

"What I wish," the moonfaced fellow said, holding up the empty bottle and eyeing it in mock disgust, "is that we had another bottle of brandy."

Chapter Six

The wind had eased by the week's end, but the temperature had dropped sharply. A light snow fell quietly throughout Lord Kittridge's drive north. By the time he arrived at Langston Hall in Suffolk he was chilled through. Snow lay over everything, softening the forbidding outlines of the dark, turreted building that had housed his ladylove since birth. His lordship spent no more than a moment, however, admiring the shadowy, snow-trimmed edifice. Shivering, he loped quickly up the steps and gained admittance.

Sandy's optimism notwithstanding, the greeting he was given by Elinor's father was not very warming. "Well, Kittridge," Lord Langston said coldly as the butler helped the new arrival off with his greatcoat, "we've three inches of snow on the ground, but you're here."

"Yes, my lord," the weary traveller answered, trying to sound cheerful. "You didn't think a little snow would deter me, did you?"

"I suppose not," his host answered enigmatically. "At least Elinor didn't give up hope of your arrival, even though I tried to discourage her."

Kittridge could not fail to notice that the house was at sixes and sevens. The front hall was piled with luggage, several footmen and housemaids were busily running about carrying articles of clothing and household goods to and fro, and there were dust covers to be seen on the sofas and chairs of the drawing room to his right. "Are you going away?" he asked in some surprise.

Before his host could answer, Lady Langston came down the stairs, carrying a birdcage in which a beautiful green-blue cockatoo was imprisoned. "Do you think Chickaberry will stand a sea voyage, Langston, or shall I give her away to—?" She stopped abruptly where she stood on the bottom step and stared at Kittridge with something like horror. "Good God!" she gasped. *"Robbie!"*

Kittridge, hiding his dismayed confusion, came forward and lifted her hand to his lips. "Weren't you expecting me, ma'am?"

"Well, the sn-snow, you s-see . . ." She gaped at him as if he'd risen from the dead. Then she clapped a hand to her mouth. "Oh, Robbie, my poor boy!" Bursting into tears, she turned, ran up the stairs again and disappeared from sight.

Lord Kittridge was not expecting to enjoy this visit, but these greetings were worse than anything he'd anticipated. He turned to his host with upraised brows. "Is something amiss, Lord Langston?" he asked. "Is someone ill? Good God, not . . . *Elinor?*"

"No, no, not at all," Langston assured him. "Don't pay any mind to Lady Langston's waterworks. She's easily perturbed. Any little change in routine can set her off."

"Change in routine? You *are* going away, then?"

Lord Langston's eyes wavered. "I think Elinor wants to tell you about it herself. She convinced me that you both deserve the opportunity for an interview in private, under the circumstances."

Kittridge eyed his host narrowly. "Circumstances? What circumstances?"

The other man looked uneasy. "Elinor will explain. Why don't you make yourself at home in the library, Kittridge? You know the way. I'll go upstairs and send her down to you."

Kittridge nodded and strode off down the hall. He found the library still habitable, with the furniture uncovered, the drapes drawn against the draughts and a fire burning in the grate. He stood before the fire warming himself as he wondered what his beloved had to tell him. Whatever it was, he realized, it would not be as devastating as the news *he* had for *her*.

He was so absorbed in his depressing thoughts that he didn't hear her step in the corridor. It was only when she threw open the door that he whirled around. She was flying across the room toward him. He had barely enough time to catch her up in his arms. "Elinor!" he breathed, holding her close.

Her arms clutched him tightly round the neck, and she buried her face in his shoulder. "Oh, Robbie, my darling!" she sobbed. "I want to *die!*"

He held her until the sobs subsided, kissing her hair and whispering soothing endearments into her ear. She was tall for a woman, so that she seemed to fit against him as if she'd been designed for him. Her body was lithe and supple in his arms. The feel of her made him weak in the knees. Whatever it was that she had to tell him could wait. All the news would be revealed soon enough. In the meanwhile he could close his mind to reality and permit himself the joy of this closeness. He'd dreamed for eight months—since his last leave—of holding her like this. As far as he was concerned, they could remain locked in each other's arms this way forever.

But all too soon her sobbing ceased, and she recovered herself enough to draw him to a large wing chair and settle him in it. Then she sat down on a hassock at his feet and took his hand in hers. "It is the end," she said, her voice thickened by pain and tears. "They are taking me abroad."

"I see," he said quietly, his eyes drinking in the beauty of her. Her face looking up at him was heart-wrenchingly lovely, her blue eyes still misty with tears, the skin of her oval face translucent, her lips appealingly swollen from her bout of sobs, her red-gold hair, only slightly dishevelled, caught up in a girlish bow at the nape of her neck and falling over one shoulder in a silken curl. But he couldn't let himself wallow in her loveliness; he had to concentrate on the problem at hand. "They know about my situation—is that it?"

"Yes. Papa heard rumors, and he went to London himself and made inquiries. I have been begging and pleading with him for weeks, saying that I did not care, that we would find a way to live, but he is adamant against you."

"Do you blame him? If you were my daughter, I would do the same."

"But I love you, Robbie." She lowered her head and heaved a sigh that trembled through her whole body. "There will never be another like you for me."

He lifted her chin and made her look up at him. "Nor for me, my love, nor for me. But circumstances have turned against us. I am saddled with debts that will take me a lifetime to pay. I can't allow you to join me in impoverishment, any more than your father can." He withdrew his hand and looked away from her pleading eyes. "It is . . . hopeless."

"We could elope, Robbie. Run off to Gretna . . ."

"Yes, we could. And then what?"

"I don't know. Something would occur to help us. Perhaps Papa—"

He stiffened. "You don't really think I would permit your father to support us. I am not a sponger."

"No, you're not. I knew you would say that." She looked down at his hand that she still clutched in hers. "Besides, Papa is not being generous. When he learned what your father had done to your estates, all he did about it was to insist that I disentangle myself from you. He never once offered to help you."

"How could he? It's not as if a few hundred pounds would solve the matter. We are speaking of a debt of thousands! He has your brother's expectations to think of. He cannot take so great a sum from Arthur's inheritance to throw away on me."

Elinor drew in a wavering breath and, dropping his hand, rose slowly from her seat. "I have given Papa a dozen reasons why helping you would *not* be throwing his blunt away. But he was not persuaded."

"Nor would I be in his place." Kittridge got to his feet and grasped his beloved by the shoulders as if he wanted to shake her. "Damnation, Elinor, you had no right even to ask it of him."

"No right?" She drew herself up in offense. "Because you haven't yet offered, is that what you mean? Are you implying that, not having the status of *betrothed*, I had not the right to plead your cause?"

He winced and pulled her to him with a groan. "No, my dearest, of course not. You have been my heart's betrothed since we played together as children in those fields behind this very house. You know as well as I that my offer was only a matter of form."

She sniffed into his shoulder. "Then, if I am truly your heart's betrothed, why had I not the right to speak to my father in your behalf?"

He held her away from him and peered at her sternly. "Because it humiliates me to have you do so. Don't you see, my love, that I couldn't be beholden to *anyone* for so great a sum? Even if it were possible for Langston to lend it to me—which it is not—it would take too many years for me to pay it back. Don't you see how such a situation would diminish me in your father's eyes and in my own? And even, in time, in yours?"

She dropped her eyes from his face and turned away from him. "Yes, I suppose I do see," she said sadly. "That's why I've submitted to parental commands and have agreed to leave for the continent. I knew in my heart you would not marry me now."

"Not would not," he corrected, his voice unsteady. "*Could* not."

"Could not." She moved to the fireplace and took up the poker. "I understand, Robbie, I really do. I know that you have many burdens . . . your mother, your brother, and now Lady Yarrow and her children, too. I would only be another one."

As she poked at the flames, he stared at her face. Her skin glowed amber in the brightened firelight. His throat burned in pain. "I would never think of you as a burden, my love. But I won't be the one to deprive you of the kind of life you've known and have every right to expect to continue."

"Yes," she said quietly. "I knew you would say that, too."

Before he could reply, there was a knock at the door. Evans, the butler, put his head in. "Beg pardon, m'lady," he said, "but her ladyship wishes to know if Lord Kittridge stays the night. And will he be wishing to have some supper?"

Elinor gave her beloved a pleading look, but he shook his head. "Thank her ladyship for me," he told the butler, "but I will be leaving at once."

"So soon?" Elinor cried when the butler had withdrawn. "Please, Robbie, can't we have just a little more time?"

"If I stayed," he said bluntly, "we would not be prolonging being together, only prolonging the good-bye. I don't think I could bear it." He took one last look at her before crossing to the door. "Good-bye, my love. You must know that I wish you every happiness."

She gave a little cry and made as if to run to him, but he held up his hand. "No. Stay as you are, there at the fire. I want always to remember you this way, with the firelight bronzing your face."

Tears spilled down her cheeks. "Good-bye, Robbie. I shall love you always."

He opened the door, but before stepping out he looked back at her. "Elinor," he asked hesitantly, "will you . . . sometimes . . . write to me?"

"I don't suppose . . ." She seemed to choke on the words. "Papa will not let me read letters from you, you know."

"I know. But—"

"I'll write, my love. As often as I can."

"No, not often. Just sometimes. To keep me sane." And he closed the door behind him, leaving her weeping brokenly for what might have been.

Chapter Seven

𝒯he one good thing about one's life being all to pieces was that it couldn't become much worse. It was with that sense of having struck rock bottom that Lord Kittridge presented himself at Mr. Jennings's office on Monday morning. He'd dressed himself in one of his new shirts and a coat just delivered from Nugee's (all purchased in the few happy days before he'd discovered what his situation was), and he'd stiffened himself for the interview to come by taking a swig of rum, something he'd never before done in the morning. His valet, Loesby, who'd been his batman in service, came upon him while he was in the act and didn't hesitate to voice his disapproval. "Since when, Cap'n, was ye in the 'abit of tipplin' in secret? An' in the a.m., too!"

"Stubble it, Loesby," his lordship had snapped. "You'll be tippling, too, I'll be bound, when I have to give you notice."

The valet had ignored the threat and merely brushed off the lapel of his lordship's new coat. "Ye kin gi' me all the notice ye want. Do ye think I'd be lettin' ye send me off when yer swimmin' in low tide? But we was speakin' of *you*, not me. I was about t' say, Cap'n, that this is the worst time fer you t' take t' drink, if ye was t' aks me."

"I'm not asking you, you muckworm. One swallow of rum doesn't mean I'm taking to drink. And you'd better start thinking about finding yourself a new post. You can't stay with me if I can't pay you."

"I kin stay so long as ye 'ave a kitchen where I kin scrounge a meal, so there ain't no use in threatenin' me," the valet had retorted, throwing his lordship's greatcoat on his shoulders and pushing him through the door. "Good luck with yer man of business. I'll tell 'er ladyship ye'll be back in time fer tea, so don't dawdle."

Lord Kittridge was ushered into Mr. Jennings's office by an obsequious clerk,

who took his greatcoat and immediately withdrew. Kittridge, in the act of placing his hat, gloves and cane on a side chair, suddenly noticed that his man of
business was not alone. Sitting on a high-backed leather chair at the right of
Jennings's massive desk was a small-boned, thin-faced, bespectacled little man
with a mass of curly auburn hair. Kittridge started in surprise. "I beg your pardon, Jennings," he said. "I seem to have intruded. Your clerk didn't tell me you
were engaged."

"No, no, my lord," Jennings said, rising, "you don't intrude. This is Mr. Oliver
Chivers, whom I've taken the liberty to consult in your behalf. He is a renowned
expert in investments and financial dealings. With your permission, I'd like to in-
vite him to sit in on this meeting. I can assure you that he will be as discreet about
your situation as a clergyman, and he may have some useful advice for us."

"Of course he can sit in," Lord Kittridge agreed as Mr. Chivers rose. "If Mr.
Chivers is acquainted with my situation, he must know that I can use all the
advice I can get."

The two men shook hands. "It's a pleasure to meet ye, my lord," Chivers said,
presenting Kittridge with his card. "I've 'eard ye spoken of for many years, and
always in the most admirin' of terms."

"Thank you," Lord Kittridge said as the three men took seats, "but as you'll
soon discover, I deserve very little admiration in matters of finance."

"Well, a man can't be expected to be expert in everythin'," Chivers said
pleasantly. "And since this muddle ain't of yer makin', my lord, there's no bla-
min' you."

Mr. Jennings, meanwhile, leafed through a pile of papers and folders in front
of him. "I'm afraid we must begin with some additional bad news, my lord," he
murmured, "for I've discovered some other debts. Your load of troubles has been
augmented, I'm sorry to say, by your sister's situation. It appears that Lord
Yarrow left some debts of his own. He dabbled in stocks, you see, and the timing
of his death was particularly unfortunate. There was a large drop at the Exchange
at just that time, and—"

"Good God!" Kittridge exclaimed, his mouth going tense. "What does that
mean for Lady Yarrow, exactly?"

"It means that the new Lord Yarrow has used the fact of the debts as an excuse to cut Lady Yarrow's already meager income even further. Leaving you that
much less with which to support the family."

Lord Kittridge put his hand to his forehead. Would this series of blows never
end, he wondered? This last blow seemed like the backbreaking straw. The total
of the family's indebtedness was more than twenty thousand pounds. And with
the estates encumbered, there was no income with which he could even start to
pay them. Meanwhile, current expenses were accumulating at what seemed to

him a staggering rate, with only his army half-pay coming in. Kittridge had no idea what to do or where to turn. He found himself at a complete loss. Even this meeting was turning out to be a disaster. What good was it to learn that he was even deeper in a hole than he'd thought?

He dropped his hand and looked from Mr. Chivers to Mr. Jennings in bewilderment. "Under these circumstances, Jennings, I don't see why you've brought in Mr. Chivers. What good is an expert on investments when there isn't anything to invest?"

"Come, come, my lord, don't lose 'eart so soon," Mr. Chivers urged, leaning back in his chair. He propped his elbows on the arms and pressed the fingers of his two hands together. He was silent for a moment while he examined Lord Kittridge from over the tops of his spectacles. "I've gone over the figures with Mr. Jennings quite carefully, an' I 'ave some suggestions. A very few, I admit, for I'll tell ye without roundaboutation that y're in a devil of a coil."

"Yes," his lordship said drily, "I've gathered that. So you *have* some suggestions?"

"A few. But you won't like any of 'em."

"If they can help me dig my way out of this hole, I'll like them well enough," the impoverished viscount assured him.

"Then let's see." Chivers took a pad from the desk alongside him and studied the figures jotted down on it. "If ye sell out everythin', the Suffolk property, the Lincolnshire estate an' the London 'ouse, ye'll come out with a small balance. Enough to provide ye with a modest income."

"How modest? Where could we live?"

"Not in London, I fear. A country cottage somewhere in the north, per'aps. But the family wouldn't starve."

"A country cottage, out of all society? That would be a drastic adjustment for my family to make. My mother and sister would be miserable in such straitened circumstances. It would be too radical a change for them, I fear. Have I any other options?"

"The other suggestion I 'ave is more risky, but the results could be, in time, a bit more promising. If ye sold the Suffolk lands an' the London 'ouse, ye could pay off some of the encumbrances on the Lincolnshire property. It's not as vast an estate as the Suffolk lands, from what I see 'ere, but it could begin to bring in an income if ye managed it well. Ye'd not be able to clear yerself of debt all at once, but with economical living, in a few years it could be done, and at least that one estate'd be yours once more. At first, 'owever, there'd be very little income remainin' after the existin' mortgage payments. Less, even, than the income would be if ye sold everythin'. 'Ere, these are my projections, based on Jennings's estimate of the estate's worth."

Kittridge looked them over, his brow furrowed with worry. "I would like to earn back Highlands more than anything. But I know nothing of estate management. Do you think I could learn—?"

"I don't see why not. If ye 'ired a proper land agent, studied land use and enclosure methods, worked 'ard and kept yer womenfolk from spending the profits on fripperies—"

Kittridge sighed. "Aye, there's the rub. How can one teach economy to women who've never thought about it in all their lives?"

"Necessity is a good teacher, my lord. If they 'ave to learn it, they will."

His lordship bit his lip thoughtfully. His sister and brother might learn, but his mother, never. And how would they manage during the early years, before the encumbrances were paid off? The family would be forced to live in even greater straits than in a cottage, for there would be less income available. It was a gloomy future he had to offer his family. His heart lay heavy in his breast. Neither of the two choices gave him much hope. "Thank you, Mr. Chivers, Mr. Jennings," he said glumly. "I shall think over what you've told me."

Mr. Jennings leaned across the desk toward the consultant. "Don't you think, Mr. Chivers, that you should tell his lordship about the third option you mentioned?" he asked.

Chivers shifted uncomfortably in his seat. "I don't know, Jennings. It's a bit awkward. And 'is lordship doesn't seem to be the sort who—"

Kittridge, who was already pulling on a glove, looked at the financier curiously. "How can you tell what sort I am, Mr. Chivers? I don't even know myself. What is it you're hesitating to suggest to me?"

Mr. Chivers peered at the fellow from over his spectacles. "It's not a pretty suggestion, I fear," he ventured.

"I am not in a pretty situation. Go ahead, man. Say what is on your mind."

"Very well." Mr. Chivers lowered his eyes to his fingers. "I take it ye ain't married, my lord?"

"No. Why do you ask? What has my marital status to say to anything?"

Mr. Chivers removed his spectacles and began to polish the lenses with his pocket handkerchief with great deliberation. "Because the fact that y're a bachelor gives ye one more option."

"Oh? And what is that?"

"Marriage, my lord. There's a great many wealthy men of industry who'd provide very 'andsome dowries for their daughters if those dowries brought— forgive my bluntness, my lord—a title into the family."

Kittridge stared at him. "Let me make sure I understand you, Chivers. Are you saying that any nobleman whose pockets are to let can arrange a lucrative marriage just on the basis of his *title*?"

"Exactly so. It's been done a number of times. Ye must surely 'ave 'eard of such alliances."

"No. I've been away for years. And even before my soldiering days I didn't pay much heed to social gossip."

"Well, ye may take my word that such marriages ain't uncommon. The cases I'm familiar with seemed to 'ave worked out well enough. The Staffords of Lancashire, for example, restored their entire estate by this very sort of an arrangement."

"Indeed?" Kittridge's eyebrows lifted sardonically. "What a mercenary time we seem to be living in, to be sure." He drew on his other glove and rose proudly from his seat. "I appreciate your advice, Mr. Chivers, but as far as this last option is concerned, I'm not interested. My title is the only thing I have left that is unencumbered. I don't think I care to put it up for sale." He picked up the papers from Jennings's desk and walked swiftly to the door. "Good day, gentlemen. Thank you for your time. When I make up my mind about what to do, Jennings, I'll call on you again."

Mr. Jennings, his mouth pursed in perturbation, jumped to his feet. "No offense meant, your lordship," he muttered, hurrying to see his client out.

"None taken," his lordship replied generously, although a wrinkle of annoyance still creased his brow.

The clerk came in with his lordship's greatcoat, and an awkward silence filled the room as he helped Kittridge on with it.

"Some titles," Mr. Chivers remarked just as his lordship stepped over the threshold, "'ave brought their owners a veritable fortune."

Lord Kittridge stopped short. "Oh?" he asked coldly over his shoulder, his curiosity warring with his pride. "And how much do you think *my* title would be worth?"

"Enough to pay off yer debts and clear the encumbrances from yer Lincolnshire estate, at least."

The sardonic expression on Kittridge's face changed to sincere surprise. He turned round slowly. "As much as *that*?" he asked.

"As much as that," Chivers said firmly.

Kittridge stared at him for a long moment. Then he came in and closed the door behind him. "Good God, man," he exclaimed, "we're speaking of a dowry that would have to be in the neighborhood of *forty thousand pounds*!"

"Yes, I know." Chivers gave an indifferent shrug. "I think I can assure ye of forty thousand."

Kittridge blinked. "I can't believe that someone would pay such a sum just so that his daughter could call herself a viscountess."

"You gentlemen who're born to the purple take yer titles lightly," Mr. Chivers answered calmly. "Only those for whom a title is inaccessible know its real value. Like ice in the tropics, if ye catch my meanin'."

"Mr. Chivers is right, my lord," Jennings put in earnestly. "There's many a captain of industry who would pay handsomely to have a nobleman grace his family tree. And many a needy nobleman has made the bargain. It isn't at all a new idea. And not necessarily a bad one, either."

Kittridge slowly removed his gloves and walked back toward the desk where the little financier was still sitting. "Are you saying, Chivers, that you have a definite offer for me?" He leaned against the desk and bent toward Chivers challengingly. "That you have someone specific in mind?"

Chivers couldn't meet that level look. "I 'ave several wealthy clients who'd be interested," he equivocated, shoving his glasses up on his nose and dropping his eyes.

"But no one in particular?" Kittridge pressed, his curiosity aroused.

"Well," Chivers murmured, "I suppose I may as well be partic'lar. After all, that's the real reason I'm 'ere." He stood up, took a deep breath and looked the viscount squarely in the eye. "Y' see, yer lordship, I myself 'ave a daughter . . ."

Chapter Eight

$\mathcal{L}$ord Kittridge, though he'd listened to Mr. Chivers's impertinent suggestion with fascination, did not for a moment give that suggestion serious consideration. The idea of selling himself and his title in exchange for a dowry—no matter how large—filled him with repugnance. Such a solution to his problem struck him as not only too easy and too vulgar but almost corrupt. There was something debauched, he felt, about any man who would consider such a plan.

Thus, having rejected that idea out of hand, he was left with only two choices for his family's future: either to sell everything and live in unaccustomed modesty on the income of the sale for the rest of their lives; or to sell all but the Lincolnshire estate and try to endure near-poverty for a few years in the hope that he could eventually coax a profit from that encumbered and thus far unproductive property. Neither of the two plans offered him anything pleasant to tell his family.

He came home from his visit to the City determined to inform them bluntly of the state of their impoverishment. It was a necessary cruelty. He had to apprise them of the hard facts at once so that they could learn to accept what would soon be their much-diminished style of life. To that end, he ordered the butler to request that the family assemble in the drawing room in three quarters of an hour, at exactly four p.m., when he would confer with them over tea.

In the meantime, he sat down at the desk in the room that had been his father's study to go over the figures that Chivers had given him. Attempting to calculate the exact advantages that one of the plans might have over the other, he picked up a pen. Its nib, he found, was impossibly dull, and he thrust his calculations aside to search for a knife with which to sharpen it. He opened the top drawer and discovered, to his horror, that it was stuffed full of unpaid bills.

He surveyed the crumpled, disarranged, confusing accumulation with a feeling of utter despair. Slowly, one by one, he studied them, sorting them into piles and jotting down the amounts on a tally-sheet. Every bill was overdue, and all of them—mostly household trivialities and ladies' clothing—were for amounts considerably larger than he would have expected. His mother seemed to have deliberately purchased the most expensive items she could find. Although she must have had some inkling of the state of their finances, she had evidently taken no steps to economize. There were, for example, thirty-seven bills for millinery alone! Why, he wondered distractedly, when one's finances were in disarray, would one even *consider* buying oneself *thirty-seven hats*?

He made a quick estimate of the total, but the sum sickened him. Could his addition possibly be right? Could his mother have spent almost *three thousand pounds* on these *trifles*? He recalculated the list, hoping that a more careful reckoning would yield a less horrendous total, but the second accounting was even worse. His fists clenched in bewilderment and frustration. *How could so large an amount,* he asked himself, *have been spent on useless, self-indulgent luxuries*?

As the fact of this new debt sank into his consciousness, his sense of helpless frustration gave way to a feeling of explosive fury. He seized the papers in an angry fist and strode across the hallway to the drawing room. "Mama," he demanded without a word of greeting, "what on *earth* is the meaning of this?"

The dowager Lady Kittridge, the only person in the family who'd thus far responded to his summons, was comfortably ensconced on an easy chair near the tea table, which was already laden with the tea things. She was about to nibble at a cucumber sandwich she'd taken from the tea tray when his bellow made her shudder in alarm. "Good heavens, Robbie, you startled me!" she gasped, her hands fluttering up in alarm. She frowned at him disapprovingly and then looked down at the sandwich which his abrupt entrance had caused to fall from her fingers to her lap. "Whatever possessed you to burst in on me like that? You made me drop my—"

"Whatever *possessed* me, ma'am?" her son exploded. "*These* are what possessed me! *One hundred and seventy-four unpaid bills*!"

"Oh, those." She shrugged, picked up her sandwich and took a dainty bite. "I don't see why you should raise a dust over them. Just send them over to Mr. Jennings. He'll take care of them."

Kittridge stared at his mother in disbelief. She was not in the least discomposed by his fury, but calmly finished her little sandwich and brushed the crumbs from her lap. She was a small-boned, delicate creature, looking at this moment—with her head tilted up at him, one graceful hand draped over the arm of the chair, and one tiny, slippered foot resting on a stool—like an exquisite porcelain figurine. Her hair was so white it seemed powdered; her complexion, once so luminous that her beaux made toasts to it, was now sadly wrinkled but still translucent; her waist was still as shapely as when she was a girl; and her graceful, slim-fingered hands fluttered like birds when she spoke. It was disconcerting to Kittridge to have to scold so fragile-looking a creature, but what else was he to do? "Damnation, ma'am," he raged, "what is Mr. Jennings supposed to 'take care of them' *with*? His own pocket money?"

The birdlike hands fluttered to her breast. "What do you mean, my dearest?" she asked, blinking up at him in bewildered innocence. "Mr. Jennings *always* takes care of the bills."

"Are you trying to pretend, Mama, that you don't know that my father left us penniless?"

Her pale blue eyes widened. "Well, I knew he was profligate, of course, and that he'd run himself into Dun territory, but *penniless*—?"

"Yes, penniless! What do you think 'Dun territory' *means*?"

"I know very well what it means. But your father never asked me to stint on the household expenses. Never!"

"Household expenses, ma'am? Is that what you call these? These are nothing but bills for gowns and bonnets and nonsense like reupholstering chairs! Nothing but *fripperies*!"

Her ladyship's elegant eyebrows rose in agitated disbelief. "Are you saying I shouldn't have purchased any new gowns?"

"That's *exactly* what I'm saying!" her son snapped. "And it's not only gowns we're speaking of. How can you have bought yourself something as expensive and unnecessary as a new barouche when there were three carriages in the stables already and you *knew* Papa's finances were all to pieces? Do you realize that there are bills here, all accumulated since his death, adding up to *three thousand pounds*? I can only suppose that you've forgotten how to *add*! I cannot otherwise explain how you could indulge yourself in such knickknackery as imported laces and French champagne and silver tea services, Mama, when we can hardly afford to pay for *tea*!"

"Not pay for tea? Really, Robbie, aren't you being a bit ridicu—?"

"Goodness, Robbie," came a voice from the doorway, "why all this shouting? I could hear you all the way down the hall." And in strolled his sister Eunice, Lady Yarrow, followed by her two little girls and their governess.

"Uncle Robert, Uncle Robert!" clarioned Della, the elder of the two children, running to embrace him. "See the portrait I've made of you!"

Kittridge, bottling up his temper, knelt down and scooped the five-year-old girl up in his arms. "Della, you minx," he said affectionately, looking at the drawing the child held up to his face, "do you really think that longshanks looks like me? And what is that you've drawn on my head?"

"It's a picture of you in your uniform, of course," the girl explained. "That's your shako on your head—with the plume, see? And this is your horse."

"And a very good horse it is, too," her uncle laughed, placing her on his shoulders and taking the other child by the hand. "How are you, Greta, my little puss? Do you and your sister stay to tea?"

"No, they don't," Lady Yarrow said firmly. "They only came down to say hello to you. Miss Roffey will take them upstairs in a moment."

"Of course they don't stay to tea," the dowager Lady Kittridge said drily. "We can't afford it."

Lady Yarrow turned a questioning pair of eyes to her mother. Eunice Yarrow was a tall, sturdily built woman whose strong features and dark coloring were inherited from her father. She had none of her mother's delicacy in her form or her manner. Her character could be summed up in one word—blunt. "What do you mean by that, Mama? You sound as if you've suddenly entered your dotage."

"Not I," the dowager declared. "It's your brother whose wits are addled. He says we can't afford tea!"

"Robbie!" Lady Yarrow wheeled round to her brother in alarm. "Are things as bad as *that*?"

Kittridge was, by this time, down on hands and knees, giving his nieces a ride on his back. "Perhaps I exaggerated a bit," he admitted, the sight of his adored nieces having dissipated what was left of his anger. "I was making a point about buying unnecessary silver. I think we can manage to afford some tea for the girls."

"Hooray!" shouted Della, clapping her little hands together delightedly. "We're staying for tea!"

"No, you're not," Lady Yarrow said sharply, lifting the girl from her brother's back and setting her on her feet. "Our teatime conversation promises to be serious . . . much too adult for you."

Little Greta began to cry in disappointment. "I want tea wiff Uncew Wobit!" she wept, hugging her uncle tightly about the neck.

Lady Yarrow pulled her from Kittridge's back. "But you can't have tea with Uncle Robert, so stop snivelling. You mustn't behave like a baby, Greta, now that you're a big girl of three. You may have your tea in the nursery." She handed the child to the governess. "Take these crybabies upstairs, Miss Roffey. I have a feeling my brother has more important matters on his mind than playing horsey with the children."

While the governess herded the girls from the room, Lady Yarrow studied her brother with a knit brow. "Jennings did not have good news, I take it," she said when the children were gone.

"No, Eunice, he didn't," her brother admitted, getting up and brushing the carpet dust from his knees.

"Are you badly dipped?"

"As bad as can be."

Eunice expelled a breath. "I'm sorry, Robbie. It was unforgivable of Papa to have done this to you." She walked thoughtfully to the tea table and picked up the teapot. "I suppose this means that all your dreams for the future are up in smo— Oh! Good God!" She froze in the act of pouring and glanced over at Kittridge with an expression of real pain. "What about *Elinor*! How will all this affect your plans in regard to *her*?"

"I have no such plans," Kittridge said shortly.

"No such plans?" Eunice put down the teapot, fixing a dubious eye on her tight-lipped brother. "Don't talk fustian to me, Robbie. I'm fully aware that you intended to offer for her . . . last weekend, I thought. What's happened?"

"I learned that I am *persona non grata* in their home. Her parents have taken her to the continent."

"Oh, *Robbie*!" his mother cried out, her hands reaching out to him in sympathy.

"How dreadful!" his sister gasped. "I can hardly believe the Langstons can be so . . . so mercenary."

"It is not mercenary to wish one's offspring to live in comfort," Kittridge said, picking up the teapot and pouring tea for her. "You would do the same in their place. Here's your cup. Sit down and drink your tea."

"I would *not* do the same," Eunice insisted, taking a chair beside her mother. "I am very disappointed in Elinor."

"So am I," his mother agreed, accepting a cup of tea from her son. "And as for Lady Langston, I shall give her the cut direct the very next time she crosses my path."

Kittridge was touched at his mother's foolish loyalty but would not permit himself to be distracted from his purpose by feelings of affection. "You'll do nothing of the sort," he said with what he hoped was a repressive frown. "It was I, not they, who cried off. I went up to Suffolk on Saturday for the express purpose of explaining to Elinor that I would not make her an offer after all. She and I agreed to call it quits. She has gone off to enjoy a Grand Tour, and I . . . well, I shall have all I can do to keep *us* fed and clothed. For me, a wife is out of the question."

His sister looked up from her teacup with raised brows. "Good God, Robbie, what nonsense is this? I still have my allowance. And, since my girls and I will be living with you, I intend to turn it over to you to add to the family income. That alone should be sufficient to keep us in necessities, shouldn't it?"

Kittridge pulled up a chair before her and gently took his sister's hand in his. "That's one of the difficult things I must tell you, Eunice. Jennings informed me that Yarrow had incurred some debts of his own. His heir intends to cut a good deal of your income to pay them."

Eunice paled. "Robbie, *no*! My Henry in debt? How can that be? Henry was not like Papa. He *never* gambled!"

"He may not have gambled with dice, my dear, but he speculated on the 'change. The market was down at the time of his death. It seems he lost more than he could afford."

"How *could* he have done something so dreadful?" Eunice cried, snatching her hand from his hold. "I can scarcely believe it! Had he no thought for me or his children?"

Kittridge shook his head. "I'm dreadfully sorry, Eunice."

"Sorry!" She got up, put down her cup and strode angrily to the window. "I shall never forgive him. To pauperize me is bad enough. But to leave his *daughters* in so helpless a condition—!" She choked back the words and stared out the window with unseeing eyes.

"Try to be fair, my dear," her brother said softly. "He couldn't have expected to die so young. When one is young, one doesn't think of death as imminent. One believes one has time to take risks. I'm sure that, if he'd lived longer, he would certainly, in due time, have made proper provisions for you."

"*If* he had lived longer . . ." Eunice shook her head, weeping silently.

"I *always* thought Yarrow was a mawworm," came a voice from the doorway.

"Gavin! There you are at last!" Kittridge strode to the door, pulled his younger brother into the room and shut the door against any other possible eavesdroppers. "You bufflehead," he said in irritation, "do you *enjoy* seeing your sister in tears? Keep your opinions about your late brother-in-law to yourself! How long have you been standing there in the doorway?"

"Long enough to get the drift," the boy declared. "We're scorched. Isn't that what you've called us together to tell us?"

Gavin Rossiter, at seventeen, was almost as tall as his brother, but his features still had the unfinished, not-quite-in-proportion look of adolescence. His nose was pronounced, like his sister's, but his eyes were as light as his mother's. His hair was almost as curly as his brother's, but it was long and fell over his forehead and shoulders in Byronic disarray. He had come down from Eton to welcome his brother home, and Kittridge had encouraged him to postpone his return until the financial situation could be sorted out.

"Yes, we certainly are scorched," Kittridge admitted, throwing an arm over his brother's shoulders and leading him to a chair near the tea table. "I hope the news does not overset you."

"You needn't worry about me, Robbie, old fellow. I won't be a burden on you. I'll even leave school, if that will help."

"What a sacrifice!" Eunice said sarcastically. She wiped her eyes and returned to her chair. "It seems to me you'd jump at any excuse to leave school."

"We shan't talk of leaving school just yet," Kittridge said. "Let's wait until we see just what our situation will be. Your schooling is the last thing I'd wish to cut off."

"Rubbish, Robbie," the boy said, cheerfully gobbling down a cucumber sandwich. "If we're going to be paupers, who needs school?"

"Well, we won't be paupers, exactly," Kittridge said, sitting down in the family circle, "but our lives will be very different from what they've been in the past." And, leaning forward and speaking with an earnest calm, he went on to explain in detail what their options would be.

He spoke quietly for a long while. By the time he'd finished, his mother was sniffing her smelling salts, his sister was white-lipped and his brother at a loss for words. Kittridge, however, looked at their stricken faces in some relief. *At least,* he thought, *the realities are beginning to sink in.*

Chapter Nine

Kittridge stirred his tea, eyeing his family from beneath lowered lids. Their reaction to the devastating news he'd just given them was crucial. If they showed themselves to be practical and courageous, he might feel encouraged enough to choose the second option: to live a few years in dire straits so that in the end they would have Highlands, the Lincolnshire property, to call their own. But they would all have to be brave and self-sacrificing to make a success of the venture. Very brave, and *very* self-sacrificing.

The family sat in silence for several minutes, trying to digest what Kittridge had just told them. Lady Kittridge was the first to break the silence. "I suppose we shall have to sell the new barouche," she remarked in a quavering voice.

"Sell the new barouche?" Kittridge echoed, his heart sinking like lead in his chest. He'd found his mother's remark unbelievably disconcerting. Hadn't she understood *anything* of what he'd just been at such pains to explain? "Not only the barouche, Mama," he said, forcing himself to speak patiently. "The entire stable must go."

"The entire *stable*?" Gavin asked, horrified. "You must be joking!"

Kittridge winced. "*Et tu,* Gavin?" he muttered under his breath.

The boy peered at him closely. "You *are* joking, aren't you?"

"No, I'm not joking. We can't afford stables. We shall manage to keep the old phaeton and a pair—the roans, I suppose—but nothing else."

Gavin leaped to his feet. "You're not implying that I must give up Prado!"

"Well, yes, I am. Prado is too valuable an animal to—"

"Damnation, Robbie, you may just save your breath," the boy declared furiously, "for nothing you can say will induce me to do such a thing! You bought him in Spain for *me,* didn't you? And now you want me to give him up! Give up Prado, indeed! It's not fair! You cannot ask it of me!"

"But I must, don't you see? We can't afford—"

"This is ridiculous!" Gavin exclaimed. "I *must* have a horse to ride. And if I must have a horse, that horse may as well be Prado."

"Didn't you understand anything I said before, Gavin? We have to give up almost everything . . . this house, the London stables, the entire Suffolk property, everything. The stables are no longer ours. They belong to our creditors. We cannot pick and choose what we can keep and what we give up. And even if we could, we can no longer afford to keep racing stock or show horses to parade in Hyde Park. Besides, we won't even be here in town."

"I don't care!" the boy cried childishly. "If I can't have Prado, you may as well take me out and put a bullet in my head!" And he stormed out of the room.

Kittridge stared after him, nonplussed. He hadn't expected difficulty from that quarter. He sighed, allowing himself to hope that when his brother's tantrum had blown itself out, the boy would come to his senses.

Eunice, meanwhile, smiled ironically. "So much for sacrifice," she muttered.

His lordship sighed and turned to his mother. She was the one he expected to be the most difficult to win over. "Speaking of sacrifice, Mama," he ventured, "I hope you realize that we shall have only a very minimal staff in our new home. A cook-housekeeper, perhaps, and a—"

"You may staff your house as you see fit, Robbie," his mother interrupted. "I realize you have a difficult row to hoe. I shall not place additional problems in your path. However, my love, you must understand that for my personal service I must have my Sophy. She has been my maid since my girlhood, so to dismiss her is out of the question. And I shall also require a hairdresser, a seamstress and at least one abigail."

Kittridge gaped at her. "An abigail, a seamstress and a *hairdresser*?" he asked in a strangulated voice. He didn't know whether to laugh or weep. It was as if everything he'd said had passed over her like an unnoticed gust of wind. "We'll be in the country, ma'am, don't you understand? You won't be going to fetes and balls. Why would you need a hairdresser?"

His mother rose aristocratically from her chair. "I have never been without a hairdresser," she declared, her fluttery hands patting her white curls, "and I am too old to change now. To move me to the country, to heaven knows what sort of hovel, is quite enough of a sacrifice to ask of me. Even *suggesting* that I do without my hairdresser, Robert Rossiter, is the outside of enough. I didn't know that my eldest son, the pride of my heart and the light of my life, could be so cruel." And she, too, swept out of the room.

Kittridge groaned and dropped his head in his hands. He hadn't expected the interview to be easy, but *this* was beyond belief. Neither his brother nor his mother seemed capable of grasping the full ramifications of this catastrophic situation. How could he make them *see*?

He felt his sister press her hand on his shoulder. He looked up at her in gratitude; at least he could count on *her*. "Tell me, Eunice, what must I do to get through to them?" he asked, his voice choked and desperate.

"Gavin's only taken a pet. He'll get over it. And I'll talk to Mama. Leave her to me." Eunice strode purposefully to the door, but there she paused. "When I came home to live after Henry's passing, I fully expected to pay my way," she said forthrightly. "I regret, my dearest, that Yarrow's heir has forced me to become an additional burden to you. I hope you know without my saying how much I appreciate your taking responsibility for me and my girls."

"Don't be foolish," Kittridge said curtly, getting up and wrapping her in a fond embrace. "We are family. We shall swim—or sink—together."

She hugged him tightly. "I don't know what I'd do without you. But I promise you, Robbie, I shan't be more of a burden than I absolutely must. I need no horses, no abigails, no hairdressers. Only Miss Roffey, of course, and a nursemaid to assist her. And I think we must have a seamstress, my love, to take care of the girls' clothing—they grow so quickly, you know. But I wouldn't keep her to myself; I could certainly share her with Mama." Not noticing the stunned look in his eyes, she patted his cheek fondly and whisked herself out of the room. Before he could bring himself to move, her face reappeared in the doorway. "And a tutor, of course, Robbie," she added cheerfully, "but that may not be a gross expense. He needn't live in, you know. We could employ a local clergyman for half-day wages, I expect. For a couple of years anyway."

Lord Kittridge stared at the closed door for a long time. Then, utterly discomposed, he sank into a chair in front of the fire and shut his eyes. It was as if he'd ridden into an ambush. Not expecting to be besieged, he'd found himself being shot at from all sides. And there didn't seem to be a place of safety, a rock or knoll behind which he could hide. He felt depleted, beaten, defeated. There was no escape for him, for how could he run away when he had five people dependent on him?

But what was he to do for them? How could he even begin to teach these innocents, who'd been pampered all their lives, to adjust to the drastic changes he was proposing? Even he, who had experienced the dangers and deprivations of war, would not find the new life easy, so how could he expect the others, who had no inkling of deprivation, to accept it? "Seamstresses," he moaned, resting his head on the back of the chair and covering his eyes with one trembling hand. "Abigails. Nursemaids. Hairdressers. They want a veritable *regiment*!"

"Per'aps not a regiment, but fer certain nine, minimum," came his man Loesby's voice behind him.

Kittridge sat up. "What?" he asked in confusion.

Loesby came round the chair and perched on the hearth in front of his lordship. "A staff o' nine," he explained. "Cook, houseman, Miss Sophy, the 'air-dresser, the abigail, the seamstress, Miss Roffey, the nursemaid, an' the tutor. Nine."

Kittridge groaned. "Might as well be a regiment," he muttered, "since I can't afford even a third of them." His eyes focused on his ex-batman's weathered face. "You were eavesdropping again," he accused.

Loesby shrugged. "The on'y way ye learn anythin' is to eavesdrop."

"Then, since you know so much, tell me how, on a captain's half-pay, I'm to set up a household of six with a staff of—how many did you say?"

"Nine. Not countin' me."

His lordship peered at his batman with sudden intensity. "Why not counting you? Are you going to take my advice and find yourself another post?"

"Not on yer life. I din't count me 'cause I don't 'ave to 'ave wages."

"Why should *you* sacrifice your wages, man? It's more of a sacrifice than anyone in my family is willing to make."

"Do ye need to ask, Cap'n? We been through a war t'gether. I ain't forgettin' that ye came back fer me when they left me fer dead after Talavera. Nor what ye did fer me at Badajoz, neither. It's more of a bond, per'aps, than fam'ly."

"Perhaps it is." He looked his ex-batman in the eye. "I know I'd feel in a damned hole if you left me," he admitted flatly.

"Well, I ain't leavin', so there's no more to be said about that. About the rest of the staff, as I tole ye, I count nine. Not a small staff, I'd say."

"No. Not small at all." Kittridge's shoulders sagged. "What shall I do, Loesby? I'm at the end of my tether."

"Act like a cap'n, Cap'n. Treat yer fam'ly like a cavalry division. Give 'em orders. Tell 'em flat out—no 'airdressers, no tutors, nothin'. Just a plain ol' couple to cook an' keep the place clean . . . an' me. Tell 'im wivout roundaboutation. This is how it'll be, an' that's *it!*"

Kittridge snorted. "That's it, eh? And if they don't heel, it's the firing squad?" He shook his head. "I don't think I can, Loesby. It just occurred to me that Mama may feel about her Miss Sophy as I do about you. And perhaps Miss Roffey means as much to my sister and the girls. If I keep you, how can I ask Mama to give up her Sophy? And the girls their Miss Roffey, eh? And Gavin his beautiful Prado, the Spanish stallion that I gave him as a gift? No, Loesby, it's too much to ask of them."

"But you 'ave no choice, Cap'n, if you ain't got the wherewithal . . ."

Lord Kittridge frowned thoughtfully and got to his feet. "Perhaps I do have a choice," he said slowly, as if to himself, "if I'm willing to swallow my confounded pride. It's the only way out of this fix."

"What way is that, Cap'n?" Loesby asked, his brow knit suspiciously.

Kittridge strode to the door. "What did I do with that card?" he muttered under his breath.

He crossed the hall in three strides, the batman at his heels. In the study, he rifled through the papers he'd taken from Jennings's office. "Here it is. Get out the curricle, Loesby, and drive down to the City at once. There's a Mr. Chivers at this address. Tell him that Lord Kittridge has changed his mind." His mouth tightened, and Loesby saw a telltale muscle twitch in his cheek. "Tell him the damned title is for sale after all."

Chapter Ten

The color drained from Cassie's cheeks. "You did *what?*"

"You 'eard me well enough, my girl," her father snapped, surprised and hurt by his daughter's reaction to his exciting news. "I've arranged for ye to wed Lord Kittridge. Why ain't ye throwin' yer arms round my neck an' kissin' me in ecstatic gratitude?"

The girl began to tremble from head to foot. "Oh, *Papa!*" she gasped, wide-eyed in horror. "How *could* you?"

Mr. Chivers glared at his daughter, angry and confused. He had achieved what he considered a brilliant success, and here was his daughter—the intended beneficiary of his triumphant scheme—behaving as if he'd condemned her to a life of hard labor in the workhouse! He realized again that he would never, if he lived to be a hundred, learn to understand her. He took his sherry from the tray Miss Penicuick held out to him and downed it in a gulp. "I 'ope, Cassie Chivers," he muttered, "that y're not goin' to put on missish airs and make a to-do about this."

The girl stared at him aghast. "You've *bribed* Lord K-Kittridge to offer for me, and you don't think I should make a *to-do?*" She sank down on the sitting room sofa, the breath quite gone from her chest. "Missish airs, indeed!" she gasped. "I think I shall *s-swoon!*"

"Don't you *dare!*" Chivers commanded. "No daughter of mine'd be so cowardly as to take leave of her senses just because 'er father gives 'er a small surprise."

Cassie shut her eyes. "*Small* surprise?" she murmured, taking a deep breath in an attempt to compose herself. "You don't know what you're saying, Papa. This is not a small surprise. It is a major crisis!"

Miss Penicuick hovered over her. "Shall I run for the sal volatile, my love?"

Cassie shook her head. "No, Miss Penny, I shan't let myself faint. But, Papa, I don't understand you. How can you have taken such a step without consulting me first?"

"I *did* consult ye. In fact, this only came about because you yerself asked me to do it."

"I?" She blinked up at her father in shock. "*I* asked you to *bribe his lordship to make me an offer*? I would never *dream* of suggesting something so monstrous."

"What's monstrous about it?" Chivers demanded, torn between fury and bewilderment. "Ye asked me to 'elp him out of 'is financial difficulties, did ye not?"

"Yes, but—"

"Well, what better way to 'elp him than this? 'E'll get every cent 'e needs and a wonderful wife as well."

"A wonderful wife?" The girl made a helpless gesture with two shaking hands. "How wonderful can a wife be, Papa, if she is not one of his own choosing? If he doesn't . . . l-love her."

"Love? What balderdash! A man choosin' a wife for love is romantic poppycock. The best marriages are made by interested third parties, not by a man an' a maid becomin' infatuated at a ball while executin' a quadrille. Marriages should be *arranged,* like sensible business partnerships."

"You don't understand, Papa." Cassie's lips trembled, and she put both shaking hands up to her mouth in an attempt to steady herself. "You don't remember about love anymore. For someone young, like Lord Kittridge, love is . . . everything."

"What?" The bedeviled father glowered at her in irritation. "I can't tell what y're sayin' with your mouth covered up like that!" Sighing helplessly, he sat down on the sofa beside her and took one of her hands in his. "What's the matter with you, Cassie?" he asked more quietly. "I thought ye'd be delighted by this news. I thought ye *liked* the fellow."

The girl's eyes filled with tears. "I d-do, Papa, that's just it. I I-like him too much to wish to *t-trap* him."

"But, confound it, Cassie, ye'd not be trappin' 'im! Ye'd be *'elpin'* 'im!"

The tears spilled over. Feeling quite incapable of explaining to her father the reasons for her abhorrence of his scheme, Cassie snatched her hand away, turned her back on him and said, quite firmly, "I won't do it, Papa, so please don't say any more."

"What's that? Won't *do* it?" He rose from the sofa, impotent rage washing over him again. "Cassie Chivers, 'ow *dare* ye say that to me? I'm yer *father*! I arranged this for *yer own 'appiness*! You will do as I say!"

"No, Papa, I won't." She did not look at him, and the words were muffled from behind the hands that covered her face, but there was no mistaking the determination of her voice.

Mr. Chivers's neck and ears reddened as his blood rose to his head in choleric anger. "I said you *will!*" he shouted.

There was no answer except a firm shake of her head, *no.*

Chivers turned a pair of frantic eyes to Miss Penicuick, as if seeking help from that direction, but the housekeeper could only shrug hopelessly. Then he looked back at his daughter's bent head. "Cassie," he pleaded in desperation, "ye *must* wed 'im. I *promised* the fellow. It was a *bargain.* We *shook 'ands* on it!"

"Then dash it, Papa, you must wed him yourself," his daughter sobbed, jumping up and running from the room, "for I never will. Never!"

"*Cassie,*" her father shouted after her, "come back 'ere! At once, do you 'ear! Damn it, girl, don't you *want* to be a viscountess? *Cassie!*"

But the girl was gone.

He stalked to the doorway. "Kittridge is comin' 'ere *tomorrow!*" he yelled, his voice thundering down the corridor. "To dinner. I expect ye to present yerself to 'im all prim and proper, do you 'ear me, Cassie? Tomorrow at eight!"

The only response came from Eames, the butler, who came stumbling up from below stairs with an expression of alarm on his usually impassive face. "Did you want me, Mr. Chivers, sir?" he asked breathlessly.

Chivers stamped on the floor in chagrin. "No, I didn't want ye," he growled. "Go away."

The butler, surprised at this unwarranted display of temper, withdrew at once. Miss Penicuick, quite unaccustomed to such theatrics in this usually peaceful household, threw her employer a terrified glance. Wringing her hands nervously, she came to the doorway and edged round him to follow her charge. "I think I . . . I'll just go and see—" she began as she stepped into the hallway.

"Just one moment, Miss Penicuick," he ordered angrily.

She jumped. "Yes, sir?"

"You 'eard what I said just now. Lord Kittridge is comin' for dinner tomorrow. See that Cassie is dressed proper an' is ready to receive 'im."

"But, sir, you know Cassie. If she's decided that this is not a suitable match . . ."

"Not a suitable match? Are ye both *demented*? The fellow is a veritable *thoroughbred!*"

"Yes, sir, I agree. But Cassie must have her reasons. And you know as well as I that she does not change her mind once it's made up. If she says she won't come down—"

"Then ye must *convince* her, do ye understand me? That's an order! She'll be down for dinner, all beribboned an' bedecked an' with a smile on 'er face, or someone standin' not ten inches from me at this moment will find 'erself *out on the street*! Do I make myself plain?"

Miss Penicuick gulped, nodded, burst into tears and ran off down the hall. "I d-don't say I won't t-try," the poor woman stammered as she mounted the stairs, "but to g-get C-Cassie to face his lordship when she has her m-mind so set against it will t-take a m-miracle. A God-sent m-miracle."

Chapter Eleven

The next day Mr. Chivers came home from the City three hours early, having been unable to concentrate for a single moment on business matters. His hair was wild, the eyes behind his thick spectacles troubled and his knees shaky. "'As she come down yet?" he asked Miss Penicuick as soon as he set foot in the house.

Miss Penicuick looked haggard. "No, sir," she said nervously, "not even once. She won't talk to me or open her door, nor has she eaten a bite since last night."

Mr. Chivers patted her shoulder. "It's all right, Miss Penicuick," he said, feeling contrite. "I'll take care of everythin'. Sorry I put myself in such a pucker and upset ye."

He mounted the stairs slowly, tasting the bitterness of defeat in his mouth. Tapping on his daughter's door gently, he mentally rehearsed his speech of capitulation. "Cassie, my love, open the door. I've decided that ye needn't wed Lord Kittridge after all."

The key turned in the lock and the door opened, but only an inch. "Do you mean it, Papa?" the girl asked, peeping through the narrow opening with eyes reddened from prolonged weeping.

"Yes, of course I do. I ain't a monster to force my girl to wed against 'er 'eart's wishes, although I may 'ave sounded like one last night."

Cassie opened the door and threw her arms about her father's neck. "Of course you're not a monster! Thank you, Papa, for changing your mind."

Chivers kissed her cheek. "But there's something ye must do for me in return," he said, leading her into her bedroom and seating her on the chaise near the window. "Ye must still act the 'ostess for me tonight when Kittridge calls."

She stiffened. "But, Papa, I *can't*—"

He perched on her bed. "Is it so much to ask? We shall 'ave a small, polite dinner, over in an hour, and then ye can excuse yourself while I tell 'im we've changed our minds. Givin' 'im dinner is the least I can do after renegin' on my bargain. Besides, I can't withdraw the invitation this late in the day."

"But surely you don't need *me* at the table, Papa. I'd feel dreadfully awkward, under the circumstances."

Her father eyed her irritably. "It'd be dreadfully awkward not 'aving ye there, don't ye see that?"

She clenched her hands in her lap. "Please, Papa, don't insist. You know how hard it is for me to . . . to speak to strangers."

"But the man ain't a stranger. 'E was yer rescuer at the linendraper's. Y're already very well acquainted."

"I wouldn't call that well acquainted."

"Well enough acquainted, I'd say, for a simple dinner. Dash it all, Cassie, why are ye makin' difficulties for me? Don't ye see that I need ye to act as 'ostess?"

Cassie felt miserable at having to refuse him, but she couldn't bring herself to accept. "Miss Penicuick will do very well as hostess. I can't do it, Papa. I just can't. Please don't keep on about it."

Chivers sighed, defeated again. What was he to do with the girl? He pushed his spectacles up on his nose and got heavily to his feet. "Very well, Miss, 'ave it yer way," he muttered, turning to the door.

"Papa?" she asked shyly as he was about to leave.

"Yes?"

"I'm . . . sorry."

"I know." He went gloomily to the door.

"Papa?"

He turned. "What now?"

"What will Lord Kittridge do now? About his finances, I mean."

"Ye needn't worry yer 'ead about that," he said impatiently. "I'll find 'im another heiress to wed. There are a good many girls with rich fathers who'd jump at the chance to snare a prize like Kittridge. I'll find one of 'em for 'im. I owe the fellow that."

Promptly at eight the knocker sounded. Chivers, who'd been watching for the carriage from behind the drapes of the drawing room window, arrived at the door ahead of the butler. He welcomed his guest warmly, shaking his hand with nervous enthusiasm as Eames took his lordship's hat and cane and disappeared down the hall. "I 'ope you've a good appetite, your lordship," Chivers said, clapping his guest on the shoulder. "My chef is from Paris an' makes the finest partridge *à la Pompadour* y're ever likely to taste."

Lord Kittridge was elegantly attired in evening clothes and, except for a tightness about his mouth, seemed very much at ease. "I look forward to sampling it," he said. "If your chef is half as talented as the architect who designed this house, Mr. Chivers, the meal will be splendid."

"Ah!" Chivers's eyes lit up. "Ye noticed the design of the facade, then?"

"I did indeed. The lines are superb. Impressive in scale but not in the least ostentatious. You are to be complimented."

Oliver Chivers beamed, his chest swelling with pride. Nothing Kittridge might have said could have pleased him more. He glanced at his guest with rueful admiration. It would have been very satisfying to have so presentable a son-in-law. Why, oh why, he asked himself, did his daughter have to be so damnably, stubbornly resistant?

It was time, he supposed, to make some sort of excuse for Cassie's absence. He took a deep breath. "I must apologize, my lord, for the fact that my daughter ain't—" But at that moment a sound from the stairway above them drew his eyes.

The befuddled father gasped in astonishment. Coming down toward them, her face lit by a shy smile, was Cassie herself. She was dressed modestly in a lavender gown with a ruffled neck and puffed sleeves, and she'd draped a lovely Norwich silk shawl over her shoulders. To her father's delight, she looked very pretty. She'd even managed to subdue her unruly hair, having pinned it back in a tight knot, so that only little tendrils had escaped to frame her face with an auburn halo. "Cassie!" he exclaimed, unable to disguise his surprise. "Y've come down!"

"Yes, Papa," she said in her quiet voice, "of course I have." She came down the last step and offered her hand to their guest. "Good evening, my lord. We are so glad you could d-dine with us."

Lord Kittridge, subduing a vulgar urge to satisfy his curiosity about his intended bride by gaping at her face, merely gave her a quick glance. About to bow over her hand, he suddenly stiffened. "But we've met, have we not?" he asked, peering at her with a puzzled frown.

"Just last week," she said, coloring painfully. "You saved me from d-dreadful embarrassment at Rollings and Chast."

The tightness of his lordship's mouth softened in a charming smile. "Of course. How pleasant to meet you again!"

Chivers, recognizing that Cassie's shyness had increased at the reference to last week's fiasco, immediately urged his guest into the drawing room. There Miss Penicuick sat waiting. Her eyes widened at the sight of Cassie in their midst, but she managed to hide her surprise. Chivers introduced her as Cassie's companion. The introduction was an ordeal Miss Penicuick survived without a gaffe. Only a slight tremor of her fingers revealed her excitement at being an ob-server of this most romantic turn of events. If it came to pass that her Cassie married this handsome nobleman after all, Miss Penicuick's dreams for her charge would have come true!

As Eames passed among them with a tray of sherries, Chivers sighed in relief. The evening had been launched without the embarrassment he'd expected. Now all he had to do was keep conversation flowing through the meal, wait until the women excused themselves and tell his lordship that he would find another bride for him in Cassie's place. The evening wouldn't be nearly as bad as he'd feared.

Dinner was soon announced, and Kittridge offered Cassie his arm with ap-propriate gallantry. Chivers, following with Miss Penicuick, felt proud of the graceful polish of his daughter's acceptance of his lordship's escort. The girl knew how to conduct herself, that much was plain. Perhaps her years at the Marchmont Academy had been of some use. He noted with a sigh that Lord Kittridge and his daughter made an attractive pair. For the hundredth time that evening he regretted the girl's stubborn refusal to submit to the arrangement he'd engineered for her. *Damn the chit,* he cursed in his head, *she doesn't know what's good for her*!

Chivers found that he had to carry on the dinner conversation almost single-handedly, for Cassie was her usual quiet self, Miss Penicuick in too dithery a state to add anything substantial, and Kittridge, though he tried to hide it, was too ab-stracted. But his lordship ate well and did not fail to praise the partridge, so Chivers did not consider the dinner a complete failure. But the time dragged by slowly, and when the wonderful apple soufflé the chef had concocted to give the repast a final flourish was at last consumed, he felt relieved that the meal was at an end.

All that now remained was for Chivers to inform Lord Kittridge that Cassie was unwilling to wed him. This announcement would not be as painful for Kittridge to hear as it would be for Chivers to make. Kittridge had no feeling for Cassie, after all. He barely knew her. What he wanted was a rich wife, and any candidate with a wealthy, willing father would do. All Chivers had to do was to inform Lord Kittridge that he'd locate another candidate within the week, and his lordship was bound to be satisfied.

When the ladies rose and excused themselves in order to leave the men to their port, Chivers got to his feet and crossed the room to open the door for them. "Thank ye for comin' down, my dear," he said *sotto voce* to his daughter as she was about to leave the room.

"Be sure to bring his lordship to the music room when you've finished," Cassie whispered back as she crossed the threshold.

"But . . ." Chivers gaped at his daughter stupidly. "That would mean y're in-vitin' 'im to make 'is offer!"

"Yes, I know," the girl answered briefly as she brushed by him.

The bewildered Chivers followed her out and grabbed her arm. "Are ye sayin' you've changed your mind?" he hissed, hardly permitting himself to hope.

"Yes." Cassie gave her father a tiny smile. "Go back to the table, Papa. His lordship will be wondering what's keeping you."

When the door of the dining room was safely shut behind him, Miss Penicuick gave an excited little scream. "Oh, my love," she cried, throwing her arms about Cassie's shoulders, "are you going to accept him after all?"

Cassie merely nodded.

"Oh, my dear, I'm so *happy*! His lordship is the handsomest, most gentlemanly, most imposing man I've ever laid eyes on! But . . ." She took a step back and, with her hands on Cassie's shoulders, peered with worried earnestness into the girl's eyes. "Cassie, you were so *adamant* before, in your refusal of him! Are you now certain of yourself? Are you *sure* you want to do this?"

The girl took her companion's hands from her shoulders and squeezed them comfortingly. "Yes, Miss Penny, I'm sure."

"I don't understand," Miss Penicuick persisted. "What made you change your mind?"

Cassie drew her shawl more closely about her shoulders and started slowly down the hall. "It was something that Papa said," she explained.

Miss Penicuick hurried after her. "And what was that, my dear?"

"He said that if *I* didn't accept his lordship, he'd have to find *another* heiress for him to wed. I decided then and there that if Lord Kittridge was determined to marry without love . . . to tie himself to *anyone,* no matter whom, so long as she could help him out of his financial fix, well, then . . ." She paused and gave her friend a wistful smile. ". . . that 'anyone' might just as well be me."

Chapter Twelve

"*Y*ou did *what*?" the dowager Lady Kittridge exclaimed when her son informed her of his marital intentions. "I think, Robbie, that you've taken leave of your *senses*! How *can* you have agreed to such a thing? Didn't you give a single thought to *my* feelings? How do you suppose I shall be able to show my face in society after my son marries a *bourgeoise*?"

Her reaction was typical of all the others. Every member of the family was appalled at the news. Gavin complained that he would have "the devil of a time explaining to my friends that my own brother is marrying a cit." And Eunice burst into tears, demanding to know how Robbie could bear facing the world after the *ton* made their odious comparisons between his lovely former-betrothed, Elinor, and the drab little nobody he intended to wed.

Kittridge kept his temper. He had made a bargain for the salvation of all of them, and although the cost to him—in the pain of lost dreams and savaged hopes—was heavy, he intended to make the best of it. He turned a cold eye on his family and merely let them know that their chagrin would be easily assuaged when they balanced the benefits each of them would derive as a result of his nuptials against the petty discomfort of accepting into the family a person they considered beneath their touch. "You, Mama, will be able to remain in the London house, with a whole staff at your disposal. Eunice, you will now be able to raise your daughters in the luxurious style you yourself enjoyed as a girl. And Gavin will be able to continue to live as he always has, even keeping his beloved Prado. None of these privileges would have been yours, I remind you, if my 'drab little nobody' had not come to our rescue. So, if you're not complete fools, you will think of the advantages to yourselves in my marriage, and you'll welcome the girl into our midst with proper warmth."

Within himself Kittridge was not nearly so sanguine about his marriage as he pretended to his family. For one thing, he couldn't put his feeling for Elinor out of his mind. He had, that very morning, received a letter from his beloved that reminded him too well of what he had lost. Elinor's letter, posted in Paris, reverberated with loneliness and loss. The magnificence of her surroundings, the adventures of travel, the excitement of seeing famous places for the first time, only made her miss him more. *I had hoped to see Notre Dame and La Chapelle with your hand in mine,* she'd written. *What joy can there be for me to see these sights without you at my side?* His throat had tightened when he'd read those words, and he'd struck his fist against his bedpost with such frustrated fury that he'd knocked it loose from its underpinnings and caused the hangings to come tumbling down about his head.

For another thing, he was troubled about this girl he'd agreed to marry. He'd thought, when he'd first seen her at the linendrapers', that she was a sweet, innocent little soul. But now he wasn't so sure, and his ignorance of her real nature made him uneasy. He felt strangely suspicious of her motives. The cause of those suspicions was the fact that she had turned out to be Chivers's daughter. It was a peculiar coincidence, and it made him so uncomfortable that he mentioned the matter to his friend Sandy.

They had met at White's and were sitting in the lounge in a pair of wing chairs, brandies in hand, gazing out through the club's famous bow windows at the strollers parading up and down St. James Street in spite of a blustery wind that was tugging at shawls and sending high top hats bowling down the street. "What's so peculiar about the coincidence?" Sandy asked.

"Don't you think it possible that this isn't mere coincidence?" Kittridge surmised. "Mightn't there be some cunning strategy lurking behind it?" Strategy had been Kittridge's forte in the cavalry; he'd been almost supernaturally adept at anticipating enemy movements. His instincts in matters of strategy had earned him much admiration. Those same instincts were at work now. They set a warning bell ringing in his head. He couldn't help wondering if the girl were up to something.

"What cunning strategy?" Sandy asked, nonplussed.

Kittridge put a hand to his forehead. "I don't know. What if *she herself* is behind the financial arrangement Chivers made with me? Having seen me beforehand and having found me useful as a protector, might she have decided that I'm an easy mark? A mollycoddle who'll be convenient to smooth her way into society?"

Sandy stirred the brandy in his glass, his eyes troubled. "Well, what did you expect? That's what that sort of arrangement is all about, isn't it? A cit's getting herself into society?"

"Yes, but if it were the father's idea, it'd be, somehow, more acceptable.

There's something *manipulative* about a girl who arranged such matters for herself. Something almost *false,* if she disguises her managing nature behind an oh-so-shy facade."

"So you think your shy Miss Chivers might turn out to be a manipulating *intrigante*?"

Kittridge peered glumly into his glass. "It is a real, if repellent, possibility."

"But only a possibility," Sandy pointed out. "Look on the bright side, old fellow. She may very well be as sweet and innocent as she appears."

But Kittridge doubted it. Sandy was eternally the optimist, but Kittridge was learning that the dice of fate rarely fell on the bright side.

Not that it mattered very much, he told himself as he got up from the easy chair and stared out the windows with unseeing eyes. If he couldn't marry Elinor, what did it matter whom he married? And if he were to be honest with himself, he'd have to admit he was as much a schemer as Miss Cassandra Chivers. Just as she was using him to win herself a title and a place in society, he was using her to get the financing he needed. Their relationship was a business matter; each expected to pay a price for value received. If the title of viscountess and the entree into society that his name provided was the price she'd set, he had no objections to paying it. It seemed little enough to pay in exchange for forty thousand pounds.

But why had she found it necessary to be underhanded . . . to keep her identity hidden until the bargain had been made? It seemed an odd ploy. Was there something more to the business than met the eye?

Well, he told himself, time would tell. Meanwhile, he made the bargain, and he had every intention of sticking to it. He would make the girl his wife, and he would be, for all intents and purposes, an honorable husband. But there was one thing he promised himself as he stood there in the window—the little schemer would get no more from him than that.

Chapter Thirteen

$\mathcal{S}$hortly before his wedding day, Kittridge asked Mr. Chivers's permission to hold a private conversation with his bride-to-be. At the appointed time, the night before their wedding day, his lordship called at the house near King's Cross. Eames admitted him, but Miss Penicuick immediately appeared behind the butler and took over his duties. Handing Eames Lord Kittridge's hat and cane, she dismissed the butler and, fluttering about nervously, began to make foolish little remarks to his lordship about her delight at the forthcoming nuptials and her concern that this visit, so close to the time of the wedding, would bring bad luck. It was not until Kittridge gave her a reassuring smile and his promise that this interview would not take long that she finally directed him to a small sitting room at the rear of the house (a room she referred to pompously as the Blue Saloon) and took herself off.

Miss Cassandra Chivers, the bride-to-be, was waiting for him. She looked quite pretty—and properly maidenly and shy—in a pale green round-gown covered with a paisley shawl. He couldn't help admiring her profusion of curly hair, which the firelight tipped with glints of reddish gold. Yet the quality that one first noticed about her was her timidity, an impression that was underlined by the heightened color of her cheeks and the trembling of her fingers. It was difficult, seeing her like this, for him to sustain the belief that her shyness was a pose, a ruse that she used to mask her manipulating nature.

She offered him a glass of brandy, which he refused. But he accepted her invitation to be seated in a chair before the fire, facing her. "Thank you for seeing me tonight, Miss Chivers," he said after a lengthy silence during which they each studied the other with surreptitious glances. "Your Miss Penicuick seems to think this interview will bring a devil's curse upon our heads."

"You mustn't mind her, my lord. She is very superstitious, especially in regard to wedding omens. If it rains tomorrow, she is bound to fall into the dismals."

"Really? Is rain a bad omen for weddings?"

"Oh, yes, my lord, it is *dire*. Have you never heard the saying 'Happy is the bride the sun shines on'?"

He shook his head. "I'm afraid I am woefully ignorant of superstitions. And of wedding omens, too. But now that you've warned me, I shall get down on my knees and pray for sunshine before I close my eyes tonight."

She gave a little gurgle of laughter. "Miss Penicuick will be delighted to hear it."

"But not *you*, ma'am?" he asked in mock alarm. "Have you no concern for the fate of our marital felicity?"

Her expression grew serious. "I must place my hopes for marital felicity on the good sense of the participants, not on the weather."

"Good for you, Miss Chivers, good for you," he said, turning serious himself. "I hope you will think it was good sense that brought me here tonight. I came because I imagine that you must find this situation of ours deucedly awkward."

"Yes," she said. "I do. Very."

"I, too," he admitted. "That's why it seems to me to be necessary that we come to some clear understanding before we make our final vows."

"Yes," she said, quietly encouraging. She sat back against the cushions, feeling a wave of relief. She had agonized all day about the nature of this interview, but now that she saw what his intentions were, her spirits lifted. He wanted to set matters straight between them. If they were to live together in any sort of harmony, they needed to agree on the rules. It was good of him, she thought, to wish to clarify matters beforehand. She peeped over at him and noted that a muscle twitched in his cheek and that his fingers gripped the arm of his chair with white-knuckled tension. She felt a stab of sympathy for him. He was as uneasy about this conversation as she was. This indication of human weakness on his part gave her more confidence in herself.

"We are strangers, after all," he went on. "And marriage is . . . is . . ."

"Intimate?" she offered shyly.

He looked at her thankfully. "Yes, exactly. I want you to know, Miss Chivers, that I have no intention of pushing those . . . er . . . intimacies on you."

Her face grew beet red. "That is . . . kind in you, my lord."

"Not at all. Intimacy, after all, is not something one can negotiate on a marriage contract. It must develop naturally, don't you agree?"

She nodded, her eyes fixed on the hands folded in her lap.

"In the meantime, Miss Chivers," he went on, "while we learn to be comfortable with each other, I'm sure that we can find ways to . . . avoid it."

There was a long, awkward pause. Then, suddenly, she lifted her head and threw him a teasing grin that was as unexpected as it was charming. "Is calling me by my given name one of those 'intimacies' you intend to avoid?"

A laugh broke out of him. "No, of course not," he said, finding himself drawn to the girl against his will. This was not a feeling he wished to encourage, having almost convinced himself that her manner was not sincere. Although he'd thus far found this conversation more pleasant than he'd dared hope and had even found the chit likable, the warning bells in his head had not stopped ringing. Her motives in this affair were not at all clear. Until he understood her nature, he would not permit himself to be an easy mark. It would take more than a small display of charm to win him over.

He sat back in his chair and crossed his arms over his chest. "You're quite right. If we're to endure a long wedded life, we can't be stiffly formal with each other. I certainly can't continue to address you as 'Miss Chivers.' Shall I call you Cassandra?"

"No, please don't," she begged. "I hate that name. Cassandra, the prophetess of doom. Would I be pushing you to too much intimacy to ask you to call me Cassie?"

"No, not at all," he said, a small smile breaking out in spite of his wish to prevent it. The girl had more spirit than he'd originally thought. He'd have to be on his guard. If he didn't keep his instincts on the alert, she might manage to manipulate him quite easily. "I'd be happy to call you Cassie if you'll agree to the equal intimacy of calling me Robbie."

"Robbie?" At the thought of using so familiar an appellation, her cheeks turned pink again. "Oh, no, my lord, I couldn't," she objected, her habitual shyness washing over her.

He noticed the quick reddening of her cheeks. "Robert, then," he suggested, admiring her ability to behave with such convincing diffidence. "You cannot continue to address me as 'my lord,' you know. Surely we can compromise on Robert until we grow more . . . accustomed to each other."

"Robert," she murmured, testing it on her tongue. "Yes, I think I can manage that."

"Then that's settled. Now, ma'am, if you please, I'd like to broach the matter that brought me here. It has to do with living arrangements. Have you given the subject any thought?"

She looked puzzled. "Why, no. I suppose I should have, but everything has happened so quickly."

"Yes. But I thought, in all fairness, that we should discuss the subject before the nuptials, in the event that there are some areas of disagreement to iron out."

"Disagreement? But why should—?"

"I assume, ma'am, that you anticipate taking up residence in the London house—is that not so?"

"I . . . suppose so . . . if that is your desire, my lord."

"Actually, it is not what I desire. What I'd really like to do is live in Lincolnshire. Your father has convinced me that the property there could, with proper management, become profitable. It is my most ardent wish to achieve that goal. With the estate making a profit, I could free myself of the remaining encumbrances on the Suffolk property and begin to give your father some return on his investment."

"But, my lord . . . Robert, it is my understanding that the money my father gave you was, in a manner of speaking, a dowry. A dowry is not an investment to be paid back, is it?"

"He may not have meant it to be paid back, my dear, but I shall feel more like a man when I've done it."

"Oh," Cassie murmured, feeling as if she'd been chastised. "I see. Then we must take up residence in Lincolnshire, of course."

"There is no 'of course' about it, ma'am. *Your* wishes must be considered, too. I would understand completely if you objected. All the women in my family prefer London to the country. After all, there is no society in Lincolnshire to compare to that in town. There might be, in Lincolnshire, an occasional Assembly dance or a dinner party with the local gentry, but there would be none of the routs, balls, galas, theater parties, opera evenings, and the other amusements with which town life abounds. So if the thought of quiet country evenings oppresses you, I'd quite understand."

"No, my lord, the thought does not oppress me. Although I've lived in London all my life, I've lived as quietly as any country girl. I shall feel quite at home in Lincolnshire."

"But that quiet life, my dear, was before you had the advantage of my name. I hope you'll not think me a deuced coxcomb for saying that, but surely your father must already have pointed out to you that your life will be quite different as Lady Kittridge. Why else did he arrange these nuptials but to open these doors to you? As my wife, you will be invited everywhere. As long as we remain in town, there will hardly be an evening—particularly in season—when you won't have half a dozen wonderful amusements to choose among. That is what removing to Lincolnshire will deprive you of."

"I'm aware of that, my lord. Please believe me when I say that I would prefer the quiet life. You must have noticed that I am not . . . comfortable in social situations."

He peered at her closely. This was not at all what he expected her to say. Did she truly wish to banish herself to the wilds of Lincolnshire? Was she sincere, or was this part of some deep game she was playing? "Do you mean it, my dear? Living in Lincolnshire would be very dull, I'm afraid. You must think carefully. I want you to be aware of every option before you make a decision. I realize quite well how much you ladies enjoy town society, and I've been struggling with this problem ever since you accepted my offer. I've even considered the possibility of your remaining in the town house with my mother while I take up a separate residence in Lincolnshire—"

Her eyes flew up to his for an instant and as quickly dropped down to the fingers she was twisting together in her lap. "S-separate residence?"

"Yes. Such arrangements are not unheard of, you know."

"Would you . . . *wish* to m-make such an arrangement?" she asked in a small voice. The suggestion had come as a blow to her. She understood that this was to be a marriage in name only, but separate residences would be no marriage at all! Why had he suggested such a thing? Was he resentful that he'd had to take her father's aid? And did that resentment include her? "Is a separate residence what you're suggesting?"

He stood up and walked to the fire. "May I speak honestly?" he asked, fixing his eyes on the flames.

"Please."

"Then, frankly, I am not. I think we should take up residence together, and for several good reasons. Firstly, I don't think your father would feel that I was living up to the spirit of our agreement if we did not. A separate residence seems to me to be an evasion of marriage rather than an entering into it, and it would surely seem so to your father. And secondly, though I know that we have agreed to . . . er . . . dispense with the connubial intimacies, I think it important that we present to the world the appearance of true wedlock. If we maintained separate residences, it would be on every tongue that we had made merely a *mariage de convenance*. That sort of gossip would be humiliating to us both, as well as a betrayal of your father's trust in me. For these and other reasons, I think we should agree on living in the same house."

She expelled a long breath. "Yes, I think so, too."

He turned his head and threw her a quizzical glance. "Do you? Then please understand, Cassie, that I intend to abide by *your* decision as to the place where we live. If you wish to live in town, I am quite ready to do so. You needn't make up your mind right now. Think it over for as long as you wish."

"Thank you, Robert. You are both honest and fair. But I don't need any more time. If the choice is truly mine, I choose Lincolnshire."

He turned from the fire and looked her in the eye. "Are you certain, Cassie?"

"Yes."

He breathed a sigh of relief. "Thank you, my dear. I'm very grateful."

She dropped her eyes from his. "There's no need for gratitude. I made the choice as much for myself as for you."

"I'm glad of that. This decision will not only help us to avoid the speculation of the *ton* as to the nature of our relationship but will also give our union the best possible start. It goes without saying that we shall spend part of every year in London. I'll not be so selfish as to keep you hidden away forever from the pleasures of town. My plan, then, if you have no objection, is to permit my mother to remain ensconced in the town house, while you and I will remove to the country except for two months in season. I'd like my brother to be with us during those months of the year when he is not in school. My sister will, I expect, remain with her daughters in the London house."

"I have no objection at all," Cassie assured him. "But as for your sister, doesn't she think the country is a better place than town for bringing up her daughters?"

"One would think so." He peered at her again in surprise. "Would you be *willing* to have them in the country with us? There's plenty of room, of course. The house is enormous, with, I believe, thirty bedrooms. But I've often heard that when two women rule one household, it makes for strife."

"Oh, no, I don't think that would necessarily be true. I should very much enjoy having children about the house, I think."

"Then I will certainly suggest it to her." He didn't notice that the words she'd just said had brought the color flooding back to her cheeks. He came away from the fire and up to her chair. Lifting her hand, he took it to his lips. "You've been more considerate than I had any reason to expect, Cassie. Your kindness has made a difficult situation more bearable. It augurs well for our future."

Cassie's hand trembled in his. "Oh, Robert, I hope so," she breathed, trying to stem the emotion that welled up in her chest so overwhelmingly that she feared it might spill over out of her eyes. "I do hope so!"

Chapter Fourteen

They were married by special license at St. Clement Danes on the Strand. The day was cloudy, with a few flurries of snow, but, as Kittridge whispered in his bride's ear, it at least wasn't rain.

It was a brief ceremony, witnessed by only a handful of people. The bride was modestly dressed in a blue walking suit and flowered bonnet and carried a nose-gay of yellow roses and white baby's breath that the groom had managed to procure for her. The dowager Lady Kittridge remarked in an undervoice to her daughter that although the bride's bonnet was far from *chic,* she was willing to allow that it was not too dreadfully dowdy.

Sir Philip Sanford stood up with his friend. The rector (a distant relative of the Rossiters) beamed as the bride's father led her to the altar, but his smile was the only one in the chapel. The dowager looked impassive; Eunice looked tragic; Gavin was utterly bored; Sandy bit his lip, disappointed that his prediction that a lucky accident would occur to keep his friend from being leg-shackled to a "manipulative *intrigante*" had not come to pass; Miss Penicuick wept openly; Oliver Chivers—who'd belatedly realized this morning, with an unpleasant start, that his daughter would henceforth be missing from his domicile—was suffering from the most painful second thoughts; the groom was stricken at heart with regrets for what-might-have-been; and the bride, to whose feelings nobody seemed to be paying the slightest attention, was terrified. This was the happy beginning to the couple's married life.

In a mere eighteen minutes, it was all over. With the papers signed and the vows taken, there was nothing left but to get through the wedding breakfast that Sandy was hosting at his hotel. With submissive sighs and a noticeable lack of enthusiasm, the wedding party moved out of the church and into the waiting carriages.

Kittridge's man, Loesby, dressed for the occasion with a top hat and a boutonniere in his lapel, organized the logistics of moving the wedding party from the church to the Fenton Hotel. For a man who'd moved mountains of equipment across the Peninsula, the job of herding the wedding party into the three carriages and leading them the short distance to the Fenton was child's play. Before the guests knew it, they were out of the wind, out of their outer garments and ensconced in the comfortable elegance of the hotel's dining room.

The buffet Sandy had ordered turned out to be lavish enough even for the dowager Lady Kittridge's taste. There in the Fenton's private dining salon, on a long table decorated with greens, were platters, trays and tureens loaded with delicacies: ham slices curled around soft cheddar; hot little rolls *à la Duchesse*; a whole, steamed salmon; eggs with truffles; delicately browned lobster cakes; oysters au gratin; cucumbers *béchamel*; fragrant orange peel biscuits; rum and apple pudding with grapes; chewy French nougat cake, surrounded by assorted jellies and creams; and the most delightful French champagne. The sight, smell and taste of such ambrosial viands couldn't fail to lift their spirits, and by the time their plates were loaded and their glasses filled, the wedding guests were almost cheerful. They even sounded quite sincere in their seconding of Sandy's toast to the health of the bride and groom.

After a while, Loesby came in and whispered something into Kittridge's ear. The bridegroom nodded and announced aloud that it was time for him to take his bride away; they had to start out at once for Lincolnshire if they were to reach Highlands without a night's stopover on the road. This announcement brought the festivities to an end, and the entire wedding party wrapped themselves up in their outer garments and trooped out to the street to see the pair off.

Emotions again came to the surface as good-byes were exchanged. The elder Lady Kittridge embraced her son tremblingly, whispering into his ear, "My poor boy, you shouldn't have done it! We don't deserve such a sacrifice!" in a shaken voice. Eunice kissed her brother's cheek and, glancing over at the "drab little nobody" who was now her sister-in-law, promptly dissolved in tears. Miss Penicuick (having decided, with Cassie's urging, to remain with Mr. Chivers, who would need his housekeeper now more than Cassie would) threw her arms round the bride in a kind of hysteria, as if she feared they would never see each other again. Sandy, painfully aware of the difference that Kittridge must see between the glorious Elinor and this shy, mousy creature who was now his bride, shook his friend's hand with energetic sympathy and promised, with a forced smile and an encouraging slap on the back, to come up to Highlands for a visit within the month. Mr. Chivers pressed an envelope stuffed full of bank notes into Cassie's hand, muttering in her ear that there wasn't a girl in the world who didn't need a bit of pin money, and adding, "If that damn fellow don't treat ye just right, y're to come 'ome at once, my love, do ye 'ear me? At *once*! And whatever it costs, I'll rid ye of 'im." In short, everyone seemed utterly miserable.

With the good-byes said, Loesby climbed up on the driver's box. Kittridge helped his bride up the steps of their heavily loaded carriage and jumped in after her. There was a great deal of handwaving as the bridal carriage (a magnificent new equipage in shiny blue with the Kittridge coat of arms emblazoned on the doors—a gift from his lordship's new father-in-law) rolled off down the street. The little group stood huddled together, gazing glumly after it. The mood that had clouded the wedding ceremony seemed to have returned in full force.

At that moment, a thin ray of sunshine broke through an opening in the clouds and shone wanly down on them. "Oh, praise be!" Miss Penicuick exclaimed in relief, sniffing into an already wet handkerchief. "The sun! That means the bride will be happy!"

"I hope, ma'am," Eunice said coldly, "that the superstition includes the groom, also."

"Of course it does," Sandy insisted with his determined optimism. "We all wish for them both to have a happy life together."

"Yes," the dowager muttered, "but it isn't very likely."

Nobody contradicted her.

Chapter Fifteen

The newlywed couple had spent only two nights in the manor house at Highlands before winter set in, in earnest and a month too soon. The temperature dropped so sharply that no one in Lincolnshire ventured out of doors unless through dire necessity. Then, after three days of freezing cold, the temperature abated just enough to usher in a snowfall of at least a foot. Kittridge, who'd planned to traverse all the grounds of the estate with Mr. Griswold, his land agent, as soon as the weather warmed, had to postpone everything. Cassie, who'd accepted the responsibility for hiring a household staff, was unable to interview any of the village lasses, for it was impossible for them to come up to the manor house. The couple had to make do with only the Whitlocks, the elderly man and wife who'd maintained the house during the years when it had been unoccupied, and Loesby, who acted as butler, valet and general factotum.

Kittridge spent a good part of each day in a small room near the library which he designated as his study, going over estate maps, blueprints and accounts. Cassie, meanwhile, tried to make habitable the few rooms they needed for daily living. With Loesby's help, she looked into all the unused rooms and made notes of which drapes, pictures, carpets and pieces of furniture were in good condition or which she particularly liked. Then she went to Kittridge's study to ask his permission to move things about. When she got to his door, however, her usual timidity took hold of her, and she knocked so shyly that he didn't at first hear her. When she was finally admitted, she told him what she'd been doing and hesitantly made her request, fully expecting a reprimand.

He looked at her in surprise. "You don't have to ask, my dear," he pointed out. "This is your house as much as mine. More, if you remember that it was your 'dowry' that made it possible for us to live here."

"That's not how I feel about it," she responded, forgetting her shyness in her determination to make him understand fully the liberties she intended to take with the furnishings. "These are things that have been in your family for generations. There is a tradition about these things, you know. In some families, the placement of a portrait or the arrangement of the Chinese vases on a mantelpiece is sacrosanct. So you see, Robert, I'd certainly understand if you'd prefer not making changes. I wouldn't wish to upset tradition."

He smiled up at her, noting that this was the first speech she'd made to him that didn't seem painfully shy. "I'm not sentimental about furnishings, Cassie. To be honest, I don't think I ever notice them. Please do as you like, and don't give tradition another thought."

Thus, happily free to rearrange the household as she wished, Cassie promptly set to work to make their rooms comfortable. With the help of Loesby and the Whitlocks, she removed and replaced the drapes in the smallest sitting room, brought in a pair of wing chairs from the drawing room, and rearranged the furniture so that all the seating would be close to the fireplace. The arrangement was especially designed so that it would be a room in which they could be cozy in the cold evenings.

That completed, they cleaned the two bedrooms from top to bottom, replaced worn carpets and hangings with better ones from other rooms, and hung various paintings—still life studies and florals, mostly, that Cassie discovered in unused rooms—on walls that had been unadorned or hung with drab, dismal portraits. Soon the bedrooms were comfortable and cheery. And although no guests were expected in this dreadful weather, they readied a guest bedroom, too, just as a precaution against the unexpected.

It was dusty, strenuous, tiring work, but Cassie enjoyed it. Not only did the work keep her feeling useful, but the resulting improvement in the appearance of their surroundings pleased her. When Robert remarked, one evening after dinner, about the cheeriness of the sitting room, she was quite overcome. The kind word from him was the reward she'd wished for.

Thus encouraged, Cassie started redecorating the Great Hall, a high, vaulted entryway large enough to accommodate the stairway, which bifurcated at the second floor and descended in two sweeping arches to the first. She and her willing assistants polished the marble floors, scrubbed and whitewashed the smoke-blackened walls, replaced the shabby carpet with a gold and blue gem of a rug she discovered in a third-floor bedroom, installed a claw-footed chaise against the south wall opposite the doorway beneath the curve made by the two stairways and removed the large, forbidding portrait of the first viscount that hung over it. Cassie confided to Loesby that she found the man's face frightening and felt the portrait gave a gloomy greeting to anyone coming in the door for the first time. She replaced the portrait with a wonderful landscape she'd found in an unused sitting room in the building's west wing. It was an early work of John Constable, the landscape painter who was creating a great stir in London these days. Cassie believed the painting to be a real treasure—a country scene with a pond and a hay wagon that was a joy to look at. She and Loesby agreed that it was a great improvement over the gloomy portrait as the first thing to greet the eye of new arrivals. "Makes the 'ole 'ouse look 'appy an' new," Mrs. Whitlock exclaimed when she saw the transformed hall. "Y're a wonder, m'lady, an' that's a fact!"

"She *is* a wonder," Loesby said to his captain that night, relating the day's events as he helped Kittridge remove his boots. "Seems t' me y're luckier in yer bride than ye 'ad any right t' expect."

But Kittridge, still unsure of Cassie's true nature, only grunted.

His lordship went to bed feeling irritable. The wind had shifted to the west and was whistling ominously outside his windows. The sound, so cold and barren, exacerbated his feeling of loneliness. It seemed to him that the already prolonged cold snap that had kept him housebound since his arrival would continue on forever. The weather, like his life, showed no promise or hope of change. Very sorry for himself, his last thought before he drifted off was to wonder disconsolately if there would ever be a spring for him.

Later that night, his lordship was awakened from a fitful sleep by a high-pitched, trilling sound that seemed like an inhuman, eerie shriek. *It's only the wind,* he told himself as he tried to burrow deeper in his bedclothes and catch at the skirt of sleep before it flitted away from him altogether. But he soon realized that the sound was not the wind. A whiny sound accompanied the blowing but was more intermittent, and its pitch was much higher. What on earth was it? It was just such sounds, he thought, that made people believe in ghosts.

Knowing that he would get no more sleep as long as that eerie wail continued, he threw off his comforter and, after lighting his bedside candle, put on a robe and slippers. With the candle held out before him, he opened his door and came face-to-face with another candle. It took a moment before he could make out that it was being carried by his wife. "Good God, Cassie," he exclaimed, "you startled me. Did that unearthly shrieking rouse you, too?"

"Yes. Isn't it awful? Mrs. Whitlock tells me it's the Rossiter ghost. She sounded rather proud of him, actually. Says he makes Highlands a real castle. She warned me that he comes calling when the wind blows from the west."

"Then, if it's a ghost, why aren't you hiding under your bedclothes, as any properly frightened female would do?"

She grinned at him over the smoky flame of the candle. "I suppose I would, if I really thought it *was* a ghost. But I don't believe in such things, I'm afraid."

"Don't believe in them?" he mocked. "What sort of unnatural female are you?"

"Unnatural enough to have grave doubts about the existence of supernatural phenomena. I suppose you must think me dreadfully prosy."

"On the contrary, ma'am. I begin to think you are unusually sensible. But if you don't believe it's a ghost, why didn't you simply turn over, cover your ears and go back to sleep?"

"Well, you see, the noise is so loud, I feared it would disturb you and everyone else in the household. So I decided to try to track it down."

"All by yourself?" He lifted his candle higher and looked closely at her face. Her eyes glowed with the flame's reflection, and he was struck by the charm of her nighttime appearance. Her unruly hair had been crammed into a large, ruffled nightcap that was tied tightly under her pointed chin, but little rebellious tendrils had escaped from the sides and back and made her look like an adorably blowsy, if elfin, scrubwoman. "Is this the shy Cassie speaking?" he demanded. "How can you pretend to be so timid and self-effacing in society and still be brave enough to go searching all alone through a large, dark house for a nonexistent ghost?"

Flustered by the sudden turn of the conversation to her own personality, Cassie colored to her ears. But she managed to answer without stammering. "People and society make me timid, my lord, not empty houses."

"Nevertheless, ma'am, it was a foolhardy intention. You are not yet familiar with the byways and passages of this enormous, cavernous edifice. What if you'd fallen down a stair or tripped on a carpet and fainted? We might not have found you for days!"

"Are you saying, my lord, that I may not go?" she asked, her voice plainly revealing her disappointment.

The wind rose at that moment, and the eerie scream so intensified in volume that it became decidedly unpleasant. "Well, we can't let that horrid wail go on forever, I suppose. Come. We'll *both* search out this ghostly shrieker."

He took her hand in his and, with a long, purposeful stride, led her down the hall. She had to scurry on her tiny, slippered feet to keep up with him, her full-skirted nightgown flapping behind her in the draughty corridor. The wail grew louder as they turned the corner to the west wing. "It seems to be coming from the corner room at the end of the corridor," he said.

He was right. When they came up to the door, they could tell at once that the sound was emanating from within the closed room. "You wait here," he ordered. "Don't move from this doorway until I come back."

"Oh, no, Robert," she cried, unwilling to be prevented from partaking in the solution of this mystery and even more unwilling to let go of his hand. "I want to go with you!"

"Very well, ma'am," he said with mock foreboding, "but if you're snatched away by evil spirits, never to be seen again, don't blame me."

The wind and the wail rose again, so loudly that she shivered. "If I'm snatched away," she rejoined, laughing nervously, "I shall return, most appropriately, in spectral form, and then you and Mrs. Whitlock can boast that Highlands has *two* shrieking ghosts in residence."

He laughed, too, but he opened the door with gingerly care and held his candle aloft for a good look within before setting foot in the room. It was one of the unused bedrooms, a large, square, corner room with windows on two walls. It was icy cold. They both drew their robes closer about them as they stepped over the threshold. Robert looked round in distaste. The room was full of cobwebs, and the air of ghostliness was emphatically underlined by the pale dustcovers that were draped over the furniture. "Ugh!" Robert grunted. "One has to admit this is the perfect place for the Rossiter ghost to haunt. Are you sure, my dear, that you still believe the ghost to be nonexistent?"

A shriek echoed shrilly through the room. "Yes," Cassie retorted bravely, "but I'll l-leave it to you to look under the b-bed."

"Thank you," he said drily. "I suppose you wish me to look under all the Holland covers, too."

"No," she said, suddenly alert. "I think the sound is coming from here. This window . . . on the west wall."

He listened. "I think you're right. Stand back, girl, for I'm about to throw open the drapes. If a transparent figure with black eyeholes is standing behind them, flee for your life, for that's exactly what I intend to do."

He flung the drapes open, releasing a cloud of dust into the air that caused them both to cough. But there was nothing behind the drapes but a large, multipaned window with a white, moon-washed landscape beyond. "Dash it all," Robert muttered, "the damnable fellow's eluded us again."

As if in response, the wail came up loud and clear. It seemed to mock them for a moment, and then it died down again. There was no doubt that the sound came from the window. Robert lifted his candle and peered at one pane after another. Suddenly the candle flame flickered and went out. "A draught," he said triumphantly. "Right—" He leaned toward the pane he was examining and ran his fingers round the frame. "—here!"

"I don't understand," Cassie said, puzzled. "What has a draught to do with it? Surely a little draught can't make such a sound."

"Wait until it shrieks again. I'll show you."

Of course, because they were waiting for it, the sound did not come for several minutes. But as soon as it rose up again, Robert put a hand flat against the pane, as if to hold it steady. The shriek stopped at once.

"It was a slight rattle in the pane," Robert explained. "The putty holding this pane in place has dried and fallen off, so there's a small space between the frame and the glass. When the wind blows strongly enough, it sets the pane vibrating so quickly that it makes a whine."

Cassie could scarcely believe it. "But . . . so loudly?"

"Yes. It's like rubbing your finger round the edge of a crystal goblet. Didn't you ever do that as a child? The action of your finger sets the crystal vibrating, and the glass 'sings.' The faster you run your finger on the rim, the shriller the sound. Eunice and I used to do it in the nursery. It made the governess frantic. Here. Try it for yourself. As soon as the wind comes up, put your hand on the windowpane."

Cassie did so. When the wind came up and the wail began to shrill, she could feel the glass vibrate.

"There," he said triumphantly. "Feel it tremble? That's what's making the whine. Now press hard to keep the glass steady."

She pressed, and the noise ceased at once. "That's marvelous," she said in amazement. "I wonder if all ghosts can be so rationally explained."

"Probably," he said, relighting his candle with the flame of hers. He took her hand and led her out of the room. "They used to talk about a ghost at the Langstons' when I was a boy . . ." He entertained her with the tale of the "chimney ghost" at the Langston estate as they strolled back down the corridor to their own rooms, relating how he'd become convinced that there was something loose in the chimney that made the ghostly rattles. He'd begged the Langstons to let him climb the chimney, but they'd refused. "I think they, like Mrs. Whitlock, liked believing that the manor house was haunted," he remarked as they came up to Cassie's door.

"Yes," she sighed as she turned to bid him good night, "I think it will be a real disappointment to Mrs. Whitlock when she learns there's no Rossiter ghost. Do you think we ought to keep our knowledge to ourselves and let the ghost wail at will whenever the wind is in the west?"

"Not on your life. I want to be able to sleep soundly at night. I shall tell Loesby to putty away the ghost first thing in the morning." He squeezed Cassie's hand. "Good night, my dear. I was glad to have had you at my side through this frightening ordeal. You've been a most intrepid adventurer tonight."

She gave an embarrassed little nod and whisked herself off into her room before he could see the blush of pleasure that suffused her cheeks. He, on his part, found himself smiling as he returned to his bed. It was the first time in weeks he'd smiled like that. Perhaps Loesby was right, he thought, as his eyes closed. Perhaps he *was* luckier in his bride than he had a right to expect.

Chapter Sixteen

*E*verything seemed cheerier the next morning. The wind had died, the sun shone and the temperature rose. Kittridge lingered over breakfast with his wife for almost an hour before taking himself off to his study. Cassie hummed to herself as she worked in her sitting room, mending a pair of gold velvet drapes for the drawing room. The future seemed to have promise after all.

But the end of the day changed everything. A carriage drove up to the door through the snowbanks just at sunset, and out jumped Sir Philip Sanford, their first visitor. He had started out for Lincolnshire just before the snowstorm and had been forced to put up at a nondescript hostelry for three boring days. "As soon as I heard that the roads were open, I came posthaste the rest of the way," he told his host as Loesby relieved him of his greatcoat. "Can't tell you how glad I am to be here at last."

"You started out before the snow?" Kittridge asked incredulously. "We'd been here less than a week. Didn't anyone ever tell you, you gudgeon, that newlyweds should be given some time alone before seeing guests? Have you never heard of a honeymoon?"

"Of course I have. But it's not as if you made a love match. I thought, under the circumstances, that you'd be glad to see me."

"I am glad to see you. I was only twitting you. And here's Cassie come down to greet you. I'll wager she's just as happy to see you as I am. It's been almost a fortnight since she's had any face to look at but mine and the servants'."

Cassie greeted their guest with shy warmth, but in truth she was not as glad to see him as she pretended. She had met Kittridge's friend only briefly, at the wedding, and felt him to be a stranger. Since strangers always made her uncomfortable, she had to strain to appear at ease. Sandy, however, was not the sort to put a hostess on edge. His moon-shaped face was cheerful, and conversation flowed easily from his tongue. It wasn't long before he won Cassie's liking, and within an hour from the time of his arrival, they were all three joking comfortably together in the sitting room like old friends.

It wasn't until dinnertime that the mood changed. They had just finished the first course, a modest offering of cabbage soup, filet of sole and buttered carrots that Mrs. Whitlock had concocted at the last minute, when Sandy remembered that Eunice had sent a packet of letters that had been delivered to her brother at the London address. He withdrew the packet from his coat pocket and tossed it across the table to his friend. While they waited for Loesby to serve the second course, Kittridge flipped through the envelopes. When he spied two large, square buff-colored envelopes, his expression changed. Without a word of explanation, he excused himself, picked up the envelopes and left the table. He did not return to the dining room. Cassie and Sandy were forced to conclude the meal without him.

By the time he did return, more than an hour had passed. Cassie and their guest had repaired to the sitting room and were making desultory conversation while Sandy sipped at a glass of port. Kittridge seemed not the same fellow that he'd been earlier. While his remarks to Sandy were friendly enough, his attitude toward his wife was formal and distant. Cassie couldn't understand it. What had happened to make him angry with her? She could only surmise that she'd committed some blunder that had earned his disapproval, but what that blunder was she couldn't imagine.

She lowered her head and sat in silent misery as Kittridge and Sandy conversed. They spoke of political events, discussed the illness of one of their mutual friends and reminisced at length about life in the Dragoons. Occasionally Sandy directed a remark in Cassie's direction, which she answered with a monosyllable, but her husband never turned his head in her direction. She endured his unkindness as long as she could, and then she excused herself and went to bed. She cried for several hours before she fell asleep.

Kittridge appeared in the breakfast room the next morning before Sandy came down. Cassie, heavy-eyed and miserable, was poking desultorily at a coddled egg. "Good morning, my dear," her husband said in an ordinary voice as he helped himself to the eggs and hot muffins that Loesby had set out on the sideboard. "I hope that Sandy's unexpected arrival did not discompose you."

"No, not at all," she murmured. "He is an easygoing guest. I . . . enjoyed his company."

"Yes, so did I." He took his place opposite her and began to eat. "I only asked because I thought you were unduly reticent last evening."

"Was I?" She looked across the table at him and took a deep breath. "If I was," she ventured bravely, "it was because I had the feeling that . . . that I had angered you."

His eyebrows rose in genuine surprise. "Angered me? You? Why on earth would you think so?"

She fixed her eyes on her egg. "Because you seemed . . . short with me."

"You're imagining things, Cassie. I don't remember being short with you, ever."

"It seemed so to me. You left the table before finishing your dinner, if you remember, and when you returned, you . . . you . . ." Here her courage failed her.

"Yes?" he prodded, studying her with a frown.

"Never mind," she muttered, reaching for the teapot. "It's not important."

"But it must be important. If my behavior offended you, you must say so. It won't do to keep silent on such matters."

"Well, Robert, if you insist on it, the truth is that you scarcely said a word to me all evening," she burst out bluntly.

"Oh. I see." He put down his fork, his brow furrowed. "I'm sorry, Cassie. I'd had some letters that . . . well, that spoiled my mood. But they had nothing to do with you, I assure you."

"Was that it?" she asked, shamed. "Now *I'm* sorry." She'd made a fuss for no reason. His letters had brought him bad news, and she'd thought about nothing but her own feelings. Now her sympathy was all for him. "I should not have taken offense. Forgive me, Robert. Was your news very troublesome?"

"No, nothing worth speaking of. Will you pass the teapot, my dear? I wonder if Sandy intends to sleep the morning away."

Recognizing that he had purposely turned the subject, she had no choice but to let the matter drop.

For the rest of the day, Kittridge went out of his way to be kind to her. Her company was requested for every activity the gentlemen engaged in; they even invited her to watch them play billiards. By evening they were so cozy together that Cassie could hardly believe her own ease of mind.

After dinner, the two friends insisted on teaching Cassie to play Ombre, a perfect card game for their circumstances, because it was three-handed. Her innocent enthusiasm for the game delighted the gentlemen, and when, at the end, she so far forgot her shyness as to give a loud curse when she lost, crying out, "Blast it, I should have played the six!" they all had a hearty laugh.

In the days that followed, Kittridge, busy making plans to renovate the farm buildings, expand the sheep herds and build new housing for tenants, found it necessary to go out with his land agent, Mr. Griswold, for several hours at a time, leaving Cassie to entertain their visitor. This task proved to be more pleasant than she expected. Sandy was always boyishly open and cheerful. And when he discovered that she'd been spending her days exploring the unopened rooms, looking for whatever small treasures of art or furnishings she could find, he eagerly requested permission to join her on her rambles.

They spent many agreeable hours exploring the house together. They dusted old paintings, peeped under Holland covers, and studied old vases for identifying marks. When they found many of their discoveries to be in an alarming state of disrepair, they decided to make a workshop of one of the third-floor rooms, where they could touch up the gilt on shabby picture frames, glue broken bits of porcelain together and refinish old pieces of furniture. The *ton* of London might have found such activities eccentric for a viscountess and a peer of the realm to indulge in, but, as Sandy pointed out, there were many among the *ton* whose eccentricities were much more reprehensible. "Besides," he added, "who in London would ever know?"

The indispensible Loesby installed a large wooden slab on two sawhorses as a worktable for them and supplied them with paints, brushes, sandpaper and tools. The two spent many hours contentedly laboring at restoring the many treasures the household contained.

During these explorations and restoration activities, Cassie found Sandy so easygoing and companionable that she forgot to be shy. On his part, Sandy discovered that the girl he'd thought too mousy and colorless for his friend was, instead, intelligent, witty and charming. Very soon, he completely forgot that he had ever thought otherwise.

One evening, after he'd spent a week in their company, Sandy announced to his friend Robbie that he'd decided to extend his stay another fortnight. "Might just as well," he explained. "I have no pressing engagements in town this month, and I'd as soon spend my evenings here quietly as dash about town, escorting insipid females to operas and balls and such."

Kittridge nodded in acquiescence. Cassie had already retired, but the two men had remained in their easy chairs at the sitting room fire. Their feet were propped up on the hearth, and they were contentedly drinking brandies from large snifters. "Stay as long as you like, old man," Kittridge said. "As far as I'm concerned, you're welcome for as long as you can endure this dull, bucolic life."

"I don't find it dull. Surprising, isn't it, that after the excitement of those long years of army life and then months of living in town, I can still enjoy the utter peace of the country?"

"No, not surprising. It's your nature, Sandy. You always see the best in everything."

"Are you saying that you don't?" Sandy studied his friend with sudden concern. "I thought you were beginning to find contentment, Robbie. Am I wrong?"

Kittridge shrugged. "I'm not discontent. I enjoy the challenge of estate management, at least so far. The days are not dull."

"But . . . ?" Sandy prodded.

His friend lowered his head. "But this is not the life I'd dreamed of."

"I know that. But, Robbie, you should consider yourself lucky. Cassie has turned out to be a gem, don't you agree?"

"Yes, I suppose so." Kittridge took a melancholy sip of his drink. "At least you and Loesby are agreed on it."

"But not you?"

"I said yes, didn't I? My wife is a pearl beyond price." He gave a short, bitter laugh. "And with a forty-thousand-pound dowry, I must consider myself fortunate indeed."

Sandy's genial face contorted into an unaccustomed glare. "She don't deserve that tone, Robbie. I think she *is* a pearl beyond price."

A shadow of pain darkened Kittridge's eyes. "Yes, I suppose she is. But you see, Sandy, I thought, once, that I would wed a diamond."

Chapter Seventeen

The weather warmed, the snow melted, and the inhabitants of Lincolnshire emerged from hibernation. Wagons again rolled on the roadways, and tradesmen appeared at the kitchen door with foodstuffs and supplies. Cassie began to interview candidates for staff positions in the household, and, with Loesby's help and Sandy's good-natured meddling, hired two housemaids, a scullery maid, an assistant cook to help Mrs. Whitlock in the kitchen, and a laundress. She left it to Loesby to engage footmen and stable help.

With the staff thus amplified, Cassie set about enlarging their living area. In addition to arranging for pleasant housing for the staff, she brightened up the dining room, readied a second guest room, ordered the new maids to clean and refresh the library and had the breakfast room repainted a sunny yellow. The only room she left untouched was the drawing room, explaining to Sandy that, since she'd taken out the best pieces for their sitting room, she was waiting for the opportunity to buy new furniture for the drawing room with the "pin money" her father had given her on her wedding day.

Sandy was still comfortably in residence when another carriage bearing guests arrived at their door. It was Eunice and her daughters. Kittridge, just returning from an outing with his land agent, was the first to greet them. "What a delightful surprise," he welcomed, picking up both his nieces in his arms.

"The girls insisted on seeing their Uncle Robbie before winter would make the trip north quite impossible," Eunice babbled, kissing her brother with warm affection. "Besides," she added, whispering with naughty malice in his ear, "I thought you would be dying of boredom by this time, stuck away here with no one to talk to but your mousy wife, so I came to save you."

But Kittridge was too engrossed in the children's happy chatter to pay her any heed.

The hallway was in veritable chaos by the time Cassie and Sandy came down from the third floor (where they'd been happily engaged in refinishing a fine old Henry Holland pier table) to see what was causing the commotion. The scene they came upon made them blink in astonishment. Mr. Whitlock and the two new footmen were running in and out, bringing in a mountain of boxes; the little girls were squealing with delight as their uncle tossed them, one after the other, in the air; the maids were scurrying about trying to help the new arrivals remove their outer garments; Miss Roffey, the governess, was attempting to calm the children's excitement; and Mrs. Whitlock was following Loesby (who himself was directing the footmen's placement of the luggage) about the hallway, attempting to discover how many mouths she would be expected to feed and when she would be expected to feed them.

Cassie hastily removed the soiled smock she was wearing and, acutely embarrassed by her stained fingers and general dishabille (especially in comparison to Eunice, who was resplendent in purple half-mourning), came slowly forward to welcome her guests. "Lady Yarrow," she said, flushing, "what a lovely surprise!"

"Ah, there you are, my dear," Eunice said, touching her sister-in-law's cheek with her own. "I was wondering where you were hiding. And *Sandy*! I had no idea you were still—" At that moment, her eye fell on the Constable painting on the south wall. "Good God, Robbie, what have you *done*?" she shrieked. "You've taken away the *portrait*!"

Cassie whitened. "The . . . portrait?" she gasped.

Kittridge set little Greta on her feet. "I don't know what you're talking about, Eunice. What portrait?"

"I think she means the p-painting that used to hang there . . . on the south w-wall," Cassie stammered, trembling in guilt and shame.

"Of course that's what I mean. The portrait of our greatgrandfather, Algernon Arthur Rossiter!"

"Oh, that," Kittridge said carelessly. "It must be somewhere about. Why all the fuss?"

Eunice stamped her foot petulantly. "But he belongs *here*! He's *always* been here. Really, Robbie, how *can* you have been so heedless of family tradition as to have taken him down?"

"*I* t-took him down, your ladyship," Cassie admitted miserably. "I didn't think . . . I'm sorry. I'll restore him to his rightful place this v-very day, I promise."

"There, you see? Nothing to fly into alt over," Kittridge said calmly, picking Greta up again and taking Della by the hand. "Cassie will set things to rights. Meanwhile, come upstairs, everyone, and let's sort out where you will all stay."

Eunice, satisfied by Cassie's promise, dropped the subject and followed her brother and the children up the stairs. Miss Roffey, Loesby and the servants trooped up after them. Cassie, shaken, just stood and watched. Sandy came up behind her and put a hand on her shoulder. "Don't take it so hard, Cassie," he said consolingly. "Eunice can be overbearing sometimes, but she's a good sort, really."

Cassie, who'd been hurt at school by just such "good sorts," was not consoled. "Is she?" she muttered dejectedly.

"Yes, she really is. I've known her for years, and I swear she can be the sweetest, most generous—"

Cassie, who'd been snubbed by her sister-in-law at their first meeting at the wedding, was not convinced. "I'm afraid you're blinded, Sandy—either by your natural optimism or by infatuation."

"Infatuation?" He drew himself up in real offense. "That's a jingle-brained thing to say."

Cassie was startled by the vehemence of his reaction. She turned to him in astonishment. "Heavens, Sandy, have I hit on something?"

Sandy began to utter a loud protest, but, too honest to maintain a pretense, stopped himself and shrugged. "I've always had a secret fancy for her," he admitted, his moon face reddening. "But that doesn't mean I condone her behavior when she acts so deucedly high-handed. She had no right to order you about. Robbie should have put her in her place. I'll have a word with him."

"No, please, Sandy," Cassie begged, a look of alarm leaping into her eyes. "Don't say anything to him. Robert is right. It is nothing to make a fuss over. You must promise not to devil Robert with this matter."

Sandy, not one who liked to indulge in arguments, promised. "But you must make me a promise, too," he bargained. "You must stop looking so Friday-faced. One would think, looking at you, that you've been bested in battle."

"I *have* been bested," she pointed out.

"Not on your life," Sandy declared. "The battle's not over yet."

Cassie smiled at him wanly. "I hope you're right. Meanwhile, for your sake, I'm glad we have Lady Yarrow's company."

He eyed her suspiciously. "If you're getting matchmaking ideas, Cassie, put them out of your mind. Eunice doesn't give me a passing thought. I'm not particularly delighted that she's here. But the children will be an entertaining addition to our circle."

"Yes, they will." She gave him a real smile at last and took his arm. "Come upstairs with me, Sandy, and let's see if we can find a suitable place for a nursery."

Sandy's promise prevented him from giving his friend Robbie a good scold. Loesby, however, was under no such constraints. "Yer sister likes t' rule the roost, don't she, Cap'n?" he remarked while laying out Lord Kittridge's evening clothes. "If I was yer wife, me nose'd be out o' joint."

"Would it indeed?" Kittridge asked absently as he buttoned his shirtsleeve. "And why is that?"

" 'Cause yer sister 'ad no right to order 'er t' replace the damn portrait, that's why. Me an' yer missus, 'er ladyship I mean, took real pains t' fix up the entryway. Lady Yarrow 'ad no right t' spoil it."

Kittridge made a dismissive gesture. "Confound it, Loesby, it's only a portrait. It doesn't spoil anything. Come, man, help me with this damnable neckerchief instead of moping about over female foolishness."

By dinnertime the forbidding portrait of the first viscount had been restored to its original place. Unfortunately for Cassie, however, Eunice's desire for restoration did not stop there. No sooner had her bags been unpacked than Eunice ordered that her bedroom be returned to its original solemnity (requiring Cassie to search for hours to find where she had stored the dismal paintings she'd taken from the room). Eunice also rejected Cassie's suggestion to locate the nursery in a bright suite of rooms with south-facing windows. She preferred instead to use the old nursery, where she'd spent summers as a child. Ignoring Cassie's shyly offered observation that the north-facing nursery might have been pleasant in the summer but might be hard to keep warm in this season, Eunice insisted not only on using those rooms, but on keeping everything in them just as they were when she was a child. Cassie, not able to bring herself to argue, felt as if she'd lost another skirmish.

During the days that followed, Eunice steadily usurped Cassie's place as mistress of the house. Having long been accustomed to running a household (her own with Yarrow and her mother's as well) without opposition, she took over the reins of household management at Highlands without giving a second thought to Cassie's superior claim to the position. Cassie, on the other hand, gave over those reins without a struggle. She had suffered humiliation at the hands of just such strong personalities at school and hadn't learned any means of survival except complete withdrawal. She thought about what Sandy had said about a battle, but she was no soldier. She didn't know the first thing about fighting. So, reverting to her earlier habits, she retired into her shell and became just what Eunice expected her to be—a mouse.

Chapter Eighteen

*W*ithin a week, Eunice had enlarged the staff by six: she'd hired a seamstress, a children's nurse, a butler, an abigail and dresser for her own use, and a drawing master for little Della. She also had taken over the selection of the daily menus, the arranging of the household staff's work schedule, and the choice of activities for the day for everyone in the household but her brother. Although there was an undercurrent of discontent in the household with this new arrangement, little was said aloud. Everyone felt that, since Lady Yarrow was only visiting for a few weeks, things would soon return to normal.

But, as Kittridge had long ago suggested, two women heading one household leads to strife. And strife was about to burst forth.

It came about when Eunice decided that the drawing room had to be made immediately habitable. She didn't see how they could exist without it. Using the little sitting room as a drawing room, as the family had been doing before she arrived, was, she declared, vulgar and gauche. She therefore ordered the footmen to take the chairs and furnishings that Cassie had removed from the drawing room for furnishing the sitting room and restore them to their original positions in the drawing room.

Cassie endured the denuding of her sitting room without a word. Sandy, appalled at Eunice's arrogance, asked Cassie why on earth she'd permitted it, but Cassie only said it didn't matter.

The work was completed in midafternoon of the very day Eunice instigated it, and she promptly put the room to use. She informed everyone that tea would be served, today and every day hence, in the drawing room.

Kittridge, engrossed in studying the intricacies of sheep breeding, was not aware of any of this. But on the day of the opening of the drawing room, he ceased his labors early and decided to go up to the nursery to spend an hour playing with his nieces. He found Miss Roffey there all alone. "Sir Philip came up and invited the children down to tea," she informed him.

He quickly ran down the stairs again. At the bottom he was accosted by a rotund stranger, who bowed with pompous formality and said, "Lady Yarrow is awaiting you in the drawing room, my lord."

"And who might you be?" his lordship demanded.

"I'm Dickie, my lord. The new butler."

"Oh? Lady Kittridge didn't tell me she'd engaged a butler," Kittridge muttered, puzzled.

"It was Lady Yarrow who engaged me," Dickie said.

"She did, did she? Seems to me I heard that she engaged a nursemaid and an abigail, too." His brows drew together in annoyance. "I think I'll have a word with Lady Yarrow," he said ominously.

"Yes, my lord," said the butler, who, though he guessed that his lordship seemed not to approve of his being hired, did not show a sign of distress in his impassive face. "You'll find her in the drawing room."

Kittridge wondered why his sister wanted him in the unused, overly large and draughty drawing room, but he set off down the hall. Before reaching his destination, however, he heard the sound of a child's laughter from the little sitting room and looked inside. He gaped in dismay at the sight that met his eyes. The room was empty of all furniture except a small table near the window. The large carpet that Cassie had installed was gone, and only a small four-by-six rug had been placed near the fire to replace it. Sandy was sitting on the rug, a teacup and saucer on the floor beside him, playing spillikins with Della, while Cassie was seated on the hearth with little Greta in her lap. She was feeding the child some hot tea with a spoon. "Good God!" Kittridge gasped. "What's *happened* here?"

"Uncew Wobit! Uncew Wobit!" Greta cried, trying to leap from Cassie's lap.

"Ah, Robbie," Sandy greeted, grinning up at him, "here you are at last! If you hadn't buried yourself away in your study all day, you'd have discovered that the drawing room's been restored. Your tea awaits you there."

"I'm winning, Uncle Robert," Della bragged, indicating the pieces scattered on the rug.

But her uncle scarcely heard her. "I don't understand," he said in confusion. "I thought, Cassie, that you prefer using this room."

Cassie threw him a nervous glance. "Eunice feels strongly that a small sitting room like this is a poor substitute for a proper drawing room."

"*Eunice* feels so? And you *agree* with her?" He ran a bewildered hand through his hair. "Then why aren't you there, taking your tea?"

"The room was too cold for the children," Sandy said, "so we took our cups and came here."

"Little Greta was shivering," Cassie added apologetically.

"I was shivewing, Uncew Wobit," Greta grinned, proud of being talked about.

Kittridge stepped over the threshold, still confused and dismayed. "Knowing that the drawing room is a draughty barn, why on earth, Cassie, did you permit Eunice to do this? I thought we were all agreed that we were more comfortable here."

Cassie didn't know what to say. "Well, you see, I . . . I . . ."

Sandy came to her aid. "When does your sister Eunice ever ask permission?" he asked sardonically.

As the situation began to become clear to him, his lordship's expression hardened. "Are you suggesting, Sandy, that Eunice took it upon herself, without asking Cassie, to rearrange this house?"

"So it seems," Sandy responded carelessly, turning back to his game.

"Is this true, Cassie?"

Cassie's eyes met his, wavered and dropped. "I don't blame her for wishing to keep the house as it was, Robert. I understand the feeling one has about the places of one's childhood. There is a tradition in houses, you know. Tradition is not something to be despised. It is, after all, one of the few links that we have to the past."

"Nonsense," Sandy said in what was for him a tone of strong disapproval. "A tradition that insists that every chair must remain where one's ancesters placed it is . . . is . . ."

"Sheer sentimentality," Kittridge finished for him. "Didn't I say before, Cassie, that I don't give a hang for such nonsensical traditions? Confound it, ma'am, this is *your* house, not Eunice's."

"But if your sister—" Cassie began.

"Good Lord, Cassie," Sandy cut in, "don't make excuses for Eunice! It's time Robbie learned the truth about his sister." He paused for a moment, looking down at where the happy Della was making the winning throw in their game, and then, while the child chortled gleefully, he got to his feet and faced his friend. "I yield to no one in my admiration for your sister, Robbie, old fellow, but she does sometimes have a high-handed way about her."

"Now, Sandy—" Cassie said in disapproval, hoping to stop him.

But Kittridge cut her off. "Am I right in assuming, Cassie, that you didn't give Eunice permission to engage that stiff-rumped butler either? Or all the other maids?"

"Well, I . . ."

Sandy glared at her. "Speak up, Cassie, dash it! Of course you didn't!"

Kittridge stared at his wife for a long, silent moment. Then, without a word, he strode over to where she sat, pulled the teacup from her hand, set it down on the hearth, plucked Greta from her arms and carried the child to Sandy. "Take the girls up to Miss Roffey, will you please, Sandy?" he asked, his mouth tight.

"But Uncle Robert, we want to play horsey with you," Della whined.

"Yeth, Uncew Wobit," Greta chimed in, "*hawthy!*"

"Later, my loves, later," Kittridge said shortly, crossing back to where Cassie still sat. He took her by one hand and pulled her to her feet. "As for you, ma'am," he said between clenched teeth, "you will come with me!"

Pulling her ruthlessly behind him, he strode out of the sitting room and down the hall to the drawing room. He burst into the room, banging the doors open with so great a crash that his sister, who'd been sitting near the tea table sipping her tea in solitary splendor, shuddered with fright, causing most of the tea to slosh over into her lap. "*Robbie!* What on earth—?"

He yanked Cassie across the room until the two of them stood in front of his flabbergasted sister. "Tell me, Eunice, do you know who this is?" he snapped.

"What?" She looked up at her brother in utter bafflement.

"Do you know who this is?" he repeated even more angrily.

"Have you lost your *wits*? Of *course* I—"

"Then *what is her name?*"

"Her *name?*" Her eyes were popping in stupefaction. "Cassie, of course. But what—?"

"Her *full name!*"

"Cassandra Rossiter *née* Chivers."

"Never mind the Chivers. Her *present* name, with title and address, if you please."

"Robbie, what is this all about? I don't understand—"

"There's nothing to understand. I want you to tell me this woman's *full name!*"

"Oh, very well! But I think, Robbie, that you've gone berserk!"

"Her *name,* please!" Kittridge thundered.

Eunice threw up her hands. "Cassandra Rossiter, Viscountess Kittridge, of Highlands, Lincolnshire."

"Ah, then you *do* know," he said, his voice dripping with sarcasm.

His sister gaped at her brother in confused frustration. "Of course I know. What nonsense *is* this?" Leaning forward, she turned to Cassie in appeal. "*Tell* me, Cassie, *please!* What is this all about?"

But Cassie seemed not to hear. She was staring up at her husband with eyes so wide she seemed mesmerized. What Eunice could not know was that Cassie was gazing at a golden knight, the same one who had done battle for her once before and was now doing it again. The look she'd fixed on her husband was one of sheer adoration.

"What this is about, sister mine," Kittridge was saying, "is your apparent ignorance of the fact this this lady, whom you evidently *do* recognize as the Viscountess Kittridge, is *my wife* and the *mistress of this house.*"

"What is the *matter* with you, Robbie?" Eunice asked in bewildered chagrin. "I am not ignorant of that fact."

"You must be. Why else would you take it upon yourself to move her furniture about and hire her servants and run her household?"

His meaning began to dawn on Eunice. She fell back against the chair. "But, Robbie, I didn't mean to—"

"Not meaning to is a very lame excuse."

"I know this is her household to run," Eunice said shakily. "Surely, Robbie, you don't believe I *intended* to . . . to . . ."

"To slight my wife?" Kittridge supplied icily. "Your intentions were good, is that what you mean? Have you perhaps heard, Eunice, of the destination of the road paved with good intentions? Frankly, I don't believe your intentions *were* good, but even if you meant well, the result was both arrogant and harmful."

Eunice had never been spoken to in such a tone by her brother. "Oh, Robbie!" she cried, quite overset. "I'm so . . . . sorry!"

"You should be. But sorries are not enough. You will make up for the damage you've wreaked, and at once. Firstly, Eunice, you will restore everything to the way it was when you arrived. Secondly, you will offer my wife a sincere apology. And, furthermore—"

Cassie placed a light hand on his arm. "That's enough, Robert," she said, low-voiced. "Eunice has already apologized. Twice."

The softness of her voice halted the outpouring of his anger. He looked down at his wife, blinking her face into focus. "Did she?" he asked. "I did not hear—"

"Perhaps you were only listening to yourself," Cassie suggested gently.

Eunice stared at her sister-in-law as if she'd never seen her before. "I *am* sorry, Cassie," she said, her eyes filling. "I never meant to . . ." But, realizing she was making the same lame excuse again, she burst into tears, rose from her chair and ran from the room.

Cassie looked after her with a troubled frown. "Go after her, Robert."

"No," his lordship snapped. "Let her weep. She deserves a little suffering."

"Then so do I, because this whole muddle is my fault, too."

Kittridge, surprised, took his wife by the shoulders and turned her to him. "How, my dear," he asked, finding himself suddenly calmed by his wife's gentle self-possession, "can this possibly be your fault?"

"Because I *permitted* her to have her way. I should have held out against her."

"Yes, you should have," he agreed, taking his wife's chin in his hand and tilting up her face, trying to force her to meet his eye. "You are my wife, Cassie. Why are you so afraid to act the role?"

She lifted her eyes to his at last and gave him a long, level look. "Perhaps because it *is* a role," she said.

His comprehension of what she'd said dawned slowly. "Of course," he muttered, feeling stunned. "How *can* you feel like a wife if our bond is largely a pretense? We are two strangers under one roof."

She lowered her head in painful agreement. "That's why it was hard for me to act your wife before a sister who is more your . . . your intimate than I am."

Sadly, he pulled her to him and rested his cheek on her hair. "My sweet Cassie! What you mean to say, in that quiet way of yours, is that, in truth, all this is more my fault than anyone's."

She stayed in his arms for a moment, savoring the tenderness of his affectionate gesture. Then, lifting her hand and brushing it ruefully on his cheek, she withdrew from his embrace. "It's not your fault that I don't feel like a wife," she said, turning and moving slowly to the door. "It's the fault of our unnatural situation. Perhaps it was all a dreadful mistake. Perhaps we . . ." She threw him a last, sorrowful look before departing. "Perhaps *I* never should have done it."

Chapter Nineteen

$\mathcal{D}$inner that night was a silent affair. Everyone looked gloomy, even the butler, who surmised that his days in this house were numbered. Sandy tried to keep up a flow of cheerful conversation, but since a monologue is difficult to maintain for very long, even he admitted defeat by the end of the first course and lapsed into silence. Finally, over dessert, Eunice spoke up. "I shall be leaving tomorrow," she announced in a tearful voice.

Kittridge put down his fork. "That," he said bluntly, "is a coward's revenge."

"Be still, Robert," his wife scolded gently. "You've said enough unkind things to your sister today. Lady Yarrow, you surely are not serious about leaving. You promised to stay for at least another week."

Eunice put up her chin. "Yes, but under the circumstances, I think I am justified in breaking that promise. You needn't worry, Robert. I will see that everything is put back as it was before I go."

"I've seen to that already," her brother retorted.

"Then you can have no objections to my departure," Eunice said sullenly.

"Only that taking your leave now sounds very much like the sulks to me."

"I wish, Lady Yarrow, you'd reconsider," Cassie urged. "We should all be very sorry to see you leave so abruptly."

"You needn't be polite to me, my dear," Eunice said proudly. "After my arrogant and insensitive behavior, you cannot pretend to wish to endure my presence among you any longer."

"But I do wish it," Cassie insisted. "No pretense."

Eunice knit her brows, puzzled. "Why would you want me to stay, after what I've done, if not for mere politeness?"

"Because I believe we will do better now," Cassie responded with a small smile. "Don't you agree? Now that the barriers between us have been somewhat breached, might we not become better acquainted at last?"

Eunice gave her sister-in-law a long, considering look. "Yes, my dear, I begin to think we might. I'm suddenly realizing, Cassie, that I have more to learn about you than I had at first believed." Wavering, she fiddled with her wine glass. "But surely Robbie has had his fill of my company," she mumbled with uncharacteristic uncertainty.

"You know better than that, my dear," her brother assured her. "And even if it were true, I would still hate to lose the company of your daughters."

"Besides," Sandy added, "you can't take the children away now. Greta seems to have a cough."

From across the table Eunice gaped at him in amazement. "You, of all people, Sandy, cannot pretend you wish me to stay."

"I?" Sandy asked, reddening. "What do you mean?"

"You haven't said a kind word to me since I arrived. You've done nothing but criticize my every move."

Sandy gave her a teasing grin. "But that was only because every move you made was misguided."

"Don't mind him, Lady Yarrow," Cassie put in. "I promise you that he wants your company as much as any of us."

"Very well, Cassie, I'll reconsider," her sister-in-law said, "but only on the condition that you stop calling me Lady Yarrow."

The awkwardness thus put behind them, they were able to spend the rest of the evening pleasantly enough. However, Eunice made it an early evening, explaining that she wanted to look in on Greta before going to bed. Sandy soon followed, leaving Kittridge and Cassie alone. In unspoken agreement, they made their way up the stairs together and headed toward their bedrooms, Kittridge so lost in contemplation that Cassie refrained from making a sound. Only when she paused at her door did he shake himself into awareness. "I've been poor company, I'm afraid," he apologized. "I haven't been able to put out of my head the things you said this afternoon."

"I wish we would all put the events of this afternoon out of our minds," she said, coloring.

"I don't. You gave us some moments of rare honesty. It was good both for Eunice and me to hear the truth for once." He took his wife's hand in his and added thoughtfully, "I thank you, too, for your gentle handling of Eunice this evening. It would have made a harmful family rift if she'd gone back to town in a sulk. Are you sure you won't mind enduring her presence for what remains of her fortnight's visit?"

"Not at all. I think she and I will get on famously together now. Thanks to you."

His eyebrows rose. "To me?"

"Of course." She smiled shyly up at him. "She won't dare to oppose me in anything more, not after you stood up to her so . . . so nobly in my behalf."

"Nobly? Do you now call my explosion of temper noble?"

"It *was* noble, Robert. You were like a . . . a knight of old, championing your lady in distress."

"Good God! Is *that* how you saw me?"

"Oh, yes!" A flush suffused her cheeks, but she admitted it anyway. "That is *exactly* how I saw you."

He peered down at her, trying to make out her expression in the dim light of the hallway that was illuminated by only a few candles set in widely spaced sconces on the walls. "Even though you used that so-noble scene as an opportunity to point out to me how far we are from being a truly wedded couple?" he asked in disbelief.

"That has nothing to do with it. The knights of old often championed ladies who were not their wives."

He grinned ruefully. "So, though I'm a failure as a husband, I make a passable knight?"

"Oh, much more than passable, my lord," she insisted, a dimple he'd never before noticed appearing in her cheek. "Quite glorious, in fact."

"Glorious!" A laugh burst out of him, but his smile immediately faded. "Cassie, my lady," he muttered, pulling her to him, "you *are* a pearl. I don't deserve you."

Startled at finding herself in his arms for the second time that day, Cassie blinked up at him openmouthed. He, on his part, was startled too. He hadn't expected to embrace her but, having done so, found himself reluctant to let her go. There was something both touching and enticing about the adoring way she was gazing up at him. The color in her cheeks fascinated him, too, with its tendency to pale or redden with the changes in her emotions. And her hair, bursting wildly, as always, from the restraining ribbon with which she'd tied it back, seemed so alive with glints of reddish light that he felt a powerful urge to bury his fingers in its curls. But in the end it was her mouth, which until this moment he'd found too full-lipped for his taste, that suddenly seemed more irresistibly desirable than anything else, and to that urge he succumbed. Forgetting for the moment all the doubts and qualms that had kept him distant from her all these weeks, he kissed her with hungry abandon.

But before either of them had a chance to realize fully what was happening, a cough from down the hall caused them to jump apart. It was Dickie, the new butler. "I beg pardon, my lord," he said impassively. "I was on my way to turn down your bed."

"Thank you, but that won't be necessary," his lordship said irritably. "My man will have taken care of that."

"Then I will say good night, my lord. Good night, my lady." With that he turned about stiffly and disappeared down the stairs.

Kittridge glared after him. "Damned jobbernowl!" he cursed. "I hope, Cassie, that you intend to sack that fellow."

"Only if Loesby is willing to continue to play the double role of butler and valet," Cassie said, feeling a joyful, if budding, confidence in herself as head of the household. "And if he is," she added with a giggle, "then I shall let Eunice do the sacking."

"Very well," Kittridge grunted, glumly aware that a special moment had been spoiled beyond repair. He turned and started toward his bedroom. "Then I'll say good night, my dear."

Cassie watched him open his door, her eyes shining. The moment had not been spoiled for her. "Good night, Robert," she whispered, her soft voice revealing no sign that her heart was singing inside her. But sing it did. If a real marriage depended on intimacy, it said to her, tonight had been a beginning.

Chapter Twenty

*W*hen Cassie asked him, Loesby admitted that he cared little for butlering. He'd never considered himself a proper butler and had no aspirations in that direction. He therefore encouraged Cassie to keep Dickie on. "I know 'e's a top-lofty sprag," the valet said with cocky assurance, "but don't ye fret about 'im, me lady. I'll take the fellow down if 'e gets too 'igh in the instep."

Kittridge made a face when Cassie told him what had been decided, but since he'd left the staffing of the house in her hands, he accepted her decision. Eunice, however, was delighted. She considered a "proper butler" *de rigueur* in a well-run household, and Dickie was just the style she liked. To show her appreciation for Cassie's concession to her wishes, she had the portrait of the first viscount removed from the Great Hall and the Constable landscape rehung, a detail that Kittridge, when he'd ordered the sitting room restored, had forgotten.

A few contented days passed, marred only by the fact that little Greta's cough persisted. But since the child was not feverish, no one was particularly alarmed. The days were busy, and in the evenings the four adults found many ways to amuse themselves. They played hearts and silver-loo until cards began to pall; they spent a few delightful hours in the music room when Cassie was discovered to be quite adept at the piano and was able to accompany Eunice, who sang the most enjoyable ditties in a praiseworthy contralto; they repaired once or twice to the billiard room, where the ladies watched the gentlemen compete; and they made companionable conversation in front of the sitting room fire. It soon became apparent that Sandy had more than a friendly interest in Eunice, and when, one morning, she put aside her half-mourning and came downstairs in a dress of gray-green muslin, he took it as a most encouraging sign. With Kittridge treating Cassie with what seemed a growing affection, and Eunice and Sandy smelling of April and May, the house was a happy place indeed.

The atmosphere took an abrupt turn, however, when a messenger arrived from town. He'd been sent by the dowager Lady Kittridge to deliver a package of letters that had been posted to the viscount's London address. Kittridge rifled through the pile while all four were seated at the dinner table. Cassie noticed with concern that his mouth suddenly tightened at the sight of two of the same distinctive, square, buff-colored envelopes that had disturbed him the last time he'd received letters from London. As soon as his eyes lit on them, he excused himself from the table and, taking the letters away with him, disappeared into his study for the rest of the evening. He didn't emerge even to say good night to his guests.

The next morning, when he appeared at breakfast, it was apparent to Cassie, if not to anyone else, that his smiles and polite demeanor were forced. And the morning greeting he gave his wife was much cooler and more remote than it had been all week. It was as if the fondness that had been growing between them had suddenly died. But before she could inquire into the reason for the withdrawing of his affection and the change in his mood, Miss Roffey came down to tell Eunice that Greta's cough had worsened considerably and that her forehead was very hot to the touch. The four ran upstairs to look at the child, hoping they would discover that the governess had exaggerated. But Miss Roffey had, rather, understated the problem. It was immediately obvious that little Greta was seriously ill.

Lord Kittridge, inquiring of Mr. Whitlock the direction of the nearest doctor, was horrified to discover that there was none closer than twelve miles to the south, in the town of Withern. And even there, the physician, Dr. Horace Sweeney, was elderly and, in Whitlock's view, not particularly praiseworthy. On the other hand, he said, there was an apothecary right down the road—a Mr. Phineas Church—who was much admired by the locals for his ability to diagnose ailments and his skill in prescribing curative nostrums. In order to leave no stone unturned, Kittridge decided to send for both. He dispatched Loesby southward to fetch the distant doctor, while he himself went for the apothecary.

He came back in half an hour with Mr. Church, a half-bald, excruciatingly thin fellow with a black-ribboned pince-nez perched on his very long nose. The apothecary examined Greta carefully. He listened to her cough with his ear against her chest, he tapped his fingers on her back, and he looked down her throat. "A putrid infection of the bronchia," he pronounced when he was done.

Kittridge and Cassie exchanged worried glances, while Eunice burst into frightened tears.

"It'll do ye no good to weep, ma'am," the apothecary said disparagingly. "It'll do ye better to set to work an' get the child's fever down. We don't want to see the infection deepen to pneumonia."

"Pneumonia!" Eunice paled at the dreaded word and tottered backward.

Sandy put a supporting arm about her. "He didn't say she had pneumonia yet," he pointed out.

Mr. Church reached for the large, black bag he'd carried in. "I'll cup 'er now," he explained, "since bleeding is a prescribed remedy for coughs. An' again tomorrow, if the fever is still high. But no more, for I don't want to weaken the child. What *you* must do, my lady, is to make the child perspire. Keep 'er warm, an' watch to see she don't throw off 'er blankets. Diaphoretic drinks will help. A hot tisane of barley water and lemon every few hours—that's the thing."

Greta moaned and tossed about in her bed, causing all eyes to turn to her. "Shouldn't she be given some mercury water?" Eunice asked fearfully, not at all sure that Mr. Church's advice was sound. "And perhaps James's Powders?"

"Quackery, ma'am, sheer quackery," the apothecary snapped. "Now stand aside an' hand me my cupping glass."

After the child was bled and Mr. Church had taken his leave, Eunice and Cassie remained in the sickroom. They covered the pale, shivering child with several warm comforters and watched as she fell into a fitful sleep. Cassie suggested that Miss Roffey be kept out of the sickroom so that she would not carry any infection to her other charge. Eunice nodded, grateful for the suggestion. Next to getting Greta well, it was imperative to keep Della from falling victim to the same complaint. And since Eunice didn't intend to leave her baby's side, Miss Roffey's assistance in the sickroom would not be needed.

The doctor from Withern arrived four hours later. Dr. Sweeney was the apothecary's opposite. He was short, potbellied and had a full head of white hair topping his apple-cheeked face. His manner, too, was the opposite of Phineas Church's, being obsequious and optimistic where the apothecary had been dour and curt. "Oh, not pneumonia," he assured them cheerfully. "She won't develop pneumonia, my word on it. With a little bleeding and a little medication, she's bound to recover."

"What medication?" Eunice asked, eager to believe him.

"Leave that to me, my lady," the doctor chuckled, patting her shoulder. "A little of this and a little of that."

"Mercury water?" Sandy probed. "James's Powders?"

"Mercury water, of course. But I prefer a powder of my own concoction, made up of ground eggshells, raw turnips, sugar candy and a few secret things."

"Quackery, ma'am, sheer quackery," Kittridge whispered into Eunice's ear.

Eunice, shaken by her brother's disparagement of the doctor, pulled Cassie aside. "Robbie thinks Dr. Sweeney's a quack," she said worriedly. "Now I don't know whom to believe."

"Neither do I," Cassie said, "but my instincts lean toward Mr. Church."

Sandy, when questioned, indicated a preference for Dr. Sweeney, an optimist like himself. Eunice, unable to reject the practitioner who offered the cheerier prognosis, elected to believe the doctor. She let him bleed Greta again, and she accepted a supply of his powder. But when he was about to force a dose of mercury water down the groggy child's throat, her confidence failed her. Mercury water was strong medicine for a child. She gave a little outcry as she stood frozen with indecision.

It was her brother who stopped the doctor's hand. Kittridge had long objected to the use of mercury as a curative. A medical man he'd met in the Dragoons had remarked to him that he'd never known mercury to deliver a proven cure. And the apothecary had not wanted to use it, either. His sister's frightened outcry was enough to push him to action. "We'll give it to her later," his lordship said, wrenching the spoon from Dr. Sweeney's hold. "Thank you, doctor, for coming all this way. My man will see you home."

Eunice didn't scold Kittridge for preventing Dr. Sweeney from further medicating her daughter, for her confidence in the elderly doctor was not strong. And it soon became obvious that even permitting him to bleed Greta had been a mistake; the cupping had weakened the child. Greta lay limply on the pillows, too sapped even to toss. Only when a cough racked her did she move. "Perhaps Mr. Church was right after all," Eunice murmured, bending over her stricken child helplessly.

Cassie, who'd believed in the apothecary from the first, remembered his advice and ran for another tisane. Happily, the hot drink seemed to soothe the invalid, and she soon fell asleep again. Eunice, now convinced that her faith in Dr. Sweeney had been misplaced, handed Cassie the envelope of powders that the good-natured doctor had given her. "You may take this concoction of eggshells and turnips and secrets," she muttered, "and toss it to the winds."

Eunice sat beside the child half the night. In the wee hours, Cassie tiptoed into the sickroom and prevailed upon Eunice to go to her room and get some sleep. She took over the vigil until daylight.

When the apothecary called the next morning, he scolded them all for permitting the child to be bled again. "I warned ye it would weaken her," he muttered, feeling Greta's forehead. "I'll not bleed the poor little tyke again. Nothing to do now but keep 'er warm. Don't let 'er kick the covers off. A mustard pediluvia, mayhap, when she's better, but the barley-lemon tisane'll do more than any quackish medicine, that I promise ye, but I can't promise any more. I'll be back to look at 'er tomorrow, for all the good that'll do. The fever'll break if it's God's will." And with that meager hope, he left them.

For three terrifying days, they watched at Greta's bedside, taking turns. Eunice and Cassie shared the nights, Kittridge and Sandy the days. Sometimes the child slept fitfully, but mostly she tossed about in a kind of stupor, her hair matted on her forehead and her cheeks ruddy with her internal burning. It broke all their hearts to see the little girl suffer and to be so powerless to do anything about it.

Sometime during the third night, Kittridge, who couldn't sleep, came in to the sickroom to see his niece. He found Cassie struggling with Greta on the bed, trying to hold the comforters over the shuddering child. "Thank God you've come," Cassie flung over her shoulder at him. "She's having convulsions."

Lord Kittridge tensed in alarm. "What can we do?"

"I'm not sure, but I think she's entirely too hot. Perhaps . . . do you think a cool cloth on her forehead—? Here, hold her while I get one."

They struggled for almost an hour against the terrifying tremors that racked Greta's little body, but after a time it became apparent that, slowly, the convulsions were subsiding. When at last Greta ceased to shake, Cassie and Kittridge expelled long sighs, as if they'd both held their breaths until they were sure Greta was safe. Then Cassie, with Kittridge's help, washed the child down and changed her nightgown, and they tucked her in between clean, dry sheets. As Kittridge spread a comforter over her, Greta's lashes fluttered. "Uncew Wobit!" she managed to croak before her eyelids drooped and she fell promptly to sleep.

"Uncew Wobit," Cassie mimicked in joyful relief, eyes glowing, "I think she's *better*!"

"Thanks to you," Kittridge said in a choked voice.

He held out his arms to her, his eyes warm with admiration and tenderness. Cassie's heart leaped up to her throat as she took a step toward him. Perhaps this would be the moment for another step toward the intimacy she so dearly craved. But at that very moment, as abruptly as the dousing of a candle flame, something in his face changed. It was as if a light within him had been instantly extinguished. Some thought or memory had crossed his mind, and, whatever it was, it effectively blocked any intention he might have had of making an advance in her direction. His arms dropped, and he actually took a step back from her.

Cassie's heart clenched painfully, and one hand, of its own volition, came up in appeal. "Robert?" she asked, bewildered.

He took her hand in his, but the gesture was awkward and stiff. "You were remarkable this night," he said, a rigid politeness diluting the effect of his admiration. "Eunice and I will always be grateful. Always." Then he kissed her hand with distant formality and was gone.

When Eunice came in the next morning, she found Greta sleeping comfortably, the ruddy color of her cheeks much less fiery and her forehead actually cool. The worn-out mother stood for a long moment at the foot of the bed, gazing lovingly at the child for whom, the past few nights, she'd prayed with fervent desperation. Then she turned her eyes to Cassie, whose very appearance had changed for her. The woman she'd considered a "mousy nobody" now seemed—after all the hours they'd spent in shared tension and fear—a wise, devoted, supportive friend. "Oh, Cassie," she sighed, embracing her sister-in-law with tremulous gratitude, tears of relief running down her cheeks, "this is the happiest morning of my life."

"I know," Cassie said, fondly mopping her sister-in-law's cheeks with a handkerchief. "Mine too." That was not a lie, Cassie realized. She was truly overjoyed at Greta's recovery. And since the possibility of happiness from another quarter was becoming more and more remote, this might very well be as much happiness as she was ever likely to find.

Chapter Twenty-one

It was not clear to Cassie, during the critical days of Greta's illness, how much Robert's gloomy mood was affected by his concern for his niece's health and how much by some other cause. But when the child began a steady, even cheerful, convalescence, and the signs of strain still showed about his lordship's mouth, Cassie knew beyond a doubt that his below-the-surface misery had another source. She tried to probe for the cause, asking him outright one morning, when they were alone at breakfast, if his letters had brought him bad news again. He again turned the subject, thus effectively cutting off any possibility of pursuing the matter.

It was a rainy morning, only a few days after Greta's fever had broken. Cassie sat staring at her husband across the breakfast table, wondering in despair if there was anything she could do to break the stalemate that her relationship with Robert had become. It was only a week since the day, so special in her memory, when, by an act of breathtaking intimacy, he'd revealed a sincere desire to transform the peculiar bond that tied them to each other into a real marriage. What was it, she kept asking herself, that had happened to cause him to back away? She knew, this time, that it was no act of hers that had deterred him. The change in him was directly traceable to the letters. But if he didn't wish to share his secret troubles with her, there didn't seem to be anything she could do about it. No matter how many ways she turned the problem over in her mind, she could discover no way to coax him to open up to her. She was at an impasse.

She reached for the teapot. "Della will be devastated by the rain," she remarked, hoping to reach him by some other route. "She was expecting to take a riding lesson this morning, but after what happened to Greta, Eunice is too frightened of the possibility of chills to permit her to go outdoors in the rain. Would you like to go up to the nursery with me, Robert? I'm sure that only a visit from her Uncle Robert will put a smile on Della's face."

Kittridge shook his head, not looking up from the paper he was studying. "I'm expecting Griswold in ten minutes. Tell Della I'll see her at teatime."

"That will be small consolation," Cassie remonstrated mildly. "In the morning, teatime can seem a year away to a child her age."

Kittridge gathered up his papers and got to his feet. "That may be, but even children must be made to realize that business must come before pleasure. First things first, Cassie," he muttered defensively as he headed out the door, "first things first."

"First things first, indeed," she mocked sarcastically under her breath when he'd gone. "And will you use that excuse, my lord, when you have children of your own?" But of course it was a silly question. The way things were going, he was not likely to have children of his own at all.

She spent the morning in the nursery, helping Eunice to keep the children busy with rainy-day activities. Playing with the girls was so entertaining she almost forgot her troubles. But after luncheon, when not only the children but Eunice, too, took to their beds for a nap, her problems returned to her consciousness in full force. Sore at heart, she headed for the third-floor workshop, hoping that some purposeful physical activity would distract her from this dreadful self-pity. Refinishing the old Henry Holland table had given her pleasure in the days before Eunice came. Perhaps it would again.

It was there in the workshop that Sandy found her an hour later. But she was not working. She'd evidently prepared for work by pushing up the sleeves of her gown and covering herself with an apron, but she was absolutely immobile. She'd seated herself on a stool at the worktable with a pot of varnish in front of her and a brush in her hand, but her eyes were fixed on the raindrops making rivulets on the windowpanes. "You won't make much progress just sitting there, Cassie," he greeted with genial raillery, but he stopped himself as soon as he saw the unhappy expression in her eyes. "I'm sorry, my dear," he apologized at once. "I didn't know— Have I barged in at the wrong time?"

She shook herself out of the doldrums with an effort of will and smiled up at him wanly. "Of course not, Sandy. I was only . . . thinking."

"They were not very happy thoughts, I fear." His voice was warm with sympathy.

"The rain depressed me," she mumbled, putting down her brush and picking up a little stick with which to stir the varnish.

"Don't lie to me, my girl. It wasn't the rain." He perched on a stool opposite her. "You needn't tell me your thoughts, of course, if you don't wish to, but I'm quite willing to give you a penny for them."

She looked at the stirring stick as if she didn't know what to do with it. "I was only thinking that . . . that I may g-go home to my father for a while."

"What?" Sandy peered at her, troubled. "Do you mean it, Cassie? Soon?"

"I don't know. In a day or two, I suppose."

"But why? Have you had a message from him? Is he ill?"

She shook her head. "No, nothing like that. It's only a . . . a whim."

"Oh, don't leave us just for a whim, Cassie. That would be cruel to your guests, you know. What would we do without you? What would *Robbie* do without you?"

Abruptly she started to stir the varnish with unwonted vigor. "Robbie would do very well without me. He probably wouldn't even notice I'd gone."

"Cassie!" Sandy exclaimed in surprise. "You don't mean that!"

The hand stirring the thick liquid slowed. "No, of course I don't," she said in a small voice. "I shouldn't have said that."

He reached across the table and took her hand. "You can say anything you like to me, Cassie," he said seriously, "you know that. You needn't guard your tongue with me. I hope you know that I am, and always will be, your friend."

"I know," she said quietly.

"Then tell me what's wrong. Have you and Robbie quarreled?"

"We never quarrel," she sighed. "I sometimes wish we would."

"Why would you wish anything so silly? What good is quarreling?"

"It has its purpose in a marriage, I think. It brings things out in the open. It shows feeling. It clears the air."

"Yes, I suppose you're right. But you can't run home to your father because you and Robbie *don't* quarrel. That makes no sense."

She looked up at him earnestly. "Does it make sense if my reason is that I'm tired of living with a stranger?"

"Robbie? A stranger?" He frowned at her disapprovingly. "How can you say such a thing?"

"Robert said it himself. And it's quite true. He shares nothing of his deeper thoughts with me. He tells me nothing of his feelings, or his cares . . ."

Sandy was surprised. "Doesn't he?"

"No. Never."

"Then perhaps he doesn't feel there's anything significant to tell you."

"But there is, Sandy. That's just it. There is."

"There is? What makes you think so?"

"He seems so . . . troubled."

"It's the estate, I suppose," Sandy speculated. "I know the responsibility of making the estate show a profit weighs heavily on him, but that's not something he would care to burden his wife with. You can't blame him for wishing to put those problems aside when he joins the family for amusement and relaxation at the end of the day."

"No, it's not the estate," she insisted glumly. "It's something else."

"What makes you so certain?"

She hesitated before replying. Then, as if driven by a need to unburden her heart, she went on. "Did you notice, Sandy, the night the messenger brought the letters from London, that Robert left the table and never returned?"

"Yes, but that was only—" He stopped himself abruptly.

"Only what?"

Sandy didn't answer. His eyes dropped from her face in sudden awkwardness.

Cassie's heart began to pound. "*Sandy*! Do *you know* why he left the table that night?"

"Well, yes," he said, studying her with a puzzled frown. "Don't you?"

"Would I be asking if I knew? Please tell me, Sandy. Was it something in those envelopes? The square, buff-colored ones?"

Sandy shrugged. "I would have thought you'd have guessed. Those letters were from Elinor."

"Elinor? Who's Elinor?"

Sandy gasped. "Weren't you ever told about her?"

"Evidently not. Who is she?"

"Damnation!" he cursed, getting up from the table in perturbation. "I've been too free with my tongue! I thought you *knew*. I thought everyone in *London* knew."

"Well, I don't, so I wish you'd stop talking in riddles and tell me."

He blinked down at her, his moon face tensing with anxiety. "I don't know if I should, under the circumstances. Perhaps Robbie doesn't want you to know. I could bite out my blasted tongue!"

"Oh, my heavens!" Cassie exclaimed, her eyes widening in sudden, painful understanding. "This Elinor is someone special to him, is that it?"

"Cassie, I . . . Must I say?"

"Please, Sandy, yes! I feel as if I've been blundering about all this time in darkness." Her large eyes looked up to his beseechingly. "Did he . . . does he . . . *love* her?"

His instinctive good nature could not resist the appeal in her eyes. "Dash it all, Cassie," he swore, sitting down and reaching for her hand again, "*someone* should have told you! They were going to be married, you see. They'd intended to announce their betrothal as soon as he was out of uniform. He had no idea, at that time, that his father had impoverished him. But when her family learned of the state of his finances, they broke it off and whisked her away to the continent."

"And that's when my father, with his forty-thousand-pound offer, came on the scene?" Cassie asked quietly.

"Yes."

"I see." She put down the stirring stick, slipped from the stool and walked to the window. "And, despite his . . . his marriage, they still correspond?"

"No. You misjudge him, Cassie. He does not answer her letters. Her family would not let her accept any communication from him in any case, I expect. But she writes to him on occasion. They broke it off quite amicably, I understand, so I suspect she only writes to assure him there's no bitterness. But the letters probably don't mean anything, Cassie. Robbie is no deceiver. You do believe me, don't you?"

Cassie stared numbly out the window. Outside, beyond the rain-smeared glass, a wet, winter-grim lawn, as misty as the clouds, stretched away to the distant horizon, so colorlessly gray that the line separating earth from sky was almost invisible. "Yes, I believe you," she answered in a voice as colorless as the view. "The letters probably don't mean anything."

Chapter Twenty-two

$\mathscr{I}$t was utterly foolish, Cassie told herself as she lay awake that night and listened to the rain, to make too much of what Sandy had told her. Nothing really had changed. She'd known when she married Robert that he didn't love her. So the new knowledge that he loved another made very little difference.

But there *was* a difference, and before the night was over she was able to admit it. Before she'd learned about Elinor, she'd been able to hope. She'd let herself believe that he would grow to love her . . . that in a month, or at most a year, he would see in her those qualities which make a man love a woman. But today she'd learned he'd already found those qualities in someone else. So now all hope was gone.

Throughout her life, Cassie's hopes of happiness had never been very high. She had dreams, of course, but the circumstances of her life had not encouraged unrealistic expectations. From her earliest years she'd been deprived of a basic source of joy: intimacy. She had not had a mother to console her childhood tears, nor loving friends to share her thoughts and feelings when she was at school. Although her father had always been adoring and indulgent, he had had to spend his days doing men's business, giving over the responsibility of her daily care to hired employees. Miss Penicuick had sincerely loved her, but the governess was too simple to fully understand how to draw out the complex thoughts of her inhibited charge. Thus, Cassie had never known true intimacy, the happiness that comes from sharing one's secret heart with another. Her life had not been joyful, nor had anything occurred before her marriage to make her believe that the circumstances would change. She'd long ago accepted the limitations of her life. She'd long ago decided to make the best of things.

It was only when Lord Kittridge had materialized so miraculously on her horizon that she'd permitted herself to dream that life might offer her more. Not at first, of course, when he'd defended her at the linendraper's. Nor when her father had first offered her the opportunity to wed him. It was only afterward, when she'd been made to understand that he was willing to marry *anyone* who could help him out of his difficulties, that she'd let herself go. She was, after all, better than just anyone. She loved him! She'd agreed to wed him in the belief (because of her feelings for him) that she could, in time, make him happy. That in time they would learn to share their deepest feelings. That in time they would become close.

With that hope she'd married him. And now she knew with certainty that it had been her life's worst mistake. Before she met him she'd at least had peace. Now she had only pain.

As the rain continued unrelentingly to beat on the windowpanes, she sat up in the dark bedroom, piled the pillows behind her and pulled the covers up to her neck. She'd made a mistake, and she had to think about what could be done about it. Certainly it could not be undone. Once a marriage was made, it was forever. Grants of divorcement were so rare that they were, in effect, unheard of. Unhappy couples could live separately, but divorce and remarriage were out of the question. Separation was, in fact, the first thing she thought of. Should she leave this house and take up a separate abode? she asked herself. Should she run home to her father? If she did, would her pain be less?

No, she reasoned after considering the possibility for a long while, running away was not the answer. It would not ease her wounded spirit to return to her childhood surroundings, and it would only pain her father to learn that she was unhappy in the life he'd so proudly purchased for her. And it would pain Robert, too. Before their marriage he'd expressed real revulsion toward the idea of separate abodes because of the gossip it would generate. He'd been glad she'd agreed to live in the country with him. If she wanted more from their "arrangement" than he could give, it was not his fault. He hadn't promised her anything more than he'd given. He hadn't promised her intimacy.

She shivered as the wind sent a flurry of raindrops battering against the windows. Was the rain keeping Robert awake, too? she wondered. Poor Robert. He, too, was suffering in silence. But he knew nothing of this internal struggle of hers. How would he feel if she left him now? He didn't love her, but he would certainly be perturbed at her defection. She was, after all, making a home for him.

Now that she thought about it, she realized that separation would not in any way be a benefit to Robert. Her departure would not bring his Elinor back to him. He would not be able to have Elinor under any circumstances. He had to live with that pain, just as she, Cassie, had to live with hers. Therefore, she realized with a start, the best thing for both of them would be for her to continue to play her role. She would be no worse off remaining here than going back to London. In fact, there were some benefits to her in remaining where she was. She could continue to make a home for Robert, to be the lady of the house, to entertain their guests and do all the little things that a woman can to help a man achieve his goals. There was much to enjoy in this country life. All she had to do was to give up her dreams of love and intimacy.

"Just give up my dreams," she repeated aloud as she slipped down under her comforters and curled into a sleeping position. Giving up those dreams would be a painful adjustment but not unendurable. She'd accepted life's limitations before. She could do it again.

Chapter Twenty-three

Not many days later, Sandy announced his intention to depart. He had neglected some business matters for too long; his conscience could no longer permit him to postpone his return to London. Besides, he confided to Cassie, he wanted to be in town when Eunice returned. He intended, at that time, to press his suit in earnest.

On the morning he took his leave, everyone in the household stood on the steps waving farewell. As soon as his carriage rolled away down the drive, a wave of gloom swept over the household. The absence of his cheery face was deeply felt by all of them, even the children. It was as if a holiday had ended, and the serious business of life would now have to be resumed.

Later that day, while Cassie worked over her embroidery in the sitting room, Eunice prowled about the room aimlessly, crossing from the sofa to the window and back again and sighing so dejectedly that Cassie felt impelled to console her. "You needn't fall into the dismals, Eunice," she said with all the good spirits she could muster. "You'll be back in town soon and will undoubtedly find Sandy waiting on your doorstep with flowers in one hand and his heart in the other."

Eunice perched on the sofa beside her. "Do you think so, Cassie? That his heart is really engaged?"

Cassie smiled over her needlework. "I think you've held his heartstrings for years. He just couldn't reveal his feelings before now. You were happily wed to Yarrow, after all. It is only since you've put aside your mourning that he's been free to reveal himself."

"But how can you be sure? His nature is so sweet and open that he showers affection on everyone. Why do you think I'm in any way special to him?"

"I am not at liberty to reveal confidences," Cassie said primly. But she followed the statement with a giggle that clearly indicated what the content of those confidences had been.

"Oh, Cassie," Eunice breathed *"really?"* This was followed by a long pause, and then, "Oh, dear!"

The second exclamation was not a joyful one. It sounded so troubled, in fact, that Cassie stopped stitching. "Goodness, Eunice, what is the meaning of that 'Oh, dear'? You're not going to tell me that *your* heart is not engaged."

"I wish I knew," Eunice said, leaning back against the sofa and tucking her legs under her. "I certainly enjoyed his company these past few weeks. And the girls have grown fond of him, too. But as for my heart . . . well, how can one be sure?"

Cassie's eyebrows rose. "Are you saying you don't know how to recognize the feeling of love? But, Eunice, you've been married! Don't you remember your feeling for Yarrow?"

"Yes, I do," Eunice said thoughtfully. "And it was equally bewildering at first."

"Then it must have been later, *after* you were wed, that you knew you loved him, is that it?"

Eunice shook her head. "It was later, after I was wed, that I knew I *didn't.*"

"Eunice!" Cassie gasped in astonishment.

Eunice gazed at Cassie with an arrested look, as if she were surprised at what had slipped from her tongue. "Good God, Cassie! I've never said that to another living soul! You, my dear, are astoundingly easy to confide in."

"Am I, Eunice?" Cassie felt a little twinge of pleasure at the compliment, for she'd never before been told such a thing. "That is very nice to know," she said, blushing as she knotted her thread and bit it off. She stuck the needle into her pincushion and pushed the embroidery frame away, her brow wrinkling in confusion. "But, my dear, I'm not sure I understand just what it was you confided to me. Did you mean that you *never* loved Yarrow? Never in all your years together?"

"Not for a moment. The truth is, Cassie, that Yarrow was a fool. Oh, he was beautifully educated and quite handsome, and he said all the right things when he went about in society, so it took me some time to see through the shiny surface to the silliness underneath. Perhaps I didn't want to see through the shiny surface. But the nature of marriage is such that one can't keep one's illusions about one's spouse for very long."

"I suppose not," Cassie murmured, mulling it over. "Marriage is so . . . intimate."

"Exactly."

Now it was Cassie's turn to sigh. "Were you very miserable?" she asked in quiet sympathy.

"Oh, no. You mustn't feel sorry for me, Cassie. I grew used to my husband after a while. I even became fond of him, in a motherly way. And then I had the children, and they quite filled my life. Mother love is a very strong emotion, you know. And when it strikes one, there's no doubt about what one feels. No doubt at all."

"Doubt such as you feel about Sandy?"

"Yes." Eunice frowned worriedly. "I feel a sincere affection for Sir Philip Sanford, really I do. But I keep wondering if this feeling will last. Good heavens, Cassie, what if I decide to wed him, and then discover, later, that I don't care for him any more than I did for Yarrow?"

"I don't know how to answer that," Cassie admitted. "The love feelings *I've* experienced have had no doubts, you see. In love matters I've felt only certainty. I may not have experienced the happiness one expects from love feelings, but I haven't experienced the doubts."

"What are you saying, Cassie?" Eunice turned herself about on the sofa to stare at the girl beside her with a sudden intensity. "These love feelings you're describing— Do you mean . . . toward my *brother*?" she asked in her blunt way.

Cassie lowered her eyes and nodded. "I've never told *that* to another living soul," she said.

"Oh, *Cassie*," Eunice cried with a heartfelt agony, "you poor dear! Tell me you don't mean it!"

"I wish it were a lie," Cassie admitted. "Or a joke. Or even a schoolgirl infatuation. But it's not."

"Not even the tiniest doubt?" Eunice pleaded.

"Not the tiniest."

"Dash it all," Eunice muttered, "I'm so *sorry!*"

Cassie met her sister-in-law's eye with a level look. "Because he doesn't reciprocate?"

Eunice bit her lip. "You know about Elinor, then?"

"I've heard." Cassie gave her a small smile. "Perhaps I'll grow used to it, as you did with Yarrow."

"Perhaps. But loving him . . . with no doubts at all . . ." She threw her arms about Cassie in a tearful embrace. "Oh, my sweet little sister-in-law, I think it will be very hard."

But Cassie didn't feel tearful. She'd known from the first that loving Robert would be hard on her. But having a sympathetic friend to whom she could reveal her feelings would make things easier. She could not be tearful when she'd just engaged in the very first intimate conversation of her life. In fact, she was startled at how pleasant it had been, in spite of the painful subjects they'd discussed. The exchange had been soothing, somehow, and full of unexpected, deep affection.

How strange! she thought. How could she suddenly feel so fond of Eunice when only a week ago she'd utterly disliked her? Moreover, she had an inner certainty that they would never go back to being strangers. No matter what happened in her marriage or in Eunice's relationship with Sandy, she and Eunice had forged a bond. A strong, durable, wonderful bond.

Eunice felt it, too. This shy little creature, her sister-in-law, had in a few short weeks become a treasured friend, while Elinor, whom she had known and admired for years, had never come nearly as close to her heart. The truth was that she was delighted that Cassie was her sister-in-law. *How strange!* she thought. She'd been wishing so hard, these past months, that Robbie could have married his Elinor and been happy. Now, suddenly, she found herself wishing that Elinor had never been born!

Chapter Twenty-four

Winter weather reappeared soon after Sandy departed, keeping all Eunice's travel plans in abeyance. Since she would not subject the children to long hours in a draughty carriage, she explained, a return to London could not be considered while the weather was so cold. The postponement of their departure pleased everyone, even the servants, for Eunice had long since given up running the household. "An' now that yer sister an' 'er ladyship 'ave become thick as thieves," Loesby reported to Kittridge, "the 'ole place 's as peaceful as Talavera after the battle."

Robert was delighted with the developing friendship between his sister and his wife. For one thing, there was no more struggle for authority between the two. For another, the strain at the dinner table to make comfortable conversation was considerably lessened by the easy flow of banter exchanged between the two women. Kittridge was especially thankful for the way Eunice's friendship had brought Cassie out of her shell, for he was well aware that his own relationship with his wife had deteriorated badly.

As far as that deterioration was concerned, he knew that he had only himself to blame. He had unwittingly encouraged Cassie, by his impetuous kiss, to believe their marriage could grow into something more than it was. But the letters from Elinor had reminded him where his heart really belonged. He had been forced to marry elsewhere, but his love for Elinor remained constant. He would not sully the memory of that love by giving even a small piece of his affections to another woman, even his wife. Elinor, who had given him her unwavering devotion all during their long wartime separation, deserved nothing less from him.

Sometimes, when he felt particularly lonely and despairing, he locked himself in his study and reread the handful of letters she'd written. He knew it was self-indulgence of the most foolish, sentimental kind, but he couldn't help himself. Perhaps if he'd been able to respond, to let out his feelings in messages to her, he could have treated her letters more casually, but the frustration of this cruel, one-way correspondence skewed his emotions. He kept imagining what Elinor was feeling, enduring waves of guilt for what she must be suffering at not having even the small solace of a word from him. When those feelings of guilt and frustration rose up in him, he found himself resenting not only the circumstances of the trap in which he now found himself but the wife who, in some mysterious connivance with her father, had entrapped him. Illogical as he knew the feeling was, he sometimes blamed Cassie for keeping him from Elinor.

There were other times, however, when he felt quite affectionate toward Cassie. There was no doubt that she sometimes charmed him. She had an unaffected innocence, an irrepressible blush that revealed every feeling and an odd-shaped but endearing little face. And when she looked up at him, adoration shining in those soft brown eyes, he had to admit that he found her hard to resist. But his conscience forced him to resist her; those few times he'd forgotten himself with Cassie made him feel almost adulterous, as if his prior commitment to Elinor had a stronger claim on his honor than his commitment to his wife.

Thus he, like the other members of the household, found many advantages in the developing closeness between Cassie and Eunice. The two women were such good company for each other that Robert was able to pursue his own interests without feeling guilty that he was neglecting them. And, best of all, their closeness made it easier for him to keep his distance from his wife.

The women, meanwhile, were busily occupied with common pursuits: They played with the children together, took companionable walks together, sat at the fire reading novels together, and even spent hours in the workshop together, Cassie having convinced Eunice that furniture restoration made a very enjoyable pastime. The friendship progressed so well, in fact, that the two women could even engage in sharp disagreements. Robert overheard them one afternoon arguing over a painting Eunice wanted to place at the top of the stairway. "That, my dear," Cassie declared firmly, "is the ugliest still life I've ever seen."

"Ugly!" Eunice drew herself up in offense. "It's by a student of *Kneller*!"

"I don't care if it was by Kneller himself. The colors are muddy and the vase is all out of proportion."

"Really, Cassie, you are quite unfair. I love the blue iris lying there beside the vase. And the drapery, here, has a very nice line."

Cassie studied the painting, head cocked, for another moment. "The drapery may be nicely done, Eunice. I grant you that. But the rest is deucedly awkward."

"Well, *I* like it," Eunice insisted mulishly, "and I think it ought to be hung."

"You may hang it if you wish, my love," Cassie said as she marched off up the stairs, "but only in your room. I will *not* have it on the top of the stair where our eyes would have to suffer it ten times a day."

As Eunice followed Cassie up the stairs, still arguing the merits of the painting tucked under her arm, Robert closed the door of his study, grinning. His shy little wife, he thought with some satisfaction, had come a long way. And for that matter, so had his sister. Their friendship was fertile soil that gave them both a healthy growth.

It came as no surprise, therefore, that Eunice decided not to return to London at all. She announced one night at dinner that she and her daughters had talked it over and had agreed that they would—with Cassie's and Robert's permission—remain for the rest of the winter right here in Lincolnshire. Robert immediately acquiesced. "We're delighted to have you for as long as you wish," he assured her. "Let me remind you, my dear, that before Cassie and I left London, I told you that you and the girls were welcome to make your home with us permanently, should you desire it."

"That was a kind gesture," Eunice responded, "but I didn't believe, then, that I could bear being away from town. I don't know, even now, how permanent our stay will be, but I'd certainly like to remain until spring."

"Have you lost your mind, Eunice?" Cassie asked later, when she and Eunice had left Robert at the table with his port and were alone in the sitting room. "You *can't* stay until spring!"

"No? Why not?" She grinned at her sister-in-law archly. "Are you tired of us already?"

"Don't be silly. But have you forgotten *Sandy*? He probably knocks at your mother's door daily to ask if you've arrived."

Eunice's smile faded. "Oh, yes, Sandy. With flowers in one hand and his heart in the other, isn't that how you described him?"

Cassie peered at her friend worriedly. "Have you decided you don't care for him? Is that why you don't want to go home?"

"I don't want to go home, my dear Cassie, because the girls and I are so happy here. And as for Sandy, I've decided that I don't want to decide. When one is a girl of eighteen, one feels pushed toward marriage for fear of finding herself, at twenty, left on the shelf. But when one is a twenty-eight-year-old widow, she can't ever be called an old maid. And being left on the shelf seems much less dreadful. So the push to wedlock is less urgent. I shall, therefore, take my own good time before giving in to a second marriage."

"Is that the reason girls get married?" Cassie couldn't help asking. "To avoid being left on the shelf?"

"Of course it is. What other reason is there to tie oneself up at eighteen? Isn't that why *you* married? You can't pretend it was for love, Cassie, for you didn't know Robbie then."

"Ah, but I did."

Eunice gaped at her sister-in-law. "You did? How? When? Why did you never tell me?"

"It's a long and silly story, which I won't tell you now, with Robert about to join us at any moment, but which you'll undoubtedly pull out of me in all its embarrassing details before the week passes. In the end, however, the tale will only prove that love is not a much better reason for 'giving in to marriage' than fear of being left on the shelf. Although in your case, Eunice," she added, patting her sister-in-law's shoulder, "if you decide you love Sandy, I think you'll have a very happy marriage indeed."

"Do you?" Eunice asked earnestly.

"Yes, I do," Cassie answered as Robert strolled in to join them, "but by all means take your own good time. Take all the time you need."

Chapter Twenty-five

With matters in his household in a state of relative contentment, Kittridge felt free to absent himself from it for a few days. The Duke of Bedford (a progressive landowner whose estates were both productive and profitable, and whose annual "sheep shearing" was an event that drew farmers and landowners from all over the midlands to his estate in Bedfordshire) had heard that Lord Kittridge was interested in developing his own herds and had generously invited him to Woburn Abbey to exchange ideas. With the assurance from his wife and his sister that they would do very well without him, Kittridge accepted the invitation and, early on a cold February morning, set out for Bedfordshire.

Cassie had risen at dawn to see him off. Eunice, however, being neither wife nor lover, had not felt any need to deviate from her usual habit of sleeping until midmorning. Thus, as soon as Robert left, Cassie found herself alone at the breakfast table and utterly miserable. She did not know why her husband's departure left her feeling so bereft, for he was hardly an affectionate companion when they were together, but the feeling persisted anyway. In order to shake off her depression, she searched about in her mind for some engrossing activity to distract herself from her gloomy self-pity.

It took but a moment for the perfect solution to burst upon her brain: This was her best opportunity to make her husband's study more habitable. She had wanted to remake the room from the first, but Robert, being in almost constant occupancy, had not permitted it. Today, however, with Robert absent, was the perfect time to start. She jumped up from the table at once and ran eagerly down the hall to the study to give it a complete examination.

Her first impression, on looking round, was that the room was much too small for its purpose. Just the few pieces of furniture it held—a one-piece secretary-and-bookcase, a chair, and a pier table under the single window—were enough to crowd the room. She would have liked to move him to a larger room, where she could fit him with a library table to sit behind, with plenty of room underneath for his long legs. But she knew he would not hear of it. He had many times insisted that this room suited him perfectly. So, with a sigh of resignation, she studied the place to see what could be done.

The fireplace took one entire wall and the window, with the pier table beneath it, another. With the bookcase-desk against the third wall and the door in the fourth, there was little she could do to rearrange the furniture. The only things that could be done were to find some way to store the maps and blueprints that were piled in untidy rolls on the pier table, cover the window with new draperies, find an interesting, masculine painting to hang over the mantel and, perhaps, to replace the secretary-bookcase with some sort of table with a larger work surface.

She looked at the high desk speculatively. It was actually a beautiful piece, the bookshelves enclosed with delicate glass doors and the whole frame topped with an inlaid arch and carved finials. It might, she thought, be the work of Daniel Langlois, a cabinetmaker of the last century whose designs she'd always admired. She would quite understand if Robert objected to its being replaced. But he must surely find the work space too cramped, and there was no possible way, underneath, for a man to stretch his legs. He would be bound to appreciate a more spacious desk, once he tried it.

To prove to herself that this desk was inadequate, she lowered the lid. As she suspected, the opened lid comprised the entire writing surface, for the area within was completely taken up with cubbyholes, all overstuffed with record books and papers. How, she wondered, could he do his work amid such a profusion of—?

Suddenly she turned quite pale. Her heart seemed to cease beating, and her blood froze in her veins. For right there, in the center cubbyhole, was a packet of square, buff-colored envelopes tied with string. *Elinor's letters!*

She shut the lid hurriedly, with the awkward nervousness of a spinster who'd opened a door and come upon a gentleman in his smalls. She had trespassed on Robert's privacy! It was in this room that he hid when he wanted to be alone. It was in this tiny place where he stored his secrets. It was here, and here alone, that he could truly be himself. She realized, with belated shame, that she should not have come in at all without asking his permission. It was his *sanctuary,* and she had no right to invade it.

She could do nothing to alter this room now, for he must never know she'd entered! She looked quickly round once more to make sure nothing had been disturbed. And then, quite ridiculously, as if she'd accidentally invaded the chapel of an alien religious sect, she tiptoed to the door.

But with her hand on the knob, she paused. Elinor's letters—the words and thoughts of the one woman whose character aroused her fascination more than any other in the world—lay right there within reach. She could, right at this moment, take them out and read them. No one need ever know.

But that was a *hideous* thought, she told herself. Cheap and vulgar and dishonest. And quite beneath her character. She could never permit herself to perform so dastardly an act! If coming into this *room* had seemed a dreadful invasion of her husband's privacy, what would reading his *most private letters* be? The very *thought* was sinful . . . sinful to the point of sacrilege! She had to leave this room, and at once!

But she didn't move. She knew, with a sickening certainty, that she was going to go back to the desk and read the letters. She simply *had* to. As ugly, as dishonest, as *immoral* as the act was, she was going to do it. It was as if some force beyond herself was compelling her. Trembling convulsively, she moved like a sleepwalker back to the desk. As she lowered the lid with shaking fingers, a horrid picture flashed into her mind . . . Bluebeard's forbidden room, where the mutilated bodies of the six wives who'd disobeyed his stricture lay strewn about in bloody heaps. Would she, too, come to the end of this misadventure to find herself, like those other too-curious wives, a dismembered corpse?

But even that repulsive image did not stay her hand. She sat down at the desk, carefully removed the letters from their niche and undid the string. Then she gingerly removed the first letter from its envelope and, bracing herself as though expecting a blow, read it through.

It was worse than she expected. Elinor Langston, she discovered, was not the sort to exercise restraint. Every pang of loss the girl experienced was expressed in detail in the lengthy document, every tear and sigh duly noted and placed in its time and setting so that the reader—Robert—might suffer too. It was as if Elinor were trying to keep him tied to her by a rope of guilt, woven strand by strand with the threads of her pain.

The next letter contained more of the same . . . and the next . . . and the next. At a dance at the Belvedere Palace in Vienna, Elinor ached to feel his arms about her. At a concert in Salzburg, the Mozart *"was a meaningless jumble of discord"* without Robert's presence at her side. At the Louvre in Paris, the mere viewing of a painting upset her. *"It was,"* she wrote, *"a portrait by Titian, called 'Man with a Glove.' It so disconcerted me because of its likeness to you, my love, particularly about the eyes and mouth, that I burst into sobs and had to be led from the exhibit—to the consternation of Mama and Papa and the amused curiosity of everyone else—and laid on a chaise in the ladies' retiring room until I could come to myself."* And after witnessing a performance of *Fidelio* at La Scala in Milan, she wrote, *"Oh, my most beloved, when I saw the lovers rewarded for their faithfulness and sent out to pursue a life of happiness, how I wished that you and I could be rewarded too. But I know it is beyond hope, and that our opera, if such were ever composed, must have a tragic end. If I were writing it, I would arrange it so that we'd be chained together somewhere in a dungeon where we would die in each other's arms. I think I prefer that ending to this terrible, interminable, boring separation we are being made to endure!"*

Cassie stared at the letters spread out before her, a wave of fury flooding over her. How could this contemptible girl dare to torture her Robert this way? she asked herself. Did she have to flaunt her self-pity in his face and make him suffer agonies of guilt?

But a second reading altered her thinking, especially the letter in which Elinor tried to face the fact of Robert's marriage. *"Mama told me yesterday that you are wed,"* she wrote on pathetically tear-stained paper. *"I cried all night. I almost hated you, but now, after some calmer thought, I do understand. You did what you had to do. I know you cannot love the despicable creature who married you for your title and whom you married for her wealth. I know, too, that your love for me remains untarnished. I admit that the tiny flame of hope I kept in my heart, the hope that we might, somehow, find a way into each other's arms, has flickered out, but the knowledge that our love will not die still burns brightly for me. It is that knowledge that keeps me alive."*

This last letter made it achingly clear that Elinor and Robert truly loved each other, and that they had been cruelly wrenched apart. Those were facts that Cassie had to face. In those circumstances, she asked herself, weren't the lovers justified in feeling pain? In being sorry for themselves? Wasn't their suffering just as pitiable as her own?

And it was *she*, Cassie, who stood between them! She was the "despicable creature" who was to blame for their unhappiness. Elinor's words jumped out from the page and struck at her soul. *I know you cannot love the despicable creature.* The very appearance of those words on the page made her cringe. But it was a final reading of the words, *the knowledge that our love will not die still burns brightly for me,* that utterly undid her, and she dropped her head on her arms and wept as if her heart would break.

The sound of the doorknob being turned froze her in midsob. With her breath caught in her throat, she lifted a terror-stricken face to the opening door. Whoever it was—Loesby or Dickie or any other of the servants—she would not be able to face him ever again. But if it were *Robert* at the door, returning by some ironically hideous quirk of fate to pick up a forgotten item on his desk, she would simply die! She would die on the spot!

But it was Eunice. "I've been looking for you all over," Eunice began cheerfully, but the sight of Cassie's reddened eyes and terrified expression startled her into alarm. "Good God, Cassie, what—?"

"Eunice, *p-please,*" Cassie begged, stammering in embarrassed misery, "pretend you haven't f-found m-me, and g-go away!"

But Eunice saw and thought she recognized the letters. *"Cassie!"* she exclaimed in shock. "Are those *Elinor's*? What've you *done*?"

"Just what you th-think," Cassie admitted, dropping her head down on her arms and beginning to sob again. "I'm the m-most d-despicable c-creature in the world!"

"Of course you're not," Eunice declared loyally, striding into the room and kneeling beside Cassie's chair. "Despicable, indeed!"

"I read all his l-letters!" Cassie wept. *"Twice!"*

"Well, it might not have been an admirable thing to do, my love, but it's not an offense that warrants a hanging."

"Yes, it is. It was a low, m-mean-spirited, ugly, d-despicable thing to do!"

"Yes, it was." She stroked Cassie's bent head. "And very human. I know I'd have done it, too, in your place."

"No, you wouldn't. You have too much ch-character."

"Not nearly as much as you, Cassie, and that's the truth. It was love that weakened you, that's all. Now, stop that weeping, take this handkerchief and blow your nose. And let's get these letters back in place before someone else comes in and discovers us."

Cassie nodded and tried to comply. She sat up and blew her nose, but when she replaced that last, cruel letter in its envelope, the tears began to flow again. "Robert must think I'm d-despicable, even if you don't," she wept, dabbing hopelessly at her eyes. "I'm the one who stands between him and the wonderful g-girl of his dreams. Me! The pathetic c-creature who had to p-purchase a husband for f-forty thousand p-pounds!"

For that Eunice had no answer. "My poor Cassie," she murmured, taking her sister-in-law in her arms and rocking her like a baby, "my poor, poor Cassie." There was nothing else she could think of to say that would be soothing, for the truth was that even at a thousand times forty thousand pounds, Robert's love could not be bought. And that one unpurchasable commodity was the only thing in the world the weeping girl wanted.

Chapter Twenty-six

*I*t did not take Lord Kittridge very long after his return from Woburn Abbey to notice a change in his wife. It was not that she was cooler to him, exactly, but that she was somehow *withdrawn*. She did not meet his eye when he spoke to her, nor did she smile up at him with that tremulous little smile she used to give when he said something kind or amusing. And when he came down to breakfast—the only time of day they were alone together—she quickly finished her tea and scurried out of the room, as if she were purposely trying to avoid any private conversation with him.

He didn't notice any change in the way she behaved toward anyone else, but to make sure his impression was accurate, he asked Loesby about it. The valet raised his brows at the question. "'Er ladyship, changed?" he repeated, peering at Kittridge as if he'd dipped too deeply in the brandy. "Not as far as I kin see. It's just like I been tellin' ye, Cap'n. She wuz a wonder from the start, an' she's a wonder still."

Unsatisfied, Kittridge applied to Eunice. He caught her on the stairs, on her way up to the nursery. "Have you a minute, Eunice?" he asked. "There's something I want to ask you."

"Of course, my dear," she said, pausing in her climb. "What about?"

"About Cassie. Do you notice any change in her? Does she seem, in the last few days, to be . . . well, different?"

"How different?"

"I can't put my finger on it. Distant, somehow."

"Distant? Not to me."

"Then you two are still as good friends as when I left for Woburn?"

"Better, I'd say."

"I don't understand." Kittridge's brow knit in puzzlement. "Then it's only toward *me* she's changed. I wonder if I've offended her. Did she say anything about it to you?"

"If she did, you wouldn't expect me to repeat it, would you, Robbie?" She turned away with a toss of her head and proceeded up the stairs. "If you want to know anything concerning your wife, my dear," she threw over her shoulder, "you'll have to talk to *her*. Don't expect *me* to be your intermediary."

Kittridge glared up at her as she disappeared round the turning of the stairs. "Women!" he muttered in annoyance and took himself off to his study.

As the days passed, his feeling that Cassie had changed toward him persisted. He told himself that it didn't matter . . . that, indeed, her coolness suited him perfectly well, under the circumstances. He'd pledged himself to remain faithful to Elinor, and this distance between himself and his wife made it easier for him to keep his pledge. When he found himself becoming snappish and short-tempered, he blamed the mood on the absence of letters from Elinor. Why, he asked himself several times a day, wasn't his mother forwarding his letters more frequently?

But as many couples learn, the Gods of Love have decreed a terrible irony in the playing out of the games between men and women: when one of the pair draws away, the other almost inevitably wishes to draw close. Thus, the more Cassie seemed to avoid Kittridge's company, the more he desired hers. He began to miss her little smiles, her cheerful morning conversation, the adoring glances he used to catch her casting at him when she thought he wasn't looking. For the first time in the months of his marriage he worked at trying to please her. He told her his plans for the day at breakfast in an attempt to keep her at the table; he brought her a pair of Wedgwood candlesticks that he'd purchased from one of his tenants; and he tried, by all sorts of ruses, to prevail upon her to remain in the sitting room at night after Eunice had gone up to bed. But no matter what he did, Cassie remained politely, unshakably distant.

At last he decided to take the bull by the horns. He tapped on her bedroom door one night after they'd all retired. She opened the door an inch and held a candle aloft to see who it was. "Robert?" she asked in surprise. "Is anything wrong?"

"No, but I'd like to talk to you, Cassie. May I come in for a moment?"

She hesitated. "Well, I . . . you see I've already undressed . . ."

"Then put on a robe. It's not so shocking a suggestion, ma'am. I've seen you in nightclothes before, if you remember."

After another moment of hesitation she let him in. In the candlelight it seemed to him she looked as delicious as she did the night they went hunting for the Rossiter ghost, with her ruffled nightgown peeping out at the bottom of her robe and her unruly hair bursting out in rebellion from the control of her spinsterish nightcap. "Thank you, ma'am," he said with exaggerated formality as he crossed the threshold.

She closed the door gingerly. "Would you . . . care to sit?" she asked, almost whispering.

"Are you afraid someone will hear us and think we are having a tryst?" He grinned at her as he lowered himself onto her dressing table chair. "I assure you that no one is near enough to hear us. And even if someone were, it wouldn't matter. We *are* married, after all."

"Yes, but . . ."

"But not quite married enough to be having trysts, is that what you're trying to say?"

She put up her chin. "I was not trying to say anything of the sort. All I intended to do was to excuse my awkwardness by explaining that I am unaccustomed to . . . to entertaining gentlemen in my bedroom."

"That much is obvious," he teased.

She sat down on the edge of her bed and folded her hands primly in her lap. "You said you wished to *talk* to me, my lord, not to twit me about my . . . er . . . inexperience."

"So I did. It's something that's been on my mind since I returned from Woburn. I wish to ask you, Cassie, quite bluntly, if I've done something to offend or anger you."

"No, of course not. What makes you think you have?"

"Something in your manner. You've changed, you know."

"I am not aware—"

"You must be aware of it," he insisted, getting to his feet impatiently. "You've been doing all you can to avoid me."

"That's silly. Why would I—?"

"I don't know." He confronted her boldly, lifting her chin and forcing her to look up at him. "That's just what I'm trying to determine."

"You are imagining things, my lord," she said stiffly.

"There! You see? It's that stiffening. You did not, before, stiffen up whenever I approached."

She turned her face away, wresting her chin from his hold. "You did not, before, approach me in my bedroom, my lord."

"And that's another thing. For months you've been calling me Robert with perfect ease, but tonight you've 'my lorded' me at least twice."

"If that's the source of your discontent, my lor—Robert, I shall try to remember not to do so again."

"Damnation, ma'am, that's *not* the source!" he burst out, pulling her to her feet. "Please, Cassie, don't be afraid to be open with me. I'd hoped that by this time we'd be dealing better with each other. What's happened to our intention to bring about some intimacy into this marriage?"

"I am n-not aware that we had such an intention," she murmured, lowering her head to avoid his eyes.

"Not aware? How can you say that? Didn't we discuss it from the first?"

"You only said, then, that you wouldn't f-force intimacy upon me."

He groaned in frustration. "Come now, Cassie, I was speaking of a later conversation, as well you know! It was when we admitted to each other that we were still behaving as strangers." He pulled her into his arms, determined to have an honest confrontation that would, he hoped, bring them to a more comfortable closeness. With one arm holding her tightly to him, he tilted her face up to his, as if to force her to remember their former embrace. "I had the distinct impression, that day, that you were *encouraging* the development of that intimacy."

"Let me go, Robert," she said, quietly firm. "That impression was false."

Her words enraged him. He was not such a coxcomb that he could have mistaken her response to his kiss. Why was she denying it now? "It was *not* false!" he declared furiously. And to prove it, he lifted her up against his chest so that he could kiss her again and evoke the remembered response.

"Robert!" she gasped, startled. *"No!"*

His eyes glittered with angry but unmistakable desire, a desire fanned by her stiff resistance. "Let me remind you of how it was," he said roughly, pushing away his awareness that the situation and the sensations he felt now were very different from the last time. Heedless of his own internal warnings and the look of utter fear in her eyes, he crushed her against him and kissed her in a way that was too urgent and too angry to be husbandly.

She struggled to free herself in spite of the sudden surging of the blood through her veins and the astonishing waves of warmth that flowed all through her. Even though she pushed with all her might against his shoulders, she could feel her body, free of the constrictions of stays and undergarments, bend back under his pressure like a slim, green tree in a storm. Her body seemed to be pursuing desires of its own, trying to mold itself to him as if it wanted nothing more than to cling to him forever. But her mind, pinpricking her with reminders that the man holding her in this most intimate of embraces did not love her, kept some inner kernel of her spirit stiff, cold and unyielding.

At first, Robert responded only to the signals of her body. Soft and pliant in her unrestricting nightclothes, she was at this moment more desirable than any woman he'd ever held. He could feel the racing beat of her heart, the heat of her skin, the sweet taste of her lips. He could have her now, he told himself, oh so easily. It was his husbandly right. He could lower her gently on the bed that stood waiting right there at his side and teach her the secrets of marital bliss.

Every lovely, lissome, warmly shivering inch of her seemed ripe for it. But his mind, too, kept nagging at him to hold back. It warned him to recognize the firm core of resistance that was keeping her, despite the passion that enveloped them both, from surrendering. He couldn't force himself on her. So after an inner struggle of what he considered herculean dimensions, he let her wrench her mouth from his. Then he set her on her feet and, feeling like a fool, released his hold on her.

Breathless and confused, they stared at each other until he could no longer bear to see the look of shocked accusation in her eyes. He turned away and leaned weakly on the bedpost. "So you see," he muttered in a lame attempt at irony, "the impression was not false."

She sank down upon the bed. "I think, my lord," she said, her voice trembling, "that you'd better go."

He turned to look at her. "Now I *have* offended you," he said, shamefaced.

She would not meet his eyes. "Yes," she said.

Her stubborn intransigence, one of her qualities with which he had no previous familiarity, brought his earlier anger sweeping over him again. "When one considers the usual husbandly privileges," he said in cold, tight-jawed self-defense, "what happened just now was a mere trifle."

"I thought we'd agreed from the first that the 'usual husbandly privileges' do not apply in our case," she pointed out quietly.

"Damnation, woman, I never intended to forgo them *forever*! I thought it was understood that we only meant to postpone them until we became comfortable with each other."

She got slowly to her feet and faced him with chin high. "And was it understood, my lord," she asked proudly, "that *you* were to decide when the time was right, or that I was?"

He was taken aback by the question. "Why, *you*, of course."

"Then my decision is that we should accept our marriage as it is, with the limitations and restrictions we placed on it from the beginning."

He stared at her in agonized disbelief. "But . . . good God, Cassie, *why*?"

She turned away. "I can't . . . I'd rather not explain."

He came up behind her and took her gently by the shoulders. "Can you give me some hope that the right time will be soon?"

"N-no," she said, her head lowered. "None."

She could feel him stiffen. "Cassie! Do you mean you wish to keep to those limitations *permanently*?"

She nodded. "We made a bargain. An exchange. My fortune for your title. We, neither of us, have a right to demand more from each other."

His hands dropped from her shoulders. "Very well, ma'am," he said, suddenly cold as ice. "If that is the way you see the terms of our 'bargain,' I shall certainly honor them. I shall not invade your room again. Good night, ma'am."

She shuddered at the slam of the door behind him. *Oh, Robbie,* she wanted to cry, *come back! I didn't mean it. I didn't mean any of it!*

But of course she had meant it, every word. She had to keep him at arm's length, or she'd not be able to endure the life she'd chosen. And she'd not be able to endure it if she gave her heart to him while he withheld his from her. What she'd just done was battle for her survival.

The scene just ended *had* been a battle, and she'd won it. Any impartial observer would surely have named her the victor. Then why did she have this empty, frightened, lonely, miserable feeling that indicated quite distinctly that she'd lost?

Chapter Twenty-seven

$\mathcal{A}$s the temperature between the lord and lady of Highlands turned chill, the temperature outside warmed. An icy February turned into a muddy March. The trees in the orchards began to show tinges of color, the lawns began to green, the air was crisp and resonated with the sound of saws and hammers as the renovation of the farm buildings began, the ewes gave birth to a number of little lambs, some new pieces of furniture for the still unfinished drawing room arrived from London, and Della's riding lessons, long postponed because of the cold, were resumed. Spring had arrived at last.

The last week in March brought not only the official beginning of the new season but a visit from Oliver Chivers. Cassie's father thoughtfully brought Miss Penicuick along with him, and the reunion was a truly joyful one. Both her father and her old governess were delighted beyond words by the apparent change in Cassie from a painfully shy schoolgirl to the confident mistress of a grand manor house. Her father almost chortled in glee at the success of his "investment."

While Miss Penicuick joined the ladies in their daytime activities, Kittridge took his father-in-law round the property and showed him the plans for its reconstruction. The grandeur of the manor house impressed Chivers mightily, as did the size of the property and the potential for income of the farms and new tenant houses. While he pooh-poohed Kittridge's claim to be able to pay him back in ten years for the "dowry"—insisting that he would not accept a penny of it—he was nevertheless proud of his son-in-law for wishing to make the attempt. "My daughter," he confided to Miss Penicuick, " 'as got 'erself as fine a fellow as ever was."

But neither Mr. Chivers nor the fluttery governess had ever developed the sensitivity to discern the subtle undercurrents in human relations. Although they extended what was to be a two-day visit to a full week, they never noticed the coolness and tension between Cassie and her husband. Mr. Chivers was even impelled, one evening at dinner, to drop a broad and vulgar hint that he expected to hear any day that his Cassie was "breedin'." Although Kittridge's jaw tightened and Cassie turned alternately rose-red and ashen white, it never occurred to her father that he'd made a gross *faux pas*. He and Miss Penicuick departed from Highlands as happy as grigs, complacently convinced that their Cassie had been granted every blessing that a beneficent God, and a rich father, could bestow.

To Eunice and Cassie, the subtle undercurrents governing Kittridge's moods were abundantly clear. As the days passed and no letters were forwarded from London, his temper grew shorter and his expression darker. It was only Loesby, however, who had the courage to berate him. "Ye needn't bark at everyone like a 'ound wi' distemper," he scolded. "Ye made yer own bed, Cap'n, so it ain't right t' blame the world if the sheets scratch yer backside."

Loesby's homily was not wasted on Lord Kittridge. He made a sincere attempt to hide his unhappiness. He busied himself with the supervision of the renovation work on the farm buildings, forced himself to be a pleasant companion to the women in the evenings and threw himself with such gusto into playing wild games with the girls that Eunice feared he would make tomboys out of them. But in spite of his efforts, Cassie could see the unhappiness deep in his eyes. She found herself wishing, for his sake, that some letters would be delivered soon. If the letters could ease his suffering, she wanted them for him.

One night, about a fortnight after her father's departure, Cassie woke up in the wee hours with a feeling that something was dreadfully amiss. A flickering light from behind the drawn draperies caught her eye. When she opened them, she discovered, to her horror, a strange, frightening red glow in the sky. Something not very far away was burning! Through the trees she could even catch a glimpse of flames!

Alarmed, she threw on her robe and ran out of her room. The halls were dark and silent. Evidently no one else in the house had noticed anything. She ran to Robert's door and hammered on it. "Robert! Robert! Wake up!"

It seemed an eternity before he opened the door. "Cassie?" he mumbled sleepily. "What's amiss? Have you heard another ghost?"

"Look out the window!" she said, trying not to sound terror-stricken. "Something seems to be on fire."

His eyes came instantly awake. Leaving the door open, he ran across the room and flung the drapes aside. "Oh, God!" he gasped. "The new barns!"

"Oh, Robert, *no*!" Cassie cried, her hands reaching out to him in sympathy. But he took no note of her gesture. He was already pulling on his boots. "If you don't mind, Cassie," he said, "go and wake Loesby. Whitlock, too. And that fool of a butler. We're going to need all the men we can find."

Cassie ran to do his bidding. Before long, everyone was up, dressed and running down across the south lawn, past the outbuildings to the site of the new structure. They all, men and women, struggled through the remainder of the night, passing buckets of water up from the nearest pond. But their efforts were unavailing. By morning the entire structure was a blackened heap of ashes.

The destruction of the new barns was a blow to Kittridge. All his efforts of the past months had burned up in the flames of that new structure. Cassie and Eunice tried to console him with the usual platitudes: that one must be grateful the work was still uncompleted and thus the barns were empty; that there'd been no loss of human or animal life; that the structure could be rebuilt. But Kittridge knew that the cost in time and money meant a major restructuring of his plans. What was worse, he didn't understand how the fire had started or what steps he could or should have taken to protect against such a calamity. Even though Griswold assured him that there was nothing they could have done, either before or during the fire, to prevent what was either an act of God or the carelessness or spitefulness of a trespasser, Kittridge's confidence in his ability to succeed in the task he'd set himself was badly shaken.

Cassie's heart ached for him during the week that followed. He seemed to have been sapped of energy, and all vestiges of *joie de vivre* were gone from his face. Every circumstance of his life seemed to have combined to defeat him, and she, loving him as she did, grieved that she was unable to ease his lonely lot. She watched from a distance as he stood staring out the sitting room window for hours at a time, his face rigid and his eyes seeing nothing but a bleak future. He did not deserve what fate had done to him, and she, who had married him because she believed she could make him happy, had failed him, too. It was not his fault that he couldn't love her. It was not his fault that she loved him too much. She would have liked to let him know that if he came to her bedroom now, as he'd done those few weeks earlier, she would not refuse to give him whatever solace he required. But he was true to his word and did not come. And she had not the courage to alter what she'd wrought.

After a week of glum passivity, however, Kittridge roused himself to action. He joined the workers in cleaning up the debris, often taking a shovel in hand and laboring with them until he was ready to drop. And he immersed himself in planning the rebuilding. His vigorous activity proved a tonic for everyone else, and soon the household was restored to normalcy.

But an event that was more likely than any other to change normalcy to cheeriness occurred on a bright afternoon in April when Cassie, Eunice and the two little girls were taking tea in the sitting room. A carriage trundled up the drive, stopped at their door and disgorged a handsome, well-dressed, top-of-the-trees dandy. Eunice, glancing out the window, gave a little shriek. "It's *Sandy!*" she cried. "He's *back!*"

"Sandy! Sandy!" the little girls squealed delightedly.

But Eunice's brilliant smile faded at once. "Oh, my heavens, look at me!" she gasped, jumping from her seat. "I've got to go up and do something with my hair!"

"Goodness, Eunice, it's only Sandy. He won't mind your hair," Cassie said, following the hurrying Eunice from the room, the girls trailing excitedly behind.

" 'Only Sandy,' indeed," Eunice retorted, starting up the stairs.

"I thought you were so full of doubts about him," Cassie taunted.

Eunice paused and grinned down at her friend. "I may have doubts about my feelings for him," she laughed, "but I don't intend to give him any reason to doubt his feelings for me."

While Dickie brought in Sandy's baggage, Cassie and the girls surrounded the new arrival in the doorway, Cassie throwing her arms around his neck in welcome, and the little girls jumping up and down in glee. The commotion had barely subsided when Eunice, resplendent in her prettiest afternoon dress and sporting a jeweled clip in her hastily brushed hair, glided down the stairs. "Sandy, dear boy," she said with complete aplomb, throwing Cassie a twinkling glance while offering Sandy her hand, "you're back, I see."

If Sandy was disappointed by Eunice's restrained greeting, he did not show it. They held a merry reunion over the teacups. Sandy, in a bantering tone, berated Eunice for failing to keep their "appointment" in London, but, optimist that he was, he didn't seem to be crushed by it. However, he announced firmly that this time he did not intend to leave Lincolnshire until Eunice agreed to return home. "I promised your mother I would not come back without you," he declared.

Cassie, at the mention of her mother-in-law, leaned forward tensely. "Did her ladyship send any other messages?" she asked, hoping to learn if he'd brought any letters from Elinor. If ever there was an appropriate moment for Robert to receive love letters, this was that time.

"Messages?" Sandy echoed, too busy filling his eyes with his ladylove to notice Cassie's intensity. "She sent affectionate greetings to you all, of course."

"Did Lady Kittridge . . . send along any letters?"

That question drew his attention. His smile faded. "A few," he said, biting his underlip.

Cassie didn't feel courageous enough to pry any further. But there was something about his response that troubled her.

She was glad when Robert finally joined them. He'd spent the day at the site of the new barn, but when he returned and learned from Dickie that Sir Philip had arrived from London, he rushed into the sitting room to greet his friend without even pausing to change from his splattered riding boots and breeches.

The gentlemen exchanged warm greetings. But Robert, after ascertaining that Sandy was in good health and intended to make a long stay, did not take many moments before he asked, "I say, Sandy, did my mother forward my letters?"

"Yes," Sandy said, "she did." He seemed uneasy as he removed a small packet of letters from his coat pocket. "I have them here."

Kittridge took the packet and, breaking the string at once, rifled through the letters hastily. There were fewer than half a dozen pieces, not one of which, Cassie noted with despair, was square and buff-colored.

Kittridge, his face unreadable, immediately begged to be excused. "I must not stay in my wife's charming sitting room in all my dirt," he said. "I'll join you all at dinner." He took himself promptly to the door. "It's good to have you back, Sandy," he added, shutting the door behind him so quickly that no one had a chance to protest his abrupt departure.

Eunice, noting Cassie's stricken face, herded her daughters to the door. "Miss Roffey will be wondering where her charges are keeping," she said. "If you both will excuse me, I'll take the girls up to her."

As soon as the door closed behind her, Cassie jumped to her feet. "Goodness, Sandy, what has happened?" she demanded, twisting her fingers together nervously. "Why were there no letters from Elinor?"

"You sound disappointed that there were none," Sandy said in surprise. "One would have thought you'd be glad."

"Then one would have been mistaken," Cassie said shortly. "You didn't do something mischievous, did you, Sandy, like getting rid of them for my sake?"

"No, of course not," Sandy said, offended. "What do you take me for? A man's letters are sacrosanct, like confessions to a priest."

Cassie's eyes fell. "Yes, of course." She got up and paced about the room, wringing her hands. "Then how do you explain it, Sandy? Elinor wrote every week for two months. Why have the letters suddenly stopped?"

Sandy shrugged. "I'm not certain, but I've heard rumors. The Langstons are staying in Italy now. They say Elinor's been seen in the company of a Venetian count."

Cassie gaped at him. "Good God! Are you suggesting she's fallen in love with *someone else?*"

"How can I tell? But the rumors and the absence of letters do seem to suggest that it's a logical assumption."

"But she *can't*!" Cassie exclaimed, stamping her foot in irritation. "The little wretch can't *do* that to Robert now!"

"But, Cassie, how can you say that? It will be good for your marriage, won't it, if Elinor and Robert forget each other?"

Cassie waved away his words with an impatient flick of her hand. "No, it won't, dash it all! Not now! He hasn't forgotten her, don't you see that? Her letters are all he has left of the life he dreamed he'd have." Tears began to stream down her cheeks unchecked. "When things go b-badly for him, he locks himself in his little study and *rereads* those d-deuced letters for consolation!"

"I say, Cassie, how can you know that?" Sandy demanded suspiciously.

"Never mind. I know. You may take my word." She dashed the tears angrily from her cheeks. "And after all the dreadful things that he's been through, to be so coldly dropped by his precious ladylove is bound to be the last straw! I won't *have* him hurt like that! I *won't*!"

Sandy stared at her in astonishment. He'd never seen Cassie so wrought up. "But I don't see what you can do about it, my dear," he mumbled helplessly, getting up and handing her his handkerchief.

"N-Neither do I," she moaned, dabbing at her eyes. "Neither do I."

He put a consoling arm about her and let her head rest on his shoulder. "Don't cry, Cassie. Tears don't do anything but redden one's—"

The door burst open. "Confound it, Cassie, did you tell that deuced butler to—?" Kittridge, taking belated note of Cassie standing in Sandy's arms, stopped stock still in the doorway, his mouth agape.

Cassie broke from Sandy's hold abruptly. She felt a stab of guilt, not for standing in Sandy's embrace (for, in truth, she'd barely noticed his arm about her), but for the tears she'd been shedding over her husband's disappointment. The last thing in the world she wanted was for him to discover her interest in his private love letters! She turned away so that Robert would not see her face. "*What* did I tell the butler, Robert?" she asked.

"Nothing, nothing," Robert mumbled in embarrassed chagrin. "It's not important. I interrupted. Excuse me." And he backed out of the doorway and shut the door.

"Good God!" Sandy exclaimed, blinking at the door through which Kittridge had just disappeared. "I think the gudgeon suspects me of . . . of fondling his wife!"

"Don't be silly. He must have seen that I was crying. I only hope he didn't suspect that I was crying over him."

"I would much prefer *that* than to have him think you were crying over *me*," Sandy muttered. "He might very well call me out!"

"Call you *out*? Why on earth would he do that?"

Sandy made a gesture of impatience. "Out of jealousy, of course."

"Jealousy?" Even in her misery, Cassie had to giggle. "It's you who's the gudgeon, Sandy. Robert wouldn't be jealous over me."

"Why wouldn't he? You're his wife."

"Yes, but you know as well as I that he doesn't love me. What do you suppose I've been agonizing about for the last quarter-hour?"

"Oh, yes. Elinor's letters . . . or rather the lack of them. I'd forgotten that for a moment." He sank down on the hearth and wrinkled his brow. "As to that, Cassie," he said thoughtfully, "I think you are needlessly overwrought. Robbie may suffer a few pangs for a time, but he's bound to get over it. Elinor's finding a new love will be the best thing for everyone in the long run. You'll see."

"Oh, Sandy," she chided, both amused and impatient, "you are truly wonderful. Always the optimist. Has there ever been a situation so dark that you couldn't find a ray of light to pin your hopes on?"

"Only when the situation involves me," Sandy admitted, grinning up at her sheepishly. "Like Eunice not coming down to London all this time. I was not very optimistic about that, I'm afraid. Tell me, Cassie, doesn't she care for me at all?"

"I'm not the one to ask, Sandy. Ask her."

Sandy's full cheeks seemed to sag. "I think I'm like you, my dear. Too shy to tell my love."

"Do you think my problem is shyness, Sandy?" She dropped down beside him on the hearth. "Am I like the girl in *Twelfth Night,* who 'never told her love, but let concealment, like a worm in the bud, feed on her damask cheek'?"

"Exactly like her," he said, shaking his head admiringly. "Couldn't have put it better myself."

"Shakespeare would be flattered," she laughed. But soon her worried frown returned. "Dash it all, Sandy, I wish my situation were as simple as that. One can overcome shyness. What one can't overcome is a love that's placed elsewhere."

"I wish I could think of some way to help," he said.

She got up and crossed thoughtfully to the door. "Perhaps I can help myself. Only promise me two things, Sandy, my dear."

"Anything. Anything at all."

"Then first, try not to be shy with Eunice."

He shrugged dubiously. "I'll try, but—"

"It won't be hard," she assured him. "Faint heart never won fair maid, as they say. But the second promise will be harder to keep. You must promise me that, no matter what, you won't say a word to Robert about the rumors about Elinor. Not a single word."

"But, Cassie, what good would it do to keep him in the dark? After all, if no letters come—"

"Perhaps they will," she said mysteriously. "Meanwhile, you must take my word that it will be best for him not to know anything about it."

Chapter Twenty-eight

*W*hen Sandy, on his way to his room to change for dinner, rounded the bend of the stairway, he was startled out of countenance by the sudden appearance of his host, who lunged out of the shadows at him and grabbed him by the lapels of his fashionable riding coat. "What did you think you were *doing*, you damnable bounder?" Kittridge demanded furiously.

"I knew it," Sandy sighed, rolling his eyes heavenward. "I *told* Cassie you'd call me out."

"And so I will," Kittridge snapped, although he was somewhat taken aback by his friend's complacency. "What else can a man do when he finds his best friend trying to seduce his wife?"

"You can loosen your hold on my best coat, for one thing," Sandy said in disgust. "I was *not* trying to seduce your wife. I was letting her cry on my shoulder. Like a friend."

"Like *a friend*?"

"Exactly."

Kittridge released his hold. "It didn't look like a friend's embrace to me," he grumbled sullenly.

Sandy smoothed his crushed lapels calmly. "I don't care how it looked to you. You're out in your reckoning, old fellow. You should think shame on yourself! If you've become so deranged that you believe Philip Sanford would seduce his best friend's wife, your vision is surely askew."

"Am I acting deranged?" Kittridge asked, feeling foolish.

"As the proverbial loon," his friend retorted flatly. "In the first place, any sane man would be able to tell that Cassie isn't the sort to play a husband false. And in the second place, I happen to be in love with your *sister*."

Kittridge ran a confused hand through his hair. "Then, hang it, why was *my* wife crying on *your* shoulder?"

"That, old fellow," Sandy said, proceeding up the stairs, "is something you'll have to ask her."

"I suppose," Kittridge muttered sheepishly, "I ought to apologize to you."

Sandy turned round and grinned down at his glum-looking friend. "No need for that, Robbie. No offense taken. I know how love can make a man loony."

"Love?" Kittridge gazed up at his friend in genuine astonishment. "Are you suggesting that I'm in love with Cassie?"

"It certainly appears so to me."

"Don't be daft!"

Sandy shrugged. "Have it your way. When it comes to these matters, I'm far from expert." He turned and continued up the stairs. "If I can't determine if Eunice feels the slightest *tendre* for me, how can I be sure about you?"

Kittridge considered the question as he walked slowly to his little study. Could Sandy possibly be right? he asked himself. Was it possible that he'd fallen in love with Cassie without realizing it? His feelings were certainly muddled enough to be the stirrings of love. Ever since the night she'd so adamantly rejected him, he'd become more and more aware of how much he wanted her. But that yearning might only be the automatic response one felt for something one couldn't have. It was certainly not comparable to the adoration he'd felt for Elinor.

He locked himself into his office and, seating himself at his desk, stared at the letters Sandy had brought him today. There was not one from Elinor among them. He'd expected to be devastated by the absence of word from her, but the truth was that he hadn't felt the expected disappointment. In fact, the only feeling he was aware of was relief. He couldn't understand it, but that word "relief" seemed to be the only one that accurately described his emotion.

He took out her letters from their cubicle and opened a few of them. His eyes roamed over the familiar words without bringing him the familiar pain. Was this another sign that he'd fallen in love with Cassie? He shook his head in self-disgust. Was he such a loose screw that he could forget his allegiance to the one great love of his life and attach himself to another in only a few months? The thought sickened him.

On the other hand, rereading Elinor's letters reminded him of the weight of guilt her outpourings of love had pressed upon him all these months. No wonder the absence of a letter brought relief. If Elinor's affection had weakened with time, or if she'd herself fallen in love with someone else, he would no longer need to feel responsible for her unhappiness! As sad as the end of their love might be, it was good to feel the weight of guilt lifted from his shoulders.

He let out a long breath and, leaning back in his chair, tried to stretch his legs out in front of him. But there was not enough room under his narrow desktop. He must, he thought, ask Cassie to find him a larger table. She had a knack for making a room comfortable. Perhaps she would agree to set her talents to work on this place.

Cassie. Even the name had a comfortable resonance. Loesby and Sandy had both been telling him for months how lucky he was to have found her. They were quite right, of course; he could see that now. But that didn't mean he loved her. Even his ridiculous attack of jealousy didn't necessarily mean he loved her, although he had to admit that, when he'd seen her in Sandy's arms, he'd felt a wild, insanely furious desire to wring his best friend's blasted neck!

He had no answer to the mystery of his muddled feelings, but one thought brought a rueful smile to his lips. *Wouldn't it be a delightful surprise,* he asked himself, *if I found myself in love with my own wife?*

Chapter Twenty-nine

*E*unice and her daughters were packing to leave. Cassie would have been heart-broken, except that her sister-in-law's reason for departure was such a happy one. Eunice was going to marry Sandy!

The decision had been made so quickly that it astounded everyone, even Sandy himself. He had followed Cassie's advice and, throwing caution to the winds, made a declaration of love that was not at all shy. "Eunice," he'd declared, pulling her into his arms, "I've been wanting to do this for ten years." And he'd kissed her squarely on the mouth.

"Sandy!" Eunice had gasped. "What does this *mean?*"

"If you don't know," he'd retorted, "I must not be doing it well." And he kissed her again, with even more fervor. It took several more of such demonstrations before she admitted, laughing breathlessly, that he'd made his intentions clear enough. By that time she knew she was his. Her doubts about her feelings for him had entirely disappeared. "I had no idea," she confided giddily to Cassie later, "that he was so . . . so *talented*!"

The day of their departure was a confused amalgam of merriment and tears. The two little girls, while very happy at the prospect of having the cheerful, moonfaced Sandy as their new father, nevertheless stood weeping among the boxes and bags piled up in the Great Hall just before their departure. They'd loved their months at Highlands, and they were thrown into despondency at having to say good-bye to their Uncle Robert and Aunt Cassie. Only the promise that their uncle and aunt would be coming soon to London for the wedding stopped their wails.

Eunice, too, was weeping at the thought of parting from Cassie. Dizzily light-headed as she was at finding herself in love after so many years, she was nevertheless heartbroken at separating from the woman who'd become her best friend. Her ambivalent feelings were clearly visible as she directed the servants in the stowing of the luggage with one hand while dabbing a handkerchief at her eyes with the other.

When the protracted good-byes were under way, and Eunice and the girls were weeping in earnest, Cassie drew Eunice away from the others and asked for a moment of private conversation with her. Eunice, surprised, of course agreed. Cassie led her to the sitting room. "Eunice," she said tensely, carefully closing the door, "I have a very great favor to ask you."

"Anything, Cassie, my love, anything," Eunice assured her, blowing her nose into an already soaking handkerchief.

Cassie put a hand into the bosom of her dress and withdrew some folded sheets of paper. "I've written some letters. Three of them. I want you to . . . to take care of them for me."

"Take care of them?" Eunice's eyebrows rose. "Keep them safe, you mean?"

"No. I mean *send* them."

"I don't understand, Cassie." She cocked her head suspiciously. "Are you up to some mischief?"

"Yes, I'm sure you will think so. They are . . . forgeries."

"*Forgeries*? What on earth—?" Her eyes narrowed. "Has this something to do with Elinor?"

"Yes. Please, Eunice, don't scold. I know what I'm doing is very dreadful, but I can't bear to see Robert so unhappy. If he learned that Elinor no longer cares, it would break his heart. So I've written these in her name. Written them *for* her, so to speak."

Eunice couldn't believe her ears. "You've written letters for *Elinor*?"

Cassie nodded. "All you need do is find the proper notepaper, copy these letters exactly as I've written them, seal and frank them, and have your mother send a messenger back here to deliver them to Robert."

"You, my love, have taken leave of your *senses*! The whole scheme is impossible. It will never work! Even with the proper notepaper, can you really believe that Robbie won't see at once that the letters are false? Why, the handwriting alone—"

"I've taken care of that. The first letter explains that she burned her hand badly with candle wax, which is why she couldn't write at all for several weeks. She is now better, but her fingers are still bandaged, so she must write with her left hand. If you use *your* left hand when you write, I'm certain we can be convincing."

"Even so, Cassie, this is *wrong*. Why should you feel compelled to indulge in so elaborate a pretense? Let him forget her. It will be better for all concerned."

Cassie shook her head sadly. "He won't forget her, any more than I would forget *him* if we were separated. Try to understand, Eunice. You and Sandy and the children will be gone. Robert will have no one left but me, and—"

"Good!" Eunice cut in firmly. "Perhaps then he will learn to appreciate you properly."

Desperate to make her friend understand, Cassie grasped her by the shoulders. "Listen to me, Eunice! Ever since he left the cavalry, Robert has had to make sacrifices. When he married me, he sold his *future,* don't you see that? And it wasn't for his own benefit. It was for the family—for *you*! It isn't fair! Can't we give him this one little gift? Doesn't he deserve to have this one bit of secret happiness?"

Eunice stared at her sister-in-law in awe. "I don't understand you, Cassie. You love him, yet you are willing to give him 'this one bit of secret happiness' with *another* woman. Why?"

"I can't bear it when his eyes get that faraway, yearning look. It makes me miserable. In a way, you know, I am the one who killed his dreams. It can't be right, can it, for a man to have no dreams? We can't change the *reality* of his life, but perhaps we can keep his dreams alive. In the dimness of his future, shouldn't we try to give him one small ray of light that he can look forward to?"

"Oh, Cassie," Eunice moaned in surrender, throwing her arms about her sister-in-law's neck, "when you speak so, you give me no choice but to do your bidding. I'll write your blasted letters for you."

They held each other tightly for a long moment. Then Eunice took the folded papers and stuffed them in her reticule. Cassie, in relief, gave her one last, fervent embrace. "Thank you, Eunice," she murmured in Eunice's ear. "I shall be forever in your debt."

"I don't want you in my debt," Eunice retorted gruffly as she went to the door, "but if the truth comes out, and this whole, preposterous scheme explodes in your face, I shall refuse to take even a *speck* of blame!"

Chapter Thirty

The messenger delivered the packet of letters in midafternoon of a rainy day a week later. Kittridge was out at the building site when Dickie accepted the packet. Cassie, who'd waited on tenterhooks all week for this moment to arrive, hid behind the curve of the stairway to await his return. She wanted to see Robert's face when he first glimpsed the letters.

It was teatime when he came home. Dickie, pompous as always, admitted him into the Great Hall and held the packet out to him. "These came from London, my lord," he announced. "A messenger delivered them at three this afternoon."

Robert, in the act of brushing the raindrops from his shoulders, froze. He stared at the buff-colored envelopes for a long moment, quite stony-faced, and then, snatching them from Dickie's hand, strode off to his study without a word. If Cassie had hoped to see a sign of gladness or excitement in his face as a reward for her endeavors, she was doomed to disappointment.

Robert, for his part, was filled with ambivalence. He hadn't thought about Elinor for days. He'd been thinking, instead, about Cassie. She, not Elinor, was his life's companion, and he'd been trying to think of ways to overcome her stubborn resistance to his advances. Now the letters brought his memories of Elinor flooding back to confuse him, and he wasn't sure he welcomed them. The past, he was beginning to realize, could sometimes become a burden. His own past was suddenly appearing so to him. It seemed to be a barricade in his advance to the future, and he had enough barricades to climb already.

Nevertheless, his feelings for Elinor were of such long-standing that, almost without thinking, his old reactions swept over him. Staring at her letters, he tried to bring her lovely face to mind, as he had done hundreds of times before. But the vision he conjured up was indistinct, and he wondered guiltily if he was even forgetting what she looked like. Sighing, he broke the seal of the first letter. The awkward handwriting disconcerted him for a moment, but soon the warmth of her words riveted his attention. The mood of the letter was different from the earlier ones. It was more gentle, and sadly reminiscent. And the last paragraph brought a clench to his heart. *"I like to imagine,"* she wrote, *"that sometimes you can feel what I feel, despite the miles between us. When my hand burned, I convinced myself that at the same moment you must have experienced a sting. One day, when I felt an unexplained tingle on my cheek, I let myself believe that you were rubbing yours and sending the touch through the ether right to me. I suppose such thoughts are foolish, but it comforts me to believe that love like ours is capable of creating small miracles. Please, my beloved, when you read this, rub your cheek and think of me!"*

Her continuing devotion, so obvious in her words, made him wince. How was it possible, he wondered, that so lovely a girl—who, with the crook of a finger, could summon a dozen suitors to her side—would keep her affection for him alive so long without the hope of any response? While he, cad that he was, was already growing attached to someone else.

The next letter made him feel worse. *"It was warm today,"* she wrote, *"and I sat on a garden bench looking up at the sky. The cloud formations irritated me, for none of them took your shape. There was one cloud like a man's head, but the nose was not yours. I began to have the silliest thoughts. I wished that I could find a brush long enough to paint on the sky. I could not paint your face, of course—even in dreams I know I am no artist—but I had this ridiculous urge to paint your name— Robert, Robert, Robert!—over and over in an arching line until, like a rainbow, it would stretch from horizon to horizon. I am growing quite demented."*

But it was something in the last letter that undid him. *"I like to remember your quirks,"* she wrote. *"They keep you real for me. I remember how you rub the underside of your nose with your right forefinger when you're about to say something you're afraid you shouldn't. Or the way a muscle right above your jaw twitches with tension when you're angry. Or the way you run your fingers through your hair when you feel bewildered. Just writing these words is enough to conjure up your face for me, and I can see you in such detail that you become palpable . . . as real as if you were standing here. It's only when I try to touch you that the vision dissolves into nothingness, and I am left bereft."*

The words made Robert groan in agony. His fingers tightened into fists, crushing the last letter into a crumpled ball. Poor, lovely Elinor! She could conjure him up in every detail, while he could scarcely remember her face. She offered him her love with such openhearted generosity that the very words with which she expressed it made his throat burn, while he lusted every day, with an ache in his loins that drove him to distraction, for someone else entirely! He was not worthy of Elinor! Or of Cassie, either, for that matter. The letters made him see himself for the loathsome toad he was. They made him hate himself.

But what sin had he committed to cause this shambles, this triangular trap that had distorted three lives? Had he sold his soul to the devil when he'd made his bargain with Chivers? But that bargain had not been the cause of Elinor's pain. His father, and hers, had done the damage long before he'd signed his devil's pact with Chivers. But even if he took the blame upon himself, it made no difference, for there was no way out of the trap no matter who was to blame. *It's as if I were cursed,* he thought as he tenderly smoothed out the paper he'd crushed, folded it and put it with the others into the cubicle. He was living under some witch's curse for which there was no antidote. Why couldn't he find a magic amulet, a wand, a wizard's potion, a virgin's kiss that would break the spell under which he was doomed to live? But no, not in this life. Only in fairy stories did the toad turn into a prince after a maiden's kiss.

Cassie, meanwhile, having no idea of the turmoil the letters had aroused in her husband's breast, basked in self-satisfaction over the success of her forgery. She'd done it! Robert had been closeted for hours in his study. If he'd found anything wrong with the letters, there would surely have been some sign of it by this time. As the minutes passed, she became more and more convinced that her letters had been a success. Robert was surely finding in them the solace he needed. Just as she wished, the letters were balm to his wounded soul. The feelings they generated would probably nourish him for weeks.

For weeks. The two words seemed suddenly to reverberate in her head. *After a few weeks, what then?* she asked herself with a start. How soon would it be before he began to look for more? What could she do then? She could write more letters, of course, but Eunice would probably refuse to commit her hand to any more forgeries. And even if she did, how could Cassie get the letters to her without being discovered? Why hadn't she thought of that before? The letters, to be effective, had to keep coming, but she had no way of accomplishing that. Yet, if they stopped coming, Robert would be in a worse case than before. What had she done?

She prowled round the sitting room, searching her mind for an answer. And right before dinnertime, it came to her. She simply had to get to London, to give Eunice a new supply of letters and convince her to keep up the pretense a while longer. It could be done, if only Robert would agree to take her to town.

At the table that evening, she looked across at him speculatively. He seemed abstracted and somewhat dazed. It gave her a feeling of rueful pride that her words—her own love feelings—had had so strong an effect on him. But the apparent success of the letters made it all the more necessary to solve the problem at hand. She hesitated to raise the subject that was on her mind, but sooner or later it had to be done. After almost an hour of complete silence, she cleared her throat. "Robert?" she began timidly.

"Yes," he said absently.

"Do you remember, that night before we were married, when we talked about settling in the country?"

"Yes, of course." He pushed his plate away from him. "What about it?"

"Do you remember saying that you would take me back to town for a month or so in season?"

He lifted his head abruptly. This was the request he'd expected from the first—her admission of her desire to mingle with the *ton,* to play the role of Viscountess Kittridge on the town! It was the purpose for which he assumed she'd married him. All thoughts of Elinor evaporated as his eyes focused on the woman across the table, his whole body tensing. "Yes, I remember," he said, watching her carefully.

"The season has already begun, you know. Do you think we might go, at least for a fortnight?"

"Well, we shall be going, you know, for Eunice's wedding."

"But that's in June. Two months away. Couldn't we . . . would it be asking too much to go now, and then again in June?"

He leaned back in his chair. "It would be too much for me, I'm afraid. The ground is to be broken for the tenants' housing strip next week. I don't see how I can spare the time."

"Oh . . . I see."

He could hear the disappointment in her voice. He clenched his teeth, trying to bring his own disappointment under control. She'd seemed so satisfied to be in the country all these months that he'd forgotten his original estimate of her motivation for marriage. But now it was clear—she *was* a *parvenu* after all. Well, if it was a life in society that she wanted, she could have it. She'd certainly paid for it. "You could go without me, I suppose," he offered, testing her.

"Could I, Robert? I do so wish to go. I would only stay a week or so."

"You can stay as long as you like," he said, a wave of disgust toward her sweeping over him. "Until the wedding is over in June, if you like."

His words struck her like a slap. She didn't understand why he'd said that. She wanted to go to town only to make the arrangements about the letters. The week away from home would seem like an eternity to her. Yet he was willing to part with her until the end of June! "Oh, no," she murmured, her voice choking up with tears. "A w-week will be quite enough."

With his mouth twisted into a sneer, he pushed back his chair and rose. *A week, indeed,* he said to himself in revulsion. Was this the creature he thought he might care for more than Elinor? What a fool he was! She wouldn't come back in a week, or even a month. Not as long as she enjoyed queening it in town! *I'll lay odds she postpones her return indefinitely,* he told himself. But aloud he only said, "Suit yourself, Cassie. It makes no difference to me." And, cold as ice, he strode across the room and out the door.

Chapter Thirty-one

*C*assie was utterly confused. As she sat over her embroidery frame in her lonely sitting room, she found herself dripping silent tears on the stitches. What had gone wrong? she asked herself miserably. She'd hoped to make her husband happy by her subterfuge, but if the letters had been, as she'd hoped, a balm to his wounded soul, she saw no sign of it. The two of them were barely speaking. Yet her portmanteau and two bandboxes stood packed and ready in the Great Hall for removal the next morning to the carriage that was to take her to London. Robert had instructed Loesby to arrange for the coachman to be at the door at seven. She was leaving. And without him.

Cassie had no real wish to go, for the terrible coldness that had sprung up between them pained her more than anything else that had happened to her. She had no understanding of the cause, but she feared that her absence would only make matters worse. But her dishonest forgery scheme, now launched, had to be continued. She saw no way around it. And to continue it, she had to go to London to see Eunice.

She wiped her eyes, wondering if Robert would join her for tea this last day before she went away. Taking tea with her was an observance he'd been avoiding for the past few days, but perhaps today he would take the trouble to join her. It would be an act of kindness that would ease her mind a little. When, just at tea-time, a knock sounded at the sitting room door, her heart leaped up to her throat. But it was only Dickie. "A message from London, my lady," he said. "The messenger said that no answer was required."

"A message for his lordship?" Cassie inquired in surprise. "How strange! His mother forwarded some letters only two days ago."

"It's addressed to *you,* my lady," Dickie said in a tone that was unmistakably disapproving. "Marked 'Private and Personal' in large letters, as you can see."

"Private and personal?" Cassie snatched the missive from him and waved him out. The pompous fellow evidently assumed that any letter marked 'private and personal' must contain a wicked message. Did the idiotic fellow think she was carrying on some sort of indiscretion? Cassie herself, however, while amused at her butler, was almost as uneasy about the contents as he was. In fact, her hands were shaking. She'd never received a letter marked "private and personal" in all her life.

It was from Eunice. *"Dearest Cassie,"* Eunice had written in a hurried scrawl, *"I hope you are reading this in Complete Privacy. And I think, when you have Finished, you should Burn this in the Fire. I've taken the Risk of writing because something has Occurred that you should know. E.L. is back in London! I'm sure you can Guess whom I mean. She is Betrothed to her Italian Conte, and I hear she has been Parading him about Town as Proudly as a Peacock. She has not yet Called on me, undoubtedly in Embarrassment over Robbie, but I expect I shall have to Face her soon. I intend to tell her that Robbie is Divinely Happy and in transports over his Wonderful Wife. What Worries me about this matter is, as you've probably guessed, the Danger to You. If Robbie doesn't hear about her before June, he's Bound to learn Everything then, of course, because you will Both be coming to Town for my Wedding! She will Have to be Invited, worse Luck, and then, in addition to Learning about her Betrothal, he might discover that She never wrote the Letters! The Fat will be in the Fire then! I only pray that Robbie may not Murder you! How you are to get yourself out of this Fix I have no Idea, but You, my Love, are Endlessly Resourceful, and I am certain you will think of Something. In the meantime, you may rest assured I am Praying for a Happy Outcome. I Remain Your Loving and Terror-stricken Eunice."*

By the time she'd finished reading, Cassie was deathly pale. She sat where she was, utterly immobilized. Eunice might believe that she was "Endlessly Resourceful," but she couldn't even think of where or how to begin to extricate herself from this nightmare. Of course, the first thing she had to do was to burn Eunice's letter, but the day was very warm and no fires had been lit in any of the rooms. With trembling knees, she marched herself down to the kitchen and, ignoring the wide-eyed stares of the astounded kitchen staff, lifted one of the stove lids and dropped the letter in. She waited until she was sure it was burned to a cinder and then marched out again with her head high. The staff might think she'd lost her mind, but if there was one thing in the world she did *not* have to worry about, it was the opinion of the kitchen staff.

Dinner that night was another silent meal. Cassie did not know how to tell her husband that she was not going to London after all. It was, on the face of it, a simple enough thing to do, but the prospect embarrassed her, especially because he'd seemed almost eager to see her go. He'd even encouraged her to stay until June! And, worse, she'd been so insistent about wanting to go! What would he make of her sudden change of heart? What excuse could she give? She was not up to telling him the truth just yet, but she could not countenance another lie. Perhaps the best thing to do would be to give no excuse at all.

She tried ten times to tell Robert that she'd changed her mind, and ten times her courage failed her. It was only when the meal was almost over that she managed it, and even then it was because Robert brought the subject up. "If I miss you in the morning, Cassie," he said in a tone of stiff politeness, "I hope you have a pleasant journey and an enjoyable stay in town."

"I'm not going," she blurted out.

"What did you say?" Robert asked in disbelief.

"I said I'm not going."

"You can't be serious!" He peered at her through the candlelight. "The plans have all been made!"

"I know," she said nervously, getting up and edging toward the door, "but p-plans can b-be unmade. I'm not going."

"But, *why?*" he demanded, pushing his chair back as if to rise.

His movement made her jump. "I changed my m-mind, that's all. I j-just changed my mind." And with that she fled from the room.

Feeling quite like a criminal, she scurried upstairs to her bedroom and shut the door. For the next hour she paced about the room, for she knew her troubles were not over. Not nearly. Elinor was back in London with a new betrothed, and Robert was bound to find out. And he was bound to find out, too, that Elinor had not written the last three letters. Cassie knew that she would have to confess to Robert what she'd done. But the admission would involve informing him about Elinor, and she didn't see how she could do that without causing him pain. Furthermore, he would be furious with her for playing so dastardly a trick on him, and she couldn't even guess what terrible form that fury would take. Even Eunice said he might murder her! She remembered, when she'd invaded his privacy and read Elinor's letters, she'd imagined herself as Bluebeard's wife— one of the six who'd been hacked to death for invading the forbidden room. When she'd first thought of the Bluebeard legend, the prospect of murder had been a sort of joke. It did not seem so funny now. She had done worse than invade a forbidden room! If her Robert became Bluebeard and dismembered her poor body, she'd deserve it!

Her wild thoughts were interrupted by a knock at the door. "Cassie, open the door," Robert ordered. "I have to talk to you."

"I'm already abed," she lied, jumping into it and pulling the covers over her to make it true.

"Dash it, Cassie, one would think I intended to *beat* you! I just want to know why you're not going to London."

"I've already told you," she insisted, not moving from the bed. "I changed my mind. It's a woman's privilege, isn't it?"

"Yes, of course. I have no objection to your staying home," he said reasonably. "I only want to know *why.*"

"I'm tired," she said. "Can't we talk about it tomorrow?"

"Oh, very well," came his voice, thick with disgust. "But I must say, Cassie, that your behavior this evening has been very, very peculiar. Well, if you're sure you won't say any more, I'll bid you good night."

"Good night, Robert," she answered in relief.

Once he'd gone, she got up and undressed, but as she crawled back into bed she knew she would not sleep. How could she, knowing that the very next day she would have to tell Robert everything? There was no way out.

Of course, she could postpone it, she supposed. He was unlikely to learn about Elinor before June. Perhaps her best course of action would be to ignore everything and let him discover the truth for himself at the wedding. She shut her eyes and tried to imagine how his discovery might take place. Robert, at the wedding, would come upon Elinor at the buffet table. "Elinor!" he'd gasp. "You are as lovely as ever."

"*Dear* Robert," she'd smile, blushing prettily, "you mustn't say such things to me. Haven't you heard that I'm betrothed?"

"Betrothed?" He would undoubtedly turn white. "You *can't* be betrothed!"

"But, my dear, I am! Since last March, when I was in Italy. There is my betrothed, over there near the window. The Italian, with the *mustachios.*"

"Since *March*?" Robert would gape at her in confusion. "How can that be? You wrote me in *April* that you still loved me! You said you wanted to paint my name across the sky!"

"I?" She would laugh a trilling laugh. "I would never have written anything so silly. In fact, I haven't written to you at all since . . . oh, since February."

Robert would stare at his beloved, wide-eyed with horror. "But who," he would wonder aloud, "would have played so dastardly a trick on me?" His eyes would suddenly narrow in comprehension. "*Cassie!*" he would exclaim, tight-lipped with fury. "Who else would be capable of such revolting underhandedness?"

And then, eyes blazing, he would confront her in front of all the wedding guests. A sword would flash in the air. There would be screams and confusion. Cassie would have to fall to her knees. "Robert, spare me!" she would beseech. "I didn't think—!"

But the sword would whizz swiftly through the air and down! The sounds of women shrieking and men shouting would drown out Cassie's last scream . . .

She sat up in bed with a start. Had she screamed aloud? She really had to get hold of herself. These imaginings were becoming too lurid for words.

She slid back onto her pillows and pulled the bedclothes up to her neck. She had to try to get some sleep, for tomorrow would be a difficult day. Since her imagined scene had made it clear that she could not subject her husband to such a humiliating scene at his sister's wedding, she would have to tell him everything herself. Tomorrow would have to be the day.

She shuddered and burrowed deeper into her pillows. *Yes,* she thought as sleep slowly overtook her, *tomorrow will be my punishment.*

Chapter Thirty-two

Whenever Loesby suspected that Lord Kittridge and his lady had had a quarrel, he expressed his disapproval by clucking his tongue, shaking his head and behaving as if his lordship had affronted him personally. "I s'pose, m' lord, ye'll be wantin' yer boots removed?" he asked icily after Kittridge had stormed into his bedroom following the exchange with his wife in the corridor.

"Since I'd rather not go to bed wearing them," Kittridge retorted, sitting on his bed and extending a foot, "yes, I'd like them removed, if you wouldn't mind."

"Much ye'd care if I *did* mind," Loesby muttered, dragging off a boot. "Some people don't seem to care about *anyone's* feelin's these days."

Kittridge glared at him. "You were eavesdropping again, I take it?"

Loesby pulled off the other boot. "Didn't 'ave to. Everyone fer miles about could 'ear ye. An' 'ow a man wot calls 'isself a gen'leman cin tell 'is lady that she's actin' *peculiar* is beyond me!"

Kittridge pulled off his coat and threw it at his valet. "Mind your own business for a change, will you, Loesby? You don't know anything about the matter."

"I know enough. She decided not t' take off fer town. Wut's so damn peculiar about that? If I wuz a lady, an' me better 'alf wouldn't go along wi' me, I wouldn't go neither."

Kittridge paused in the act of unbuttoning his shirt and stared at the fellow speculatively. "Do you think *that's* her reason? That I wasn't going along with her?"

Loesby shrugged. "Wut else?"

"There are any number of other possibilities. But I don't intend to stand here and argue the matter with you. You always defend her, anyway, no matter what I have to say. So you can just take yourself off, you bobbing-block. I've seen enough of you for one day."

"Don't ye want 'elp wi' yer breeches?"

"I can undress myself, thank you. Good night!"

But after the valet departed, Kittridge didn't bother to finish undressing. He threw himself upon his bed in his stockinged feet, still wearing his half-unbuttoned shirt and his breeches, and, with his hands tucked under his head, stared up at the ceiling. He had to think. This undeclared war with Cassie was getting on his nerves. Every time he believed he was beginning to understand her, something would occur to overset him. He'd believed, at first, that she was a conniving *parvenu*. Then, after the early months here at Highlands, he'd begun to believe she was sincere in her expressed desire to live a modest country life. She seemed to take to it so well. He'd even begun to think of her as rather a jewel—a "wonder" as Loesby liked to call her. But the other day, her request to run off to town, just when the work on the estate was getting into full swing, returned him to his original suspicions. Then this evening, as if on purpose to upset him again, she boldly announced that she didn't want to go to London after all. What on earth was he expected to make of *that*?

To make matters more confused, he still suspected that he'd fallen in love with her. Nothing she did, no matter how annoying or reprehensible, had the power to loosen her growing hold on him. Even Elinor's recent and quite wonderful letters hadn't managed to free him from the subtle, inexplicable allure that Cassie seemed to exert on him. What was wrong with him? How could he have permitted this devious and manipulative female to lure him from his pledged loyalty to his first love?

It surprised him that even the recent letters had not brought him back to his earlier state of mind. None of the letters Elinor had written before had moved him as much as these. They made Elinor seem more gentle and touching, and a good deal less sorry for herself. She seemed, somehow, to have matured. Why, then, hadn't they made a difference? Why hadn't they weakened the growing hold that Cassie had on his emotions?

Perhaps it was because the change in Elinor's style of writing made her seem, suddenly, a bit unrecognizable. He couldn't hear her voice in the words any more. And the strange handwriting added to the confusion. It almost seemed as if someone else had written those letters. Even the way Elinor had said his name sounded unfamiliar. What was it she'd written? *I had this ridiculous urge to paint your name across the sky—Robert, Robert, Robert!* She'd never called him Robert before. From early childhood she'd always called him Robbie. Everyone called him Robbie except . . .

He sat up with a start, a shocking idea flashing across his brain like a lightning bolt. Everyone called him Robbie except *Cassie!*

The idea, once it burst upon him, took over his mind with the crystal clarity of truth. *Elinor hadn't written those letters at all! Cassie had!* He could even hear Cassie's voice saying the words! He didn't know how, and he certainly didn't know *why,* but he was as sure as his name was Robert Rossiter that Cassie had done it. And as the conviction grew that he'd stumbled on the truth, a knot formed in the pit of his stomach, and, slowly, a fury such as he'd never known burst out and spread like a poison to every part of his body. He wanted to take a chair and heave it through a window. He wanted to smash the walls with his fists. He wanted to feel Cassie's throat in his two hands and squeeze it until she went limp and lifeless in his hold. Yes, that was it! He wanted to *murder* her!

Maddened with rage, he lit a candle with shaking hands. Then he plunged down the stairs to his study, pulled out the three letters and stormed up again, the candle in one fist and the letters clenched in the other. Using his shoulder to batter his way in, he crashed through Cassie's door.

Cassie, curled into a ball under her bedclothes, had just dozed off when the crash woke her. She sat up, shuddering in terror as Robert, eyes glittering with rage in the eerie light of his single candle, strode to the side of her bed. "What, ma'am, was the meaning of *this?*" he snarled, holding up the letters before her.

"R-Robert?" she stammered, not sure whether the threatening apparition standing over her was a vision from a nightmare or Bluebeard in the flesh.

"Yes, it's 'Robert.'" He shook the letters in her face. "Well, ma'am? Explain, if you can, why you wrote these damned letters!"

"Oh, heavens," she gasped, turning ashen, "how—?"

"Never mind how! I am a dozen ways a fool, but did you think me such a dupe that I could be humbugged by these . . . these inept imitations?"

"Robert, *please!*" she begged, sitting up and edging along the headboard away from him in sheer terror of his white-lipped rage. "Don't go on! I didn't intend—"

"Didn't intend what? To humbug me?"

"Well, no . . . yes . . . I m-mean . . . not exactly . . ."

He slammed down the candle on her bedside table. "What sort of craven evasion is *that?*" he demanded. "*Of course* you intended it! When someone signs a letter with a name that is not one's own, the intention *must* be to deceive, isn't that so?"

"Yes, but—"

"And you *did* write these, did you not? And you did sign Elinor's name to your fraudulent creations?"

"Yes," she answered in a hoarse, shamed whisper. "Yes."

He stared at her, her admission of guilt killing the last hope, hidden somewhere deep within him, that he'd accused her wrongly. "How could you?" he asked with unmistakable loathing, dropping the letters from his hold as if releasing something noxious. "What have I ever done to you to make you wish to make a mockery of my private sorrows?"

"Robert!" she cried out, agonized. "You *can't* believe that I meant to mock you!"

"What else am I to believe? The more I think about it, the more repugnant the act becomes. I never intended for you to know anything of Elinor's existence, since it was not a matter that had anything to do with you. But you learned of it somehow—Eunice's glib tongue, I have no doubt. And having learned of it, you couldn't just let it be. You had to interfere—is that it? You somehow discovered that she wrote to me, although I don't know how—" Just then, another hideous awareness broke upon him like a blow to the jaw. "Good God!" He glared down at her with increased revulsion. "You must have stolen into my study, opened my desk and *read her letters*!"

Cassie shut her eyes in utter humiliation, unable to face the burning hostility in his. "Oh, Robert, I'm s-so . . . *sorry,*" she mumbled helplessly, dropping her face in her hands.

"Sorry!" He spat out the word with utter disdain. He pulled her hands from her face, grasped both her shoulders and lifted her up until her eyes were on a level with his. "Never mind your 'sorry'! What I want to know is *why*!"

Tears welled up in her eyes. "I thought . . . I only w-wanted . . . for you to be h-happy."

"Happy!" He gave a mirthless, disbelieving snort. "I'd like to wring your blasted neck!" he ranted. "If you're going to keep on *lying,* you surely can do better than that!"

Her eyes looked pleadingly into his. "It's the truth, I swear. What other reason—?"

He shook his head. "I wish I knew." He dropped his hold on her and let her fall back upon the pillows. Their eyes met, hers wide with acute, tormented remorse and his narrowed with such bewildered antipathy that she had to turn away and bury her face in the pillows.

"All these months I've wondered what sort of woman it was I've married," he said after a long silence, his voice now quieter but infused with scorn. "I've never been able to understand you. It didn't seem possible that you, with your oh-so-gentle manner and oh-so-modest demeanor, would agree to shackle yourself to a stranger merely for the sake of calling yourself a viscountess. But I could think of no other motive. Yet you came to live here, far away from any society among whom you could preen yourself with your new title. And you won everyone over, even Sandy, who'd once described you—before you put him in your spell—as a 'manipulative *intrigante*.' You even had *me* believing I was falling in love with you. What a damn fool I was! You *are* a manipulative *intrigante* after all! You first wrested control of the household from Eunice—and so cleverly, too, that you now have her eating out of your hand. And now, I suppose, it is *I* whom you want to control, although how you intended to manage it with forged letters from Elinor is beyond my puny understanding. As to the why of it, it is all too subtly devious for me. But all at once I find I don't care anymore. I don't *want* to understand. I just want to take myself out of here, before I choke on my disgust of you!" And with those cutting words, he slammed out of the room and left her to her shame.

Chapter Thirty-three

Robert drank all of an almost full bottle of brandy before falling on his bed. He hoped that getting himself soused would help him forget the devious little schemer to whom he was leg-shackled. He fell asleep hugging the empty bottle to his chest. Several hours later, deep in a dream in which he was holding Cassie tightly against him and trying desperately to make out the words she was murmuring softly into his chest, he felt someone tugging at what he was holding in his arms. He opened his eyes to find Loesby trying to take away the empty bottle while glaring down at him with a pinched-mouth expression of disgust. "So ye're awake, are ye?" the valet sneered, removing the bottle from his lordship's suddenly unresistant grasp.

Robert shut his eyes again. "Someone's hammering inside my head," he mumbled miserably.

"Serves ye right," Loesby retorted unsympathetically, stalking to the windows and pulling back the draperies with such loud force that his lordship groaned. "Do ye wish to wear wut ye slept in, me lord," he asked, his nose wrinkled in revulsion, "or do ye wish to change?"

Robert put a hand to his aching forehead. When his valet called him "me lord," it always meant trouble, but his head pained him too much to exert himself to find out why. Besides, he had troubles enough. His last words to Cassie were still reverberating in his brain and making him feel like a bounder. In his sleep his brain had been actively recalling to his consciousness the many occasions when she'd seemed so completely sweet and charming that it was hard to believe that she could be the devious schemer she had seemed last night. She'd committed a serious transgression, true, but he hadn't given her sufficient opportunity to explain. He'd said many unkind things that he was now sorry for; the hammer blows in his head were not the only things making him feel sick.

Somehow he knew that he would not feel better until he spoke to her again. All he wanted now was to go to her room and talk things over calmly.

He lifted himself up from his pillow, groaning with the effort. "I'll change later," he told the valet. "Just hand me my boots."

"Wut fer?" Loesby asked scornfully as he took a clean shirt from the chest of drawers. "Do ye think ye're goin' somewheres?"

"Yes. I'm going to see my wife, if you don't mind," his lordship retorted, pulling himself erect by hanging on the bedpost.

"Ye'll 'ave to run pretty quick," Loesby said. "She's miles away by now."

Robert felt his chest clench. "Miles away?"

Loesby nodded. "Sent fer the carriage at seven this mornin'. Said she'd changed 'er mind again and was off to town. She looked mighty red-eyed about it, too, if ye ask me."

A feeling of desolate emptiness swept over him. "Did she leave a message? A note?"

Loesby shook his head. "No, but I found these in 'er room, tossed in the grate." He gave Kittridge a sly look as he handed him the three crushed, buff-colored envelopes. "Fished 'em out just before the maid set about lightin' the fire."

"I suppose you think you've earned my undying gratitude for that," Robert growled, stuffing the letters into his pocket. "Well, you haven't. Don't think I'm not aware that you read them. I have as much privacy in my life as a damned fish in a jar!"

Crestfallen and angry, he ordered Loesby out of the room and lowered himself slowly back down on the bed. Cassie was gone. His wife had left him. Was her departure supposed to be a punishment? And if so, was it meant for him or for herself? Well, at least he knew the answer to that. *She* might have been red-eyed, but *he,* he acknowledged as he put a shaking hand to his hammering head, was sick unto death.

A few days later, however, he'd recovered not only his health but his rage. He'd spent the time of his recovery dwelling on his injuries. His wife had injured him by her inexplicable invasion of his privacy. His sister had injured him by supporting his wife against him, for he'd soon deduced that it was Eunice who'd been enlisted to post the fraudulent letters. Sandy and Loesby had injured him, too, by siding with Cassie all the time. He'd been wounded to the heart by all of them!

By the time three days had passed, his rage was full-blown. He was furious that Cassie had left without a word. He was furious that he'd even *considered* making it up with her. He was furious that he was unable to put his mind to anything else. Something had to be done to release all the fury pent up inside him. "Send for the phaeton, Loesby," he ordered suddenly. "I'm going to settle things once and for all. We're going to London!"

Loesby, who'd been glowering at his lordship for three whole days, broke into a smile. "Well, well," he chortled, rubbing his hands together in approval, "*now* ye're talkin'!"

Chapter Thirty-four

The first person who greeted Lord Kittridge on his arrival at Rossiter House in Portman Square was his brother Gavin. "So, Robbie, you've finally come back to town, have you?" the lad asked, not even pausing on his way out the door. "That's splendid."

"Just a moment, Gavin," his elder brother said, catching his arm. "Why aren't you at school?"

"I've been sent down. But I'm too busy to go into details now, old fellow. I'm off to Tattersall's to look at a roan. See you at dinner."

Kittridge looked after his brother with a troubled frown. The boy was wasting his life, and no one seemed to be in the least concerned about it. He was about to call after him when his mother suddenly appeared, descending the stairs with her delicate grace. "Darling!" she exclaimed in delight. "We weren't expecting you until the nuptials. What a lovely surprise!"

He kissed her cheek. "You look thriving, Mama," he said. "Planning a wedding must agree with you."

"I wish I could say the same for you, my dear," his mother said, peering at him keenly as she took his arm and strolled with him to the sitting room. "You've shadows under your eyes, and you're looking too thin. I knew that your marriage to that *bourgeoise* would undo you, no matter what encomiums Eunice heaps on her."

"See here, Mama," Robert chided while he handed her over the threshold and into an easy chair, "I won't have you casting aspersions on my wife. If I look worn, you may blame it on the fourteen-hour drive from Lincoln—"

"Robbie!" The scream came from the doorway, and in flew Eunice in a flurry of ruffles and flounces. She threw her arms round his neck ecstatically. "What

are you doing here? We weren't expecting you for weeks! How lovely that you came so soon! Where's—?"

He removed her arms from about him with icy formality. "Never mind the effusions, ma'am. I'm sure you'll understand that, under the circumstances, I don't care to speak to you. Please be good enough to inform Lady Kittridge that I'm here."

Eunice blinked at him in stupefaction. "Do you mean Mama? She's sitting right behind you."

"Of course I don't mean Mama. I mean my wife, as you very well know."

"Your wife? *Cassie?* Isn't she with you?"

It was now Robert's turn to look stupefied. "She left Lincolnshire several days ago. Do you mean she isn't here?"

"I knew it," his mother said with some satisfaction. "You've quarreled. I knew the marriage was a mistake. I said so from the first."

"Oh, Mama, do be still," Eunice snapped, glaring down at her. "Your baseless judgments do you no credit. Cassie is too good for your idiot son, if you ask me. Now be a dear, Mama, and do go away. Why don't you see to Robbie's baggage or make sure his room is ready? I want to talk to Robbie alone."

"Eunice, really!" her mother exclaimed, rising in offense. "I have as much right to hear what the new Lady Kittridge has been up to as you do. More, in fact."

"It might be best, Mama, to do as Eunice asks," Robert said. "I have a few words to say to your idiot *daughter* that are not fit for a mother's ears."

The dowager Lady Kittridge looked from one to the other of her offspring with raised brows, poised to debate them both. But then, capitulating with a shrug, she turned on her heel and sailed proudly from the room, muttering under her breath that it was a mistake ever to have bred them.

Eunice rounded on her brother as soon as their mother was gone. "What do you mean, a few words not meant for a mother's ears? Have I done something to offend you?"

"Don't play the innocent with me, ma'am. I know about the letters."

"Oh!" Eunice's eyes fell. "I *told* Cassie it was a terrible idea. But how on earth did you find out?"

"I'm not such a fool as you both seem to think. I can tell the difference between Elinor's style and Cassie's."

"Yes, I thought you might. Cassie has so much more . . . sincerity." She looked up at her brother with a troubled crease in her forehead. "I suppose you and Cassie had a dreadful row over it."

"You suppose correctly."

"And she's run off? You must have been horrid to her."

"Wouldn't you have been, in my place?" he snapped. "It's a bit degrading, to say the least, to have one's privacy invaded and one's inner feelings mocked by one's own wife . . . and one's own sister."

"Mocked?" Eunice gaped at him. "What are you talking about?"

"Isn't that what motivated you both? I admit that I find the whole incident too confusing to comprehend. But you, Eunice, have too strong a character to let Cassie manipulate you into doing something you believe is wrong. So I don't know what else could have convinced you to agree to such a despicable deception. What else could your purpose have been but to have a vulgar laugh at my expense?"

"You *are* a fool, Robbie. Do you know Cassie so little that you can believe she did this just to laugh at you? And do you know me so little, too?"

He stared at his sister in confusion. "Then why on earth—?"

"To make you happy, confound it! What else?"

"To make me *happy*?" He ran his fingers through his hair in frustration, feeling as though she were speaking gibberish. "That's the same nonsense I got from Cassie. What would possibly make you believe that forged letters could make me happy?"

Eunice shrugged. "I don't know any more," she admitted, sinking down on the sofa as she tried to reconstruct the logic of Cassie's little scheme. "Cassie was very convincing at the time. Elinor had stopped writing, you see, and you were glooming about the place, looking as if you'd lost all chance of salvation. Cassie said you'd sacrificed your future for us, and it wasn't fair that you had no sunshine in your life, or some such nonsense. She was almost poetic about it. I suppose I was carried off on the tide of her emotion."

"Are you saying that you both believed that letters from Elinor would bring *sunshine* into my life?" Robert asked in disbelief.

"Well, *didn't* they?"

He gave a snorting laugh. "All they brought was a sense of guilt. It seemed to me that while Elinor was remaining loyally attached to me, I was disloyally building a life without her."

"*Really,* Robbie?" Eunice smiled broadly and drew a deep, relieved breath. "Then may I conclude that the latest news of Elinor won't pain you?"

"How can I say until I know? What news?"

"Your lost love has gotten herself betrothed to an Italian count."

His eyebrows rose. "Has she, indeed? Is that why she stopped writing?"

"Is that your reaction?" Eunice shook her head in amusement. "And to think we were so afraid of breaking the news to you!"

"Well, you needn't be so deucedly gleeful," Robert said sourly. "The news doesn't have me dancing in the streets. It doesn't puff up a man's pride to learn that he's been superseded in a female's affections."

Eunice laughed. "My dear brother, you are as inconsistent as a child. I needn't remind you, need I, that you can't have your cake, etcetera? Isn't the loss of a bit of masculine pride worth the loss of the guilt?"

He sighed. "I suppose so. But all this talk of Elinor has distracted us from the more important question. Where on earth has Cassie gone?"

"Back to her father's, I assume."

Robert jumped to his feet. "Yes, of course! I should have thought of that myself. Somehow I always assumed that she'd come here, so that she could play the grand lady and go running about with you and Mama to all the balls and routs and galas."

"*Cassie?*" Eunice gave her brother a look of disgust. "She doesn't give a fig for such things. I think, Robbie, that you have much to learn about your wife."

"So it seems," he said thoughtfully as he headed for the door.

"Do you intend to go to King's Cross to find her?"

"Yes. Right now." But he paused in the doorway. "Eunice," he said, his brow wrinkled in bewilderment, "I still don't understand. Why would my wife wish to make me happy by giving me love letters from, supposedly, another woman? It doesn't make sense."

Eunice threw him a strange, almost pitying smile. "Doesn't it, my dear? Think about it. Think about it hard. And if I were you, I wouldn't go seeking Cassie until the answer was absolutely clear."

$\mathcal{R}$obert did not take his sister's advice but rode over at once to King's Cross and hammered with the knob of his cane on the Chivers' doorknocker. Eames, the butler, answered the door and was about to admit him when Miss Penicuick loomed up in the doorway and barred his way. "Her ladyship is not at home," she said firmly.

"Come, come, Miss Penny," Robert cajoled. "You and I both know she is. Eames as much as admitted it."

Miss Penicuick glared at the butler. "Then he exceeded his authority, my lord. Her ladyship told us all, quite distinctly, that if Lord Kittridge called, she was not at home."

"Oh, she did, did she? Then, Miss Penny, will you please go up and tell her ladyship that I have come to apologize? Perhaps that will convince her to admit she's at home."

Miss Penicuick looked dubious. "I'll tell her, my lord, but you know Cassie. She doesn't change her mind easily once it's made up."

"Yes, I've noticed that. But do try."

The attempt was not successful. Miss Penicuick repeated that her mistress was "still not at home," and closed the door before he could say another word.

Robert tried again an hour later. This time Miss Penicuick opened the door only a crack. "Perhaps her ladyship has returned by now," he suggested, smiling charmingly at the eye that peeped out at him.

"No. Still out," Miss Penicuick insisted.

"Tell her I must see her . . . on a matter of immense importance. Enormous importance. Please, Miss Penny. It's a matter of . . . of life and death."

"I'll try again," Miss Penicuick said with a sigh, unable to resist him.

Lord Kittridge cooled his heels on the doorstep for fully fifteen minutes. But when the housekeeper returned, the answer was the same. Not at home.

Kittridge went back to Portman Square in a rage. "If she doesn't want to see me," he snarled at his sister, whom he passed on the stairs on his way up to his room, "then the devil take her! I'm going back to Lincolnshire tomorrow. I have more important things to do than to hang about on her damn doorstep!"

"I told you not to call on her until you understood her better," Eunice said. "Did you think about the answer to your question?"

"I've given the whole business too much thought as it is!" Robert declared. "*I'm* not the one who pried into matters that don't concern me. *I'm* not the one who forged letters! How have I suddenly become the penitent, standing about with my hat in my hand waiting for absolution?"

Eunice shrugged. "I have no idea," she said callously, proceeding down the stairs. "Go back to Lincolnshire, then. No one here will stop you."

Robert shut his bedroom door and threw himself down on the bed. What was his sister trying to tell him in that annoyingly enigmatic way? That he loved Cassie? He'd discovered that already. That fact had become clearer with each passing day. But that didn't explain why Cassie had forged the letters. That was the enigma, the answer to which seemed to be the crux of his confusion. Why had Cassie done it? Why had she peeped into his private letters? Why had she written him love notes from another woman? What had she hoped to gain by it?

Before he'd left Lincolnshire, he'd crammed Cassie's three letters into an inside pocket of his coat. He got up from the bed, pulled them out of their storage place, removed them from their envelopes and laid them, side by side, on his bedside table. He read them over, and then over again, but if they held an answer, he could not see it.

They were, however, an interesting puzzle in themselves. Cassie had composed them by pretending to be Elinor—putting herself in Elinor's place, so to speak. But she'd never even met Elinor and didn't know anything about her. So where had the ideas in the letters come from? They had to have come from Cassie herself, of course. But where had she learned about those feelings she'd expressed? Had she been in love before? Were these memories she'd stored away from an earlier experience? Had she herself once tried to touch her lover from a distance, "through the ether," as she'd put it in her letter? Had she sat on a garden bench and yearned to paint her lover's name across the sky? Had she conjured up his face, that face with the muscle twitching in the jaw? But, wait! That face described in the last letter—wasn't that *his*? All those "quirks" she'd so carefully detailed, weren't they his quirks? And hadn't she described them just as a lover would?

"Good God!" he exclaimed aloud, staring at the letters in front of him with wide eyes. Could *that* be it? His heart began to hammer in his chest as it occurred to him for the first time that Cassie might have been expressing her own feeling toward *him*! Could she really love him, even though she'd kept him at arm's length, even though their marriage had been a business arrangement, even though he'd kept himself distant from her for Elinor's sake?

Not trusting himself to answer, he ran out of his room and down the hall to Eunice's room. "Eunice, may I talk to you?" he asked, banging on her door.

"Of course, you gudgeon," she answered. "Stop that hammering and come in."

She was sitting at her dressing table, rubbing a strange greenish liquid on her face. "It's called Balm of Mecca," she explained, laughing at his shocked expression. "It is made up of all sorts of magical ingredients, like lemon oil, crushed cucumbers and tincture of turpentine. It is guaranteed to make my complexion as youthful as a schoolgirl's if I use it every day for a month. I intend to be a glowing bride a month from now."

"You'll be a glowing bride whether or not you use that stuff," he said, perching on her bed. "But I didn't come here to talk about complexions. Tell me, Eunice, were you hinting this afternoon that you believe Cassie *cares* for me?"

"Any fool could tell that in a moment," Eunice said in her blunt way.

"Oh, God!" Robert breathed, feeling a glow of joy in his chest.

Eunice beamed at him. "Fool!" she said affectionately.

He eyed her askance. "But I still don't see why, if she really loves me, she would want me to receive letters from *Elinor*."

"For some people, Robbie, love is more a matter of giving than taking. I think that Cassie would hand Elinor over to you on a silver platter if she could . . . and if she thought it would make you happy."

He expelled a long breath. "Damnation, Loesby was right. I *don't* deserve her."

"But she deserves you, so you'd better win her back."

"How am I supposed to do that," he asked, turning glum, "if she won't even see me?"

"Oh, you'll find a way," Eunice said airily. "Now, get out of here and let me get on with making myself ugly so that I can be beautiful. Good night, my dear."

Yes, he told himself before he fell sleep that night, *I'll find a way.* Life had suddenly opened up for him this unexpected new chance for happiness, and he'd be more of a fool than he even thought he was if he failed to grasp it.

The next morning he was on Cassie's doorstep early. "Miss Penny," he said to the housekeeper confidently, "just give her this note. She'll see me then."

He'd spent half the night writing it. Love letters were not in his line, so every word had come hard for him. In the end, he'd had to plagiarize some of hers. *Dearest Cassie,* he'd written, *it has slowly dawned on my sluggish brain that I am one of those lucky husbands who truly loves his wife. I have wanted to tell you so for a long time, but many foolish and quite imaginary impediments seem to have gotten in the way. I am not skilled at expressing my feelings, so I can only say that I've been trying since you left me to conjure up your face, but when I try to touch it, the vision dissolves into nothingness. Do not, I beg you, leave me so bereft.*

He hummed under his breath as he waited for Miss Penicuick to return. His pulse raced at the prospect of their imminent reunion. He would take her in his arms in so passionate an embrace that—

"Sorry, my lord," Miss Penicuick said, handing him back his note unopened. "Her ladyship is still not in."

Robert reddened in anger. "She would not even *read* it?"

"No, my lord. She said that any written communications could reach her through her father."

"Oh, she did, did she?" he muttered furiously, ripping the note in half and then in half again and throwing the pieces on the ground. "You may tell her for me that the note was for her eyes or for no one's!" And he stalked off to his curricle and drove furiously away down the drive.

When he'd put a couple of miles between him and her father's house, he grew calmer. Perhaps it might be a good idea at that, he thought. He would pay her father a visit at his office. Mr. Chivers would be on his side. Perhaps he might be able to help.

But Chivers's greeting was not warm. "I can't 'elp ye, Kittridge," he said flatly. "The girl is too cut up. She doesn't wish to live with ye anymore."

"But dash it all, Chivers, we're *married*! And what dreadful thing did I do to her, after all? Fell into a rage because she read some private letters, that's all. Many a man, finding himself in my place, would have done much worse."

Chivers shrugged. "I don't say ye're at fault, Kittridge. In my eyes ye seem a perfectly amiable fellow. But I'll admit to ye that I don't understand these new-fangled notions about love and romance and all. Cassie's got it in 'er 'head that marriage doesn't work without love, and per'aps she's right." He looked up at his son-in-law in embarrassment. "She's confessed to me that yer marriage isn't . . . wasn't . . . er . . . consummated."

"Has she?" Kittridge asked carefully, wondering what his father-in-law was getting at.

"So I've an appointment to see a solicitor. To ask about the possibility of annullin' the marriage, ye see."

"Indeed?" Kittridge managed to keep his expression impassive.

"Ye needn't poker up that way," Chivers said. "I won't ask fer the return of the settlement. Ye tried to keep yer part of the bargain, so the money's yours."

"Hang the money!" Kittridge's mind suddenly began to race. A scheme to win his wife back came rushing into his mind. It was shocking in its vulgarity, but it might work. "I'm not concerned about the money," he repeated. "But you're wasting your time with solicitors, Chivers. No one will believe you. Your daughter didn't tell the truth. The marriage *was* consummated."

Chivers blinked up at him in surprise. "What's that ye say?" he jumped angrily to his feet. "I'll 'ave ye know, Kittridge, that my Cassie doesn't lie!"

His lordship smiled coolly and picked up his hat. "I am also known for telling the truth. Your daughter and I lived in the same house for five months. Who do you think is more likely to be believed?"

He sauntered out of the office and down to the street. It was a lovely day. He smiled to himself as he saw Cassie's face in his imagination. He pictured her reddening in indignation as her father recounted the conversation he'd had with her husband. Robert didn't know what action her indignation would lead her to take, but he hoped it would bring her rushing to Rossiter House to confront him. That confrontation was what he hoped for. It would be all he'd need.

He was still smiling to himself as he approached Bond Street. The street was busy with shoppers, but Kittridge took no notice of them. His head was so full of plans that he didn't hear his name called until someone hissed in his ear, "Robbie! Wake up! It's I!"

He turned and found himself face to face with Elinor. She was a vision in a high feathered hat and a green and white striped walking dress. She seemed taller than he remembered, but her red-gold hair and translucent skin were as remarkable as ever. "Elinor!" he gasped. Recovering quickly, he bowed over her hand. "I'd heard that you'd returned from the continent. And that you are receiving best wishes on your betrothal."

She blushed. "Yes, I am. As a matter of fact, Mama has stopped in at the stationer's just behind you to order the cards for the wedding. I escaped from her because I caught a glimpse of you and wished to . . . to speak to you. Who knows when, if ever, we shall get such a chance as this to be private."

He smiled at her gently. "There's not much need to be private, is there? I think that what we have to say to each other has already been said."

Her eyes misted. "Oh, Robbie, I . . . I suppose so. Have you missed me, my dear? I've missed you dreadfully, especially at first. Mama was right, though. One does get over things after a time."

"Yes," he said.

She looked at him tenderly. "Have you gotten over me, Robbie?"

He hesitated, wondering how to answer her. He couldn't help studying her, trying to remember how she'd felt in his arms the night they'd said good-bye. It had seemed to him then that her tall, shapely form was a perfect fit for him and that there would never be another who would feel quite so thrilling in his arms. But that hadn't turned out to be true. He'd found another girl, of a very different size, who was even more thrilling. But Elinor was looking at him now, half coquettishly and half earnestly, waiting for an answer to her question, and he had no wish to give her an unkind one. "I've thought of you more often than you can imagine," he said with perfect truth.

She smiled tremulously, pleased with his answer. "I used to think of you all the time. Until Paolo. He swept me quite off my feet, as they say."

"You're happy, then. I'm glad for you, Elinor."

"Thank you, Robbie. I'm glad, too. Everything has turned out well after all, although for a while I didn't believe that it would. After all, we'd loved each other for so long."

"Yes," he said, wondering how she would feel if he admitted that matters were turning out well for him, too.

"By the way," Elinor continued excitedly, "did Eunice tell you that Paolo and I shall live in Florence in the winters? I think I shall like that. It's so lovely there. But we plan, every year, to be in London for the season. Shall you be glad to see me, if we meet sometime this way?"

"Of course," he said politely, suddenly wishing for this stilted conversation to end. Elinor had become too self-absorbed to be interesting, he realized with surprise. She'd twice queried him about his feelings for her, to make certain she still held a string on his heart, but she'd not asked once about his wife or if he was happy. Now that their feelings for each other had died, they had little else to say to each other. Elinor now seemed a distant acquaintance, someone with whom conversation was a strain. He was glad when her mother emerged from the stationer's, forcing Elinor to whisper a hurried good-bye and bustle off.

By evening he'd already forgotten the encounter. He had other things on his mind. He'd calculated that Chivers would have returned to his home by six and would certainly have told Cassie about his conversation with her odious husband by seven. It was now eight, and Robert was sitting at the dinner table with his mother, Gavin, Eunice and Sandy. He was waiting tensely for Cassie to come bursting in on them, wondering if he'd miscalculated her reactions. She might be too shy, even now, to take the action he hoped she'd take.

But just as the possibility that she would not come was becoming a real fear, the dining room doors were thrown open and Cassie, heedless of the butler who came scurrying up behind her, stalked over to Robert and slapped his face.

One of the footmen dropped the roast. Eunice gasped. The dowager Lady Kittridge screamed. Gavin exclaimed, "I *say*!" And Sandy cried out, "Cassie! What on earth—?"

Robert, grinning broadly while holding his tingling cheek, got to his feet. "Good evening, my dear. What has impelled the shy Lady Kittridge to break in on us and create such a dreadful scene?"

"You know very well, you . . . you blackguard!" she said, coloring to her ears but going on with her prepared accusation anyway. "How dared you tell Papa that you . . . that I . . . that we . . . ?"

"That we *what*?" he taunted.

"That we consummated the marriage!" she finished, her fury making her daring.

"My dear young woman," the older Lady Kittridge reprimanded, "how can you speak of such things now? We are at *dinner*!"

"Your son," the enraged Cassie snapped, wheeling on her mother-in-law, "is a blasted *liar*!"

"Who, *me*?" Gavin asked, bewildered.

"No, you nodcock," Robert corrected. "Me."

"He is not!" Eunice declared loyally. "You know how much I adore you, Cassie, but I won't have you calling Robbie names."

"He's never lied to me," his mother said with finality.

"Good God!" Sandy said, his belief in Cassie's sincerity causing him to eye his friend with suspicion. "You wouldn't lie about a thing like that, would you, Robbie?"

Robert laughed aloud. "Yes, I would. I did. And I will again."

Everyone stared at him. Cassie was completely taken aback. "You admit it?" she asked in disbelief.

"Yes," Robert said, taking her hand and grinning down at her, "I admit it openly. Before all these witnesses. But I will not admit it outside this room. I intend to keep on lying . . . to your father, to his solicitors and to anyone else who tries to nullify our marriage."

"Robert!" Cassie gasped, wrenching her hand from his grasp. *"Why?"*

"*Why*? How can you ask? I love you! I shall declare to my dying day that we are well and truly wed, in the sight of God and all this company. So you may as well give up, my love, and come home."

"I will n-not come home!" Cassie declared, bursting into angry tears. "I will never g-go home with a man who l-lies about such things. You d-don't love me! I don't know why you're saying that you do, but you don't."

"But he *does*," Eunice cried. "He *told* me. Why won't you believe him?"

"How can you say that, Eunice," Cassie asked, dashing the tears from her cheeks, "when you know as well as anyone that it isn't true?"

"But—" Eunice began.

"Confound it, Cassie," Robert said, grasping her shoulders in desperation as his confidence in his ability to sweep her off her feet rapidly dissipated, "can't you unmake your stubborn mind for once and *listen* to me? I love you!"

"You needn't pretend anymore," Cassie said, pushing him away. "Papa will not renege on his business agreement with you, so you don't need me. Your money is safe."

Robert's face whitened. "This has nothing to *do* with the blasted money!"

"Hasn't it?" Cassie turned and faced him, erect and defiant in spite of her trembling lips and tear-streaked cheeks. "I heard you speak the t-truth to me that last night in Lincolnshire. You said I d-disgust you."

"Cassie!" He stared at her in agony. "I never meant it. I was crazy with anger and confusion. You can't believe that I—!"

She held up her hand. "No more, please, Robert! I can't b-bear it. Let us go our separate ways. It will be better so." And she went quickly out the door.

"Cassie!" Eunice ran forward as if to catch her. "Wait!"

"Let her go," Robert said in despair, sinking down on his chair and dropping his head in his hands. "It's no use. I married her for her money. As long as that damnable forty thousand pounds stands between us, she'll never believe me. Never."

Chapter Thirty-six

$\mathcal{R}$obert disappeared from the house in Portman Square for several days, and when he returned he had a long conference with Sandy. Then, the next morning, he called his family together in the sitting room. "I have some things of importance to announce," he said quietly. "They may not be pleasing to you, but there will be no argument. All the decisions I've made have already been implemented, and they are final. I've decided, you see, that I cannot keep the forty thousand pounds that Mr. Chivers gave me. So I've made some difficult financial decisions that will enable me to return the money to him. First, I've sold the Suffolk properties. Since I'd already paid off the debts on them, I realized a goodly sum. Second, I sold this house to Sandy. Hush, Mama, there is no need for you to fall into hysterics. He and Eunice will be happy to have you remain in residence here with them for as long as you wish, provided, of course, that you don't let your penchant for reckless expenditure get out of hand. Sandy is generous, but he's not a mogul. If you become extravagant, I've instructed him to ship you out to me in Lincolnshire where, you can be sure, the opportunities for extravagance are extremely limited. You, Gavin, since you obviously have no love for school, will come to live in Lincolnshire with me. There is no point in protesting, for my mind is made up. We cannot expect Sandy to take charge of you when he has Eunice's two girls to raise, to say nothing of whatever offspring he and Eunice may have in the future. Besides, I intend to set you to work learning farming and estate management. With your instinct for horseflesh and love of animals, I think country life may suit you better than you think. For the rest, I've been given a generous loan by the Duke of Bedford, who is interested in my plans for my herds. This will enable me to keep Highlands, at least as long as I can make it a paying enterprise. Since that won't be easy, and I will be hard-pressed for years to pay him back, I am counting on your help, your encouragement, and your good wishes."

At the same time that Robert was making this announcement to his family, Chivers was making an unaccustomed trip home from his office in midmorning to bring some bewildering news to his daughter. "I don't know what to make of it," he said to Cassie, perching on the sitting room sofa and drawing her down beside him, "but Kittridge came to see me early today and returned all the money."

Cassie paled. "*Returned* it? How could he?"

"I'm not certain of all the details. For one thing, 'e sold the town 'ouse to Sir Philip Sanford, 'is brother-in-law-to-be. And, for another, 'e sold the Suffolk properties."

"But *why?*" Cassie jumped up in agitation and began to pace about, the flounce of her morning gown swishing about her ankles. "The Suffolk lands would not have brought enough to pay you and the debts on Highlands as well."

Chivers gaped at his daughter in astonishment. He hadn't been able to interest her in financial matters in twenty years of trying, but Kittridge had done it in five months. "How do you know that?" he demanded.

"Robert explained it to me. Don't tell me he sold Highlands, too! It would break his heart!"

"No. It seems 'e procured a loan from some other source. A duke, I think."

"It must be Bedford," Cassie surmised, sighing in relief. "The Duke of Bedford likes Robert's ideas about raising sheep. But why is Robert doing all this, Papa? He can't be thinking that the return of the money will free him to marry again. Doesn't he know that the solicitors told you that nullifying our marriage would be impossible?"

Chivers shrugged. "I don't know what 'e knows. I don't know what 'is motive is. All I know is that the fellow appeared at my door and plunked down a bank note for the entire amount. *"Tell Cassie,"* was all 'e said."

"Tell C-Cassie?" She stared at her father openmouthed. "He said *that?*"

"That's what I'm tellin' ye. What do ye think 'e meant by it?"

"I don't know," she said, but her eyes widened and her cheeks turned bright red.

"If ye don't know," her father snapped, "then why're ye blushin'?"

"I don't know," she insisted, suddenly turning and crossing quickly to the door. "All I know is that you shouldn't have taken the bank note. You made an agreement, and the money is rightfully his."

"Is it my fault the cod's 'ead wouldn't take it back?" he asked in irritation, following her out of the room just in time to see her flounce disappearing round the turning of the stair. "What was I to do? Tear the damned note up?" he shouted up the stairs. "And where are ye runnin' off to?"

"Nowhere, Papa." Her voice floated down to him from the upper floor, sounding cheerier than it had since she'd come home. "I just thought I'd better change my dress."

Less than an hour later, Lord Kittridge appeared on the Chivers's doorstep. Eames, as soon as he saw who it was, signalled for Miss Penicuick to come to his aid. She stepped up to the doorway. "Here again, are you, my lord?" she asked, blocking the door.

"Yes, here I am," his lordship said to the housekeeper pleasantly. "May I ask if Mr. Chivers has come home from the city this morning?"

Miss Penicuick looked surprised by the question. "Yes, he has, but he's gone back to his office."

"Good. Now, Miss Penny, one more question. Are your instructions to inform me that her ladyship is not at home still in effect?"

"Yes, my lord. Still in effect."

"Then I'm sorry to have to take liberties, ma'am," Kittridge said, "but it's a matter of necessity." He placed his two hands on her waist and lifted her bodily out of his way.

"Now see here, my lord," Eames said, stepping into the breach, "you can't shoulder your way in like—"

"Yes, I can," Kittridge said, fixing a threatening eye on the butler. "I'm very handy with my fives. Would you like a taste of them?"

"No, my lord," the butler mumbled, stepping away hastily and holding Miss Penicuick back, too.

Kittridge crossed the hallway in three strides. "Where is she?" he asked over his shoulder.

"In her room," Miss Penicuick said in tearful surrender.

"And her room is—?"

"Upstairs," the butler admitted, giving Miss Penicuick a helpless shrug. "Second door on the left."

Kittridge mounted the stairs two at a time. When he found the door, he didn't bother to knock. He merely burst in, startling his bride into emitting a small scream. "Robert!" she gasped, turning red.

She was sitting at a small writing table near the window, looking utterly delicious in a light blue gown with a deep lace ruffle at the neck. Her unruly hair was tied back with a blue ribbon, and the sun behind her head lit her curls with such delightful glimmers of gold that he almost didn't notice her attempt to cover something on her table with her hand. "Well, my dear, I'm here," he said, crossing the room to her. "If your father gave you my message, I imagine you were expecting me."

"I was not expecting you at all," she lied.

"Really? And I thought that pretty blue ribbon was for my benefit. What a disappointment. But tell me, my love, what is that paper you're trying so hard to hide from me."

"Nothing," she said, shifting nervously in her chair. "It's nothing."

He made an abrupt dive for it and snatched it from her hand. When he saw what it was, his face lit with a broad grin. "My love letter!" he exclaimed. "However did you find it?"

"Miss Penny picked up the pieces," she admitted, "and I . . . pasted them together."

He pulled her to her feet and into his arms. "But I thought you didn't believe my declarations of love."

She hid her face in his chest. "I wanted to b-believe them," she said in a small voice. "And I believe them now."

"Of course you do," he laughed, lifting her chin. "Any girl would believe a man's declaration if he backed his word with forty thousand pounds."

"It was a grand, but much too expensive gesture, Robert," she said softly. "Let Papa tear up the note."

"Not on your life. We shall do very well without it. Without that blasted dowry, we can embark on a proper marriage, based on those 'newfangled ideas of love and romance' that your father says you so adamantly believe in. The truth is that I believe in them, too."

"But . . . do you truly love me, Robert? In spite of having to give up Elinor because of me?"

"Elinor?" he asked. "I don't remember any Elinor. I haven't really remembered her since the night you and I went hunting for the Rossiter ghost. And if you doubt me, I have some irrefutable proof to offer." And he lifted her high on his chest and kissed her so soundly that she grew dizzy in his arms.

She wound her arms tightly round his neck and surrendered to the long-postponed joy of indulging in a completely unreserved embrace. No longer did she have to hold back. The result was so breathtaking for them both that they had to pause and recover themselves before indulging in a second, and then a third. By the time he let her go, all they could do was gaze at each other besotted with joy. "When did you first know you loved me?" he asked, smoothing back the wild curls from her forehead tenderly. "Was it when I stood up for you against Eunice?"

"Oh, no," she confessed shyly. "It was long, long before. Before you even knew my name."

He held her off and stared down at her with eyes narrowed. "How can that be?" he asked dubiously.

She wrapped her arms about his chest and hid her face in his shoulder. "It was when you stood up for me at the linendraper's, remember?" she whispered. "I've loved you ever since."

He expelled a long breath. So *that* was why she'd married him! It had nothing to do with being a viscountess or making her way in society. He tightened his hold on her and pressed his lips to her hair. "I *don't* deserve you," he murmured. "But I promise you, my love, that I will never again make you sorry you married me."

It was a long while before Robert remembered the main purpose of this invasion of her room. "Get your wrap, my love, and let's be off. We're going back to Highlands right now."

"Oh, but I can't!" she exclaimed. "Not so soon. I must prepare Papa, and make arrangements, and pack my things, and order some furnishings for the drawing room, and have a fitting for my gown for Eunice's wedding, and—"

"That's just what I expected," he said in disgust. "Do you realize, Lady Kittridge, that we've been married five months and have not yet had a honeymoon? Any sane person would agree that five months is the outside of enough. That's why I took an oath that I would not go back to Lincolnshire without you. So will you or nill you, you are coming home with me *now*!" And without giving her a moment to object, he lifted her off her feet and threw her over his shoulder.

She gasped for breath as he clambered down the stairs. "Robert, have you gone mad?" she cried. "Put me down!"

"I will, my love," he promised, "as soon as you're safely locked inside the carriage."

But Miss Penicuick, who'd been standing at the bottom of the stairs wringing her hands ever since his lordship had burst in, began to scream. "What are you *doing*?" she cried. "Someone, *help*! My Cassie is being *abducted*!"

"Out of my way!" Kittridge ordered, brushing by the hysterical housekeeper.

"Cassie, my dearest!" Miss Penicuick shrieked. "What shall I *do*?"

Cassie gave her a cheery wave as Kittridge carried her out the door. "Nothing, Miss Penny. Everything's fine, really. Lovely, in fact."

Miss Penicuick, breast heaving in dismay, followed them to the door. "But where are you *going*? And *what* shall I say to your *father*?"

Kittridge, having arrived at the carriage door, set Cassie on her feet. "Tell him that we've gone to consummate our bargain," he said, grinning down at his bride.

"Oh, Robert, hush!" the blushing Cassie ordered, putting a hand over his mouth. She looked up at Miss Penicuick and waved again. "Good-bye, Miss Penny. Just tell Papa that I've gone back to Lincolnshire. That message will be quite enough."